D0786818

NOVELS BY WILLIAM D. MONTALBANO AND CARL HIAASEN

A Death in China   *1984*
Trap Line   *1982*
Powder Burn   *1981*

A DEATH IN CHINA

A DEATH IN CHINA

William D. Montalbano and

Carl Hiaasen

ATHENEUM   NEW YORK   1984

Library of Congress Cataloging in Publication Data

Montalbano, William D.
  A death in China.

  I. Hiaasen, Carl. II. Title.
PS3563.05377D4   1984   813'.54   83-45496
ISBN 0-689-11448-6

Published simultaneously in Canada by McClelland and Stewart Ltd.
Composed by Maryland Linotype Composition Company,
Baltimore, Maryland
Manufactured by Fairfield Graphics, Fairfield, Pennsylvania
Designed by Mary Cregan
First Edition

FOR DANIEL JOSEPH MONTALBANO
AND CARL ANDREAS HIAASEN

In 221 B.C., China came to be ruled by the formidable Emperor Qin Shi Huangdi, whose dynasty was China's shortest, but arguably its most important. It was Qin who unified the feudal country. He built a road system, organized a central government, standardized Chinese language and coinage, and it was he who ordered construction of the Great Wall. Qin's hope for China's future was tied to a belief in his own immortality; to achieve that end, he was both ingenious and brutal, and when he finally died, he was interred in a giant tumulus near his capital of Changan, now the modern city of Xian. In the last decade, no archaeological dig has aroused more world interest than that involving the tomb of Qin Shi Huangdi, the Son of Heaven. . . .

From a lecture by Dr. David Wang
St. Edward's College, Ohio

A DEATH IN CHINA

PROLOGUE

Changan, China, 213 B.C.

"WHERE IS CONFUCIUS?" the emperor demanded.

Princes, nobles, councillors, generals, diplomats, servants and eunuch-ministers mimicked the emperor's angry mien. Square-jawed, flint-eyed, they stared at the cluster of old men whose robes and formal bearing marked them as scholars. Silence wrapped the throne room. It was not a question to be answered. Everybody knew Confucius had been dead nearly three hundred years.

"Is Confucius in heaven? Where is heaven? What do your books tell you? Is he a bush, or a river, or a bird that flies through the forest? Does he live still? Tell me, scholars."

The eldest scholar, gnarled as the cane he clutched with both hands, responded in a voice that held no fear.

"Where the master is we cannot say. But his spirit is among us men."

"You know nothing!" the emperor snapped. "Am I then just a man, like any other?"

"You are foremost among men, and more," answered a

3

councillor named Li Su in prayerlike incantation. "You are Qin Shi Huangdi, August Sovereign, the Son of Heaven. You are the Emperor of the Middle Kingdom."

"Have I lived as other men?"

The ritual required a general to answer: Men Qian, the emperor's best.

"Your feats have surpassed all others."

The emperor allowed himself a smile and cocked an eye; a parody of surprise.

"You have unified the Middle Kingdom," the general continued. "You have given us a great wall, stretching many months' journey, from the great ocean to the desert to protect us from the barbarians. So wide six horsemen may ride abreast. So tall and so strong that it will never be breached."

"So I am not just any man, am I? I am the Son of Heaven, ruler of the mightiest empire. Tell me, scholars, in your wisdom: Is that not right?"

The old man ran a clawed hand through his wispy beard.

" 'Let the prince be prince, minister be minister, father father and son son.' So it is written," he said.

The royal fingers kneaded an elaborate bronze chalice, and a serving boy, unnoticed, carefully poured more wine.

"They are all men. Men die. But I am different; the Son of Heaven. I shall not die. My body may stop, but I shall not die. I shall be *immortal*."

There were none to vouchsafe the emperor a response. The eldest scholar folded his hands around the cane and stared out over the exquisite royal city, where five palaces and fifty temples drowsed in the summer sun.

"I have heard the criticism of the scholars," the emperor said. "They ridicule my dealings with sorcerers and alchemists. They deny immortality because it is not written in their books.

"Scholars! It is not enough for an empire to be strong and orderly. No, they insist as well that the emperor must also be a sage, must also follow the teachings of Confucius, *who is not here*."

The eldest scholar replied softly, as though rebuking a child. " 'To govern is to set things right. If you begin by setting

4

yourself right, who will dare to deviate from the right?' That is what Confucius said."

"I am the Son of Heaven and I have set things right in this world as I will in the next. You have seen my preparations. They have taken more than thirty years." The emperor cocked his head. "Did you not believe what you saw?"

"I believe in the majesty of the work I saw," the old man said evasively.

"Majesty? Yes, my old friend." The emperor nodded. "Majesty indeed. A mountain whose insides have been carved into the shape of the cosmos by hundreds of thousands of workers who have labored a lifetime. I have made a generation of peasants dig through subterranean streams and seal them off with bronze to create a burial chamber where I shall rule for eternity. Palaces, pavilions—with fine vessels, jewels, stones and rarities. With quicksilver I have created the waterways of the empire, the Yangtze and Yellow rivers, and even the great ocean itself, and made them flow mechanically. Perfect models. And above I have depicted the heavenly constellations, and below, the geography of the earth. All this you have seen?"

"Yes," the old scholar answered.

"And the vaults?"

"Yes."

"Majestic, would you say? Large vaults surrounding the mountain, filled with clay soldiers, thousands of them; infantry, archers, charioteers and generals. Each carrying a real weapon." The emperor's eyes flashed.

"Your celestial army," the scholar said.

"It will protect my perpetual reign." The emperor emptied his cup. "And having seen my tomb and my army, scholars, can you still deny my immortality?"

There was a long pause then. Every eye was riveted on the small group of scholars before the throne. After the pause, the eldest replied.

"Ideas, like Confucius, are immortal. Men die."

"Fools!" the emperor screamed.

The next day, four hundred and sixty wise men, gathered

5

from all corners of the empire to assay the emperor's immortality, were made to watch as soldiers burned their books.

Then they were led to a deep pit not far from the emperor's celestial kingdom. From atop the steep sides of the pit jeering peasants shoveled clods of thick red earth. Most of the scholars kept their dignity. A few cursed and one or two of the younger ones cried. Before noon, they were all buried and dead. But then, three years later, so was the emperor, laid to rest under the perpetual vigilance of his fierce clay soldiers.

CHAPTER 1

Peking, August 1983

THE HIGH-CEILINGED LOBBY seemed carved in time, socialist testimony to yesterday's barren promises. A wine-red carpet crawled like a stain toward the horizon. Improvident columns that were neither attractive nor altogether round highlighted bile green walls. The furniture was of blond wood and indeterminate proportion. Waist-high counters cluttered every inch of wall space, each chockablock with white-coated workers. Some were accountants, some receptionists, some managers. Most were watchers.

Tom Stratton threaded through a knot of noisy Americans. He skirted a gaggle of Japanese clustered around a guide waving a flag. He neatly sidestepped a functionary listlessly pursuing a fifty-pound steel vacuum cleaner. Reaching the stand where an empty-eyed girl protected trays of almost fresh fruit, Stratton bought two apples. She weighed them on a digital scale and made change of his one yuan note with an abacus.

"*Ba lou*," Stratton told the elevator operator in phrase-book Mandarin. He was eventually deposited on the eighth floor.

The room was a monstrous little brother to the lobby, but already, after a week, it seemed like home. Stratton kicked off his shoes and padded into the bathroom. The hot water tap snuffled and growled, barked and hissed. On past experience, the chances that the water would be hot when it finally appeared were exactly one in two.

Stratton ate the apples and fingered leaves of tea into a thin-walled mug. Tenderly, he added water from a thermos on the night table, then threw back the red velvet drapes to let in the last rays of sunshine and sprawled on the bed. It was one hell of a place, Peking. Stratton had not decided whether to love it or hate it. The city sprawled in all directions, a flat, dusty, one-story town punctuated by brick chimneys thrusting toward the smog like phallic exclamation marks. Graceless monuments of revolutionary architecture dwelt alongside exquisite, gold-roofed survivors of the city's imperial past. Stratton scissored off the bed to watch the evening rush hour flow past a hundred feet below. He had just calculated the bicycle flow at nearly five hundred per minute when the room door flew open.

"Comrade! The chairman wants to see you right away."

"Hello, Alice." Stratton stifled a grin behind the tea mug. She had become a China groupie, a parody in blue cotton. The pants Chinese women wear with shapeless abandon strained across Alice's ample rump. The jacket was buttoned to the neck and fashionably wrinkled. The flat-brimmed hat bulged in a frustrated attempt to contain a mass of bottle-blond hair. Clinging precariously to the cap was a sheet metal button, red on white. AAAH, it said.

"You could pass for a native," Stratton mocked. Alice Dempsey was not his favorite woman.

"Bought it all at the Friendship Store. Why didn't you come with us?"

"I felt queasy."

"Baloney!" she snorted. "Every chance you get you slip away from us. What have you got against art historians any-

8

way? I'll bet you don't even wear your badge, do you?" She rolled her eyes up toward her own AAAH. American Association of Art Historians.

"It's a fine group, very nice folks," Stratton said with forced politeness. Alice Dempsey was ugly as sin and as annoying as a rash, but she did have wit and will enough to be a prized member of an excellent faculty in California.

"Fact is, I'd rather walk around than ride on a bus."

"Well, it's rude to our Chinese friends. The guide, little Miss Sun, is always asking about you: 'Where is Professor Stratton?' At least don't forget about the acrobatic show tonight."

"Sure, Alice."

Stratton's heart had not been with the tour since he had bumped into Daivd Wang outside the Summer Palace, just as if they had been on Adams Street in Pittsville, Ohio, or at one of those *ad hoc* seminars Wang had loved to lead at St. Edward's, stockinged feet curled to the fire in the old library.

It was Stratton's first time in Asia in more than a decade, and he had still not worked out to his own satisfaction why he had come. Asia was a dead letter. Had he come because a a two-week package tour of the People's Republic was cheap and exotic? Or because it would spare him dull hours of summer research at the small New England college where he taught? Not that, either. The research would have to be done, sooner or later, one way or the other; long nights followed by a slim volume only initiates would read. The job was waiting when he got back. Say he had come to escape the shards of a divorce that still hurt, a year later. Was that the real reason? Part of it, maybe, but only a lesser part, if Stratton was in the mood to be honest with himself. Carol was gone and he did not really miss her, although sometimes he ached to be with the boy.

Boredom. That was closer to the truth, wasn't it? His friends would know it intuitively. Stratton had worked hard to become a scholar. He was a legitimate historian, an able professor of emerging reputation. And . . . so what? Passing

9

years that dulled the senses, blank-faced students in vacuous procession. What next, Stratton? Mid-life crisis. Male menopause. Maybe there was no next.

So he had come to China. To throttle the boredom. No, there was something deeper. He was also testing the scar tissue, the way an athlete will gingerly measure the recovery of an injured limb. Something else, too. Thomas Stratton, as he alone knew, had come to weigh the man he had become against the one he had once been.

At Peking Airport, standing before the immigration officer in white jacket and red-starred cap, visions of yesterday had come flooding in with a gush he had battled to control. The man had fingered his passport without interest.

"Is this your first time in China?" the inspector had asked in slow, careful English.

"Yes," Stratton had lied. "Yes, it is."

"You are perspiring. Are you ill?"

"No. It is hot."

The man had stamped his passport and Stratton had sought the refuge of protective coloration in the gaggle of art historians.

Stratton shook his head at the memory and sipped his tea.

That night he skipped the acrobatic performance. Too bad about little Miss Sun. Once Stratton was sure his tour mates had left in the green-and-white Toyota minibus in which all tourists in China seemed to live, he went looking for dinner. On the way, he conducted prolonged negotiations with the white-jacketed floor attendants. If there was a telephone call for Professor Stratton, could they transfer it to the restaurant? It might work. Even if it didn't, it was not crucial. If punctilious David Wang called once unsuccessfully, he would either leave his number or call again.

The restaurant—foreigners only—was a purely functional place of round tables, soiled tablecloths, spotted silverware and spicy food in the inevitable blue-and-white crockery. The tour group ate three meals a day there, Western for breakfast and Chinese for the other two—a procession of savory dishes that appeared unordered.

Stratton settled into a small table and began leafing through

10

a purple-covered issue of the *Peking Review*. About two paragraphs into the cover story, a gob of wet white rice caromed off the red plastic sign that proclaimed his table 37. From two tables away, Stratton's assailant grinned evilly, gap-toothed and green-eyed. He was about seven years old and his chopstick catapult was poised for another round. A second child carefully probed the innards of the sugar bowl with a spoon. There were two, no, three, others in tenuous custody of a pretty woman in her thirties and a great bear of a man with a bushy red beard. Stratton intercepted the next gob with his menu.

"Kevin!" the woman jerked the missile commander around to face his dinner.

"I'm sorry," she told Stratton. It was something she had said before.

The bearded man looked up from a dam of napkins that encircled a lake of spilled soy sauce.

"Somehow it was easier at McDonald's. Sorry," he said.

"No problem. Actually, he's a pretty good shot."

From the waitress, Stratton ordered Sichuan chicken with peanuts, noodles, vegetables and a beer.

"Qingdao beer."

"Qingdao *mei you*." She pronounced it "may-o."

"What kind do you have?"

"Peking."

"Okay."

"Hey, baby, that's a bad mistake," the bearded man called from his chaos. "Peking beer tastes like it was passed through a horse. Tell her you want Wu Xing." He wiggled a green bottle in front of him.

"Wu Xing," Stratton told the waitress.

Stratton abandoned the last hope of a quiet meal when something began gnawing his leg. He carried it, squirming and squealing, back to its tribe.

"An escapee, I think," Stratton said, handing it to the woman.

"Oh, Tracey! Again, I'm sorry."

"That's okay. I'm used to kids. My sister has four."

"Spend a lot of time with them?" the bearded man asked.

11

"Never go near the little bastards."

"Can't imagine why. Why don't you join us, since we've ruined your dinner anyway? I'm Jim McCarthy. This is my wife, Sheila. I've never seen the kids before."

McCarthy, it turned out, was one of about twenty American reporters resident in Peking, a correspondent for a big East Coast newspaper. He had an office in a hotel and an apartment in a compound on the eastern side of the city where foreigners lived in Western-style buildings behind high brick walls erected and patrolled by the Chinese government to keep Chinese out.

"You here for long?" McCarthy asked.

"Another couple of days."

McCarthy rolled his eyes.

"Jim is not a great China fan," his wife explained.

"Yeah, one day I'll write a book. 'Hold the May-o' it'll be called. It's the national sport. If you want something, they haven't got it—beer to interviews. *Mei you.*"

After dinner, Stratton marveled at the texture of the city as he walked along a broad tree-lined avenue that ran past the Temple of Heaven. The dark summer streets bustled with life. Where puny street lamps cast wan patches of light, people gathered in loose, friendly groups to escape the heat. Almost all were men, in old-fashioned undershirts. They squatted to gossip or to play cards. The few cars rode with parking lights only, wary of the swirling stream of hard-to-see bicyclists, who used no lights at all. A young couple conducted public courtship on the stone steps of a government office building. From one alleyway, Stratton heard the muffled click of mah jongg tiles, and from a window, the beat of Western rock music from a cheap tape deck. Like headlights, mah jongg and rock music were forbidden in Peking that summer; the headlights so that bicyclists would not be blinded, the ancient game and the music because they were decadent. It pleased Stratton to realize that people still pursued their own muses on summer nights, and to hell with the Party and its rules.

The aim of Stratton's walk was a downtown park built on an artificial hill. The park itself was nothing special, but the circumstances of its construction were testimony to the siege mentality of Chinese communism. Perhaps forty feet high and a quarter mile around, the hill had been built entirely by hand, one bucket at a time, by volunteer workers who had scooped it from underneath the foundations of the city. In every shop, every factory, every school, Stratton had read, a well-oiled door led down to a network of tunnels. It was the most elaborate bomb shelter in the world, and it had taken more than thirty years to finish.

Bombshelter Park, as Stratton had silently dubbed it, was closed. As he strolled back toward the hotel, he thought of David Wang.

He owed much to the old professor. Wang had sensed the disillusion, no, the despair, that Stratton had brought with him to the tiny college in rural Ohio. Stratton had been running from Asia when he arrived at St. Edward's for graduate studies. Despite Wang's considerable reputation, Stratton had avoided his courses. Still, he had found himself attracted to the gentle and patient teacher. They had become friends, then confidants, and on the bright morning when a changed Stratton had strode forward to receive his Ph.D., no one could have missed the fatherly gleam in David Wang's eyes.

They had drifted apart, more by circumstance than design. With Stratton teaching in New England, rural Ohio had seemed increasingly remote. It had been two years since they had seen one another. Until Peking. Stratton, avoiding his brethren art historians for the first time and feeling particularly exultant at being alone, had stood, back arched, head up, to study the magnificent lakeside arcade of the Summer Palace.

The voice had come from behind him.

"They say she was a fool—profligate—the empress dowager, squandering national riches on a marble boat when she should have spent the money to build a modern navy."

Stratton would have known the voice anywhere, and the professorial restatement of conventional wisdom that was meant to be challenged. He had replied without turning around.

"Perhaps she knew more than most people give her credit for."

"How so?" asked the voice.

"She may have understood that, even with modernization,

13

the Imperial Navy would have been no match for the barbarian fleets. She foresaw the end of dynastic China and, instead of sending more young men needlessly to their deaths, decided to create that which would give her pleasure in the realization that the end was coming for her kind." It was, Stratton thought, an inspired improvisation.

"Mmmm, an interesting theory," the voice had conceded, "but in the end, I would think history correct in judging her a foolish spendthrift."

"Me, too," said Stratton, turning around to embrace David Wang.

Together, they had strolled the lake, finding amid the crush of Chinese visitors a seat aboard the ludicrous and beautiful boat the Empress Ci Xi had ordered built a century before.

Wang seemed immune to time, Stratton thought. He had looked fit and every bit the elegant, prosperous tourist in tattersall shirt, gabardine trousers, polished loafers and Japanese camera. As always, Wang looked a trifle owlish behind his thick glasses with gold frames.

"I keep hoping that if I put off everything long enough, the publisher will forget about the book contract," Stratton had joked to explain his presence. "But how about you, David? Aren't you the man who once told me never to look back, who persuaded me at a tough time in my life to lay the past aside for good and get on with life?"

"I would be distressed if I thought you were really as dogmatic as you sound, Thomas," Wang had chided. "But of course you are teasing, and, yes, I was the one who always said that the United States was my country, China just the place I happened to be born. But then I changed my mind. It is an old man's right, you know, to change his mind."

"Why?"

"Two things, really. For one, I am retired, you know—"

"No, I didn't. If I had known, I would have come to wish you well."

"Well, it was just a quiet leavetaking, no ceremony. Of course, I expect to stay in Pittsville and keep my hand in now and then." David Wang had smiled. Only death would ever

14

take him from the college and the town where he had been an institution for nearly forty years.

"The second reason is that I have a brother. I had not thought much about him all these years and then suddenly there was a letter inviting me to China. In the end, I came. A good idea, I guess."

Stratton had caught an uncertainty in the old man's voice.

"Is something wrong? Anything I can help you with?"

"I'm just a bit bewildered is all. Call it culture shock. You know, when I got off the plane, I was nearly too nervous to speak Chinese."

"I know the feeling."

Wang had touched Stratton's arm then, and they had both remembered the night by the fire in Wang's farmhouse when an angry and confused young man had spilled the bitter dregs of senseless war.

"My problems are nothing compared to the dilemmas you once had, believe me," said Wang. "But it would be nice to talk about them. I'll tell you what: I'm going to Xian to see my brother tomorrow. He's a deputy minister, you know. I'll be back around dark on Wednesday. I'll call you then. If you can break away from your tour, I'll show you the real Peking and we can talk as we walk."

"I wouldn't miss it."

Wednesday night Stratton returned from his walk to Bomb-shelter Park about nine thirty. David Wang never called.

CHAPTER 2

ALICE SCOLDED. Little Miss Sun, the China Travel
International Service guide, implored timidly. Walter Thomas
—or was it Thomas Walters?—a foppish Egyptologist from
the Midwest, spoke vaguely of "fraternal kinship," whatever
that meant. Stratton endured. When the atmosphere turned
bitchy, he shrugged and walked away. The White Pagoda and
a refurbished lamasery were not on his agenda that day. Stratton watched without expression while his colleagues, suitably
armed with cameras in black leather cases and sensible shoes,
obediently flocked onto their minibus under Miss Sun's set-
piece smile. Then he went up to his room and squeezed forty-
five minutes of exercise from the cramped patch between the
cracking wall and iron bedstead. When, near ten o'clock, David
Wang still had not called, he prowled the gloomy hotel corri-
dors until he found the room that Jim McCarthy used as an
office.

Dust blanketed stacks of books and haphazard piles of
newspapers that overburdened a loose-jawed table. It carpeted
the dials of an expensive radio atop a gray filing cabinet. It

16

lay like virgin snow on the bright yellow shade of a lamp meant more for Sweden than China.

McCarthy lolled in a swivel chair, desert boots comfortably atop the burnished top of a huge partners' desk that Stratton identified instantly as a valuable antique.

Mechanically, McCarthy was ripping strips from a newspaper, laying them in a corner of the desk and tossing the discards in the general direction of a big straw basket.

"Hey, baby," McCarthy lured Stratton from the doorway. "Make yourself a cup of coffee. Or there's some Qingdao, if it's not too early for you." The massive head gestured toward a box-sized refrigerator on the floor.

"Thanks." Stratton spooned Brazilian instant into a hotel cup identical to the one in his room, then added hot water from an identical pitcher.

"You teach art history. And karate, right?" McCarthy called.

"Why karate?" Stratton laughed.

"Sheila was admiring your whipcord body. I had a whipcord body, too—until I came to China." McCarthy patted his belly. "Is it fun, teaching?"

"I like it, I really do. It's not as exciting as being a foreign correspondent, but you do get hooked into the research. You find one piece here and another there and pretty soon you don't know where the hours went. Then, too, the vacations are nice and long. Most summers I go out west and help a friend of mine run a wilderness company for tourists—whitewater rafting, survival hikes, sissy climbing, that kind of thing. I should be out there now, instead of screwin' around here. But I really wanted to see China. Five cities, twenty-one days."

"Yeah, everybody ought to see it. Once. I wish I had—shh . . ."

McCarthy waved for silence and Stratton heard a familiar litany lancing through static.

". . . off the wall into the corner . . . Remy is in and Evans is around third . . . throw is to second but Rice is safe with a stand-up double . . . That'll be all for . . ."

"A baseball game?"

17

McCarthy laughed

"Last night's game. We're thirteen hours ahead of the East Coast, remember. There's a game on almost every morning—Armed Forces radio."

"Pretty nice, if you're a fan."

"Naw, not me. Only been to one game in my life. My father took me to Briggs Stadium when I was a kid. About the third inning there was this foul ball and I reached up to catch it, you know, like on television. Broke two fingers. Never went back."

"If you're not a fan, why do you listen?" Stratton teased.

McCarthy heaved himself upright and planted both feet on the floor. Stratton, from the other side of the desk, imagined without seeing the spurts of dust.

"It's China, baby. In China, I'm a baseball fan because it helps kill the morning. In China, I read five or six newspapers a day and cut out things I might use six months from now, but probably never will. Savin' bits of string, but never finding the spool. For correspondents, China is purgatory, baby. The thing about this place that drives you crazy is that there are no facts; a billion people and not one goddamned fact. Did you know that everything here is a secret until it is published, even the fucking weather forecast?"

"Then what do you do for news?"

"I worry a lot." McCarthy grinned. "Particularly on Thursdays; that's when stories for the weekend paper are due. Today they want a political piece, ugh. I don't understand what's goin' on—that's normal—but I have reached the solemn conclusion that neither do the Chinese."

"Like how?"

"Like something big is bubbling beneath the surface. There are lots of little signs: people being suddenly reassigned or demoted, or simply disappearing—they could be forcibly retired, or dead—nobody knows. No one will talk about it."

"A power struggle," Stratton offered.

"Don't you know it. This place has been a circus since Mao died; probably before, too. When Deng came in with his pragmatists, the old hard-line Maoists got pushed aside. Now I'd say that the hard-liners were getting their own back."

18

"Most of the people who are being knocked down are the ones that Deng made respectable again?"

"That, for sure. But more than that." McCarthy lit a cigarette. "There's a hard-ass campaign under way right now against Chinese having anything to do with foreigners. You know the old song: 'We welcome your technology, but no blue jeans, please.' The idea that the decadent West will contaminate the heroic masses has been around for a long time, but now it's worse—ten times worse—than I've ever seen it."

Stratton was surprised.

"People have certainly been very nice to us. I've seen no hostility at all," he said.

McCarthy nodded.

"Right. The average guy is more interested in Western ideas and culture than ever. He hears the Party's antiforeign line and says to hell with it. But the guys who are getting axed are those whose jobs require the most contact with foreigners. They're falling like tenpins." McCarthy threw up his hands in mock despair. "Who's doing it? Does it means some sort of new madness like the Cultural Revolution is brewing? That's what my editors ask. And all I can do is to quote Confucius' greatest line."

"What's that?"

" 'It beats the shit out of me, baby.' "

Stratton laughed.

"I'll get out of your hair, but let me ask a quick question. I was supposed to meet a friend of mine today, a Chinese-American professor who's here on a personal visit. He never showed up. How do I go about tracking him down?"

"You sure he's here in Peking?"

"Almost. He was supposed to come back yesterday from Xian."

"Plane probably didn't fly. The national airline only flies when the weather is good. No joke."

"That's probably it. Still, I'd like to try. He's a very old friend of mine and I'd hate to miss connections."

"I could have the interpreter call the hotels, but it would be a waste of time. The one constructive suggestion I can make is that you ask about your friend at the American Embassy. If he's an academic type, they should have some record of him, an itinerary."

"Who could I ask?"

"The culture vultures would be most likely to know, but they are turds to a man. Try the consul, Steve Powell. He won't know, but he's the kind of guy who could find out."

"At the consulate?"

"Never on Thursday mornings. Steve plays tennis every Thursday. Over at the International Club, the courts they call the Rockpit. Do you know where it is?"

"I've passed it."

"I have to go out, but you're welcome to use the corporate bicycle."

"Corporate bicycle?"

"No correspondent is complete without one," said McCarthy, fishing a small key off a large ring. "Downstairs at the bike rack, license number oh-oh-two-seven-two. It's black, like all the rest of them. Do you know how to get there?"

"I have a map, thanks. Do you ride much?"

"Only in the line of duty."

Seen from a hotel window or a tourist bus, the infinite procession of bicycles is one of China's most impressive sights. On every major street, broad lanes are reserved for bicycles. Even in downtown Peking they outnumber the trucks and cars by a thousand to one. Alice and her friends rhapsodized about the bicycles. They could talk for hours, insulated in the air-conditioned bus, of the silent, measured stream, as massive and as unstoppable as the Yangtze. They found in the bicycles a symbol of the progressive New China. At faculty teas it would, no doubt, sound quite profound.

Stratton learned some different things before he had wobbled two blocks. For one thing, the Chinese bicycle, copy of old English Raleigh though it may be, is more tank than scooter. It weighs a ton, steers hard and pedals harder. McCarthy's corporate bike had no gears, and by the time Stratton passed the old imperial observatory he was sweating. What astonished him most, though, was the chaos into which he had plunged. Bicycles, he decided, as a pert young thing nonchalantly cut

20

him off and he swerved to avoid a three-horse cart, were the ultimate bastion of Chinese individualism. To outsiders, the cyclists might look like an army of blue ants. To somebody who pedaled among them, the Chinese all had fangs. They veered without warning. They knifed through lanes of cross traffic with terrifying, expressionless élan. Chinese flirted as they rode. They hawked and spat. They sang and cursed.

The left turns were worst of all. The first time Stratton tried to make one he found he could not maneuver into the left segment of the bike lane in time. The second time he saw no way of getting across the oncoming flux of trucks and bikes. The third time he tensely negotiated the turn in the protective shadow of an old man who looked only straight ahead and miraculously emerged unscathed.

Twenty-five minutes later, Stratton pedaled past the iron gates of the International Club. He locked McCarthy's bike near a willow tree and walked to the tennis courts. Two players volleyed steadily on a pocked asphalt surface that looked as if it had not been repaved since Peking's last earthquake.

Stratton leaned on a chain-link fence and waited for a break in the game. It came on a gorgeous drop shot that brought one of the players, a stocky blond, lunging fruitlessly to the net. His opponent, a sandy-haired man in his early thirties, shouted in a southern accent: "Good try!"

"Mr. Powell?" Stratton called.

The sandy-haired player ambled to the fence. Stratton introduced himself. He told the American consul about David Wang.

"Mr. Stratton, I usually don't hear about American citizens in China unless they get in some sort of trouble. Professor Wang is a man of some distinction, however, and I'll bet the culture folks have his itinerary."

"Yes, well, Jim McCarthy said—er—suggested . . ."

Powell smiled. "He said, 'Those culture vultures are cross-eyed, close-minded sonofabitches,' " he drawled in fair imitation. "Well, I suppose he's right. Tell you what, soon as I polish off Ingemar here, I'll make a couple calls."

Powell was an excellent tennis player and he ended the game with a fierce flurry. With a towel around his neck and

21

his racket under one arm, he led Stratton into the main building of the club.

Stratton waited in the lobby while Powell used the phone in an adjoining booth.

"They're checking on your friend," he reported when he came out. "Have you read *Too Late, the King*?"

"Yes, of course." Stratton was impressed. It was not David Wang's best-known book, but it was his best work.

"I admired it very much," Powell said. "Clear, sharp, almost lyrical. We've got a copy in the library here."

"He's a special man. Very talented," Stratton said.

"Tell me more." Powell spread out the towel and sat down on an old leather chair.

"God, by the time I met David in the early seventies he'd already been around forever. He was born here in China, of course, but came to the U.S. to study just before World War II broke out. He never went back. By the time I entered graduate school he was famous in academia for his scholarship. I was"—Stratton hesitated—"just getting interested in Asian art. So it was natural to gravitate to Dr. Wang."

"He was originally from Shanghai, right?"

Stratton nodded. "An entrepreneurial family of the old sort. It had been making money, from salt or silk, opium or tea, from time immemorial. Toward the end of the nineteenth century both of David's grandparents, who were business rivals, I guess, got modern. David's father went to Columbia. His mother, who had studied at the Philadelphia Conservatory, was about fifteen years younger. When David's time came to go off to school in the States, he was still a teenager. In the normal course of events, he would have gone home and, as the eldest son, taken over the business."

"They were hardly normal times, were they?"

"No. Civil war between the Communists and the Nationalists. Invasion by Japan. Then the knockdown years until the Communists finally won in forty-nine. I would guess that David's father told him not to come back until it was all over. And then, of course, the wrong people had won—if you were a Shanghai millionaire. David bounced around, quietly accumulating degrees; money was never a problem, I gather, and

22

at the end of it all, there was nothing to come back to—the Wang empire was just one more victim of revolution. Whether he was cut off from his family or broke with them I don't know, but he never mentioned them. He settled in at St. Edward's and never left. I suppose he—"

"Excuse me. That'll be my boys." Powell caught the phone on the second ring. Stratton stared out the window at weeping willows in the overgrown courtyard.

When the consul returned, Stratton sensed there was no news.

"We've got Dr. Wang listed at the Heping Hotel. The culture officers had invited him to call or come by when he got back from Xian, but so far no one's heard from him. Maybe he just decided to spend an extra day or two at the digs."

"Maybe so," Stratton said, unconvinced.

"Our fellas are a little disappointed, too. They're looking forward to meeting your Dr. Wang. You know about his brother?"

"David told me he was a vice minister or something."

"A *deputy* minister, Mr. Stratton. Deputy minister of art and culture. A big gun. His name is Wang Bin. He's in charge of new archaeological digs and the big museum here."

Stratton said, "Maybe I'll just drop by David's hotel to see if there's a message for me. What was the name again?"

"Heping," Powell said. "It means 'peace.' It's a nice place, off the usual Peking trails. I can draw you a map . . ."

"No thanks. David would be pleased if an old student proved intrepid enough to track him down. In the meantime, if you hear anything, could you call me? I'm at the Minzu."

"Sure," Powell said. "Good tracking."

Stratton nearly missed the hotel. It was tucked away in a lane barely wide enough for one car. Stratton left the bicycle in a parking lot near Wangfujing, Peking's main shopping street. An old woman with a can affixed a wooden marker with a number on the handlebars, handed him a paper receipt, and took a fee from among the aluminum coins Stratton displayed in an open palm.

It was a smaller hotel than the one he was in, and more graceful. Stratton did a full circle in the lobby looking for the front desk. There was the usual assortment of work spaces, but none of them identifiable. Finally, he chose one at random.

"Excuse me, could you tell me the room number for a guest named David Wang. He's American."

Three desks later a hunchback with a gray Mao jacket and some English took Stratton's request into an inner office. Through the open door Stratton could see him staring farsightedly at what was obviously a handwritten guest register. Just as Stratton was succumbing to the sinking feeling that Wang had registered in his Chinese name—which he didn't know— the hunchback emerged. He had obviously found something.

"You wait," the man ordered.

Stratton watched curiously while the man trundled into a second office. There he spoke animatedly with another man whose face Stratton could not see.

It seemed to Stratton they were arguing.

Finally, the second man appeared alone. He had a hook nose and an obvious habit of command.

"The Wang man is not here," the Chinese said in labored English.

"Couldn't you check again? I'm a friend of his."

"Not here." The man turned away, walked back into his office and closed the door.

Perplexed, Stratton cycled slowly back to his own hotel. He had been lied to. Of that he was certain. Hook Nose had known something about "the Wang man" that he had chosen not to tell. Why would a hotel in Peking deny the presence of a guest?

Stratton was still thinking about it when he got back to his room.

The phone was ringing as he walked in.

"David?"

It was not David.

"Mr. Stratton, this is Steve Powell, at the consulate."

"Oh, hello. I went to the hotel and they claimed never to have heard of any David Wang—"

Powell interrupted brusquely.

"Mr. Stratton, I am sorry to have to tell you this. David Wang is dead."

24

CHAPTER 3

Tom Stratton could smell the smoke. He could taste the cordite. He could see the gray shape, feel its struggle, hear its scream. He could sense the impatient clatter of the helicopter, hovering, waiting, anxious to be gone. Fire. Run. Run to the chopper, its rope ladder slowly dangling, the only lifeline he would ever get. Drop. Fire. Run from a black night and a devil-scorched patch of earth, all memory and no meaning.

Run, captain. Rope swaying. Lungs burning. Side burning as the black medic cut away the cloth and applied a salve. Eyes burning, exhaustion and shame, in the cramped cabin of a blacked-out aircraft carrier.

"You're sure there were no prisoners?" A man, a colonel, trying to be professional, sounding only disheartened.

"No POWs." A dirt-poor commune with a PLA company stationed on its fringes.

"Intelligence was so damn sure about the prisoners. They said there were American prisoners."

"Not anymore."

"How did they get on to you?"

"We made a mistake."

"Your team?"
"Gone, all gone."
"How long did they have you?"
"Not long."
"Bad?"
"Real bad."
"So what'd you tell 'em?"
"Said I was an East German, training with their Viet friends."
The colonel laughed at the idea.
"How'd you get away?"
"I got away."
"It was supposed to be a quiet recon."
"It wasn't quiet."
"Shit, you're telling me. Their radio is already screaming to high heaven. They say thirty-eight 'innocent peasants' are dead."
"Most of them were soldiers."
"They blame us; probably they'll get one of their pious friends to raise hell at the UN."
"Why shouldn't they blame us? We did it, didn't we?"

Stratton wrenched himself from a tangle of sodden sheets. His watch said 5:47. It was still dark in Peking. His eyes felt gummy, his mouth wooden. He glanced at the bottle of whiskey he had bought the night before in the hotel lobby. Less than half full, and still open.

He had not drunk like that for a long time. And he had not hurt like that for a long time. David Wang's death had triggered reactions and dreaded memories he thought he had buried for good.

From the street below came the muted whir of cyclists, harbingers of the morning rush hour. Stratton rejected his body's urging for sleep. His mind would not sleep. Naked, he lurched to the bathroom and turned on the hand shower, hardly noticing that the water was stone cold.

A wrinkled woman with blue-rinse hair and stiff new Hong Kong sandals sat across from Stratton in an anteroom at the

26

U.S. Embassy. Sitting next to her, but obviously on a separate mission, was a slender middle-aged man with a leathery face, a smoker's face. He carried a suede valise.

"How is *your* tour?" the old woman said to Stratton.

"Not too good," he said hoarsely. News of David Wang's death had left him numb. Sadness itself was slow in coming. Another old friend dead and—as in Vietnam—Tom Stratton was a long way from tears. Instead he fought a deep, dull melancholy.

"We have a lovely guide," the wrinkled woman said. "Her name is Su Yee. Her great-grandfather helped to build the Great Wall."

Stratton managed a polite smile.

"Where are you from?"

"New York," volunteered the smoker. "I'm an art dealer."

"I'm from Tucson, retired there from Chicago," the woman reported. "My husband used to be a stockbroker."

Together they awaited Stratton's contribution. "I'm a teacher," he said finally. "I teach art."

"Asian art?" asked the man with the leathery face.

Stratton did not reply.

The art dealer hunched forward, and Stratton shifted uncomfortably. There was something felonious about the man. He was dressed well enough, but the fine clothes didn't match the tiny brown rodent eyes that scoured Stratton from head to toe in quick appraisal.

"Do you know much about Sung Dynasty sculpture?" the art dealer asked. His voice dropped to a clubby whisper. "I'm trying to cut a deal with some government types down in the Sichuan Province. They've got a little gold mine of a museum down there, but I can't persuade them to part with any of their artifacts."

"This is our first trip to China," the old woman interjected.

"Mine, too," Stratton said, glancing at the door to the consular office. Surely it would not be much longer.

"Where's your hotel?" the art dealer pressed. "Maybe we can get together for a duck dinner." He laughed a Rotary Club laugh. "Look, I've done a lot of work in Western Europe, the Mideast, even Russia. But this is new territory, and

I don't know whose back needs scratching. Maybe we could help each other out."

"I don't see how," Stratton said.

The man held out his hand. "My name's Harold Broom."

Stratton guessed that Broom was the sort of man who carried business cards in his top shirt pocket, and he was right.

"I'm always looking for experts. Especially free-lancers," Broom said. "The more I know, the more I can take home." The smile was as thin and hollow as the voice. "And the more I take home, the more I spread around."

"No thanks," Stratton said. "I'm here on pleasure, not business.

"Too bad."

"I have a passport problem," said the old woman with blue-rinse hair. "I can't find my passport. I may have left it at the opera. My husband said there should be no problem, but I told him this isn't Europe. A passport is probably more important here. This *is* a Communist country."

"Yes," Stratton said. He was miserable.

The door opened and an American secretary beckoned. Steve Powell sat at a small desk in a tall room with one narrow window.

A gray file cabinet stood in one corner. On a table, in front of a cracked leather sofa, was a stack of American magazines.

"I'm sorry for making you wait," Powell said. "I've spent the last two hours wrestling with the Chinese bureaucracy. It is intractable on the most routine matters. You can imagine the problems we face with something like this."

"Can't be much worse than ours," Stratton said.

"Oh, but it is," Powell said cheerily. "Infinitely worse. I could tell you some incredible stories . . ."

"What happened to David?" Stratton asked. "When I went to his hotel all the manager would say is, 'Mr. Wang not here.' "

Powell nodded. "When you ask a question of a Chinese, expect a very literal answer. The man was telling you as much of the truth as you requested. Professor Wang became ill Tuesday night and was taken from the hotel."

"But David told me he wouldn't even be back in Peking until Wednesday evening."

Powell shrugged. He slipped on a pair of tortoiseshell glasses and opened a file. Stratton noticed that it was the only item on the desk. Powell was a neat young man.

"Tell me what happened to David," Stratton said impatiently.

"Death by duck."

Stratton's face twisted.

"Sounds funny, I know," Powell went on, "but that's what we call it. It's a new China syndrome: Aging, out-of-shape American tourist comes to Peking, hikes and strolls through the Forbidden City and climbs the Great Wall until he's blue in the face. Then he gorges himself on—what else?—rich Peking duck, gulps liters of Lao Shan mineral water and promptly drops dead of a myocardial infarction."

"A heart attack, that's all," Stratton said.

"Sure," Powell said. "Death by duck. We're had dozens of cases. It has nothing to do with the duck, I assure you. Just too much food, too much exertion. Might as well be Coney Island franks."

"Just like that." Stratton's voice was tired and low.

"After dinner, Dr. Wang apparently felt sick to his stomach. Several guests apparently saw him go up to his room. Two hours later one of the cleaning boys went in and found him there in bed, unconscious but still alive. Two medical students came and took him to a clinic nearby. The doctors apparently worked very hard but it was too late."

"It's all *apparently* this and *apparently* that. Aren't you sure?"

"Of course. I use that word as a reflex," Powell said uneasily. "This information comes from the Chinese government. I can't vouch for it a hundred percent, but on a matter like this, I see no reason to challenge the facts. It is, as I said before, fairly routine. Tragic, to be sure, but still routine."

"This is a maddening place," Stratton said. "The people at

the hotel might at least have told me which hospital he went to."

"They probably didn't know," Powell responded. "It took *me* five phone calls to find out. It was a small but very modern clinic on Wan Fu Jing Street. It has everything most hospitals in Peking don't have—the machines, I mean. I'm sorry for the confusion, but if you've spent much time in Asia, you come to expect it."

Stratton nodded. He knew something of Asian confusion.

"Why," he asked, "was there such a delay in reporting the death to the embassy? Is that routine, too?"

The delay, Powell explained, was another matter. He opened a desk drawer and withdrew a new file; he put the first file away. Professor Wang's death was not treated as those of other American visitors, the consul continued, because of Wang's relation to a high-ranking Chinese official.

"It was a homecoming for Professor Wang, and apparently was a very moving reunion with his brother. In this file I have a note from the deputy minister himself—a rare communication, believe me—and it describes Professor Wang's visit to Xian, and his return to Peking with his brother. That night, unfortunately, he suffered his fatal heart attack."

"The deputy minister was notified before the U.S. Embassy was?"

"He *was* Professor Wang's brother, after all. And in his position, Wang Bin certainly would be entitled to all the information regarding his brother's death. Once that information was delivered to the deputy minister, we were officially notified. Please don't make more of this than is warranted." Powell sighed. He took off his glasses and put them on the desk. "I was up half the night trying to reach David Wang's relatives back in Ohio."

"There are none," Stratton said emptily.

"So I learned. No wife, no kids, just a roomful of books and paintings."

"And a garden."

Powell glanced at his wristwatch. "I asked you to come this morning because Wang Bin requested it. Apparently the professor told his brother of your friendship and of your mutual

30

interest in Chinese art and culture. For obvious reasons, Wang Bin will not be able to attend his brother's funeral in Pittsville. But he would like someone to accompany the body back to the United States."

Stratton rubbed his temples with both hands.

"In his note here," Powell said, "Wang Bin suggests that you would be the perfect escort. Let me read you this one part: 'It would mean a great honor for the memory of my brother if Mr. Thomas Stratton could accompany David's body to his homeland for burial in the manner so requested by my brother. I realize that this would be an inconvenience and a hardship, but it would advance the friendship between our great peoples. Please convey this humble request to Mr. Stratton, and please assure him that he will be able to complete his visit to China at any other suitable time, as a welcomed guest.'

"The deputy minister wrote that himself, in English," Powell said.

Stratton stood to leave. "Tell the deputy minister I'll be happy to accompany David's casket to the United States."

"Excellent!" Powell was pleased with himself.

Stratton asked about the body.

"It won't be ready for transport for a few days."

"Where is it?" Stratton asked.

"One of the city hospitals. Capital Hospital, I believe."

"You're not sure?"

"I can find out." Powell was defensive again. "I'll leave word at your hotel. But, as I said, I'm fairly sure it's at Capital. That's where it was sent for the autopsy."

Stratton motioned toward Powell's file. "The autopsy results?"

"Oh no. The stuff on the heart attack I got by phone this morning. Through official channels . . . Anyway, the body will be taken to the Peking Airport Monday morning."

"Fine," Stratton said. At the door, he turned again to Powell. "I'm curious, though. Is Wang Bin certain that his brother wished to be buried in the United States? Perhaps, after all these years, he wanted to be buried here, in China."

Powell was a little perturbed. "I really couldn't say. I as-

31

sume his brother would know. And besides, nobody is buried in China anymore. Nearly everyone is cremated. It's a helluva thing, Mr. Stratton, but it's true. Apparently there's no more room for any bodies—especially in Peking."

The important man rode in the back seat of the black limousine. At each side sat a trusted comrade whose function, simply put, was to do as he was told.

"The train is late," said the limousine driver, who wore thick eyeglasses and gripped the wheel tightly with bony hands.

"As long as everything is safe, I don't mind," said the important man.

"I talked to the workers in Xian this morning," volunteered the man at his left side. "They assure me that, as before, the crate was placed in a separate boxcar."

"With a guard?"

"Several guards, Comrade."

The driver steered the limousine along the special lanes used on Peking streets by privileged travelers. The bicyclists gave wide berth to the long black car.

"You have done well."

"Thank you, Comrade."

Then, in a voice so low the driver could not hear, the man said, "Has anyone asked questions?"

"No," replied one of the escorts, whispering. "No one."

"Excellent." The important man gazed out the window of the speeding car and thought how fortunate he was, in these times, to have someone he could trust.

CHAPTER **4**

ALICE DEMPSEY knocked on the door at eight sharp the next morning. At eight thirty, she knocked again. Stratton grunted.

"Surely, you're not still in bed!" she said through the door. "We leave for the Great Hall of the People in ten minutes."

Stratton groped for his watch. "I'll catch up," he mumbled.

He dressed and went downstairs to claim a cup of tepid American coffee in the hotel restaurant. Then he set off on foot for the Heping Hotel.

It had occurred to Stratton that David Wang's belongings would have to be gathered for the sad trip home—clothes, cameras, textbooks, souvenirs, and the ever-present journal. Wang was not a mellifluous writer, nor was he poetic, but he wrote down all he saw. His journals were meticulous, sponge-like and even a bit silly; once he had visited Disney World in Florida and returned, sheepishly, with fifty-seven pages of diary. Tom Stratton felt a duty to recover his old friend's things.

Everything about Stratton attracted the eyes of the Chinese —his height, his blond hair, his thick reddish mustache. In

Vietnam it had been much the same. He remembered the clutter and chaos of Saigon, the heady taste and thrill of war, the horror, the ultimate revulsion: bitter, black fear. Stratton waded like a bushy mutant among hundreds of Chinese in the broad streets, a pale stalk shooting up from blue fields. He thought back to the flippant, soft-life description of academia he had foisted on Jim McCarthy. A self-justification.

"I am an obscure college professor because that is as far as I could get from guns and killing," Stratton should have said. "I haven't got the balls to do anything else. I lost my pride, and something more, one terrible night a long time ago."

At David Wang's hotel Stratton was greeted by a polite young clerk who spoke poor but passable English.

"I am a friend of the gentleman who got sick here the other night," Stratton began. "I came for his things."

Stratton expected a discussion, but the clerk merely smiled and led him upstairs. The door to David Wang's room was not locked. "No one sleep here for three nights, I think," the clerk said.

The room was small, the walls white and recently repainted. Chinese tourist hotels are not luxurious by European standards, but they are functional. A blue woolen blanket was smoothed across a single bed, and a chest of drawers had been carefully dusted. Two fresh hand towels hung on a hook near a chipped water basin.

The room was ready for a new guest. There was no sign that David Wang had ever slept there.

"Do you remember Professor Wang, the man who stayed here?" Stratton asked the timid clerk. The man nodded vigorously. "I came for his things. Where are they?"

The clerk shook his head.

"His clothes, his books . . ."

"Men came and took things. Comrades clean the room, that's all."

Stratton checked the closet and found three wire coat hangers on a dowel. Stratton went through the bureau. In one drawer he found two handkerchiefs and a pair of blue cotton socks. One of the handkerchiefs was monogrammed with the initials D.W.

"The men left with suitcase," the clerk volunteered.

"When?"

"The day after Mr. Wang got sick."

Somebody tapped on the open door.

A small-shouldered American in khaki walking shorts stood in the hallway. He was gray-haired and pink in the face; around his neck hung a pair of small Nikon binoculars.

"Are you a friend of Dr. Wang's?" he asked Stratton. "My name is Saul Weinstock. I was here Tuesday night when he got sick after dinner."

Stratton stood up from the bed and introduced himself. "You were in the restaurant?"

"No, but I was in our room downstairs when I heard the commotion. A cleaning boy found Dr. Wang and shouted for help. That's when I ran upstairs. I'm a retired physician. Had a general practice in Queens for thirty-one years. My wife and I are on a world tour. We met Dr. Wang on a walk through one of the municipal parks."

Weinstock told Stratton that he had seen David Wang late Tuesday afternoon, shortly after his return from Xian.

"He was tired, but he seemed in good health. We asked him to join us for dinner because we wanted to hear all about the reunion with his brother, but he declined. He promised to join us for breakfast on Wednesday morning."

The clerk excused himself. Stratton closed the door and motioned Weinstock to sit on the bed.

"Was David still alive when you got here?"

"I'm not sure, Mr. Stratton. Let me tell you what happened, because it's been bothering me a great deal. After I heard the room boy shouting, I ran up the stairs. As you can see, I'm not a young man. But still, it couldn't have been more than two minutes.

"Yet already there were two men in the room. They identified themselves as medics—at least that's what they told the hotel manager. I told them I was an American doctor, and I showed them my medical bag. But it was no use, Mr. Stratton, because they wouldn't let me in. One of the men stood there, at the door, blocking the way. The other was here at the bed, leaning over Dr. Wang. Now I saw some movement

35

in the professor's legs, and I'm almost positive I heard him say something in Chinese."

Stratton asked, "Was he in pain?"

"Yes, it sounded that way. I begged to go in and help, but the hotel manager insisted that I go back to my room. The medics said everything was under control. After a few minutes, they came out with Dr. Wang on a stretcher. A blanket was pulled up to his neck. His eyeglasses were sort of propped on his forehead, and his eyes were closed. I think he was still breathing, but I couldn't be sure. His color was very poor. His face was gray. I followed the medics downstairs to the car," Weinstock said.

"They had a car?" Stratton was surprised. Three-wheeled bicycles customarily served as delivery wagons and ambulances in the city.

"Not just a car," Weinstock added, "a limousine. They put the litter in the back and roared off. And that was something else that bothered me. There's a clinic just three blocks down the street, near the Dong Dan market. It's a very modern facility by Chinese standards; it was included on our tour. I saw the cardiac unit myself—not great, but adequate for a heart attack. Yet the medics drove right past it, never even slowed down."

"Maybe it was closed for the evening."

"I don't think so, Mr. Stratton."

"Strange, isn't it?" Stratton mused. "Do you know who David had dinner with?"

"It was a small banquet in a corner of the dining room; all the people were Chinese."

Together they walked down the stairs. The whole hotel smelled of turpentine and cheap new paint. On the second floor, Weinstock paused on the stairwell, as if making up his mind. "Mr. Stratton," he said. "I've got something in my room that you should see."

Gerda Weinstock was caking her cheeks with makeup when the two men walked in; she let out a tiny shriek and fled into the bathroom.

"She hates for anybody to see her until she gets her face on," Weinstock whispered. With bony knees rubbing on the

36

wooden floor, he hunted under the bed. When Weinstock got to his feet, he was holding a black medical bag.

"Once a doctor, always a doctor," Stratton said.

Weinstock shook his head soberly. "No, this isn't mine. This is what the medics left behind in Dr. Wang's room. This is what I wanted to show you. I found it on the floor, near the bed. I opened it because I was curious. Professional curiosity."

Inside, lying in a shining heap, were dozens of identical gadgets: a small tool, perhaps three inches long, with a small arm that swung out on a tiny hinge and flipped over to form a lever for the thumb. Pressing the lever made the sharp U-shaped jaws of the tool open and close silently.

"Do you know what these are?" Weinstock asked incredulously.

"Fingernail clippers," Stratton muttered.

"Fifty-four sets," the American doctor reported. "Made in China."

"I'll be damned," Stratton said.

"Some medics," said Saul Weinstock. "Some goddamned medics, huh?"

Stratton asked to keep the medical bag.

"Sure, just don't tell them where you got it. Please," Weinstock implored. "My wife and I don't want to get kicked out of China before we get to see Tibet."

"You're damn right!" came a voice from the bathroom.

Steve Powell lifted the doctor's bag from his tidy government-issue desk and shook it. The nail clippers clattered metallically inside. "You've got to admit it *sounds* authentic," he said to Stratton. Then, with a dry laugh: "Welcome to China, my friend."

Stratton ignored the consul's invitation to sit down. "I don't think this is funny," he said.

"Understand something, Mr. Stratton. These 'medics' who attended to your friend at the hotel—of course they weren't real medics. Forget the bullshit you've heard about the phenomenal modernization of Chinese medicine. It's still backward as hell. And try to find a fucking veterinarian in this

37

town! The embassy wives have to send their precious French poodles to Hong Kong for a lousy distemper shot.

"These guys who took Wang to the hospital were, at the very most, first-year students. They could have been janitors just as easily. The doctor bag is a prop, as you no doubt figured out. They were lackeys. Their only job was to get the patient to a hospital."

Stratton asked about the clinic three blocks from the hotel. "It's supposed to be very good," he said.

"Maybe it is," Powell said, "but David Wang was the VIP brother of a deputy minister. The Chinese knew who he was, where he was and what he was doing. When he got sick, they took him to Capital Hospital, one of the most advanced hospitals in Peking, whatever 'advanced' means here."

Stratton sat down. "Yesterday you weren't so sure."

"Since then I've received a full report from Wang Bin's office."

As proof, Powell displayed a file folder. "You're probably wondering what happened to Professor Wang's personal effects." Powell rose. "Come with me. We'll do our own inventory."

The two men walked to a cordoned-off area of the embassy building. Powell flashed a plastic identification card at a Marine guard, who opened a gate to a stale vault. The consul used a tiny key to spring a metal drawer on a bottom row of locked cabinets. He removed three paper bags. Each had been marked in black ink: "D. Wang, Pittsville, Ohio."

"The Chinese authorities collected these from Professor Wang's room. They may have overlooked a couple of things, but I think you'll find most of Dr. Wang's valuables are intact."

Stratton dumped the contents on a small table in a dimly lit corner of the vault: underwear, shirts, pants, a white sun visor, an extra pair of eyeglasss, a Nikon 35-mm camera, a bottle of Excedrin, three tombstone etchings on rice paper, four books about China and Chinese dialects, three rolls of unused film and a shaving kit.

"Wasn't there a suitcase?"

38

"I suppose it was just too large for the drawer," Powell said. "Does everything else seem in order?"

"No," said Stratton. "Where is David's journal? He always wrote in a thick diary with a leather binding."

"His brother has it. Wang Bin asked us for permission to read through David's writings. We saw no reason to object. He has promised to return the journal before the body is sent to the States."

Stratton said, "And David's passport?"

Powell adjusted his glasses and pawed through the items on the table. The Marine stood stiffly at the door of the vault, his back toward the two men.

"It's not here?" Powell asked lamely.

"No." Stratton watched the consul's composure drain. The cool eyes fluttered.

"It must be here," Powell said. "Something so important."

"What are the regulations in a case like this?"

"Our regulations, or theirs?" Powell grumbled as he fished in the empty pockets of David Wang's neatly folded trousers. "Jesus, this is unbelievable. Just what I need. You say you went through the room as well?"

"Nothing much," Stratton said. "Socks, handkerchiefs. What happens if you can't find the passport?"

Powell had given up. He stuffed the sad remnants of David Wang's life into the paper bags. "Well, if we can't find it, then I have to write a report. That's about it. I'll have a few forms to fill out." He eyed Stratton with annoyance. "What *should* happen? I mean, Christ, the man's dead, isn't he? He doesn't need a passport anymore. A corpse travels on a bill of lading."

Back at the consul's office, Stratton waited while Powell checked another office for David Wang's passport. Stratton sat in a chair directly across from Powell's empty desk; there was a different file on top now. It was light blue. Stratton could see his own name on the tab. Instantly, he reached for it.

"Sir?" A woman's voice, behind him. "Sir, please don't. That's confidential, for Mr. Powell only."

Stratton faced a young woman who had emerged from an

39

adjoining office. She had long auburn hair and brown eyes, and wore a dark blue dress with a round white collar. "You don't have to sneak a peek," she teased. "You know what's in there. Want some coffee?"

"Please." When she came back—"Watch it now, the cup's very hot"—Stratton asked, "Where did that file come from?"

"Washington. By telex. It's routine. It would please both governments to know that the person we're sending home with Dr. Wang's remains is not a smuggler or a thief or a fugitive of some sort. It's just a routine check."

"That's a pretty thick file," Stratton noted, "for routine." The coffee was much too hot to drink, but it smelled glorious.

"You're a war hero," she said. "The Pentagon writes books on its war heroes. In your case, they were happy to pass it along. Proud even. Langley, too."

"Step right up and read all about it. Hurry, hurry."

"Sometimes Steve prefers a little synopsis," she said, ignoring the sarcasm. "It saves time if I'm familiar with the material. Don't worry, I've got clearance on stuff like this."

"You know *my* name, what's yours?" Stratton asked.

"Linda," she answered. "Linda Greer. I'm vice-consul."

Linda Greer. He looked at her for a moment and wondered. This hardly seemed the time, but . . . the only women he had talked with for days had been Alice and her gaggle, and little Miss Sun. Right now, he certainly could use some company.

"Would you like to have dinner sometime?" he tried.

"No, thank you, Mr. Stratton."

"A movie?"

"The embassy movie doesn't change for another two weeks, and I've already seen it four times. Besides, you're leaving for the States on Monday morning."

Stratton sat back in the chair and tested the coffee again. Well, it was what he'd deserved. Linda disappeared. Powell walked in and crisply stationed himself at the desk.

"I'll be looking into the passport matter. I hope to have some sort of explanation by the time you leave."

"Monday morning," Stratton said.

"Linda told you. Well, good. Did she tell you the itinerary? It's Hong Kong, San Francisco, Cleveland. The body stays on the plane in Hong Kong, but you'll have a customs layover in California. We're trying to get a diplomatic waiver from Washington on that now."

Stratton did not react outwardly. Powell shifted.

"Do you have a suit and tie?" the consul asked.

Puzzled, Stratton said: "I have a tie and a blazer. I suppose it's good enough for Pan Am."

"And for the deputy minister as well," Powell said. "He'd like to see you tomorrow morning. Nine o'clock. Any taxi at the hotel will take you. Here's the address."

Powell walked Stratton to the door. Stratton got the impression that this was a vital part of his job, walking tourists to the door.

"Linda says you were at Man-ling."

"Yes," Stratton replied.

Powell asked, "Was it as bad as they say?"

"Worse," Stratton said as he walked out. "I'm sure it's all in the file."

CHAPTER 5

IN THE HOTEL COURTYARD, amid gleaming rows of
Chinese-made automobiles that looked like boxy stegosaur-
uses, off-duty waiters played uproarious catch with a red
Frisbee. Stratton sat on the stone front steps, elbows on his
knees, palms supporting his face, a brown study. He watched
without seeing. David Wang was dead and he did not know
how to mourn him. Wang had come late to Stratton's life,
and yet for a time Stratton had felt closer to him than he had
ever felt to his own father. Stratton had the feeling, without
really knowing, that he had been but one of a number of private reclamation projects Wang must have quietly undertaken
over the years at St. Edward's. In Stratton's case, it had
worked. Wang had molded a scarred young officer—no, that
was a euphemism; a cynical young killer—into the shape of a
civilized man who could honestly savor poetry and the whisper
of breeze on a pine branch. Who could sleep deeply and rise
remorseless, without scrabbling for a cigarette and a gun. Who
could even, more than a decade later, return to China, feeling
legitimate, almost comfortable, as a genuine if unheralded
and rough-hewn college professor.

But Wang had worked too well, had he not? Stratton had

42

slipped away from him, further every year. Two disparate clouds that had met improbably, intermingled and then sailed away to different horizons. Had he been back home teaching, word of David Wang's death might have provoked a few minutes of sharp but distanced regret, then hurried cancellation of classes and a trip to the funeral, complete, surely, with the trappings of a Catholicism that Wang knew and loved as much as the priests who would recite the final incantation. Here it was different. Was it cruel for Wang to have died in his native China? Or was it poetic? Regardless, Stratton felt grievously hurt by his death and fiercely protective of the body that lay somewhere in Peking, being prepared for a journey home. How banal, yet how true. In their last gossamer encounter, David had seemed so well. . . .

An insistent horn snapped the reverie. Stratton levered up off the steps and strode into the parking lot. The passenger door of a tan Toyota opened invitingly. As he slid in, his gloom began to lift.

"I'm glad you changed your mind," he said.

Linda Greer smiled. She had changed into a beige shirtwaist dress, a fetching advertisement for her long, bronzed legs that scissored with a rustle of unseen silk as she expertly maneuvered the car into bike-laden streets.

"Usually when I say 'no,' it's because I mean 'no.' When I say 'no' and mean 'yes,' I am not above confessing my mistake. One look at your face in there, and I could tell you needed someone to talk to. And I am sorry about your friend."

He gave her a curious look, then settled back against the seat. She swung the car quickly around a yellow-and-red bus bursting with empty-faced workers on their way home, then pulled sharply behind a three-wheel motorbike spewing a noxious trail of black smoke.

"Ugh," Linda said. "And the Chinese wonder why the air is so bad."

They drove past the majestic Qianmen, once the front gate of a walled Peking. Linda turned to enter the gigantic square named after the gate. Stratton's guidebook said it was ninety-eight acres.

"Postcards hardly do the place justice," Linda remarked. "You could land a plane in here."

In the vastness of the square, a handful of Chinese on their haunches nursed kites through the light summer air. The handmade kites—frogs and princes, fat fish, and a clever troop of tiny sparrows suspended from the same string—danced against the backdrop of the Forbidden City, the network of palaces that had housed imperial dynasties for six hundred years. On the left stood the stark white mausoleum where the rubber-looking remains of Chairman Mao lay under glass. Beyond the mausoleum rose the Great Hall of the People, more massive than majestic.

"The museums," Linda said, pointing. "History on the right, the Museum of the Revolution, appropriately, on the left."

"They're huge. You could lose an army in there."

"That's fitting, too. The people across the street"—she waved a cool hand toward the Great Hall—"they're perpetually worried about losing a country."

"Many things are sacred in China, of course, but not history. History is for rewriting. Take poor Emperor Qin. For centuries, history officially shat all over Emperor Qin." Linda pronounced it 'Tsin.' "He was always the example of the most savage dictator, a kind of Chinese anti-Christ. He was the nut who commissioned the sculpture of seven thousand clay soldiers to guard him in the afterlife. And he was the maniac who once ordered four hundred Confucian scholars buried alive because they wouldn't admit that he was smarter. Buried alive, can you imagine? But in the new history, that's all forgiven. Qin is the man who unified China and so he's a hero—rehabilitated two thousand years later. And his celestial army is a national treasure. What the hell, easy come, easy go . . . Hey c'mon, Stratton, come back to me, huh?"

Normally, she would have had all his attention. Linda Greer was more than a passably attractive woman. Quick, witty, assured. Stratton had made a fool of himself over that kind of woman more than once. The setting she had chosen

44

for dinner added to her allure, as she undoubtedly knew, as she tossed off crystal-clear Mandarin to a smiling waitress.

They sat on an ancient balcony overlooking a moat at the rear of the Forbidden City. It was, Linda had said, the oldest restaurant in Peking. The food, particularly a kind of shaved beef that was the house specialty, was superb. The fiery *mao tai* she had ordered when they arrived smelled like distilled sweat socks, but went down smoothly and kicked like a mule. The Great Wall white wine, heavy and a trifle too sweet, had initially doused the *mao tai* fumes, but, by the second bottle, subtly fanned them. Stratton should have felt mellow, but all he really felt was sadness.

"Tell me about Wang Bin," he said, in an effort to rouse himself.

"A year younger than David," Linda began. "A perplexing man. His pedigree in the Party—and that's what counts in China—is impeccable. Madame Wang, his mother, was one of China's earliest and most vociferous revolutionaries."

Stratton was surprised. "I knew that David's father was a man of substance in Shanghai, but I can't recall that he ever mentioned his mother."

"She was quite a lady. She had the two boys, and then gave herself—physically as well as ideologically—to the Revolution. In the early days, Mao and his friends could always be assured of a warm welcome at the Wang mansion on the Bund in naughty old Shanghai. By the time Papa Wang discovered his wife was more than a salon radical, it was too late. She had left and taken Bin with her. That must have been soon after David went abroad, because in the normal course of events Bin would have followed close behind.

"Madame Wang become the mistress of one of Mao's chief lieutenants. She actually made the famous Long March. And Wang Bin went with her, every step of the way, one of Mao's teenage soldiers. By the time the Communists won control of the country in 1949, Wang Bin was a distinguished veteran, an up-and-coming young man."

"Fascinating," Stratton said, as a mental light clicked on. "In another year, he might have gone off to school with David and none of it would ever have happened. And two years earlier that might have been David's story, too, although I can't imagine David raising his hand to strike even his worst enemy—if he ever had one."

"Like most of Mao's soldiers, Wang Bin's education had been shut off by war—although I guess most of them would never have had much schooling anyway," Linda continued. "Bin would probably have stayed in the army and become one of those semiliterate genius-generals that still run the armed forces, but Mama Wang took a hand. He entered the University of Peking and became a major figure in the Party there."

"That must have seemed pretty tame after what he had been through. What'd he study, theology?" It was a pale joke, but a joke nonetheless.

"Fine arts, if you can believe that. Of course, he didn't stay long. During the Korean War somebody remembered that he spoke English—for the past two centuries all Shanghai Wangs have apparently spoken English—and back into the army he went as an interrogator of captured Americans. After that, there were a succession of jobs, mostly Party positions of increasing influence, although he did have an occasional artsy job here and there. I guess that's what did him in."

"Did him in?"

"Yes, sir. In the mid-sixties, along comes the Cultural Revolution—you know, Mao's attempt to revive a revolution that was choking on its own red tape. It was incredibly destructive madness, of course, turned the Chinese universe topsy-turvy for nearly ten years. In the midst of it, Wang Bin just vanished. Turned out he had been attacked by the Red Guards because he was an intellectual—crime enough in those days. He apparently spent four or five years slopping hogs in a commune out west. Didn't get rehabilitated until the mid-seventies."

"And now he's back on the track again."

"Well, not exactly." Linda Greer chose her words with care. "He is a powerful man. It looks as though his culture job is a kind of front for deeper Communist Party activities. He's rumored to have his own little band of enforcers to patrol his domain. You've heard about the political struggle that's going on around here, I'm sure."

"A little." McCarthy had given him a beginner's lesson. Stratton wished he had paid more attention.

"Well, as far as we can figure out, all the guys Wang Bin has ridden with over the past thirty years are being systematically shot out of the saddle."

"But not him," Stratton anticipated.

"Not him, at least not yet. Maybe not ever, who knows? He should be struggling for his political life and instead, while all sorts of political shit flies, he invites his long-lost brother to come from America—that certainly could be used against him—and spends all his time assembling an archaeological exhibit nobody but us cares much about."

"An overture to old Uncle Sam, right?"

"Maybe. I wish I knew."

Stratton emptied his glass, and refilled both of theirs.

"How long have you been a spook, Linda?"

Linda Greer blushed.

"I'm not. I'm a vice-consul."

"Sure you are."

"Not convinced, huh?" she tried again.

"Try that on some little old tourist lady who has lost her luggage."

"About five years, if you must know. And I am not a spook. I am a case officer."

"Then get off my case, officer." He watched her hackles rise.

"What do you mean by that?"

He reached across and took her hand.

"Linda, it took me all of five minutes to figure out that you didn't pick me up just because of my sad face, but I only just now realized exactly what it is you want. Linda, I was recruited and trained and conned and sent to the wolves by guys who were playing nasty games while you were still in Pampers. This is what I would call a transitory recruitment."

"Okay, wiseass, how does it go?"

"Something like this. Could Mr. Stratton, who is known to us and thought, on the basis of previous service, to be reli-

47

able, interject into his conversation with Wang Bin tomorrow questions that might establish Comrade Wang's view of the United States, such as: How does Comrade Wang foresee the development of relations between our two great countries in this time of great international stress? And, providing Comrade Wang seemed receptive to that particular conversation, perhaps expressing veiled admiration for the United States, a second approach might be made. And perhaps a third, and a fourth, each one a little deeper until one day somebody, say a beautiful, art-loving vice-consul, would hold her breath and try to recruit Comrade Wang." Stratton stared out over the sleeping canal. "Actually, it's not a bad gambit."

"Gee, thanks."

Stratton thought aloud. "Let's see, if Wang will deal and he wins this current round of intrigue, you're in clover— you've got a source at a high level. And if he loses, Wang might be persuaded to accept asylum in the United States— 'defect' has a nasty ring to it, don't you think? He would be a man with a grudge against the guys who forced him out. He would provide great inside intelligence up until the time he left, and knowledgeable guesses about how things might go from there."

Linda Greer assayed a wan smile. "You could have been a great one, Stratton. It's all there in your file."

"And does the file also say that I left in such disgust that, if I had stayed, I probably would have blown my head off?"

"Or somebody else's."

"And no doubt the file also says I am now a straight-and-narrow, almost middle-aged college professor who hardly ever does anything more adventuresome than jaywalking?"

"That, too."

"So why bother?"

"A spur-of-the-moment thing. Nothing we set up. We thought the fact you deliberately came to China might mean you were bored, but we were willing to let it go at that. No contact. But suddenly you have natural access—much better than any of us could ever get—to a major player in the Chinese drama. So we thought we'd try—although we had a hunch you'd say no."

48

"And all this while I was supposed to think I was here in this romantic setting because of your vast powers of sympathy. Or was it my dashing figure and rugged good looks?"

She had the grace to smile.

"Stratton, Thomas Henry. D.O.B. et cetera, et cetera. Married the former Carol Webster, pediatrician. Rancorous divorce after nine years and one child, Jason, age six. . . ."

"He's nearly eight."

"Okay, Mr. Rugged Looks." Linda Greer took his hand with both of her own. "Will you do it, Tom?"

"What's in it for you, Linda? Little gold star on that pretty forehead? Big desk at Langley, maybe. One case is all it takes, right? I know how it works."

"Do you really?" She was hurt. Stratton instantly regretted the nasty jabs.

"How do you think I got this job, Tom? I got it because I'm good, and I've got some guts. And I've risked my ass once or twice, literally. I'm no war hero, and maybe I don't have your scars, Tom, but I've got a few little nightmares of my own. No ribbons, no plaques on the wall, just some pretty rotten dreams. And, yes, I want out of Peking. I want to work in a place where the twentieth century has arrived, where I can leave the city without a dog tag or a babysitter, where I can have a *life*, like a normal woman. So the answer is yes, I want this case. I want *him*. Wang Bin."

"Linda, I'm sorry . . ." But nothing gave way. No tears, no rage. Just a trace of color in her cheeks—and again the question.

"Tom, will you do it? Please."

"No," Stratton said. "I've already got my ribbons, remember?" A bloody stage, a pitchfork, a scream. He remembered.

"Nothing I can say or do to change your mind?"

"No."

"Shit."

They did not speak of it again. Leaving the restaurant, Linda Greer once again became an earnest tour guide. She drove competently on parking lights, dipping here and there into seemingly unpeopled alleys. Stratton had lost all sense of direction by the time Linda wheeled through a gate set in a twelve-foot brick wall. She nodded to two armed soldiers posted there, as though to trusted doormen.

"The diplomatic compound," she announced. "This is where I live."

Stratton waited.

She killed the motor and half-turned in the driver's seat. Her arm crawled up Stratton's shoulder and around his neck.

They kissed.

"That would be delightful, but the answer is still *no*."

"Mata Hari goes off duty after dessert," she murmured. "Besides, Peking is a lonely post, and you aren't bad-looking—in an almost middle-aged, professorial kind of way. You think you're the *only* one who needs some company?"

Stratton didn't believe a word of it, but he went.

CHAPTER 6

SHE DROVE ALONE through the night. The great city slept. Waxen pools of light marked a twenty-four-hour dumpling restaurant that was a nocturnal refuge of the young men and women who drove the number-one buses; a mindless twenty-mile route, back and forth endlessly, along Changan, and nary a turn. Her groin ached deliciously. Her mouth felt bruised. Maybe she had fibbed about going off duty, but she'd told the truth about one thing: she *had* needed the company. Peking was not exactly swarming with available American men. She yearned to be back in bed, but the digital clock on the dashboard read 3:15. Linda Greer was late.

She had roused Stratton with a lie, saying her reputation would be ruined if the night guards' report showed that a visitor to Miss Greer's apartment had not left. He had gone willingly enough—a goodbye kiss and a hug.

Her route led through the northern quarter of the city, and she knew it by heart. She turned right at a corner marked by a dusty bicycle shop and flashed her lights before a gray metal gate set firmly into the usual Peking-anonymous concrete wall. The gate creaked open at the urging of an old man in worker blue. She—or some other consular officer—was expected on duly appointed diplomatic rounds.

After nearly a year in Peking, she still did not understand why the Chinese had to do it in the dead of night. Was it distaste? Or left-over superstition that had survived the arrival of the Communist era? She had asked, at first, but all of her questions had been answered with a shrug. This is how it has always been done. After a while, she, too, had learned to shrug. By embassy tradition, it was a job reserved to the junior member of the consular corps. If that happened to be a woman, who also happened to be an intelligence officer, too bad. In another month, a new junior vice-consul would report for duty and Linda Greer would drive no more by night in Peking.

There were no preliminaries. The Chinese had no more liking for this chore than she.

"I am Miss Greer of the American Embassy. Where is Mr. Li?"

"Mr. Li is ill tonight. My name is Mr. Hu."

Linda nodded. Hu's on first, a pockmarked man with a cowlick. She was glad she had worn a skirt. Her panties were damp with the aftermath of love; no, of good old-fashioned, hard-and-fast sex. For a wild moment Linda imagined driving to Stratton's hotel, rushing to his room on some pretext and . . . no, that would never do. That ruggedly aloof professor with the scarred body and great stamina was not for keeping; strictly a half-night stand. Still, it was better to think of him than to contemplate her late-night diplomatic duty.

"I believe there are two," she said primly, waving a pair of manila folders.

Mr. Hu nodded. It was not unusual. The average was about twelve a year, but they tended to cluster in the peak tourist months. Twelve ducks.

The inner room was chilly, smelling of things Linda Greer never thought about. The welder, too, was new to Linda. She thought of asking Mr. Hu if the entire crew had been changed, but didn't bother.

"Friedman, Molly R., Fort Lauderdale, Florida," she read from the file.

52

Mr. Hu gestured. The lid was open. Linda looked, nodded.

"Wang, David T., Pittsville, Ohio." Her own voice seemed strained.

"We have already begun on that one."

"I am required to see it first."

"You were late."

"That is procedure."

"It is very hot."

A Chinese standoff. Linda could insist. They would shout and argue and, finally, with ill grace, they would probably snap the welds and open the lid. Linda had a sudden vision of herself, screaming like a harridan in Mandarin in the foreigners' morgue in Peking at the deadest hour before dawn. She shivered and surrendered.

"Very well," she said.

Mr. Hu nodded. The welder, a stocky, middle-aged woman, twirled a knob and ignited her torch.

Then, as procedure dictated, Linda watched in the eerie, smoking blue light of cascading sparks as the welder worked methodically, up one side and down the other. When she had finished, Linda checked to make sure that the labels were correct—that was really the most important part of her night's work. Neither coffin would be opened again, but it would never do to dispatch heart attack victim Wang—Stratton's friend—to Florida, or obese Mrs. Friedman, victim of complications of a broken hip on the Great Wall, to Ohio.

Linda Greer walked with cowlicked Mr. Hu to a small office. There, with a pen and a seal, she testified, in parallel English and Chinese documents that Linda May Greer, consular officer of the United States of America, had witnessed the sealing of two caskets and certified their contents. She drove home in the breaking dawn, trying to think of sex, but the images would not come and the effort left her feeling dry and brittle.

The setting was exactly as Linda Greer had predicted.

"It's a ritual, Tom. All official meetings in all parts of China are staged exactly the same way," she had said. "Maybe it's something they borrowed from the Russians early on—or from the emperors—but it is literally a case of 'See one, you've seen them all.' "

Wang Bin had sent a car to the hotel. A Red Flag, no less, one of those dying-breed hand-tooled lustrous black limousines that are such a conspicuous status symbol in China that they have their own relaxed set of traffic regulations. The driver wore white gloves and had no English. He deposited Stratton at the apex of a circular driveway at the entrance to the museum. A young man with bottle-bottom glasses sprang for the door.

"Welcome, Professor Stratton. My name is Mr. Zhou. Comrade Wang is waiting for you. Follow me, please."

They passed quickly through a marbled lobby bristling with watchers, turned left immediately, and left again at the first doorway.

The formal reception room was just as Linda had sketched it: long and narrow, filled by two lines of parallel overstuffed chairs and sofas in gray-brown wrapping. Between them ran a set of low coffee tables. Before each seat was a flowered tea mug, an ashtray and an ornate wooden box of tea leaves. On the wall was a large mural of the traditional dwarfed-by-nature theme.

Inside the doorway stood Wang Bin, a gently rounded ghost of his brother. From a few steps away, the resemblance to David was startling; nonplussed, Stratton faltered at the door. Wang Bin motioned him in kindly.

As they shook hands, Stratton saw the differences. Wang Bin's face seemed leaner and older than David's; the hair was shorter of course, but also thinner, and more liberally dashed with gray at the temples. The deputy minister's bearing, in a crisp gray Mao suit with a black mourner's band on one arm, was rock-hard military. But the greatest difference welled in the eyes. To look at David Wang's almost-almond eyes was to have seen wisdom, humor, compassion. In Wang Bin's eyes Stratton saw intelligence, strength—and something else. A certain intrepid determination that had no doubt stood him in good stead all these years.

Stratton and Wang sat at right angles in adjoining chairs and the interpreter took up a priest-at-confession pose to one side.

54

Stratton's last private meeting with a Chinese official had been with a snarling, saucer-faced man who'd punctuated shouting questions with blows from a rubber truncheon. When the time had come to leave, Stratton had shot him, twice.

Wang Bin was speaking. Stratton leaned forward attentively, letting the sibilant Mandarin wash over him in uncomprehended waves. A girl in pigtails and a white jacket materialized. Gently, she eased the top off Stratton's tea cup and added boiling water from a thermos. She soundlessly recovered the cup. Tea leaves had already been placed in the cup.

". . . to meet a distinguished scholar such as yourself and hopes you are enjoying your stay in China," the interpreter hissed.

"Please tell Comrade Wang that I am pleased and excited to be in China. It is a fascinating country and my trip has been very educational."

A pause for translation. Wang's response. Then the translation floating back toward Stratton. An agonizing way to communicate, he reflected, about as lively as geriatric shuffleboard.

"Comrade Wang asks if this is your first trip to China."

"Tell Comrade Wang that, yes, this is my first trip. I have always wanted to come before, but it was too expensive." Stratton had told that same lie dozens of times. He would die proclaiming it. And why not? The first time he had come without a passport.

"Comrade Wang asks, What cities besides Peking have you visited?"

The conversation meandered like the Yangtze for nearly fifteen minutes; three offers of cigarettes, two cups of tea and banalities uncounted. Stratton let it wander. It was Wang Bin's ball park, and if he was in no hurry, neither was Stratton. The art historians had voted unanimously to spend their last morning in Peking—a rare, unprogrammed three hours—on a return visit to the Friendship Store.

"Comrade Wang says his brother spoke well of you to him. He said you were a treasured former student and a distinguished professor. Comrade Wang says he is pleased."

Stratton smiled.

"Tell Comrade Wang that David had many spiritual children like me and that some of them are truly distinguished. I am not, but I mourn David as I would my own father."

When the translation ended, Wang said something to the interpreter that brought him to his feet. Stratton, too, started to rise, thinking the colorless encounter ended. Wang stopped him with a gesture of his mourning-banded arm. When the door closed behind the young interpreter, Wang lit a cigarette and blew smoke at the ceiling.

"I would like to speak of my brother, Professor Stratton. I believe we can dispense with protocol," he said in nearly accentless English. Stratton did not comment on the language shift. Wang had never allowed the interpreter to complete a translation of anything Stratton had said.

"You will be returning with my brother to the United States, the land he made his nation. Many people will ask about his death. I will tell you, so you may tell them."

"I would like to know."

"Let me start with life, Professor Stratton. That is where all death begins, does it not? In life? Once we had been close, my brother and I, close in that special way that only brothers know. I can still see the cobblestone courtyard in Shanghai where we would play.

"We took our piano lessons and studied our math and our English and when no one was looking we would sneak away to play by the river. We loved the river. So much life, excitement. Once we saw a knife fight between two sailors. Then came the day for my brother to leave. Back to the river, but this time in rickshas with trunks and my brother in a Western suit. We tried not to cry, but we cried and my father was angry. At first my brother wrote every week. After my parents had done with them, I would take those letters and read them until they entered my memory. But already the Revolution was beginning, Professor Stratton, and the letters became more infrequent. Soon I left with my mother to join the people's struggle. I heard no more from my American brother for many, many years. Some good years, and a few that were very bad. For several years my job was to collect night soil in a big barrel that I pushed on a cart. Do you know what night soil is?"

56

"Human excrement, collected for fertilizer."

"Yes, I am glad to see that you have done your lessons, Professor. Human excrement, to be collected by leaders in punishment when the Revolution is betrayed by fools. I know you have read of the Cultural Revolution, Professor, but it was worse than anything that is written about it. Much worse. Then came some good years, and now . . . who knows?" Wang Bin slipped some tea and lit a fresh cigarette from the butt of the old. "My brother . . . one may lose touch with a brother, but one never forgets him. Brothers are part of you, like parents. I have heard that when parents go to visit their grown children in America, they are asked to pay for their meals, Professor Stratton. Is that true?"

"Certainly not."

"I thought not. It is a lie then, published in our newspapers to make people less envious of America. Revolutions require many lies, you know." Wang Bin smiled without mirth.

"One day, I decided to write my brother. I cannot tell you why, exactly, except that he was my brother and we are—were—old men. That must have been three years ago; a friend in our embassy in Washington got me the address. At first, the letters were respectful, distant, like the opening moves in a game of chess. But, eventually, they became letters between two brothers. I invited David to come for a visit. Hundreds of thousands of overseas Chinese have returned for visits to their families in the past few years, from America, Canada, Europe, everywhere. Did you know that?"

"It must have been very emotional, your reunion with David."

"Oh, yes, it was. A wonderful experience, happy and sad. Last week, when I saw my brother for the first time in nearly fifty years, I wept. So did he, although Chinese do not display their emotions publicly. Americans are much more open about that, aren't they?"

"Yes, I suppose so."

"As David—that was not my brother's given name, but that is what he asked me to call him—as David may have told you, I was unfortunately not in Peking when he arrived, but in Xian, a city in the west. Do you know it?"

Stratton shook his head.

"A beautiful city where the emperors lived when Peking was still just a village. So David flew to Xian and there we reunited. We wept, and laughed, and at night after dinner we would go to his room, drink tea and remember; be little boys again."

"Did he show any signs of being sick?" Stratton asked.

"Only the excitement, at first. But then, perhaps it was the day before we returned to Peking, he complained of pains in his chest. We sat for a while and then continued our walk; we were in a park. He took a little pill, I think, and when I asked him if something was wrong, he laughed and said he had some trouble with his heart, but that it was not serious. His doctor had joked, David said, that the problem was just grave enough for him to take two or three little pills a day for the next forty years."

"I hadn't known that," Stratton said.

"Well, he tried to do too much, you see. He was so excited about being in China again and being with me. He tried to do too much, rushing everywhere. I tried to slow him down, but you know how David was. . . ."

"Yes. Were you with him the last night?"

"At the beginning. Some of my colleagues here had arranged a special banquet for us in honor of my brother—a Peking duck banquet. You will forgive my patriotism, Professor Stratton, but I am assured by men who know that Peking duck is the single finest dish in the world. It is also, for Chinese people, quite expensive. My brother and I were both moved by my colleagues' gesture. It was a wonderful meal, one I shall remember always. Afterwards, I went with David back to his hotel, but I did not join him for tea. I had a meeting."

Wang Bin's eyes again strayed to the ceiling.

"Someone came for me there to say that David had been stricken. I rushed to the hospital, but the comrade doctors said he was dead when he arrived. Heart, they said."

"I'm sorry," said Stratton.

"Your embassy has inquired about David's passport. The comrades at the hospital told me that intravenous solution had

58

spilled on the passport during the attempt to save David. An apprentice, not knowing what it was, threw it away. He will be punished."

Stratton sipped some of his own tea. He had the overwhelming sensation that he was being lied to, fed a carefully contrived script. But what was the lie? And, more important, why?

"Tell me about America, Professor Stratton."

The request caught Stratton off guard.

"Well, how—I mean—what would you like to know?"

"I would like to know something of the truth, something between the lies of the Revolution and the lies of the American Embassy. It is not often that a senior Chinese official may speak frankly with an American without someone present to listen."

Better natural access than any of us will ever get, Linda Greer had said. Well, why not?

"I am partial, of course, Comrade Minister, but it is one of the few places on earth where a man is actually free. Think what you like. Do what you like. Which is not to say that it is a nation without problems. Many people never think at all, and even more talk without having anything to say. It is a beautiful and powerful and vigorous and violent country."

"Yes, I have always admired the vigor without understanding the violence."

"You must come to visit."

"I would like that, but my duties here and"—his hand waved at the window, toward the Communist Party headquarters across the massive square—"elsewhere do not permit it. But tell me about my brother's America. Tell me about the special place he will be buried."

"The Arbor," Stratton said. David's pride.

Soon after he had appeared at St. Edward's as a young assistant professor, David Wang had bought an abandoned dairy farm on the outskirts of Pittsville. When he hadn't been teaching, he'd begun to work the land. Not to farm it, or forest it exactly, but to manicure it, to build it into a place of beauty according to his own orderly view. David had planted stands of pine and maple, birches and oak, as well as exotic trees he grew from seed. A clear stream bubbled through the Arbor into an exquisite formal lake on the lee side of a gentle hill. David Wang had done most of the work himself, with simple tools. When he hadn't been in the classroom, he could be found on his land or deep in an armchair in the old white clapboard farmhouse that had no locks on the doors.

Over the years the town had grown; tract houses now flanked the Arbor on two sides and an interstate lanced through an adjoining ridgetop. But nothing molested the tranquillity and the beauty of David Wang's oasis, and nothing ever would. Gradually it had become part park, part botanical garden, a place of fierce civic pride. Stratton could remember spring weekends when sixty people, from rough-hewn farmers in bib overalls to shapely college girls in cutoffs, would appear at the Arbor as volunteer gardeners. And how many St. Edward's coeds, over the years, had surrendered their virginity on an aromatic bed of pine needles? Stratton smiled at his own memories. Anyone was free to wander the land, and no one dared molest it. This was where David Wang wanted to be buried.

Stratton spoke haltingly at first, and then with a rush of details. The Arbor was a place of both beauty and meaning.

Wang Bin displayed such lively interest that for an instant Stratton wondered, absurdly, whether the deputy minister believed that his brother had willed him the land. Everybody in Ohio who knew about the Arbor also knew that David Wang had publicly promised it to the college.

As he talked, Stratton mentally weighed what he knew about David's death against what Wang Bin had told him. There was something . . .

And then he had it.

". . . would liked to have enjoyed it at David's side," Wang Bin was saying.

"Yes, of course." But what did it mean, damn it?

Wang Bin looked at Stratton sharply, as though he had divined the wandering of a perplexed mind. From the table he took a leather-bound volume that looked like a diary. He handed it to Stratton.

60

"Here, this is my brother's journal. Apparently he was addicted to writing something nearly every day. I was interested in his first impressions of China. I would be grateful if you could take it with you." Wang Bin rose. "And I am in your debt, Professor Stratton, for agreeing to accompany David's body. I am sure your presence will smooth the formalities. I am assured that the body has been prepared to the most exacting standards."

"Yes, of course."

"I know little of such things, Professor, since corpses are cremated in China, but I believe my brother would have appreciated a simple ceremony as quickly as it can be arranged. For my part, I think it is particularly fitting that he be buried in the Chinese coffin in which he makes his last journey."

"That should be no problem. But, look, about my accompanying the body. I'm not sure . . ." Stratton wanted some fresh air, some room to think.

"Why?" Wang Bin asked sharply. He made no effort to hide the strength behind the question.

Stratton improvised.

"This has been very emotional for me. The thought of David's body riding in the cargo hold of the same plane . . . I'm not sure that I'm up to it."

"It is all arranged, Professor. My car will call for you in ample time for the flight. Everything is taken care of."

"But . . ."

"You must." Stratton could taste the menace.

Later, Stratton would not remember leaving the museum, or whether he walked back to the hotel or had been driven. What he remembered with clarity was sitting on the bed, staring out the hotel window, puzzling, and the lie—and wondering why.

If you were a man in your sixties with serious heart trouble, would you go to China, where tourism is rigorous and health facilities are primitive by American standards? Perhaps, if it was to see a long-lost brother.

But, if you did go, would you remember those life-giving pills that you had to take two or three times a day "for the

61

next forty years"? Of course. And if you took them with you, would you take them for the entire trip and a reserve supply, just in case? Again, yes.

And there logic exploded. Stratton had examined David Wang's effects with care. The only medication he had found was an unopened bottle of Excedrin.

CHAPTER 7

GRASS, like nearly everything else in China, is subject to political interpretation. Historically, the Chinese have taken a dim view of grass. In Peking's parks, the dirt is swept daily since cleanliness is prized, but gardeners relentlessly uproot any tuft of grass. Grass breeds disease, generations of Chinese have been taught. Additionally, Communist doctrine teaches that grass is decadent since it is usually associated with leisured classes and generates exploitation—one man hiring another to cut it.

In the pragmatic years, though, when the town fathers of Peking were allowed to gaze at their city without ideological blinders, they recoiled at what they saw. Peking, capital and presumed showcase of the most populous nation on earth, was a mess—overcrowded, disorganized, dreadfully polluted.

An emerging generation of Chinese environmentalists has sought to repair the wreckage by planting trees and, yes, grass. But history does not die without a fight. So it is that on some weeks students at Chinese elementary schools can hear a lecture one day from an earnest ecologist on the virtues of

63

grass and another from a functionary of public health on the merits of its destruction.

Tom Stratton, amused by the ongoing struggle between tradition and modernization, had early on spotted a fresh plot of grass on the shoulder of a new highway overpass near his hotel.

It was on this hard-won and possibly temporary bit of green that he sat cross-legged in the heat of a summer's afternoon to read David Wang's journal.

AUGUST 10.

Peking overwhelms me, and it is only my second day. Walking the streets, I realized how cluttered and musty my memories have become. As a child, I visited this city a dozen times, and for all these years, I have carried visions of its history and art, visions of brilliant colors and vibrant people.

Yet that is not what I have found so far. What has struck me, instead, has been the crush of masses of people—all seemingly in a hurry and all almost faceless amid the brownness of the city. Each block seems to have at least one noisy factory. Brick chimneys spew so much filthy smoke that hundreds of Chinese customarily wear surgical masks, called koujiao, *to protect their throats and lungs from infection. For a city with so few automobiles and trucks, I have never seen, or breathed, such foul air.*

I suppose that this is one of the prices that the government has chosen to pay for industrialization, and I must admit that I have seen several great technological accomplishments. This morning, for example, I made a trip to the Grand Canal, which stretches eleven hundred miles to Hangchow. It is the longest man-made waterway in the world and many Chinese believe that it is more of a masterpiece than even the Great Wall.

During my childhood, however, the Grand Canal never was fully utilized because it had become blocked with silt and impossible to navigate at many key ports. My father told me it had been that way all during his life; my grandfather, too, could not remember the Grand Canal in its prime.

Yet, I learned, under the Communists the canal has been

64

redredged during the last twenty years and is now thriving from Peking to its terminus. The economic benefits of this must be incalculable for cargo transport, as well as agriculture. Yet I fear that the human costs of the intense restoration program also were incalculable; in that area, my guide provided no information.

Tomorrow I meet my niece for the first time. Of course I am nervous, but I am also nervous about seeing my brother again. With so much on my mind, it has been difficult to absorb and appreciate the changes in this ancient place.

AUGUST 11.

The most disturbing thing just happened. When I returned to my room, I discovered that someone had searched my belongings. Nothing was missing, but several things are out of order. My passport, which I had left under a pile of undershirts, had obviously been examined and replaced. I found it in another drawer. I complained to the room attendant, but he seemed uninterested. In all, it has been a stressful day.

This morning, at the former Democracy Wall, I struck up a conversation with a young man whose father had once been prominent in the Communist Party. Perhaps because the man could see by my clothing that I was an overseas Chinese, a huh chiao, *he spoke with surprising candor.*

He told me that his father had once enjoyed a promising career, that he had risen in the bureaucracy from a street cadre to being a Party officer of some standing. One night, while dining with several comrades at a restaurant here in Peking, the Party man recited a poem that he had written to celebrate the Cultural Revolution. It was an amateurish but lively verse that extolled Mao and glorified the progress of the Party. The last lines of his father's poem, the young man told me, said:

> *And in the radiant future, all China's children*
> *Will sing in freedom and dance in universal happiness.*

Several weeks passed, the young man recounted, and then his father was suddenly arrested by the army. He was stripped of his Party membership and charged with counterrevolu-

65

tionary behavior. At his trial, the prosecutors charged that the man's poetry encouraged laziness and immorality. Why? Because good, strong Party workers would never have the time, or desire, for song and dance. Such frivolous things, the prosecutors said, belong only in the theater.

The man, whose name was Cheng Hua, was never given a chance to speak in his own defense. He was not even permitted to introduce the complete poem into evidence to demonstrate his loyalty and love for the government.

Cheng was sentenced to eight years in a prison camp. His son told me he is not allowed any visitors, but letters are delivered once every two months. One of his father's closest friends is the man who turned him in, the young man told me. This story made me profoundly depressed.

At lunchtime I met my niece, Kangmei. She is a beautiful girl of twenty-three, slender, with a luminous smile and a very quick mind. Unlike most Chinese women, she likes jeans and silky shirts—from Hong Kong, she told me. She was fascinated by my descriptions of the United States, so much so that I could scarcely get her to tell me anything about life in China. Of her father—my brother—she said little. "He is a man of power and achievement," Kangmei said—but, of course, this I already know.

She described her studies at the Foreign Languages Institute and impressed me with her flawless English. In a few months, she will graduate and assume a prestigious job as a government translator. Kangmei said she is looking forward greatly to the travel opportunities, and to meeting more European and American visitors.

Finally, near the end of our lunch, I asked my niece about the young man whom I had met at Democracy Wall. I told her his sad story.

"Such events were not uncommon," she remarked. "The boy's father was very unwise to reveal his poem, even to friends. Within the Party, many cadres rise and prosper by informing on fellow workers. Everyone should be cautious."

"But it seems so wrong," I replied.

"Your outlook is different," Kangmei said. "We who live

66

here understand. There is freedom only for the old men who exploit the Chinese people."

As we talked more, I learned that my niece is a woman of firm opinions. She possesses a keen, questioning intellect— and I am heartened by it. We promised to meet again after I had seen Wang Bin.

AUGUST 12.

Today I walked down the Avenue of Eternal Tranquility, toward the western wall of the Forbidden City. I had a notion to visit the palaces, but first I stopped to buy a knitted hat from a vendor named Hong.

I noticed that one of his legs had been removed at the hip. Because of his youthfulness—he appeared about thirty—such a handicap seemed unusual. I asked him if he had been in a bicycle accident, which is common in the city.

Hong smiled and said no, he had lost the leg as a teenager. The year was 1966. His father was a prominent scientist. One of his colleagues, a Party member, was very jealous. He accused Hong's father of secretly passing scientific papers to pro-Western publications in Taiwan.

The Red Guards came to the scientist's apartment. Hong, who was seventeen and full of fire, took a punch at one of the intruders. The youth was quickly knocked to the floor, and beaten so badly with the butt of a rifle that his leg bones were shattered. His father was put in detention for eighteen months, and was freed only after his accuser was arrested— for lying about the loyalty of another fellow worker.

Hong told me that he bears no ill will toward the Red Guards. I find that difficult to believe.

Later this afternoon, I had a marvelous surprise by the lake at the Summer Palace. I ran into an old friend, Thomas Stratton. He once was a student of mine at St. Edward's, and now teaches art history at a college in New England. Tom is visiting China with a group of art historians and he is understandably eager to break away from the entourage as soon as possible.

I promised him a personal tour of Peking, as soon as I re-

67

turn from Xian. There's some wonderful Qing hung *porcelain on display in a state gallery near the Heping. I think we'll stop there first.*

Tomorrow is the biggest day of my trip. In the morning, I fly to Xian where I am to meet my brother at eleven sharp. After lunch, we will tour the archaeological site of the tomb of the Emperor Qin.

I'm thrilled about visiting this historical dig, but I'm even more excited about seeing Wang Bin again. He is only a year younger, but history and political fortunes have cast us centuries apart. Even without knowing him, I fear that we will be the inverse of each other. Perhaps not. Perhaps the journey backward to our Chinese childhood is not so great. It is easy to remember little Bin's face as a boy. But it has been fifty years since we were together in my father's home. And, in that time, I have not seen so much as a photograph. His invitation was so unexpected that I didn't know how to respond.

I think it will be a powerful reunion.

Tom Stratton closed his friend's journal and walked thoughtfully back to his hotel.

The words faithfully belonged to David, and reading them freshened Stratton's grief. It was so typical of his old friend, he thought, to be moved more by the people of Peking than its art or scenery. David Wang had not returned for the temples and tombs of China, but for the people like Cheng and Hong. Each day had brought new faces, new chances to learn: What is it really like? What have I missed? Should I have come back sooner?

But David Wang was a circumspect man; not all of what he saw and heard would be recorded in his notebook—of this Stratton was sure. The professor had probably altered the names of the Chinese to protect them from reprisals. He had also carefully refrained from political commentary that could backfire against his brother, the deputy minister.

But the journal ended too abruptly.

It contained no mention of David Wang's trip to Xian, or of his reunion with his brother. Stratton was baffled, for the professor unfailingly wrote in the notebook each night before going to bed. Why—full of such emotion, and dazzled by exotic sights—would David have forsaken this habit while on this most important trip?

Opening the journal again in his room, Stratton flipped to the last written pages. Something caught his eye. He retrieved a metal fingernail file from his luggage and slipped it between the pages, pressing toward the spine of the notebook. The binding easily gave way, and the pages separated in loose stacks.

Stratton ran a finger across the inside borders of the paper. It felt sticky. He held one page to his nose. The glue was pungent, and new. Someone had pried Wang's journal apart, and then glued it back together so it would appear undisturbed. No ragged stubs revealed where the missing pages had been.

It was a professional job, Tom Stratton thought. Almost perfect.

"Every time I see you, you're riding solo," Jim McCarthy said with a cannon laugh. "Your tour group really must be wall-to-wall losers, huh?"

Stratton accepted McCarthy's offer of a bottle of Peking-brewed Coca-Cola.

"Almost like home," the newsman said. "Now where did you want me to take you?"

Stratton said, "The Foreign Languages Institute."

"And what," McCarthy said, "do you plan to do there? Stare at the walls? Pose for pictures with a few soldiers outside the gate? It's a restricted area, baby. No Yanks allowed. It's definitely not on the tour, yours or anybody else's."

Stratton told McCarthy about David Wang.

"Death by duck, right? That's what Powell said, I bet."

"Yes," Stratton replied. "How did you know?"

"Because the bastard ripped the lead off one of my stories to steal that phrase. Fucking cretins at State, no imagination. Suppose I should be flattered."

"So there really is such a thing?"

"Sure." McCarthy pried open the Coke on a desk drawer handle and guzzled half. "Just your basic tourist burnout,

69

really. The Peking roast duck dinner gives it a nice twist, though. I wrote the story two years ago and the stats have held up. Quite a few elderly Americans die every year in the great China adventure, but it's not a trend that gets much publicity. I remember one old geezer who arrived lugging a heavy suitcase and went home inside it."

"Huh?"

"His wife had him cremated and continued the tour—said he would have wanted it that way."

Stratton blanched.

"Hey, Stratton, I don't mean to sound like a total prick about it. I'm sorry about your friend, really I am. But what's it got to do with the Foreign Languages school?"

"David's niece is a student there."

McCarthy whistled. "It's a tough school to get into."

"Her father is Wang Bin, a deputy minister. David's younger brother."

"Right, I remember now."

"The girl saw David shortly before he left for Xian to meet Bin. I want to talk to her, just to make sure everything was all right." Stratton decided not to mention the journal or the passport.

McCarthy said, "I'm not exactly a low-profile character in this town. More like the Jolly Red Giant. With me at your side, you don't stand a fucking prayer of getting in.

"But I tell you what. Go with my driver. He'll take you to the gate and haggle on your behalf. He speaks some English and he's worked miracles for me, but don't get your hopes up. You might have to settle for leaving a note—and then it could be another four weeks before you get an answer. I'm not kidding. Watching this government in action is like watching a bad ballet performed in molasses."

Stratton sat in the backseat trying to look important while McCarthy's driver argued with a guard at the Foreign Languages Institute. After several minutes, the driver, Xiu, shuffled to the car with a furrowed brow.

"It is not possible, Mr. Stratton."

"Why not?"

70

"He says it is a study hour. The students are in their dormitories and cannot be disturbed."

Stratton sighed. "Tell him I am a friend of the family. I have come to offer my condolences at the death of her uncle. I will be most insulted if I am not permitted just a few minutes."

Xiu nodded somberly and tracked once more toward the gatehouse. He came back smiling. "A few minutes, Mr. Stratton. Can you wait?"

Soon, a young woman appeared. The guard motioned toward the car and spoke rapidly. Then he waved stiffly at Stratton.

David Wang had not embellished his journal; his niece, Kangmei, was indeed a beautiful woman. Her jet-black hair, daringly long by Peking standards, fell past her shoulders. Her eyes were bright, and her features were elegant, almost regal.

"I was a good friend of your uncle," he began.

"Yes. Stratton," she said. Her eyes worked on him.

"David was a good man, a great scholar," Stratton said. "I felt I needed to—"

The guard shifted his feet and peered up into Stratton's face.

"You wish to talk?" Kangmei asked.

"If it's possible."

"It is."

"At my hotel?"

"Not a good choice, Mr. Stratton." Her English was excellent and self-assured. "Meet me in an hour at the Tiananmen Gate. Don't tell anyone. Have the driver take you back to the hotel, then walk."

Stratton eyed the guard anxiously.

Kangmei almost smiled. "Don't worry, they don't speak a word of English." Then she was off, her hair bouncing lightly. It was a Western walk. A wonderful walk.

Stratton was ten minutes early. Kangmei arrived precisely on time, the trait of a good Chinese. She parked her bicycle in a guarded sidewalk lot and locked it.

71

"Just like Boston," Stratton said.

"Excuse me?"

"Thieves, I mean."

Kangmei shrugged. "Bicycles are expensive. Come with me, Mr. Stratton. We are going on a tour of the Forbidden City."

"But I had hoped to talk—"

Again her eyes stopped him. "Please," she said, "we will talk."

At an imperial red kiosk, Stratton paid for his ticket with ten fen. Kangmei spoke to the cashier in Chinese and was allowed to enter without paying.

"I told her I'm your guide," she explained, escorting Stratton through the broad entrance tunnel. "I saw my Uncle David two days before he left for Xian. We had a very nice talk. He was very thoughtful."

"He mentioned you in his journal," Stratton said as they walked. "He was very impressed."

"Oh." She paused as a crowd of Chinese tourists passed them, chattering. When it was quiet, she asked, "Was he important in the United States?"

"Yes, in his field. And popular. He had many friends."

They approached a group of Americans, Kodaks clicking. They were led by a Chinese guide with her hair pulled back in a prim bun.

Kangmei said, in a louder voice, "This is the Meridian Gate, the entrance to the grounds of the Inner Palaces. It is the biggest gate in all the Forbidden City, built in the year 1420 and restored again in the fifteenth and seventeenth centuries. Every year, the reigning emperor would ascend to the top of this structure and announce a new calendar for the people of China . . ."

Stratton applauded. Kangmei blushed. "Please don't make fun," she whispered. "You must behave like a tourist and I like a guide. For me to be with you under any circumstances would be very serious."

The competing tour group moved away. Kangmei walked Stratton across a paved courtyard to a marble bridge over a clear, slow-moving stream.

"The *Ji Shui He*," she trilled.

72

"Did you and your uncle talk about politics?" Stratton asked.

"A little. He seemed to understand that China cannot be analyzed in a week, or understood. I don't think that's why he came, Mr. Stratton. Some of his questions could never be answered. They are not relevant anymore. Not to my generation." A family of alabaster ducks splashed noisily in the stream.

"They were good questions, just the same," Stratton said.

"Yes," Kangmei said softly. "Very good. It was odd, seeing my uncle. He looked very much like my father; there is an alertness about both of them. Uncle David was more direct, of course. My father cannot afford to be so candid. Not with all the rumors of a new political campaign. We live with that concern, and it makes people like my father more cunning than David. No one can be sure what the future holds, so we must constantly be watchful. This, Mr. Stratton, is the Hall of Supreme Harmony."

A group of Chinese schoolchildren swarmed around them. A plump teacher in a blue Mao tunic recited a history lesson and the children listened attentively.

"The statues on the terrace are made of bronze," Kangmei said in her drone-guide voice. "On one side are storks and, on the other, giant tortoises. A sundial on the eastern side of the terrace represents righteousness and truth; on the west side is a grain measure, which symbolizes justice . . ."

"Did you memorize all this stuff?" Stratton said under his breath.

"We learn English at the Institute," Kangmei explained when the school tour was gone. "Those who perform well may someday become translators. The very best will receive diplomatic assignments. And travel." She ran a girlish hand through her hair, and Stratton noticed for the first time the glint of red nail polish, expertly applied. "So the answer is yes, I memorized this 'stuff,' " she said acidly.

They climbed the stairs and entered the hall. The columns were extravagantly carved with gilded dragons. In the middle stood the emperor's throne, surrounded by incense burners.

"How did David feel about seeing your father?" Stratton asked.

73

"The first time we spoke, he was very excited."

Stratton took her elbow. "The first time? You saw David more than once?"

"Yes," Kangmei replied. "Once before Xian, and the night of his return."

"The night of his heart attack?"

"The night he died, yes," she said.

"And how did he seem?" Stratton pressed.

"Upset. I guess the reunion was a disappointment. He and my father argued. There were bitter words. The tour of Xian was cut short by a day and the two of them returned to Peking."

"What did they argue about?"

"I'm not certain." They were alone in the Hall. It was too dark for pictures so the Americans had moved on, a fidgeting, pink-faced horde.

Kangmei said, "Do you listen to music at home?"

"A little," Stratton answered, off balance again.

"The Rolling Stones. Do you listen to the Rolling Stones? A friend of mine, another student at the Languages Institute, got an album smuggled to her from Hong Kong. It's a Rolling Stones album; during *xiu-xi*, our daily nap breaks, we sometimes sneak down to the music room and play it on the phonograph. The name of the album is *'Goat's Head Soup.'* Does that have special meaning in America?"

Stratton laughed. "No, not at all. Do you like the music?"

"Very much. It's good dancing music. My friend and I dance together when we play the record. We have to be careful, though. We could be expelled over something like that." Kangmei's voice dropped. "I would love to have more records."

They walked down marble steps and faced another pavilion. "As an art expert, you will appreciate the exhibit in this hall," Kangmei said. "Bronze chariots and their warriors, taken from the Han tombs."

"No, thank you," Stratton said. "It's time for me to go."

They retraced their steps toward Tiananmen. Kangmei kept her eyes on the pavement.

"Mr. Stratton, David and my father argued about the arti-

74

facts at Xian," she said. "David did not go into detail. But he said that my father was doing something wrong. Immoral was the word my uncle used. He was horrified his brother would attempt such a thing."

"He told you this—"

"After dinner last Tuesday night. He had left a message for me at the dormitory. I rode to the hotel after my father and his group had left. I met Uncle David in the lobby."

"He seemed in good health?" Stratton asked.

"Fine. Just angry. As we walked down Changan Avenue, he stopped to curse at the cadres who were following us. My father's little watchdogs. Uncle David walked right up to them and called them something nasty in Chinese," she said, blushing. "I admired his courage. The cadres said nothing. They just disappeared into the crowd."

"Some pages were missing from David's journal. And his passport is gone," Stratton said.

"Oh," Kangemi said.

"Something's wrong with all this. Do you believe your uncle died of a heart attack?"

"I have not thought about the how, Mr. Stratton. His life is over, and I'm sad. I wish I had known him better and longer. I'm very sorry that he and my father quarreled."

After they left the steps of the Forbidden City, Kangmei walked briskly to the lot where her bicycle was parked.

"Thank you for meeting me," Stratton said.

Kangmei nodded as she lithely swung onto the bike. "I'm glad that you are going with Uncle David's body. It's a long trip back to America and it is only right that he should be with someone who cares."

I cannot bury my friend so easily, Stratton thought, and not under a cloud of riddles.

"I'm sorry, Kangmei, but I won't be going after all," he said. "My tour group leaves for Xian tomorrow, and I've decided to join them."

Her expression never changed. It didn't have to.

"Tourists always take the early train," she said, and rode away.

CHAPTER 8

S T E V E P O W E L L offered hot tea all around. Linda Greer
shook her head politely. The station chief said yes to a small
cup. The Marine who served them closed the door carefully
as he left.

"What do you make of it?" Powell said.

Linda scanned the note once more, then passed it across
the table to the station chief. It was the handwriting of a man
who was trying hard to be neat, but obviously would have
been more comfortable with an academic's scribble:

"Dear Mr. Powell,

*"Please inform Deputy Minister Wang Bin that I have
changed my plans and, therefore, will not be able to
accompany David's body back to the United States. I
regret the inconvenience this might cause, but such a
journey would be too emotional for me at this time.
When I return to the United States, I will pay the proper
respects to my dear friend at his gravesite in Ohio. In the
meantime, I've decided to join my tour group on the trip*

*to Xian this morning. David Wang would understand
and I would hope his brother does, too.*

*"Sincerely,
Thomas Stratton."*

The station chief tossed the note on the table and shrugged.
"Linda?"

"He's bummed out. Just doesn't want to make the long
flight with his buddy's corpse," she said. "Can you blame
him?"

"That's the way I read it, too," Powell said. His tone suggested that the meeting should be over. The station chief
didn't budge.

"Shit, if it's such a big deal, we can send a Marine back
with the body, can't we?" Powell asked.

"Finding an escort is not the problem," the station chief
said impatiently. "The problem is Stratton. He's not the kind
of guy we want running all over China without a tether. He'll
get in trouble. He'll get *us* in trouble."

"He'll be all right," Linda said. She glanced at Powell, who
was obviously in some distress.

"I can call him now," the consul offered. "Lay on the
guilt. Tell him it will be an international insult if he doesn't
go home with the professor's body. He'll understand. He
knows the system; I saw his file. He used to be a pro."

"He used to be a killer," the station chief muttered. "Now
I wish you hadn't hit on him about Wang Bin."

"It was your goddamn idea," Linda Greer snapped. "I told
you he wouldn't go for it. All it did was get his antennae up."

The station chief, a gray-skinned man with baggy eyes and
thin dark hair, nodded tiredly. "It was a risk," he conceded.
"And I take the responsibility."

Powell was getting frantic. "I don't understand."

"It's not important now," the station chief said. "What is
important is that Wang Bin is going to be pissed off at a time
when we don't want him pissed. He's going to suggest that
Mr. Stratton has offended the People's Republic and is not so
welcome here anymore. He's going to want to know more

77

about Mr. Stratton and we cannot afford to let him find out *anything*. Is that clear, Powell?"

"Man-ling was a long time ago," the consul remarked.

"To the Chinese, it might as well have happened last night," the station chief said sharply. He leaned back, waiting for another remark from the consul.

"Steve, it's a matter of lousy timing, that's all," Linda Greer intervened. "Stratton could have helped us with Wang Bin, but he didn't want to. Now he's headed off to the countryside, upset about his friend's death, suspicious when there's no reason to be—"

"It was a goddamn heart attack!" Powell said in exasperation. "I told him, death by duck."

"I know," Linda said.

The station chief stood up. "Powell, see if you can smooth Wang Bin's feathers. Apologize on behalf of the embassy. Tell him Stratton meant no offense. Offer a fucking dress guard of Marine escorts if you have to. And remember, we want the old guy to *like* us. Just in case.

"Linda, you think your dinner friend will really stick with that tour group?"

"I think so," she answered coldly, trying not to blush. The Company kept track of everything, didn't it?

"Any other reason he'd go to Xian?" the station chief asked.

"History," Linda Greer replied. "That's all."

The Americans piled their luggage on the steps of the Minzu Hotel. Stratton offered polite good-mornings to Alice Dempsey, Walter Thomas, and the other art historians who milled and paced and tested their cameras on passing Chinese. Naturally the gaggle of brightly dressed foreigners attracted a crowd outside the hotel, and Stratton was mildly embarrassed. He melted back into the lobby to wait for the bus.

"Are you coming to Xian?" It was Miss Sun, the pert, ceaselessly cheerful tour guide.

"Yes, I'm looking forward to it," Stratton replied.

"Yesterday you missed beautiful White Pagoda," Miss Sun

said. It was not a reprimand, but there was concern in her voice.

"I'm sorry," Stratton said. "I had a personal matter."

Miss Sun seemed embarrassed. "I did not mean to intrude in your business, Professor Stratton."

"It's quite all right. Your English is coming along very well, Miss Sun. You've been practicing," he said warmly.

The tour guide smiled gratefully.

"Tom's going to be a good boy, aren't you, Professor?" Alice Dempsey had a way of inserting herself into conversations that made Stratton want to punch her. "I promised Miss Sun I'd keep an eye on you at Xian, Tom. If you'd read the tour book, you'd know about the travel restrictions outside of Peking. Can't just go roaming the hills, digging for pottery and chatting with the townsfolk. You'll get us all in hot water."

Stratton scowled. "Don't worry, Alice."

"Mr. Stratton?" A thin man with thick glasses and a fresh-bought Mao cap called out across the lobby. It was a man Stratton knew only as Weatherby, an art history teacher from a small college in San Francisco. Weatherby was delicate, anemic-looking; he approached in tiny, diffident steps.

"Tom Stratton?"

"Yes."

"There are two men out front who say they've come to pick you up," Weatherby reported.

"Here we go again," Alice Dempsey muttered.

"I do not understand," Miss Sun said, her voice rising.

"Me neither," Stratton said. "There must be a mistake."

"They've got a car," Weatherby said dramatically.

Stratton walked out of the lobby and down the steps. A jet-black Red Flag limousine was parked in front of the hotel. Two cadres in starched blue uniforms stood near the front bumper, talking in whispers. At the sight of Stratton, they turned and bowed slightly, from the neck, in unison. When the cadres looked up, they wore official smiles.

"Where is your luggage, Professor?"

"On its way to Xian."

"Oh. Very bad." The taller of the two wore thick eyeglasses

79

set in heavy black frames. His teeth were crooked and yellow.

The other cadre, a plump young man with fat rubbery lips, said, "Mr. Stratton, we came to take you to airport."

"But I'm going to Xian by train. With my group."

The cadres conferred, brisk Mandarin whispers.

"We take you to airport," repeated Crooked Teeth, unsmiling. "Plane leaves for America."

In Chinese, Miss Sun asked, "Where are you?"—the equivalent of an American, "Who do you work for?"

"Ministry of Culture," Fat Lips replied curtly, and then again in English for Tom Stratton's benefit. "Deputy Minister Wang Bin sent us." And then more, to the tour guide, in Mandarin.

"He says you are scheduled to fly back to America with the body of your friend," Miss Sun said to Stratton. "I very sorry, Professor. I did not know of this tragedy. I did not know that the deputy minister had made this request of you."

"Miss Sun—" Stratton began.

"Comrade says your plane leaves soon," she said. "I'll get your suitcase from the bus—"

"No!" Stratton said. "Miss Sun, please tell the comrades that I sent a message to Deputy Minister Wang this morning, informing him of my change in plans. The U.S. Embassy was notified at the same time. Everything is fine. I don't wish to leave China today. I wish to stay with the group."

Miss Sun translated. Fat Lips frowned and traded glances with his partner. They replied breathlessly, together: This is a most urgent matter. The deputy minister is anxious. Mr. Stratton is expected at the airport soon; we know nothing of any messages to the embassy. Our task is to take the professor to the plane. There is no other choice.

Miss Sun understood. "*Wei*," she said neutrally, and walked away.

Stratton saw that the other Americans were filing into the Toyota bus for the ride to the train station. From a window seat in the first row, Alice Dempsey glowered out at him.

"We take you to airport," Crooked Teeth announced with cheerfulnesss. "Come now."

80

"No," Tom Stratton insisted. The cadres were well trained in the Chinese art of stubbornness. The next stratagem, he knew, would be guilt. Americans were suckers when it came to guilt.

"We must go," Fat Lips said worriedly. "It would be bad not to go, Professor."

"Arrangements are ready for you," the other cadre added. "The deputy minister—"

"It's impossible, comrades. Thanks just the same, but my bus is about to leave." Stratton turned away and hurried along the sidewalk. The green minibus was idling. The driver tapped on the horn three times.

"Coming!" Stratton shouted, breaking into a trot.

Then he felt an arm on his sleeve. Angrily, he whirled to face Crooked Teeth. The other cadre jogged a few steps behind, puffing.

"Come now," Crooked Teeth said. This time is was a command, and there was nothing polite about it.

"What is this?" Stratton demanded.

Inside the tour bus, the Americans watched the confrontation with shock. Stratton towered over the cadres, shouting down into their impassive faces.

"Fuck off!" is what he said.

"My God," sighed Alice Dempsey.

"He's nothing but a troublemaker," mumbled Walter Thomas. "He's going to spoil this for all of us."

"He's a little upset, that's all," Weatherby said. "He's just upset about his friend."

The other Americans craned for a glimpse of their colleague haggling with the government cadres. Miss Sun quickly moved to the front of the bus and whispered to the driver: "Go now."

As the tour departed for the railway station, Alice Dempsey saw Stratton being guided down the sidewalk toward the limousine, a resolute Chinese at each elbow.

"I missed the fucking bus," Stratton was growling. "Get your hands off me, comrades."

"All is arranged," Crooked Teeth said as they walked.

Stratton sneaked a backward glance over his right shoulder

81

as the minibus turned down Dongdan Street and disappeared. Fat Lips slipped away from Stratton's side long enough to open the door to the cavernous Red Flag.

"Okay," said Fat Lips, with a shove.

"No okay," said Stratton, uncorking a nasty left jab that snapped flush in the cadre's face. Fat Lips fell backward like a domino. His head cracked on the rear fender.

Instantly, Stratton stumbled forward, gasping. His right side cramped from a kidney punch; he caught himself with both hands on the Red Flag and spun around. Crooked Teeth coiled in a crouch, snarling. His cap was on the pavement. Other Chinese pressed in a growing circle, yammering excitedly. The fight did not last long.

Crooked Teeth feinted a punch, then spun forward on one leg, aiming a powerful kick at Stratton's neck. It was a prosaic maneuver, and Stratton deflected it from memory. Deftly, he seized the cadre's ankle in midair, and seemed to hold him there—flustered and grunting—before delivering a decisive punch to the poor man's testicles. Crooked Teeth fell in a blue heap, bug-eyed, semiconscious.

Instinct warned Stratton to run, but he could hardly move. The bystanders formed a wall—hundreds of them, packed shoulder to shoulder in front of the hotel. Soon the police would arrive.

Sideways, Stratton edged through the heaving crowd with deliberate slowness. Stratton resolved to keep calm, to stop the fear from reaching his eyes, where people could see it. Obviously, the Chinese in the street were confused; some hastily moved out of the tall American's path, while others stood firm, scolding. The worst thing would be to run, Stratton knew, so he held himself to a purposeful walk; a man with someplace to go.

After three blocks, Stratton appropriated an unlocked bicycle and aimed himself on a wobbly course toward Tienanmen Square. He had no map and very little time. The Square was the heart of Peking, a central magnet, lousy with tourists. Somebody there surely would be able to tell him the quickest way to the trains.

Inexorably, Stratton was drawn into a broad, slow-moving

stream of bicycles. He had hoped that the clanging blue mass would swallow him and offer concealment—but his stature and blond hair betrayed him. Among the Chinese he shone like a beacon.

From somewhere a car honked, and the cycling throng parted grudgingly. Stratton dutifully guided the bike to the right side of the blacktop road. He heard the automobile approach and he slowed, expecting it to pass. Instead it lingered, coasting behind the two-wheeled caravan.

Puzzled, Stratton turned to look. It was the Red Flag limousine, so close he could feel the ripple of heat from its engine. Crooked Teeth was at the wheel, fingers taut on the rim; his battered eyeglasses were propped comically on his nose. He looked like Jerry Lewis.

Next to him sat Fat Lips, gingerly daubing a scarf to a gash on his forehead. Neither of the cadres showed any anger, only eyes hardened in determination.

Stratton pedaled like a madman. He weaved and darted from street to sidewalk, stiff-arming cyclists who dawdled and elbowing himself a narrow, navigable track through the horde. The tin bells on a hundred sets of handlebars chirped furiously in protest as Stratton plowed through a lush pile of fresh cabbages. In a racer's crouch, he doubled his speed, his chin to the bar. He gained precious yardage while the Red Flag braked and swerved, dodging Chinese pedestrians who had raced into the street to retrieve mangled vegetables.

Finally, Stratton broke free of the mob and barreled into the cobbled vastness of Tienanmen Square. Behind him the limousine came to a jerky stop on the perimeter road. The cadres got out and stood together, smaller and smaller as Stratton pedaled on.

Then came small voices. Dozens of them crying, *"Buzhen! Buzhen!"* Stop. And then Stratton remembered: Bicycling is strictly forbidden inside the great square. Quickly he dismounted. He found himself in a sea of schoolchildren, dressed in blue and white uniforms with brilliant red scarves. They walked in formation, bright-eyed, singing, toward Mao's tomb, stealing secret glances at the tall foreigner with the Chinese bicycle. The youngsters had stopped shouting the

83

moment Stratton dismounted. He smiled apologetically and set a course for the ornate main gate at the far end of the square. Looking back, he no longer could see the limousine. Perhaps his escorts finally had given up.

"You, mister!" A young Chinese waved at Stratton. A plastic badge identified him as a guide from the China International Travel Service.

"Please no ride bicycle in the Square," he said firmly.

"I'm very sorry," Stratton said. "I am late for a train. Can you tell me which way to the railway station?"

The young guide pointed east. "Left at the Tienanmen. About five blocks."

"Thank you."

"Where is your suitcase?" the guide asked.

"At the train. I overslept," Stratton said.

The guide eyed him curiously. "You need a ticket to enter the station."

"It's in my luggage." Stratton waved, moving off. "Thanks again."

"Is that your bicycle?" the guide called.

Stratton waved again and kept walking. His eyes fanned the crowds for a sign of the two cadres. The square was immense. Still, Stratton knew, he could hardly be invisible.

In the center of Tienanmen, at the Monument to the People's Heroes, a class of teenaged boys listened to a political speech. Someone had placed a wreath of red and gold paper flowers at the base of the statue. The speaker paused briefly while Stratton passed, then resumed an ardent, high-pitched denunciation.

Finally, Stratton reached the tree-lined avenue bordering the end of Tienanmen. It had taken twenty minutes to cross the great square. He mounted the bicycle, praying that the train would be late in departing.

Pedaling quietly, he was absorbed quickly into the flow of traffic. The bright sun gave life to the brown buildings, and the trees shimmered green. Stratton's heart beat cold when the big car roared up behind him. He was incredulous; the resourceful cadres wore their familiar expressions.

Recklessly, Stratton broke from the pack and veered south

84

down a side street. With the limousine close behind, he raced through the Old Legation Quarter, gracious Colonial-styled embassies long since converted to warehouses, clinics, banks —buildings to serve the workers. And, between them, drab and monotonous apartment buildings, sterile and new, lifeless in the shadow of the Forbidden City.

He tucked the bike down an alley so narrow that his knuckles scraped against the flaking walls. The cadres merely circled the block and waited at the other end. Crooked Teeth tried to position the limousine to block Stratton's path, but the American managed to skitter by, jumping a curb so violently that the basket snapped off the bicycle and clattered to the pavement.

"Stop!" Fat Lips cried in English.

But Stratton heard a train. He was back in the safety of traffic. Ahead, a busload of tourists turned south. Stratton followed. The railway station was but two blocks away. Another whistle blew.

This time it was the cadres who found a propitious side street. The railway-bound minibus passed, with Stratton not far behind. Crooked Teeth punched the accelerator.

By the time Stratton spotted the long black car, it was too late. The Red Flag clipped the bicycle's rear tire. Stratton spun clockwise. He hit the pavement to the sound of glass tinkling around him. A headlight. Through half-open eyes he watched the twisted bicycle skid away, kicking up sparks as it bounced.

Stratton forced himself to his feet. He had landed brutally hard on his right shoulder. The sleeve was in shreds, and his arm was bloody. His left hand felt for broken bones.

"Now!" said a triumphant voice behind him. "Time for airport."

Stratton lurched into a run.

"No, no!" Fat Lips scuttled back to the limousine. "Stop!" he yelled as Crooked Teeth started the car.

And Stratton did stop—when he got to the bicycle. The chain had been torn from the sprockets and hung from the hub of the rear wheel. He picked it up.

The limousine pursued with a needless screech of the tires.

85

Stratton stood motionless, his arms at his side. This time the cadres showed no sign of slowing down.

Stratton's left arm shot up and windmilled above his head. The steel bicycle chain hit the Red Flag like a shot, and pebbled the glass in the cadres' faces. The car weaved erratically through the cyclists, hopped the curb and parked itself violently around the trunk of a Chinese elm. The radiator spit a hot geyser into the branches.

Stratton trudged the last leg to the train station in a stinging fog.

"You're darn lucky the train's late. What happened to your arm? What was all that fuss back at the hotel?"

"Nice to see you, Alice," Stratton muttered.

The group was gathered fitfully outside the entrance. There had been the usual delays. Miss Sun had gone inside to make the necessary inquiries. The Americans were outnumbered by large groups of Chinese travelers who waited patiently with cardboard suitcases. A crate of two hundred live chickens perfumed the air.

It was Weatherby who came up with a first-aid kit. Stratton was grateful for the disinfectant and bandages.

"What happened?" Alice repeated.

"I had a little bike accident."

"You're lucky it's just a scrape," Weatherby said.

"You don't know the half of it," said Stratton.

Miss Sun bounced down the steps. "Okay, we go now," she said brightly.

Then she saw Stratton. "But you went to the airport."

"No. I straightened everything out."

"You come to Xian?"

"Yes," Stratton replied. He knew it wasn't what little Miss Sun had wanted to hear. She had pegged him as a troublemaker back at the hotel. "You have my ticket?"

"Yes, Professor," she said, scanning the promenade for some sign of the diligent cadres.

"Then let's go," Stratton said.

Miss Sun led the way. Once inside the railway station, the art historians filed up a long escalator toward the trains. Stratton made it a point to be first.

The train to Xian was half full. As the Americans walked along the platform toward the soft-class cars, Stratton glanced up at the faces of the Chinese who were already aboard.

An old man with an elegant gray beard, squinting at the tourists. A plump matron with a baby on her shoulder and a toddler in her lap. A dour soldier.

And a stunning young woman with long black hair, tapping gently on the dingy window. Stratton smiled.

Kangmei.

From his private office in the national museum, Deputy Minister Wang Bin could gaze at the Forbidden City, a grand horizon, serrated by the gold-tiled rooftops of a dozen ancient temples.

His thoughts were sour. History taunted him. The architecture was inspired, ripe with passion. The city was full of such masterpieces.

But where did they come from? The ages, Wang Bin reflected sadly. The dynasties. Where could one find such imagination now? And, worse, how could it flourish?

The thin man in the stuffed chair waited until the deputy minister turned from the window. "I'm deeply sorry we were not successful," he said in Chinese. "The cadres were clumsy, and their actions were dangerous. I would punish them but . . ." He clasped his hands together.

"Both dead?" Wang Bin asked.

"One, yes. The other is badly injured."

Wang Bin asked, "Did Stratton leave on the train?"

"Yes," the thin man said. With nervous hands, he lit a cigarette.

"Liao and Deng are on their way to Xian?"

"The plane leaves in an hour," the thin man reported. "Their documents are in order. No questions were raised. Officially, they are joining the inventory team at the tombs."

Wang Bin rigidly walked to the sparse desk and sat down. His voice tightened. "This is very delicate, you understand, Comrade Xi? Stratton has put us in a fragile posture. He is no ordinary tourist, I assure you."

Xi was soothing. "Deng is a trustworthy man. Have you

87

ever known him to fail? In two days the threat will be gone, I am certain."

"I hope so," Wang Bin said, rising. "Now send in my visitor."

"The embassy has sent Miss Greer. She wants to apologize formally for Mr. Stratton's inconsiderate change of heart. They have even offered to send an American soldier back with the casket." Xi grinned. "It's ironic, isn't it?"

"A thoughtful gesture," Bin said sarcastically.

The deputy minister was halfway to the door when Xi reminded him: "Comrade, your mourning band. Don't forget."

CHAPTER 9

"ONE OF HISTORY'S most pathetic lines was uttered in this city," J. Paul Prudoe was explaining. "It occurred in 1911, as the last dynasty, the Qing, was falling. The Qing were Manchu, of course, and the majority of Han people hated them as barbarian invaders. The Manchus imposed their rule in Xian with an army of occupation that occupied its own quarter of the city. When the people rebelled against the Manchus in 1911, there was a fearful slaughter. Many Manchus died. There was an English hospital here then and a few Manchus wound up there with dreadful self-inflicted wounds.

"An English doctor asked one of the wounded soldiers—his name is not recorded, alas—why he had attempted to slit his own throat. The soldier replied: 'Because the wells were full.' "

J. Paul Prudoe, erect in a stiffly pressed safari shirt and hair-by-hair perfect Van Dyke with an artful sprinkling of gray, paused for effect. He surveyed the room. Around him, twenty-three art historians waited expectantly.

" 'The wells were full.' Starting with the commanding general, an old man who realized that defense was hopeless, the

Manchus had thrown themselves down the wells to avoid capture. The wells were thirty-six feet deep, and when they were full, a warrior's only honorable escape was to slit his throat. Subsequently, of course, the city is famous for the so-called Xian Incident, when the Communists caught Chiang Kai-shek in a farmhouse during the Civil War, but let him go. During the last days of that war, the giant man-made hill —the tumulus of Emperor Qin, dead for more than two thousand years—was literally an armed camp, fortified with machine guns and snipers. How the muse of history must have smiled at that."

J. Paul Prudoe was the envy of America's art historians. He spoke with the zeal of a revivalist, the slick, contrived passion of a corrupt politician. His presence on the tour, tramping through museums and riding the buses like any ole AAH, was the celebrity magnet that had drawn so many of his nominal peers to China in the first place.

Stratton, slouched and alone at the rear of a reception room in Xian's Renmin Daxia Hotel, disliked Prudoe's showmanship as much as he despised his pop art scholarship.

"Now that I have your attention," Prudoe went on, preening, "let me talk about the Xian that really interests us, or Changan, as it was called then."

Stratton slurped his tea loudly enough to draw annoyed glances and an unspoken reprimand from Prudoe himself. Pompous ass. Stratton tuned out.

They had arrived before dawn, twenty hours from Peking. Twice Stratton had walked through the train looking for Kangmei. Twice guards had turned him back from the hardclass section of the train reserved for Chinese only.

But she had found him on the platform at Xian. They had shared a few quiet minutes in a corner of the terminal as the train disgorged its passengers with billowing steam and a slumbering pace.

"I have come to help," Kangmei had said.

"But . . ."

"You want to know what happened to make my father fight with my American uncle. So do I. Alone you will never find out. I can help."

90

"How? How can you even be here? Don't you need a special pass?"

"Listen to me, Thom-as," she said with sober, almost childlike earnestness. "In China, many things are possible for Chinese. Not for foreigners"—she tapped him lightly on the chest—"but for Chinese."

Stratton smiled. She was proud of herself.

"China is the most wonderful land on earth, Thom-as, but it has been betrayed too many times. Everywhere there are old men who rule only because they are old, or cruel, or because they are friends of other stupid old men."

The crowd on the platform was beginning to thin. From somewhere near the terminal entrance, Stratton heard a petulant woman—it could only be Alice Dempsey—in full bay. "Now where can he have gotten himself to?"

"The old men sit on the young," Kangmei continued. "They are jealous because we have studied and they have not. They cling to power, betraying China and their own Communist ideals. These tired old men are everywhere, Thom-as. And everywhere there are also angry young people who believe in the New China. There are millions of us. We talk not to the stupid old men, not to the government, or the Party. We talk to one another. In Peking, in Shanghai, in Canton, here in Xian—everywhere. My friends and the friends of my friends. They will help me to help you."

"Stratton? Ah, there you are. Will you come on, please? Everyone is waiting. How can you be so rude?" Alice Dempsey's bray carried across half a hundred Chinese heads and echoed off the vaulted terminal roof.

Kangmei grabbed his arm.

"Go, Thom-as. In two hours, I will come to your hotel. Be ready."

With an empty smile for Alice, Stratton had docilely ridden the bus to the tourist hotel.

". . . at Ban Po, a few miles out of town, we will see a well-preserved village belonging to the Yang Shao culture from about 6000 B.C. Xian did not come into its own, though, until the third century before Christ. The famous Emperor Qin, who unified China and built the Great Wall, had his capital here. We'll visit the new digs around his tomb east of the city . . ."

It certainly was something to think about, Stratton reflected. If anybody could actually harness the energies of the educated Chinese young people . . . no, "harness" was a bad word. "Unfetter" would be better. Unfetter the young millions, let them think and act and build without the constraints of a revolution grown old before its time. Would they yank China headlong, breathless and excited, into the twenty-first century, or would they produce some monstrous new revolution? The last time the young had been mobilized, it had been by Mao, and that little adventure—the Cultural Revolution—had cost China a decade of development and a generation of young people who discovered too late that being revolutionary too often meant being uneducated as well.

Two thoughts occurred to Stratton simultaneously. The first was that if Kangmei was willing to help him, then she was openly at odds with her own father. The second was more chilling than revealing: If Kangmei's network of disaffected young people was any more than a nebulous and idealistic dream, if it had any form at all, any organization that posed the slightest threat to the state or to the Party, then it was only a question of time until authority in all its multi-bludgeoned wonder fell on it like a ton of bricks. Such was the historic international lesson of communism. Hungary, Czechoslovakia, Democracy Wall, Solidarity . . .

". . . successive dynasties built successive capitals in and around present-day Xian. At the beginning of the Tang Dynasty, Changan was a metropolis of over one million people, six miles square and girded by stout walls breeched by eight gates. The Tang palace was nearly a mile square inside the city and protected by a wall nearly sixty feet thick at its base. Enough remains to keep us more than busy for the two days we have." An avuncular smile.

Stratton knew exactly what he wanted to accomplish in Xian. It had been his reason for not flying home with David's body: He wanted to know what had happened between the two brothers and if, by any means, it could have led to David's death.

92

Stratton must have sighed aloud, for it drew J. Paul Prudoe's ire.

". . . forest of steles, pagodas, pottery and a celestial army. Professor Stratton?"

Stratton stood up. "May I be excused, please, Mr. Prudoe? I have to go to the bathroom."

He left the art historians to mutter at his insolence and walked out into the early morning sunshine. In the courtyard of the hotel, draped around the open door of a gray Shanghai saloon, stood Kangmei.

"Are you Professor Stratton?" The smile was dazzling. "Good morning, and welcome to Xian. I am Miss Wang and this is Mr. Xia. We are your guides. Please get in."

The rail-thin Mr. Xia, it turned out, was a legitimate China Travel Service guide. That he was one of Kangmei's young allies went without saying, for she too wore the same guide's red identification pin on her white cotton blouse. Kangmei's friend smiled a lot and spoke little, although his English proved to be quite good. Xiao-Xia, she called him.

Leaving the hotel, they drove through handsome, wide streets with little traffic. At one clutter of shops, Stratton did a double take. There on the sidewalk, in English, was a sandwich board announcing "Xian's First Exhibition of Abstract Art."

"I never saw anything like that in Peking," Stratton said. Kangmei and the guide laughed. The third Chinese, the driver, was a lugubrious soul with sharp features. He gave no sign of understanding, no English.

"And you never will," chirped Kangmei, radiant with excitement. "Abstract art—what would the old men say to that? That it was counterrevolutionary, of course. Here it is different. Remember, Thom-as, that the farther you get from Peking, the more relaxed are the people and the easier the rules. I would like to show you the south someday, where my mother's family lives. You would think Peking was in another country."

"There are fewer police here," confirmed Mr. Xia, the guide.

They drove toward what seemed to be the center of the

city, a giant tower that stood as a high-hatted civic sentinel.

"Where are we going?" Stratton asked.

"That is for you to decide," Kangmei replied. "But you must see the Bell Tower. It is very old, very famous." She gestured ahead.

"Once it was the center of the Tang imperial city, in about the ninth century," said Mr. Xia in reflexive patter-for-tourists. "It was restored again after Liberation. From the second story, there is a fine view of the city—"

Stratton cut him off. "Kangmei, what I really want to know is what your father and your uncle fought about. I want to go to some of the places they might have gone together; someone might have heard something. I will see the sites of Xian some other time."

"I see," she said doubtfully, and lapsed into a lengthy exchange of Chinese with Mr. Xia.

"It will be difficult, Thom-as. There are so many places. And what do we say?"

"We say that I am a friend of the distinguished American brother of Deputy Minister Wang. Anything like that will do, and there can't be all that many places. What exactly is your father's responsibility here?"

She thought about that one.

"He is everything and he is nothing. There are many cultural places in China, and they are usually controlled by local authorities. Until the old men in Peking get interested in one of them. Then it is my father's job to carry out their wishes. At least, I think that is how it works. My father does not confide in young daughters."

"All right. Between you and Mr. Xia, you must be able to think of some things special here that have interested the old men in Peking. That is where we go."

"It is a good plan, Thom-as," she said. There followed another Mandarin interlude. "There are five or six such places."

They visited the historical museum, a fourteenth-century temple, a thirteenth-century drum tower and Big Goose Pagoda south of the city, originally built early in the seventh

94

century by the Tang, or was it the Sui? They walked the Ming city walls, and visited the neolithic site at Ban Po. Dynasties and centuries began to run together for Stratton. At each stop, Stratton and Mr. Xia would do a quick tourist round and Mr. Xia would ask to see the comrade in charge so that a distinguished American visitor could pay his respects. None of the comrades seemed overworked. To a man, they all poured gracious tea and exchanged compliments interminably. Three of them knew of Comrade Wang from Peking. None had ever met his distinguished brother. By midafternoon, Stratton wondered whether his patience or his bladder would burst first. Kangmei attended none of the interviews. Instead, she wandered around, "talking to the young people," as she put it. It was hard for Stratton to know whether she was devoted more to seeking information or to recruiting for her cause.

"So much for the Taoist Temple of the Eight Immortals." Stratton sighed as he sank back into seat cushions already dank with his sweat. "Now what?"

"The Qin ruins to the east of the city. It will take us about thirty minutes to get there, Thom-as." She ran light fingers across his cheek. "Do not be discouraged."

They drove through an intensely cultivated valley, past communes that seemed rich by Chinese standards. Suddenly, the car turned sharply onto a narrow strip of asphalt that looked as if it had been laid as an afterthought. Through gaps in the fields of chest-high corn, Stratton could see a large cone-shaped hill off to the right.

"That is Mount Qin, the tumulus," said Mr. Xia. "It was looted three years after the emperor's death, when the dynasty fell. It took an army three days and three nights to carry away treasure from the tomb. The new excavations have not reached it yet, so it is not known what the grave robbers may have left. The current excavations are all here, to the west of the tumulus."

"What's that?" Stratton nodded toward a squat, two-story building with a big chimney about a quarter mile off to the left.

95

"That is a factory belonging to the commune. They make Tiger Brand sewing machines." Mr. Xia smiled. "The factory wants to expand, but the local authorities will not allow it because it is not known what is buried around the factory, or even under it. The factory owners say they do not care about old things: It is the commune's land and the commune has an obligation to provide a good life for its people."

"Sounds like the kind of squabble we have at home between environmentalists and developers," Stratton said. "What happened?"

"The dispute went all the way to Peking. There is no decision yet," said Mr. Xia.

Stratton turned to Kangmei. "By 'Peking' does he mean your father?"

She nodded.

To honor a cruel emperor reviled for two thousand years, but latterly proclaimed a hero, the Chinese had created an instant museum.

Kangmei vanished in search of young co-conspirators. Mr. Xia led Stratton into a large building with a vaulted roof that looked like an airplane hangar. Once inside, the guide went off to look for an official with whom Stratton could drink tea. Alone, Stratton pushed through two polished doors and into the main chamber.

It was like changing centuries.

Stratton stood about fifteen feet above the dig in a skylight-lit hall the size of a football field. His first thought was that it was the cleverest and most awesome museum he had ever seen. To protect the excavation while simultaneously exploiting the discovery as a tourist attraction, the Chinese had simply erected the museum over the dig.

Below Stratton, in roofless chambers that extended in four files, lay the Emperor Qin's celestial army. Stratton stood on a concrete platform, which was shaped like a square U with two wings stretched out parallel along the files. In the pit, a modern army of Chinese technicians worked with brushes, dust pans and hand shovels. Stratton stared into the chamber where three hundred clay soldiers stood.

They were magnificent. He had seen pictures, of course—

96

who had not?—but even that foretaste had left Stratton unprepared for their true majesty.

The figures were life-sized, nearly six feet tall. They had been molded from gray river clay by master craftsmen, dead for twenty-two hundred years. Stratton stared with breathless fascination at the nearest warrior, a kneeling archer. The detail was extraordinary.

The archer wore a topknot, pulled tightly to the left side of his head and held with a band. Stratton could count the hairs.

The archer's ears clung close to his skull. The eyebrows were high and stylized, as though they had been plucked. The nose was broad, classically Chinese. The warrior had affected a finely combed mustache and a tuft of hair on his chin. On the face, mirthless and resolute, were flecks of blue and red paint mixed two centuries before Christ was born.

The archer wore a studded jerkin that reached below his waist and ended high on the biceps. It afforded protection from sword slashes, while at the same time allowing mobility with which to wield a bow. Below the waist, the emperor's soldier wore a skirtlike loincloth, leggings and stout, square-toed sandals.

Nearby, a second archer wore the same uniform, but his face was different—rounder, a trifle older, no mustache. Every soldier, Stratton noted with awe, had a different face—in eternity, as in life.

Stratton paced the arms of the platform. Here lay a terracotta arm jutting out from the red clay. And there, a headless torso, being dusted by a young woman with intense concentration. Toward the back of the vast hall, new chambers had been carefully outlined in chalk, but had so far been unmolested. Working at their current painstaking pace, Stratton reckoned, it would take the Chinese technicians at least another ten or twenty years to exploit the dig completely. Stratton was fascinated. He could have stayed for hours. Too soon, Mr. Xia was at his side.

"Director Ku will see you for a few moments, but you must hurry. It is nearly closing time."

Reluctantly, Stratton followed him out of the chamber.

"Mr. Xia, do you realize that this might be the most important archaeological discovery of this century?" Stratton asked.

"Yes, so many American friends have told us. The soldiers excite them very much, but there are many other discoveries as well."

"Can I see them?"

"I am sorry, but only the soldiers are open to the public."

Director Ku was a roly-poly individual with a ready smile and the callused hands of a worker. Stratton squatted on the inevitable overstuffed chair and tried not to drink the tea.

The pleasantries went quickly enough. Ku, Stratton suspected, was not a man to keep his dinner waiting. Even the set speech that seemed to come with every Chinese official's job seemed to sail by: the discovery had been made in 1965 by peasants digging a well. During the Cultural Revolution, not much happened. Since then, the work had proceeded systematically, entirely in the hands of Chinese specialists; no foreigners were welcome. Test excavations were still being dug. So far, scientists had positively identified an armory, an imperial zoo, stables, other groups of warriors, the tombs of nobles sacrificed to mark the emperor's death, the underground entrance to the tumulus and exquisite bronze workings, including a chariot two-thirds life-size.

"I did not know about the bronzes," said Stratton. "Can they be seen?"

"They are in Peking," came back the translation. Stratton saw what he thought was a flash of annoyance on the director's lined face. Annoyance at the question? No, more likely at the thought that Xian's precious treasures had been preempted by the central government.

"Explain about my friend and his brother, Xiao-Xia, but this time don't ask if they were here. Say that my friend told me he would always remember the hospitality he received here."

At the translation, Ku's face lit. He reached into his breast pocket and extracted a silver ballpoint pen.

"The director says he remembers your friend very well. He

calls him the 'gentle professor' and shows you the pen he was honored to receive as a gift," said Mr. Xia.

Bingo. But now what?

"Ask the comrade director if it would be possible for me to see the special excavation that my friend and his brother visited. Be sure and use Kangmei's father's name."

That provoked a quick exchange in Mandarin before Mr. Xia finally said: "He asks if you have permission."

A direct hit. "Tell him yes."

Mr. Xia looked quizzically at Stratton.

"Do you really have permission?"

"Of course."

Stratton barely concealed his impatience at the Mandarin that followed. If he could see what David had seen, he might understand why the brothers had quarreled. Ku, who obviously took no pains to hide his own distaste for Peking, might even tell him. For him, Peking probably meant Wang Bin.

"The director regrets that the excavation is only opened when Peking advises him that an important visitor is coming. He regrets that the responsible officials in Peking did not inform him you were coming, but, he says, perhaps in a day or two it will be possible."

Damn. What that meant was that the director would check with Peking.

"I would be grateful," Stratton said. "Ask him if my friend—"

"The director also apologizes, but explains that he now must supervise the closing and meet with the technicians to discuss tomorrow's work schedule," Mr. Xia interjected.

"Shit," said Stratton. It escaped. Mr. Xia looked perplexed. Stratton flushed. "Say we are sorry for interrupting his work. Thank him for his hospitality and say we will return to look at the special excavation when the details have been arranged."

Darkness was falling and large numbers of workers had already left the site on a wheezy bus by the time Kangmei returned to the car.

"It happened here, Thom-as," she erupted. "My father

and my uncle had an angry discussion, shouting. A young worker told me; he is a cousin of a friend of mine who also studied languages."

"What was it about? Why did they argue?"

"I do not know. My friend could not speak long. But later I will see him. He will tell me then."

"Kangmei, that's terrific."

Kangmei bubbled excitedly as the car returned to the old imperial city. After darkness had fallen, and she was sure Mr. Xia would not see from the front seat, she grasped Stratton's hand and clasped it tightly.

Stratton ate alone in the restaurant of the sprawling hotel complex, careful to time his arrival and departure to miss the art historians. To his astonishment, the food was awful. He retired to his room with wizened tangerines and a bottle of mineral water. He was half asleep, near ten o'clock, when the phone rang.

"Thom-as," she said without introduction. "In two minutes, you must walk to the end of the corridor with the vacuum bottle in your room and ask the floor attendant for more hot water."

Stratton understood; he was to be a decoy. "Are you sure that's wise?"

"Please."

Stratton obeyed, remembering to empty the thermos. The attendant, drowsing over the color pictures in a back copy of *Time* that a tourist must have left, smiled and obligingly padded into a kitchen with the bottle, leaving the hall unwatched.

When Stratton returned to the room, Kangmei was waiting. She embraced him. Her tongue played a sparrow's tattoo against his teeth. It was Stratton who broke the embrace.

"Kangmei . . ." he said uncertainly.

"It is so exciting," she said. "My friend told me everything, Thom-as, everything." She sat on the narrow iron-framed bed, leaving Stratton standing absurdly above her, thermos suspended.

"Would you like some tea?" he asked weakly.

"Yes, please."

100

Stratton turned and busied himself elaborately with the tea leaves. He tried to ignore the rustlings behind him. Was she getting into bed?

"Here is what happened," she began. "My friend saw it. There is a special place near the emperor's tomb, Thom-as. It is not controlled by the workers there, but by Peking directly —my father—and it makes all the Xian people very angry."

"What kind of a place?" Stratton asked.

"My friend called it a special place. No one may go there without permission. When my uncle came, my father took him there. My friend was there to help; it is covered with reeds and cloth most of the time. My father and my uncle went down into the hole on a ladder, into a long tunnel. They were gone a long time. When they came out again, they began to argue. My father tried to grab my uncle's camera. 'No, no!' my uncle kept saying. My father grew very angry. They shouted. Then my father ordered the hole covered and they drove away."

Stratton was thinking furiously. If the chamber with the common soldiers was an international sensation, then Wang Bin's private dig could be a literal gold mine. Stratton had a vision of gold swords encrusted with jewels, of bronze and gold helmets, chests of gems: an emperor's legacy.

"My father wanted my uncle to help him steal something, Thom-as, didn't he?" It was the voice of a little girl.

"It's possible," Stratton said. He turned, a full teacup in each hand.

Kangmei lay naked on the bed. The light from a single dim-watted bulb painted her the color of brushed ivory. She wriggled, and the shadowed V between her legs became a beckoning S. She reached for him, arching her back.

"Kangmei, we can't . . ."

"Thom-as," she whispered. "Do you know what Kangmei means in Chinese?"

"Mmm?"

"It means 'Resist America,' Thom-as. My father was very patriotic before he become a thieving old man. Shall I resist America, Thom-as?"

Her little-girl laugh broke the spell.

101

"Kangmei," Stratton said more sternly than he felt, "you are David's niece, and I'm nearly old enough—"

"To what?"

"To know better," he said. She was a spectacular woman, and certainly older than some of the students with whom he had dallied in his early years as a teacher. "You are very beautiful, and I want to," Stratton said lamely, "but it would be wrong. Do you understand why?"

Kangmei seemed to wilt. Stratton, feeling a fool with a teacup in each hand, watched as tears sparked in her eyes. She clawed for the sheet and drew it up to her chin.

"Oh, Thom-as, I meant nothing wrong, but you . . . there is so little time, and I am very excited. Also a little frightened."

"So am I," Stratton said, and kissed her lightly on the forehead.

She took the tea, and he sat primly by her on the bed, stroking her hair as an uncle might, or a lover-to-be. When at last Kangmei fell asleep, Stratton curled stiffly in a hard-bottomed chair, wondering if he yet knew enough to lay murder charges against her father.

CHAPTER 10

THE MEN named Liao and Deng moved away from the streetlight and into the shadows. Their discussion was brief, disturbed.

"You are sure it was her?" Teng asked. He was the older of the two; brawny, leather-faced, he wore his Mao cap pulled tight on his head, the brim snug on his eyebrows.

"I am certain," Liao replied. "This changes everything." He lit a cheap cigarette and glanced across the street at the hotel. His eyes moved up the wall to an open window. A faint bulb gave a burnished light to the inside of the room; no shadows moved. Liao was hatless; his black hair was cropped extremely short. In a robe, he could have passed for a Buddhist monk. His round face was youthful, but humorless.

"When she leaves . . ." he said.

"And if she doesn't?" Deng asked. "Perhaps we should contact Peking."

"I don't think we should wake the deputy minister." Liao shook his head.

Deng scowled. "This foreigner is important."

103

"That's why we're here."

"But so is the daughter important. It is a grave matter," Deng insisted. The brim of his cap bobbed as his brow furrowed. "We can't wait all night. I say we grab the girl. As for the American, we have our instructions."

Liao sighed. He had an intuition about complications, and this assignment troubled him. "We'll have to report this to her *dan-wei*."

Deng said, "Why? Let Lao Wang handle it. He is her father." And then he thought for a moment and said, "You are right. We must report it. Even if the deputy minister tells us not to." Deng and Liao had heard the same rumors. Today the old man was a power broker, but he could just as easily be shoveling cowshit in Hunan tomorrow.

"We do as we're told," Liao said finally, "and a little more. The deputy minister does not have to know whom we talk to. China comes first."

Stratton drowsed, half-sleeping, in the hard chair. When he heard the doorknob jiggle, he figured it was one of the floor attendants. They all had passkeys, and no compunction about barging in on the slightest pretext.

It would not be wise to be found in the same room with a Chinese woman. Stratton padded barefoot across the floor and reached for the door. Two men stood there in the darkness. One held a sack of some kind in his right hand, away from his body.

"Yes?" Stratton said, stiffening.

The young man bowed, then rammed the heel of his hand into the tip of Stratton's nose. The American fell in a heap, gurgling blood.

From the bed, Kangmei yelped and sat up. The men stared silently at her naked figure before they closed the door behind them.

Stratton awoke in darkness, heaving for air. His nostrils were clogged with blood, and his face was clammy and wet. Two strips of industrial tape had been pasted across his mouth, forming an X that nearly blocked his desperate breathing.

He was in a closet. He smelled clothing—his own—and the

104

canvas from his duffel. Through throbbing eyes, he noticed a weak sliver of light at the base of the door, near his feet.

Stratton tried to move. His hands were free, but his legs were bound tightly at the ankles. Voices, male and female, seeped through the door. The conversation was singsongy Mandarin, and Stratton understood none of it. The male voices were cold and conspiratorial and the female voice was full of fear. Kangmei.

He struggled to his knees, grunting, using his hands to feel in the blackness. If these thugs were so efficient, he wondered, why hadn't they tied his hands as well? Why leave him free to explore the darkness for a way out—

And then one of Stratton's hands found what it was supposed to. It was as big around as a baseball bat, yet taut and rippling. It was smooth to the touch, not oily, and it made a hushing sound as it glided across the floor of the dark closet.

Stratton froze, and the amplified beat of his heart filled his ears. The creature had stopped moving; it was not bothered at all by the darkness.

Stratton cowered. He felt that the thing could actually sense his pulse, and feel the heat of his terror.

"You are stupid men. Leave me alone!" Kangmei clutched the cotton sheet to her neck. Her knees were drawn protectively to her chest.

"Your father sent us," Deng said from under his brim. "Not for you, Kangmei, but for your American friend. He is a dangerous man, an enemy of the state. He is trying to use you to obtain information that would harm the deputy minister."

"Lies!"

"We did not know you were with him," Liao said in a nervous whisper. "And you can be sure that we will not make a public matter of this . . . incident."

Kangmei's eyes flashed toward the closet, and the knot of hemp rope that secured the door.

"You know what would happen if this episode became known," Liao continued. "You would lose your place at the language school. There might even be punishment at a labor camp for rehabilitation."

"What do you want?"

Deng nodded toward the closet. "The foreigner is our only interest. If you need to know more, ask your father. We are here to do a job. I am sorry that you had to become involved in this, Comrade."

"Think of the shame and embarrassment for the deputy minister," Liao said.

"Thom-as was a friend of my uncle. He is an art teacher on tour," Kangmei said. "That is all."

"We see what we see, Comrade," Liao said.

Kangmei flushed.

"Put on your clothes. You will come with us and say nothing of what happened here," Liao said.

"And what is happening?" she demanded.

"Very unfortunate," Deng said. "Mr. Stratton, the American tourist, purchased a rare poisonous snake from a street vendor. His plan was to smuggle it out of China to the United States. It was a king cobra, the most terrible snake in the world, Comrade. Zoos in America would pay handsomely for a specimen—and the one *meiguoren* wanted to smuggle was certainly large and healthy."

"Unfortunately," Liao broke in, "the American was careless. The snake bit him. He fell forward, shattering his nose on the floor—see here." With a blue canvas shoe, Liao daubed at a blood smear on the wood.

"But the fall didn't matter," Deng said. "He probably was dead already. One drop of the king cobra's venom can kill a horse."

Kangmei stared at the empty sack in Deng's hand and began to whimper. She dressed with her back to the cadres.

"Come now, we will take you away," Deng said. "In the morning, we will notify the deputy minister. If you behave, my friend and I will leave the explanation of this up to you. It is not our place to tell the deputy minister that his daughter is a common whore."

"A traitorous whore!" Liao barked, pushing her toward the door.

"But Thom-as!" Kangmei cried.

106

"We will come back in a little while," Deng said, "to arrange things."

"Yes," Liao said with a satisfied smile. "The snake will require special attention."

Tom Stratton inched into a corner of the closet and balled up like some gangly, naked autistic child. He ached and he itched, but he dared not stretch or scratch. Every motion was a clue, and every tiny noise a magnet for the huge killing machine that shared his darkness.

He knew a little about cobras: that their vision was excellent, their sensory reflexes keen, all filtered through a magical flicking tongue that could find a rat or a lizard or a camouflaged toad in the blackest of Asian jungle nights. Man was not prey; he was an enemy. The cobra, Stratton knew, would not attack unless cornered and threatened.

It was a small closet, but Stratton gladly surrendered most of it to the reptile. During the argument outside the door, it had moved back and forth, brushing silkily against his feet and legs. Occasionally, its shadow crossed the floor in such a way that it obliterated the crack of light beneath the door. In those moments of total darkness, Stratton would close his eyes, for he feared an unseen strike at his face, and strained to listen for the cobra's breathing. He could hear nothing. In and out, the tongue was reading him, measuring him, taking his temperature . . . all in silence.

It was a superb creature, a mystical creature.

When the door to the hotel room closed, and Kangmei and her captors were gone, the snake seemed to settle down in a corner of its own. In his mind's eye, Stratton could see its thick olive coils—and the hooded head, motionless and erect.

After an hour, Stratton decided that the snake was as relaxed as it was ever going to be. He edged on his buttocks across the dusty floor, inches at a time, pausing several moments between moves. From the corner where he imagined that the cobra slept there came no sound.

Stratton eased himself up to the door. His right hand spidered slowly across the wood until it found the knob. He

107

twisted and pushed—but the door would not budge. Stratton tried again, this time with his shoulder as a buttress. The door held fast. The problem was breaking it down without arousing the cobra.

Stratton's knees cracked loudly as he struggled to his feet. The ankle ropes had been a cinch, even in the darkness. If he could just get out of the goddamn closet, he would be free.

He was careful not to move his legs; instead, he pivoted from the waist up, ramming the door with his upper body. Stratton could feel the hinges weaken. He rammed again, a bayonet-thrust without the sword. And once more with all of his hundred ninety pounds.

On Stratton's third try the snake struck. He heard the hiss and felt the passing breath. Stratton froze. The cobra struck again, biting air. Six inches to the left and the fangs would have pierced Stratton's groin.

The cobra was angry. The sweat, the heat of human exertion, the blood racing through Stratton's body as he pounded the door—all this had ignited the snake's primal reflex.

Instinctively, Stratton jumped to his left, crashing into a suit of clothes that hung from a dowel. The snake followed. Once, ssshhhhhh, in the air. Again, closer, a deadly sibilance two inches from Stratton's ear. And once more, higher and longer . . .

Stratton pressed his head against the wall; he held himself there to stay out of range. Now he heard a different sound. The cobra was struggling in front of him, thrashing wildly in the folds of clothing. Stratton knew instantly what had happened. Its fangs were hung in the fabric. The beast was stuck like a dart on cork.

He reached out and found the snake. He grabbed it like a rope, working upward, hand-over-hand toward the frantic lethal head. Stratton found the cobra's hood. It seemed enormous, but it folded smoothly in his grip. Stratton kneaded his way to the head.

Both hands yanked the cobra down to the floor of the closet. Squeezing its neck with all of his strength, he threw his body on the writhing coils. The cobra took twelve and one-half minutes to die. Stratton knew. He counted every second.

"Thomas! I hear you in there." Alice Dempsey paced the hallway outside the hotel room. Her voice dripped with annoyance. "You missed breakfast again, and you're about to miss the bus." Alice despised disorder; Stratton embodied it. In her mind, she had already composed a stern letter to his dean. The trip was a farce as far as Stratton went. He had disappeared for days at a time. He had openly taunted his colleagues. He had insulted the Chinese and even fought with them, for God's sake. Stratton would live to regret his inexcusable behavior.

"Come on!"

Alice knocked again. This time the door swung open on its own. Two Chinese strangers stood there. One wore a Mao cap pulled down low over his eyes.

"Where's Mr. Stratton?" Alice demanded. She sensed trouble.

The man with the cap shrugged and said nothing.

"Do you understand English?"

The other man, younger than the first, shook his head no. Alice took a step inside. The bed had been slept in, but the room held no sign of Stratton. The drawers in the bureau had been drawn half open. The closet door was ajar—it too was empty—but something caught Alice's eye: a length of heavy rope hung from the outside doorknob. In one corner of the room appeared to be another length of rope, brownish green in color, and glossy, as if it were made of plastic. Curious, Alice stepped forward for a closer look.

She let out a hoarse scream when she saw that the coil of rope was actually a large dead snake.

The man with the Mao cap pointed to the reptile and then tapped his chest proudly.

"You killed it?" Alice gasped.

The man nodded excitedly and pointed at his friend. Then he performed a brief pantomime, clubbing at the floor with an imaginary truncheon. Then he pointed at the cobra again and grinned.

109

Alice returned a nervous smile. "Well, you both are very brave. But where has Mr. Stratton gone? Have you seen him?"

The men's faces went blank.

"*Weiguoren*," Alice said, laboring over each syllable.

"*Wei*," answered the man in the Mao cap. It was as good as a shrug.

Alice bowed goodbye and left the room, grumbling. No one on the bus would believe *this*.

Stratton poured himself a large cup of hot tea and drank it quickly; the train would lurch to a start any second, and he didn't want the steaming cup to spill in his lap. That the soft-class compartment was unoccupied was his second stroke of luck this morning. The first had been talking his way onto the Peking-bound train. His papers showed that he was not routed back to Peking, and the clerk at the station had noticed the discrepancy at first glance. She had called for an interpreter, who had explained that Stratton could not leave Xian until the date prescribed on his papers. Stratton had responded with a hideously graphic story about food poisoning from some bad snails; he even interrupted the discussion and run to the restroom, pretending to be sick. It was a good performance, and both the clerk and the translator had solemnly agreed that he should return to Peking at once for rest and medical treatment.

Now, alone on the train and seemingly safe, Stratton had time to think. David—dead at the hands of his own brother. Kangmei—arrested, maybe worse. Then there was the deputy minister, Wang Bin—frightened enough to order the murder of an American tourist. But why?

At the dig, Kangmei's friend had observed Wang Bin struggling for David's camera. This puzzled Stratton, for the site had been photographed extensively, and the pictures had been published throughout the world. Evidently David had found something extraordinary—something forbidden.

The inventory of his belongings provided by the American Embassy listed three unexposed rolls of film. To Stratton, the

110

explanation was simple: Wang Bin had confiscated all the film his brother had shot during his homecoming.

A shrill chorus of military music exploded from a scratchy speaker in Stratton's compartment. He groped for the dial and tried to turn it off; the marching song faded, but it would not die. He glanced at his wristwatch and noticed that the train was already ten minutes late for departure.

Stratton was uneasy. Next time, he knew, Wang Bin's methods would be less diabolical, but more dependable than a killer snake. Once back in Peking, Stratton would make a beeline for the embassy and enlist Linda's help.

A waiter knocked lightly on the door of the compartment. He brought Stratton a hand towel and a small lumpy pillow. Stratton thanked him and said, "Are we leaving soon?"

"Soon," the waiter answered politely. He stared at Stratton's swollen nose as he backed out.

"Is there some kind of mechanical problem?"

"Soon," the waiter repeated, disappearing.

Through the window Stratton scanned the empty station ramp. The train was loaded. Any minute now . . . he sighed, and stretched his legs on the long seat.

Stratton toyed with his newfound scenario. Wang Bin had invited his brother to China, hoping to recruit David into a smuggling scheme. As a courier, perhaps, for ancient artifacts. Or maybe Wang Bin simply needed a trusted person to act as a broker for the priceless contraband back in the States.

Together they visited the Qin tombs. Wang Bin gave David the grand tour—maybe more. David took some pictures. Wang Bin made his pitch, but David rebuffed him. The deputy minister was enraged, panic-stricken. Stratton could easily imagine Wang Bin's reaction if David had threatened —as he probably did—to report his greedy brother to the authorities in Peking.

Stratton recalled Kangmei's conversation with her uncle on the night of his death: *He said that Wang Bin was doing something very wrong. . . . He was horrified that his brother would attempt such a thing.* Yes, the old professor's indignation would have been volcanic. And what if, Stratton won-

111

dered, David had learned something so scandalous that it could have sent the deputy minister to prison?

Wouldn't that be enough to make one brother murder another?

Stratton finished his tea and set the empty cup on the table. The train still had not moved, but in his ruminations Stratton had forgotten his impatience.

He was sure now. He had figured it out.

To Wang Bin, it must have seemed a simple scheme, wonderfully pragmatic. Faithful brother David returns home from his China trip, a sword or vase or delicate clay mask packed in his personal luggage. The proper-looking receipts would be provided, of course—and where would one ever encounter a customs officer expert enough, or bold enough, to challenge such artifacts?

Once safely in the United States, any large museum would pay magnificently and ask precious few questions. David would be delighted for his cut, however small. After all, who can retire comfortably on a meager university pension?

As for the rest of the money, Wang Bin's share: a bank draft to a numbered account in Zurich, and from there, a transfer to Hong Kong. There were a few creative ways to get it actually back into Peking, but Stratton figured that Hong Kong would have been close enough for the deputy minister.

A neat scheme, Stratton thought, until David Wang balked. Then there was only one thing his fearful brother could do.

Stratton stood up and stretched. Powell would never believe it. With Linda Greer, he had a better chance. By now, she would have learned of his escapade with the cadres in the Red Flag limousine. Her feelers would be out on the street; friendly eyes would be looking for him. Stratton figured that Wang Bin was not the only person who now wanted him out of China.

He was not frightened for himself, but he worried for Kangmei. Because of who she was, she probably would not be killed. Still, her life could be ruined. There was no telling what her penance would be. In Kangmei's case, Stratton reflected sadly, there would be no one to intervene.

112

Someone tapped on the door.

"More tea?"

"No, thank you," Stratton said, surprised at the sound of hard-learned English. "Can you tell me when we're leaving?"

The door opened. "Now," said the man in the Mao cap. He pointed a Russian-made pistol at Stratton's face. The American raised his arms. Liao followed Deng through the door.

The three men stood awkwardly together in the small compartment, Stratton awaiting directions. He could not believe they would shoot him on a crowded morning train.

"Where to?" he asked after a few moments.

"Off train," Deng said, but he didn't move.

"Nose broke," Liao said with a perceptive sneer. He pointed at Stratton's face.

"Yeah, well, I'm sorry about your pet snake," Stratton muttered.

Deng lowered the pistol from Stratton's head and held it at waist level, trained on the American's midsection.

"I'll go quietly, don't worry," Stratton said. The Chinese traded glances. "How long are we going to stand here?" Stratton asked.

"Go now," said Deng, pulling the trigger.

The bullet lifted Tom Stratton and propelled him backward into the wall of the compartment. His head cracked against a steel bunk and he rag-dolled forward into a heap on the floor. Day became night. The Chinese demons screamed in Stratton's ears until his mind went limp and cold in a terrible sleep.

CHAPTER 11

"WE'VE GOT a pair of nasty little problems on our hands, don't we?" The station chief drummed his pudgy gray fingers on the desk. He let out a sigh of disgust. "Wang Bin *and* Stratton."

Linda Greer was reading a file. She wore glasses, forcing herself to fix on the words. She fought off despair.

"Why did the deputy minister want your friend out of the country so badly? Think of it: We tell him quite politely that Mr. Stratton will not be accompanying his brother's body back to the United States—and what does he do? He sends a couple of goons to the hotel. Why?" The station chief did not wait to hear any theories. "Because he *knows*. Linda, somehow Wang Bin got hold of Stratton's service record. He knows about Man-ling."

Linda shook her head slowly and set the file on the desk. "It's more than that. It's got to be."

"Damn, the coffee's cold already. Why does it have to be more than that?"

"Suppose Wang Bin knows about Stratton's brief incursion back in 1971," Linda began. "Wouldn't it be easier, and more

114

effective, to make a formal request: 'This man is an undesirable and we would like him to leave China at once'? A sticky little deportation problem, nothing more. We've handled stuff like that in the past. Now this," she said, motioning toward the file, "is pretty clumsy, sir. Chasing Stratton all over the city with a goddamn Red Flag, then trying to run him over in the street . . . that's not the style of this bureaucracy, sir. It's too messy. Reckless. Something like that might happen in Moscow—"

"In a blue moon!" the station chief huffed.

"—but never in Peking. The police or the PLA could have captured Stratton in a matter of minutes."

The phone rang once. The station chief spoke briefly and hung up. "So what are you saying, Linda? That this was a private matter between Wang and Stratton? An informal abduction?"

"Something's going on, and it's damn sure not just a matter of honor. My guess is that Wang Bin sent those two clowns to grab Stratton, not to kill him. But when it looked as if he would get away, they panicked and tried to run him down."

"Now one is dead and the other's a cabbage. Jesus!" The station chief grunted as he flipped through his copy of the file. "And our Mr. Stratton is missing in action. What a fiasco!"

Linda Greer said nothing. The possibilities were too depressing.

The station chief looked up and asked, "Think they caught up with him at Xian?"

"Yes."

"Me, too. Think he's dead?"

"Probably. We had someone interview some of the other Americans on that tour. They saw Stratton at the hotel yesterday morning, but he didn't stay with the group."

"Naturally."

"He left with two Chinese, a young woman and a man."

"And?"

Linda took off her glasses and folded them. "This morning, when one of the Americans went to Stratton's hotel room, he was gone. Gone without a trace. The woman who discovered

115

him missing is the same one who gave us the story about the snake."

The station chief smiled slightly, remembering the bland entry in the file, rated "very reliable."

"Ah, that would be the busybody Mrs. Dempsey. She also found the Chinese in Stratton's room. Just tidying up, I suppose. What kind of snake?

"She didn't know," Linda said. "By the time our people got there, the room was clean. There was a little blood on the floor, though. Most of it had been scrubbed away—"

"Was there enough to—"

"Yes. O positive. Same as Tom's." Linda Greer felt very tired. She wanted to go back to her apartment and soak in the bathtub. She wanted to cry.

"Oh dear," the station chief muttered. He gazed out the window; the setting sun painted the tiled roofs of Peking a burned yellow and turned the haze into a pale lemon curtain.

"I took the liberty of filing formal inquiries with China Travel, the tourism bureau, and the others. . . . I don't expect to hear anything, but at least we're on the record as far as procedure goes."

"Yes," the station chief said. "Good thinking. Let's meet again tomorrow. Noonish. In the meantime, say nothing to Powell. I'm sure he's picked up whispers about that insane goddamn bicycle chase, so just tell him we're checking it out."

Linda Greer collected her purse and briefcase, and headed for the door.

The station chief cleared his throat. "Linda," he called in a softer voice. "I'm sorry about Stratton."

"Thanks."

"What do you suppose he was after?"

"I haven't the slightest idea," she replied truthfully.

For three days the freight train creaked south through plains and farmland, skirting the rugged mountain ranges that rule China's interior. The trip was hot, the train old and plodding, led by a spanking new steam locomotive.

Tom Stratton lay in a boxcar that smelled of ammonia and

116

cow manure. His arms and legs were trussed, and a burlap sack had been tied loosely over his head and upper torso. A dirty wad of gauze had been tightly taped over the nearly circular wound in his thigh. Deng's aim had been perfect; the small-caliber bullet had missed Stratton's hip bone and passed harmlessly through the fat of his upper leg. The blow on the head that had come with the fall had been a bonus for Deng and his partner; it had then been a simple matter to explain the unconscious American tourist being carried off the train in Xian. He had fallen in the compartment and badly cut his leg. He needed medical attention immediately.

Tom Stratton woke hours later to the clanging of rails, the lurching of the boxcar, and the tickle of a small animal scampering across the sack that cloaked his head. It was night. His thigh ached painfully. Stratton guessed that his bunkmate was probably a rat, and he rolled over to frighten it away. His head twirled and his ears rang as he moved; undoubtedly he had been sedated. He lay still and inhaled vigorously, the burlap puckering at his mouth with each breath. The stale air was heavy with musk, but in it there was a sweet tinge of wheat and maize. Stratton's stomach growled in recognition.

Eventually, he squirmed into a sitting position, propped up against a sack of what smelled like potatoes.

It was a small moral victory. Sitting up, Stratton felt a little less helpless. He wondered why they hadn't just killed him. No esoteric stuff—cobras and the like—just a good old-fashioned bullet in the brain. He felt slightly nauseous but resolved not to throw up in the sack. As the hours passed and his body cried for water, Stratton began to pray that they would not leave him there to die in a vegetable car with a horde of hungry goddamn rats.

The panel door of the boxcar clattered open and daylight exploded in Stratton's face. He had managed to work himself out of the burlap, in the darkness, but could see nothing. Now the sudden brightness blinded him. Rough hands yanked him upright by the hair. A terse command in Mandarin, and then in English: "Drink!" Stratton gulped strange-tasting water from a wooden mug. Within minutes, he grew dizzy and passed out.

Deng and Liao were in a foul mood; neither had relished a trip to the south. Peking, with its fine restaurants and all its cadre privileges, was infinitely preferable to a muggy peasant farm village. Down here the lines of authority were less clearly drawn, Deng grumbled; respect seemed to diminish with each kilometer away from the Imperial City. At every stop there had been questions: Where are your papers? What are you doing here? Where is your *dan-wei*? In his agitation, Deng handled the sleeping form of Tom Stratton with something less than gentleness.

"I thought we would be finished with this in Xian," Liao said as they heaved Stratton onto a flatbed truck. "The orders changed. I wonder why."

"A good question for the deputy minister," Deng said. "He will be here soon."

Wang Bin leaned back and blew a smoke ring toward the ceiling. "Tell me about the American."

"I will not," his daughter said hotly.

"You will! You are too old to spank, Wang Kangmei, but you are of an age where other punishment can be more terrible. You still have a future today, but there is no guarantee. Tomorrow, who knows? I would not be the first senior Party official to forsake an errant child."

Kangmei folded her arms across her breasts and stared at the floor.

"Did you sleep with him?"

"He told me all about Uncle David. He wished to see the tombs at Xian, the dig you are so proud of. What harm was there in showing him?"

"He asked many questions, did he not?"

"Not as many as I asked him. Father, I was merely curious. About Xian, about my uncle. I was distraught because he died only days after we first met. Can you understand that?"

"Did you—"

"No! I did not sleep with Stratton."

118

"Deng and Liao told me you were in his room." Wang Bin's eyes dropped. "Naked in his bed."

"They are vicious liars, Father. They came to *my* room, and dragged me from my own bed. They took me to Stratton and began to interrogate us. They hit me, Father, and said terrible things. Stratton tried to stop them and they beat him up, and locked him in a closet—"

Wang Bin raised a hand. "You are a foolish girl, and a bad liar. For that, I suppose, I should be grateful. Your eyes confess everything, Kangmei. Now I ask you: What of the family honor? Whoring with a foreigner—such behavior aggrieves me, and insults the entire Wang family. I shall not mention what it would do to your mother."

"I *told* you—"

"It probably will not be possible to keep this quiet for very long. Today the loyalties of Liao and Deng belong to me; tomorrow, who can say?" Wang Bin watched his daughter's eyes grow moist. Her posture remained erect, and her face defiant. "Kangmei, this fascination you nurture for America has become a dangerous and disturbing thing. You are in serious trouble. This Thomas Stratton is no simple tourist. He is a cunning man, a former soldier. He has been to China before, and he has killed Chinese. He is a spy, Kangmei, and you, his tool. The shame you have brought to our family . . . it saddens me."

"No!" Kangmei cried. "You are wrong, Father. Stratton was a friend of my uncle, that it all. He mourns David Wang as a friend mourns, deeply and sincerely. This I know. I've done nothing shameful—"

"That is enough," Wang Bin said coldly.

"No!" Kangmei was on her feet, shouting and crying at once. "How can you treat a daughter like this? The thugs who beat me, attacked me in my bed—*they* should be in jail, not me. Yet I am dragged from my room, tied up, gagged, and thrown in a dirty cell with dangerous criminals. Why, Father?"

Wang Bin laughed shortly and stubbed out his cigarette. "Your pitiful cellmates hardly qualify as dangerous criminals. They are petty thieves, my daughter, that's all. They're being

119

punished for pilfering from the archaeological sites—nothing valuable: trinkets, really. But it is important to set an example for the others. Stealing cannot be tolerated at such historic places. However, these people are not truly dangerous, so stop the tears."

Kangmei asked, "Must I go back to the cell?"

Wang Bin circled the small desk and slipped an arm around his daughter's trembling shoulders. "No," he said. "We're going on a trip."

Kangmei pulled away and faced her father. "Where?"

"South," he replied, "to a small village. Kangmei, there is something you must do for me—and for yourself. To erase what has happened is impossible. But it is still possible for you to repent, to have a future, and perhaps even a good position in China. You *must* do as I say."

"And if I refuse?"

Wang Bin raised his hands in a gesture of feigned indifference. "Then I will not hesitate to put you on the first train to Tibet, where you can grub potatoes for the next five years."

Tom Stratton awoke to the hum of flies circling his head. His cheek pressed against an earthen floor, and the cool smell of clay filled his nostrils.

As he righted himself, the bleak room spun briefly. His arms and legs were free. His thigh throbbed, and by the dismal condition of the bandage, Stratton knew that his captors had not changed the dressing.

His cell was spartan: a single wooden chair, straight-backed, handmade, with a crude hemp seat; a solitary bare light bulb, fixed in the rafters; a large ceramic bowl, crusted with stale rice and scum, buzzing with insects; and a single window, at eye level, crisscrossed in a loose pattern with barbed wire.

Tom Stratton was alone. He paced the dimensions of the room at eight feet by twelve. The heavy door was made of intransigent timber. Stratton knew it would never yield to his shoulder.

Peering through the window, which measured about a foot square, Stratton expected to see a military compound with marching squads of People's Liberation Army soldiers, or at

120

least some uniformed police. Instead he saw a newly paved road and a large parking lot half-filled with trucks and bicycles; beyond that, a banana grove carpeted an entire hillside. A lorry painted dark PLA green trundled down the two-lane road and stopped in the parking lot no more than fifty yards from Stratton's cell. He watched a quiet but affable procession of Chinese jump down and form an orderly group. The men wore sturdy gray or brown slacks, starched shirts open at the neck, while the pigtailed women wore loose-fitting pants and white cotton blouses. Their clothing was too fancy for work. Stratton assumed that the visitors were local tourists.

The truck rattled off, and the Chinese marched dutifully toward the building in which Stratton was being held. They crossed only a few feet from his cell, talking in pleasant tones, until they finally passed out of Stratton's sight.

He decided that his dungeon definitely was not part of a regular Chinese jail.

Stratton moved to the corner of the room that garnered the most light from the small window. There he peeled off the soiled bandage and examined the bullet hole in his right thigh. The dime-sized wound was black and scabbed, but the vermilion halo around it announced that infection had set in. Stratton's only piece of clothing, a short-sleeved sports shirt, was rancid from the long train ride, and of no use as a sponge. Reluctantly, he rewrapped his injured leg with the same dirty gauze, and sat down to wait for his keepers.

They arrived without pleasantries, an hour before dusk; three men, lean, unremarkable, impassive at first. They wore no uniforms, which surprised Stratton. One of them, who carried a rifle with a bayonet, motioned Stratton out of the cell.

He was led to a small courtyard whose boundaries were marked by tangled hedges. Red bougainvillea plants radiantly climbed the walls of the otherwise drab buildings that formed the complex. The place reminded Stratton of a monastery.

The men stopped in the middle of the courtyard. Stratton faced them. He was naked from the waist down, and filthy. His mustache was flecked with clay, and it smelled.

"Could I have a pair of trousers?" Stratton asked.

121

His escorts glanced at each other. They spoke no English. The one with the rifle suddenly raised it to his shoulder and aimed at Stratton's dangling genitals.

"Pah! Pah!" he barked, pretending to pull the trigger. "Pah! Pah! Pah!"

His comrades sniggered. The rifleman lowered the gun and his face grew stoic once again.

Stratton lifted his arms from his sides. "You missed," he said, pointing. "See?"

Self-consciously, the escorts averted their eyes. From across the plaza came the sound of many voices. Stratton realized that the workers at the compound had been summoned to witness a public humiliation—his own.

As the Chinese filed through the courtyard, they bunched into a confused knot at the side of the half-naked American, standing at attention in the day's final shadows. A few jeered. Others laughed and pointed. Then, some of the women became upset and began to leave. The men also soon wearied of the spectacle.

Stratton was too exhausted to be embarrassed, but the three guards wore satisfied smiles.

After the workers had gone, the men took Stratton outside the compound to an alley. One of them twisted the handle on a water faucet, and a stream of cold water shot out. The man with the bayonet pointed at the swelling puddle.

Stratton obligingly stripped out of his shirt and removed the bandage from his thigh. He squatted beneath the faucet and closed his eyes. The frigid water was invigorating, but his injured leg stiffened in protest. While his feet and his buttocks rested in the murky puddle, Stratton was careful to keep the wound clean. He pressed his scalp to the mouth of the faucet, and let the hard water rinse the grime from his hair.

"*Gou!*" commanded one of the watchers. Enough.

Stratton stood up and smoothed his hair back. Then he slipped into his shirt.

One of the escorts held out the rag that had served as his bandage.

"But it's too dirty," Stratton objected.

The man with the gun stared back blankly. Stratton

122

wrapped the fetid gauze around his upper leg and tied it with a small knot.

With a sharp shove to the small of his back, Stratton was directed to his cell. One of the jailers followed him inside just long enough to ladle two scoops of rice into the food dish, and to replace a rusty tin can full of water on the earthen floor.

The door closed heavily, and night swallowed Stratton's room with a humid gulp. Outside, in the tropical orchards, birds whistled. The hills were dotted sparsely with yellow lights from distant communes.

Stratton waved the flies off the bowl of rice, and put a cold lumpy handful in his mouth.

He decided that the march to the water faucet had been a good sign. Certainly the bath had not been meant for his benefit, so it could mean only one thing. Soon he would have a visitor.

Probably an important visitor.

CHAPTER 12

J I M M c C A R T H Y parked in a dark corner of the crowded lot at the Peking Hotel. His station wagon was fire-engine red—the journalist's mobile protest against the drab sameness of Peking. Every now and then, when China weighed too heavily, McCarthy would roll down the windows, plug in a Willie Nelson tape as loud as he could stand it and—gawkers be damned—cruise at high speed into the ancient hills around the city.

McCarthy made sure the driver's door was unlocked. He trudged up the circular driveway and through the automatic doors that admit foreigners only to Peking's best hotel. To the left of the lobby lay a broad marble passageway that had been converted with plastic tables and chairs into a brightly lit lounge. The Via Veneto, denizens called it sarcastically. The cafe, a grudging Chinese concession to the influx of foreigners that had accompanied the late '70s opening to the West, had, perforce, become the center of social life for transient foreigners in Peking. Sooner or later, everyone wound up drinking instant coffee at the ersatz cafe. McCarthy had interviewed a movie star there, an ice skater and a famous

124

novelist, each one of them self-impressed and self-righteous— *doing* China.

That night there was only a middling crowd. McCarthy nodded to a pair of African diplomats. He chatted briefly with some members of a British lawyers' tour and watched in amusement while well-heeled businessmen of three nationalities sniffed around a lady banker from New York. She had lived in the hotel for two years and would die there on full expenses, if the Chinese allowed it, having long since discovered one of the secrets of revolutionary Peking: It is nirvana for ugly Western women. In New York, the lady banker would have trouble getting a tumble in the raunchiest singles bar. In puritan Peking, without local competition, she never slept alone. McCarthy ordered a cognac at the bar and watched the circus.

After about ten minutes, he walked back to the car and drove toward the poorly lit northern quarter of the city. On an empty side street, he pulled to the curb.

"Come out, come out, wherever you are," he called.

From the backseat, a passenger untangled himself from the folds of a car blanket and climbed into the front seat.

McCarthy lit a cigarette, watching in the rearview mirror as the side lights of another car appeared. Things they never teach you in journalism school, he reflected sourly.

As the other car approached, it slowed. Its headlights flashed, bathing the station wagon from behind. McCarthy reacted.

The station wagon surged from the curb with a peel of rubber, dumping McCarthy's passenger awkwardly between seat and door. McCarthy turned right. The other car followed. For ten tense and silent minutes, he played hide-and-seek until at last he found the main road that tourists took to the Great Wall. His foot went to the floor. The following car, Chinese-made, more for touring than sprinting, dwindled and finally disappeared. McCarthy relaxed.

"It's nice to see you, Little Joe. How're things?"

The passenger smiled, dangling a child's sandal from its strap. In the dashboard half-light, it looked like a dead white hamster.

125

"I found this in the blanket."

"Shit, I've been looking for that for two weeks. Thanks." McCarthy passed over the pack of cigarettes. "Sorry for the bumpy start, but we had friends."

The passenger dragged deeply, opening the window to let the smoke escape.

"It is no surprise."

He was a slender youth in his twenties with a tousled thatch of black hair and sharp cheek bones. He wore a cheap open-necked white shirt and baggy olive-green trousers. A schoolboy's satchel sat primly on his knees. Over the past year, since a casual meeting at an art exhibition arranged by the American Embassy, the shy youth had become McCarthy's best Chinese source.

"Shall we go to my place for a few drinks and some music? The kids are all asleep, Little Joe." It was a name the boy had assigned himself. McCarthy didn't know his real name, or where he lived. He knew only about the young man's dreams and that his information was good.

"Tonight is bad, Lao Jim. The army, the police, the watchers all have instructions to be particularly alert about contacts with foreigners."

Among foreigners who knew any Chinese willing to risk it, the procedure for getting a guest into the walled diplomatic compound was almost routine: bundle them down in the back and drive smiling through the gate. The PLA soldiers seldom did more than wave; in the winter, they simply peered out from their hut and wrote down the special license numbers reserved for *weiguoren*. Except for taxis with passengers, normally registered vehicles were forbidden to enter the compound.

At first, Little Joe had been reluctant, and then thrilled, at the prospect of cheating the security system. In recent months, he had become more cautious, resorting finally to hurried phone calls to arrange meetings at "the usual place"— the hotel parking lot.

"How are things, Little Joe? Are we hearing the same rumors?" McCarthy coaxed.

The youth lit a fresh cigarette from the butt of the old.

126

"Special security units are being assigned to the embassies—uniformed and plainclothes—beginning two days from now. I think they expect some attempts to defect."

"Why?"

"The old Maoists are winning control. They will purge several hundred officials in Peking in the next week. Did you hear that rumor?" Little Joe not only spoke good English, but also had a subtle sense of humor, rare in a Chinese. He was a friend to be treasured.

"Among others," McCarthy lied.

"Well, I have seen the list, and it is true."

"Any names I would recognize?"

"Possibly." He named two or three. "Most of them, though, are second- or third-rank people, administrators and—how do you call it?—technocrats."

"What have they done?"

"Just like the others who have already been purged. They are skilled at what they do and have great experience in dealing with foreigners. The Party thinks they are more loyal to their own jobs, or to their ministries, or to their foreign friends, than to the Party itself. The Party allows no other lovers, as you know, Lao Jim."

"Is it true? About their loyalties?"

Little Joe laughed. "What do you think?"

"I'd say yes. A lot of people dislike the dull old men."

"You are right. It is not their loyalty to China that is the problem, but their reliance on the Party. The people I am talking about run factories that are profitable or bureaus that are too modern. They make decisions without asking the Party each day if it is permitted to eat rice for lunch."

"I know the kind of people you mean."

Little Joe nodded. "Yes, they are the best of China and the young people who work for them are fantastically loyal—these men are seen as the true future of the New China."

"To purge them will have a great effect on morale, won't it?"

"Will you never understand China, Lao Jim?" The Chinese laughed at his own question. "They will be purged not because they are efficient, but because they are corrupt. That is what the accusations will say, and that is what many people will believe. That Manager Hu used his position to enrich himself; that he stole money, or the factory's car; that he accepted gifts or bribes from foreigners; that he had a foreign bank account; that he smuggled goods from China under false documents. The list of charges is endless. The Party can say anything it likes. No guilt is necessary. The accusation is enough—for the Party."

McCarthy saw what was coming.

"No good news for you, huh?"

"I have been denied permission to travel—no families of leading cadres may go abroad to study any longer. That is the ruling."

"I'm sorry."

Little Joe had worked three years to pass the exams and polish his English. When McCarthy had first met him, the young man had boasted of a scholarship offer from an American university. "I am going to study language and literature," Little Joe had said. "Can you lend me some books to read before I go?"

It had been a year of yes-maybe-come-back-tomorrows. And then the bureaucracy had reneged.

"I have been assigned to work in the Number Five Locomotive Factory. I am to be a cook."

"Jesus, that's awful." They were on the tree-shaded street where Little Joe usually got out. McCarthy stopped the car and reached around for a package on the back seat. "It's easy for me to say, but try not to be discouraged, Little Joe. Keep reading and studying. Here, take a look."

McCarthy flipped on the dome light and the Chinese quickly riffled through his gifts—back copies of *The Economist*, *Time* and *Newsweek* and some paperback books.

"I couldn't find *Twelfth Night*, but I got *Merchant of Venice*. And here's one by Graham Greene, *Monsignor Quixote*. It's great."

"Quixote . . . Cervantes, right?"

McCarthy nodded.

"Well, he wrote in prison. I guess I can read in prison." Little Joe gestured. He meant everything around him.

128

"*Zaijian*," said Little Joe, and vanished into the night.

Pensively, McCarthy drove home. Poor bastard, he thought, another one of the good young ones being devoured. But a damned good source. Apprentice cook he might be, but Little Joe was still the son of a general.

"I trust the accommodations are satisfactory," Wang Bin said from the doorway. "I would be offended if such a distinguished guest were not comfortable."

Stratton stared dully at him from a pile of dirty straw at the far corner of the room.

Bathed in sweat, he rolled clumsily to a sitting position.

Wang Bin sneered. "Your leg is all bloody. You should be more careful, Professor."

"Fuck you."

"Stand up."

"I can't."

On mincing steps, as though afraid of dirtying his highly polished shoes, Wang Bin advanced into the room until he stood over Stratton. His foot lashed out, striking Stratton's shin. Stratton bit back a moan.

"That is just the beginning, *Professor*." He spat as he spoke, hitting Stratton between the eyes. "I regret only that I shall not be present for the end. It was planned for Xian, but you were lucky. A train station is too public, and a bullet is too merciful for a man who rapes my daughter."

Stratton felt the spittle course down his face. He tensed for a spring. Movement caught Stratton's eye. Framed in the doorway stood one of the jailers, a pistol leveled at Stratton. With an explosion of breath, he allowed his body's tension to dissipate. Revenge alone was not enough. There must also be escape. There would be another time.

"I will tell you where you are, since you will never leave," Wang Bin said. "It is a museum on the outskirts of the city of Nanning. It is a backward place, Nanning, but it has some lovely Ming Dynasty pottery."

"You know where you can put your pottery."

"Oh no, Professor Stratton, there are better uses for it. For you, there is no use at all. Except as an example of revo-

129

lutionary justice. Has anyone listed your crimes for you? No? An oversight, I'm sure."

Wang Bin rocked with his hands behind him, a student reciting his lessons.

"You are accused of theft: of the personal effects of my distinguished brother. You are accused of murder: of one of my trusted drivers in Peking, and of assault against another, who may still die."

Wang Bin's voice was rising in pitch, like a factory whistle.

"You are accused of kidnapping my daughter." He spat at Stratton again. "And of rape of my daughter.

"You are guilty of all charges, *Professor*." Wang Bin's face was flushed. "The sentence is death. There is no appeal. People's justice. Do you know how executions are carried out in revolutionary China, Professor?" Wang Bin's mouth twitched. "The condemned man is forced to kneel, with his hands tied behind his back. His executioner stands behind him. At the signal, the executioner advances one step, brings up his gun and in one motion, delivers a killing shot to the back of the head. Sometimes a pistol is used, but in your case, I think a rifle is more appropriate. A rifle leaves no room for mistakes."

"It will never happen," Stratton said slowly.

"You think not?"

"I know it. You are bluffing. This isn't a real jail, and you have no authority. This is your operation, *Deputy Minister*, and yours alone. The Chinese government has nothing against me—but a great deal against you."

"I am a servant of the Revolution," Wang Bin said, self-mockingly.

"You serve only yourself. You are a thief and a murderer."

"Stratton, you are like so many of your countrymen, much noise but no wisdom. You know nothing."

"I know that you have been stealing artifacts from the dig at Xian. I know that you asked your brother to help you smuggle something out. He refused. You argued, and later you killed him in Peking. Poison, I would say. There will be evidence, you know. Poison stays in the bones; any pathologist can find it. It remains only to exhume the body."

130

Wang Bin laughed.

"Fool! You understand nothing. My brother was of great assistance to me, yes, although he did not know it. I did not need him to smuggle contraband, Professor, but to bring me something. Something perfectly legitimate. He did it willingly."

"I'll bet."

"There is one other thing you should know, fool: My brother is not dead." Wang Bin hurled the words with ferocity.

"He's dead and you killed him. You can lie to me, but I doubt if your own government will be impressed. I have written a letter—everything I know about David's death, including the fact that you killed him. It is somewhere safe. If something happens to me, then it will be opened and forwarded to the Chinese government."

Wang Bin paused to consider.

"A letter, perhaps, with one of the members of your tour group, given to him before leaving Xian."

Stratton said nothing. That is what he might have done—if the document really existed.

Then Wang Bin smiled and Stratton knew his desperate ploy had failed.

"I think the letter is your invention, but if it exists, it cannot trouble me. For me, the time is ready. And your time is finished, *Captain*."

Stratton looked at the arrogant Chinese without expression.

"Does it surprise you to hear your old rank? It should not. We are thorough people, we Chinese, patient people with long memories. We have files for everything. There is a fat security file in Peking with your name on it, and a black ribbon across it. The ribbon is a special distinction. It means kill on sight. So, in addition to all your other crimes, you are a spy. It will be a great pleasure to kill you, a service to the Revolution—my last gesture."

"How?" Stratton was too nonplussed to invent a denial.

"How did we ever know the name of the dashing captain of intelligence in Saigon who always undertook the most dangerous infiltration missions? The hero of many medals who led raids into North Vietnam and, once, even into China?

"How simple Americans are! Heroes are never truly anon-

131

ymous, Captain, and soldiers can never be trusted with secrets. Can they? Think back to Saigon. Many Americans knew the true identity of the secret 'Captain Black.' Can you believe they never talked? To their girls, to friends when they were drunk. It took some time, the file says as much. But within a few months, North Vietnamese intelligence knew you were Captain Black. After your raid into China, they shared their information—we were allies then, remember. The Vietnamese wanted you very badly, and after your slaughter of innocent peasants, so did we. Too bad you left Saigon before the assassination teams could find you."

"You got the wrong guy," Stratton said without conviction.

"I think not. Your death, at least, is something for which the Revolution will thank me. Goodbye, Captain. I hope you will find hell even less hospitable than China."

Wang Bin stormed from the makeshift cell. Stratton heard the heavy wooden bar fall against the door. He lay for a long time on the fetid ground, thinking, listening.

Then, painfully but surely, he pulled himself to his feet. He hurt, but not as badly as he had led Wang Bin to believe. Teeth clenched, moving with the jerky uncertainty of an old man, Stratton began a series of painful limbering exercises. As he bent and swayed, Stratton replayed the conversation with Wang Bin. If the mind is too occupied to register pain, then there is no pain.

The man was angry, and he would be merciless. That was the bottom line. Yet there had been bits of information within the conversation that Stratton might use. He began to gnaw at them.

He was in the south of China. What he had seen of the vegetation Wang Bin had confirmed. Guangxi Province. Stratton tried to superimpose the train ride on a map of China. South for three days. He couldn't be far from the coast. If he could get to the sea and steal a boat . . .

There had been puzzling things, too. David's unwitting role had been to bring something, Wang Bin had said. That was an obvious lie. The brothers had argued in Xian only after David had learned that Wang Bin wanted him to smuggle.

132

"My brother is not dead," he had said. A second lie, even more senseless than the first. Of course David was dead—he had been murdered.

There was a third riddle. Stratton's death was to be "my last gesture" to the Revolution. What could account for that strange phrase?

Gingerly, he began a series of knee bends. Down-two-three-four. His leg howled in protest. Why tell lies to a condemned man? Senseless. Unless . . .

"Oh, Jesus."

Stratton spoke aloud to the emptiness of his cell, the words forced from him by sudden realization. What if Wang Bin had been telling the truth?

Stratton saw it then. Not entirely clear, but in terrifying outline. Solid, diabolical, imminent.

On one point, Wang Bin had been right.

Stratton was a fool.

In frustration, he hammered at the walls of the cell. Then he snapped a leg from the wooden chair and with its point began to scrape at the crude mortar between the bricks. It was irrational, and he knew it. Still, it was not a time for reason. It was a time for fury. Stratton scraped like a man demented.

Wang Bin sat with his legs crossed in an overstuffed armchair, waiting for his tea to cool. On the table before him sat four vases, each exquisite, each more than five hundred years old.

An aide in bottle-bottom glasses came silently into the room. He sprang forward to light the deputy minister's cigarette.

"Will we be needing our guest any longer, Comrade?" the aide asked quietly.

"One more day, I'm afraid, Lao Zhou." Wang Bin was perturbed. "I wish it could have been done on the train. If only his embassy had not started asking questions. I *must* know what he told his people, if he told them anything. One more day . . . then he must vanish completely, do you understand? No trace."

133

"It will be done. He is a dangerous enemy of the state." The frail-looking young translator with weak eyes was the most sadistic killer Wang Bin had ever encountered.

"You will tell me everything he says. It is vital . . . to the Revolution," Wang Bin said. "I would like to be there myself, but I must return immediately to Peking. Go make the arrangements."

When the aide had gone, Wang Bin extracted a green and white envelope from the breast pocket of his Mao jacket. The telegram had arrived with breakfast and he knew its contents by heart.

YOU ARE REQUIRED TO APPEAR BEFORE THE DISCIPLINARY COMMISSION OF THE PARTY.

It gave a time and a date: tomorrow.

He had been expecting it. And it might have come sooner. Once again, it seemed, those idiots in Peking were determined to wrestle long-suffering China back into the Middle Ages. A few months before, such a summons would have paralyzed Wang Bin with terror—as it was intended to do. But he had foreseen it this time, and he was ready. Now there was just fleeting irritation at the dreadful cost to the nation and his own comfort. Let them writhe, he thought. Let them devour their own entrails if they wish. Comrade Deputy Minister Wang Bin would never again collect night soil.

This new peace of mind had its price, of course: an odious alliance with the American art dealer Harold Broom. His name had come to Wang Bin from an underground buyer in Hong Kong. Broom had been highly recommended, not for his taste—he had none—but for his resourcefulness. It was a trait that Wang Bin had come to appreciate, though he could not help but despise Broom for his crude arrogance.

Their short relationship had been curt, clandestine and efficient. So far. A visa problem smoothed over. A travel permit expedited. Quiet favors.

Yet there were watchers everywhere, Wang Bin well knew. He doubted that the Disciplinary Commission had learned the truth about Harold Broom, but such news would not shock him. He was ready for anything.

134

By the time the aide returned to confirm the travel arrangements, Wang Bin had already decided.

"We will take the first one and the fourth one," he said, pointing to the smallest of the four vases.

"Yes, Comrade Deputy Minister. But the comrade director of the museum will be very upset. They are among the best pieces."

"Tell him they are for permanent display in a place of honor in Peking."

"Still, he will not like it."

"Tell him it is for the good of the people. The Revolution demands it."

"Very well, Comrade Deputy Minister. But he is a hard man. He will want a receipt."

A hard man who thinks a receipt will protect him.

"A receipt," said Wang Bin. "By all means. Have the director prepare a receipt and I will sign it."

CHAPTER 13

HAROLD BROOM arrived ten minutes early at the gleaming white mansion in the River Oaks section of Houston. He leaned against his rented Lincoln for five minutes, admiring the tall pillars and polished marble steps. At the door he was met by a Mexican houseboy in a stiff high-collared waiter's jacket, who motioned him inside. He led the art dealer up a spiral oaken staircase to a second-floor office where the customer waited.

"Well, hi there!" the Texan said. Even by Houston standards he was young for a millionaire. He wore a flannel shirt, pressed Levi's, lizardskin boots and the obligatory cowboy hat with a plume. When he shook Broom's hand, he gave a disconcerting little squeeze before he let go.

Broom sat down and said, "This is a helluva homestead."

The Texan grinned. "You like it?"

"Oh yeah." Broom noticed three king-sized television screens mounted on one wall, each flashing a different program. The corners of the office were occupied by stand-up

136

stereo speakers. The Texan kept a video display terminal on his desk to watch the Dow Jones; behind his chair, Broom noticed, stood an arcade-sized Pac Man machine.

The Texan jerked a thumb at it. "Bored with it already," he said. "I've got an order in for an Astral Laser."

"Swell," Broom said. It was sickening: all this money and no brains. "Could I have a drink?"

"I don't see why not." The Texan poked an intercom button near the phone and shouted, "Paco! Two bourbons pronto."

"It's *Pablo*," a teenaged voice replied with unmasked annoyance.

The bourbon was excellent. Broom savored it, while the Texan sucked it down loudly. "Nectar," he said. "Pure nectar!"

Broom reached into the suede valise on his lap and extracted a glossy black-and-white photograph. He glanced at it before handing it across the desk to his host.

"There it is," Broom said with parental pride. "The real McCoy."

The Texan was radiant. "Broom, you've outdone yourself, I swear to God. I know better than to ask how you did it."

Broom took this as a compliment, and he forced a modest smile.

"If it arrives in this condition, it will be . . . awesome." The Texan clicked his teeth, as if leering at a centerfold.

Broom said, "The photograph was made moments before we packed it. I took the picture myself. That's the genuine item, and it's all yours. Guaranteed."

Pablo poured more bourbon. Broom drank up, basking in luxury and triumph. He was elated to be out of China.

"Harold," the Texan said, "I've gotta be sure. This is the only one?"

"Absolutely," Broom lied. If the Texan only knew.

"The price is—"

"Two hundred and fifty thousand now. Another two fifty on delivery. And don't worry. I'll be delivering it myself."

"You damn well better," the Texan growled, reaching for

137

his checkbook. "For the kind of commission you're getting, Broom, you damn well ought to show up pulling a ricksha."

The *xiu xi* is China's most revered institution. Indeed, a worker's right to rest is enshrined in China's constitution. Nowhere does it say that all China shall sleep between noon and 2 P.M., but that is how it seems. If the Russians ever come, it will be at 1 P.M., when only the rawest Chinese recruits will be awake to oppose them. In Peking, office workers sleep on their desks. In the countryside, peasants sleep in the fields. If airplane crews find themselves on the ground at noon, they will not fly again until after lunch and a *xiu xi*. The more senior a cadre, the better-appointed and more private the place of his *xiu xi*, and the longer he sleeps.

The Disciplinary Commission had cited Wang Bin for 1 P.M. It was a calculated insult, and he knew it. At noon, Wang Bin lunched with senior aides in a private room of the staff restaurant at the Peking museum that was his headquarters. Conversation was furtive. One or two of the men who had been with him the longest mentioned things that had occurred in the Deputy Minister's absence in the south: The Qin exhibition had been dispatched to the United States on schedule. From Xinjiang in China's desert west, the museum was to receive the mummified corpses of two soldiers perfectly preserved in the dry air these six hundred years; they would require a special room with stringent humidity controls.

Mostly, though, the aides avoided meeting Wang Bin's eyes. Their discomfort amused him. They knew. Deliberations of the Party are secrets closely held. But when the ax is about to fall, everybody knows. Peking becomes a village in those times. When the arrival of soup signaled the last course, Wang Bin pointedly looked around the table, studying his aides individually, making no secret of it. He was rewarded with the sight of six heads, bent uniformly, like acolytes, slurping their soup, seeing only the bowl. He wondered which of them had informed against him, and which would give testimony—if it came to that. The answer was obvious, and it saddened him: all of them. Poor China.

138

Rising, Wang Bin raised a tiny crystal glass of *mao tai*.

"To long life and happiness," he proposed. "*Ganbei*."

"*Ganbei*," the aides responded, and each drained the fiery liquor in one swallow.

"*Xiu xi*," said Wang Bin. He found savage delight in the uncertainty that caused. One of the aides even looked at his watch. It was precisely one o'clock. So they even knew the time. Spineless sons of a turtle.

Wang Bin slept deeply on a daybed next to his office for more than an hour. The train from the south had been crowded and slow, arriving in Peking just after dawn, and he had rested little. Again and again, he had replayed the climactic acts of the drama he had forged. It would work, as long as he could keep time on his side. He had not expected the Party's summons so soon. Another day or two might have made all the difference. Wang Bin sighed with finality and prepared to meet his inquisitors.

Precisely at 3 P.M., Wang Bin presented himself at a side entrance of the Great Hall of the People. To those who knew it existed, it was the most dreaded doorway in Peking.

"You are late," said a severe young receptionist without preamble.

"I was detained on the people's business. Please tell the comrades that I have arrived."

"You will wait," the young man instructed. "The comrade will show you where."

He gestured to an orderly who led Wang Bin to a high-ceilinged reception room big enough for fifty people. It was empty, except for one straight-backed wooden chair in the precise center of a beige carpet. Wang Bin nearly laughed aloud. It was so transparent.

"Bring tea," he snarled to the orderly.

No tea came, nor any summons for nearly two hours. By the time Wang Bin was led into a red plush room usually reserved for Central Committee meetings, the two-wheeled afternoon rush hour gripped Peking.

Once more, intimidation. Another crude chair facing a long, highly polished table where three men sat: two wizened

139

Party cadres and a PLA general, to lend authority. The army, after all, belonged not to the nation but to the Party, by decree of the same constitution that had enshrined the *xiu xi*.

Wang Bin knew all three men. The two Party ancients were willows, professional survivors who had devoted an empty lifetime to swaying back and forth with changing political winds. The general was something else again. Wang Bin had soldiered with him once, when they had both—like their cause—been young and strong.

The three old men comprised the Disciplinary Commission. To their right sat a younger man in his forties. His black hair leapt impulsively from his skull. His eyes burned with the unmistakable fire of a zealot. The prosecutor. At a desk of their own sat two sexless women stenographers.

"You may sit," said the elder of the two Party hacks. That made him the president of what was technically a commission of inquiry, but only by euphemism. It was as close to a trial as Wang Bin would see, if he was smart. Everybody in the room knew it. Everybody also knew that Wang Bin had already been found guilty of whatever it was they were about to charge him with. All that remained was the sentence.

"I prefer to stand, Comrade," said Wang Bin.

"You will sit," snapped the prosecutor.

"Oh, let him stand if he wants to. What difference does it make?" The general sighed from a mouth half-hidden by a hand that supported his face.

"Proceed," said the president.

"This is an inquiry by the Disciplinary Commission of the Communist Party of the People's Republic of China against Wang Bin, Party member since 1937, expelled in 1966 and rehabilitated blameless in 1976."

The prosecutor read like an automaton in a high, singsong voice.

"Based on information received, and from direct observation, the Party accuses Wang Bin of conduct inimical to the best interests of the Party and the state."

Wang Bin tensed. How much did they know? Everything hinged on the innate stupidity of the bureaucracy. They would list the charges chronologically, with the most recent first,

140

Wang Bin knew, to shake the confidence of the accused by showing how vigilant and up-to-date the watchers could be.

"One. You are accused of meeting secretly, privately and without authorization with a foreigner for purposes inconsistent with the best interests of the Party: namely, Harold Broom, an American citizen; five counts.

"Two. The same accusation applies to another American, one Thomas Stratton, with whom you met secretly in your office in Peking in violation of the Party code of correct conduct.

"Three. You are accused of misuse of Party property, namely one Red Flag limousine, damaged severely while assigned to you.

"Four. You are accused of the misuse of Party funds in paying for a decadent art exhibition attended by foreigners in state property, namely a museum, under your custody.

"Five. You are accused of conspiring against the best interests of the state and the Party in personally securing an entry visa for an American citizen, namely David Wang, without authorization, and of abandoning your post to travel and to meet secretly with David Wang.

"Six. You are accused of receiving unauthorized gifts from a foreigner, namely propaganda materials from the Embassy of France . . ."

Wang Bin stared at a streak of grease on a chunky window behind the commission table. He tried to remain detached. He tried to keep from laughing. The "propaganda materials" had been a set of art books for the museum library.

And how typical. The Party, in a frenzy of self-consuming self-righteousness, could not see fire, but invented smoke. What he was accused of was making his ministry fairly open, semiefficient and less backward than most in the Chinese government. His true guilt was unmentioned, unknown, invisible to zealot cadres who found termites in healthy trees, but never noticed that the forest was burning. Wang Bin fought back a sneer. If you really knew my crimes, comrades, my friend the general would end this charade with a single shot—and I wouldn't blame him.

It was amazing. The prosecutor seemed immune to breath-

141

ing. He read without pause, increasing shrillness his only concession to an indictment of forty-seven different crimes over seven years.

"Forty-seven. You are accused of meeting privately with a foreigner, namely Gerta Hofsted, in the dining room of the Peking Hotel and charging your ministry for the meal when in fact it was paid for by the foreigner."

My, my, how thorough. A lunch seven years before with a West German anthropologist. She had never noticed when he pocketed the receipt, but obviously a waiter had.

The prosecutor shut up as suddenly as he had begun. Wang Bin remembered a joke a Russian had told him back in the days when Russia and China were allies. About the factory worker who left every night carrying a heavy load of sand in a wheelbarrow. The KGB knew he was stealing something. They tasted the sand. They sifted it. They sent it away for analysis. The results were conclusive: plain old ordinary worthless sand. It took them months to realize the worker was stealing wheelbarrows. Marxist myopia.

"One other matter has come to the attention of this commission," said the moribund cadre who sat next to the president. "It is not within the province of this investigation since the accused is not a Party member, but it does reflect on the failure of Comrade Wang Bin to inspire his own family to live according to Party principles." The cadre sucked, hollow-cheeked, at his tea.

"The commission has evidence that Wang Kangmei, daughter of Comrade Wang Bin, left her unit without permission, that she traveled without permission to the city of Xian, and that there she engaged in sexual relations with a foreigner."

"She was abducted," Wang Bin blurted, and instantly regretted it.

"This commission is forwarding the relevant testimony to the Public Security Bureau for action," the cadre intoned without expression.

That was the cue for the prosecutor. He jerked back to his feet.

"In view of the seriousness of the charges, I call for a full trial and a sentence of life imprisonment at hard labor."

142

It was a formality. Still, in the calculated silence that followed the prosecutor's demand, Wang Bin began to sweat.

"The commission agrees with the prosecutor's request," said the president.

Again, the old men allowed a cruel silence to build. Wang Bin braced for the sound of the door opening, the rush of air, the footsteps of the guards summoned by a buzzer beneath the table.

"However," the president began.

At last! Wang Bin felt a sudden release.

"In view of Comrade Wang's long service to the Party, this commission will waive a trial in exchange for Comrade Wang's admission of guilt, a self-criticism, his removal from all state and Party posts and his reeducation through labor in . . ."— he consulted a printed list in front of him—"Jilin Province."

It was a sentence of slow death. Manchuria. Backward and cold, so bitterly cold and primitive he would not survive two years there.

"Jilin," said the second cadre.

That left the general.

"Hunan," said the general. "And as an office worker. He is an educated man."

Hunan was backward, too, but warmer. To work there as a bookkeeper on a commune would be dull, but not dangerous, almost like retiring. Such were the fruits of a fifty-year friendship between men who had once fought together.

The two hacks dithered for a while—Jilin was what their paper decreed—but the general proved implacable.

"Hunan." The president surrendered. "You have twenty-four hours, Comrade, in which to inform the commmission whether you wish a trial or will accept the Party's mercy."

Wang Bin squared his back and strode from the room.

Twenty-four hours. He had counted on that. It was time enough.

CHAPTER **14**

STRATTON'S makeshift chisel splintered after only an hour. A cone-shaped pile of concrete dust and a faint groove in the mortar were all he had to show for his furious scraping. There was no way out of the cell. Stratton snapped another leg off the wooden chair and rubbed one end back and forth across the rough wall until a sharp point was formed. Then he buried the stick in a corner. Another corner was used for defecation. A third corner he reserved for sleeping.

He curled up, facing the wall, and shielded his eyes with one arm. That night, for the first time, the jailers had left the light bulb burning in the rafters; insects darted and danced around it. Stratton closed his eyes and thought of his parents. For thirty-one years his father had driven a UPS truck in Hartford, while his mother had reared five children. Now the Strattons were retired, living in a small apartment in Boca Raton, Florida, entertaining grandchildren and feeding the ducks in a man-made lake behind the high rise. Tom Stratton had visited his parents only twice in their new home. He telephoned once a month from wherever he was. He had prom-

144

ised them postcards from Peking, but of course he had forgotten. They wouldn't be worried, not Dale and Ann Stratton. They knew their youngest son. The restless sort, his mother used to say. Pity the poor gal he marries, and pitied she had.

The flat horn of a truck jolted Stratton into daylight. He unfolded, stretched his arms, and watched through the window as the first morning visitors arrived at the small museum. It had been more than a day now since his keepers had brought fresh rice or water. Stratton was famished. He considered pounding on the door on the remote chance that he had been forgotten, but rejected the idea. He knew he was a VIP. Whatever awaited him had been carefully planned by Wang Bin.

The day passed slowly, and Stratton napped intermittently, using sleep as a substitute for food. Finally, late in the afternoon, he heard footsteps in the hall outside the cell. He sat up, and shrank into the shadow of the cleanest corner, his sleeping corner.

Two men entered the cell. Stratton recognized one of them as a jailer, one of the men who had paraded him to his public bath.

The other was a wan, slightly built Chinese who wore bottle-bottom eyeglasses. He squinted at Stratton until he became accustomed to the light.

Each man carried a large tin bucket.

"Stand," ordered the man with the eyeglasses.

Stratton obeyed. The two men heaved the liquid contents of the buckets on the floor in a large puddle at Stratton's feet. The odor assaulted him and he tried hard not to gag.

"Pig manure," said the same man, again in clear English. "Kneel."

"Why?"

"You will not argue. You will not ask questions. You will do as I say. You are unfit to speak in this room. You are unfit to stand. So you will kneel, and you will be completely silent."

Stratton did not move. The man with the bottle-bottom glasses circled him disdainfully, eyeing the American as if he were a roach.

145

"You have broken this chair!"

"No, it fell apart."

"Liar!"

"Liar!" shouted the jailer, chiming in.

"An accident," Stratton repeated.

"My name is Comrade Zhou," said the man in the glasses. "We have met before."

"Oh, yes. You were Wang Bin's interpreter in Peking," Stratton said.

Zhou lifted the mangled two-legged chair as if examining it. Then he swung it over his head and brought it crashing down on Tom Stratton's shoulders. Stratton pitched forward, face down into the warm pig dung. A small hand seized his neck, and another clutched his hair. Roughly, he was jerked off the floor, and propped on his knees like a mannequin.

"I will repeat this one more time," Zhou said. Now he was squatting in front of Stratton, glaring into the American's dripping face. "You are unworthy to stand in the presence of any Chinese citizen, do you understand? You are worse than the shit on this floor. You are a murderer, a thief, a destroyer of Chinese property, a corrupter of young women, a spy . . . and, I think you should know, Stratton, that you have no secrets here. We know everything about you!"

Stratton made no response. He breathed through his mouth only. He closed his eyes. He fought to neutralize all his senses, one by one.

"We have come here to give you the opportunity to confess your crimes, Comrade Stratton. Do not be afraid, and do not be foolish. Many thousands of Chinese have profited from such expurgation. They lived to tell about it, however. I cannot promise the same for you."

"What is this, a struggle session? You're sick," Stratton said.

Zhou nodded. "Ah, you've heard of this. You have read about it, I suppose, in some perverted imperialist book. China is the subject of many books in your country. China is a popular subject among American scholars. You came here posing as a scholar, did you not?"

"I am a tourist."

"Liar!" It was the jailer again. He knew the script.

"Do not continue with these lies," Zhou said. "I know your country very well, Stratton. I know the American people. I even know the language. I studied for two years at Yale University." Zhou laughed. "It's amusing, in a way. In the many years since my return to China, I have never once had the opportunity to interview an American criminal. You are my first. I am grateful to Comrade Wang Bin for the chance to serve China in this way. He tells me you are a treacherous spy."

"He is mistaken, Comrade Zhou. I am merely a friend of his brother."

"You are a liar," Zhou replied.

"Liar!" screamed the jailer. It was the only English word he knew.

"Liar!" Zhou yelled.

"No."

"Now it is time to confess," Zhou said. He left the cell, and returned shortly with a handwritten Chinese document. "Please sign this now."

"What does it say? Could you read it to me?" Stratton said, stalling.

"Of course." Zhou motioned at the jailer, who slogged out of the cell. He and another jailer returned carrying three wooden chairs. One was placed directly in front of Stratton, and that is where Zhou sat. The first jailer took the second chair, to Zhou's left, but equidistant from the kneeling American. A third chair was placed on Zhou's right. It was empty.

"You have been found guilty of numerous crimes against the state," Zhou began. "This is the list. It is lengthy.

"To begin with, you lied on your visa application. You said you had never been to China before, Stratton. Therefore you are charged with presenting false information to immigration officials.

"Secondly, you are charged with the theft of personal articles belonging to Mr. David Wang. These items were stolen from Mr. Wang's hotel room in Peking nearly one week ago."

Stratton stared at the earthen floor and shook his head.

"You are charged with the murder of Huang Gong, a limousine driver in Peking who was killed while serving the state. Additionally, you are charged with the attempted murder of another comrade, Ni Zanfu, who was seriously injured in the same tragic episode."

"They tried to run me down," Stratton protested.

"Liar!" screamed the interrogators in unison.

"There are two more crimes which are the most serious," Zhou went on. "One of them is the abduction of Wang Kangmei, the daughter of the deputy minister. We will discuss that in a moment. But I first should like to ask you about the crime of espionage against the People's Republic. On March 18, 1971 . . ." and Zhou began to read the document: " 'Thomas Stratton, then a captain with the Special Forces Intelligence section of the United States Army, illegally entered the Chinese town of Man-ling with a squad of armed soldiers and assassinated thirty-eight innocent peasants.' "

Zhou paused and glanced up from the paper. "You came back to China this year for the purpose of continuing your terrorism and trying to recruit Chinese citizens for your criminal espionage. You are a dangerous agent of the United States government, and you must be punished according to the laws of the Chinese state. Now . . . are you willing to confess to your crimes, Mr. Stratton?"

"I cannot, Comrade Zhou." Stratton stared at the frog-eyed face. Zhou's thick eyeglasses looked like a cheap prop for some stand-up comic, but there was nothing funny in the Chinese eyes. He waved the document contemptuously.

"Perhaps we should review each charge separately—"

"My answer would remain the same. Not guilty. I am not guilty of anything."

Zhou nodded at the jailer. The jailer's leg shot out, and his boot caught Stratton flush in the Adam's apple. He toppled backwards into the slop, moaning, choking, gulping air. He grabbed impotently at his throat with both hands.

After a few moments, the jailer yanked Stratton to his knees.

"Have you caught your breath?" Zhou asked.

Stratton's mouth moved, but only a dry rattle came out.

"It is a question of honor, then?" Zhou pressed. "You will

148

not confess because your pride rebels. We know something of honor in our country, too, Mr. Stratton. I cannot tell you how many men and women have knelt before me and resisted the truth because of honor and pride—no matter what the evidence, no matter what kind of punishment awaited them. I have seen many men—some of them weaker than you—resist for days. Three, four days, even longer. It was remarkable. No food, no water. They knelt there, wetting themselves and soiling themselves and suffering . . . yet, they insisted, no matter what, that they, too, were innocent. I have to admit that I came to admire some of those comrades even after I executed them, Mr. Stratton.

"The choice is yours. Would you prefer to be admired for your valor? Or would you instead care for some warm food, and cold water. And perhaps some medical treatment for your leg? Clean clothes? A bath?"

Zhou did not smile. The jailer waited for another signal.

"One man lasted six days with me," Zhou said. "His was a political crime, truly insignificant compared to yours. I was prepared to send him to one of the far provinces for two years. Farm labor on a rural commune. It would have been a fair sentence, had he confessed. But he, too, spoke of honor. Even after three days, when we boarded the windows. It was summer, very hot and still. He was old and sick. We took away all the food, of course. By the fifth day, he was drinking his own urine. On the sixth day, I threw a live river rat into the cell and he ate it raw, tail and all. So much for honor, Mr. Stratton."

Stratton could not think for the pain; each idea seemed to sting the inside of his brain. Cowering on his knees, never had he been so helpless. His captors did not have a gun, nor did they need one. Stratton was the weakest man in the cell, and all three of them knew it. All he could do was drag it out, and hope for the pain to pass.

"Do you see why you are unworthy to stand? After hearing the list of your crimes, do you now understand?"

"What if I were to confess to some of the charges?" Stratton asked in a raspy voice.

"No!" Zhou barked. "Not good enough. The crimes are

149

related. One leads to another. It is impossible to be innocent of some and guilty of others. It is either day or night. Justice must be distinct, and clear, and indisputable. Otherwise there would be no respect for laws. So if you confess, you will confess to all of it. You *will* be truthful."

"How long have you worked for Wang Bin?"

"Shut up!"

"Are you paid well?" Stratton's tone was soft, boylike.

"I work for the state."

"Then where is your uniform?"

"Quiet!" Zhou snapped. The jailer did not understand the words, but he listened tautly, in expectation.

"Have I been convicted by the state?"

"Yes. The deputy minister pronounced—"

"No, I said by the *state*." Stratton was breathing easier, although his throat felt bruised and swollen. "If this is a state prison, then where is the PLA?"

Zhou smiled darkly. "You would feel more at home with soldiers? It would bring back old memories for you, I'm sure. That is too bad. There are no PLA here. And this is not a trial, Stratton. The trial is over. All that remains is for you to accept your conviction and acknowledge your crimes. We expect no more from you than we would from a Chinese criminal. The truth is, the deputy minister has more patience with you than I."

Zhou stood up. He spoke to the jailer, who left the cell immediately. "The smell in here is very bad. I am not certain if it is the pigs or you, Mr. Stratton. I am going outdoors for a few minutes for some fresh air, and perhaps a cold beer. In the meantime, the other comrade will give you something to think about. Then we will resume."

Zhou hitched his trousers and walked out. Stratton sagged back on his heels. He glanced longingly at the corner where he had concealed his makeshift weapon, but within seconds the jailer had returned, flinging the door open. He spoke sharply in Chinese to someone else in the corridor. Stratton rose to his knees and looked up. There, in the doorway, stood Kangmei.

* * *

150

Not for the first time, the old professor wondered at the futility of man. He had dedicated his life to the proposition that all mankind's creations should be appraised not just for their beauty or ingenuity, but for what they revealed about the mystery of the human mind. And now, so late in his life, to face the mystery of true evil. No Chinese artist could ever express such a horror—the betrayal of history, of art itself, of one's own brother.

It was a secret David Wang had never asked to know, but knowing, he could not let it die with him.

He was not a man of action, but he had ruminated long enough. He was certain that escape was possible. He had studied the primitive lock on the door of the Peking attic that served as his warm prison. He had even secreted a spoon that his slovenly jailers had missed, and he had bent it so that it could be prised between the door and the rusty jamb to lift the latch. David Wang was both exhilarated and frightened by the possibilities.

It had taken two days—a drugged two days—before he had come to his senses. He remembered a big dinner of roast duck, then sipping tea alone in his hotel room afterward. And then nothing—until he awoke as a captive.

For six days, David Wang had analyzed the routine of his keepers until he had identified the flaw. After his supper was delivered each day, the jailers all ate together, loudly, in a large kitchen at the end of the hallway. They never returned for the tray in less than an hour, on one occasion, they had not come again until the next morning.

An hour was plenty of time, David Wang figured, to break out, slip away from his brother's museum and lose himself in the streets of Peking. The guards had dressed him in an old-fashioned undershirt, more gray than white, baggy blue trousers and cotton shoes. In the darkness of the street, he would be indistinguishable from millions of other Pekingese.

He would walk to the American Embassy if he could. Failing that, David Wang decided, he would approach the first policeman he saw and ask for help. The policeman would not believe his story, of course, but he would take him in, just the same.

151

David Wang would find someone to tell: *My brother is committing a terrible crime against China, against humanity. I have seen it in Xian. He must be stopped.*

David had reached this conclusion with sadness. His important brother was a criminal. For days he had expected Wang Bin to appear at the attic to explain, to apologize, to disavow any knowledge of David's imprisonment. Then he had prayed that Wang Bin would come in repentance, denouncing his own crazed scheme, begging forgiveness. David would have given it, willingly, and returned to the United States without saying a word.

On the third day, David Wang had shouted at his jailers, demanding an audience with Wang Bin. The jailers had laughed at the old man.

By the fifth day, a new thought had occurred to David, and he came to fear that Wang Bin *would* appear. Death itself did not frighten him, but he did not want it like this, in Peking, at the hands of his own brother.

David convinced himself that the only perilous part of the escape would be finding his way out of the museum. In dim lighting, his weak vision suffered from a loss of depth and distance. He would have to move slowly, maybe too slowly.

After the jailers brought the dinner tray that night, David meticulously counted one hundred and twenty nervous seconds before he slipped the latch on the door.

The corridor was poorly lit. At one end, light seeped from a room where the jailers dined raucously. Peering intently, David Wang could make out a doorway that appeared to lead to a flight of stairs. His confidence rising, he tiptoed along the hall until he reached the door and his feet found the first flight. Cautiously, he began to descend.

The stairwell was dark. David felt his way like a blind man—one hand groped the grimy wall, the other clung to a cold metal handrail. Would it be four flights, or five? He tried to remember the size of the building from the day he had first visited the museum as his brother's honored guest.

After two flights, David Wang stopped to rest. A reassuring stillness wrapped the museum; the only sounds he heard were his own shuffling, tentative footsteps. At the third land-

152

ing, David's questing hand encountered something tall and wooden. At the same instant, his foot kicked something bulky and metallic. David dropped to all fours and used his hands to identify the objects: a ladder and a chest of tools. He found the handle of the tool chest and lifted it. Not too heavy. He would take it with him as protective coloration. It might be just the thing to get him out the back door and into the street.

Suddenly the lights in the stairwell snapped on. From above came agitated shouts, and the rumble of feet on the stairs.

For a few precious seconds David Wang was paralyzed, rooted and tremulous as the din escalated. Only when the first young cadre appeared at the top of the stairs did he act.

With a desperate jerk, David toppled the ladder. It fell in front of his pursuer. As David lunged for the door on the landing, the cadre hurdled the ladder easily. A hand clamped David by the shoulder. He spun around and breathlessly shoved—nearly threw—the tool chest into the cadre's gut. The young man staggered backwards and doubled up. When his heels hit the ladder he tumbled down the stairs in a groaning somersault.

David Wang did not wait to see his enemy stop rolling. He was already anxiously exploring the second floor of the museum. It was a large room, dominated by rows of display cases, dimly perceived, their contents a mystery. If only there were someplace to hide, and if only he could see it. Across the gallery was another doorway. David Wang did not particularly care where it would take him. He ran for it. His gait was the huffing half-waddle of an old man, no match for the athletic cadres who streamed behind him.

David was but halfway to the door when he realized that he would not make it. He meant to stop, to gather himself and surrender with dignity. Instead, he lost his balance and skidded into a glass display case housing a collection of seventh century bronzes. David Wang and the exhibit went down together with an ear-splitting crash.

When his wits returned, a circle of young men was standing over him. He expected that they would scream at him, perhaps jeer, or even beat him. But they did not. Rather, the cadres simply led David back to his attic cell with the impatience of peasants who have frustrated the ungainly escape of a commune mule.

Later, the keepers even brought the old scholar tea and dumplings to replace the dinner he had fled. This time the spoon was plastic.

In another cell, hundreds of miles away, Tom Stratton shakily faced a contrived tribunal. The jailer returned to the chair on Zhou's left. Zhou himself sat down next, his back straight, his face unreadable. Kangmei wordlessly took the chair on Zhou's right. Her long hair had been braided in pigtails, and her Western clothes had been replaced with standard Mao blue. Stratton searched her eyes for a clue, but Kangmei looked away.

"Nice room, huh?" Stratton said. "This is what I get for taking the American plan."

"You are to remain silent," Zhou warned, "until these accusations are read. Then you will be permitted to state your confession and sign it. Then sentence will be declared. Wang Kangmei?"

"Yes, Comrade Zhou."

"Do you see the man named Thomas Stratton in this room?"

"Yes, Comrade."

"Describe him," Zhou commanded.

Kangmei studied the half-naked Stratton for several moments, up and down, and this time it was he who looked away.

"He is an American. He is tall and light-haired. With a mustache."

"And what is he doing now?"

"Kneeling, Comrade Zhou."

"And what is he wearing, Wang Kangmei?"

"A shirt, a torn shirt."

"Filthy? Unclean?"

"Yes, Comrade."

"And what else? What else is he wearing?"

"A bandage. A filthy bandage." Kangmei glared scornfully down at Stratton. "And that is all, Comrade Zhou. He has no other clothes on."

"And do you find him . . . attractive?"

"No! He is disgusting. He is a pig. A pig and a liar."

"Liar!" shouted the jailer. He propped one of his shoes on Stratton's bruised shoulder. "Liar! Liar!" Stratton pushed the foot away.

"Kangmei, what crimes did Mr. Stratton commit against you?"

"He asked me to come to his hotel room in Xian. He said he wanted to give me something that belonged to my uncle, David Wang, who had died in Peking. He said it was something of great sentimental value."

Zhou said, "Did you believe the lying pig Thomas Stratton?"

"Yes, Comrade. I believed him."

"What happened when you went to his hotel room in Xian?"

"He held me against my will. He abducted me. He beat me. He said my father, the deputy minister, represented all that was evil about the Communist Party, and that he must be destroyed."

"So," Zhou said, "he threatened to kill a Chinese deputy minister. What else did he say?"

"Thom-as Stratton admitted that he is an agent of the imperialist United States government, and that he was sent to China to encourage terrorism and disrupt the efforts of the loyal workers."

To Stratton's surprise, Kangmei did not recite her indictment in monotone. Rather, her tone was impassioned, the words seemingly spontaneous. Her eyes seemed to glisten, but whether in rage or sorrow Stratton could no longer be sure.

Zhou said, "What did you do when you heard Stratton denounce your father?"

"I argued with him, Comrade. I became angry. I told him he was not worthy to visit our country, and that I was going to report him to the Public Security Bureau. When I tried to

155

run out of his room, he grabbed me by the arms and threw me down on the floor. Then he kicked me between the legs . . ."

"No!" Stratton bellowed. "Kangmei, please, I know what's happening, but—"

Zhou motioned to the jailer, who swiftly moved behind Stratton and dug a knee into the small of his back. Then he seized Stratton's hair and yanked back so that Stratton was forced to stare up at the roof, his neck stretched tight. Zhou scooped a handful of rancid manure from the floor and dropped it into Stratton's face. He retched.

"You will remain silent from now on," Zhou said mildly. Stratton stared back with dead eyes. His face was chalky.

Kangmei continued her story: "Stratton gagged me so I could not scream. Then he tied me to the bed in the room."

"Then what?"

"He ripped my clothing off . . . and raped me."

"Several times?"

"Yes, Comrade Zhou. Several times . . . and once in a terrible way."

Stratton grimaced. A horsefly landed on one cheek, beneath his left eye. Even as it bit him, Stratton made no move to brush it away. His arms hung like butcher's meat.

"Finally I was rescued when two comrades came to the hotel room. They must have heard me fighting back. Stratton escaped, but at least my ordeal was over."

Stratton gazed sadly at Kangmei, and shook his head back and forth with determination. Her eyes never softened.

Zhou said, "Kangmei, do you now see the folly of your actions? Do you understand why the government discourages contact with foreigners, especially decadent Americans? They are a menace to the state, a threat to everything we are working for. They are not to be trusted, and never to be believed. Stratton is a model of this—a murderer . . ."

"Murderer!" Kangmei agreed.

"A thief, a corrupter . . ."

"A thief!" she yelled in a suddenly shrill voice that startled Stratton.

"A rapist," Zhou concluded.

156

"Rapist!" Kangmei cried. "A murderer and rapist!"

"You were deceived," Zhou said.

"Yes, Comrade, and I am truly sorry. He seemed sincere and I believed him. I was blind, like a man who suddenly loses his sight and becomes confused."

Stratton wasn't looking when she said it, but he heard Kangmei's voice crack.

"Blind, Comrade Zhou," she repeated. "Nearsighted. Clumsy. Foolish."

Stratton stiffened. He tested the muscles in his arms and legs with invisible isometrics. He hurt everywhere, but he willed himself to be ready.

"Blind," Kangmei said softly. "Blind, blind, blind!" And with that, she plucked the bottle-bottom glasses from Zhou's eyes and tossed them across Stratton's cell. They landed in the worst corner. Insects scattered.

Zhou was utterly bewildered. The jailer shouted a question in Mandarin. Stratton did not wait for the answer. He rammed a fist into the side of Zhou's head, spilling the inquisitor off the chair into a writhing heap.

Stratton grunted to his feet and stood rubber-legged, facing the jailer. The man dove for Stratton's waist and brought him down. They rolled together in the fetid slop; the jailer, clawing for Stratton's throat and eyes; Stratton, weak and nauseous, using his long arms and his weight to entangle his wiry attacker. Kangmei stood to the side, crying nervously.

"In the corner," Stratton yelled. "Dig! By the window."

The jailer hung on Stratton's back, arms clenched around his neck in a fierce choke-hold. Stratton held his breath and rolled over.

Kangmei dug feverishly. Her hands uncovered the crude three-foot spear Stratton had fashioned from the leg of the chair. In another corner, Comrade Zhou groped pathetically for his eyeglasses in the excrement.

In the middle of the small cell, only Thomas Stratton was breathing normally. The jailer, pinned beneath him, was slowly suffocating in the muck. Stratton reeled to his feet and snatched the weapon from Kangmei.

Somehow Zhou had found his precious glasses and now

157

he was at the door, pounding loudly. His black hair was matted, his clothes stained and sodden.

"Comrade. *Tongzhi*!" he cried.

Stratton's handmade bayonet tore through the inquisitor's chest. He collapsed making noises like a leaky bicycle tire, a death wheeze.

"Thom-as, I am sorry. I am so sorry." She was sobbing. "He made me do it."

Stratton put a finger to his lips. For several moments, he listened at the door. "We must hurry," he whispered. Kangmei dabbed at her eyes. Self-consciously she turned away as Stratton slipped into Zhou's trousers. When she turned back, Stratton held her by the shoulders and said, "Your uncle is alive."

"Oh, Thom-as!"

Stratton tested the door of the cell. It was unlocked. The corridor was empty. Kangmei took his hand and together they ran.

CHAPTER 15

"IDIOTS! My orders are to be followed. When I say that a man must be guarded, I speak for the state and for the Party. I must be obeyed. You listen to stupid rumors like old women, and you behave as donkeys. I am still the deputy minister, and I still command here."

Wang Bin burst into the attic cell. In a pregnant moment, much was said between the two brothers, but no words were spoken. David Wang looked up at his brother quizzically.

"It is not what it seems," Wang Bin said finally. "I will explain later . . . and apologize. Now we must go quickly. Here, put on these, there is a chill."

The deputy minister handed his brother a well-cut gray Mao suit with a mourner's band pinned to the sleeve of the jacket, and a pair of vigorously polished black shoes, one-half size too small.

"Please, hurry, David. We must go."

Befuddled, unspeaking, David Wang dressed and followed his younger brother into the night. Wang Bin walked briskly. He had but thirteen hours left.

* * *

159

"What do you mean you can't drive?"

"I was never permitted to learn . . . it was not my job," Kangmei stammered. "In this country, we have drivers—"

"Get in," Stratton said.

The truck was a bad Chinese imitation of a bad Russian flatbed, but it was the only vehicle in the museum's parking lot with keys in the ignition. Stratton's original plan had been to hide under some lumber in the truck and let Kangmei navigate the escape, but now he had no choice. Night was on his side, but not much else. Any half-blind idiot would see that the driver of this truck was not Chinese. Stratton turned the key and urged the transmission into first gear. The clutch yelped like a dog on fire.

"This is terrific," Stratton muttered as they trundled down the two-lane blacktop.

Kangmei gave him a puzzled stare. Stratton laughed and reached out for her hand. "Never mind," he said. "Where to?"

"A very safe place," she answered, "but a long, long way, Thom-as. Eighty kilometers."

Stratton flicked the headlights on and tried to hunch down as low as he would go in the driver's seat. Kangmei found a dirty canvas cap under the seat, dusted it off and stuck it on Stratton's head.

"I'm worried about you," he said after a few minutes. "If we get stopped, I'm running. You tell them I kidnapped you and stole the truck. Tell them you never saw me before. I want you to promise."

"No," Kangmei said quietly. "I will not lie again. My father made me say those things at the struggle session. I am very sorry. He told me you were a spy."

"Did you believe him?"

"No." She looked at him pridefully. "It wouldn't matter if you were."

The sluggish truck picked up speed alarmingly on a long downhill stretch. A quarter-mile ahead, Stratton could make out a group of commune workers, trudging home down the middle of the road. He pressed on the horn and they parted slowly. Their ox, however, was disinclined to yield the right of way. Stratton honked again and pumped the brakes slowly.

160

Incredibly, the barn-shouldered animal turned to face the noisy intruder.

"Oh, shit," Stratton said. As the truck bore down on the ox, Stratton leaned hard on the horn. At the last second, he cut the wheel and steered onto the shoulder, around the ox and its peasant entourage. In the rearview mirror, he saw several men shake their fists at the truck. Kangmei trembled next to him.

"Sorry," Stratton said sheepishly. "They acted like they own the road."

"They do," Kangmei said evenly.

The unlit road was newly paved in some sections, pocked and dangerous in others. The hill countryside was lush with citrus stands, cane fields and banana groves. Here and there the night was broken by a commune's lights or the pinprick headlights of a distant truck, but mostly Kangmei and Tom Stratton were alone. Stratton recounted his confrontation with Wang Bin in the museum cell.

"But how could my uncle be alive?" Kangmei asked.

"Because your father is planning something, and he needs his brother—at least for a while," Stratton conjectured. "When he's done, I think Wang Bin *will* kill David. We don't have much time. Kangmei, it's important that we get out of China so I can contact the State Department. Hong Kong would be the best."

"An overnight train from where we are going," she said. "But you have no papers. How will you leave China?"

"Can we go tomorrow?"

Kangmei did not answer right away.

"If I return to Peking, your father will have me arrested," Stratton said. "There is nowhere I can go but out. There's nothing I can do here for David."

"The place I'm taking you is very safe, Thom-as."

"For me, maybe. Think of your uncle. If the U.S. Embassy only knew he was alive. Kangmei, we could call them in the morning—"

She shook her head glumly. "Where we are going, there are no telephones."

"Do you believe what I'm telling you, that David is alive?"

Kangmei said, "I don't know. It is hard to accept." In the darkness, Stratton could not see the tension on her face, but he could sense it.

The boundaries of the mountain road became indistinct as it snaked through acres of tall pines. When the truck rattled past a plywood sign erected at the foot of a hill, Kangmei sat up and grabbed Stratton's elbow.

"Slow down, Thom-as. The sign says there is a police stop ahead. One half a kilometer."

Stratton quickly downshifted, pulled off the road and dimmed the lights. "We'll never slip through with me at the wheel," he said, turning to Kangmei. "How'd you like a driving lesson?"

Her eyes surveyed the simple dashboard instruments with trepidation. "I don't think so," she said.

"You've got to. Come here, sit closer and I'll show you." Stratton kept his foot on the clutch and ran through the gears one time. "Hell," he said, "my father drove one of these tanks for thirty years. How hard can it be?"

Kangmei practiced with the truck idling.

"That's good," Stratton encouraged. "Remember to watch the speedometer needle. When it gets to here, shift into second. And here, third. When we get to the checkpoint, press the clutch pedal with your left foot, and put your right foot on the brake. You'll have to use most of your weight because the drums on this truck are nearly shot. The important thing is to slow down smoothly so we don't attract attention."

"There is no one else on the road at this time of night," Kangmei remarked. "The police certainly will ask questions."

"I'll be hiding in the back. There's a bundle of wood and some old vegetable crates back there—"

"Thom-as, I don't have my identification papers. They might arrest me."

Stratton got out of the cab. Kangmei moved into the driver's seat.

"Make up a story," Stratton said, scouting the foggy highway. In both directions it was quiet, deserted. "Tell them you're on the way to get medicine for the commune. The regular driver is sick."

162

Kangmei's hands explored the steering wheel. "What if they don't believe me?"

"How many policemen will there be?"

"One, perhaps two at the most. It is so late . . ."

Stratton was thinking. He removed the dusty driver's cap and placed it on Kangmei's head. Gently he tucked her silken pigtails underneath it. "There! You look like a teenaged boy."

She glanced down at her chest.

"Well, almost," Stratton said. He climbed into the flatbed and concealed himself in the rummage and lumber. "Okay," he called from the back. "Let's go."

The truck lunged forward, then coughed into a stall. Kangmei tried again with the same results. The third time the clutch engaged perfectly and the truck found the pavement. Stratton smiled to himself.

Kangmei drove slowly, eternally grateful that the stretch of road was straight so she could devote all concentration to mastering the transmission.

As the truck crested a small hill, Kangmei noticed a swatch of yellow light below. Half in panic, she mashed both feet on the clutch and let the truck coast. Gradually the details of the small police station became clear: a white booth, with a Chinese flag posted on the tin roof. Three bulbs hung from a slender wire; one lit the building and the other two a zebra-striped gate that blocked the road. Inside the booth stood a man in a blue-and-white uniform. He seemed not to notice how the truck stuttered downhill, Kangmei fighting for the brakes.

She brought it to a stop with a brief screech of the tires. The policeman, who had been dozing on his feet, glanced up sharply and peered out the window of the booth.

As he approached, Kangmei shook her hair out from under the cap.

"*Ni nar?*" the policeman demanded—the universal inquiry of Marxist China.

Kangmei gave the name of a commune not far from her own birthplace. She told the policeman she was a barefoot doctor there.

"Are you a driver too?" The policeman eyed her. He did

not have a flashlight so he stood very close, sticking his head through the window of the cab. In the flatbed, Tom Stratton held his breath.

"No, Comrade, I am not a driver. This truck is assigned to the commune." Kangmei made up a common name. "Children are sick, and so is the regular driver," she went on. "We have run out of medicine and I am going to get some more at the clinic in Chungzho." She fumbled in her blues for an imaginary piece of paper.

The policeman shrugged and waved her on.

"*Xie xie, ni,*" Kangmei called in the earnest tones of a heroic worker. She pressed the accelerator, lifted her foot off the clutch—and promptly stalled the truck. Heart pounding, she wrestled with the stick shift. First gear. She could not find first gear. Again she tried to move the truck and again the engine died. *Don't flood it,* Stratton prayed from beneath the lumber and crates.

The policeman laughed and ambled back to the truck. "I hope you are a better doctor than you are a driver," he said. "Let me try."

"No, Comrade, I can do this," Kangmei said defiantly. "I must do this myself—for my commune." She turned the key, and from under the hood came a dying whine.

"Too much fuel in the carburetor," the policeman diagnosed. "Wait a few minutes and it will be fine." He opened the door to the cab. "Would you care to come in for a drink of tea?"

Kangmei reached for the door and slammed it. "No," she said sternly. "I must hurry, Comrade. I told you, the children are very sick."

Stratton had no idea what was being said. The slamming of the truck door alarmed him. Through the slats of the crate above his head, Stratton could see nothing but stars and wispy clouds. Gradually he levered himself up, turning his head slightly to gain a view of Kangmei. Suddenly the woodpile shifted and one of the vegetable crates fell, banging on the steel flatbed.

The policeman jumped at the noise. "What!" he said. "What

was that?" He walked to the back of the truck and peered into the rubble of cargo. "Are you alone, driver?"

Kangmei twisted the key and jerked on the stick shift with all her strength. This time the engine responded, and the truck surged forward.

"There, I did it!" she exclaimed.

The flustered policeman dashed ahead of the truck to lift the zebra-striped gate before it could be demolished.

"*Xie xie, ni*," Kangmei sang out as she drove past.

Stratton waited several miles before sitting up in the flatbed. Then he tapped on the rear window of the cab and signalled for Kangmei to pull over. She surrendered the driver's seat with a sigh of relief.

"Your father must be a very skilled man, to drive a truck like this," she said. "I am sure it is a most important job."

"Well, it doesn't exactly put you at the top of the social ladder in America," Stratton said. "I'm not sure what you told that cop, but you must be a wonderful actress. And your driving isn't bad for a beginnner. My old man would approve."

Kangmei shyly turned away. Stratton tenderly stroked the back of her neck; her skin was warm velvet.

"Are there more road checks?"

"I don't think so," she replied distractedly. "None that I remember."

"Are you tired?"

"Just a little, Thom-as. You are the one who needs to sleep."

Stratton cruised slowly through the hillsides until he found what he was looking for. He drove the truck off the asphalt and steered it down a washboard track until it was out of sight from the road. He parked and turned off the lights. Tall trees swallowed them into shadows.

"We can nap here for an hour, but no more. We must not be on the road after the sun comes up."

"Yes, we must finish the journey tonight." Kangmei took Stratton's hand and led him through the trees until they found a clearing. They lay down together on a natural mat of pine

165

needles, ivy and crisp cedar leaves. Stratton closed his eyes; his mind fell, spinning through the clouds toward sleep. He barely felt Kangmei's hands, gently pulling his shirt off. He heard her soft footsteps fade into the forest.

He quivered out of sleep when the cold water drenched his thigh.

"Ssshh. Lie still, Thom-as." She sponged his face with a rag and kissed him on the forehead.

"There is a brook nearby, with clean water." Kangmei washed the bullet wound in Stratton's leg. She had pulled his trousers off. In the grayness of deep night, he lay pale and limp.

"We will see a doctor tomorrow," she whispered. "He will treat the leg properly."

Stratton smiled and reached up to capture her hand. Tenderly he kissed it. She looked down at him for a long moment, a young woman of timeless wisdom.

"Yes," Stratton said at last. "Please."

In silence, Kangmei stripped. Suddenly she was astride him, a velvet presence. She moved gently at first, back and forth, until she found his lips, and then his neck. Stratton closed his eyes and held her fiercely as she sank down on him again and again.

Later, when they were in the truck again, Kangmei revealed her secret. It was as if she had saved it for Stratton, saved it for the end.

"After they dragged me from your room in Xian, I was delivered to the police," she began. "They were told I had been caught pilfering at a market. I was thrown into a cell with three other women. Each had been accused of stealing items from the Qin burial vaults. They were not mere peasants, but trusted workers on the site. Petty thieves, my father called them. Their arrests were part of a new campaign—banners, leaflets, announcements on the loudspeakers—all arranged by my father to show the ministry that he was cracking down against pilfering. It was a charade, Thom-as."

"But I saw a big article in the *People's Daily*," Stratton broke in.

166

Kangmei said, "Certainly there is a problem with stealing, but only a minor problem. The artifacts are worth a fortune by Chinese standards. One of the women in my cell admitted that she had stolen a bridle from one of the bronze horses. The bridle was made only of stone beads, not gold or silver. Still, she was able to sell it to a street peddler for a hundred yuan. The peddler probably sold it to a tourist for three or four times as much. Such things do happen."

"In our country, too."

"But, Thom-as, something bigger is happening at Xian. If these prisoners were telling the truth, then I know why Uncle David quarreled with my father. I know what he had found out. During the past several months, the Qin site has suffered three major thefts—the crimes are so enormous that they would create a terrible scandal in Peking. There would be a large investigation by the *Ke Ge Bo*. People would go to jail, or worse."

"What was stolen, Kangmei?"

"Soldiers. Three soldiers, Thom-as, on three different occasions. A spear carrier, an archer and a charioteer. They are among the most priceless treasures in Chinese history, buried with the Emperor Qin—and now missing."

"My God." Stratton's mind juggled the pieces of the puzzle. "David found out!"

"I think so," Kangmei said sadly. "That is why I do not think he is still alive, Thom-as, no matter what my father told you."

"No, don't you see? Wang Bin needs David more than ever now. He needs him to get out. It's only a matter of time before Peking discovers this theft, and your father knows this. There is nothing left for him to do but run."

Stratton coaxed more speed from the recalcitrant truck. Once Wang Bin learned that Stratton had escaped, he would act quickly. Quickly enough, and there was a good chance he would never be caught.

"Kangmei, what could your father have done with the clay soldiers?"

"You assume that it was he who stole them."

"I am certain," Stratton said.

167

Kangmei swallowed to keep back the tears. "The women prisoners said the same thing. The rumor is that he smuggled them out of the country. To America."

"How?"

"I do not know," she said wearily. "Something so large and so delicate as a statue—it would be very difficult, Thom-as, even for Wang Bin. Every box or parcel destined for your country would be subject to automatic inspection, especially if it came from a government office. The Party has been watching my father closely. Some of the old men do not approve of the way he has handled the Qin project. I'm sure they are jealous of the publicity."

"Wang Bin would never ship the artifacts directly to the United States," Stratton agreed. "The risk would be too great. Boxes like that would never clear U.S. Customs without a search." Then it struck him. "Unless . . ."

"What?" Kangmei asked.

"Oh, God." Stratton could not bring himself to say it aloud, a theory so horrible with black irony, so devious that it could be the only explanation of how a Chinese deputy minister could actually steal the storied Celestial Army, one soldier at a time.

CHAPTER **16**

THE CAR was a Shanghai, requisitioned without explanation from the ministry motor pool, and it veered without grace through empty streets, a whining gray shadow. Decades before, in the army, Wang Bin had briefly driven a truck. Since then, it had been beneath him to drive at all. David Wang slumped against the passenger door with the empty gaze of a vexed old man.

"Why?" he asked again.

"I have tried to explain. It was for your own protection, brother, I promise you." The strain of driving overwhelmed Wang Bin's English. He had lapsed into the Shanghai dialect of their childhood. "The radicals . . . the madmen, they are coming back, grabbing for power. I am one of their victims."

"You caged me like an animal."

"Only to save you . . . from the madmen."

David Wang shook himself like a dog awakening. He squinted at his brother in the pale reflection of the windshield. Like watching a mirror. A mirror of lies.

"It was not the 'madmen' who drugged me and jailed me. Not the Party, or any radicals. Just you, brother. Only you."

"It was not my choice or my liking, I promise you. I had to make you disappear. They . . . they were going to arrest you."

"Nonsense. You invited me to China as a pretext. Somehow my presence was important to your conspiracy. But I still do not see—"

"A wish to see the brother that was robbed from me. That was the only conspiracy, I swear it."

"And I was so glad to see you, at first. Like seeing myself again, seeing what I might have been like, living another life in another country; the product of a totally different society, a revolution. It moved me to see you, my brother, more than I can explain."

"And I, too."

Ahead, the road wound darkly toward the northern hills.

"But how fragile are our illusions, how quickly dispelled. It was in Xian. One single day of joy, discovery. And then, disillusion when I saw what you had done."

"Forget Xian," Wang Bin hissed. "It is not important. It has nothing to do with you."

"At first I imagined you wanted me to help you steal. I photographed what you did not want me to see and you took my camera away. Your carefully sculpted mask slipped then and I realized that you are my brother only in name. It is well that our father is dead."

"You do not understand."

"Oh, yes, brother. I have seen it, and touched it, and tasted its majesty. What you are doing is a crime against China, against all of us. I will not allow it."

Wang Bin spared a glance from the road, expecting to see his brother's hand on the door handle, ready to bolt. It was what he feared most. But David sat with his arms folded, staring straight ahead, a self-righteous plodder chewing on a puzzle. Wang Bin despised him.

"Where are you taking me?" David Wang demanded.

"This road goes to the Great Wall and to the Ming Tombs. I am taking you somewhere you will be safe."

"I would be safe in Peking, except for you."

"You must understand," Wang Bin exclaimed with all the

170

conviction he could muster. "They were going to arrest you . . . as a spy."

"I? A spy? Can you not invent something less transparent?"

"It's true, I swear it. Hundreds of Chinese return here each year and disappear. The government believes that once a Chinese always a Chinese. You may carry some other passport, but it doesn't matter. I heard from friends in the Public Security Bureau that you were to be arrested. Perhaps it was only their way of getting at me. But when I heard about it, I became desperate. I could not tell you. Since you have not lived in China, you cannot understand how things are. In desperation, the only thing I could think to do quickly was to hide you; to keep you safe until I could find a way to help you leave the country."

"And that is where we are going now? On an empty road to nowhere in the middle of the night? To keep me safe? To get me out of the country?"

"Yes."

"My brother, we are both old men, but neither of us is stupid. If you tell me the truth, I will try to help you. We can go to the embassy. I have important friends at home. It is not too late. Look, it is nearly dawn. Let it be the first dawn of a new life for you, my brother. I implore you. I will help."

Wang Bin never faltered. Cautiously, he directed the car across a long causeway that breasted a dry river. They entered an avenue lined with giant stone animals in pairs: camels, lions, elephants.

"This is the entrance to the Ming Tombs," Wang Bin said.

"I have seen the pictures."

"Very well, we will talk as brothers. Tell me what you think. Perhaps you are right. Perhaps it is not too late."

They were near now. Wang Bin needed only another few minutes. Of the thirteen tombs, one had been excavated and was open to tourists. The other twelve were in disrepair, their dusty grounds impromptu picnic sites for bored foreign residents of the capital. Wang Bin turned onto a narrow strip of asphalt running to a modern reservoir built in a gentle valley beneath the hillside tombs.

David Wang rambled on, but the words had become

171

irrelevant now, like the memorial chants in the aftermath of battle. Wang Bin stopped the car on a rocky beach at the shore of the reservoir. The half light of false dawn shadowed a half-dozen wooden rowboats lying face down above the high-water mark. There was no sign of life.

Wang Bin shut off the engine. Carefully, he set the hand brake.

"Your words have great impact on me, brother," he said. "I am beginning to see my mistake, an excess of pride. Let us talk further in the fresh air. It is quite beautiful here. It is not often in China that a man can be alone like this."

Wang Bin stood with his back to the car, facing the dark, still water. He fished among the larger rocks for a flat stone and sent it skimming.

"Only two jumps. Do you remember how as boys we would skim stones in the river? Five jumps, six jumps. Anything seemed possible then."

"I remember," David's voice came from behind.

"Things are more complicated now."

"Yes, they are. Neither of us is as strong as we were once in Shanghai."

"It is true."

They fell silent, watching tiny wavelets lapping at the beach stones.

It was David who spoke at last. A voice of infinite sadness.

"I have thought it through. I understand why you invited me to China, why you held me captive. And why you have brought me here. I know now what it is that only a brother can do for you, no one else. I understand your plan for him."

"Tell me."

"He is to be your essential victim. You must murder him."

Wang Bin never turned. Unseeing, he spoke to the waters.

"Yes. I must murder him."

With a tremendous shove, David Wang pushed his brother into the shallow water. Then, clumsily, he began running along the beach toward a workman's shack that beckoned from the distance. David had not run far when he lost his footing on the loose stones and pitched forward with a groan.

It was then his brother caught him from behind.

172

Stratton's forearms ached from steering the hard-sprung truck over what seemed an endless series of unseen hills. The pitted road twisted, like a snake. In the tepid glint of light from the dashboard, the gauge that Stratton had decided was for gas rested on its bottom mark. The one next to it—temperature?—seemed to be rising. He nudged the girl at his side.

"Wake up, Kangmei. It will be dawn soon and the truck will not go much farther."

"I was not sleeping, Thom-as, just resting." She stretched and ran her hands through the mass of tangled black hair. "Have we passed a river?"

"On a very shaky bridge, about ten minutes ago."

"Good. We are almost there."

"Where is *there*, Kangmei?" She had been coy about that since their escape. A safe place where they would be with friends, she had said.

"It is a commune, Thom-as. We call it Bright Star. It is the home of my mother's family. I lived there during the Cultural Revolution when my father was being punished. My uncles are among the commune leaders. They will protect us."

Stratton nodded. It had to have been something like that. He riffled through the possibilities. A commune in a backward province more than a thousand miles from Peking, and probably a century in terms of control. Once they had taught him a great deal about communes, the central fact of life for eight hundred million Chinese. The instructor's voice came back to Stratton. He had been a Spec/6, dragged from a Ph.D. program to war. Shared reward for shared work, a Marxist replacement for rural villages dominated by landlords. Now there were no more landlords, only work brigades and production teams tilling common land.

What had resisted revolution was the social makeup of the communes. Almost all who lived on a commune in China were descendants of people who had lived there centuries ago. Nearly all the children born there would also die there in toothless old age. The continuity of families remained stronger than the caprice of a distant state.

Kangmei would be safe. The family would close around

173

her, shutting out inquiries from cadres who, knowing the system, would not press too hard. She would be safe, but also empty. What kind of life would it be for an intelligent, vivacious young woman, calf-deep in paddy muck, courted by half-literate bumpkins? Whom would she talk to? Whom would she love? Kangmei deserved better than that. Stratton made himself a private promise: She would have it. Somehow. One day.

But would the commune shelter him as well? Probably, for a time, anyway.

"Kangmei, we're in Guangdong Province, right? How far from the coast?"

"No, this is Guangxi. And we are many hours from the sea, many hills and many people."

Guangxi. Memories worse than the cobra.

"Look, I think it would be better if—"

She had outthought him.

"You would never make it to the sea without help, Thom-as. And my family will be very proud to hide you, and to help you escape, especially when they see the wonderful gift you are bringing them."

"You?"

She laughed, a mountain stream.

"Oh, they will be glad to see me, too. But it is the truck they will prize most."

"The truck."

"But . . . how will they account for it?"

"They will hide it while they let all other production teams know that they have saved enough money to buy a used truck. Then one day it will appear. Imagine the celebration; the other teams will be so jealous."

"I see," Stratton said in quiet wonder.

"You will be a hero, Thom-as. My hero." She slid across the seat and kissed him with flashing tongue.

They left the truck in a copse of trees on a hillside capped by an ancient pagoda. Kangmei, bubbling with the excitement of a little girl on Christmas, led him to the hilltop. It was nearly light by the time they reached the top.

"Down there," she said, gesturing to a mist-shrouded valley.

174

"That is Bright Star. My family lives in the houses near the school. Soon you will see."

With exaggerated care, she installed him on a bed of needles beneath some pine trees, about a hundred yards from the dirt path that wound into the valley.

"No one will see you here. Rest. My uncles and I will come back around lunchtime, when everyone is sleeping. It will be safe then for you to come down. It's not far." She looked at him through almond eyes without end. "You will wait for me, Thom-as. Please?"

"I will wait." He hugged her. "Here, a gift for your family." He handed her the leather-yoked keys of the truck.

When she had gone, Stratton lay with his head pillowed in his arms and watched the sky turn blue. As the tension drained from him, aches replaced adrenaline. It had been a long time since he had been this tired. Stratton surrendered to sleep.

When he awoke it was already late morning. The sun, approaching its zenith, oppressed the pine grove. It had brought sapping humidity and a winged holiday for insects of every stinging phylum. Stratton relieved himself against a tree and crawled onto an outcropping of rock that looked onto the valley, trying not to think how hungry he was.

A picturebook scene. The commune was comprised of what had apparently been four separate villages in the space of several square miles. Around each cluster of single-story wood homes well-trod dikes led to paddies of rice. In the northern quadrant lay a bright green field of what could only have been sugarcane. To the east was a well-kept citrus grove. A patchwork of small private plots lay on the fringes of the communal fields. The nearest settlement, the one to which Kangmei must have gone, was arranged around a carp pond. The only building of substance was a low, ramshackle structure with a thatched roof and a fresh coat of whitewash. Stratton decided it must be a combination school and office for the production team.

The fields and earthen streets of the village swarmed with people. Stratton watched a double file of schoolchildren, hand-in-hand, parade in a swatch of color toward a dusty soccer field where some teenagers desultorily kicked a ball.

175

Stratton counted two trucks and a handful of three-wheeled contraptions that looked like misshapen lawn mowers. "Walking tractors," Kangmei called them.

The scene was peaceful and, by Chinese standards, an advertisement for rural prosperity. Stratton noted the slender cable on thin poles that dropped into the hamlet and spread ancillary arms toward a few of the nearest houses; by rule of thumb in China, if electricity has spilled down to individual production teams, a commune is well off.

At the base of the hillside path there appeared a supple girl and two stocky men in peasants' garb. As they began to climb, the girl waved diffidently, a fleeting, offhand movement, like shooing flies. Kangmei had found refuge.

Stratton decided to wait where he was. Idly, he began to trace the power line out from the settlement, across the fields and back toward its origin.

It was a mistake.

In almost the precise center of the valley, sheathed in trees, lay the administrative headquarters of the commune, the hub of which the four production teams were spokes. Stratton could see a dingy white water tower and, amid shadows, the perimeter walls of what once had been the landlord's house. He made out a strip of macadam and along it some shops, a vegetable market and a fair-sized building with a half-domed roof that might once have been a 1930s movie theater.

Stratton saw without seeing the red-starred flag that hung limply from the building. He saw a chimney thrusting unnaturally from among the trees and knew without knowing that it belonged to a homespun woodworking factory that made grapefruit crates and slatted folding chairs. He saw a glint of water through the trees and knew that, except in the rainy season, the river that flowed there could be safely forded by men five feet ten or taller.

Stratton groaned aloud. In an instant of black despair, he cursed the luck that had forsaken him in rags among Chinese pines.

He rose to run.

Before him stood Kangmei. Smiling at her side were two

176

erect, honey-colored men of late middle age with the same subtle, alluring facial structure that Kangmei had inherited.

"Thom-as," Kangmei said gravely, "these are my uncles. They will help us."

They were Zhuang, members of a race more Thai than Chinese that had settled in the southern hills in the mists of time. The Zhuang survived in modern China as the country's largest minority. Kangmei's mother was Zhuang, her father, Wang Bin, a member of the majority Han. The combination was what made her so striking. Stratton should have realized it before.

I know all about the Zhuang. They taught me that, too, Stratton wanted to yell, and wondered about his sanity.

Kangmei stared in open-mouthed concern.

"Thom-as! What is the matter? There is no danger. These are my uncles. They—"

"What is the name of this fucking place?"

"Thom-as!"

"Goddamn it. Tell me." He took an involuntary step toward the girl and the two peasants closed around her.

"I told you. We live in Bright Star."

"That's not the right name. I know. Tell me in Chinese."

The two peasants began talking angrily. Kangmei interrupted them with a stream of local dialect that seemed to mollify them.

"Thom-as, I have told them that you are feverish and hungry and very tired. But you must be polite to them, please."

"I'm sorry." Stratton grappled for composure. "Tell me the real name, please. I want to hear it."

"We live in Bright Star," she said slowly, as though instructing a slow child. "Over there is Sweet Water, and there, Good Harvest, and there, Evergreen. Why is it so important?"

"And the place in the middle? Where the factory is, and the water tower?"

"That is where the cadres live, and some soldiers. It is not important. Our people go there only when they must—for Party discussions, to buy shoes and bicycle tires."

"What is it *called*?"

177

"It is called Man-ling."

"Man-ling, yes, Man-ling. Oh, sweet Jesus."

Stratton sank to his knees and buried his head in his hands. The peasants' hostility surrendered to concern. Kangmei sprang to his side.

"Thom-as, do not weep. Come, you will be safe. My aunts will cook special food. There is a warm bed and a doctor for your leg. Yes, a doctor . . . you can trust him. He is a friend of my uncles'. Come, please. It is not far to walk."

"I can't. I must not."

"Please, Thom-as. Please. Soon there will be too many people. Already there are rumors about things that happened last night. . . . Please."

"No. No. No," Stratton muttered in an anguished litany that was a warrior's penance.

He was too weak to resist when Kangmei and her uncles levered him to his feet and led him blindly down the gentle hillside into yesterday.

The general came late.

He had lunched too long—a farewell banquet for a retiring colleague: sea cucumbers, suckling pig, whitefish, pigeon, shark's fin soup, tree fungus for dessert, and torrents of *mao tai*. The colleague, eighty-four years old, a Party militant for nearly half a century, had never cracked a smile.

The general rebuffed chastising glances from the two civilian members of the tribunal with a short nod and settled noisily into his padded chair. He spared hardly a glance for the gray-haired man disintegrating before the prosecutor's tongue-lashing. He thumbed briefly through the docket on the polished wood desk before him. The man was a musician of some sort.

The general did not know him. He ignored the stream of accusation and thought of his own son. The surveillance reports were quite concrete: The boy had been meeting foreign journalists, hanging out at the International Club, perfuming his hair, reading Western magazines. He had even, apparently, bedded a diplomat. The general would not have minded that, but the omission of the diplomat's name, nationality and sex—certainly a calculated omission—could mean only the worst.

The young fool had been a mistake from the beginning, a winter child by the general's third wife when he was already fifty-seven. The boy had inherited his mother's looks, but not a scrap of common sense. He wanted to study in the United States. In the dawning Chinese political winter he might as well declare his intention of walking on the moon. The general dozed off, deciding that the boy would have to go into the army. If he let the Public Security Bureau have him, the boy's mother—another mistake, she cackled like a chicken—would make the general's life impossible.

". . . compose and play unauthorized, bourgeois, decadent and immoral music.

"Twenty-six. You are accused, during the visit of foreign guests, to wit, the Berlin Philharmonic Orchestra, of playing foreigners' instruments without authorization and of demeaning the prestige and honor of the People's Republic by publicly suggesting that they were of a quality superior to those made in the People's Republic . . ."

The general roused himself for the climax. When the prosecutor asked for life imprisonment, the musician fainted. The general watched expressionless. He had seen that before, and stronger men wet their pants. When guards had roused the musician and the president offered to commute the sentence to self-criticism and twenty years at a state farm in Qinghai Province, the idiot actually seemed grateful.

Qinghai, on the unforgiving Tibetan plateau. One of the loneliest, coldest, most savage places on earth. If he was still alive in six months, it would be a miracle. Soft-handed wretch.

When the president intoned "Qinghai" he looked over at the general with arched eyebrow, as though inviting an objection, a local joke. The prosecutor smothered a smile.

Silently, the general assented. He had never liked musicians.

After the last of that afternoon's accused had been dismissed, the prosecutor summarized the results of the day before.

Normally, while the tribunal members smoked and sipped fresh tea, the prosecutor would report that all of the senior comrades given twenty-four hours to mull their fate had volunteered to accept lesser sentence rather than to contest the charges.

That afternoon was different. Head down, voice muted, almost embarrassed, the prosecutor began reading:

"The following comrades who appeared before the Tribunal yesterday have agreed to self-criticism and reform through labor: Wu Ping, Sun Liu . . ."

Surprised, the president riffled through the papers before him.

"Wait until I find the list, Comrade," he demanded with raised hand. "Very well, proceed."

When the prosecutor had finished—after repeating some of the names as many as three times to accommodate the president, whose hearing was not what it had once been—he remained standing.

Slowly, lips moving, the president read through the list of names he had checked.

"The list is complete except for Comrade Wang Bin," the president said at last.

"Yes, Comrade President."

"He demands a trial?" The president was incredulous.

"No, Comrade President."

"What then?"

"I do not know, Comrade President."

"What are you saying?"

"Comrade Wang Bin has not reported to the Tribunal within the time afforded him, Comrade President."

The prosecutor was frantic. Such a thing had never happened before.

"Why has he not reported?"

"I do not know, Comrade President."

"Where is Wang Bin, Comrade Prosecutor?"

"I do not know."

"It is your job to know."

"It is the job of the Public Security Bureau. I have asked them."

"What do they say, idiot? What do they say?"

"Comrade Wang Bin is missing. He has not been seen anywhere since last night. There is no trace of him. The Public Security Bureau—"

The president surged to his feet with the sudden furious energy of a man fifty years younger. He slammed his fist on the desk, scattering papers and upsetting his tea.

"Find him!" the president roared. "Find him and bring him to me, Comrade Prosecutor. Do it now!"

The general belched.

CHAPTER 17

T H E Y W A L K E D by the river, a nurse and her patient.

Stratton's confidence was returning with his strength. He had slept for nearly twenty-four hours, a half-life in which he had grayly drifted around reality without ever reaching it: sober-miened women scrubbing him; a middle-aged man probing gently at his leg; wondrous soup, piping hot, that tasted of the earth and scissored through the pain. And the beautiful woman who sat by him, whispering reassurance. That, he would never forget.

When Stratton had at last surfaced, tears of relief belied Kangmei's fixed smile.

He had reached out for her clenched fist and gently pried open the fingers.

"I'm all right. Really I am," he had comforted.

"I was afraid, Thom-as. So afraid."

Later, watching him wolf down a mound of rice with scraps of chicken, she had seemed like a little girl again.

"You must listen, Thom-as. To my mother's brothers I have said that you are a good man who is being pursued by evil men; nothing more. They are simple peasants, but good,

182

and strong. They will not betray you. To the rest of the people in Bright Star my uncles are saying that you are a foreign expert from Peking who has come to show us new ways to grow better rice. I am your guide."

"I don't know anything about rice." Except what paddy mud feels like, wet, consuming.

"That is not important. When the people of Bright Star learn that you are *our* rice expert, they will not speak of you to members of the other production teams, or to the cadres at Man-ling. You will be safe then, do you not see?"

"I must not stay here, Kangmei," Stratton had insisted weakly. "I must try to help David."

"Yes, Thom-as. My uncles have cousins who work on the railroad. They think it would be possible to get you to Guangzhou."

Guangzhou in Chinese. In English, Canton, China's sprawling southern metropolis across the border from Hong Kong. Canton was still China, but from all he had read of it, the city was also a curious East-West hybrid infinitely more relaxed than Peking. In a teeming and sophisticated city where foreigners were no novelty, he had a fighting chance.

"Guangzhou would be fine."

He slept again, and when he awoke it was midafternoon. Kangmei laughed when he tried on clothes smelling of strong soap that had been neatly stacked alongside the bed. The trousers bottomed out four inches too soon. The shirt went across his shoulders, but only the bottom two buttons would fasten.

"These are the biggest we could find, Thom-as. But you will never be a peasant. Come, let the people see their new rice expert."

Along the river there was a kind of promenade, a path of beaten earth flanked by shade trees. Stratton smiled at the peasants they met and tried to look knowledgeable.

"This is the end of Bright Star," said Kangmei. "Over there is Evergreen."

She gestured to the far side of the brown river, flanked on both sides by steep banks. The water flowed swiftly and looked deep.

183

"And beyond Evergreen is Man-ling, right?"

"Yes." She led Stratton to a spot where the promenade had been widened to include a graceful copse of palms. He sat beside her.

"This looks to me like Bright Star's lovers' lane," Stratton remarked.

"I do not understand."

When he had explained she smiled.

"It is true that many young people come here at night and that they do not always discuss politics."

They kissed.

And then she asked the question that Stratton had dreaded.

"Why are you afraid of Man-ling, Thom-as?"

It was not so much that she deserved to know. To his surprise, Stratton discovered that he wanted to tell her.

"I was there once. In a war. While you were a child."

She sat quiet for a time, tracing circles in the dirt with a stick. Stratton stared down at the river.

"Was it very sad, Thom-as?"

"Yes."

"I would like to know." She spoke to the stick.

He told her.

March 18, 1971

A black sergeant in plainclothes had brought the summons to the Saigon villa Stratton shared with Bobby Ho. An hour later, they were in a briefing room protected by concentric circles of invisible guards.

A squat, sweat-stained colonel abandoned an uneven struggle with a balky room air conditioner.

"Captain Black," the colonel said, shaking hands with Stratton.

"Captain White. Congratulations." The colonel gave Bobby Ho's hand an extra pump. He had been a captain only for six days, but no one outside the room was even supposed to know that Bobby Ho was in the army. Deniability, they called it. Officially, Stratton and Ho were civilian psychologists on contract to the government: studying stress.

184

"Rested up? Everybody's talkin' about it."

On the last one they had been close enough to see the lights of Hanoi.

"This one should be even more fun." He passed across aerial photos. "The Chinks are involved in this little old war, up to their slanty assholes."

"Who is that, Colonel?" Bobby Ho asked quietly. Stratton stifled a grin. Bobby Ho's parents ran a pawnshop in San Francisco. They had raised their son to be an American, but there was no way you could tell by looking at him. Vietnam had intercepted Bobby Ho between Stanford and medical school. He wanted to be a pediatrician, and he spent a lot of his time and most of his money working with some French nuns who ran a clinic near the village. When the army made him White for missions that didn't exist to places that were never named, Bobby Ho hunted with uncommon skill.

The colonel had the grace to color.

"The Chinese. The Chinese are teachin' the Viets how to brainwash our boys. Remember what they did in Korea? I was there, man. The last thing you wanted to happen was to get captured by the Chin—Chinese. They turned people inside out; tell you Ike was a faggot and make you believe it."

The colonel poked a pudgy finger at the aerial photos.

"What we hear is that the Chinese are trainin' Viet interrogators in that building there in the middle of the picture. They got about a dozen of our POWs up there as guinea pigs."

"Where is it—the village?" Stratton asked.

"Jesus, I just told you. It's in China."

"Shit," said Bobby Ho.

"We supposed to go in and get them?" Stratton asked.

The colonel nodded. "Yeah, go get 'em out and fuck Chairman Mao. Does that offend you, Captain White?"

"Not a bit, Colonel," said Bobby Ho.

"What's the name of this place?" Stratton asked.

"Man-ling it's called. You guys see Joe and the boys. They got it all worked out, pictures, models, the whole shootin' match, just like usual." The colonel's eyes assumed a faraway cast. "If it was me, I'd take about four gunships and hit 'em so hard and so fast they wouldn't have time even to find their

185

little red books. That's the only way to win this war, hard and fast. That's how I'd do it, if it was me."

Hot air. Stratton would write the operational orders and the colonel knew it.

"If it was you, I'd stay home," said Bobby Ho.

They took one chopper off a quiet carrier high up in the Gulf of Tonkin. Stratton, Ho and four sergeants. Captain Black was traveling light. If he needed help, it was only minutes away in the air behind them.

For a landing zone, Stratton had chosen a paddy about three miles east of the village. He had wanted the farmland and the village between the chopper and the PLA camp that lay a few miles to the west. Intelligence said a regular infantry company used the camp. Intelligence had not said why it believed the nowhere village called Man-ling had been chosen to brainwash POWs.

They landed in driving rain and gusting wind, ankle-deep in water—killers dressed for the country in dark, rough civilian clothes without nationality. In the distance, at night, they might pass for peasants. Close up it would be harder. Stratton's peasants bore a Russian AK-47, Chinese grenades, a silenced East German pistol, a Thai killing knife and a cyanide capsule. On his back, each man carried a folding bicycle. They looked superficially like Chinese machines, but were half as heavy and twice as fast. Stratton had insisted. A question of image: See a man on a bicycle and you assume he lives nearby and knows where he is going. He belongs.

The same reasoning had ordained the timing. It was midnight, and the helicopter would return one hour before dawn unless Stratton called earlier. They might have come later, but anything moving in the Chinese countryside between midnight and dawn would alarm sentinels accustomed to seeing nothing move at all. Even midnight was cutting it fine, Stratton knew, but he had not dared come until the village was asleep.

They watched in silence as the chopper clawed for the clouds on muffled engines. It was the seventh time Stratton had endured that particular parting. The seven loneliest moments of his life.

186

Even in the mud, the bicycles worked like a charm.

They were the only thing.

A sentry materialized, wraithlike, from the shelter of a tree about a mile from the village. PLA.

The sentry hollered something that was lost in the wind. Bobby Ho, riding point, head down, waited until he was within ten yards of the man, until the pistol would bear. He answered in Chinese.

Maybe the man had heard the helicopter. Maybe Bobby Ho said the wrong thing. The sentry coiled, unslinging his rifle. From their shelter by the tree, two more wet soldiers emerged. The six Americans slithered off their bikes into the mud like a satanic rank of marionettes.

It ended quickly, but one of the sentries managed a single shot. It ricocheted like flat doom through the blackness.

For five breathless, unbearable minutes, Stratton's team crouched by the road, safeties off, ears aching, praying. No one came. The sentry had died in vain.

Bobby Ho tried to break the tension.

"These Chinks ain't even tryin'," he whispered in jocose mimicry of the fat colonel. It didn't sound funny.

The single guard at the head of the village main street died in silence for his sloth. He must have felt the blade administered by a saturnine Puerto Rican named Gomez, but he never saw it. Stratton left Gomez and a fireplug Tennessean named Harkness to watch their back door.

They met the boy a few minutes later, creeping through such stillness and total absence of color it gave Stratton the eerie sensation that the entire village was a two-dimensional fantasy.

Bobby Ho flushed the boy from a pile of rags in the imperfect shelter of a shop doorway. Panofsky grabbed him, roughly clamping his jaw. The boy wriggled, a minnow in the maw of a shark. Stratton saw the knife come up and winced.

"Wait!" Bobby Ho hissed. "He can't be more than twelve, all skin and bones."

The knife wavered. Panofsky looked over at Stratton. Everybody knew the rules. It wasn't even a judgment call. Stratton made it one. It was Bobby Ho's play.

Panofsky's eyes flashed with anger.

In a sibilant, harsh undertone, Bobby Ho tongue-lashed the boy in Chinese. Stratton watched the boy's eyes: flat, emotionless. They showed intelligence, but no surprise, no curiosity. And most of all, no fear.

At length, the boy nodded. Bobby Ho stepped back.

"It's all right."

Again Panofsky looked at Stratton.

"Let him go," Stratton said. Sometimes you break the rules.

The rag boy massaged his neck. With arrogance that could only have been inherited, he turned his back and stalked away, vanishing within seconds up an alley on pencil legs that seemed unequal to their sixty-pound burden.

"I told him we are on a secret training exercise with foreign friends, and that if he ever interrupts the PLA again, I will personally shoot him and everybody in his family."

"I hope he believed you."

"He believed me."

Panofsky snorted. Bloomfield grunted. Stratton sent them up to the far end of the main street to share their scorn.

Lights burned inside an old movie house that now featured Mao slogans on its sagging marquee. Bobby Ho prised open a side door. They cached the Kalashnikovs in the shadow outside; assault rifles are useless for close work.

Inside, the building smelled of molding concrete, stale tobacco and rancid bodies. Wooden chairs, neatly arranged, filled the pit of the theater. Empty, every one of them. The stage had been divided into four separate rooms, each with double doors facing the audience. All the doors were closed. From behind one set rose a high-pitched monotone that gave Stratton goose bumps.

". . . Delano Roosevelt . . . Harry S. Truman . . . Dwight David Eisenhower . . . John Fitzgerald Kennedy . . . Lyndon Brains Johnson . . . Richard—"

"*Baines*," a deeper voice interrupted. "Lyndon Baines Johnson."

The first voice resumed, a record returned to its groove: "Lyndon Baines Johnson . . . Richard Milhous Nixon . . ."

The voices were Chinese. Stratton looked at Bobby Ho,

who gave an elaborate shrug. A teacher and his student. What else could they be?

Stratton gestured and Bobby Ho nodded. He would check the area around the stage and watch Stratton's back.

The basement, intelligence had said. The prisoners are held in the basement. They are paraded upstairs for onstage interrogation classes.

Stratton found the stairs without trouble. He went down with a gentle rush until he came to a stout wooden door. He nudged it open with his boot and let the pistol precede him.

Blackness. Absolute. And a terrible smell: fresh soap thinly overlaying the smell of fear and anger. Stratton let a cone of light from his Czech torch play around the room, and came within a heartbeat of firing at a sound in the far corner. Two rats, red-eyed and territorial.

It took Stratton fifteen minutes to explore the basement thoroughly. Six cells. Stratton toured them, one at a time. In the fourth, scratched into the cheap concrete, a lover's testament had survived its author: "Rick & Connie Houston '70." With the leaden movements of an old man, Stratton visited the remaining two cells. In the last one, he found traces of blood the cleaners had missed. They had come too late. How long? A day? Two? Stratton would never know and never forget. He ran the back of his hand across his lips to moisten them and tasted ashes. He had only another instant to mull his disappointment.

From above came the unmistakable sound of boots hammering the tired floorboards. Not furtive. Authoritative boots.

Stratton listened from the head of the stairs. Two men, speaking Chinese. Plus the student and his professor. At least four. He and Bobby Ho had played against worse odds than that.

From the back of the theater came Bobby Ho's voice. Stratton understood none of the words. He understood too well what they meant. The tone was enough: arrogant, strong, with a touch of exasperation. An officer's voice, informing more than explaining.

Bobby Ho was playing the cover story, singing loudly enough to alert Stratton.

189

The cover was pretty much what Bobby Ho had told the ragged boy: He was a PLA officer down from Peking on a training mission with East Germans en route to North Vietnam to help the heroic struggle there. It was not a bad story. There were plenty of Caucasian instructors with the Viets, even some Germans. In the jacket of his pocket, Bobby Ho had a set of orders that looked like the real thing.

It might have worked. But it didn't. Three or four voices speaking at once drowned out Bobby Ho. The shouts grew louder. Wood smashed. Bodies fell. Stratton didn't hear Bobby Ho again until he screamed.

Stratton rammed through the door with the pistol ready. The neatly ordered folding chairs lay in matchstick piles. In their chaos stood four Chinese, two uniformed, the other two in bureaucrats' white short-sleeved shirts, their red books of quotations clutched protectively. As Stratton's eye recorded, his brain raced to establish target priority. The student and his professor were unarmed. Shoot last. The other two both had pistols. One was pressed against the head of a kneeling Bobby Ho. Its owner was screaming at Stratton.

Stratton let his gun arm come down, slowly, with emphasis. He reversed his grip on the pistol. Holding it by the butt, he walked toward the Chinese.

"*Vas is los?*" Stratton demanded in his own officer's voice.

The man with Bobby Ho barked something that brought the student and professor to life like wind-up dolls.

"Comrade Commissar Wu . . ." they began together.

". . . instructs you to put down the gun and to raise your hands," concluded the professor.

Stratton forced a rictus grin.

"English. *Nein. Deutsch.*" He tapped his chest. "*Kamerad.*"

After a cursory search, they tossed Stratton into one of the rooms on the stage. He was alone for twenty-seven minutes by his watch. An important eternity. He listened to them working on Bobby Ho. The shouts became one-sided, the screams dwindled to pathetic groans.

When they came for Stratton, they brought Bobby Ho unconscious. Stratton tried not to look at him.

There were still four of them. No one had left, so without

190

phones, they had made no attempt to spread the alarm. Stratton asked himself why. Were they swayed by the cover story? Or were they simply in a hurry, trying for good information before seeking help?

The commissar was a lean, gray-haired man in PLA green with red tabs and a four-pocket tunic reserved for officers. The other uniformed man, balding and pot-bellied, wore the blue and white of the police. Stratton marked him as a local.

The policeman did the heavy work. He jabbed Stratton in the belly with a truncheon. When Stratton involuntarily clammed forward, the policeman struck him on the head.

The professor screamed: "How many men in your unit? Where are they? What is your mission? Talk or die, imperialist running dog!"

"Deutsch."

It lasted about ten minutes. The policeman enjoyed his work. An expert, a fat man with bad breath, who stung without maiming. Stratton rolled with the blows and calculated his chances. The student, nearest the door, held a Chinese carbine with familiarity. The professor was unarmed. The policeman had his club and a holstered pistol. The commissar held a heavy Chinese military pistol.

Stratton, fighting the pain, babbling in the few words of German he knew, realized that Captain Black was finished. Sooner or later they would alert the PLA garrison outside of town and that would be that.

Then the Chinese made their mistake.

From the night came the sound of small arms fire. Stratton heard the pop of Chinese weapons and the crack of the AK-47s. The PLA already knew. The shooting flustered the Chinese. The commissar spoke in English for the first time.

"There is no time for this. Pick up your friend."

Stratton stared dumbly. Only when they all began to shout and wave did he allow himself to understand.

He picked up Bobby Ho the way a mother bundles an injured child. Blood from Bobby's mouth ran off the shoulder of Stratton's jacket. There was a jagged hole where his teeth had been. Stratton held his head gently and pressed him close. Bobby Ho rasped a final sentence into Stratton's neck.

191

"It was the kid . . . sorry, Tom. . . ."

Bobby Ho spun from Stratton's arms and lunged for the student. The carbine, shockingly loud in the small room, cut him in half. Impelled by momentum that the bullets did not reverse, the corpse of Bobby Ho collided with his killer.

The commissar was too slow. A bullet from his pistol plucked at Stratton's ribs. Stratton's open palm drove the commissar's nose into his brain.

Then Stratton had the pistol. He shot the policeman twice, and then the student as he writhed to free himself from Bobby Ho's last embrace. The professor burst from the room, vaulted off the stage and darted among the chairs, a frenzied hurdler. Stratton shot him in the back.

Outside was a holocaust. Two trucks burned at the far end of the street, and along either side civilians spilled from single-story hutches whose thatched roofs burned with a hungry crackle. The PLA had arrived in force. Stratton counted eight or nine rag doll figures in army khaki sprawled around the trucks. Stratton saw Panofsky go down hurling a grenade. Bloomfield dove after him. He didn't make it.

Screaming, waving his assault rifle to scatter peasants who seemed more curious than frightened, Stratton headed back up the street the way he had come. Two knock-kneed soldiers emerged from an alley. Stratton took them with a short burst. He ran back to where he had left Gomez and Harkness. An old man brandishing a cane appeared from nowhere. Stratton clubbed him with the rifle.

He found Harkness's body propped against a tree, and then Gomez, firing methodically at dancing shadows from behind a low concrete wall.

Together they broke away from the village and into the black, beckoning fields. Stratton's wound bled freely. Every step was a fresh souvenir of defeat. After about fifteen minutes he could go no farther. He huddled in an irrigation ditch, Gomez beside him. The Chinese had paused at the edge of the village. To regroup, to await orders, or simply to separate soldiers from civilians. It made no difference. They would come soon enough.

192

"What a fuck-up," Gomez growled.

Stratton gasped for breath, wincing with pain.

"Did you call for help, for the chopper?"

"Bloomfield had the radio," Stratton whispered.

"Shit. I got no ammo left."

Stratton checked his own rifle. One magazine remained.

"They're all around us, Captain. I can feel it. And the civilians are worse than the fucking soldiers. Crazy bastards. One guy came at us with a cleaver."

Stratton knew what the next question would be, and he dreaded it.

"How are we gonna get out of here, Captain?"

"Pickup is in about thirty-five minutes," Stratton gasped. "Do you think you can find where we left the beacon? It can't be more than a mile or so."

"I can find it."

"Go. I'll stay here and keep them busy till the last minute. When the chopper comes I'll be right behind you."

"Sure," Gomez muttered in a way that meant it would never happen. "*Adios.*"

"Good luck," Stratton called, and waited alone to die.

The bugs were bad. He ignored them. Every time he shifted, his jungle boots squished in the mud. He held perfectly still. The second hand crawled around the face of his watch like a turtle with palsy. He willed himself not to look at it.

The flames were dying now, but enough light remained to make the village a perfect target. The Chinese recognized that. They could not know how large was the force opposing them, and they were in no hurry to find out. Stratton blessed their fear.

Stratton heard officers hollering and the whine of new trucks arriving, but it was nearly twenty minutes before the first infantrymen burst from the closest buildings and dove for cover. They were in range, but Stratton did not fire. To fire was to die.

He waited another agonizing five minutes. Then he crouched and with all his strength hurled the last grenade as far as he could off to the left, away from the route of escape. The night

193

ignited once more: the grenade, followed by Chinese carbines, firing blind. Tracer bullets streaked along the treeline like orange meteors.

Stratton slithered from the ditch and trotted for the landing zone.

He had nearly made it when he heard a grunt and the thrashing of a desperate struggle about thirty yards ahead. In the moonlight he saw a figure wielding a pole, a ghostly jouster.

A scream pierced the night, and then a terrible, expiring "*Madre . . .*"

Stratton crashed forward like a murderous boar, the Kalashnikov on full automatic. Before him, squat gray shapes rustled away. Peasant killers. Systematically, Stratton cut them down. One. Two. Three. Four.

It had not been a pole, but a pitchfork, and it had impaled Gomez as he lay on the moist earth beside the homing beacon that would bring the rescue helicopter. Gomez was dead when Stratton reached him, the pitchfork deep in his chest.

Mindlessly Stratton knelt by his friend's body and activated the ultrasonic beacon. Already he could hear the invisible helicopter, waiting for the signal. From behind he heard whispers from approaching Chinese soldiers as they skittered between clumps of cover.

Stratton glanced down at Gomez and smothered a moan. He passed a grimy hand across parched lips. All he could do was wait; it would be a very near thing. Wait in silence for deliverance, for the sight of the rope ladder peeling out of the chopper's belly. Pray that the chopper came before the Chinese found him.

Stratton heard a noise and knew instantly that the helicopter would come too late, an eternity too late.

It was a squelch in the mud, and he whirled to face it. Another gray shape, only a few yards away. It had been watching him; he should have sensed it.

Stratton sprang forward, his hand working on the Thai blade at his belt. The shape had no gun or he would already be dead. But it could scream, and if it screamed, he would be discovered.

194

In three frantic bounds he reached the peasant. It was a young woman. She cried out and backed away, her eyes wild. The distant throb of the chopper blades grew louder. A minute or two, maybe more.

The woman turned to flee.

Let her go?

But she would scream. He knew she would scream. She ran in awkward steps, her arms around her belly. Stratton swiftly caught her, sobbing. Not this time, Bobby Ho. Not again.

With his left hand Stratton jerked back the girl's head, and the fire's glow shone on the flesh of her neck. He killed her with a single savage thrust.

Still she screamed, a thin, piteous wail lost in the clatter of the descending helicopter and the confused shouts of the Chinese soldiers. She screamed for her life, and that of the child who lay heavy within her. Two senseless deaths.

Thomas Stratton did not care.

CHAPTER **18**

STRATTON'S THROAT was dry, his voice rough. He felt himself winding down like a cheap clock.

"Like it was yesterday," he said. "I still dream about it. It still hurts. I murdered them. The woman, the baby . . ."

Kangmei worried a deep furrow with her stick.

"It is a very sad story, Thom-as," she murmured at last.

"I'm sorry."

"Men should not fight, Thom-as. They should live in peace and build beautiful things. Man is for good, not for killing."

"I wish I could believe that."

"Oh, but it is true. For every evil old man like my father, there are hundreds—many thousand—who are true and loving. Leave your unlocked bicycle at their door and it will be there tomorrow, and the day after. Those are the Chinese people, Thom-as. Not my father, not commissars who play with people's minds."

"Your Uncle David is a good man."

"Yes, I could see that."

"Until today he was the only person who had ever heard my story."

196

"Thank you."

"I wanted you to know. It was important . . ."

"I understand. I am not a witch, like one of the old women in Bright Star, but I have seen the sadness inside of you."

"Kangmei, I . . ."

Stratton let the thought drift away. He watched the swift river, as muddy as his own thoughts. He felt light-headed and empty. And yet purged, as though retelling the horror would at last allow him to file it in some dusty mind bin, where it belonged.

On the far side of the river a young woman led a file of nursery-school children toward an old wooden footbridge. A flock of pigeons alighted in the trees around them. The palm leaves glinted with fleeting gold in the brief tropical dusk. Soon it would be dark, and a few hours after that he would be gone. Kangmei's family had found a friend of a friend who was a conductor on the overnight train to Canton. Tomorrow the vestige of Captain Black would take over. Canton would be no problem. It was tonight that hurt. Stratton wanted the ghost of Man-ling banished as quickly as the Chinese railroads would allow. He wanted to get to Hong Kong, and from there to save David Wang. But he did not want to leave the strong and idealistic woman at his side.

He was assembling the question when Kangmei spoke. Again, she had anticipated him.

"Have you ever loved, Thom-as?"

"Yes, sure," he said, but he could not separate the images of a clichéd decade: blondes and Titians, quiche and Perrier, trim-cut ski jackets, designer sheets. Carol, who had proved a more devoted doctor than wife, more brittle than beautiful, a better diagnostician than mother.

"No," he said. Not like this.

"I loved once," she said, so far away, so fragile he wanted to gather her into his arms, but dared not molest her privacy.

"A gentle boy, not tall and strong and handsome, but short and plain. One leg was shorter than the other and he limped. His face was so round you thought it was the moon, and he could not see well, so he wore heavy glasses that always slid off his nose and broke. There was no place he could hide:

197

People would point and say, 'Oh, how ugly.' But when they saw what he wrote, no one laughed anymore. His poems were beautiful, like the morning sun creeping along an open field. His poems were as simple as the birds in these trees and as pure as those children across the river.

"He was a happy boy who did not mind being ugly. He laughed at his bad luck and lived for the hours when he could write his poetry. During the days he worked as an electrician in a big factory. At night he would compose in a workers' dormitory. At first he showed his poems only to his friends. That was when he was happiest. He gave poems to his friends as gifts and then showed them to other friends until finally other writers saw them, writers who work without Party control. He gave poems in secret to his friends at the factory and finally the top cadres of the factories saw them, too. The writers went to him and said, 'Write of life. Be freer.' The cadres of his unit went to him and said, 'You have great talent. You must write of the workers' heroic struggle.'

"My friend was a happy man who wanted everyone to share his joy. So he wrote for the writers about larks and joy, and he wrote for the cadres about the beauties of blast furnaces and socialist progress. At first both were very pleased. 'More,' they said. 'Write more.' So my friend wrote more, and more, until he could hardly remember whether the next poem was supposed to be about the glorious fulfillment of factory quotas, or every man's right to find his own truth.

"Then one day my friend said, 'No more.' He went to the writers and to the cadres and told them, 'I must write for me, not for you. What I write for you is not me, and it is not good.' They both became very angry, the writers and the cadres. They felt my friend had betrayed them. They yelled and screamed at him. The factory gave him the most dirty and dangerous jobs. The writers no longer invited him to tea or to walk in the park. My friend became very unhappy. Soon he could not write at all—not even for himself. He would limp around the city looking for inspiration, his great moon face empty, like a man whose father has died. He wrote nothing. All this happened the year that I loved him."

198

Kangmei smiled through tears. "That is my sad story, Thom-as."

"I'm sorry, Kangmei. Is your friend still in Peking?"

"He is beyond Peking."

"What happened?"

"One day at the factory he picked up two heavy cables in his hands and rubbed them together. They were full of electricity. Perhaps it was an accident. . . ."

"I'm sorry." A temporizing banality.

"I love you, Thom-as."

"I was trying to say the same thing. Come with me, please. We'll find a way to Hong Kong. America is a strange country, I know, but you will like it. If you don't, we can come back to Asia. Anywhere you want . . ."

"No, Thom-as, no. This is my country. China is where I belong."

"But you will be hunted here. You have sacrificed everything for me. Your school, your family . . ."

"I have done what is right."

"That will not protect you."

"My relatives here will protect me now. Later, I will find my protection in the millions of young people who believe in China, and who believe as I do. I have talked to you about them and I have seen how you looked at me—like an uncle looks at a young girl who says she can walk to the moon. I am right. You will see."

Damned if she wasn't mad, twin points of color blazing from her cheeks.

Stratton tried not to sound patronizing.

"Kangmei, let's not argue. I believe in your vision, but I want to be with you. If a man and a woman can find love—isn't that enough?"

"I, too, have thought about that. I am . . . confused. A part of me wants to go with you, but another part insists that I stay. So I will stay and I will think. I—"

"Look!" Stratton was on his feet, pointing. On the far side of the river, bellowing in fear, blind with pain, ran a pig. In the failing light, Stratton could see the stream of blood that

199

marked the pig's passage and, in distant pursuit, a peasant with a knife. Running pig of Chinese commune-ism. A weak joke.

There was nothing funny about the running pig.

It veered onto the narrow dirt promenade that paralleled the one Stratton and Kangmei had walked on their side of the river. Striking from behind, the dying pig tore through the line of schoolchildren like a berserk bowling ball. The youngsters flew to the left and right. Most were simply shuffled. Stratton saw one trampled. A peasant woman in black dumped a load of laundry from her head and kicked viciously at the pig. It staggered off the path. The young teacher who had been leading the children screamed. Around her frightened, crying children needed immediate attention and reassurance. But that was not the worst of it. Two of the children—they could not have been more than three years old—tumbled down the steep bank and into the river. First the boy, then the girl. They made twin ripples.

"Aiyee!" Kangmei screamed.

Across the river, Stratton could see men running. Behind him, too, there came the sound of feet. They were all too far away. And in minutes, the rescuers would need flashlights if they were to be of any use at all.

Tom Stratton threw himself down the bank with a rush that left his leg yelping in protest. He entered the water in a long, flat dive.

The river tasted of mud. Stratton angled upstream, fighting the current. It was his only chance. Wait until the water brought the children to him.

Stratton had three enemies in the warm, pungent river. First was the current, stronger than it had seemed. It tugged and caressed, unyielding, eternal. Treading water, trying to ride as high as possible, Stratton knew he was barely holding his own. If he was pushed downstream he would travel roughly at the same speed as the children who even now should be, must be—God, where were they?—approaching him. They would certainly drown then.

Second was the light. Precious little remained. If he did not

200

find the children while he could still see, he would never find them.

Third was his strength. His leg, he felt sure, was bleeding again. The bicycling motion in the water reminded him how badly his body had been abused by Wang Bin's thugs. He hadn't much stamina.

People dotted both banks now. He saw one man running up with a ladder and another setting a match to a kerosene lamp. On the Evergreen side a middle-aged man with a coil of rope was purposefully making his way down the embankment. Stratton wondered how long the rope was. He would know when the man reached the water's edge.

But where were the children? He couldn't see . . .

"Thom-as! Swim to the right." A banshee's command. Kangmei. Smart girl. She had stayed up on the embankment where the elevation expanded her vision. She had never taken her eyes off the children from the moment they hit the water. For the first time Stratton felt a surge of hope. Obediently, he swam right, challenging the current.

"Four meters . . . three meters . . . two meters . . . now! Now! Now!"

Still, he almost missed it, a bundle of color that was on him before he saw it. Stratton grabbed. Missed. Grabbed again. He pulled the child by the hair until its face came clear of the water. He could not tell if it was the girl or the boy, but it was alive, feebly fighting his grasp.

"Right again. Now! You must hurry!"

Stratton windmilled right with one arm, clutching the child tightly with the other. Within seconds the arm felt as though it would wrench from his socket. He seemed rooted.

"Faster! Faster!"

Stratton swallowed a mouthful of water. He gagged. He wanted to scream. *I'm swimming as fast as I can.* He wanted to rest. *I never said I was Superman.* He wanted to tell her, *I love you.* Stratton swallowed more water.

The little boy whimpered as he swept past, a chick peeping. Got ya, you little bastard. Gotcha. He grabbed the boy by the collar of his shirt. His strength failing, the children clutched to his chest. Stratton pumped his legs ruthlessly, fighting off extinction for three flickering candles. It was dark now. And he was so tired. He must rest. Tomorrow he would finish. . . .

Talons that felt like steel yanked Stratton's hair. He cried out.

The stocky man had not thrown the rope. He had tied one end to the trunk of a dead tree and the other around his waist. Mercilessly, the stocky man pulled again at Stratton's hair, gasping in Chinese.

"All right, all right," Stratton protested. "You win, take one."

Clumsily, a splashing *pas de deux* for the blind, they transferred one of the children from Stratton to the man on the rope. His arm free, a fiery, tremendous, unbearable weight suddenly lifted, Stratton grasped the man's shirt. Willing hands reeled them in. Tom Stratton felt as if he were flying.

CHAPTER **19**

HAROLD BROOM put on his most expensive tailored suit—navy, with a fine ash-gray stripe—and plunged into the muggy Washington afternoon. He flagged a taxi at 14th Street. Six blocks was too damn far to walk on a hot day in your best suit.

The curator was waiting in a private office. It was a Monday, and the museum was closed to the public.

"Hello, Dr. Lambert."

The curator nodded. "You have the photograph?"

Broom gave it to him.

"I asked for an infantryman," Lambert remarked with a scowl.

"Not available," Broom said curtly. He didn't like Lambert at all; he didn't like experts in general.

"When was it dusted?"

"Two, three months ago," Broom answered. "I'm not sure."

Lambert grunted.

Broom said, "If it's the quality you're worried about, don't bother. It's been stored in a dry place, safe from the elements."

The curator unfolded a schematic of the Qin tombs. The

drawing illustrated each of the eleven columns under excavation. The location of the archers, the chariots, the spearmen and the armored infantry was noted in pencil.

"Which vault did this one come from?"

"I have no idea," Broom said. "That's my partner's end of things. And what the hell difference does it make? You know exactly what you're getting, friend. There's seven thousand of these buggers underground in China, but this is your only chance to get your hands on one."

"It's history," Lambert said stiffly.

"History, my ass. It's an investment."

"You're revolting," the curator said in a hoarse voice.

"I'm also late for a plane. I want the down payment right now—that is, if you're still interested."

"Oh, I'm interested, Mr. Broom. But first: How many of these have you and your *partner* smuggled in?"

"This is the only one."

Lambert's eyes turned to ice. He stood up. "Good day, Mr. Broom. You're welcome to come back when you've sobered up."

Broom sighed. Lying to the crazy Texan was one thing; he should have known better with Lambert. He signaled the curator to sit down.

"There's three of them," Broom said, his voice low.

"And the other buyers?"

"Some junior oil tycoon in Texas who doesn't know Qin Dynasty from Corningware."

"Who else?"

"An Oriental restaurant guy down in Florida. I think he's going to put the soldier next to his salad bar."

"That's it?"

"Yes, I swear."

"I'll find out if you're lying," Lambert promised. "How much?"

"Seven fifty."

"Six hundred," Lambert said. "Three hundred now, the rest on delivery. If it's damaged when I open the crate, you won't see another penny—so I suggest you wrap it in heavy quilts and pack it in styrofoam. So . . . we have a deal?"

204

"Shit." Broom grimaced.

Lambert smiled. "Good. Now, when can I expect delivery?"

"A week, maybe more. You're number three on my list."

"But why?" Lambert cried.

"Because the others already paid us," Broom said, rising, "and their checks cleared."

Lao Fu had lived more than eighty years amid the monuments to dead Ming emperors. As a boy, he had witnessed the fall of China's last dynasty. For Lao Fu, the Communists were newcomers; when he thought about them at all, it was as emperors with different names. What difference did it make? A man lived and worked and, if he was lucky, his children cared for him until he died. At Sunrise Commune, Lao Fu was a man of distinction. There was nothing he had not known about ducks, and little he had forgotten. Had he not three times personally traveled more than fifty li to Peking to hear successive generations of chefs praise his ducks? Didn't the young men of the commune still come to him for advice when their foolish practice of force-feeding the ducks made the birds sick? Lao Fu was a man who possessed wisdom. So it was that the commune leaders chose not to know of the pastime that had, once a week, occupied Lao Fu for nearly half a century. Who would invoke bureaucratic injunction to an old man who could not read?

On a summer's afternoon, Lao Fu walked to the reservoir that nestles among the Ming Tombs. He borrowed a rowboat from the caretaker. With a small net, each perfect knot tied by patient hands, Lao Fu went fishing for carp. He fished in secret places.

When he returned that day, Lao Fu left a plump brown fish in the boat where the caretaker would find it and carried two others home to his family. At dinner, everyone praised his skill. They devoured tender white flesh. Lao Fu did not eat, refusing even the eyes and the maw, the most succulent and honored pieces that were his right.

Afterward, his eldest son asked Lao Fu if he was sick.

"I will die soon," the old man said.

205

"You are healthy and strong. You will not die for many years."

"My time is gone. There is too much I cannot understand."

The eldest son thought of the new commune television set, of the noisy diesel tractors, of the experiment to produce more ducks by keeping the lights burning in their roost. Each of these things he had carefully explained to his father. But it was difficult.

"What troubles you, Father? I will try to help."

"What lives in the water?"

"Fish."

"What lives on the land?"

"Man and the other animals."

"Is it still so?"

"Yes, my father."

"You are wrong."

"How am I wrong?"

"Today I fished a man."

They brought Stratton tea, and a hair-curling local moonshine. They wrapped him in a blanket. A doctor came and, clucking, dressed his leg and gave him a shot of antibiotic with a needle meant for horses. They produced clothes that almost fit, and a pair of rope-soled sandals. People pressed around, all talking at once. They smiled and bowed. They shook his hand and pounded his back. Stratton let it happen.

He had been bundled onto the back of a truck, he and the waterlogged stocky man, peasant women cuddling the two little bodies and, it seemed, half the commune, a tight-pressed gesticulating horde.

Where else would they go but to the seat of power, the headquarters of the commune, the site of the local dispensary?

They had come to Man-ling.

Shivering in the humid tropic night, Stratton viewed himself as though from another dimension. Could it have been inevitable? All this time, all these years? Karma? Fate? What else could account for it? Of all the villages on the planet, he had been returned to the one that had seared him and stained him and left him a man of palpable sadness.

206

To that village was he led back, bearer of two tiny corpses. Fresh bodies for Man-ling. I am your plague, don't you see? I have only to come and people die. Forgive me. I am sorry. This time I did my best. I tried. Now, please leave me alone. There are ghosts here who frighten me and of which I shall not speak. I want to leave.

Someone handed him a bowl and a pair of chopsticks. Eat, they gestured. He ate. Face buried in the bowl, he could not see. It was better not to see.

The dispensary was new, single story and freshly white-washed. It contained six beds, some rudimentary medical equipment and windows that opened onto the village main street. The view was of an old movie house across the street. Weary and sagging. In passing headlights, Stratton could see where bullets had marched up the facade. The movie house was as quiet, as dingy and as terrifying as it had been the first night he saw it. They had not even painted it.

Imagine.

After all these years they had not even painted it. His mind had seen the building thousands of times. And always he had imagined that it was white again, that someone had come, orders had been given, workers had arrived, and paint had covered the scars. White paint.

But his nightmare had deceived him. No paint. No clean-up, fix-up, paper-it-over. It was the wrong country for that. China. Let the scars be seen. The people's struggle. Stratton wondered if Bobby Ho's body still lay on the stage.

Kangmei arrived at last and, with her, a measure of sanity.

She hurled herself at him, burying her head in his chest. Stratton's rice bowl went flying. From the spectators came laughter, nervous and polite. Women in the New China did not embrace foreigners, in private or public.

"Oh, Thom-as, you are so brave. So brave."

He kissed the top of her head.

"The children?" he asked, dreading the answer.

"The boy is well, Thom-as. The girl . . . the doctors are still working."

One for two. It could have been worse.

"Kangmei, can we go now? We have to talk." She felt so good in his arms.

"No, we cannot. There are very many people. Now you are *everyone's* rice expert. They want to express their thanks."

"I just want to be alone with you."

"The train will be here in less than one hour."

He had forgotten.

"An hour?" He had so much to say to her.

The Chinese seized on Kangmei as their link to Stratton. They pushed and shoved and jostled for her attention. She yelled something in her struggle-session voice, and the crowd quieted. The semblance of a line formed.

"They will come individually to greet you. They want to take you across to the old theater where there is more room, but I said you were too weak. Also, I have told them to say only a few words and leave you to rest. Once they have left, so can we, not before."

"Let's get it over with." Stratton fixed a smile on his face.

A ruddy-faced man with iron gray hair appeared, speaking forcefully.

"This is the boy's grandfather," said Kangmei. "On behalf of his family, he extends his most grateful thanks and wishes you a speedy recovery. It is his wish that you will be guest of honor for a banquet once you are well."

"Tell grandfather that I am pleased to have been of assistance and that I would be honored to meet his entire family—when I am recovered."

An uncle replaced the grandfather. Then cousins and aunts, the boy's mother, fighting back tears, even neighbors. Stratton thought it would never end.

"Kangmei, let's get out of here."

"This is a Zhuang tradition and, for you, a great honor. We cannot offend these people."

A few minutes later, while a portly man whose relationship to anyone seemed only dimly established spoke at length in a politician's growl, Kangmei said suddenly:

"You are very handsome."

"Did *he* say that?"

208

"He says all the usual things. *I* say that."

"Come with me, please, to America."

"I cannot."

"I love you."

"This man is the best friend of the boy's mother's second sister and he wishes to convey to you . . ."

Stratton noticed a commotion at the door. Three men came in. Peasants made way for them.

"The leaders of the commune," Kangmei whispered.

Stratton nodded. Their bearing alone made that clear.

The commune president wore an impeccable white shirt outside his belt. His were the first clean fingernails Stratton had seen all day. The vice-president was a me-tooer, handsome and suave. They were both Han Chinese, their lighter skin and sharper features distinguishing them immediately in the room of Thai-like Zhuang. They came forward smiling, hands outstretched.

"Comrade president explains that he was at a regional meeting and has only just returned. He has heard of your bravery and would like . . ."

The third man in the delegation was old and fat. He had a cruel saucer face that made smiling a parody. He walked with a cane. The sleeve of his jacket was pinned neatly to his right shoulder. The absence of the arm, and the limp, gave him a sinister, off-balance appearance.

". . . regrets that the comrades in Peking had not informed him of the arrival of such a distinguished guest or he would have come personally to Bright Star to welcome you," Kangmei translated. "Don't worry about that, Thom-as. After tonight no one will ever ask for your papers and he will be afraid to ask Peking why they did not tell him."

The saucer-faced man's smile had vanished. He rocked back and forth on his cane. He shuffled to the left and right to measure Stratton from different angles. Stratton's eyes never left him.

". . . will offer a banquet of welcome and thanksgiving within the next few days and pledges full cooperation of all of the commune work brigades and production teams in your work. You have only to ask—"

"*Kuei*!" The word can mean either ghost or devil. In this case, it was doubly apt.

Screaming, the old man lunged with the cane, jabbing with it as more than a decade before he had jabbed Stratton with his truncheon.

Time had not been kind to the old man. Stratton easily parried the blow. He wrenched away from the cane, sent it spinning to the far corner of the room, and tried to look aggrieved.

The old man's voice cracked with fury. His eyes bulged. The muscles in his neck corded. He threw himself on Stratton, splintering the chair. They rolled to the floor, the old man striking repeatedly with the only fist Stratton had left him.

Stratton covered up protectively. He did not fight back. It would not last long. It didn't. The peasants pulled the old man off and built a human fence between him and Stratton. Stratton didn't even bother getting to his feet. Instead, he scrambled over to the wall and leaned against it, waiting for what he knew must come.

Quivering, weeping, the old man shouted in a high, reedy voice. Within seconds a hush had fallen over the dispensary waiting room.

Kangmei translated. She needn't have bothered.

"The old man was the head of the Public Security Bureau in Man-ling for many years—the top policeman. He knows you. He says you are an American spy who came to spy and to kill. Everybody will remember the night, he says. The night of the heroic people's victory. The old man says he saw you then. He talked to you. You killed cadres. You shot him twice, once in the leg, once in the arm." Kangmei's voice jumped an octave, almost falsetto. "He says—"

Stratton had heard enough. He dug his nails into Kangmei's arm.

"That's enough, Kangmei. Tell the comrade that I understand his distress, but that he is mistaken. I have never been in China before this month. I have never been in Man-ling before. I have never been in a war. I am a rice expert. Say it calmly. Make it sound true."

210

When she had finished, the old policeman began again, but the president of the commune silenced him. The president's apparent perplexity mirrored expressions around the room. Whom to believe? What to do? The Zhuang, Stratton sensed, were with him. The Han cadres would probably side with the policeman. They were vastly outnumbered, but they had what counted most: authority.

The commune president ran a hand across his brow and seemed on the verge of speaking when a tall man appeared wiping his hands on a towel—the doctor who had bandaged Stratton. The doctor spoke quietly to one of the Zhuang near the door. The man's face lit up, and he began chattering loudly. In an instant, the entire room was abuzz. Stratton watched the one-armed policeman say something to a slender young man who nodded and hurriedly left the room.

A new crop of smiles blossomed among the peasants, and fresh tears. One woman fainted. In the hubbub, Stratton had to yell to make himself heard.

"What is going on?"

Kangmei squeezed his hand. She was smiling and crying.

"It's the little girl. They thought they had lost her, but now she is breathing well and seems to be out of danger."

"Thank God." For the nameless little girl, and for Thomas Stratton.

One of the peasants who had ridden on the truck with Stratton addressed the commune president.

"He says your goodwill and good intentions are plain for anyone to see and, while he does not dispute Comrade Ma's word, he believes the comrade is mistaken. He says you should be allowed to return to Bright Star now with the thanks of the commune for your heroism."

Kangmei finished her translation amid an assenting chorus from the Zhuang peasants. The commune president chose not—or dared not—to affront the majority. He nodded slowly and Stratton could almost see him thinking: to hold Stratton on the unsupported word of an overwrought old man would anger the peasants. To release him cost nothing. Tomorrow they could always bring him back in. Stratton sensed that the

211

man was the kind of political bureaucrat who would most of all prefer to make no decision at all. If Stratton were to disappear from the face of the earth, so much the better.

Favoring his leg, Stratton used the wall as a crutch to gain his feet. Kangmei stood at his side.

"Say something graceful and let's go."

Before she could speak, the old policeman fired a fresh stacatto burst.

"He says he knows how people are tired of the memories and the obsessions of an old man who will not forget. But he begs for patience. There is another witness, he says, one who will say positively that you're a murderer and a spy. The witness will come soon."

The commune president sighed resignedly. He would humor a trusted old colleague.

The president spoke briefly and courteously to Kangmei.

"He asks if you would please remain for another few minutes, even though you are tired, so that this matter may be finally resolved without further affecting our friendship."

Stratton shrugged. It was a sugar-coated command, but the worst was over. Mentally, he ticked off the witnesses who had seen his face that other night in Man-ling. Besides the policeman, only the commissar, the professor and the student. All dead. The policeman should have been, too. There had been no other witnesses.

They left Stratton and Kangmei alone then, side by side on wooden chairs in a corner of the room.

"The train will be leaving soon," said Stratton.

"There is still a little time. Would you like some tea?"

"Yes, please."

She was back in a minute with gossip and two steaming mugs.

"The witness is a schoolteacher, a young man who is very bright, but is of poor family background."

"What does that mean?"

"His father, or perhaps his grandfather, was a landlord or a capitalist. That means he cannot go to the university or join the army or belong to the Party. So he is a schoolteacher."

A lovely system, Stratton mused. Convict a man for his

212

ancestors' crimes. For how many generations? He sipped his tea and watched shadows from an overhead lamp play across Kangmei's lovely features.

And then Stratton knew who the witness would be. His cup fell, set free by stricken fingers.

"Thom-as, your tea!" Kangmei exclaimed in alarm. "You are shaking. What is wrong? Shall I get the doctor?"

"No, no," he said. And thought for the second time that night of Bobby Ho.

The young man entered the room with quiet poise. The policeman limped over and spoke urgently with him, gesturing at Stratton, the hatred unmasked. The president said something to the young man and so did one of the peasants. Lobbying, Stratton supposed.

The young man dragged up a chair and sat directly in front of Stratton—mute reviewer of a one-man play. They stared at one another across three feet and eleven years.

The rag boy had added weight to the skin and bones, but not much. The face had filled, but still it spoke of suffering. The body had remained as insubstantial as it had looked the night Bobby Ho's quixotic, absurd, fatal gesture had spared one life and cost many more. The inborn pride had not changed, or the cold, calculating intelligence in the masked obsidian eyes.

Stratton knew he was finished.

There was eloquence in the poker gaze of the grown-up rag boy. His identification was as certain as Stratton's. He, too, like the tormented old policeman, like Stratton, still dwelt in the debris of horror.

Did he also weep, alone at night, for friends so brave? Did he dream terrible dreams of acrid tracers and bullet-stitched buildings that should have been white? Did he still gnaw at desolation? And what had he suffered for a peasant woman and her unborn child? He hadn't felt the knife go through her neck.

Stratton waited for the denouement. Captain Black riffled methodically through escape scenarios. The dice roll, man. Nobody lives forever.

But at least make him work for it.

213

You bastard. Stratton stared at the rag boy. You chicken-shit son of a bitch. We let you go. I could have ended your pitiful knitting-needle existence with a nod, but instead I let you go. In return you killed my friends.

"It was the kid . . . Sorry, Tom. . . ."

Stratton plumbed the Chinese, seeking the man behind the intelligent eyes. He found nothing. And then he made a decision. We both of us should have been dead these eleven years, son of a bitch. Call in the cards. It was a simple decision. It refreshed Stratton and gave him strength. The instant the rag boy raised his voice in accusation, Captain Black would kill him. One dead man kills another. Justice in Man-ling. To finish what had been neglected that night in the rain. I'm sorry, Bobby Ho.

Stratton was sizing the blow when he saw what he had not dared hope to see.

The Chinese eyes spoke plainly. I know you. I have you. You are mine.

And then, the final message:

A life for a life.

"Bushi," the man spat in an unexpectedly deep voice.

He stalked from the room.

"Thom-as, he says it was not you," Kangmei cried.

"Of course not."

Babbling peasants erased the tension. Minutes later, Stratton and Kangmei were alone in the back of a jeep. Stratton had departed without pity for the old policeman, agape, blubbering alone in a corner of the room.

Rest in peace, Bobby Ho. You were right and I was wrong, all this time, all these years.

CHAPTER **20**

"Open your suitcase, please."

"It's locked."

"Find the key and open it," said U.S. Customs Inspector Lance P. Dooley, Jr. He strained to be polite. His boss was working the next aisle.

"But the key is in the suitcase," whined the young man in Dooley's line. "I packed it by accident. I'm sorry, officer." The man had just debarked from Pan American Airways Flight 7, Peking–to–Tokyo–to–San Francisco. He wore blue jeans and a Van Halen concert T-shirt, with Day-Glo lettering. His black hair was long and straight, tied in a ponytail. Dooley studied the face. Malaysian, he decided. The passport confirmed it.

"Sir, I want to take a look in your suitcase. Either you find a way to open it, or I will. We have special tools," Dooley said. "Hardly put a scratch on it, you watch."

"But it's a brand-new Samsonite," the young man objected.

"So it is."

Behind the young man a haggard procession of travelers stretched and sighed and muttered their annoyance at the

215

delay. Second in line was a stocky, handsome Chinese man in his sixties. His hair was neatly combed, and he wore gold-rimmed eyeglasses that gave his features an intent, scholarly cast. His clothes fit somewhat loosely: beige slacks slightly wrinkled from the long flight, a knit canary-colored sports shirt buttoned all the way to the neck, and a dark brown sweater with a monogram on the left breast.

The Chinese man carried only one piece of luggage, a cumbersome old suitcase exhibiting thirty years' worth of scuffs and dents. The man did not hoist the suitcase to the conveyor belt, but kept it at his feet, one hand firmly on the grip, as if it were a Doberman on a leash. He seemed transfixed by the argument in front of him.

"You can't just break into my suitcase," the young Malaysian insisted.

"Sir," Dooley said, "if you decline to have your luggage searched here, we will escort you to a private inspection room where we will not only search the suitcase, we'll ask you to take off your clothes—and we'll search some more. Which do you prefer?"

Dooley's supervisor glanced disapprovingly at the long line at Dooley's aisle. Dooley got the message and tried to step it up.

"The key, sir?"

The young man fidgeted. Dooley nodded to a couple of other customs agents, who had been leaning against a square pillar. They stepped eagerly to the front of Dooley's line.

"Okay, okay. I'm not hiding anything. Let me see if I can get this open." The Malaysian played with the latches on the Samsonite and it popped open. "Go ahead, see for yourself. Just clothes and some junk I brought back from Singapore."

"Do you live in Singapore?" Dooley asked as he picked through underwear, socks, snapshots, toothpaste, a packet of condoms.

"No, I live here in Frisco," said the young man. "Lived here since I was ten. My father still lives in Singapore. I got two brothers there, too. I go back five or six times a year."

This was the talking phase. Dooley smiled to himself. He took his time. It was here somewhere.

216

"I'm a chef," the young man volunteered. His eyes were glued to Dooley's hands, sifting and exploring. "It's a Chinese joint off Market Street. Li-Siu's. Have you been there? I make good money. And I send half of it home every month—"

"What's this?"

"Film. Kodak film."

Dooley studied the two yellow packages. The end flaps of one were creased, and off square from the carton.

"I bought those here, before I left."

"Really?"

"I didn't take as many pictures as I thought I would." The Malaysian grinned nervously.

Dooley opened one of the film cartons and removed the black plastic containers. He snapped one of the caps and looked inside. The two agents behind him edged closer. The Chinese man, waiting in the customs line, craned his neck to get a glimpse.

Dooley showed the inside of the canister to the two agents. Gingerly he probed with his pinky finger; it came out covered with what looked like flour. Dooley tasted it with the tip of his tongue. Then he popped the top back on the container.

"Heroin," he said.

"No!" exclaimed the young Malaysian. "You're kidding."

"High-speed film, all right," one of the agents growled.

The Malaysian was led away, squirming. A third agent appeared and confiscated the Samsonite and the film packages.

"Sorry for the delay, folks," Lance Dooley said to the rest of the passengers. "We'll move right along now. Next?"

The Chinese man wrestled his huge suitcase to the conveyor belt. Quickly, almost frantically, he opened the latches.

Dooley looked at the passport. "You are returning from the People's Republic of China. Is that right, Dr. Wang?"

"Yes, sir."

"Says here you've got some scrolls and some pottery." Dooley was reading from the customs declaration form.

"That's right."

"Worth about?"

"One hundred dollars. Approximately."

Dooley opened the suitcase. The scrolls were on top—

217

inexpensive but delicately painted wall hangings. You could find them all over the place on Fisherman's Wharf.

The pottery had been carefully wrapped in several layers of Chinese newspaper. Each piece was packed for protection between stacks of clothing. Dooley unearthed two large parcels.

"Vases."

"I'll be careful with them, Dr. Wang." Dooley peeled the newspaper away, making a lame effort not to rip it.

Cobalt dragons writhed on the body of each vase, beneath a crest of ornate blue scrolling, a field of peonies and, nesting there, a mallard. The vases were identical.

"Very nice," remarked Lance Dooley.

"Imitations, I'm afraid, but lovely bookends. For my office at the university."

"How much did these cost?" Dooley asked.

"Sixty-five dollars. A tourist shop in Peking."

Dooley set the vases on the conveyor belt, next to the suitcase. "Dr. Wang, could I see the sales receipt for these?"

"Certainly, it should be right here." He sorted through a billfold. "That's odd. I can't find it. See here—the receipt for the scrolls—"

Dooley gave it a cursory glance and handed it back.

"I keep all the receipts in the same place. It must be here . . ."

"Do you recall the name of the store?"

"No . . . no, I don't. But it was printed on the receipt."

Dooley's boss shot him another glare from the next aisle. "Lance you got another one?"

"No, sir." Dooley could take a hint. Quickly he rewrapped the vases in their paper cocoons and placed them back in the suitcase.

"Where is your final destination, Dr. Wang?"

"Ohio. Pittsville. My flight doesn't leave until tomorrow. I can search for the receipts this evening . . ."

"That won't be necessary," Dooley said. "How long were you in China?"

"Three weeks, approximately. Eighteen days, I think."

"Have a good trip home, Dr. Wang. Next, please."

218

Later, on his lunch break, Dooley sat down at a video display terminal in a small gray office and typed the name and passport number of David Wang into a U.S. government computer. He also typed the port of entry, the date of entry and his own identification number. On the single line allotted for general remarks, Dooley typed: "Queried China pottery/ blue-and-white vases (2)."

Dooley pressed the "store" button, and turned his attention —and the remainder of his lunch hour—to the mountain of paperwork generated by the capture of the Malaysian scag mule.

Danny Bodine stuffed his hands in his pockets as he stood in the doorway of the Dong Fang Hotel. Outside a hard gray rain pelted the city of Canton. Things could be worse, he told himself. It was the typhoon season. Traffic crawled on the slick streets and bicycle riders pedaled at double speed, their heads wrapped in newspaper or crinkly plastic rain hats. Everywhere people clustered in doorways, waiting for a break in the downpour.

Maureen and Pam had scheduled an excursion to White Cloud Mountain. Danny had hired a cab for the trip—but there would be no sightseeing today.

A cargo ship docking on the Pearl River sounded its horn, piercing the shroud of rain. Danny was afraid his wife was about to suggest a trip to another museum.

"Let's go to a teahouse," he said, a preemptory strike.

"For lunch? I'm hungry, Danny."

"Me, too." It was Pam, Maureen's sister, fresh from her morning makeup marathon. She looked pretty damn good, Danny had to admit.

From somewhere out in the rain, a bedraggled American came bounding up the steps of the Dong Fang. He excused himself as he passed Danny, Maureen and Pam in the doorway. Pam watched him in the lobby, his blond hair matted and dripping. He wore thin, ill-fitting cotton clothes.

"Wonder where *he's* been," she said.

"One of those swell tailor shops near the river," Danny said.

"Be nice," said Maureen. "Maybe he's with a church group."

As Danny had feared, the three of them wound up at the Guangdong Provincial Museum.

When they returned to the Dong Fang three hours later, the American stranger was still in the lobby. Danny and Maureen paid no attention and went up to the room, but Pam sat down next to him in a high-backed leather chair. "What are you reading?"

"Oh, just travel brochures," said Tom Stratton, smiling. "It's all I could find."

"Are you a tourist, too?"

"Sort of."

"We came from Denver—me, my sister and her husband. He works for an oil company that's got an office in Hong Kong. He'll be there a couple of months, I guess. Maureen and I are going back to the States day after tomorrow."

"Oh? I am too," Stratton said. "Are you at this hotel?"

Pam nodded. She liked his smile, but he looked—well, like he'd come off a three-day bender. In Denver she'd never approach a man who looked quite so worn out, but this wasn't Denver.

"I'm on the eighth floor," Stratton lied. "Eight twelve."

"We're in seven eighteen," Pam said, then added, for clarification, "It's quite a big suite."

Stratton told her that he taught art history. Predictably, she had never heard of the college. "It's a small place," Stratton explained, "but very peaceful."

"It sounds nice," Pam said. She was thinking about the flight home; maybe they could sit together, she and her new friend, if Maureen wouldn't mind.

"What oil company does your brother-in-law work for?"

"Rocky Mountain Energy Corporation," Pam said. "Danny's a vice-president. I don't think he's too crazy about Asia, though. He's heavy into domestic shale."

"Oh."

"What are you doing for dinner?"

Stratton shrugged. "Nothing special."

220

"Why don't you join us, Tom? We're all going to the Ban Xi. Have you ever tried quail eggs?"

Stratton shook his head.

"It's supposed to be a beautiful restaurant. You can eat on a houseboat. Danny won't mind if you come—he'd kill for some male company."

"That's very nice. I could use some company, too." Stratton caught her glance after he said it. "What time?"

"We'll meet you here at about seven, okay?"

"How about if I meet you at the restaurant? I'm waiting for a telex. Besides, it'll take me a while to clean up."

"Fine, we'll see you there about seven thirty." Pam stood up and said brightly, "Maybe the rain'll stop by then."

"Let's hope so," said Stratton, hating himself.

He snuck into the People's Republic's only hotel sauna and baked for ninety minutes. The heat was luxurious, soporific; wisps of steam curled off the tiles. The grit and dust of Man-ling washed away. Stratton closed his eyes; as exhausted as he was, he could not even doze. Training—that's where the feeling came from. Pack your gun and put your conscience in a drawer.

And love? Where do you put that? No training needed. It just happened. It can even happen when you are fighting for your life.

The ache in Stratton's belly was more than simply hunger.

In the unsprung jeep, they had embraced clumsily, kissing, chattering toward calm after the dispensary confrontation.

"But why, Thom-as? Why? If the young man knew who you were, why did he not say so?"

"*I'll* never ask him, but I can guess."

"Tell me."

"I'd rather kiss you. I think you are wonderful."

"No more kisses until you tell me."

"Let's say the rag boy—now the young teacher—has given a lot of careful consideration to what happened that night, like I have, and the policeman. I think he came to realize over the years that he was a dead man who had been reprieved by one of the evil invaders he had denounced."

221

"So he lied."

"I think he was trying to apologize."

"And the fat old policeman. He—"

Stratton stopped her with a kiss.

"Kangmei, I don't want to talk about it anymore. I want to talk about you, and about me. About us. I love you. Please come with me."

She ran cat's-paw fingertips across his jaw.

"I must try to do what I believe is right, my brave Thom-as. Would you respect me if I did not?"

"Respect! I'm talking about love. I want you with me. I need you."

"And I you. But I must try. And I must think. Perhaps one day I will see that you are right; that, as you say, harmony between a man and a woman is really what is most important."

"And then?"

She smiled.

"And then I will confess to you what I feel now, but must resist: that I, too, am empty without you."

"If that happens, will you tell me, please?"

"Yes, I will tell you. I promise."

"I will come back to get you."

"No, Thom-as."

"Why not, damn it?"

"Because." She squeezed him tight enough to hurt and bit playfully at his ear. "Because," she murmured, "I do not wish to witness a war between our two countries."

The train was waiting. At the station, like a schoolboy fighting a curfew, he had scribbled his address on the back of a yellowed old timetable.

"Write to me, please."

"I love you, Thom-as."

A smiling conductor who spoke only with a warning finger at his lips led Stratton to a darkened soft-class compartment and locked the door.

All the way to Canton the rails whispered her name.

*   *   *

222

Stratton laid aside his reverie and the sauna precisely at seven thirty-five. Dressed again in the strange-fitting commune clothes, he took the elevator to the seventh floor and padded the carpeted hallway until he found room 718. He knocked sharply. No one answered.

Stratton found one of the floor attendants sorting cakes of soap.

"Excuse me, but I seem to have locked myself out of our suite. Seven-one-eight. The name is Bodine. My wife is down at the hairdresser."

"I help," the attendant said. The master key hung from a chain on his cloth belt. The attendant unlocked the door to the darkened suite and Stratton went to work.

He shed his clothes and concealed them beneath a mattress on one of the beds. From Danny Bodine's closet he selected a navy blue necktie, a pin-striped business shirt and a pair of dark trousers. The clothes fit almost perfectly; Stratton had guessed as much when he had first noticed the American oil-man in the hotel lobby. Even Bodine's black wingtips felt snug.

Stratton removed a blue suitcase from the closet and opened it on the bed. Haphazardly, he tossed in a suit, a couple of shirts, another pair of slacks. One could not very well leave China without some luggage.

In the bathroom he borrowed Bodine's cordless Remington.

Danny Bodine was a second-drawer man—that is, the kind of traveler who hides his most precious valuables in the second drawer of the bureau, instead of the top, in the belief that this will outfox the burglars of the world. A jet-setter's illusion.

Stratton triumphantly located Bodine's passport under a stack of jockey shorts. Next he guessed that the oilman's emergency cash would be either carefully taped on the underside of the drawer, rolled into his socks, or divided in equal sums between the two hiding places.

Again, Stratton silently congratulated himself. A pair of black nylon knee socks yielded three hundred dollars and two hundred yuan. Stratton took only the dollars. Traveling expenses—he had lost everything in Xian.

223

Before he left Bodine's room, Stratton checked his watch. It was barely eight o'clock. He picked up the telephone and asked the switchboard operator to ring the Ban Xi restaurant. It took five full minutes for a waiter to locate "the American woman named Pam" and lead her to the phone.

"Hi," said Stratton. "I've got some bad news: I don't think I'm going to make it to dinner. I'm sorry for all of the trouble."

Pam was disappointed and curious.

"Did you get your cable?"

"Yes, and that's the bad news. I've got to go back to the States tomorrow," Stratton said. "For a funeral."

"I'm so sorry."

"I'm the one who's sorry—for all the inconvenience. Could I have your address? I'd like to write after we get back." This time he was telling the truth. Stratton wrote down her address in Denver.

"I'm going to send you something," he said. Something the size of a man's suitcase, he thought. Bodine would be thrilled to get his wingtips back, not to mention the three hundred bucks.

"You're missing a great dinner," Pam said. "I skipped the quail eggs and ordered something called 'fragrant meat.' It's very tasty, Tom."

"Dog meat," Stratton muttered.

"What did you say?"

"Never mind. Good night, Pam."

The rain had stopped. Stratton left the Dong Fang Hotel by foot, carrying Bodine's suitcase as nonchalantly as if it were a briefcase. He strolled past a city park, lushly landscaped, its circular ponds ringed by orchids. A young Chinese couple sat together on a bench, whispering in the twilight, touching each other's hands. On a downhill sidewalk, slick from the rain, Stratton was startled by a throng of teenagers who flew by on roller skates, giddy with speed.

At the Guangzhou Railway Station he had only an hour to wait for the train to Hong Kong. Bored immigration inspectors barely glanced at the passport.

224

CHAPTER 21

THE TAXI climbed haltingly toward Victoria Peak through the morning rush-hour snarl. On all sides, Hong Kong howled at Tom Stratton; a glitzy, avaricious, sequined city, a century from Peking, light-years from Kangmei's bucolic Bright Star. It seemed impossible that they shared the same continent, let alone the same blood. Below, the famous harbor, tickled by the prows of a thousand boats, glinted gold in the early light.

The driver braked to a stop at the foot of a steep hill. Behind the taxi, a long line of cars bunched up, honking—gleaming Subarus, BMWs and Jaguar sedans, all seemingly driven by serious, thin-lipped businessmen. Stratton scrambled out of the cab, dutifully toting Bodine's suitcase. On the hillside sat the United States Consulate, square-windowed, flat and uninviting. It reminded Stratton of a cut-down version of the Boston City Hall except for the forest of antennae prickling from the roof.

Stratton lugged the suitcase up a winding flight of steps. By the time he reached the black iron gate, his injured leg throbbed in misery. He was intercepted by a young Marine in a white hat and a starched blue-and-khaki uniform. Stratton asked to meet the station chief.

"Sir?"

"The head spook, Sergeant. It's an emergency."

"Wait here, please, sir."

Stratton sat down in a waiting room, paneled with fine honey-colored wood. The sound of typing chattered from behind a closed door. Stratton's shirt clung to his back, and the cool breath of the air conditioner brought goose bumps. With one foot Stratton slid the suitcase across the waxed floor into an empty corner.

"Sir!" The Marine was back. "Mr. Darymple."

Mr. Darymple was a young man with perfectly sculpted black hair that looked to Stratton like it had been parted with a laser beam. Stratton pegged him as an idle subordinate.

Darymple held out a slender hand and introduced himself as the assistant administrative officer.

Stratton said, "I need to see the CIA station chief."

"I'm not really sure whom you mean." Darymple smiled officiously. "Perhaps I could help."

"Very doubtful," Stratton said. "I've just spent the last week or so getting the shit kicked out of me in China."

Darymple expressed concern. "You'd like to report an incident?"

Stratton sighed. "An incident, yes. Go get your boss and I'll tell him about it."

"Could I have your name?"

"Stratton, Thomas. Tell him I was classified Phoenix."

Darymple stiffened. "Here?"

"No, Saigon. 1971. Go ahead and check, but hurry. Then go tell your boss I need a line out, right away."

Darymple said, "He'll want to see your passport."

"It was taken from me in Xian."

"Then how did you . . . excuse me, Mr. Stratton." Darymple walked out of the office in long, hurried strides.

The trick was to give them enough to chew on so that they would help, but not too much. Stratton knew what it meant to get the agency involved; he also remembered the not-so-friendly competition between stations. The boys in Hong Kong

226

would want to claim him as their own. Peking could tag along for the ride, of course. Hong Kong probably would want to make an actual *case* of the whole thing. This, Stratton knew, he could not afford, nor could David Wang. There was no time for tedious little filemakers like Mr. Darymple.

When Darymple returned, he was accompanied by a beet-faced man in his early forties. "This is our chief political officer."

"Whatever you say."

The beet-faced man turned to Darymple and said, "That'll be all, Clay."

When they were alone, the CIA man said, "Tell me what's going on."

"I need to speak with your counterparts in Peking," Stratton said. "An American citizen is about to be murdered."

Linda Greer was clipping an article about rice production from the *People's Daily* when the buzzer went off. She snatched a notebook from the top of her desk and hurried to the station chief's private office. He was on the phone. He motioned her to a chair.

"She's here now," the station chief was saying. "I'm going to put you on the speaker box."

"Linda?" Stratton's voice cracked and fuzzed on the Hong Kong line. "Linda, can you hear me?"

"Tom!" She could not mask her elation or astonishment. When Stratton had vanished without explanation, Linda was certain he had been killed. She had blamed herself; after all, Wang Bin had been her target. The station chief had sent a curt note: *No record to be kept of your contact with Stratton.*

Yes, Linda had agreed, no record. But now Stratton had surfaced, and for the moment she didn't give a damn about her precious case file or all the cables to Langley.

"Are you all right?" she asked.

"Torn and frayed," he said. "Nothing serious."

"We had people out looking," Linda Greer said. The station chief shook his head disapprovingly. The message was: Don't say too much.

"Well, I appreciate the concern," Stratton said drily, "but

I imagine the trail got pretty cold at Xian. You've probably figured out that this wasn't a government operation."

"What do you mean?" asked the station chief.

"It was Wang Bin's personal project. No army, no *Ke Ge Bo*, just his own private goons. He did it that way for good reason, the same reason he wanted me out of the picture."

"Tom, haven't you heard—"

"Let him finish!" the station chief barked. Linda Greer opened the notebook on her lap, mocking the pose of an obedient secretary. The station chief scowled.

"Start with what happened to you at Xian," he instructed Stratton.

"Forget what happened to me," Stratton said impatiently. "You need to get to Wang Bin as soon as possible. Call the ministry and leave a message. Tell him I'm alive. Tell him I know about David—"

"What about David?" the station chief asked.

"If you folks have any decent sources at all, you probably know what's been happening at the Qin tombs in Xian. During the past few months several large artifacts have been stolen."

"What kind of artifacts?" Linda said.

"Soldiers."

"*The* soldiers?"

"The emperor's death army," Stratton said. "Didn't you know?"

The pause on the Peking end gave Stratton his answer.

"How many did you say, Tom?"

"I didn't say how many. I said several."

"The ministry mentioned pilfering," the station chief said. "Pottery, jewelry, trinkets—small stuff. Didn't say anything about the soldiers. How would you do it, Stratton? And what in the world would you do with them?"

Stratton laughed harshly. "You guys ought to try to get out of Peking once in a while. It'd open your eyes."

Linda Greer was thinking ahead of her boss. "For money," she said. "Wang Bin was getting out."

"Exactly," Stratton said excitedly. "He's a smart man, like

his brother, and the future was plain: all his old comrades dropping like ducks in a shooting gallery. Wang Bin knew it wouldn't be long before they took away his limousine and made him the number-three tractor mechanic at some commune in the sticks. That's a long fall from deputy minister, and Bin didn't want to take it. Linda, he's your pet project. It fits, doesn't it?"

"There were rumors," she acknowledged, "rumors that he was in trouble."

"But were there rumors of defection?" the station chief asked.

"I'm not talking about defection," Stratton snapped. "I'm talking about disappearance. Remember that Wang Bin is a wealthy man from his smuggling enterprise. The clay soldiers are worth . . . who knows? A fortune, certainly. The best market is the United States, and I'll bet that's where the bank accounts are—a fabulous nest egg. But how does Bin get to it? How does such a well-known official escape from China? By boat, or plane . . . or scaling the fence at Kowloon? No. All too risky. And think of all the noise and hoopla if the spooks this side of the border get hold of him." Stratton winked amiably at the beet-faced man across the rosewood table.

"No, Wang Bin would want to go quietly. Wouldn't you, if you had a couple hundred thousand U.S. dollars squirreled away?"

"Getting out would be nearly impossible," Linda Greer said.

"Suppose he had a passport," Stratton ventured. "A legitimate U.S. passport—with a photograph that seemed to match."

"How?" the station chief demanded.

"Oh, God," Linda sighed. "His own brother."

"I've heard enough," the station chief said. "Stratton, you're out of your mind."

"Tom, go on," Linda said.

"Check your files. I had Steve Powell try to run down David's passport a few days after he supposedly died. Oddly enough, no one could find it—but it was Wang Bin who provided the explanation, remember? He said David's passport was destroyed accidentally at the hospital."

Linda Greer recalled Powell's memo about the incident, a two-paragraph brush-off.

Stratton said, "What happened to David's belongings, the stuff in the vault at the embassy?"

"I assumed it went home with the body," Linda replied.

"Who picked it up?"

"A driver. From the Ministry of Art and Culture."

"Don't you see?" Stratton exclaimed.

"It was simple protocol, Tom. Wang Bin was David's brother and he wanted to handle things. We could hardly argue, especially after you welched out of the funeral flight. We aren't in the business of insulting foreign governments."

"I understand, Linda, but think . . . *think*! Instant wardrobe, instant identity, a ticket to the States—it adds up. Picture the deputy minister in David's eyeglasses—could you tell them apart? Would immigration ever question the passport photo? No. It's one goddamn perfect plan." Stratton's voice cracked.

Yes, perfect, thought Linda Greer, except for one thing. She spoke soothingly. "It's a good theory, Tom."

Stratton was in a fury. She was patronizing him.

The station chief said, "I think it's a crazy goddamn theory and it's time to cut the shit. Whatever Wang Bin was up to, it doesn't matter anymore."

"Listen to me," Stratton insisted. "David Wang is alive! His brother intends to murder him any day, any second."

"No, Tom," Linda said, shooting a glance at the station chief. "Maybe the deputy minister *was* planning something big . . . but it doesn't really matter anymore—"

"You keep saying that . . ."

"—because Wang Bin is dead."

From Hong Kong came only static. Linda Greer glanced anxiously at her boss. She leaned closer to the phone speaker. "Tom? Did you hear what I said?"

Stratton battled waves of nausea. His head sagged to the rosewood table; sweat beaded on the back of his neck. He raged silently, the private agony of a terrible failure. Now he knew; it was too late.

"Tom?"

"How?" came a hoarse voice from Hong Kong.

"Drowned," the station chief reported. "An old fisherman snagged the body in the Ming reservoir. The Public Security Bureau found a capsized rowboat near the shore. We got wind of it yesterday afternoon. Today the government newspapers say it was an accident. We hear differently."

"Oh." Head bowed, Stratton mumbled through clenched hands.

"We hear it was a suicide."

Stratton laughed sadly. "What?"

"Suicide," the station chief repeated, with emphasis. "Wang Bin was due to appear before the Disciplinary Commission earlier this week. Obviously his number was up, and he knew it. So he cashed all his chips. No fancy stuff—phony passports, secret Swiss accounts, all that Hollywood bullshit—just good old-fashioned Chinese honor. In this country, anything beats total disgrace, and that's what Wang Bin was facing. So he chose to die an honorable man. That way, at least, all the brass show up at your funeral."

"Will there be a state service?" Stratton wondered.

"Yeah, and you're not invited. Party types only, mid-level flag wavers, we're told. Courtesy, but no fanfare. And, Stratton, no flowers."

"Have you seen the body?" Stratton demanded.

"The coffin is *closed*. For God's sake, he'd been in the water a couple of days. Do I have to spell it out to you, Stratton? The man looked like a bloated carp."

"Please, that's enough," Linda Greer implored. "Tom, are you all right? I know you've been through hell—maybe I ought to fly down."

"No, thanks, I'm fine. If the nice folks here will just get me a new passport, I'll be on my way." The beet-faced man at the oblong table nodded helpfully; it would be a relief to book this yo-yo on the next Pan Am. "Phoenix" indeed.

Sitting in Peking with the station chief, talking into a squawk box to an unseen face across the continent, Linda

231

Greer could say none of the things she wanted to say, and none of the things that mattered now. Stratton was safe, somehow returned from the files of the dead, and for that she could be happy. But there was something else, something troubling about his theory . . .

"It's over now, Tom," she said softly. "Whatever happened between your friend and his brother is finished. I'm sorry about everything."

It was only after Stratton hung up that Linda Greer realized what the loose end was: the soldiers. Stratton had never explained about the clay soldiers. He'd never told her how Deputy Minister Wang Bin had done it.

As night shrouded Victoria Peak, a galaxy of bare-bulb lights sprinkled the hillsides of Hong Kong. Jim McCarthy sat in the Foreign Correspondents' Club, sipping gin, imagining a shanty-porch view of the ravenous blast furnace of a city. The poor looking up on the rich; the rich too busy to look down. Once McCarthy had written a feature story about three Hong Kong families who shared a tiny attic in the heart of the city—ten adults, six children, no running water, not even a ceiling fan to stir the air. After he filed the piece, an editor called to ask how many Hong Kong Chinese actually lived like that. Hundreds of thousands, McCarthy had told him; it was right there in the story. The editor told him they were looking for something a little more offbeat, a little sexier. And so the next day the newspaper sent McCarthy off to do a feature on the manufacture of counterfeit Rubik's cubes. That story made the front page.

McCarthy ordered up another gin-and-tonic. Cursing the idiots—that's what R-and-R is for. Get it out of your system, Jimbo.

The club was bustling and noisy with journalists hell-bent on a night of sloppy decadence—British, Australians, New Zealanders, a Frenchman, even two American network guys. Behind the huge padded bar, stone-faced Cantonese bartenders poured quickly and expertly. As the night wore on, McCarthy knew, the ratio of water to booze would escalate in proportion to the patron's inability to tell the difference. McCarthy, who could hold his liquor and appear to when he couldn't, kept a close eye on the Tanqueray bottle behind the counter. The instant the bartender made a secret move for an off brand, McCarthy would lunge for his throat.

At the big table in the center of the club, one of the American network guys was screaming at the French magazine freelancer. Vietnam again, McCarthy thought. Every time he was in the place there was a fight about Nam. Almost everybody in the club had covered the war, some of them with a fanaticism otherwise reserved for the World Series or slot machines. Everybody had a story, everybody had a theory, everybody had a pain. The walls of the club had become a Nam shrine: headlines, photographs, tributes to fallen colleagues like Larry Burroughs and Sean Flynn. When Nam had been hot, Hong Kong had been the jump-off point for journalists. The club had been electric then, swirling with stories of war; the war had been the story, and even besotted Fleet Street could focus on it. Now the story was China, McCarthy reflected, huge, ungainly, enigmatic, unsexy China. There was only so much you could write, so many telescopic shots of the Great Wall, before the guys on the desk started hollering for more Rubik's cubes.

McCarthy guided himself to the men's room. Standing at a urinal, he observed that in the eight months since his last visit, there had been only one addition to the wall graffiti: a strikingly accurate likeness of Lady Diana, reclining languorously. The Aussies, McCarthy decided, it had to be. As he was admiring the steady hand of the artist, the door swung open and McCarthy was joined by another man.

"Remember me?"

McCarthy studied the face in the mirror. "Stratton, baby! Gimme a second here and I'll be right with you."

"Take your time," Stratton said.

"Hey," McCarthy said, zipping up, "you don't suppose the princess is really double-jointed?"

"Not like that, Jim."

To make room for Stratton at the bar, McCarthy gently

233

shooed a buxom prostitute who had costumed herself like Marilyn Monroe in *Some Like It Hot*. Stratton immediately claimed the barstool and ordered a Budweiser.

"Heresy!" McCarthy exclaimed. "Every time I see you you're ordering the wrong beer. What brings you to this seedy place?"

"You do," Stratton said. "I need your help."

After leaving the consulate, he had walked for hours through Hong Kong, dazzled and disoriented, distracted from the city's raucous vitality by his own despair. Stratton mourned for David, and for Kangmei. Once, in an alley market where old crones cooled their feet in vats of live shrimp, he had spotted her, swaying through the crush of people, an ebony trail of silken hair. He had run, hurdling racks and side-stepping vendors, until he had caught her, taken her by the elbows, turned her and seen a stranger's face. The young woman had smiled shyly and backed away, but Stratton had been too sad to apologize.

He had taken a tram to the Peak, and from a windy plat-form imagined China unfolding beyond Kowloon. Some-where, David's body. Somewhere, Kangmei. As the sun set, the grand harbor had shimmered and then in darkness evap-orated to a vast black hole. The famous floating restaurants sparkled like stars, bobbing on a windy night. For an hour Stratton had clung to the solitude of the Peak until ghosts had caught up with him, and he had gone looking for Jim McCarthy.

"I called the bureau in Peking. They said you'd be here for a couple of weeks."

"Sheila and the kids fly in tomorrow," McCarthy said. "I can't wait to see 'em. Hell, another night or two alone in this town and a hard-drinking Irishman might buy himself some serious trouble. Like Peroxide Lucy over there. You ever see a Chinese with a wig like that? This club is a regular Mardi Gras, just what you need when you're fresh out of China."

"Your clerk had a pretty good idea you'd be here."

"She's a doll. I'd trust her with my life." McCarthy sus-piciously eyed the bartender, who was pouring another gin. "Tom, I was just thinking about you yesterday. Your friend,

234

the old professor who died, wasn't his name Wang? Well, his brother, the honcho deputy minister of whatever, died this week, too. Did you hear about it?"

"Yes. Supposedly drowned."

"Dressed in full uniform, resplendent Mao gray, according to some of our embassy boys. Ironic, isn't it? The old guy had a black mourning band pinned to his sleeve. The big whisper is suicide."

Stratton started to say something, but reined himself. "Are you doing a story about it?" he asked McCarthy.

"Naw, I don't think so." McCarthy looked up from his drink. "You think it's worth a story? I dunno, you might be right. The death of two brothers—one American, one Chinese. The ultimate reunion! The desk might go for it. They're slobbering for human interest stuff."

A screech came from the big table in the middle of the club. McCarthy and Stratton looked over just in time to see one of the American network correspondents punch the French freelancer in the nose.

"Bravo, baby!" McCarthy called out. "Hoist the flag right up his ass!" He turned back to Stratton. "I'm not so sure about this Wang story after all . . . maybe I'm just not in the mood to write." McCarthy sighed. "I'll feel a hell of a lot better when Sheila's here."

They drank together for half an hour, eavesdropping on the slurred debates and laconic come-ons, watching the fog turn to cotton over the harbor. Finally McCarthy said, "What was it you needed from me?"

"A list."

"Of what?"

"Remember the story you wrote on 'Death by Duck'? You told me about it—about all the American tourists who die over here . . ."

"I did the story two years ago, Tom. You want a list of all of them?" McCarthy could not mask his curiosity.

"Not all of them. I want a list from the last four months, a list of every American who died in China. Can you get it?"

McCarthy shrugged. "No sweat. All it takes is a phone call."

235

"What else is available?"

"Ages, hometowns, occupations. That's about it."

Stratton leaned forward. "Hometowns are all I need. How big a list are we talking about?"

McCarthy shifted on the barstool. He was not accustomed to being grilled. "A small list, Tom. A half-dozen names, at the most. I'm just guessing. I really haven't been following the death-by-duck box score since I wrote that one story."

"But you *can* get the list?"

"Sure, Tom." McCarthy fingered his fiery beard. "But I've got to ask why. I'm not too drunk to listen."

Stratton stood up. "I can't tell you, not now."

McCarthy smiled. "Someday?"

"Maybe," Stratton said. "It's possible."

"That's good enough for me."

Stratton slapped a Bodine twenty-dollar bill on the counter and motioned to the flinty-eyed bartender. "Good God, don't be a fool and leave the whole thing," McCarthy hissed. "He's been pissin' in the drinks all night."

Stratton laughed and shook the newsman's hand. "I'm at the Hilton. My flight leaves at about noon tomorrow."

"Hey, you're talking to an ace foreign correspondent," McCarthy roared. "You'll have your list by ten sharp."

Stratton walked back to the hotel room and stood under a steaming shower for twenty minutes. The melancholy and bitterness gradually receded to a remote corner of his mind; he began to feel galvanized, perversely exhilarated by what lay ahead. One race was finished, and he had lost. Another was beginning. This time the track was his.

236

CHAPTER **22**

STEVE POWELL caught up with Linda Greer in the hall outside the embassy conference room.

"Did you win today?" she asked amiably.

His hair slick from an after-tennis shower, Powell nodded with an air that said no contest. "The dust was murder out there. Took some top spin off my serve." He propped his briefcase on one knee and opened it. The yellow cable was on top of a stack of files.

"Here," Powell said, handing it to Linda. "It arrived this morning from San Francisco."

Linda read the cable twice and went cold.

"Whatever it means," Powell said, "I don't think I ought to mention it at the staff meeting."

It means Tom Stratton was right, Linda thought.

Powell said, "Some guy with two Ming vases makes it past customs and immigration using David Wang's passport. Strange: Didn't the late, great deputy minister tell us that the passport was destroyed?" Powell snapped the briefcase shut. "The question now is, Who was this guy? And how the hell did he get the passport?"

The passport. *No*, Linda told herself, it *can't* be true.

"Maybe the deputy minister swiped it, then turned around and sold it," Powell theorized, "like he was selling everything else. There's quite a few Chinese who'd give anything for a U.S. passport. Your old buddy Bin could have found himself a rich customer."

Powell watched Linda's expression carefully. She was ashen.

"I guess you'll have to cable customs," she said finally. "They'll want some kind of report."

"I've got to let them know the guy was illegal, and screw the damn vases."

Linda lowered her voice. "Steve, can you wait on it? Two or three days, tops. I need a little time, a head start."

"For what?"

Powell could never know, nor could anyone else at the embassy. It would remain her secret because it had been her mistake. Angrily she flashed back to that night at the for-eigners' morgue. She had not recognized the welder who had bent over David Wang's coffin, nor had she protested when the odd Mr. Hu had declined to open it for the requisite inspection. *I am required to see it first*, she had said. *You were late*, he had replied.

Now she knew why Mr. Hu had sealed the coffin so swiftly: it must have been empty. David Wang had been alive. Then.

"Steve, I can't say much. Maybe when the boss gets back from Singapore. All I can tell you is that this"—Linda waved the cable—"is very serious. Extremely serious. Can I count on you?"

Powell smiled. " 'Course you can. Took customs three days to get us a wire from Frisco . . . might just take another three days for them to get an answer. Fair is fair."

Linda squeezed Powell's arm and whispered a thank-you.

The staff meeting was soporific and Powell droned through the agenda—new guidelines for visa requests, an upcoming visit by an undersecretary of state, still more travel restrictions for American tourists leaving Peking. . . .

Linda drifted in a rough sea. Stratton was right: she had lost the deputy minister. Not merely lost him, but let him

238

slip away like an eel. He was cunning, but was he the murderer that Stratton claimed? It added up, all right. The mystery coffin at the foreigners' morgue, the "official" drowning at the Ming reservoir, the hasty Party cremation—and now San Francisco.

The sonofabitch had done it, bought his way out of China with the blood of his own brother.

Now Wang Bin was free. Stratton knew. And he would find out where to look. And when Stratton caught up with Wang Bin it would all explode. There was no avoiding it. My secret, Linda thought, my failure. "One case is all it takes, right?" Stratton had said at that long-ago dinner. Yes, one case was all it took for glory—or for demotion down to some backwater, shuffling papers for the rest of her life. All those years fighting those stupid patronizing male smiles just to get somewhere—and now this. There'd be nothing left to save.

". . . and finally," Powell was saying, "I got a call yesterday from one of our friends in the fourth estate. He wanted another update on our deaths-by-duck, so I presume we'll be reading about it in the next week or so. I'm sure the travel agents back in the States will be thrilled to tears."

"Excuse me, Steve, who—" Linda began.

"Jesus, what else can they write?" piped one of the preppy junior officers. "Didn't the Chicago *Tribune* and the Boston *Globe* do big take-outs year before last?"

"Yeah. So did AP," Powell grumbled. "But I had to give out the list, it's a public record."

"Steve!"

Powell was startled. "Yes, Linda."

"Excuse me, I was just wondering who it was who called." Her tongue was chalky; her heart pounded.

"McCarthy. Jim McCarthy from the *Globe*."

"He's the one who did the first story," interjected one of the junior officers, hoping that someone would remark on his keen memory.

But it was Linda Greer's memory that stabbed at her, jolted her back to the first day Tom Stratton had walked into the embassy. Jim McCarthy had been the one who had sent him; Stratton had said so.

239

She was sure it was no coincidence. McCarthy wouldn't be updating his story, not so soon. Oh, he wanted information, all right, but not for a newspaper story. For a friend.

"Linda, is there a problem?" Powell asked. "We gave Jim a full list the first time around. Interviews, too. No one said there was a problem."

Linda smiled. "Oh, no problem. I was just curious." She thought her voice sounded tremulous.

Powell seemed not to notice. "It's really nothing," he said. "McCarthy just wanted to know how many Americans had died here over the last couple months. I gave him the names. No big deal."

"Sure," Linda said agreeably. No big deal. Jesus, if Powell only knew. "Is that all for today?"

In the hallway, she could scarcely keep from running toward her office. Now she knew everything. She knew that Stratton's plan was already in motion, and it spelled disaster for her.

In a bleak way, it was funny, she reflected. It all came back to the goddamn morgue—*her* job, too. An awful little job— late at night. A simple detail, really. Or one would think. But Linda had botched that, too.

She would have to leave immediately for the United States. Sick leave, Linda would call it, or an illness in the family. There was no time to fight the bureaucracy.

Tom Stratton would have to be stopped.

Wang Bin would have to be caught.

She had to get to one of them before they got to each other. And she had to do it alone.

Wang Bin, Stratton—her responsibilities, both of them. That's what you're here for, the station chief had told her. That's what you're good at. Do what you have to, he had said—not warmly—but get them where we want them. Keep them there.

Gone was not where she wanted them.

Getting them back was the only thing that would save her career.

There was no time to worry about breaking a few laws.

* * *

240

A warm breeze from Tampa Bay ruffled Stratton's hair and stood him up as he walked across a broad, green lawn that seemed to ramble all the way to the water. Wheeling gulls bickered high above and a dour pelican plunged into a school of mullet. The splash startled the old man who had been pushing a lawn mower around the tombstones.

"Hello!" Stratton called.

The old man cocked his head. He glanced up to the sky, wondering if one of the noisy birds had actually shouted to him.

"Here! Hello!" Stratton yelled over the mower's engine.

The old man spotted Stratton and muttered a grumpy acknowledgment. He turned off the mower and pulled a handkerchief from the belt of his trousers.

"I'm looking for the grave of Sarah Steinway," Stratton said.

The old man noticed that Stratton carried a modest spray of flowers.

"Are you a relative?" he asked.

Stratton said he was a nephew. "I came all the way from New York."

"Jesus H. Christ," the old man said, shaking his head. "I'm sorry to hear that."

He led Stratton along the water to a footpath that took them up a gentle man-made hill. On the other side was a stand of young pine trees that formed the boundary of the cemetery's newest lot.

"If you'd have come tomorrow most of it would have been cleaned up," the old caretaker said apologetically.

"What are you talking about?"

"Come on."

Stratton followed him to the gravesite. Many of the plots were recently turned; others remained untouched, the gravestones bare—prepurchased, Florida-style.

They walked to the end of a long row before Stratton saw what the old man meant. The caretaker stopped and pointed up and down the column of graves. "Look what they did!"

"They" had gone amok, toppling the headstones, shredding the flowers, trampling and thrashing the soil. On one grave sat a mound of rotting garbage, with bright blue flies buzzing obscenely. Another was peppered with broken whiskey bottles. Still another grave had been defaced with bright crayons. Stratton bent over the granite slab and read:

> *There was an old geezer named Saul*
> *Who dropped dead in the Hillsborough Mall*
> *His wife called a cop*
> *Then went back to the shop*
> *So she wouldn't miss the sale, after all*

"Cute," Stratton muttered.

"It's sick," the old caretaker said. "Teenagers, that's all."

One double headstone read: "Eva and Bernard Melman." Beneath the names, smeared in burgundy, was a Nazi swastika. In dripping letters at the base of the tombstone, someone had painted the words MORE DEAD JEWS.

Stratton stepped closer to study the vandalism. After a few moments he turned to the caretaker and asked, "Did you call the police?"

"Of course. They sent a man. So what? What can they do?"

The old man moved forward and pointed with his foot to an area around the Melmans' granite slab. The dirt was dark and moist and loose, as if a shovel had been plunged into the ground and withdrawn.

"I figure they were interrupted by a car," the old man speculated.

"What about Aunt Sarah?" Stratton asked.

The caretaker pointed to the next headstone on the row:

Sarah Rose Steinway
1919–1983

The only mark of vandalism was another swastika, this one drawn in orange crayon between the "Sarah" and the "Rose."

"Look at that," Stratton said disgustedly.

"That'll come right off, mister. I can get it with some turpentine, or some real strong acetate. Won't harm the marble, either. I'll clean it off this afternoon."

Stratton set the flowers on the grave and stepped back to

242

the footpath. The caretaker took a deep breath. "It's impossible to guard a place like this twenty-four hours a day. You understand, don't you? We're just a small cemetery—I mean, we've got a watchman, but he's old and he doesn't hear so well."

Stratton was only half listening. He concentrated on the Steinway grave. The sod around the marker was puckered in several places, and badly gashed near the headstone.

"When did all this happen?"

"Either last night or the night before. See, I don't get around to this side every day. I mow it three times a week, though, and if there's a visitor like yourself, or the men who came a couple of days ago, then I'll bring 'em here to show the way."

"What men?"

"They brought flowers for your Aunt Sarah there . . ." the caretaker began.

A lovely touch, Stratton thought.

"How many men?"

"Two. Said they were good friends of the deceased."

The old man dabbed at his neck with the handkerchief. "I'm trying to remember their names. One of them was a thin fellow, about forty-five, fifty maybe. Had black hair. Dressed kind of bright for the cemetery. The other guy looked Japanese. He didn't say much. Last time I saw them they were just sitting on the bench, talking quietly. I'm glad they weren't here to see what happened to their flowers."

Stratton found two motels within a half mile of the small cemetery. He went first to the Holiday Inn. The young junior-college student at the registration desk was helpful. He allowed Stratton to study the check-in cards going back for seven days; there were no Oriental names registered. Stratton asked the young desk clerk if he remembered an American and a Chinese staying there. The clerk shook his head no.

"And I probably would have noticed them," the clerk said. "This is the slow time of the year. A lot of our business is lunch hour." He winked.

Across the street at the Bay Vista Court Stratton was

243

greeted by an attractive, middle-aged woman with frosted hair and a warm smile.

"Carl Jurgens," he said, holding out his hand. "Apex Car Rentals."

"I'm Mrs. Singer," the woman said. "How can I help you?"

"Well, a few days ago we rented a car to two fellows. A red Oldsmobile, brand-new. When they picked it up at Tampa Airport, they wrote on the rental agreement that they'd be staying here at your place. I've got a copy of the rental papers in the car."

Mrs. Singer nodded. Stratton could tell that she was curious.

"Anyway," he said, "they stiffed us. Dumped the car at a Grand Union over on Dale Mabrey."

"I still don't see how I can possibly help."

"Simple, Mrs. Singer. Just tell me if they were here, and maybe let me have a look at the registration cards—to see if they left an address, or a phone number. The ones they gave our people were phony, of course. Maybe they paid you with a credit card. Now that would be great."

Mrs. Singer stood up and smoothed her dress. "How much did they get you for?"

"A hundred and ninety-four," Stratton replied. "It's not Fort Knox or anything, I know . . ."

Mrs. Singer smiled. "It's a lot of money. I understand, believe me. We've been burned a few times ourselves." She pulled a Rolodex wheel across the counter and thumbed through the cards. "What were their names?"

"One was an Oriental man, a Chinese. His name is Wang. W-A-N-G. Like the computers."

Mrs. Singer nodded vigorously. "Yes, I remember him. Here." She unfastened a three-by-four card from the Rolodex. "They stayed one night. Room forty-one, no phone calls. Paid with a Mastercard. Here's a copy of the charge slip."

Stratton read the name: Harold Broom.

Broom . . . Broom? Then he had it: the overbearing art broker he had met at the consular office in Peking. What was it he had said: *This is new territory, and I don't know whose*

244

back needs scratching. Maybe we could help each other out.
Hey, pal, wanna buy some artifacts?—it was almost that blatant. Broom was a soulless cretin, the perfect confederate for the deputy minister of art and culture.

"Are these the men?" Mrs. Singer inquired.

"Yes. This is very good."

"But they weren't driving an Oldsmobile, Mr. Jurgens. They drove a white van—like a U-Haul, only white. Mr. Broom did all the driving."

A van, of course. Prosaic but practical—a modern hearse for an eternal warrior.

Mrs. Singer asked, "Do you rent vans like that?"

"No, only cars. Perhaps they got the van after they ditched our Oldsmobile. Well, the important thing is that these are the fellows I'm looking for."

She gave Stratton a coy look. "I might be able to help. Mr. Broom asked to borrow a phone book—we don't keep them in the rooms anymore. They just get stolen. Anyway, I let him borrow the telephone book. Then he walked over to that pay phone and called Delta Airlines. He made reservations for today to New York. La Guardia, I think."

Stratton wanted to hug her.

He drove to a Holiday Inn on the other side of St. Petersburg and checked in. It was almost dusk. He turned on every light in his room, slipped out of his shoes and sat down at a wobbly desk. From another pocket in his suit jacket, Stratton took the piece of paper that Jim McCarthy had delivered to him in Hong Kong. The list was typed under the letterhead of the Boston *Globe*. It said:

U.S. citizen deaths May–August 1983:

Steinway, Sarah	5-10-83	Canton	St. Petersburg, Fl.
Mitchell, Kevin P.	6-22-83	Xian	Baltimore, Md.
Bertecelli, John	7-4-83	Xian	Queens, N.Y.
Friedman, Molly	8-14-83	Peking	Fort Lauderdale, Fl.
Wang, David	8-16-83	Peking	Pittsville, Ohio

With a blue felt-tip pen, Stratton circled the name of John Bertecelli, who had died on the Fourth of July in Xian. Bertecelli's body now lay somewhere in New York. Probably

245

Broom and Wang Bin were already there, and maybe already at work.

Stratton thought: I ought to leave right now. There is no time to do what I had planned. Catching them will not be easy, even with the right grave.

The right grave.

Stratton contemplated his macabre odyssey. Chasing the coffins was a shell game. Five caskets, three Chinese soldiers. Scratch off McCarthy's list the name of David Wang, whose "death" at the Heping Hotel had been staged after the theft of the warriors. That left four possible caskets.

Stratton had arrived in San Francisco with a simple strategy: geography. He could think of no other logical way to go at it. He had booked a flight to Miami where he had planned to begin the search, moving north, following his death list.

Molly Friedman had been first. A death notice published in the Fort Lauderdale *News* had announced that Molly was at rest at the Temple of David Mausoleum in Hallandale. A brief memorial service had been held four days after her sudden death in Peking. Rabbi Goren had kindly presided.

Stratton had found his way from the newspaper offices to the Temple of David. Bearing a small parcel of flowers from a Moonie working the stoplights on Federal Highway, he had been greeted at the door by a small balding man dressed in a dark wool suit. "Molly Friedman, please," Stratton had whispered, and the greeter had led him down a chilly hallway with high granite walls. They had entered a huge vault bathed in purplish light that filtered from stained-glass panels set high in a rectangular ceiling.

The balding man had consulted a small, leatherbound directory. Then he had taken ten steps forward and pointed high up the wall. "There," he had whispered, "G-one-two-oh."

Stratton had squinted to see the name. Molly Friedman's remains lay seven rows up, on a granite ledge—in an urn. A Chinese urn.

"Your flowers," the greeter had whispered. "We can arrange them."

"That will be just fine," Stratton had said. Two hours later he had been on a plane to St. Petersburg.

And now the trail was red hot. Stratton rocked the chair, gripping the cheap desk by its corners. He was jittery, restive. How easily all the old hunting instincts had returned. He envisioned the icy-eyed old Chinese prowling a foreign graveyard, a remorseless night bandit. Why not go to New York tonight? Stratton thought. The grave of John Bertecelli waited. He could end it there.

Stratton thought of the old caretaker with the lawn mower at the St. Petersburg cemetery. He thought of the stinking garbage on the graves, the bloody swastikas, the vulgar poem —all doubtlessly the work of Harold Broom, relishing his role as a teenage vandal. If Wang Bin was a man to be feared, Broom clearly was a man to be hated. And not to be taken for granted. What if the despoliation was a double-blind, a misdirection on the off chance someone was following them? Unlikely, but . . .

Stratton resolved not to leave St. Petersburg without seeing the evidence with his own eyes, erasing what little doubt remained. He would do the work swiftly and neatly, leaving no clues.

He changed into jeans and a black T-shirt, and tied on a pair of Puma jogging shoes. At an Army-Navy store a few blocks from the motel, Stratton purchased a heavy-duty flashlight and a portable screw-down shovel. At midnight, he headed for the graveyard near the bay.

Stratton parked in a municipal lot not far from the gate. Carrying the shovel under one arm, he melted into a stand of pines and scouted the cemetery on foot. The caretaker had mentioned a security guard; Stratton found him in a matter of minutes. He was sitting in a compact car, reading a magazine by the dome light—a silver-haired black man, wearing the usual rent-a-cop uniform.

Stratton crossed behind the guard's car, running low to the ground. He chose a path through the trees and scrub and purposely stayed clear of the water, which shimmered revealingly with the lights of Tampa. After about a hundred yards, Stratton flicked on the flashlight.

The caretaker had worked earnestly to clean up Broom's foul mess. The trash was gone, and most of the glass had

247

been swept up. The old man had scrubbed the Melmans' grave marker until only a shadow of the swastika was visible. He had obviously devoted equal energy to the stone of Sarah Rose Steinway, although the orange crayon had proved stubborn. The Nazi emblem had become a permanent greasy smudge between the "Sarah" and the "Rose."

Stratton unfolded the shovel and tightened a bolt at the neck. He began to dig with short, powerful strokes. There was no slab on the grave, only a layer of new sod. Below the grass, the earth was moist and soft. It gave way easily—too easily for a three-month-old grave.

For ninety minutes Stratton dug. He expected that the coffin had not actually been interred six feet deep, and he was right. He was only up to his armpits in the hole when the shovel bit struck metal. He dropped to his knees and cleared the rest of the dirt by hand. At the foot of the coffin, Stratton carved out a trench for himself. He stepped down and bent over so far that his chin nearly met the lid. In the darkness he fished like a raccoon for the corners of the coffin.

Stratton got a good grip and stood up with an involuntary grunt. The coffin came loose of the earth. Stratton backstepped out of the grave, dragging the thing half out of its cool pocket until it rested at a peculiar angle—head down, feet toward the sky.

Stratton was panting. He scoured the pines and the cart paths for headlights. His hands trembled and he wiped them on his jeans. He thought it obscene to use dirty hands for this. Obscene, but not inappropriate. With the point of the cheap shovel he gouged the seal of the coffin, and the lid flopped open with a cold click.

Stratton took a deep breath and aimed the flashlight.

The coffin of Sarah Rose Steinway was empty.

The cheap cotton lining bore the indentation of a rigid human form. Something sparkled microscopically against the fabric. Stratton ran a finger lightly along the inside of the casket, as if tracing the spine of the invisible dead.

In the beam of the flashlight, Stratton examined his fingertip and noticed a powdery film of red-brown clay. The ancient dust of another grave, another violated tomb.

248

CHAPTER **23**

THE CAB RIDE from La Guardia was no more harrowing than a spin through downtown Peking, and Wang Bin rode in unperturbed silence. He grunted once when a sleek black limousine cut sharply in front of the taxi, and jumped slightly in his seat at the sudden blast of a trucker's horn. But it was the vista of Manhattan, seen from the Triborough Bridge, that left him breathless. At first glimpse Wang Bin leaned close to the window and stared at the vast skyline marching along the river, molten in the pink light of the late afternoon. The city was like nothing the deputy minister had ever seen.

Harold Broom glanced over and smiled with a superior air. "Hey, Pop, the cabbie is Russian. How about that?"

Broom had taken to calling Wang Bin "Pop," an annoying term that the deputy minister did not understand.

"Didya ever think you'd be riding with a Russian through the streets of America?" Broom roared at some dim irony while Wang Bin watched out the window in fascination as the skyline swallowed them.

The two men checked into a small, comfortable hotel on

Central Park South. Broom did all the talking—to the cabbie, to the doormen, to the desk clerk, to the rental car agent. Wang Bin had nothing to say; New York was richer and more bewildering than he had ever imagined. Compared to that of Peking, even the air was a tonic. The crowds of walkers were garish, and certainly less orderly than the Chinese, but the Americans were equally hurried and wore the same expressions of determination. And the automobiles were boggling— more cars than Wang Bin believed existed in all of China, stacked on every street, inching forward with horns blaring. The noise jarred his nerves.

Wang Bin stood at the window of the fifth-floor hotel room and watched a hansom cab clop down the street toward the Plaza Hotel. On the sidewalk at Columbus Circle, a ragged group of men and women waved placards and shook their fists. Two policemen stood at the corner, chatting calmly. Wang Bin could not understand why they did not hurry to arrest the demonstrators. He decided that the officers must be waiting for reinforcements.

Broom groomed himself in the mirror. "So what's it gonna be tonight, Pop? Studio 54?"

Wang Bin scowled at the joke. "I am tired."

"Okay, no disco. But we gotta eat," the art broker said.

"I want to rest before we work."

"Look out there, old man. That's the greatest city in the world. Don't you want to have a good time?"

"I am tired."

"Hey, Pop, let's celebrate a little. We're rich, remember? You and me, we're on a roll now. Packed our little pal off to our Florida buyer yesterday—that's one down, two to go, and money in the bank." Broom rubbed his hands together hungrily and gave the deputy minister another one of his winks. "Let's see the sights!"

"You go ahead," Wang Bin said, stepping away from the window. "I want to sleep."

The deputy minister was dressed for the graveyard when Harold Broom returned at one in the morning.

"Hey there, Pops, you missed a good time." Broom weaved

250

across the room and eased down on the sofa. He kicked off his shoes and scratched at his feet.

"You are drunk," Wang Bin said angrily.

"Don't worry, partner." Broom struggled out of his clothes without assistance, but Wang Bin had to guide the art broker's arms and legs into the dark gray coveralls that they had selected as their grave robbers' uniform.

"Didya see the *Post* tonight?" Broom babbled. "It made the headline on one of the back pages: VANDALS DESECRATE JEWISH GRAVES AT FLORIDA CEMETERY. Just a little story, no big deal, but they printed part of my poem. Even had a photo of one of the headstones."

Broom stretched out on the sofa and groaned feebly.

"It's time to go now," Wang Bin said, standing over him.

"In a minute."

"Now!" said the deputy minister, grabbing Broom's arm.

The art dealer easily shook himself free and pushed the old man away. "Don't fuck with me, Pop! I got a tiny headache right at the moment so I'm gonna rest. I'm the driver, 'member? We go when I say."

Wang Bin sat down only when he heard Broom start to snore.

Tom Stratton slouched glumly in the Eastern Airlines lounge that overlooked the main runways at the Tampa–St. Petersburg Airport. A long line of jets sat in the slashing rain, the wing lights flicking red and white and red again, the pilots waiting for the weather to clear. Stratton's flight to New York had already been delayed thirty minutes.

Stratton was on his second beer when he got the idea for a modest head start. He found a nest of deserted pay phones in the main lobby near the gift shops.

In a neat brownstone in one of the better neighborhoods of Queens, Violet Bertecelli cracked her shin on a coffee table as she fumbled in the dark for the telephone. When she finally found it, she was in too much pain to say a gracious hello.

"Do you know what the hell time it is?"

"Is this Mrs. Bertecelli? Mrs. John Bertecelli?" asked a fuzzy voice.

"Yes. Yes, it is. Is this long distance?"

"Yes, ma'am," Tom Stratton said. "I apologize for calling at such an hour, but it's morning here in China—"

"What? You're calling from China?"

"Yes, ma'am. Peking. I'm Steve Powell, with the United States Embassy. I handled the arrangements after your husband's unfortunate . . ."

"Death," Violet said helpfully.

"Yes, of course, back in July. That's the reason I'm calling, Mrs. Bertecelli. I'm not exactly sure how to go about telling you this, but in recent months there have been reports of irregularities in the shipment of human remains from China back to the United States."

Violet said, "Johnny died of a coronary."

"Yes, I know. But we've had complaints from a couple of families about the quality of the metal on the coffins. In the case of one poor fellow, the hinges snapped off and the lid came loose."

"The coffin was just fine. It was actually very nice. Did you pick it out yourself, Mr. Powell?"

"No, ma'am."

"Well, it was lovely. Everything was just fine with Johnny. They sent him to Riordan's Funeral Parlor and he was buried out at St. Francis with his ma."

"That's excellent," Stratton said. "And our files show he was laid to rest in plot E-seventy-seven."

"No, sir, that's wrong," Violet said. "It's plot number one-sixty-six. I remember 'cause one-sixty-six was Johnny's best-ever score in the bowling league. That's how I remember the plot number."

"I'm sorry, Mrs. Bertecelli, you're absolutely right. I see it here now, right in the file. Plot one hundred sixty-six.

"Thank you, Mrs. Bertecelli. That was St. Francis Cemetery?"

"That's right. Grand Central Parkway, Queens."

Tom Stratton hung up the phone and hurried to the nearest Eastern ticket counter. The video monitor now showed that his flight to Kennedy Airport would not depart until two in

252

the morning. Dejectedly Stratton walked back to the lounge and ordered another beer and stared out the window to the runways, where the jets still waited in the rain. He prayed that it was storming like hell in Queens.

Wang Bin sat down in a heap on the ground. His chest heaved, and he could feel drops of sweat trickling into his eyebrows. He watched furiously while Harold Broom grappled with the coffin, muttering obscenities from the dank hole where he worked. The sky was cloudy. Cars and trucks raced by on the parkway, drowning out the other night noises. Headlights from the scattered traffic would suddenly turn the tombstones yellow, and cause an eerie dance of shadows across the hillside.

"We need assistance," Wang Bin declared.

"We need a backhoe," Broom growled. "The dirt down here is like concrete." He tossed down the shovel and tried swinging the pick. The musty earth around the coffin crumbled away in hard clods, but the box itself held fast where it had been buried under a chorus of Hail Marys. "Get down here and help me lift," Broom said.

But the two of them—Broom, nauseous and half-drunk; the deputy minister, exhausted, his thin arms cramped from the shoveling—could budge the coffin only a few inches and no more.

Broom glanced at his watch. Four in the morning. Time was running out. Wang Bin was right: They needed help.

"Stay here," he said, fishing for the keys to the rental car.

Wang Bin was too tired to object to being left alone, but after Broom had been gone half an hour, he began to worry. What if the fool never came back? What if he got scared and abandoned him? Enough money had been collected already to finance a very comfortable life for a man like Broom . . . and where would that leave Wang Bin?

He stood up and stretched his aching arms and legs. The headlights from the highway caught him square in the eyes and he turned away grimacing. In the opposite direction the sky was tinged orange by the incredible lights of Manhattan.

253

Wang Bin doubted if he could ever grow accustomed to life in this city; he understood now why David had chosen a rural place, a small and orderly place. A manageable place.

Not far away, a dog barked excitedly.

Where was Broom?

The deputy minister regarded his American partner as a truly despicable man. He had not understood the vagaries of Broom's behavior at the graveyard in Florida, only that the desecrations had been meant as a ruse to confuse the police. The art broker had assured him that no one would check the coffin after they had buried it again, and he had been right. But it was the way Broom reveled in the vandalism that Wang Bin found so utterly repulsive. He would shed himself of the man as soon as possible, and now . . . now he was stranded in a cemetery, desperately hoping that Broom was greedy enough to come back. Wang Bin needed Broom and this, too, was a foreign emotion. In China, he had been provided everything he needed; here, without his title, absent of his authority, he felt helpless and common. To defer to a man like Broom was disgraceful, but, for now, quite necessary.

Wang Bin's heart raced at the sound of an automobile winding up the road toward St. Francis Cemetery. An involuntary smile came to his lips when he saw Harold Broom, flanked by two tall, slender figures, trudging down the hill.

"Pop, say hello to Tyrone and Charles."

Wang Bin nodded but caught himself before he bowed. Tyrone and Charles were both angular black teenagers, but they appeared very strong. Tyrone sported a red ski cap and Charles was dressed in a white-and-green sports jersey of some sort. It occurred instantly to Wang Bin that the two strangers could handily overpower him and Harold Broom and steal the treasure themselves.

"These gentlemen were testing the back door of a liquor store down the street," Broom was saying. "Good thing I happened to see 'em before they got into real trouble. They said they'd be happy to help."

"For how much?" the deputy minister inquired.

"Hundred bucks apiece," Broom said.

254

Wang Bin said nothing. Broom shrugged. "Whaddya want at four in the morning, Pop? I didn't have time to take out an ad in the goddamn *Times*. They look like good workers to me. Right, boys?"

Tyrone shrugged and Charles said, "What the hell is this deal?" He gestured at the open grave. "What's the fuckin' story? I ain't messin' with no stiffs."

"Me neither," Tyrone said.

"I'm not asking you to *mess* with a stiff, pal. I'm asking you to help us get the coffin out of the ground. A little manual labor, that's all. Won't kill you, take my word for it."

"Don't seem right," Charles said, peering into the hole.

Broom said, "Fine! You don't like it? Then beat it. Get the hell out of here!"

Wang Bin looked at him sharply.

"I didn't know you guys were a couple of pussies," Broom said. "Shit. For two hundred bucks I'll go find a couple of *men* to help with this."

As Broom waved his arms theatrically, Charles calmly seized him by the back of the neck and said, "Shut up, you greasy jive mo'fucker. Give us the bread and we'll dig."

The art broker huddled with Wang Bin as the two teenagers wrestled with the coffin. "You got to know how to talk to these people," Broom explained.

"I don't like them," Wang Bin whispered.

"Of course you don't."

"I don't trust them."

"Relax, Pop."

Broom hopped into the grave. Within minutes, he and the two teenagers had hoisted the coffin of John Bertecelli from the hole and laid it on the ground. Tyrone sat down on a headstone and said, "So who's in it, Dracula?"

"I don't want to know," Charles said. "Let's split."

"No, man, I want the dudes to open it."

"You can go now," Broom said. "Thanks for the help, fellas."

"Open it, man!"

"No."

255

"Okay. I'll open it." Tyrone lifted the pick and windmilled it at the coffin. The lid skewed from the hinges. Tyrone kicked it off with one of his basketball shoes.

"Shit," he said. "It's a mummy!"

Swaddled in plastic, a Chinese spearman stared through wise eyes into the firmament.

Broom stepped forward and said, "That's enough. You've seen it, now get the hell out of here."

"What's it worth?" Charles asked, leaning over the coffin, hands on his knees.

"Let's haul it out of there," Tyrone suggested. "You get that end—"

"No!" Wang Bin said.

The black teenagers looked up to see the old man pointing a chrome-plated pistol at them. They noticed that his arm was rigid. Charles chuckled and fumbled with the statue.

"Why you so uptight?" Tyrone said to Wang Bin. "This mummy must be somebody special for you, that right? Is this your old man?"

"Tell your friend to let go of the artifact," Wang Bin instructed.

"He ain't gonna break it."

The crack of the pistol got the dog barking again. Charles wriggled on the damp ground, clawing at his right arm. Tyrone was speechless.

"Oh shit, Pop," Broom said in a husky voice. "We've got to get out of here."

"I agree," the deputy minister said. "Mr. Tyrone, would you please help Mr. Broom carry the artifact to our car? If you make trouble, I will shoot your friend again and again until he is dead."

By this time Charles was sobbing, and his New York Jets jersey was sticky with fresh blood. Tyrone gingerly lifted the Chinese spear carrier by the head while Broom—suddenly sober—carried the other end. The two unlikely pallbearers tenuously made their way up the hillside, weaving among the tombstones. Wang Bin held the pistol steadily on his captive and wondered sourly if this was going to be the only way to gain people's obedience.

256

The first cop on the scene was a patrolman named Sanderson, who borrowed a spool of kite string from one of the neighborhood kids and cordoned off the gravesite using four other tombstones as corner posts. The total effect, Sanderson noted with self-satisfaction, was to convey the impression of an actual crime scene. All that was missing was the chalk silhouette.

Tom Stratton arrived by cab at 7:15 A.M., a haggard presence among the rabid, coffee-hopped reporters. Because he was carrying a fresh spray of flowers, Stratton was immediately marked as a grief-stricken relative and besieged with questions. Who would want to steal Mr. Bertecelli's body? Had a ransom note been received? Did Mr. Bertecelli practice satanism? How was the widow holding up?

Stratton deflected his interrogators and was relieved when a plump brunette woman identified herself as Violet Bertecelli and began to tell her sad story to the mothlike newsmen. The moment also offered a breather for Officer Sanderson, so Stratton walked up and asked what had happened.

"Some assholes ripped off a corpse here, which is grand theft, presuming the item taken has a value in excess of one hundred dollars. We're looking for two or three perpetrators, at least one of them armed with a pistol." Sanderson shrugged. "Who knows what to think? You want my opinion? Kids. Maybe it's some kind of sick fraternity ritual. Else it could be 'Ricans. They're all into that witchcraft shit. Voodoo, eatin' chicken heads. Could be that. Hey you! Get out of the fuckin' hole!" Sanderson waved his nightstick at a photographer. "Get out of the goddamn grave. What are ya, some kinda sick hump?"

"Somebody said there was an ambulance here," Stratton remarked.

"Yeah, that's the odd thing." Sanderson took out his notebook and read from the top page. "Victim's name was Charles Robinson, aged seventeen. Long juvenile record for b-and-e, shoplifting, boosting bicycles. Nothing like this."

"Was he hurt badly?"

"Naw, you know them people. You got to shoot 'em in the

asshole to do any real damage." The cop laughed. "You a relative of Mr. Bertecelli or what?"

"No, I brought some flowers for my grandmother's grave. It's up the hill a ways. I was just curious, that's all."

"Well, the little shit was shot in the arm. He'll live. I'm pretty sure he was involved in the whole thing. He's not talkin', naturally. Says he was walkin' by the graveyard on his way to church when some crazy Chinaman shot him." Sanderson shook his head admiringly. "You got to give these douche bags credit for imagination. Fuckin' weird, even for Queens."

The retinue clinging to Violet Bertecelli suddenly moved with her to the edge of the damaged grave. She stared at the broken casket and began to wail, accompanied by the sibilance of a dozen motordrive Nikons.

CHAPTER 24

THEY DROVE SOUTH. Broom was careful to stay at fifty-five, and even so he could not keep his eyes off the rearview mirror. He was ragged and nervous. A shooting had been the last thing he had expected. The Chinaman had balls, that was for sure—how the hell had he gotten that gun?

As always, Wang Bin rode in silence. In contrast to Broom, the deputy minister was placid, almost serene. He seemed to pay particular attention to other cars. The brighter and newer they were, the more he stared. One time, when a black Porsche flew past them, Broom thought he noticed Wang Bin smiling.

He's like a little kid, the art dealer thought. A little kid with a chrome-plated .38.

"I am hungry," Wang Bin said.

Broom found a Burger King. He used the drive-in lane, braking as they pulled abreast of a plastic menu board.

"What do you want?" he asked the deputy minister.

Wang Bin squinted at the colorful menu sign for a long time. A young girl's voice cracked on a speaker box and said, "Good morning, can I help you?"

Wang Bin sat back, startled.

259

"Tell her what you want," Broom commanded.

"Tell who?"

"The girl! Tell her what you want to eat!"

"I see no one." Wang Bin looked above and beneath the sign. "Who is speaking?"

"Welcome to Burger King, can I help you?"

"It's a bloody microphone, Pop!" Broom leaned out the window and shouted: "Two Whoppers, two fries and two coffees!"

After Broom paid for the food, he parked the car in the shade of a maple tree. He tore open his hamburger carton, took two bites and said, "It's a good thing I'm your partner. Otherwise you'd fucking starve in this country."

Wang Bin meticulously unwrapped his hamburger. He lifted the bun and examined the meat. He was overpowered briefly by the hot smell.

"Go on, eat," Broom said. "We've got a long ride."

Wang Bin forced himself to take a bite, and chased it down hastily with black coffee. "I would have preferred to wash myself before—"

"Sorry if I offended your Oriental hygiene, Pop. After all this is over, I'll take you to Hong Fat's for real won ton soup."

Wang Bin said, "I would like an accounting of the moneys."

"Finish your lunch. We'll talk about it later."

Wang Bin sipped at the coffee, but found himself longing for tea. Broom was impudent, and shamefully greedy; this the deputy minister had known from the first day. Now, in the final stages, it came down to trust. Wang Bin studied his oily partner as Broom gnawed on a french fry. In a cold rush it struck him how foolish he had been. Broom was his chauffer, his travel guide, his interpreter, his caretaker; Wang Bin needed him. There was no doubt.

Yet Broom did not need *him*. Not anymore. The soldiers had arrived. The buyers were in place.

Coldly, Wang Bin began to see himself as excess baggage. "What of the money?" he asked again.

"We've been through this."

"Once more, please."

"All the accounts are in the name Henry Lee. That's both

260

of us. We're both Mr. Lee. Both signatures are good at all the banks. As of today we got money in Texas and Florida. Lots."

"You said the spearman is for a Washington museum."

"The curator of an important museum. An expert," Broom muttered. "He would only agree to three hundred thousand, C.O.D. No money down."

That extinguished Wang Bin's faint hope that Harold Broom might be an honorable man. Broom was a liar. Wang Bin knew there had been a substantial down payment on the Chinese spear carrier. He had found the deposit slip in Broom's wallet, three hundred thousand dollars at the Riggs National Bank in Washington. The date on the deposit matched the date Broom had met the curator.

Wang Bin sighed. If only David had been cooperative, there would have been no need for an alliance with Harold Broom. If only David had agreed.

Now he was dead, and Broom was on his way to being a millionaire.

"Three hundred thousand for the spear carrier is an insult," Wang Bin declared.

"I agree, Pop. But the buyer has me over a real barrel. He heard about the other soldiers—don't ask me how—and accused me of cheating him. See, I'd promised him an exclusive. I *had* to. Anyway, when he heard about the other two soldiers he almost threw me out of the museum. I had to do some fast talking to jack him back up to three hundred, believe me."

"Find another buyer."

"It's too late."

"Why?"

"Because we're hot now," Broom said urgently. "The papers will have fun with our noisy escapade last night at St. Francis'. And if that little spade you plugged decides to talk, we could be in trouble." Broom jerked his thumb toward the trunk of the car. "I'm going to unload Charlie Chan on a train to Texas this afternoon. After that, just one more. Then we split the money and disappear, the sooner the better. By the way, where did you get that gun?"

"I purchased it last night, while you were sleeping off the liquor."

"Where?"

"In a place where people speak in my language."

Broom grinned, a yellow half-moon. "Chinatown! You old son of a bitch."

Wang Bin turned away.

"Eat your french fries, Pop. I've got a couple important calls to make, then we'll be on our way. Can't keep the customers waiting."

Broom sauntered down the street to a corner telephone booth. Wang Bin collected the lunch debris and placed it in a trash can outside the Burger King. He stretched his legs and breathed deeply of the summer day. He felt the butt of the pistol dig into his midriff, and he adjusted the gun a fraction in his waistband. From the highway overpass came the now familiar din of speeding traffic. Wang Bin thought how pleasant it would be to find a place untouched by the big road and all its relentless noise. A city of bicycles had certain advantages.

Harold Broom returned to the car with a pinched look on his face. He refolded the spiral notepad in which he had scribbled the vital phone numbers and slipped it into his pocket.

"I've got bad news, Pop," he grumbled. "Real bad news."

For nine hours Tom Stratton kept his place in the amphitheater. In throngs the tourists came and went, cameras dangling, children bounding up and down the marble steps. Twice an hour one audience replaced another, yet Stratton held his place, watching the lean young men in their dark blue uniforms. He glanced now and then down the gentle hill where Kevin Mitchell was supposed to be buried.

Eighteen times Stratton watched the guards change at the Tomb of the Unknowns. The cameras clicked most often when the guards faced each other and presented arms. There were three or four different Marines, working in shifts. Despite the heat and humidity, each man looked crisp and fresh as he strode to the marble crypt. For Stratton, the drill was his clock. From the amphitheater he had a clear view of grave 445-H, third row, fourth from the end, a small white cross in a sea of crosses, geometrically perfect.

Perfect, Stratton mused. Perfect was always the way the military wanted its men, but in war that was impossible. In death it was easy; dead soldiers can march precisely as desired.

Stratton thought of Bobby Ho, and wondered morbidly what had become of his friend's body after the massacre at Man-ling. Had the Chinese buried it? Burned it? Displayed it as a trophy? Perhaps they had fed Bobby's flesh to the starving dogs and cats of the village.

Arlington was for heroes.

Bobby ought to have a place here, Stratton thought. If not his body, at least his name. Wouldn't take much space, and God knows he was more of a hero than most of the men planted in the sea of crosses that rolled toward the Potomac.

The last tram of the day sounded its horn, and the tourists thundered from the amphitheater. Stratton rose from his spot, as if to follow, but instead took a different path downhill, and melted into the trees to wait for nightfall. He sat down at the base of an old oak and took out a pair of small Nikon field glasses. From his new vantage, Stratton could read the name on the cross:

Lt. Kevin P. Mitchell, USAF
B. 11-22-29
D. 6-22-83

A fighter pilot, World War II and Korea. Medal of Honor. After the wars Mitchell had joined Boeing as a test pilot and later became a captain with Pan Am. He'd died on a vacation to China—a heart attack, the U.S. Embassy had reported, while riding a bus to the Qin tombs at Xian. Death by duck.

Baltimore was where the family had wanted the coffin sent—a family plot, Stratton had learned, where one of Mitchell's brothers was buried.

Arlington had been an afterthought, Mrs. Mitchell's idea. A real honor, the family agreed. The Medal of Honor ought to count for something.

But Baltimore was where the embassy had sent the coffin, and Baltimore was where Broom and Wang Bin would go first, Stratton reasoned. He would wait for them at Arlington—days, weeks, whatever it took. How they could dream of ever trying it here . . .

Someone was walking among the graves.

Stratton panned with the binoculars along the crosses until he froze on the figure of a woman, dressed in black. Dusk was cheating him of the finer details. She was tall and wore a veil. Chestnut hair spilled down her back. She walked slowly, elegantly, stopping every few steps to study the names on the crosses.

She was young, Stratton decided, younger than the soldiers who lay buried in Section H. Too young to be a widow.

The woman in black stopped walking when she came to grave 445. She stopped to read the inscription. Then she reached out and touched the cross with her right hand. It began as a light and sentimental gesture, and from a distance would seem nothing more than a sad moment. But through the field glasses Stratton could see that the woman was not merely touching Kevin Mitchell's cross, but *testing* it, pushing on it with discernible force. Then she stood up straight and with a quickened pace made her way out of the rows of graves to a footpath. There was something familiar . . .

Stratton followed at a distance. He was careful to stay in the grass so his steps would not echo. Arlington was nearly empty now. The trams had stopped running and the tourists had gone back to the city. The woman in black walked alone, no longer in the gait of a mourner. Her heels clicked sharply on the pavement, and the sound dominoed along the tombstones.

"Hey there!" Stratton called.

Self-consciously she slowed, then turned as Stratton ran up. She looked at him and smiled. "So *there* you are!"

"Linda!" Stratton said.

"How'd I do?"

"I like the dress. Black becomes you. What are you doing here?"

It was a pointless question. She knew. He knew.

She kicked out of her high heels and said, "These things are killing me. Come on, walk me to the car."

"I can't."

She took his arm. "Come on, Tom, they won't come at night. They'll never find it at night."

"You're wrong, Linda. How did you know—"

"The same way you did. I had to play catch-up, that's all. I should've listened to you before, Tom, and I'm sorry. I didn't see what was happening—but even if I had, I'm not sure it would have made a difference."

"Nobody would have believed it, least of all your boss."

"Wang Bin was my case. The last couple of days I've had a lot of time to think about how I could have caught on sooner." She did not tell Stratton about the foreigners' morgue in Peking. She was afraid he had already figured it out.

"Are you here alone?" he asked.

"For now," she said.

"Me, too. And I'm staying."

He started back up the hill and she followed. "Tom!" she called. "I'm ruining my goddamn stockings. Slow down. Listen to me, they aren't coming tonight. They think the coffin is in Baltimore—"

"They've beaten me twice already. This is my last chance."

"Tom, be serious. I'll have some people here tomorrow. When the bad guys show up at the gate, we'll arrest them."

"What makes you so sure they'll use the gate?"

"Once they realize where the coffin is buried, they'll give up on it. They'll never try to dig this one up. Christ, it's *Arlington*, Tom. They can't possibly get away with it."

"This way," Stratton said, leaving the asphalt path and winding through a stand of tall trees. "I've got a good view from up here."

Linda Greer sat next to him under the oak, tugging the black dress down to cover her knees. She had hoped he would notice, but he didn't. He offered her a thermos of coffee.

"This is like summer camp," she teased. "Are you really going to stay here all night?"

"Why not?"

Linda edged closer until her cheek touched his shoulder.

"Might as well make the best of it," she whispered. "It's a soft night, isn't it?" Stratton nodded but did not look at her. "Tom, relax—it's like I'm snuggling up to one of those damn gravestones."

"I'm sorry."

Stratton trained his eyes on Kevin Mitchell's plot. A lemon moon, nearly full, was rising behind the capital across the river. The silent cemetery became a sprawling theater of shadows; the crosses turned into tiny soldiers with arms extended, whole battalions frozen on the hillsides in calisthenic precision.

"I stopped at the Kennedy grave this morning," Stratton said.

"Which one?"

"Both of them. That's where all the tourists go. I'd never seen them before, only pictures."

Linda said, "I took my little sister a couple of years ago. She cried."

"Last year some guy fell into the flame and died," Stratton said. "He got drunk and pitched face down into the Eternal Flame. They found him the next day, burned to death. When I saw the story in the paper, I had to wonder about that guy. What was he thinking about that night? Why did he come here, of all places? I could just see him standing there in front of the President's grave, after all the goddamn tourists were gone. I could see him crying. Sloppy drunk tears. Staring at the flame and crying like a baby. Then it made sense: If you want to be sad, this is the place. Look out there, Linda. Look at them all. So many you can't even count them. I think this must be the saddest place of all. I think the guy knew exactly what he was doing."

Linda kissed him gently on the neck. Nothing. Stratton was loaded like a spring. She wondered sadly if their night in Peking had left any tender echo. It would make her job so much easier if it had.

"Can I ask you something?" Stratton said softly. "Are you here to stop them—or me?"

*   *   *

266

Harold Broom had had about all he could take from the snotty Chinaman. Being cursed in Mandarin was not so bad, but now Wang Bin had begun to call him "fool" to his face, as if it were part of his name. Broom was not a violent fellow, but now he shook his fist at the man in the passenger seat and said, "Shut up before I punch you in the nose!"

Wang Bin merely grunted.

"It's not my fault," Broom said for the tenth time. How could he have foreseen that Mrs. Kevin Mitchell would change her mind about the funeral? How could Broom have known that her husband's coffin would wind up at Arlington instead of the old Mitchell family plot in Baltimore, which would have been just as lovely. It would have been a cinch.

"Son of a turtle!" Wang Bin snapped.

"These things happen."

"How are we to find Mitchell's grave?"

"Simple," Broom said. "We aren't. There's acres of soldiers at Arlington and not all of them are dead, Pop. They've got crack Marines with very nasty rifles—not peashooters like yours. No way we're going to try to dig up that coffin."

"But this cannot be!"

"Oh, but it is. Your precious Chinese warrior can rest forever. He'll be right at home, believe me. I'm not risking a trip to jail."

The deputy minister snorted. "I must have the third soldier."

"Pop, don't be greedy. There is no way we can pull it off. You want to get shot in the back? Those Marines are genuine marksmen, Pop, and you're old and slow."

Wang Bin stared straight ahead at the highway. "It can be done," he said. "And if it cannot, at least I want to see for myself."

Broom surrendered. They stopped at a camera store in Crystal City and purchased a couple of cheap 35-mms. This way, the art broker explained, they'd look like everybody else on the blue-and-white trams that chugged through the cemetery. Broom also bought a large canvas shoulder bag to conceal the collapsible shovel and two hand picks. "This is

267

insane," he grumbled. "And if anything goes wrong, you're on your own."

"Meaning what?" Wang Bin asked.

"Meaning I never saw you before in my life."

It was mid-afternoon when Broom drove down the Jefferson Davis Highway toward the national cemetery. He turned left past Fort Myer, then right again on Arlington Ridge Road. He drove half a mile and pulled the car up on a curb. "Get out now," he ordered Wang Bin. "Try to be useful."

The deputy minister silently followed the art dealer on a long sidewalk up a slope, through the gates of Arlington and onto a motor tram. The Chinese and his canvas shoulder bag sat down with a conspicuous clatter. The tram wound slowly up the hills. Wang Bin gazed in wonderment at the burial markers that seemed to march on forever.

"All soldiers?" he whispered to Broom.

"Yes. The Fields of the Dead, they call it."

"How many?" Wang Bin asked.

"Thousands," Broom said. "I checked with a guide back at the office and our friend is supposed to be resting in Section H. Grave number four-four-five. I got a map, but I'm not sure it'll help."

"We have nothing like this in China," Wang Bin marveled. "There is no land for such a place. All our dead are cremated."

"You build temples, we make graveyards. Each to his own."

Wang Bin took a deep breath. "Like Xian, in a way. This is your Imperial Army, is it not, Mr. Broom?"

Stratton spotted them without the field glasses.

They emerged from a copse at the foot of a hill, perhaps one hundred meters from Lt. Kevin P. Mitchell's white cross. They found the footpath and walked side by side, Mutt-and-Jeff silhouettes. Once they stopped to confer, and Stratton noticed the beam of a small flashlight as they bent over together, pointing. A map, probably. They resumed walking, with Broom leading the way.

Stratton slipped away from the oak tree where Linda Greer

268

slept, curled on a damp bed of leaves. He moved in a familiar half-crouch, using the trees and the dappled shadows to hide his advance. He stopped only to watch them, pace them, and anticipate their path up the hill to Section H.

Stratton got there first. He chose a spot slightly downhill, across the footpath from Mitchell's grave, in an older section of the cemetery. Here a six-foot granite marker paid homage to a four-star general and one of his three wives, and it was here that Stratton easily concealed himself.

He had already decided against a confrontation among the tombstones. The park police would arrive swiftly, to be sure, but what would they have—a couple of prowlers? No, it was better to let Harold Broom and Wang Bin finish their task. The evidence would be obvious, and afterwards the ghouls would be pegged as criminals.

Part of Stratton's decision owed to logic, and part to curiosity. He wanted to see if they would really try it.

Whispering, Broom and Wang Bin passed above him. The two men shuffled off the footpath and began probing grave markers in Section H. Stratton rose from his knees—dampened by the grass—and peered over the general's headstone.

He heard a voice counting: "Four-fifty, four forty-eight . . ."

And another: "It is here."

The flashlight threw a skittish beam from the ground to the trees to the crosses. Stratton crept out of the tombstones, sliding caterpillar-style along the earth until he reached the paved footpath. From there, braced on his elbows, he studied the grave robbers.

Wang Bin struggled out of the canvas shoulder bag and turned it upside down. The shovel and picks landed with a sharp clink against one of the white crosses.

"This is fucking insanity," Broom muttered.

"Where are your Marines?" Wang Bin chided. "It appears we are alone. You dig first."

"We're going to wind up in Leavenworth!" Broom said.

"There is a fortune beneath your feet. Now dig."

Grudgingly, Broom assembled the portable shovel. He removed his knit golf shirt and draped it across the arms of Kevin Mitchell's cross. As Broom poised at the edge of the

269

grave, Wang Bin took one step back and folded his hands at his waist.

"Keep your eyes open!" Broom instructed. He planted his shoe on the shovel and rammed it into the moist green sod.

The exhumation went on for two hours. Stratton watched the shadows trade places, and measured their progress by the muffled grunts and curses, some in Chinese, some in English. Otherwise Arlington was perfectly still, save for the changing of the guard at the Tomb of the Unknowns.

Stratton felt himself dozing when the sound of muffled voices arose in Section H. The flashlight snapped on, and he was able to see both of them: Broom, shirtless, sweaty, up to his waist in the pit; and Wang Bin, toweling his own forehead, exhorting Broom from the edge of the grave.

Then the flashlight went black.

Stratton squinted, waiting for his eyes to readjust. When he focused again, the two shadows were moving with belabored haste, a blur of pick and shovel, flinging dirt back into the grave. Then Wang Bin himself dropped to his knees and pressed ragged squares of green sod back into place, like so much carpeting.

"Let's get out of here," Broom said.

Wang Bin took the feet of the ancient soldier while Broom cradled its head. They walked without light, an odd and halting procession made easier by the perfect geometry that ruled the Fields of the Dead.

Fascinated, Tom Stratton did not move at first, but merely watched them recede among the graves.

Then he was on his feet, padding quietly behind them at a distance of fifty meters. When they reached an iron fence, Stratton dropped to one knee and raised the field glasses. Broom went over first, ripping his golf shirt. Wang Bin followed, grimacing with the exertion. The soldier was brought over on a precarious makeshift pulley, fashioned from two long ropes. Through the binoculars, Stratton noticed that the artifact had been carefully wrapped in a canvas bag.

Stratton scaled the fence easily, and followed the men along a deserted road. Fearful that they might wheel around and spot him, Stratton clung to the trees and hedges.

270

"Faster!" he heard Broom say. "We're almost there."

Ahead, parked on a curb, was a car. Stratton ducked into a grove of young trees. He did not move again until he heard the sound of the car doors.

Then Stratton stepped to the middle of the road, twenty meters from the car. The trunk was open. Beside it stood Harold Broom and the smaller figure of Wang Bin, their backs toward him. Stratton drew a .45-caliber pistol from his belt and took aim at the base of Wang Bin's skull.

It was an easy shot. Even in the dark he'd never miss. David Wang's murderer would die instantly—die without knowing who had claimed revenge.

Behind Stratton, something rustled in the trees.

Wang Bin whirled, his face a fright mask. At the sight of Stratton the fear vanished in a portrait of pure hate.

Another noise. Wang Bin slowly raised a finger, as if to point. Broom's arms fell to his side.

Footsteps. Stratton's pulse hammered. He held the gun steady. Someone was there, beside him. He turned to see.

The pain hit Stratton high in one leg. It seared like a snakebite, racing up his thighs, burning through his lungs until it choked him. The gun dropped from his hand. Stratton spun down like a top, clawing at his leg, his throat, mashing the heels of his hands into his eye sockets.

Even as he lay there rasping, the galaxy exploding in his skull, he was aware of someone standing over him.

The last thing Stratton heard was the faraway voice of the deputy minister.

"Miss Greer, it is very good to see you again."

CHAPTER **25**

A LL THE NEXT MORNING, Dr. Neal Lambert waited.

Harold Broom phoned at eleven. "All set," he had said. "Be ready at noon."

But noon came and went, and Lambert's excitement soon dissolved into panic. He paced the halls of the museum. He told himself not to worry; people like Broom were *always* late. They were incapable of common courtesy.

At six the museum closed. Lambert sank into the chair behind his polished desk and ranted out loud. Every few minutes he would dial the number that Broom had given him, only to be reminded by a very bored answering service that, no, Mr. Broom had not called in. Would he care to leave a number?

Lambert grew despondent. Broom was a greasy twit, but would he dare sell the Chinese soldier out from under him? And was he resourceful enough to locate a new buyer on such short notice? Doubtful, Lambert assured himself.

He wrung his hands and stood at the window of his office, gazing down the mall toward the Washington Monument.

272

Gravely he thought of his three-hundred-thousand-dollar down payment. Then he thought of something worse: someday, years from now, walking into another museum, maybe Renner's in Atlanta or that bastard Scavello's in New York, and discovering his own Chinese warrior on grand display in the main room.

No, not even Broom—his minimal reputation at stake—would stoop so low, Lambert concluded. Something else must have gone wrong. The possibilities were numbingly depressing. He picked up the telephone and tried again.

Tom Stratton awoke in the back of a taxi. He was dizzy, queasy, babbling.

"Easy, bud," the cabbie said. He led Stratton up the steps of the Hotel Washington and into the arms of a doorman.

"I took a twenty off you, okay?"

Stratton nodded foggily.

"What happened?" the doorman asked.

"Some broad called. Told us to go get this drunk out by the cemetery." The cabbie glanced down at Stratton. "That's where I found him, crawling around on all fours like a mutt."

Stratton groaned.

"Better get him up to his room," the cabbie advised, "before he urps on your nice carpet."

Stratton lay alone, dreaming of coffins. Slowly the pain drained from his limbs, but cotton clung to his mind. He could hear the sound of a city outside his window. A police siren. Screeching tires. A jet roaring down the Potomac. The noise crashed over him, triple amplified. His ears rang. His head felt like plaster.

He had to get up. Hours crawled by.

A maid rapped on the door.

"Not now," Stratton mumbled.

He had to get up. *Move.* Open your eyes.

The room was bright. The clock on the bedstand said eight o'clock.

"Jesus Christ." He had spent a full day in bed.

He made a wobbly journey to the shower. He found a

273

crimson dot on his leg, still tender from the hypodermic injection. He stood under the hot water for twenty minutes, letting his blood wake up.

Sorting out the reality from the nightmare wasn't easy. Just where did Linda Greer fit in now? She had zapped him with something—elephant tranquilizer, it felt like. Why? And where was she?

On her own, that's where. No Langley, no Peking. Wang Bin had become a personal project, but why? And how personal?

Stratton was angry, restless and, above all, baffled. She had let them get away. For whatever reason, that's what she had done. It was one truth that had survived the horrible night.

Stratton toweled off and pulled on a pair of jeans. He called room service and ordered a big stack of pancakes, three eggs and a pitcher of black coffee.

His options were dismal. He could run to the State Department and lay it all out. Someone very polite would call China, and someone in Peking would reply—very tersely—that the body found in the Ming reservoir *was* positively Deputy Minister Wang Bin; that no clay soldiers were missing from the Xian excavation; that no visa had ever been issued to an American named Harold Broom. That's what the Chinese would say—because they *had* to. They would admit nothing, because they could never permit themselves to be seen as fools.

And that would be it.

A better option would be confiding in old friends at the CIA. But what proof could Stratton offer? Vandalized grave plots? Hardly a red-hot trail.

It all came back to Linda. Was she in league with Broom and Wang Bin? Or was she trying for that solo coup that would edify her career—bringing the old Chinese bastard in from the cold? He remembered their dinner talk in Peking. Yes, that was probably it.

Either way, the lady had guts. Wang Bin was a killer, not easily induced, coerced or charmed. With some defectors it was easy. Bring them in gently. Pay them. Pump them. Pay them some more. A new name, a new passport, off you go.

274

Linda was wrong if she imagined it would be that simple with the deputy minister. He was the ultimate pragmatist.

Maybe she knew that. Maybe she was way ahead of him. I'm the one who's fresh out of clues, Stratton thought ruefully.

He wolfed down his breakfast and went downstairs. He bought a copy of the *Post* in the lobby and walked out into the sticky heat to think. There was an empty bench on the mall near the Smithsonian, and Stratton sat down. Hearty joggers and lean cyclists flew by him, a reminder that he did not yet have his strength back. The sidewalks swarmed with foreign tourists who seemed to walk twice as fast as everyone else.

Stratton imagined himself back in Tiananmen Square, where the order and propriety that ruled Chinese history seemed also to govern those who came to celebrate it. Here in Washington, among the functional granite monuments to democracy, there was a holiday festiveness; in China, among the wildly extravagant temples, sobriety.

To Stratton's eye, it was not merely a culture gap, but a canyon. Chinese tourists traveled thousands of miles just to stand where the emperor's scholars had once gathered in the Hall of Supreme Harmony. In Washington, people lined up for blocks to watch the Treasury print money. Talk about awe.

If Americans seemed transparent, the Chinese mind was opaque. For Stratton this had become tragically obvious, first at Man-ling—a fatal grant of trust to a young boy—and now, with humiliating emphasis, at Arlington.

Stratton would never forget Wang Bin's face as Stratton had aimed the gun. Such magnificent defiance. Stratton would have liked him to have begged for his life, but he would have settled for one tear from the steely bastard. A tear for his own brother.

Yet all that had shone in the deputy minister's eyes had been an iron, immutable spirit. Stratton despised it.

He sat on the bench, watching a group of young girls from a parochial school chase a runaway kite, their plaid skirts beating together as they ran. Their laughter trailed off after the kite string.

Stratton opened the *Post*. The front section was clotted

275

with the usual turgid political news. Stratton dismissed it and turned to the local pages to see if there was any mention of the grave robbery. There, on 10-C, a headline midway down the page grabbed his attention: ART BROKER FOUND DEAD IN BURNING AUTO.

The article was an Associated Press report from Grafton, West Virginia:

> Two persons were found dead Monday at the scene of a single-car traffic accident on Shelby Road, two miles south of Grafton.
>
> Police said the victims were discovered in a burning automobile after the car apparently had run off the highway and crashed. Grafton Police Sgt. Gilbert Beckley said that rescue workers who reached the scene were forced to wait for the fire to subside before approaching the car.
>
> Authorities have identified one of the victims as Harold G. Brown, an art dealer from New York. Police said Broom carried business cards listing him as an associate of the Parthenon Gallery and the Belle Meade Exhibition Center in Manhattan.
>
> The second victim found in the car carried no personal belongings and has not yet been identified, police said. The accident was reported by a Greyhound bus driver who passed the scene but did not stop.

Tom Stratton stuffed the newspaper into a trash basket, bought himself a lemon ice, and jogged exultantly back to his hotel.

Gil Beckley was not what Stratton had expected. He was not a middle-aged hillbilly with hemorrhoids, but an athletic young cop with a Jersey accent and two junior college diplomas on the wall. If Beckley felt it was beneath him to work traffic accidents, he hid the resentment well. In fact, he seemed pleased to meet this angular, quiet man who had arrived with information about the Shelby Road fatalities.

Stratton introduced himself and said, "I read about the accident this morning in the *Post*."

276

"That was the *official* version," Beckley said.

"What do you mean?"

"The two people in that car didn't die in any wreck. They were shot. Classic murder-suicide, I'd say."

Stratton was dazed.

"When you called, you said you knew something about the passengers," Beckley prodded. "Can you help us out?"

Mentally Stratton dusted off his story.

"Harold Broom was doing business with a good friend of mine. They'd been traveling together for the last week or so."

"Had you seen them recently?"

"Yes," Stratton said. "Day before yesterday. In Washington. They rented a car."

"So you think the other victim could be your friend?"

"I'm afraid so," Stratton said. "That's why I drove straight over here after I saw the story in the paper."

"We appreciate it," Beckley said. From a bottom drawer in the gray metal desk the policeman withdrew a stiff brown envelope. "How's your stomach, Mr. Stratton?"

Stratton took the envelope. His hands trembled. He scratched at the gummed flap.

He wasn't acting anymore.

"What was your friend's name?" Beckley inquired.

Stratton pretended not to hear. *Be there*, he said silently.

He slipped the photographs from the envelope. They were black-and-whites, the usual eight-by-tens. The top picture captured what was left of Harold Broom after he had been dragged from the smoldering car. His clothes dangled like charred tinsel. His chest and face were scorched; the flesh on the upper torso was scabrous. The face was raw, frozen in a death scream. The eyelids had burned away completely, leaving only a viscous white jelly in the sockets. Broom's outreached arms had constricted into the common rigor mortis of burn victims—elbows sharply bent, fists clenched in front of the face, as if raising a pair of binoculars.

Tom Stratton took a deep breath. He felt clammy.

The next two pictures, taken from different angles, were also of Broom.

277

"The next one," Beckley said, watching closely. "That's the one you're interested in."

Stratton looked at the photograph and nearly gagged. Through the din of his own heart pounding he barely heard Beckley shouting for someone to bring a glass of water.

The pictures slipped from Stratton's hand and drifted to the floor . . . Broom lying by the road, Broom face-front, Broom from the waist up . . .

And Linda Greer.

Stratton covered his eyes and moaned. His face burned.

Beckley stood at Stratton's side, a hand on his shoulder. "I'm very sorry," the cop said. "Have some water. You'll feel better."

Stratton scooped the photographs from the floor and, without looking, handed them to Beckley.

"Mr. Stratton, can I ask your friend's name?"

"That wasn't him," Stratton croaked.

"Him?" Beckley was bewildered. "But just now—"

"My friend is a Chinese man. Wang is his name."

"Judging by your reaction to that photo, I thought for sure that the girl was the one—"

"No. And I'm sorry I frightened you."

"Well, it was a pretty goddamn frightening picture," Beckley said. "I'm sorry you had to see it. Still, it's better to know one way or another. Did you recognize the girl?"

"Never saw her before." Stratton drank some water. "You say it was murder?"

"Lover's quarrel, the way I figure it. The girl was a one-nighter, a fiancée, a hooker—we'll nail it down eventually. She got it first, back of the skull, two rounds. Then Broom aced himself, once in the right temple. The gun was a cheap thirty-eight. We found it on the front seat between them."

Beckley reached into the same drawer that held the photographs. He slid a piece of notebook paper across the desk toward Stratton. "We found this in a briefcase that was tossed in some bushes near the car."

The suicide note had been written meticulously in black ink, each letter capitalized:

278

"DARLING I AM SORRY, I COULD NOT ALLOW YOU TO LEAVE ME. THIS WAY IS BEST."

One glance and Stratton knew who had written it. *I could not allow you to leave me.* Much too clumsy for a fop like Harold Broom.

"What about the fire?" Stratton asked.

"An accident. Here's what I figure: Broom pulls off the highway in a passion. Takes out his gun, plugs the girl, writes his farewell note, then checks himself out. Bang. Leaves the engine running and the goddamn catalytic converter overheats. Catches fire. The whole thing goes up in blazes. That's Detroit for you."

Stratton said, "I'd better go now."

"You knew this Broom character?"

"I met him only once or twice."

"A real asshole, right?"

Stratton shrugged. "I couldn't say." Suddenly he was in the line of Beckley's fire: time to go.

"What about your friend, the Chinaman?"

"I . . . I guess he's all right."

"I'd really like to talk to him," Beckley said, "your friend, the Chinaman. I'd like to keep it nice and friendly, too. Subpoenas are such a pain in the ass."

"I understand," Stratton said. "When I talk to him, I'll be sure to have him call you."

"Right away." Beckley tugged at his chin. "And you've got no idea about the dead girl?"

"No," Stratton replied. "I'm sorry."

I am sorry.

Beckley led him back through a maze of dingy halls in the police station. As he reached the front desk, Beckley realized he was walking alone. He backtracked and found Stratton at the door to the property room. Staring.

"It was in the car," Beckley explained. "Wrapped up in the trunk. Didn't even get singed."

Rigidly Stratton approached the Chinese soldier who stood noble and poised, an unlikely centerpiece amid the flotsam of crime—pistols, blackjacks, bags of grass and pills, helmets, stereo speakers, radios, jewelry, shotguns, crowbars. Each item, Stratton noted, was carefully marked.

The ancient Chinese warrior, too, wore a blue tag around its neck, an incongruous paper medallion.

"What do you think?" Beckley said.

Stratton was overwhelmed. He couldn't take his eyes off the imperial soldier.

"Well, I'll tell you what *I* think," the cop said after a few moments. "I think it's the damnedest-looking lawn jockey I ever saw."

CHAPTER 26

STRATTON spent the night in Wheeling. He slept turbulently, racked by old dreams and new grief.

First David, and now Linda.

He tried to convince himself that it wasn't his fault. They had argued under the oaks at Arlington: Stratton for vengeance, Linda for patience. Wang Bin was worth more alive than dead, she had said. "He's an encyclopedia, Tom. Do you know what he could do for us?"

"Do you know," Stratton had countered, "what he's already done?"

But she had been determined, and Stratton had underestimated her.

Now she was dead, and Wang Bin was dust in the wind, a clever phantom. Stratton was sure he'd already grabbed the money, and with the money came boundless freedom—comfort, respectability, anonymity. That's the way it worked in America. That's what the deputy minister had counted on. In his mind's eye, Stratton pictured the cagey old fellow in his new life—where? San Francisco, maybe, or even New York; an investor, perhaps, or the owner of a small neighborhood business. Maybe something more ambitious: his own museum.

Stratton was desolate in his failure. Without clues, without even a scent of the trail, he had nowhere to go.

Nowhere but home, back to doing what he should have been doing all along. And before that, a detour. A couple of hours was all he needed, a moment really. A chance to say goodbye to the man who had meant so much to him, and whose murder he had been unable to prevent. A taste of better times, something enduring and warm for a lifetime of cold dreams.

Stratton got an early start and reached Pittsville by noon. The moment he passed the city limit sign he pulled his foot from the accelerator, a vestigial reflex from his days as a student. Speed trap or not, the town was still gorgeous.

It was green and cool and hilly, a sleepy old friend. Stratton wished he had never left.

He stopped for lunch at the village sundry, not far from St. Edward's campus. The counter lady, a grand old bird with snowy hair and antique glasses, remembered him instantly and lectured him on his lousy eating habits. Stratton cheered up.

The campus had changed little, and why should it have? The enrollment stayed constant, the endowments generous but not extravagant. Ivy still climbed the red-brick bell tower, and the bells still rang off key. The narrow roads were as pocked as ever, and the college gymnasium—now called an Amphidome—still looked like a B-52 hangar.

Stratton discovered he was in no hurry. He was home. He allowed himself to be led by sights and sounds. On the steps of the cafeteria, a shaggy folksinger strummed a twelve-string and sang—Stratton couldn't believe it—Dylan. Stratton dropped a dollar into the kid's guitar case and strolled to the post office to read the campus bulletin board. It was another St. Edward's tradition.

"Roommate wanted: Any sex, any size. Must have money."

"Need Melville term paper within ten days. Will pay big bucks, plus bonus for bibliography. Reply confidential."

"I want my Yamaha handlebars back. $200 firm. No questions."

Stratton shook his head. Nothing had changed.

282

"You lookin' for work, young man?" came a gruff voice from behind. " 'Cause we sure don't need any more liberal agitators on this campus!"

Stratton immediately recognized the voice. "Jeff!"

"*Mr.* Crocker, to you." Crocker beamed and threw an arm around Stratton's shoulders. "How are you, Tom? You look like hell."

"You too."

"Editors are supposed to look like hell. It's in their contract."

"Yeah, well, I've been driving all day and I'm beat."

They walked the campus, making small talk. Crocker had been a reporter for the local newspaper when Stratton had been a student at St. Edward's. Now he was executive editor.

"They even let me teach a journalism class out here."

"God help us," Stratton said with a ghost of a smile. "The *National Star* comes to Pittsville."

They gravitated to the beer cellar in the basement of the cafeteria. It was five o'clock, still early for the campus drinkers, so Stratton and Crocker had no trouble finding a quiet booth.

Halfway through his first beer Crocker said, "I kind of expected to see you at the funeral."

"I couldn't come, Jeff. I was in China."

"With David? When it happened?"

Stratton told him what he could.

"It was such a shock," Crocker said. "The irony. After all those years, to return—only to die."

"He told me he was writing new lectures."

"Yes," Crocker said. "We did a feature story before he left. David always felt there was a thirty-year gap in history, at least for him. By going back he hoped to fill that empty space so he could bring his students up to date. The way he talked, the trip was purely a scholar's survey . . . hell, we all knew better, Tom. You should have seen how excited he was." Crocker polished off the beer. "He was packed two weeks before the plane left. Isn't that the David Wang we knew?"

"Orderly, to the extreme," Stratton said fondly.

"Yup. It was so sad. The service was very lovely."

"I would like to have been here, Jeff. You know that."

"Have you been up there yet?" Crocker motioned with his head. Stratton knew where he meant.

"No, not yet. I'll walk up in a little while. Is the house still open?"

"They decided to lock it up after David died. To protect his library as much as anything." Crocker winked. "The key's in a flowerpot on the porch."

"Thanks."

"On my way back to town I'll tell Gulley you're up there, so he won't get all worked up and send a squad car when he sees the lights."

Stratton said, "I'll only stay a little while."

"Stay as long as you want," Crocker said. "Don't cheat yourself."

Outside, darkness had gathered swiftly under a purple quilt of threatening clouds. Stratton set out for the Arbor with a quick stride, freshened by the cool stirrings of the birch and pine. All around him students lugging books hurried to beat the rain. Past the biology building, which looked and smelled like a morgue, the campus ended and the old trees gave way to a sloping, blue-green valley. All this had once been pasture, part of the old dairy David Wang had purchased after his arrival at St. Edward's. The valley was narrow and sharply defined, and halfway up the far slope Stratton could see the trees, David's trees, a lush wall of maple and pine and oak. At the top of that hill was the old farmhouse. Beyond that, on the downslope past another tall grove, was the bluff where David's coffin lay, near a lone oak. Stratton had no desire to visit the gravesite. An empty place, it mocked him in his nightmares.

The house was something else again—all the hours they had spent together there, the student and his teacher. It was there Stratton had shared his private agony—Man-ling—and tried to explain it over and over until David had gently touched his arm and said, "I understand, Tom. War."

"Murder." Stratton had wept. "*Murder*."

"I understand, Tom."

284

And from the confession had come a silent bond more powerful than any in Stratton's life. Often in the evening the two of them would sit on the porch, sipping tea, watching the hillside go dark. Stratton learned to talk of other things, and finally the nightmares went away. Because of David, Stratton had left St. Edward's a man reconciled to his past.

Now the wind came in fits, slapping at the leaves of the trees. Stratton jumped a clear brook and bounded up the hill in a rush toward the old clapboard house. He clomped onto the wooden porch at full tilt.

For a few moments he stood there, facing the Arbor, trying to catch his breath. The cool wind raked through his hair and made him shiver.

It was almost nightfall.

Stratton found the flowerpot on a freshly painted window-sill. The house key lay half buried behind a splendid pink geranium.

The key fit easily, but before Stratton could turn it, the door gave way. Crocker was wrong. It had not been locked.

Stratton groped in the darkness, cursing loudly when his knee cracked against the corner of an unseen table. His hand found a hanging lamp and turned the switch.

He stood in the middle of David Wang's library. Ranks of books marched from floor to ceiling. There was the burgundy leather chair with the worn and discolored arm rests. There was the giant Webster's on its movable stand; David would drag it all over the house, wherever he happened to be read-ing. And there in one corner was the newest thing in the room, a grandfather clock. Never on time, never on key, it had been a recent gift from the faculty club.

Stratton felt warm and safe in this place.

His eyes climbed to a high spot in one of the bookcases where David had tenderly arranged several framed photo-graphs of his family. Stratton moved closer and stood on his toes. One picture in particular intrigued him: two young men at the waterfront, arms around each other's shoulders. They could have been twins, they looked so much alike. Both young men in the sepia photograph smiled for the camera, but those smiles told Stratton which of them was leaving Shanghai Harbor that day. David's smile was bright with hope, his brother's strained with envy.

"Yes, it was a sad farewell."

The voice cut through Stratton like a blast of arctic air. He had no time to speak, no time to turn around. He heard a grunt, and then his skull seemed to explode, and he felt himself falling slower and slower like ashes from a mountaintop.

CHAPTER **27**

THE PHOTO ALBUM had a royal blue cover and a gold stripe. It was old and worn, with tape for hinges. The album contained faded black-and-white pictures, a half century old, of wicked, life-giving Shanghai. There were photos of New York in the 1930s as well, of a self-conscious young man in stiff white shirt and broad necktie posed before municipal landmarks: Grant's Tomb, the spanking new Empire State Building.

The album had been David Wang's favorite.

He would sit at his desk in the old farmhouse and turn the well-remembered pages. Before a man can understand where he is going he must first come to terms with where he has been. Sometimes David Wang found refuge in the album when he had a visitor. From it he would extract lessons that matched the problem the visitor brought. Once Thomas Stratton, nerves jangled, memories still too fresh, had sat before the cumbersome old farmer's desk and watched David Wang finger the pages to the accompaniment of a gentle, wise man's monotone.

"Ah, Shanghai, what a city it was, Thomas. A cauldron of

the very best and the very worst there is to life. Luxury un-
bounded. But for most, inconceivable misery. Too much misery. It had to change, but alas, it took the Communists to do
it. We are all a bit like Shanghai, aren't we? We all change.
Every day we are different. And if we are smart, smarter than
the Communists, we do not destroy the good. We destroy the
bad, edge it out slowly but surely—ruthlessness, cruelty, in-
justice, rash behavior. We build on what is good, like the
body repairing a wound, forcing out the infection, replacing
good for bad. Why, I remember as a boy in Shanghai . . ."

Through a cotton wool of pain and confusion Thomas
Stratton watched David Wang again at his desk, again with
the album in his delicate, thinker's fingers.

But it was not David. Not even the dulling ache in his
skull would allow Stratton to believe that. There was no cup
of jasmine tea at David's elbow. Instead, a coil of rope,
serpentine and menacing, lay on the scarred old desk. There
was no crackle from the old fire or soft glow from a desk
lamp, only the rattle of an old-fashioned kerosene lantern
perched anachronistically in one corner.

David Wang did not sit at his desk. David Wang was dead.

At David's desk, defiling his memory, his goodness, sat his
brother. His murderer.

Stratton would have sprung but for the bonds that held
him, hand and foot, to the old Harvard chair.

"He was a fool, my brother," Wang Bin said. "An arrogant,
intellectual romantic, a superior being who lived in a cage of
his own making—too smug to come to terms with reality. No,
reality might have been disordered, unpleasant, and that
would never do, would it? Of course not. Best to ignore it,
then. A fool . . . but you do not agree, Professor Stratton?"

"What are you doing here?" A wounded plea. Stratton
barely recognized his own voice.

"I could tell you I came for sentimental reasons. David told
me about this place, and what it meant to him. And all you
see around you in this room, Professor, are the memories of
a childhood we shared. I could tell you I came here to see all
this, to taste these old memories . . . but that's not the reason."

Wang Bin eyed Stratton. "There is a more practical reason for me to be here."

"Let's hear it."

"Soon enough, Professor." Wang Bin walked slowly around the desk. Knots bit into Stratton's flesh. He would break the chair. It was only wood.

Stratton saw the punch coming out of the corner of an eye; there was nothing he could do. A knobby fist smashed into his cheekbone. Stratton tasted blood.

"My brother," Wang Bin said calmly, "was a fool who could see the truth but chose to ignore it. Even as a child he was a sanctimonious fraud. One year older he was, that is all. Is that a century? Does one year bestow wisdom? Ah, but how David loved to play the elder, he the superior and I the inferior, the ignorant younger brother. My mother and father, they were fooled by him, like everyone else. . . .

"Once I broke a vase, a beautiful Ming vase. It sat there on a polished wooden table, beautiful and ludicrous. And I broke it, perhaps even intentionally. I smashed it into a million pieces." Wang Bin paused, with a curious smile. "Like all children, I was afraid of what my parents would do. So I told my mother that a deliveryman—an old man who brought fresh crabs to the house—had carelessly broken the vase with his sack. She believed me. But that was not good enough for my brother. He went to Mother and said, 'It was I, your eldest son, who broke the vase, Mother. Bin is only trying to protect me. I take responsibility.' Did they beat him? No, of course not. 'What an honest boy you are,' they said.

"And did David then beat me, or mock me to show me how much braver he was? No. He never said a word, nothing, as though by making me wallow in my shame I would drown. Just as he never said a word to me those days when I would skip my piano lessons and come back only to find him playing *my* exercises, so that downstairs my mother would hear it and think how dedicated I was, just like my elder brother."

Stratton said, "Why are you here?"

Wang Bin sat down once more at the desk. "We have time for that, Professor, plenty of time."

289

Stratton worked the knots at his wrists. "So you were a jealous little brother," he prodded. "That's your explanation."

"For murder?" Wang Bin seemed amused. "No."

"How could you hate him so much?"

"I am not sure I did. Not at the end." His voice was level, emotionless. "The day finally came for my big brother to leave for the United States. How sad was my mother, how proud my father. All the servants wept, and I wept, too. I wept for the joy of it, Professor Stratton. He was gone and I would be the elder son. My parents thought I wept from sadness. How I fooled them! My father took me aside and said, 'Bin, do not weep. You must be strong and brave like your brother and in another year, perhaps two, you will join him to study.' I never would have gone. To follow him. In anything. *Never*. How little my father understood of me, or of China.

"When my mother left for the Revolution I joined her instantly. Here was something my brother could not do, or my father. To fight a revolution. War is very exciting, Professor Stratton. Do you remember how the skin tingles, the senses race? I was barely sixteen—imagine, not yet sixteen!— and I would call my soldiers and say, 'Comrades, we must take that bridge. The people's struggle demands it.' And they would say, 'Yes, Comrade,' and they would march with fifty-year-old rifles into artillery and machine-gun fire. They would die unflinching, uncomplaining, with a mindless zeal that someone like you would admire. I loathed their stupidity. And I loathed the Revolution, too. Loved and loathed it.

"It should have been a bright dream, a dream so great my brother could never have known its like. Instead it was a theater of the absurd. 'Yes, Comrade, we will go off and die because the people demand it.' Is it heroic to roll in the mud like a pig when you can be clean, or to march through snow in bare feet when you can ride? It was a peasant's revolution. The peasants won. And ever since, in their bungling, they have disgraced the heritage of the nation with the most splendid history of all.

"The imperial times! The dynasties! That was when China

290

was great. That is when I should have lived." Wang Bin spoke with a trace of sadness. "In the times of the emperor."

"You'd fit right in," Stratton said. "A greedy old man who murdered his brother for profit."

"My brother. My *brother*."

The thumb and forefinger of Stratton's left hand were mobile now, and with them he feverishly worried the knots.

" 'Dear elder brother,' " Wang Bin recited in mockery. " 'I think of you often after all these years, so many miles away. I should like to see you before I die. It would be wonderful if you could come to China. . . .'

"And so he came, with his cameras and his loud synthetic clothes. 'You must help me, brother,' I said. 'I must leave China for reasons that you would not understand, and I must take with me what is my due.' I showed him my treasures in Xian. He stood beside me and looked at them."

"Clay soldiers, that's all."

Wang Bin stared at Stratton scornfully. Through the heavy drapes a gust of wind rattled the windows and Stratton heard the sudden assault of rain on the glass. He used the sound to mask his movements, tilting the chair just a fraction to give his feet greater purchase against the ropes.

Wang Bin said, "The soldiers are toys for children, a pittance. In Xian I showed my brother the real treasure. Even he was left speechless by its majesty.

" 'You must help me,' I said to him. 'With the soldiers we will have enough money to live in splendor wherever we choose. I ask but two things of you: That you allow me to hide you here in China so that I may leave the country on your passport. After two weeks you have only to go to your embassy to say that you lost your passport, and they will give you a new one. Then, once we are together in the United States, you can help me recover the soldiers and sell them. Is that too much to ask of a brother, after all these years? Help me, please. I have lived more than once as a peasant. I cannot live like that again. I will not.' "

"You should've known what his answer would be," Stratton said.

Wang Bin nodded. "He said, 'It is wrong what you are

291

doing, it is a crime. I cannot help you.' " The deputy minister shrugged.

"So you killed him." Stratton's thumb was abraded and hurt painfully. He wished he had longer fingernails. Keep him talking. Above all, keep him talking.

"I did not plan to murder him," Wang Bin said. "I had his room searched, and I had him followed because I was afraid he would rush to his embassy like an old woman. In the end I did kill him, but because I had no choice. In his death was the only means of accomplishing my escape and saving my treasure."

Stratton said, "You're a weak old man, Comrade. Even in death your brother intimidates you. Listen to yourself—the lies, the jealousy, the way you pervert his memory."

One of the knots came loose. The pressure on Stratton's right wrist eased; he twisted it back and forth within the growing circle of rope.

"But that's your stock in trade, isn't it, *Comrade* Deputy Minister? The perversion of history. That's why we're here."

"Ah, yes." Wang Bin smiled a winter's smile. "My artifacts."

"And your coffins!"

"They make excellent shipping crates." Wang Bin folded his hands but looked impatient. "Don't tell me you mourn the tourists, Professor. I did not kill them all. The first, a fat capitalist, died quite naturally. Death by duck, your embassy called it. A clever name for a common occurrence, I learned. And it gave me the idea. His was the first coffin."

The rope rubbed raw against Stratton's wrist. Feeling flooded back into his fingers. Another minute . . .

"You couldn't have done it all alone."

"Certainly not. I had many trusted associates—a doctor for the lethal poisons, welders for the caskets, diggers, of course. Fortunately they understood that I was directing a secret project for the Party. That lie was necessary, you see, to assure their complete loyalty and their perpetual silence."

"And your buddy, Harold Broom. Was he, too, working for the glory of the Party?"

"Broom was a worm, a drunken cheat. I chose him only

292

because David would not cooperate. Broom cheated me about money, and then he conspired with the Greer woman."

"Poor Harold," Stratton sneered. And poor Linda.

Another twist. Just one more. Make the fist small. Slide the rope over . . . there! Stratton's right hand was free. He clawed at the knot on his left wrist, blessing the rain pummeling the house.

"The Greer woman was another worm, wasn't she?" Stratton said harshly. "Well, she was the only who could have saved you, Comrade."

Wang Bin looked quizzically at Stratton. "It is not my salvation that brings us here, but your death. You must die as Miss Greer had to die. The difference is that you are troublesome and she was dangerous—more dangerous than you because she was smarter. She did not come as you have, thrashing about, making great noise and great threats. She did not care about smuggling or murder. Or morality, Professor. She had only one goal: information. I respected that. She was not like the professor of stupidity who seeks revenge for a pompous friend, or perhaps merely wants to cleanse himself of past sins. . . ."

Wang Bin allowed the phrase to dangle, watching Stratton.

"Did you think that I did not know about the pregnant peasant woman who was slashed from her throat to her belly? It had to be you. You were the only invader who escaped from Man-ling."

"I don't know what you're talking about."

"Oh yes, you know. Your face says so. You would have lived longer, Stratton, if you had been less impulsive and more clever. Miss Greer was very clever; she must have been a good spy. The way she dealt with you, for example, quickly and noiselessly, outside the cemetery. Then she rode with us, Broom and I, bought us dinner, talked . . . and made her proposal. It was very civilized. 'I know everything,' she said, 'about your brother and the soldiers. I know everything and none of it matters. If you come with me and talk to us—tell us what you know—you may keep the money and remain in the United States under our protection.' "

Wang Bin paused for effect, like one of the professional

293

storytellers who nightly enthrall the old men at dank tea-houses in provincial China. Stratton was picking up speed; his left hand was nearly free.

When Wang Bin resumed, he had become another person, a canny old grandfather. "For Harold Broom, who would have sold his mother, it was as though Miss Greer spoke from the heavens. He choked on his chicken dinner. 'Me too?' he asked. 'No prosecution?'

"Miss Greer smiled. She had a lovely smile, Stratton. Did you notice that? She smiled at Mr. Broom and said, 'Of course. You, too.' And I said, 'Miss Greer, this is a very fair offer. I can be of great assistance to your government. But please tell me so an old man will know your thoughts: What will happen if I refuse?' Miss Greer looked very sad. 'We would have to arrest you and deport you to China,' she said. 'but I am sure that will not happen. . . .' "

The rope came free. Stratton bunched it in his left hand so that it didn't fall to the floor. He calculated the distance from chair to desk. It would have been easy, except for his feet, still bound to the chair. If he launched himself pogo-style he might—just might—reach far enough to grab an arm, the shirt, the neck—anything would do.

Wang Bin said, "Of course I gave Miss Greer my consent. 'I realize when I have been defeated,' I said. 'Your terms are very generous and I accept them. Let us leave now.'

"Broom could not contain his glee. Miss Greer seemed surprised—it had been so easy. And after that, who could deny a confused and defeated old man the right to sit alone in the back seat with his thoughts? Miss Greer, you see, was not as clever as she thought. She never looked for a gun—and the price of that mistake was death. The world will think she died as Broom's lover, mistress to an international crime."

Wang Bin glowed in self-satisfaction: another victory, among so many.

Now. It had to be now. Stratton tensed to spring.

Too late.

Wang Bin must have had the gun on his lap the whole time. There was no other way he could have leveled it so quickly.

294

It was a fat, black .45, the kind the United States government issues its agents. Linda Greer's gun.

"Stratton, you have been maneuvering your hands as I spoke," Wang Bin said quietly. "If you move again, I shall shoot. I can do it, believe me. I spent many more years in the army than you did."

Stratton sagged, full of self-disgust.

"It's hard for me to believe you could actually be David's brother, or Kangmei's father," he said. "You have dishonored your country, your ancestors, your family, all in the name of greed."

"Ah, Kangmei, my lovely daughter. She excited you, yes? You were not the first, I assure you. It was probably she who made possible your escape. I should have foreseen such a thing, but it is too late. China's system will deal with her—for that, the system is efficient."

"This country's got a system, too," Stratton said. "You'll get caught, Bin. The spooks—Linda's friends—will snatch you up and turn you inside out. You'll tell them everything, too. You won't be able to help it—drugs, sensory deprivation, shock. When they're finished, you'll be as dead and dusty as your goddamn clay soldiers."

"I don't think so, Professor."

"Believe me." Stratton fought to keep his voice steady. "I'll make you a better offer than Linda Greer did. Go now. Run. Get out of here. I'll give you twenty-four hours before I come looking, and then it'll just be me. Alone. No police."

Wang Bin's response was icy, bemused. "I think not, Stratton. No one is looking for me now, and no one will. I drowned in Peking, you see. Drowned before I could see my ministry dishonored by two thieves—imperialist American running dogs who looted the treasures of the people of China. Harold Broom. And Linda Greer. When she is identified, and the emperor's soldier is found in the car, her superiors will understand where her true loyalties lay: she was a thief. I was very careful, Stratton. I provided all the pieces to the puzzle: the soldier, the suicide note and the list."

"What list?"

"The list of Mr. Broom's buyers, of course. Wrapped up

295

with the soldier, in the trunk of the car. You look surprised."

"No," Stratton said. But he was. Sgt. Gil Beckley hadn't
mentioned the list—he was an even better cop than Stratton
had thought.

"I had no need for the customers anymore, Professor. The
money is quite safe, and so am I. All clues point to Mr.
Broom and Miss Greer. There will be no pursuit. But you
must accept that on faith, Stratton. I have already anticipated
your own quiet removal."

"People will look for me . . ." But Stratton saw that it was
useless.

Wang Bin had won.

Thomas Stratton would be the last sacrifice of an ancient
funeral rite.

With the speed and deftness of a snake—a cobra—Wang
Bin's hand flicked the coil of rope from the desk. A noose
settled over Stratton's head.

Wang Bin hauled Stratton, wheezing, until he was suspended almost horizontally between the desk and the heavy
chair which held his feet. He squirmed and grunted, lamely
pawing at the rope on his neck.

"Something else I learned in the army," Wang Bin said.
"Careful, Stratton. The harder you struggle, the worse it will
be."

Stratton felt the rope slacken and instantly he was on the
floor, heaving. His shirt was soaked with cold sweat.

"Your original question, Professor Stratton: Why am I
here? It's very simple. I am here to borrow some tools."
Wang Bin stood up. One hand held the gun. With the other
hand he fitted a shapeless, faded hat—David's gardening hat
—onto his head. "There is a shovel out on the porch. You
will carry it."

Wang Bin wrapped Stratton's tether around his right fist
and pulled hard.

"Now we shall go for a walk, Mr. Stratton. There is something you must do for me before you die."

296

CHAPTER 28

THE PUPPET dangled waist-deep in a grave.

His shovel bit through sodden red clay made heavy and unstable by rainwater that sluiced into the pit. The puppet dug by the dancing light of two hurricane lamps, abetted by stalks of lightning that made him think of deranged Chinese characters.

The rain had stopped, but it would come again. Such was the promise of distant thunder, alien battalions marching, and of the brusque summer wind that chilled without cooling.

The puppet dug awkwardly, his head erect, the position enforced by the rope that arched from his neck over a limb of a lonely oak, and into the darkness below.

In that darkness stood Wang Bin, a furtive scout.

"Kuai-kuaide!" he barked above the wind. "Faster!"

Wang Bin jerked the rope, yanking the puppet's head, forcing a fresh sob through lips that begged for air.

Thomas Stratton was dying.

He was dying with cruelty and calculated humiliation that no Western mind could fashion.

297

He could dig, and die when he finished; a shot from Linda Greer's revolver.

He could refuse to dig and die now at the end of a rope, swinging as lifeless as yesterday's shirt.

But he could not die with any dignity, any pride. They had been stripped from him by the murderer who supervised his agony.

Professor of stupidity.

Wang Bin had been right. Stu-pid, stu-pid, stu-pid, muttered the wind through the Arbor.

The solution had been there all the time. In the grave of David Wang. It had been there from the beginning, and Stratton had not realized it.

The puppet did not dig to satisfy Wang Bin's sadism, nor merely to create his own eternal shroud.

He dug because there was something to recover from David's grave. Not an empty coffin, as Stratton had assumed, or even another carved soldier.

It was to his brother's coffin that Wang Bin had consigned his real treasure.

What was it?

Stratton was too dazed even to speculate. He dug mindlessly, an ashen marionette.

"Slack," he gagged. "More slack . . . I can't breathe."

The rope eased a grudging fraction, and in the next aching instant Stratton's shovel struck the lid of the coffin. The clunk was unmistakable, and it brought Wang Bin bobbing forward to perch at the lip of the grave.

"Careful!" he commanded excitedly. "*Xiao xin*, fool!"

Gradually Stratton uncovered the coffin lid, the cheap Chinese metal streaked with moisture and freckled with incipient rust. Like a teacher bestowing reluctant favor on a backward child, Wang Bin paid out rope to allow Stratton more movement.

Shovel plunging, the puppet dug his way around the coffin from corner to corner.

"*Huang di*," Wang Bin said, a reverent whisper.

"What is it?" gasped Stratton.

"Do not stop now, Professor. You are about to have the history lesson of your life."

Wang Bin positioned himself at the foot of the grave. The barrel of the pistol poked from his shadow, an ominous telescope on Stratton's midsection.

"Pull it out now," the deputy minister said. "Be careful."

Stratton staggered to the gentle slope of soil at the peak of the grave. He squatted in the mud, wrapped both blistered hands around the head of the coffin and pulled it toward him. The metal was slick, and Stratton's purchase poor.

The coffin edged a few inches from its bed and then slid back as Stratton's legs flew out from under him. The rope stopped his fall, but left him choking and scrambling in a tortuous pushup pose.

Wang Bin played out the rope and Stratton collapsed, prying with nerveless fingers to loosen the noose.

He lay there for what seemed like a long time, his lungs devouring draughts of fresh air. His brain teetered between blackness and reason.

"Pull, you must pull again," came the thin, ice-pick voice of his captor. "Pull, donkey. Pull."

Stratton levered himself to a sitting position, encouraged by a fresh jerk on the rope. "I can't," he cried. "I need air."

Wang Bin fired once. The bullet slapped into the mud between Stratton's knees.

The puppet lurched back into the grave. Moments later he had dragged the coffin out of the pit onto the muddy slope, bracing it there with a heavy rock.

Wang Bin inched forward along the side of the open grave. "Now break the welds, Professor. Use the point of the shovel." The rope hung loosely from his left hand now. The time for donkeys was nearly over.

Stratton found the welds soft and accommodating; a child could have fractured them. The lid of the coffin sprang open. Unbidden, Stratton stripped away a protective layer of gray quilts. Then he slumped against the grave wall to stare.

Russian dolls, he thought dully, a game of Russian dolls— one inside the other.

299

"What is it?" Stratton murmured again.

The gleam of Wang Bin's smile was visible in the darkness. "It is beauty, Professor—or can you no longer recognize it? It is beauty. It is history. It is mine."

Inside the coffin that was never meant for David Wang lay another coffin, cushioned by green quilts and chocked with fresh-cut wood.

The smaller coffin was exquisite, a masterpiece of lattice-work gold studded with gems—diamonds, rubies, pearls—that sparkled even in the sallow lantern light. It was like nothing Stratton had ever seen. Beauty and majesty unsurpassed.

"I know what it is," Stratton marveled. So this was the deputy minister's private excavation at Xian. No wonder David had raged. A crime against humanity, he had called it.

Indeed, it was more than that.

"Open it." The eyes of the old man flashed in triumph. The voice was placid, confident. "Open it, Stratton. There are latches on the side."

Stratton opened it.

He looked, then spun away and retched into the grave.

"*Huang di*," Wang Bin said. "Son of Heaven. Ruler of the Middle Kingdom. Beloved ancestor."

It was the Emperor Qin.

He lay as serenely as when his vassals had placed him at the heart of his colossal tomb, protected by his army of ceramic soldiers. Twenty-two hundred years ago.

The ultimate artifact.

Thomas Stratton had never imagined anything so macabre. It was hideous, a loathsome caricature of life, a rotted monster that did not belong on this verdant hillside, David's place.

No one would ever know what secrets the emperor's alchemists had employed to prepare him for eternal reign. But they had failed. They had not cheated time, but perverted it. A mummy can have dignity, like a man making his own grave. Wang Bin's emperor had none. It was a green-tinged parody of empty sockets, spore-covered bones, shreds of dusty silk and a rictus grin.

For this abomination men had died. David had died. Stratton would die.

Drenched, fatigued, bleary, Stratton looked up at Wang Bin. "Why?" he ask feebly.

"Think, Professor. As a student of history, as an observer of mankind." He held the rope and the gun where Stratton could see them. "You know what this is, Professor. It is the most cherished archaeological treasure in all China. Its value is both symbolic and very real. It is—truly—priceless. My government—" Wang Bin caught himself, smiled self-consciously. "Excuse me, my *former* government will do anything to recover this artifact. It will do anything, in fact, to conceal the circumstances of the theft. You see, Stratton, in China the scandal would be more of a calamity than the actual crime. There is no limit to what my former colleagues might do to prevent such a thing."

"So you're a blackmailer, too," Stratton said derisively.

Wang Bin stiffened. "I am not familiar with that term," he replied, testing the rope with a sharp twitch. "However, I do intend to seek what is due to me after a lifetime of devotion."

"The soldiers weren't enough?"

"Think, Stratton. There are seven thousand celestial soldiers. There is only one imperial casket. There is only one . . ." His voice trailed off in the night. His eyes fell to the grave, gazing at the withered creature within.

Stratton watched the gun and waited.

"By now they know," Wang Bin said smugly. "The comrades know of my achievement. They know what they must do, for I left precise instructions. The men who would have purged me are the same men who will beseech me for this treasure. They will pay enormously for my future comfort, and for my silence. And, in return, I will give them back their precious little corpse."

"And then you disappear?"

Wang Bin nodded. "I disappear from history. My name will never again be mentioned in Peking. Those who worked with me . . . I cannot say what will become of them. The

301

comrades who pursued me, however, will certainly suffer. They were too slow and much too stupid. Their defeat and humiliation is my vindication, Stratton. That much even you can understand."

Stratton understood. He understood why the celestial soldiers were not enough. He understood the genius of the crime, the genius of the vengeance.

And he knew why Wang Bin—so small and unimposing—frightened him so.

"Close the coffin now," the deputy minister ordered. "Remove it from the grave."

"I can't."

The rope cracked. Stratton was on his toes, then peddling in the air, gulping for breath. Then he was on his knees, on all fours. Dizzy. Dying.

David, help me.

"Now," said the brother. "Remove the emperor's coffin!"

"No."

For this Thomas Stratton would not die.

With all his strength he hurled a wet handful of dirt in Wang Bin's face and dove across the grave with a scream.

Sometimes you have to take a shot. It was something you were taught but never spoke of. Sometimes the only remote chance is to give the enemy one shot and hope to survive it. Bobby Ho had remembered, there on the bloody stage at Man-ling.

Diving low, Stratton survived because Wang Bin made a mistake. Logically, he should have jerked on the rope with all his weight; that would have snapped Stratton's neck.

But Wang Bin chose the gun instead. He fired reflexively, and missed by a hair's breadth.

The bullet scored the top of Stratton's shoulder and exploded in the grave behind him. When Stratton hit Wang Bin, the almond eyes were riveted in horror—not at his assailant, but at the coffins.

Then they fought along the rim of the pit. They fought like the maniacs they were, with hands and feet and teeth: Stratton younger, heavier, but exhausted; Wang Bin possessed of unquenchable fury.

302

Stratton finally saw it—a slow-motion frame—as they teetered on the lip, Wang Bin's hands like talons on his neck.

The bullet meant for Stratton had found another target: the emperor's skull. After twenty-two centuries his warriors had failed him. A traitor's gunshot had reduced the legend to an anonymous pile of powdered bone.

Not for that.

I will not die for that.

With power he had never known, Tom Stratton ripped free of Wang Bin's clinch. With the heel of his right hand he delivered a killing blow beneath the old man's chin, a blow that would paralyze the nervous system in the microsecond before it broke the neck.

Stratton hurled Wang Bin into the grave and fell back in the mud.

It was the rain that roused him—fresh rain, thunder and the wind that scoured his wounds, pierced his lethargy. Stratton was sick again. Then, as recognition returned, he cautiously crawled to the edge of the grave.

Wang Bin had joined his emperor forever.

He had crashed on his back into the coffin, smashing beneath him the delicate, lacework-gold bier. The impact had jarred the coffin off the rock and sent it sliding down the slope, back into the muddy tomb.

With a grunt, Stratton reached down and slammed the lid of David's casket, sealing the two sleepers. Then, determinedly, ignoring throbbing limbs and a bloody shoulder, Stratton set to work.

He had been digging for ten minutes when he heard the sounds. Stratton wiped the water from his eyes and paused to listen: branches chattering in the wind. What else could it be?

Stratton had covered the entire coffin with a foot of wet red earth when he heard it again.

Faint raps. Then a clawing, a muffled disturbance: the scuttle of rats in a barn.

It came from the grave.

Wang Bin was alive.

303

His body quivering, the rain cascading off his back, Stratton bent for a long and horrible moment over the shovel.

Rap. Rap.

"No!" Stratton screamed. "No! No, you!"

He shoveled relentlessly then, with black fear and desolate conviction. Dig. Lift. Throw. Dig. But don't think. Lift. Never think. Throw.

Stratton had no memory of finishing. There was but an hour until dawn when he levered the headstone back into its silent place, tucked a shapeless old gardening hat in his back pocket, and left the rain to wash away his traces:

✝

David Wang

1915–1983

Teacher and Friend

Rest in Peace

EPILOGUE

IN LATE SEPTEMBER, Thomas Stratton took his students to the Boston Museum to see a traveling exhibition of terracotta soldiers from the Qin Dynasty. They were impressed.

In October, he read a story in the Boston *Globe* that amused him:

China Won't Disturb
Tomb of First Emperor

By James X. McCarthy
Special to the Globe

PEKING—Chinese officials have a message for the Emperor Qin Shi Huangdi, dead these 2,200 years.

Rest in Peace, Emperor.

The emperor is remembered by history as the man who first unified China. In his spare time he built the Great Wall and buried alive Confucian scholars who dared to suggest that he might be mortal.

Since his death (natural causes) in 210 B.C., the emperor has lain under a gigantic man-made mountain near the central Chinese city of Xian. The area around the tomb has become one of the world's great archaeological digs, yielding more than 7,000 life-sized, priceless terracotta soldiers and horses who guarded the tomb as an imperial guard of honor.

Scholars had hoped that the Chinese, who are anxious to capitalize on the find as a tourist attraction, would soon begin excavations of the tomb itself.

Sorry, it won't happen any time this century, says scientist Gao Yibo.

"We are reluctant to open the tomb itself," he said in an interview. "To dig faster does not mean to dig better. We must work slowly to evaluate what we already have, and to preserve a legacy for archaeologists of the future."

Painstaking evaluation and reconstruction of the existing finds, which lie in three giant pits about two-thirds of a mile from the emperor's tomb itself, will take at least until the end of this century, said Gao.

"We leave the emperor himself to our children. He will be safe in the ground until we are ready for him," said Gao, who this month became the new deputy minister in charge of all of China's archaeological discoveries and the museums that display them.

Continued on page 16

In November, Stratton won permission from a bemused college administration, which had regarded him as a popular underachiever, to teach a course in Asian history, literature and philosophy. Stratton's detailed prospectus outlined what he called the Wang Syllabus.

In December, two visitors came. Stratton was expecting them.

"I'm Tony Medici, this is Jerry Flanagan. We're from the Smithsonian," said the dark one, a rangy man with sharp, veteran's eyes who wore a button-down shirt. The young one had red hair and a scowl he probably practiced in the mirror.

"I'm Mother Goose. Sit down."

"That'll save a lot of pointless bullshit." Medici grinned.

306

"We understand you have some information about Chinese artifacts . . ."

"Three big ones, to be exact," said Flanagan.

"That's what I said in my letter."

"Yeah, I saw it. We'd like those items back."

"How badly do you want them?"

"Hey, if you even *know* we want them you're in deep trouble. National security. We can put your ass away for a long time."

Stratton ignored the redhead. Medici was the pro.

"How bad?" he asked again.

"Well, it is a matter of some concern. We've searched, of course. Even got a hint that maybe one of our . . . uh, that a government employee might have been mixed up in it. You might even know the lady."

Stratton gave him nothing.

"How bad?"

"All the way up to the White House, since you ask. You got 'em?"

"I know where they are."

"How much?" Flanagan snapped.

"They're not for sale."

"What then?"

"A swap."

"For what?"

Stratton told him.

Medici blew air between his teeth. "I don't know if we want the merchandise that much."

"It's up to you."

"I mean, that kind of thing . . . it's out of style, isn't it, Stratton? These days we don't just sneak in . . ."

"You do it or I do it."

"I don't believe this," said Flanagan.

"Shut up, Jerry." Then to Stratton: "I'll have to check."

"There's a pay phone down the hall."

Stratton went back to marking papers. The redhead fidgeted.

"You an art teacher?"

"Something like that."

"Never did much for me in college."

"I know."

"When Tony comes back we'll probably drag you out of here in handcuffs. I'd like that, *Professor*."

Medici was back in twenty minutes.

"You've got a deal," he said without preface, measuring Stratton with curiosity.

"What!"

"Shut up, Jerry. There are some conditions, though."

Medici consulted a notebook. "First, we get *our* friends' merchandise back. Then we go lookin' for yours. It'll take some time."

"I know."

"There's something else." Medici read slowly from the notebook. "You must promise not to undertake, organize or direct any incursion into the People's Republic of China, or attempt in any way to enter the People's Republic under your own or any assumed identity, for any purpose."

"Tony, who *is* this guy?" Flanagan whined. "What's going on?"

"Anything else?" Stratton asked.

Medici mumbled. Stratton barely caught the words.

"They said to say please."

Flanagan coughed.

Stratton said, "Tell them I agree."

He handed the agents two sheets of paper. The name of Sgt. Gil Beckley was written on the first.

"Who's this?" Flanagan said, frowning.

"A cop in West Virginia. Be nice to him. A piece of your merchandise is locked up in his property room. He's also got a list that you'll find very interesting."

Broom's roster of stolen warriors and their buyers. It had been found in the trunk of the car with the last Chinese soldier, exactly as Wang Bin had planned. Stratton had phoned Gil Beckley to make sure; the next day, Stratton had written his letter to Washington.

"What kind of list?" Flanagan demanded.

"The best kind. Short and simple. It'll help you find what you're looking for." Not just the imperial artifacts, Stratton

308

thought, but Linda Greer, too. She deserved much more than a pauper's grave.

The second paper Stratton handed to the agents was as good as a map. Medici studied it briefly.

"Okay, brother, you got it. We'll be in touch."

Stratton walked them to the door. Flanagan left, shaking his head. Medici paused.

"I was in Nam," he said. "Fourth Division Lurps. We heard stories . . . well, I'm proud to know you."

Stratton said good-bye. He walked back to his desk and opened the middle drawer. The envelope was stained, dog-eared. It carried a Hong Kong stamp.

He did not open it. He did not need to. He knew what was inside. Six words that spelled two lifetimes.

"Thom-as, I cannot live without you."

One of the first group of American reporters to be based in China since World War II, William D. Montalbano served as Peking bureau chief of the Knight-Ridder Newspaper chain from 1979 to 1981. Montalbano, forty-three, has reported from more than fifty countries on five continents and is regarded as one of the foremost authorities on Latin America in the United States press. He is now El Salvador Bureau Chief for the *Los Angeles Times*. His major awards include the Ernie Pyle, Tom Wallace, and Overseas Press Club Awards, and the Maria Moors Cabot Prize.

Carl Hiaasen, thirty-one, is an investigative reporter for the *Miami Herald*. In 1981, he was part of a *Herald* reporting team that won two national journalism awards for a series of articles about smuggling and corruption in Key West. His reporting honors also include the Heywood Broun and National Headliner's Awards.

Montalbano and Hiaasen are also coauthors of the novels, *Powder Burn* and *Trap Line*.

THE
ROAD TO
RECOVERY

THE
ROAD TO
RECOVERY

How and Why Economic Policy Must Change

ANDREW SMITHERS

WILEY

Registered office
John Wiley & Sons Ltd, The Atrium, Southern Gate, Chichester, West Sussex, PO19 8SQ, United Kingdom

For details of our global editorial offices, for customer services and for information about how to apply for permission to reuse the copyright material in this book please visit our website at www.wiley.com.

Library of Congress Cataloging-in-Publication Data

Smithers, Andrew.
   The road to recovery : how and why economic policy must change / Andrew Smithers.
        page cm
   Includes bibliographical references and index.
   ISBN 978-1-118-51566-2 (cloth)
   1. Economic policy.   2. Financial crises–Prevention.   I. Title.
   HD87.S59 2013
   339.5–dc23
                                        2013026697

A catalogue record for this book is available from the British Library.

ISBN 978-1-118-51566-2 (hbk) ISBN 978-1-118-51567-9 (ebk)
ISBN 978-1-118-51569-3 (ebk) ISBN 978-1-118-74524-3 (ebk)

Set in 11.5/13.5 pt Bembo Std by Toppan Best-set Premedia Limited
Printed in Great Britain by TJ International Ltd, Padstow, Cornwall, UK

Contents

For Jilly, with love and admiration

Foreword

by Martin Wolf

Andrew Smithers is a truly remarkable man. He brings to his analysis of the economy and financial markets a combination of abilities that is, in my experience, unique. Notable in this list are intelligence, eclecticism, pragmatism and independence. Andrew is devoted to the facts, is never impressed by status and possesses both deep knowledge of financial markets and a penetrating understanding of economics. Above all, he has an apparently uncanny – indeed, downright infuriating – tendency to be right.

Yet, in truth, his tendency to be right is not uncanny at all. Andrew is so often right not just because he has great intellectual abilities but because he cares about being right. His record is a triumph of character. He has the abilities of a first-rate academic. But he has never been one. He is, as a result, liberated from what he justly condemns as the "scholasticism" of academic economics.

When I look back on my many discussions with Andrew over the last quarter of a century, I find myself reminded of Bertrand Russell's remark that "Every time I argued with Keynes, I felt that I took my life in my hands and I seldom emerged without feeling something of a fool." I feel the same way about debates with Andrew. But however foolish Andrew may frequently have made me feel, I know how much I have benefitted from his insights. Alas, I would have gained even more if I had paid his views even more attention than I did.

I first became aware of Andrew's exceptional qualities when I met him in Tokyo in the late 1980s, where he was then working

for the late lamented S. G. Warburg. I learnt much from him at
that time about what was happening in the Japanese corporate
sector and particularly about the implications of the extensive cross-
holdings of shares.

Yet Andrew's analysis first transformed the way I thought in the
mid-1990s. It was then that I read his work for Smithers & Co., his
recently founded research house, on the correct way to value stock
markets and the emerging bubble in US stocks. I found this analysis
both brilliant and persuasive. It influenced my writing on the stock
market throughout the decade. The fruit of this work was subsequently published for a wider public in March 2000, perfectly
timed for the market peak, as *Valuing Wall Street: Protecting wealth in
turbulent markets*, co-authored with Stephen Wright of Cambridge
University.

Andrew's introduction of "Tobin's Q" (the ratio of the market
value of equity to the replacement value of corporate net assets)
into the valuation of stock markets was a profoundly important idea.
It was a theoretically better-grounded complement to Robert Shiller's cyclically adjusted price earnings ratio. To me, the idea was an
eye-opener. It would have been an eye-opener to the rest of the
world, too, if more people had been willing to pay attention. But
it is hard to persuade people to change their minds if their salaries
depend on remaining un-persuaded.

In making this point, too, Andrew introduced me to the idea
of "stockbroker economics". That is the art proving that assets are
always cheap, however expensive they may actually be. But the
purpose of stockbroker economics is, he noted, not wisdom, but
sales. In the 1990s stockbroker economics needed to show extraordinary imagination, as stock prices soared, on occasion even suggesting that no equity risk premium was needed.

A particularly significant contribution of *Valuing Wall Street* was
the book's demonstration that the efficient market hypothesis does
not hold for the stock market as a whole, even though it does hold
for the relative values of individual stocks. The stock market does
not follow a random walk, but shows serial correlation, instead. In
other words, markets show trends. Sometimes they become increasingly overvalued. At other times they become increasingly under-
valued. Such bubbles can persist, partly because the cost of betting
against long-term market overvaluation is prohibitively high. In the

case of housing markets, it is effectively impossible to bet against overvaluation.

This argument demonstrated that, contrary to the conventional wisdom of economists, it was not only possible for markets to enter bubble territory but also possible to know when they were doing so. Andrew's conclusion was that central bankers were profoundly mistaken in refusing to identify and prick bubbles, relying on cleaning up the mess afterwards instead. In *Stock Markets and Central Bankers: The economic consequences of Alan Greenspan*, which was published in 2002, Andrew argued that the policy of doing everything to avoid recessions was a big mistake, partly because it created asset price bubbles. On the contrary, he argued, the only way to avoid the occasional huge recession was to accept frequent small ones.

I was not fully convinced of this proposition in the early 2000s. But subsequent events have, yet again, proved Andrew right and the world's central bankers (and me) wrong.

Andrew's ability to be both out of the mainstream and right (the former being, almost certainly, a necessary condition for the latter) was shown in smaller matters as well as such big ones. Throughout the 2000s, Andrew argued that UK fiscal policy was far too loose. On this, once again, he has been proved right. Along with that argument went the view that the UK and US were saving and investing too little, a failing that was masked by their (temporary) ability to run large current account deficits and so import capital-intensive manufactures. This argument, too, looks increasingly relevant and persuasive.

Readers should approach the present book, which Andrew has suggested may be his last, with this remarkable history in mind. Most will find its arguments uncomfortable. But they will also find them trenchant, original and brilliant. Above all, if history is a guide, they are likely to be proved largely correct.

The book's most original argument is that the "bonus culture" is creating a far bigger economic disaster in the US and UK than almost anybody has realised. Because leveraged options on the share price are such a large portion of their compensation, managers run their businesses not for long-term profit but for short-term return on equity. They achieve the desired outcome by buying back shares, so shrinking their equity base, and raising prices, so boosting profit margins. As a result, companies both over-save and under-invest. In essence, managers are rewarded for extracting short-term rents, while running their companies into the ground. One consequence is that US and UK businesses are becoming more leveraged, not less, as many assume.

This development, argues the book, puts governments in a dreadful dilemma. Without continued huge fiscal deficits, demand is likely to collapse. But these fiscal deficits may have to continue indefinitely. That threatens to rekindle dangerous expectations of high inflation. The problem, then, is that deficient private sector demand is structural, not merely cyclical. Policymakers consequently find themselves navigating between the Scylla of inflation and the Charybdis of depression.

To realise how Andrew reaches these and other disturbing conclusions, one needs to understand his starting point. His views on what has gone wrong in economies emerge from his ideas on what has gone wrong with economics. He states that the two major deficiencies of modern academic economics, a reliance on mathematical models which are sometimes untestable, and an insufficient attention to data, have become major obstacles to the introduction of sound policies. Overreliance on elegant models and indifference to data on how economies work are, in Andrew's view, fundamental to everything that has gone – and continues to go – wrong.

More broadly, the book focuses on six challenges.

First, it argues that the excessive level of debt needs to be brought down. Over time the tax treatment of debt must be changed, since it encourages companies to have dangerously high leverage.

Second, while the build-up of debt creates conditions for financial trouble, it requires a trigger to set off actual crises. That trigger is usually a fall in asset prices. Policymakers need to devote far more attention to the valuation of assets. In addition, argues the book, "quantitative easing" encourages the overvaluation of assets and so should be slowly reversed.

Third, the fiscal deficits of Japan, the UK and the US must be brought down without creating another recession. This requires that greater attention be given to the counterparts of these deficits, which are the cash surpluses being run by businesses and by other countries. What are needed therefore are reductions in fiscal deficits in Japan, the UK and the US, which are offset by rises in fiscal deficits in the rest of the world. Above all, there must be a rebalancing of the global pattern of current account deficits and surpluses.

Fourth, the reason fiscal deficits are likely to be needed is that the business sectors of Japan, the UK and the US now run cash surpluses that will not disappear without big changes in policy.

Fifth, banking is still a mess. Major reforms are needed to reduce the risks that the industry runs and to ensure that it becomes properly competitive. Among those reforms must include much higher equity and a complete separation of market making from retail banking.

Finally, argues the book, the need for better economic understanding is not only limited to Keynesians and monetarists. It is ever more needed among the anti-Keynesians, whose policies seem to rule the eurozone.

In addressing these six challenges, Andrew provides thought-provoking analyses of the consequences of corporate incentives. He analyses the mistakes of central banks in the run-up to the crisis. He discusses the fragility of banking. He looks closely at the excesses of leverage. He justifies the Keynesian response to the crisis, but argues that the wrong countries have, yet again, chosen to go in this direction. Meanwhile, Germany's failure to understand the need for higher demand is undermining the ability of the eurozone to escape from its economic mire.

In all, the book is a characteristic delight: wide-ranging, full of fascinating information, provocative and dismissive of those whom its author views as incompetent. Intellectually, Andrew takes no prisoners. Readers will often want to disagree. I myself am unpersuaded on a number of important points: I am not convinced that large fiscal deficits bring imminent risks of higher inflation or higher inflation expectations; I am not persuaded that quantitative easing is dangerous in the current circumstances; and, again, I am far from sure it will be possible to eliminate the bonus culture, even if it is as damaging as Andrew argues.

Yet, even when I disagree, I remember an important lesson of my experience: I am almost certainly going to be proved wrong.

This book is a feast. Enjoy the spicy food it provides.

Martin Wolf, Chief Economics Commentator,
Financial Times

1

Introduction

The world economy is badly managed and thus doing badly. The financial crisis caused the most severe recession since the depression of the 1930s. The fall in output has been arrested but the recovery has been disappointing. If neither the crisis nor the weak rebound were inevitable, we must be suffering from policy mistakes. Either economic theory is sound but being badly applied or it contains serious weaknesses. In this book I will seek to explain what has gone wrong and the steps needed to put the world economy back on track for a sustained recovery.

The errors of policy have their sources both from failures to understand and apply the parts of economic theory which are sound and from failures in the generally accepted theory, which policy-makers have sought to follow. The economic policies of the euro-zone fall into the first category. For the zone as a whole, short-term fiscal policy should be aimed at expanding rather than contracting deficits, and my view is probably shared by a majority of economists. But there are two areas where, I think, theory has failed. The first lies in misunderstanding the causes of the crisis and thus the policies needed to prevent its repetition. The second is the failure to recognise, and thus be able to remove, the obstacles that currently prevent sustained recovery in Japan, the UK and the US.

With regard to the crisis, there are many issues over which the views of economists diverge, and many of the points I will be making are shared by others. At the moment, however, I seem to be more or less alone in my identification of the problems currently impeding recovery, a situation which I hope this book will change. If I am correct, the vast bulk of the current debate on economic policy is misdirected and new policies are needed to produce a more satisfactory recovery in terms of both its speed and its sustainability.

I aim to convince the reader that the financial crisis, the great recession which it produced and the failure to generate a strong recovery are all the results of policy errors in the management of the economy, and I will rely heavily on data in my task of persuasion. I will use many charts because these are often the easiest way to communicate the data's messages. They will also provide pictures as I am mindful of Alice's comment, when looking at her elder sister's book and about to nod off to sleep to dream of Wonderland. "What is the use of a book," she remarks, "without pictures or conversations?"[1] Even in the form of quotations, I have been able to include only a limited amount of conversation, but to compensate for this and console readers for its absence, they will find plenty of pictures.

[1] From Chapter 1 of *Alice's Adventures in Wonderland* by Lewis Carroll.

2

Why the Recovery Has Been So Weak

We are now suffering from a weak and halting recovery. Chart 1 shows that among G5 countries only in Germany and the US has real GDP risen above the level that was achieved in the first quarter of 2008. Both the UK and the US provide examples of how unusual the recession has been, both in terms of the slowness of the recoveries and in the depths of the downturns. It has taken longer to recover to the previous peak in real GDP than on any previous occasion since World War II. Indeed, there are claims that the UK recovered more quickly in the 1930s than it has after the recent recession.[1] The US took four years from Q4 2007 to Q4 2011 to recover to its previous peak and the UK after four and half years has still not recovered to its Q1 2008 peak. In both countries the loss of output from peak to trough was the greatest seen in the post-war period, amounting to 6.3% of GDP for the UK and 4.7% for the US.[2]

---

[1] *"A funny way of firing up the locomotive"* by Sam Brittan, Financial Times (17th January, 2013).
[2] The worst previous post-war recessions were during the first (*c.*1973–1976) and second oil shocks (*c.*1979–1983); neither their length nor their duration was as severe in either country as the post-shock recessions.

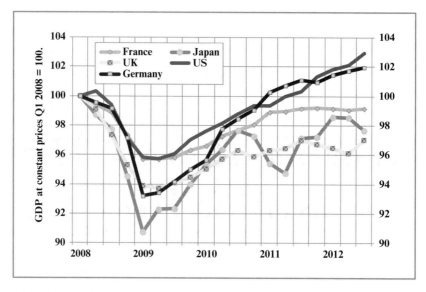

Chart 1. The Weak Recovery of G5 Countries.
Sources: National Accounts via Ecowin.

The weak recovery has occurred despite the most aggressive attempt at stimulating the economy, in terms of both fiscal and monetary policy, that has been tried since World War II.

Interest rates were kept low in wartime, but then rose and have now fallen back to their lowest post-war level in nominal terms (Chart 2).

The pattern is similar, though more nuanced and less marked in real terms. Chart 3 shows that for both the UK and the US interest rates were very low in real terms after the war and after the oil shock, owing to high rates of inflation. With these exceptions, current real interest rates and bond yields are at their lowest post-war levels.

Chart 4 shows that the pattern was the same for other G5 countries. Both real and nominal rates are exceptionally low and the fall in real rates is only constrained by the relatively low levels of inflation.

As Chart 5 and Chart 6 illustrate, the Japanese, UK and US governments' deficits have all risen to over 10% of GDP in recent years, while Germany's budget is currently balanced. France's deficit

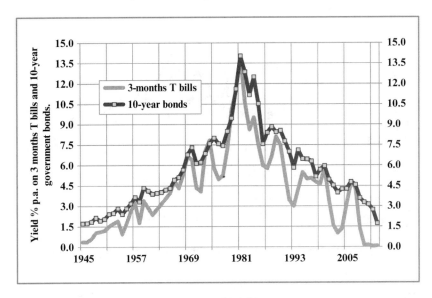

Chart 2. US: Interest Rates & Bond Yields.
Sources: Federal Reserve & Reuters via Ecowin.

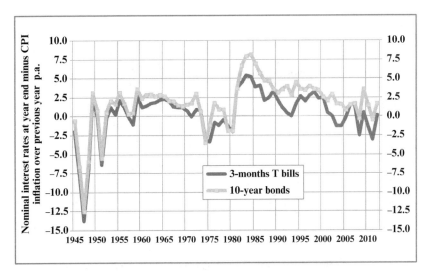

Chart 3. US: Real Interest Rates & Bond Yields.
Sources: Federal Reserve, Reuters & BLS via Ecowin.

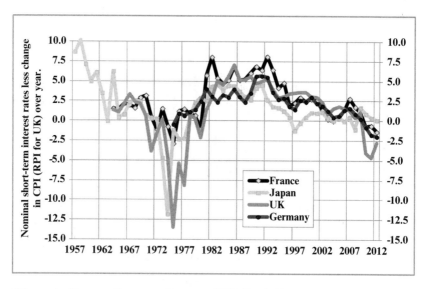

Chart 4. France, Germany, Japan & UK: Real Short-term Interest Rates.
Sources: Reuters & Federal Reserve via Ecowin.

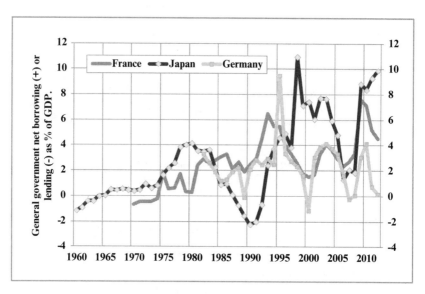

Chart 5. France, Germany & Japan: Fiscal Deficits.
Source: OECD via Ecowin.

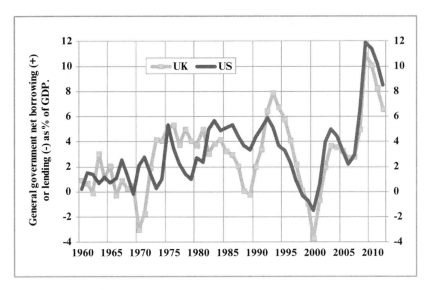

Chart 6. UK & US: Fiscal Balances.
Source: OECD via Ecowin.

peaked at 7.6% of GDP and is thought to have fallen to 4.5% of GDP in 2012.

Large deficits have not therefore been successful in generating strong recovery. Nor has the growth of individual economies been associated with the size of their deficits. Japan, which has the largest current deficit, shares with the UK the wooden spoon for recovery, and Germany with no deficit has achieved the best recovery alongside the US.

Neither fiscal nor monetary policy has therefore been successful in creating the growth rates that are generally assumed to be possible. It follows that either the growth potential is less than assumed, the policies are correct but have not been pursued with sufficient vigour or the policies are ill considered.

My view is that the policies have been the wrong ones and, although I am not alone in thinking this, my reasons seem very different from those of other economists who share my conclusion. At the centre of the disagreement that I have with those who favour more stimulus is why the economy remains weak. The central issue is whether it is due to short-term, temporary problems, which are

termed cyclical by economists, or structural ones which last longer
and tend to be more intractable. The key difference between my
views and the proponents of more stimuli is that I see today's problems as structural which need to be addressed with different policies,
while those who favour continuing the current medicine but upping
the dosage assume that the problems are purely cyclical.

On the other hand I do not agree with those who see the
structural problem as being a lack of output capacity. This in my
view is overly pessimistic. There seems to be plenty of unused capacity in terms of both labour and capital equipment; the problem is
that there are structural inhibitions to this capacity being used,
without creating inflation. We are not being held back by either a
simple cyclical weakness in demand or a lack of capacity to grow:
we have a new structural problem that we have not encountered
before.

As I will seek to explain, the key structural inhibition that is
preventing the spare capacity which we have in both labour and
capital equipment from being fully used is the change in the way
company managements behave, and this change has arisen from the
change in the way managements are paid. There is abundant evidence that a dramatic change has taken place in the way those that
run businesses are paid. Their incentives have been dramatically
altered. It should therefore be of no surprise that their behaviour
has changed, as this is the usual result of changed incentives.

For the economy as a whole, incomes and expenditure must be
equal. No one can spend more than their income unless someone
else spends less. If one company, individual or sector of the economy
spends more than its income, it must find the balance by selling
assets or borrowing from somewhere else, and the company, individual or sector that lends the money or buys the asset must spend
less than its income. A cash flow deficit in one sector of an economy
must therefore be exactly matched by a cash surplus in another. I
am not here making a forecast but pointing to a necessary identity
and one which it is essential to understand in order to comprehend
the nature of the problem that we face in trying to bring government budget deficits under control.

Although much that is forecast is not very likely, almost anything
in economics is possible, subject only to the essential condition that
the figures must add up. This is always important, and often neglected

by forecasters, but it is particularly informative when a large reduction in fiscal deficits is essential. This is because any reduction in fiscal deficits must be exactly matched by reductions in the combined cash surpluses of the household, business and foreign sectors. When the deficits fall, the cash surpluses of these other sectors of the economy must fall by an identical amount. The OECD estimates that in 2012 the UK and US economies had government budget deficits, which are also known as fiscal deficits, equal to 6.6% and 8.5% of GDP respectively. To prevent a dangerous and unsustainable situation arising in which the ratios of national debts to GDP are on a permanently rising path, these fiscal deficits must be brought down to about 2% or less of GDP. It follows, as a matter or identity, that the surpluses in the household, business and foreign sectors of the economies must fall by around 4.6% of GDP for the UK and 6.5% for the US from the level estimated by the OECD in 2012.

One of the major lessons of history is that economies must from time to time adjust to large changes and can do so without disaster, provided that the speed at which they are required to adjust is not too rapid. It will therefore be very important to make sure that there are smooth rather than abrupt declines in the fiscal deficit and thus in the matching declines of other sectors' cash flows. Unfortunately, ensuring that the adjustment is smooth is also likely to be very difficult. This is partly because the economy is unpredictable and partly because political decisions are often wayward. But it is also because the impact is likely to fall mainly on the business sector, and, if the hit is too sharp, companies are likely to respond by reducing investment and employment, thus causing another recession. The probability that a reduction in the fiscal deficit will fall most heavily on the business sector is shown both by past experience and from considering the contributions that are likely from other sectors.

In the past, changes in the fiscal balances of the major Anglophone economies have moved up and down with fluctuations in the business sector's cash flow, as I illustrate in Chart 7 for the UK and for the US in Chart 8.[3] On historical grounds, therefore, the

---

[3] The correlation coefficient between business cash flow and the fiscal deficit is 0.71 for the UK and 0.83 for the US. In each case we measure the relationship for the whole period for which we have data, which are annual from 1987 to 2011 for the UK and quarterly from Q1 1960 to Q3 2012 for the US.

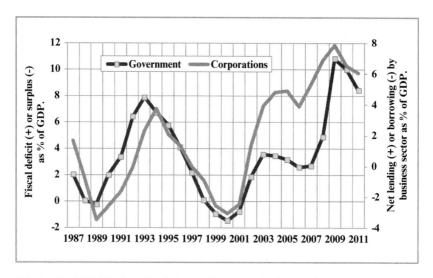

Chart 7. UK: Budget Deficits & Business Cash Surpluses Go Together. Source: ONS (EAOB, NHCQ & YBHA).

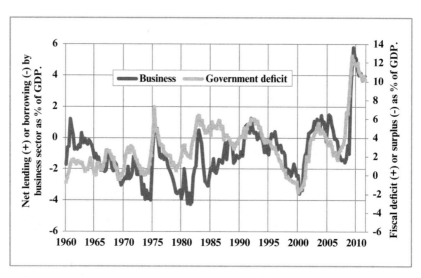

Chart 8. US: Budget Deficits & Business Cash Surpluses Go Together. Sources: NIPA Tables 1.1.5 & 5.1.

Table 1. Business Cash Flow Surpluses (+) or Deficits (−) as % of GDP (Sources: ONS & NIPA)

UK		US	
1987 to 2001	−1.65	1960 to 2001	−0.85
2002 to 2011	4.54	2002 to 2011	3.34

scale of the reductions required in the fiscal deficits means that large compensating falls in the cash surplus of the business sectors will be needed.

As Chart 7 and Chart 8 show, companies in both the UK and the US are currently running exceptionally large cash surpluses. It is the existence of these surpluses as well as their size which is unusual. As Table 1 shows, until recently companies have tended to run cash deficits. It is only over the past decade that companies have been producing more cash than they pay out, either to finance their spending on new capital investments or to pay out dividends.

The regular cash deficits shown before 2001 are the expected pattern. The business sector normally finances itself partly from equity and partly from debt. The extent to which companies finance their business by debt compared to equity is called their leverage. If, for example, half of companies' finance comes from borrowing and the rest from equity, the ratio of debt to equity will be 100%, i.e. debt and equity will have equal values. There are limits to the extent that companies can finance themselves with debt. Their leverage rises as the proportion of finance from debt rises, and as this ratio becomes higher so does the risk that lenders will lose money when the economy falls into recession. This puts a limit on the extent to which companies can finance themselves with debt, but this limit is not fixed. If lenders don't find that they are experiencing losses from bad debts, they assume that current leverage ratios are conservative and are willing to lend on the basis of even higher ratios of debt to equity. But this is a dangerous process, because high leverage increases the risks of a financial crisis and the risks that it will cause a deep recession.

Leverage can vary a lot over time, and I will be showing later that business debt had risen to unprecedented heights prior to the financial crisis. It has since fallen a little but remains nearly at record levels and it is almost certain that it is still dangerously high. We should therefore wish to see leverage falling and thus see equity providing a higher proportion of companies' financial requirements than has been the case in recent years.

It is easy to see how the growth of the economy can be financed by a mixture of equity and debt. In a long run stable situation the leverage ratio will also be stable. If debt and equity each provide half the capital needed, this will also be the ratio by which new investment is financed. However, the proportion of new investment that needs to be financed with equity will always be a large one. If, for example, over the long-term, investment is financed 60% by debt and 40% by equity, rather than 50% by each, the leverage rises sharply. In the first example debt will equal 100% of equity and in the second it will be 150%. This measure of leverage would thus be 50 percentage points higher than if the proportions financed by debt and equity had remained equal. In practice things can be more complicated, but the broad outline is nonetheless clear. Over time the capital stock must grow if the economy is to expand and, over the long-term, companies must therefore add to their equity capital at a steady rate. This equity capital is equal to the value of companies' assets less the amount that they have borrowed to finance them and is also known as net worth.

Equity rises from operations if companies pay out less than 100% of their after-tax profits as dividends and falls if they pay out more. Equity can also be increased by new issues and will fall if companies buy back their own shares or acquire other companies using cash or debt. Companies either run down their cash or increase their debt when they buy back their own shares, and this often occurs when they acquire other companies. It is possible to finance acquisitions with the whole cost being met by equity through companies using their own shares. In recent years companies have been using debt to finance acquisitions of their own and other companies' shares to a much greater extent than they have been making new equity issues and they have also, of course, been paying dividends. By adding up the sums of money spent on buybacks, acquisitions and dividends, and deducting any amount raised from new issues, we know the total amount of cash that companies are paying out to shareholders.

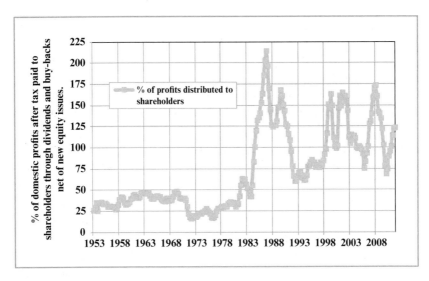

Chart 9. US: Percentage of Profits after Tax Paid to Shareholders through Dividends & Buy-backs.
Source: Federal Reserve Z1 Table F.102.

As I show in Chart 9, US companies, according to the official data, have in recent years been paying out in cash more than 100% of their domestic profits to shareholders. They probably don't know that they are doing this as the figures they publish as their profits are usually overstated and, as I will show later, amount to more in aggregate than the profits that are shown in the national accounts. Such a high level of cash distribution could last for some time, particularly if inflation were to be rapid, as this would reduce the real value of debt incurred in the past while the real value of companies' investments in plant and equipment would be unaffected. But rapid inflation is not stable and brings with it the need for a large expansion in working capital, which is one of the reasons that inflation has not in the past been associated with a decline in the ratio of debt to GDP. Indeed, as I will show later, the ratio of debt to GDP has not, between the end World War II and 2008, shown any sign of slowing whether inflation has picked up or fallen back.

Distributing more than 100% of profits to shareholders in cash, through a combination of dividends and buy-backs, which as Chart 9 shows is the current situation, may continue for some time, but it is not a stable situation.

Looking ahead, we can be sure, or at least as sure as anything can be in economics, that the UK and US fiscal deficits must fall and that this must be accompanied by a decline in companies' cash flow. Such a fall must come either because companies invest more or because they save less. If they invest more, they will need to pay out less money to shareholders in order to prevent their debts rising even faster than they are at the moment. If they don't increase their capital spending, a decline in their cash flow will mean that their retained profits must fall. Even if they don't cut their dividends, a fall in retained profits will mean a fall in profits.

When profits fall, companies usually distribute less in dividends, particularly if the fall takes place over several years and is not restricted to a relatively mild and short-term drop. So companies will probably cut dividends if profits decline. Any fall in dividends will increase the extent to which the fall in retained profits is reflected in a fall in total profits. There can be temporary factors that mitigate the speed at which leverage rises and this can defer the speed at which other adjustments have to be made. For example, last year the value of companies' real estate rose, according to the Flow of Funds Accounts ("Z1") published by the Federal Reserve. But without such fortuitous help companies must, at the current level of profits, cut back the amount of cash they distribute to shareholders or their leverage ratio will rise. If profits fall, they will have to cut back even more on the amount of cash they spend on dividends and buy-backs.

When governments manage, at last, to cut back on their budget deficits, companies' cash flow is going to fall. It is most likely that we will return to the usual situation in which a business runs cash deficits rather than surpluses. When this happens there must also be a large fall in the amount of cash that companies distribute to shareholders either through dividends or buy-backs.

I can see no realistic way in which it will be possible for the budget deficits of the UK or the US to come down to a sustainable level, without a large fall in business cash flow. As dividends move over time with profits, this fall must come from some combination of rising investment and falling profits. This poses a problem because falling profits naturally discourage companies from investing. Fortunately, history shows that the combination of higher investment and lower profits is possible, provided that the fall in profits is not rapid.

There are three ways in which profits change. One is that businesses can pay more in interest, either because interest rates rise or because they have increased their leverage. Another way is for them to pay more in tax through a rise in the rate of corporation tax. The third way is that they can have lower profit margins.

As leverage changes quite slowly, and interest and corporation tax rates are unlikely to change much while the economy remains weak, a fall in profit margins is going to be the main way in which profits will fall back. Fortunately, declines in profit margins have often, in the past, been accompanied by rising investment, provided that the falls in profits have taken place quite slowly.

I illustrate the usual lack of any connection between profit margins and business investment in Chart 10. From 1929 to 1939, the two moved together, but from the end of World War II until

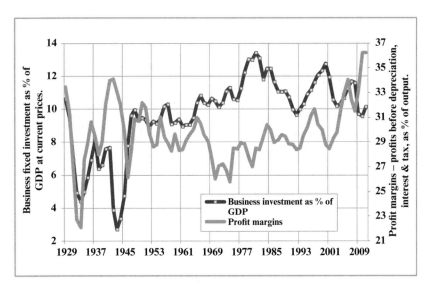

Chart 10. US: Business Investment and Profit Margins.
Sources: NIPA Tables 1.1.5 & 1.14.

Table 2. Correlation Coefficients between US Corporate Profit Margins and Non-residential Fixed Investment as % GDP 1929 to 2011 (Sources: NIPA Tables 1.1.5 & 1.14)

	Contemporary	Investment one year later
1929 to 2011	0.02	−0.03
1947 to 2011	−0.14	−0.07
1929 to 1969	0.11	−0.01
1970 to 2011	−0.24	−0.09
1929 to 1939	0.84	0.89

1980, profit margins were trending downwards while business investment was rising, and since 1980 things have moved in the opposite direction, with profit margins rising and investment falling back. The obvious inference is that investment can rise independently of changes in profit margins, provided that these do not change too quickly, and this conclusion is supported by statistical tests.

In Table 2, I show the relationship between profit margins and business investment and I compare the way they have risen and fallen in the same year. As a check to see if a change in profit margins has a delayed impact, I also compare changes in margins with changes in investment a year later. The statistics show that there has been no long-term relationship covering the whole period for which data are available from 1929 to 2011, or any shorter term one during the post-war period. There was, however, a strong relationship during the decade from 1929 to 1939. As this was the period when profit margins narrowed sharply, it is reasonable to conclude that investment can rise despite declines in margins, provided that the falls are not too steep.

Economic policymakers face the difficult task of bringing down the fiscal deficit to a manageable level without throwing the developed world back into recession. An essential requirement for this is to bring down profit margins slowly while at the same time encouraging companies to increase their investment in plant and equipment. As Table 2 shows, history suggests that this can be achieved, but it has become much more difficult than before because companies, at least in the UK and the US, behave differently today than they did in the past. The change is recent having become clear only over the past decade. It is thus a 21st-century phenomenon.

Companies in both the UK and the US are behaving in a different way today from the way they used to do and in a different way from companies in other major economies. The evidence for this change is very strong, but I have found that it is difficult to get the subject discussed and it is not yet therefore generally acknowledged by economists.

The behaviour of companies depends on the decisions of their managements, and although these can change for a variety of reasons, including fashion, the most likely cause, and the one that applies in this instance, is that they have incentives to behave differently. Over the past 20 years, there has been a profound change in the way that management is paid. Basic salaries have shot up, but bonuses have increased even faster, to the point where they dominate the incomes of the senior people running firms. The average length of time for which senior management hold onto their jobs has also fallen and those who wish to get rich, and there are very few, if any, that don't, have a great opportunity to do so but only a little time.

Since the future is unpredictable, managements have to take decisions on the basis of inadequate information. Different types of decisions involve different types of risk. A decision to invest in more equipment is usually necessary to enable companies to increase output, at least over the longer term, and to reduce their production costs. When investment is made, the equipment that is installed embodies the latest available technology, but as technology improves new investment is usually, though not always, needed to improve productivity.[4] Expenditure on new capital thus enables companies to grow over time and to lower their production costs. It reduces their long-term risks, as if they fail to invest when other companies are doing so they are in danger of becoming less competitive and losing market share. But these long-term potential benefits, even if hopes are realised, come at a short-term cost. Investment requires

---

[4] I do not wish to underrate the scope for improvements in productivity that can come from learning on the job, which is admirably set out in *The Free-Market Innovation Machine* by William J. Baumol, Princeton University Press (2002), but major improvements require new plant in which new technology is imbedded.

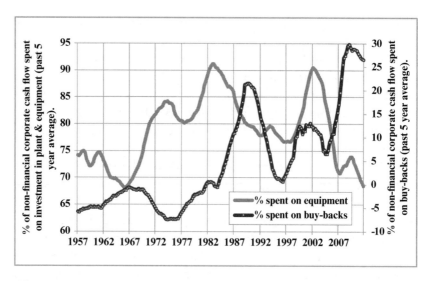

Chart 11. US: Management Prefers Buy-backs to Investment in Plant & Equipment.
Source: Federal Reserve Z1 Table F.102.

money, and even when debt is cheap, this money cannot be used both for long-term investment and to buy back shares.

Faced with this choice, managements today have a much greater incentive than they had in the past to prefer buy-backs to investing in new equipment, and Chart 11 shows that they are responding to the change in incentives. Since 2008, the proportion of cash flow invested in capital equipment is the lowest on record and the proportion spent on buy-backs is at or near its highest level.

Managements must also take decisions about their companies' pricing policies. In the short-term a decision to hold or increase prices is unlikely to result in lower profits. Profits will usually fall when prices are cut, because the improvement in sales is unlikely to be sufficient to offset the short-term impact on revenue. A failure to cut prices can on occasion be even more damaging to profits. But while this is often the case over the long-term, since it is liable to cause a loss of market share, it is less likely in the short-term and only occurs in the short-term when the volume of sales is highly sensitive to the price demanded. This is the case for commodities, where one producer has to accept the market price and cannot sell his product at all if he seeks to charge more than that. But the volume of sales is seldom very sensitive to price in the short-term for most goods and services. It is only when demand is so weak that there are many businesses with abundant spare capacity that buyers can easily switch large orders to other suppliers when their existing sources seek to keep their prices high. It is therefore common for a failure to cut prices to be the lesser of the two evils in the short-term, and the greater of the two over the longer term and, of course, future benefits are always less certain the more distant they are. The risks of holding up prices vary among businesses. They are most clear in the case of standard items where the products of two companies can be readily compared with each other, such as diesel fuel of a set grade. But it is much more difficult to compare prices of two restaurants where the table service and cooking quality cannot be the same. Decisions about prices are similar to those about investment in that the short-term and long-term risks involved are different. Maintaining or increasing prices runs the risk of a long-term loss of market share, while reducing them runs the risk and usually the probability of a cut in short-term profits.

As bonuses have come to dominate their pay, senior managements have changed the way they assess the risks that they take. The size of bonuses depends on the assumed success of the management. This is usually measured either by changes to earnings per share (i.e. the profit after tax as a ratio of the number of shares outstanding, which can rise if profits go up or the number of shares falls) or the ratio of profits after tax to net worth (i.e. the return on corporate equity, known as the ROE), or by an increase in share prices. The result of the increased importance of bonuses and the use of these measures of performance is that managements are now less inclined to take short-term risks, such as cutting profit margins, and more inclined to take the longer-term risks involved in lower investment and the possible loss of market share that will result from higher margins. Bonuses rise when profits get a short-term kick from higher prices and usually when acquisitions of other companies are made, because the increase in the added interest payments on the new debt, after tax, is usually less than the increase in the profits after tax of the company acquired. It is similar with buy-backs, which usually increase earnings per share. These benefits depend on the fact that companies pay corporation tax on their net profits, after the cost of interest payments has been deducted. This encourages companies to use debt rather than equity to finance their businesses. As our current problems are largely due to the excessive building up of debt, allowing interest to be deducted as an expense before the liability to corporation tax is calculated is both dangerous and absurd.

Not investing usually involves little short-term risk, but a considerable longer-term one, while maintaining profit margins is the exact opposite. Its long-term risk can be great as it makes a loss of market share more likely, but it is much less risky in terms of the impact on profits in the short-term than allowing margins to narrow. Management weighs up these risks in terms of their own interests, and changes in the way they are paid have changed their assessment of these risks. As a result companies invest less and have higher profit margins than they would have done in similar circumstances before the bonus culture so dramatically changed the way managements were paid.

It is therefore likely that the behaviour of companies will have altered as management incentives have changed and the data show that this is exactly what has happened. There are three important ways in which we can observe this transformation.

One dramatic illustration of how managements behave differently today compared with formerly is in the way US companies publish their profits.

Whether bonuses depend on changes in earnings per share, return on equity or share prices, management is paid more if profits rise sharply in the short-term than if they are stable. It therefore pays management to have very volatile profits. When new managements arrive they will wish the profits to be low and then rise sharply. Even when management is not changed, the basis on which bonuses are paid is often rebased. The excuse made is that managements will not have an incentive to try hard if a fall in profits has made the achievement of their bonus targets unlikely.

It therefore pays management to have volatile profits. Chart 12 shows this has been the result. In the chart I compare the changes in the earnings per share published by listed companies included in the S&P 500 index, with changes in the profits after tax of US companies shown in the national income and product accounts (NIPA). The chart shows that the volatilities of both were very

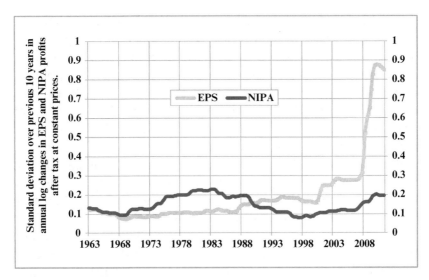

Chart 12. US: Volatility of S&P 500 EPS Compared with Volatility of NIPA Profits after Tax.
Sources: Standard & Poor's, NIPA Table 1.14 & BLS.

similar until about 2000, when the volatility of published profits rose dramatically and over the past decade has been more than four times more volatile than US profits after tax, as shown in the NIPA.[5]

I have not been able to find long-term data to test whether the rise in the relative volatility of the published profits of listed companies is limited to the US. I have not therefore been able to judge whether there has been a similar divergence in the volatilities of profits as shown in the national accounts and those published by quoted companies in France, Germany, Japan or the UK.

[5] I have measured volatility in real terms so that the results are not affected by changes in the rate of inflation. The measure of volatility is the standard deviation over 10 years of the log changes for each quarter over the previous 12 months for both EPS on the S&P 500 and profits after tax from NIPA Table 1.14. I have used 12 months' rather than one quarter's figures because there are no seasonal adjustments to the EPS data on the S&P 500 and using quarterly figures would confuse the picture by introducing some season volatility. The first 10-year period for which data are available is that ending Q1 1963 and the most recent that ending Q4 2012.

The marked ways in which profits published by companies have differed from those in the national accounts can only be possible if there is considerable scope for companies to adjust the profits they publish. This has always existed but has certainly become greater in recent years, owing to the change in accounting from "marked to cost" to "marked to market". If assets are recorded at their cost of production, then the profits published will in general be very similar to those found in the NIPA. Under "marked to market" accounting, profits can be marked up through increasing the assumed value of an asset, even without that asset needing to be sold. When this happens there will be large differences in the profits published by companies and those published in the NIPA.

In Q4 2008 companies in the S&P 500 published large losses. In the national accounts, profits were lower but they still amounted to $100 bn after tax. The difference between the change in published profits and those in the NIPA was largely due to write-offs. These are only found in the profits published by companies and have no equivalent in the national accounts and occur when companies decide to write down the value of their assets. Since profits over time are the difference between recorded costs and sales, these write-downs in the profits published by companies amount either to an admission that profits have been overstated in the past or to a promise that the managements will seek to overstate profits in the future.

It is very important for many people, including policymakers as well as investors, to understand the difference between the profits published by companies and those shown in the national accounts. I shall therefore be discussing the problem in more detail later. At this stage, however, it is worth noting that it is much more likely that the national accounts will provide a better guide to the true profits being made by companies than anything published by the companies themselves. National accountants do not have the incentives that encourage those in the private sector to misstate them. No bonuses are paid by the Bureau of Economic Analysis, which published the NIPA, if GDP or profits rise. There is also an important check on the validity of NIPA profits, which has no counterpart in any check that can be made on the truthfulness and accuracy of the profits published by companies. GDP can be calculated in three different ways – through measuring output, income or expenditure – and the result must always be the same whichever system of measurement is used. There can be discrepancies between these different measures, but these are always small and if they were large would alert the national accountants to the probability that something was being badly measured. Profits are an important part of the total income of a country. In the US, broadly-defined profits before depreciation, interest and tax payments amount to around 15% of GDP, and if profits in the national accounts had fallen in Q4 2008 by as much as the decline in the published profits of companies, there would have been a far greater, and indeed generally incredible, fall in the recorded output of the economy and the spending of individuals and business.[6]

The change in the way the profits of US companies are published, from marking to cost to marking to market, has several bad consequences. First, it makes the figures even less reliable than they were before. Second, it makes it probable that in the next serious downturn in the profits recorded in the national accounts there will a much greater fall in the profits published by companies. This is because it is in the interests of management to accentuate the volatility of the profits they publish. Falling profits are usually accompanied by falls in the stock market and as the next fall in published profits is likely to be much greater than the fall in the profits shown in the national accounts this is likely to accentuate the extent of the next major stock market decline and thereby increase the risks of another financial crisis. Since companies probably believe, or at least half believe, in the validity of the profits published by others even if not in the ones they publish themselves, this is likely to reduce even more than before the level of business investment and thus add to the depth of the next recession.

It used to be said, "He was dropped on his head when young and believed what he read in the Sunday newspapers." Today it would seem appropriate to include company profit and loss accounts along with the Sunday newspapers.

[6] On reasonable but necessarily rough assumptions, the fall in GDP in Q4 2008 from Q3, which was recorded as 2.3%, would have been more than 12% had the published profits of companies given an accurate guide to the true change in GDP.

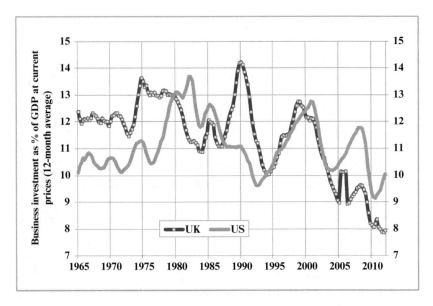

Chart 13. UK & US: Business Investment.
Sources: ONS (NPEK & YWBA) & NIPA Table 1.1.5.

Another way in which corporate behaviour has changed is in the level of spending on plant and equipment. Business investment normally rises and falls with the strength of the economy. Recently, however, in both the UK and the US investment has been on a declining trend, as Chart 13 shows, and has been lower in each cycle than would otherwise have been expected. There has been a downward trend in the level of investment, in addition to the swings expected because of the ups and downs of the economic cycle.

If managements take a long-term rather than a short-term view they will favour investments which boost the long-term strength and viability of their company; if they take a short-term view they will prefer to spend cash on share buy-backs. Comparing the amount of money which companies have spent on these two different forms of investment is therefore a way to judge managements' time horizons. The data, which I show in Chart 14, give a strong indication that managements have been taking an increasingly short-term view when deciding whether to invest in their companies' long-term futures or to return cash to shareholders.

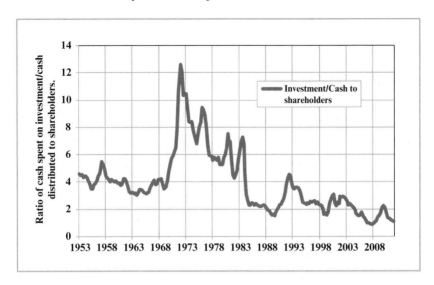

Chart 14. US Non-financial Companies: Management Horizon – Long-term vs Short.
Source: Federal Reserve Z1 Table F.102.

The increasingly short-term horizon used by UK and US managements with regard to their decisions on capital spending has resulted in the fall in business investment relative to GDP that I illustrated in Chart 13. However, as investment rises and falls with the cyclical state of the economy these fluctuations need to be disentangled from the underlying trend. In order to do this Chart 15 compares, for the US, the level of business investment with the "output gap", which is the estimate, made in this instance by the OECD, of the cyclical state of the economy.

In 1981 and in 2009, the US economy was, according to the OECD's estimates, operating at a similar and rather low level of its potential. Over the same period, business investment fell by three percentage points of GDP. Chart 15 therefore supports the view that business investment has not just followed its usual pattern of rising and falling with the swings in the cycle, but has been declining on a trend basis as well.

Chart 16 makes a similar comparison for the UK and shows the same pattern with investment rising and falling with cyclical

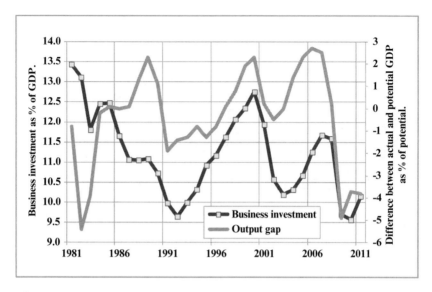

Chart 15. US: Business Investment & Output Gaps.
Sources: OECD Economic Outlook Vols 64 & 90 & NIPA Table 1.1.5.

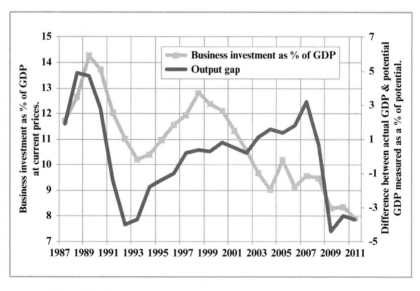

Chart 16. UK: Business Investment & the Output Gap.
Sources: ONS & OECD Economic Outlook Vols 68 & 90.

changes in the economy, but also showing a falling overall trend. For example, business investment was more than two percentage points of GDP lower in 2011 than it was in 1993, although the OECD estimated that the output gap was the same in both years.

It is of course possible that current estimates of the output gap are wrong. The impact of this depends on the direction in which the estimates err. If the output gap is less than calculated then the level of underinvestment is even greater. It is only when the output gap is even greater than estimated that the current level of investment can be considered in line with past corporate behaviour. But if this were the case then, as I will be explaining in more detail later, inflation would be falling at a faster rate than forecast, but it has been greater rather than weaker than expected. In so far as the OECD's estimates of the output gap are criticised, the overwhelming direction of the criticism is that they are overestimating the output gap. It is therefore extremely improbable that the weakness of current business investment can be explained by assuming that the output gap is much higher than the level assumed by the OECD.

Economic theory holds that for mature economies the share of output going to labour or to capital is stable over time and will therefore rotate around a stable average. This theory is supported by the data, particularly for the US, where we have data annually since 1929 and quarterly since 1952, which I illustrate in Chart 17. Standard statistical tests confirm that US profit margins have been "mean reverting".[7] US profit margins are currently at their highest recorded level and thus likely to fall substantially.

The prospect of falling profit margins is naturally unwelcome to investment bankers, and I have seen several papers by analysts arguing either that they are not high or that they will not fall. In none of the papers that I have read do the authors refer to the underlying economic theory let alone seek to show that it is wrong. This reticence can be attributed either to the fact that the analysts are ignorant of the theory or to the hope that their readers are. Kind people will wish to assume that ignorance rather than an attempt at deception lies behind this reticence.

---

[7] These are set out in Appendix 1.

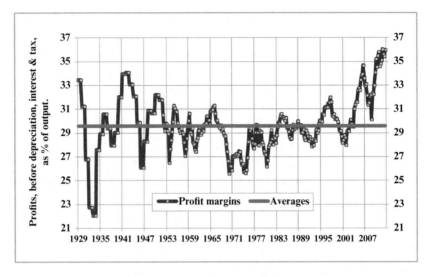

Chart 17. US: Profit Margins 1929 to Q3 2012.
Source: NIPA Table 1.14.

Just as GDP can be measured in terms of output, income or
expenditure, so the output of companies has to equal the income
of those who produce it. This income must, in some proportion or
other, go to those who provide the labour and those who provide
the capital. The theory requires that the share going to labour, by
way of employee compensation, and the balance, which is the share
to profits, should be stable over time. The labour share and profit
margins, which together must add up to 100% of output, must both
vary around their average. When profit margins are above average,
they will tend to fall over time. When they are low, they are likely
to rise. Both the labour and the profit share of output thus tend
to be pulled back to their average. They are therefore mean
reverting.

The theory that profit margins are mean reverting depends on
one single assumption, but the claim is a valid scientific statement
since it can be tested and, as the tests show, will be proved robust.
The assumption is that employing more people or increasing the
amount of capital will, over the short-term while there is no change
in the available technology, reduce the efficiency of production. In

the event that more people are employed and there is no change in the amount of capital, output will rise but it will rise by less, proportionately, than the increase in the numbers employed. In these circumstances the productivity of labour, which can be measured either as the output per person or per hour worked, will fall. In a similar way, adding to the stock of capital without employing more people can increase output, but not proportionately as much as the increase in the amount of capital. This situation, in which adding one factor of production, either capital or labour, disproportionately to the other, reduces the overall level of efficiency and is said to lower "total factor productivity" and is described as showing diminishing returns to scale.

As technology improves, real wages will also rise and the increase will match the improvement in labour productivity that results from the introduction of the new technology. But the return on capital does not rise over time as productivity improves. For example, we have data for the US going back to 1801 which show that the real return on equity has been stable and mean reverting around 6%. Over the same period we have had a very large rise in labour productivity and real wages.

If this assumption of diminishing returns to scale is sensible, and it seems to me to be very hard to argue against it being so, then it can be easily shown that the share of the income and thus of output that goes to labour or to profits will be stable. As Chart 17 showed, this has seemed to work in practice as well as in theory for the US.

Getting data from other countries is more difficult. I show in Chart 18 the data for the UK. These are worse than those for the US as they only seem to be available on an annual basis and are only available since 1987 and up to 2010. Nonetheless, the data fit my assumption that companies' behaviour has changed, since UK profit margins are currently only slightly below average at a time when output is depressed, being in Q2 2012 7.8% below the level recorded for Q4 2007.

In Chart 19, I show the data for non-financial companies in France. This has the advantage of being available quarterly from 1955 to the end of 2011 but applies only to non-financial companies. This is an important limitation as there is no reason according to theory that profit margins should be stable if the data are restricted to results from non-financial companies.

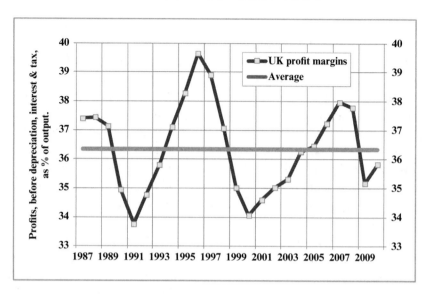

Chart 18. UK: Profit Margins 1987 to 2010.
Source: ONS via Ecowin.

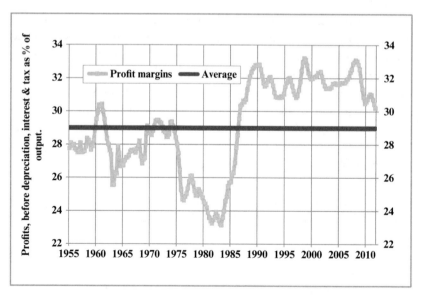

Chart 19. France: Non-financial Profit Margins.
Source: INSEE via Ecowin.

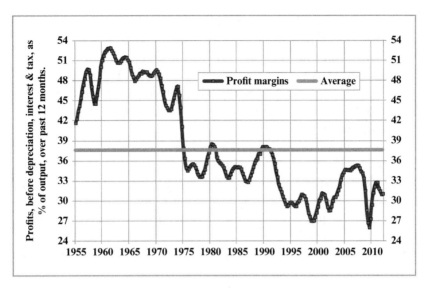

Chart 20. Japan: Non-financial Profit Margins.
Source: MoF quarterly survey of incorporated enterprises.

In spite of these limitations, the data for the UK, US and France are generally supportive of the theory that profit margins are mean reverting.

The only other country for which, as far as I am aware, good long data on profit margins are available is Japan (Chart 20). As in the case of France only data for non-financial companies are known and they illustrate the caveat that I mentioned above, which is that the stability of share of output going to labour and capital applies only to mature economies. By the end of World War II, 50% or more of Japan's productive capital, plus 90% of its merchant marine, had been destroyed, but the population had grown, despite the terrible loss of life.[8] The supply of labour had risen while educational standards had been, at least, maintained. The ratio of labour to capital had thus risen sharply whether employment is judged solely by numbers or allowance is made for the educational skills of the labour force. The resulting shortage pushed up the return on capital well above

---

[8] See Table 10.4, Chapter 10 of *The Cambridge History of Japan: Vol. 6*, edited by Peter Duus, Cambridge University Press, (1988).

its long-term equilibrium level. When the data series starts, a decade after the end of the war, the profit share of output was very high, which made investment very rewarding, so that spending on new capital amounted to between 30 and 40% of GDP. The economy grew rapidly as the supply of capital was brought into line with the supply of labour and the profit share fell, till today where it is a little below the US level.

The available data on profit margins are thus consistent with the theory that they are mean reverting. But the speed with which they revert to their mean and the precise level of this mean are uncertain. One reason is that the cost of capital in this context can vary and with it the readiness of management to substitute labour for capital or vice versa also varies. The balance of preference given by companies to the employment of more labour or more capital is known as the coefficient of substitution. The cost of capital is not simply determined by the cost of debt and equity and the cost of capital equipment; other forms of capital are needed for production and the cost of land in particular varies from country to country and within a country over time.

Companies' willingness to invest in new capital will depend not only on the managements' objective assessment of its cost to the company but also on their expectations and on the perceived cost to the management in terms of the impact it will have on their remuneration. As I have explained the change in the way managements have become paid in recent years with the increasing emphasis on bonuses has changed their perception of the cost of capital when used for investment in plant and equipment. Money spent on buying shares will boost managements' bonuses more than money spent on capital equipment; so for those who make decisions about how much to spend, the perceived cost of such investment has risen, even though interest rates have fallen sharply. The coefficient of substitution has thus changed and profit margins have risen in response to this change.

The change in management incentives through the dramatic increase in the size of bonuses is likely to have changed management behaviour not only with regard to investment decisions but also with regard to pricing policy. Managements are therefore likely to have sought to widen profit margins. If they have been successful, this will have shown up by profit margins, in recent years, not only

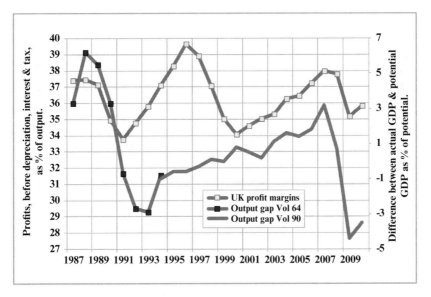

Chart 21. UK: Profit Margins & the Output Gap.
Sources: ONS & OECD Economic Outlooks.

fluctuating with the cyclical strength of the economy but also having risen, at least for the time being, relative to those cyclical fluctuations.

Chart 21 for the UK and Chart 22 for the US show that experience matches these expectations. In both countries profit margins have been rising and falling with cyclical changes in the output gap, but there has also been a marked rise in profit margins relative to the cycle.

In the US profit margins are wider than ever before even though the economy is weak, and in the UK margins are relatively robust despite the cyclical position of the economy.

France and Japan are markedly different from the UK and the US. As Chart 23 and Chart 24 show, profit margins in both countries have been on a declining trend in line with a similar trend in terms of the output gap. Whereas profit margins in the UK and US are higher than expected from their past relationship to cyclical changes in the economy, it does not seem that any similar change has occurred in France and Japan.

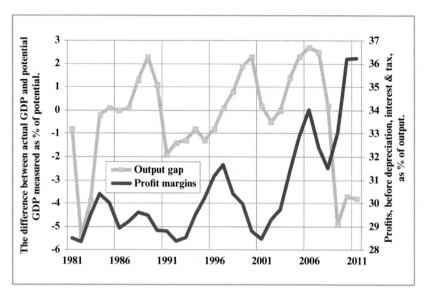

Chart 22. US: Profit Margins & the Output Gap.
Sources: NIPA Table 1.14 & OECD Economic Outlooks Vols 68 & 90.

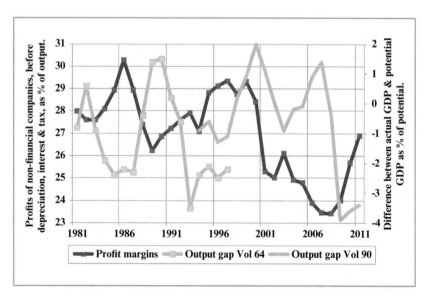

Chart 23. France: Profit Margins & Output Gap.
Sources: INSEE via Ecowin & OECD Economic Outlooks.

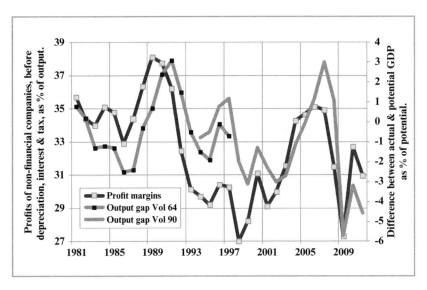

Chart 24. Japan: Profit Margins & Output Gap.
Sources: MoF Quarterly Survey of Incorporated Enterprises & OECD
Economic Outlooks.

French profit margins seem to have been less influenced by the
cyclical changes in the output gap than those of other countries. I
am uncertain as to why this should be, but one possible explanation
is that government has a much greater influence on the pricing and
wage policies of companies than is found in other countries, both
because the French state is a large shareholder in many important
companies and because there is greater public interference in employment conditions. It may also be partly due to France's membership
of the eurozone, which is not yet sufficiently integrated for labour
costs to be mainly driven by the zone as a whole, but where there
has probably been a greater degree of integration regarding prices.
France in this respect has probably suffered less than the Mediterranean members of the zone; if their labour costs had responded
more to the conditions in the eurozone as a whole and less to the
individual circumstances of different countries, the problems of the
eurozone would have been a great deal less than they have been.

Taking into account the past relationship between business cash
flow and fiscal deficits, or comparing the current positive cash
flow of the sector with the deficit that seems inherently natural,

the business sector is likely to take the brunt of any improvement in fiscal deficits. It is possible to imagine ways in which the full burden would fall on the foreign and household sectors, but this is unlikely to happen, and it would certainly be dangerous for policy to be based on such hopes or forecasts. Equally, however, it is important that the whole burden of adjustment does not fall on business. The latest NIPA data available to me, which for the US are the 12 months to 30th September 2012, show that the business sector had a cash surplus of 3.1% of GDP and the fiscal deficit was 8.9% of GDP. If the deficit were to fall to 2% of GDP and the full burden of the compensating adjustment were to fall on the business sector, then its cash flow would have to fall to −3.8% of GDP and the change would be 6.9% of GDP. As the profits after tax and dividends of the US corporate sector over these 12 months are equal to 3.1% of GDP, any likely combination of falling profits and investment would be incompatible with anything other than a severe recession.

As Chart 25 shows, the business sector had negative cash flows in the 1970s and in the early 1980s, similar to that of 3.8% of GDP, which it would suffer if it bore the full burden of a reduction in

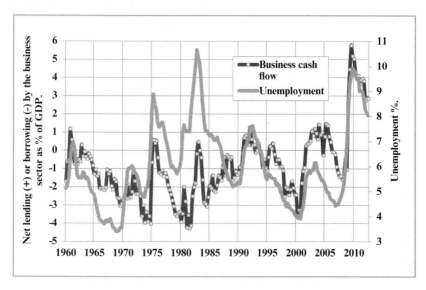

Chart 25. US: Business Cash Flow & Unemployment.
Sources: NIPA Tables 1.1.5 & 5.1 & BLS.

the fiscal deficit from 8.9% to 2% of GDP. On both occasions these very weak periods of business cash flow were followed by sharp rises in unemployment. A similar low level of cash flow is likely to have a much worse impact today because the change would be so much greater, because the business sector habitually ran negative flows in the 1970s and 1980s, while business has become habituated to a much easier time in recent years.

It is therefore essential that the improvement in the fiscal deficits of the UK and the US should not fall on their business sectors alone. This means that either the foreign or the household sectors must have lower cash surpluses.

In the years ahead it is unlikely that households will be able to make much of a contribution to offsetting the decline in the fiscal deficit. If they were to do so, it would create imbalances that would themselves present future problems of adjustment.

The cash flow of the household sector is the difference between the sector's savings and investment. In economies that have growing populations, such as the UK and the US, the sector will in equilibrium have a positive cash flow. It will thus be a net lender to the rest of the economy. Only if the sector has a positive cash flow can households' ownership of houses and pension assets rise in line with the growth of the economy. I have shown that the corporate sector naturally runs a cash deficit and this must be balanced by cash surpluses in other sectors. If the public sector runs even a small cash deficit, then cash surpluses will have to be found in the household and foreign sectors. To avoid foreigners owning an ever-increasing proportion of a country's wealth, the household sector must run a significant cash surplus.

Chart 26 shows that in the US the household sector has, on average, run a cash surplus over the years since 1960 when the data series start. The chart also shows that the surplus over the past 12 months has been below its average level and well below the average from 1960 to 1998. In the subsequent decade the recent housing mania was at its height and the sector ran an exceptional and clearly unsustainable cash deficit.

Current data for the UK, which are only available since 1987 and are set out in Chart 27, show that the cash surplus of the household sector is less than 1% of GDP and thus even below the current US level.

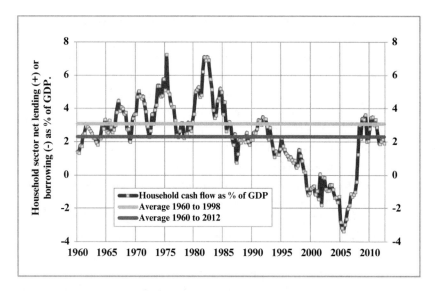

Chart 26. US: Household Sector Cash Flow.
Sources: NIPA Tables 1.1.5 & 2.1.

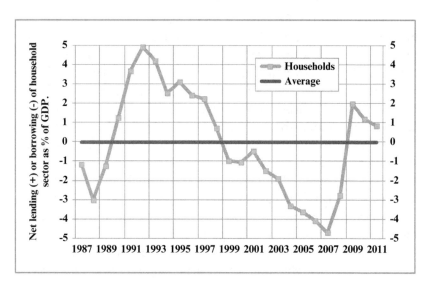

Chart 27. UK: Household Net Savings as % of GDP.
Source: ONS via Ecowin.

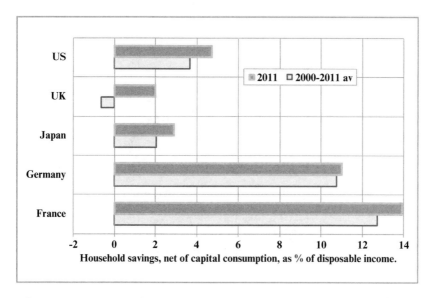

Chart 28. G5: Household Savings.
Sources: OECD Economic Outlook Vol 91 & ONS.

In both the UK and the US the household sectors have low savings' rates, whether measured by the standards of other G5 countries (Chart 28) or by their own history (Chart 29), and very bad balance sheets; their liabilities have fallen back a little in recent years but are still over 100% of disposable income (Chart 30).

Households' investments consist for the main part in paying for the construction of new houses. Housing investment is low in both countries and should pick up, but households will probably need to find part of the additional finance needed to buy more new houses by increasing their savings. In the past they could often rely on debt to finance 100% of the cost of a house, but one result of the financial crisis is that this is now seldom if ever possible. Currently, both household savings (Chart 28 and Chart 29) and investment (Chart 31) are low and it is probable that both will rise. It is, however, likely that housing construction is more depressed in the UK and less so in the US than would appear by comparing the current level of output with historic averages. Prior to 1980, UK households relied heavily on rented accommodation provided by the public

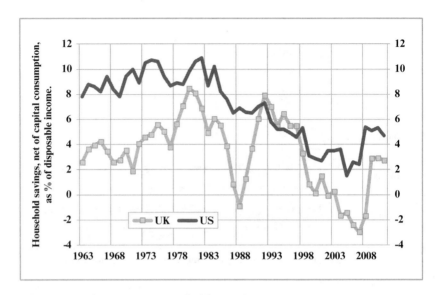

Chart 29. UK & US: Household Net Savings.
Sources: ONS & NIPA.

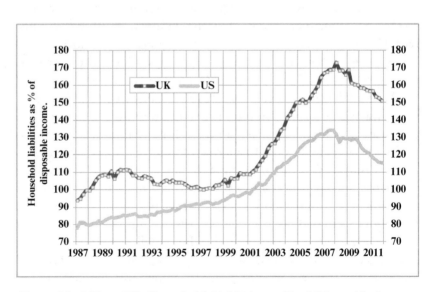

Chart 30. UK & US: Household Liabilities as % of Disposable Income.
Sources: ONS & Federal Reserve.

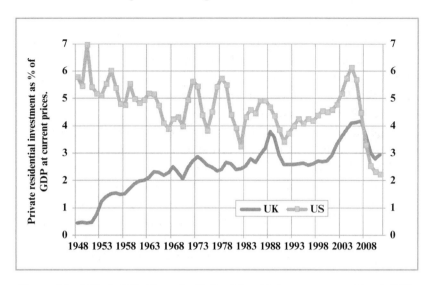

Chart 31. UK & US: Household Residential Investment as % of GDP. Sources: ONS (DFDF & YBHA) & NIPA Table 1.1.5.

sector, which was a major investor in housing, so the current level of private sector investment is more depressed than would otherwise appear from the chart. In the US household formation and the demand for housing is on a long-term declining trend and the high level of housing construction in the run-up to the crash of 2008 is likely to have created an excessive level of inventory, in terms of unsold and repossessed houses. It therefore seems likely that housing investment will naturally rise in both countries, in the case of the UK to above its historic average and in the US to below. These levels will of course also be influenced by unpredictable elements such as government interference through planning permissions, in the UK, and by interest rates.

I expect, however, that household savings in both countries will rise, partly to help finance the rise in investment. It is unlikely that the household sectors in either the UK or the US can afford any marked fall in their current cash surpluses, which represent the small differences between their current level of savings and investment. A rise in household savings is necessary if household investment is to rise, unless the cash flow of the sector can fall even further below its average and likely equilibrium level.

I am not making forecasts as to the level of household cash flow in either the UK or the US for any particular year. I am simply seeking to show that over time a significant fall in these sectors' cash flows is not something that should reasonably be expected and that it would be reckless for policymakers to assume that it would occur while the current fiscal deficits are reduced.

Since a fall in the fiscal deficits must be exactly matched by falls in the cash surpluses of other sectors and we should neither expect nor hope for any significant reduction in the small surpluses currently being run in the UK and US household sectors, it follows that there will have to be large declines in the cash surpluses of foreigners and business. (Foreigners' cash surpluses are the same as a country's current account deficit.) A massive fall in these sectors' cash flow will thus be needed to match the reduction in fiscal deficits.

There is a widely held view that the wish to deleverage is holding back demand in the UK and the US. In the case of both households and companies, the poor state of balance sheets makes this assumption seem at first sight reasonable, but it does not seem compatible with the low level of household savings or the sectors' cash surpluses.

In neither the UK nor the US would it be sensible to hope or expect household sectors to reduce, over the medium-term, the low levels of positive cash flow that they currently enjoy. It is, however, no more sensible to hope that the burden of reducing their fiscal deficits of GDP could be placed solely on the business sector. As I showed in Table 2, the level of business investment appears to be unaffected by the relatively small changes in profit margins which have occurred in the post-war era, but it fell sharply in the 1930s when profit margins fell sharply. The impact of falling business cash flows is therefore likely to depend on whether the impact comes from rising investment or falling profit margins.

I have argued that if the burden falls too heavily on profit margins it will cause a recession and that we cannot sensibly expect households to alleviate this by their cash flow falling significantly. The impact of an improved fiscal balance needs therefore to be shared between the foreign sectors and business sectors with the latter reducing its cash flow by higher investment as well as lower margins. Business investment depends not only on profitability and

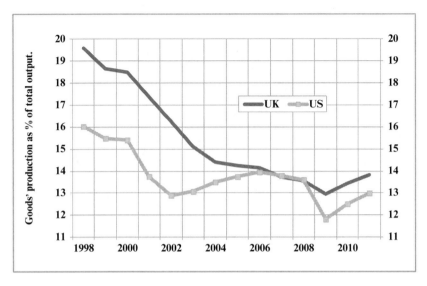

Chart 32. UK & US: Goods' Output as % of Total.
Sources: ONS via Ecowin & NIPA Table 6.1D.

optimism but also on whether demand is increasing for the output of goods or services, because the amount of capital required to increase the output of goods is about 70% greater than that needed to produce the same rise in service output.[9]

Domestic demand is primarily for services rather than goods. As Chart 32 shows, goods' output constitutes only 14 and 13% respectively of total output in the UK and the US. However, as Chart 33 illustrates, goods represent 65 and 75% respectively of international trade of the UK and the US. For trade balances to improve either domestic output must replace imports, or exports must expand. Whichever occurs, there will be a rise in the demand for domestically-produced goods and as their production is capital intensive this will lead to an additional rise in investment, which largely takes the form of goods. An improvement in trade balances will thus stimulate investment and thereby reduce the degree to which profit margins will need to fall with the deterioration in business cash flow.

[9]The evidence for this is set out in Appendix 2.

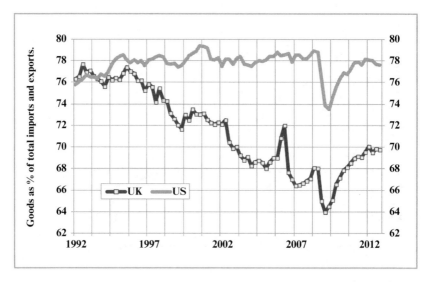

Chart 33. UK & US: Goods as % of Total International Trade.
Sources: ONS via Ecowin & NIPA Table 1.1.5.

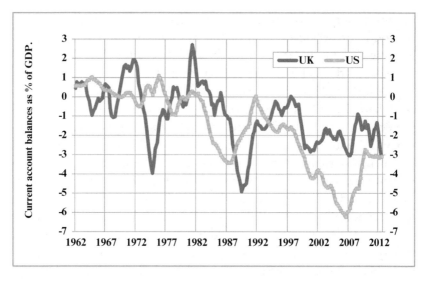

Chart 34. UK & US: Current Account Balances.
Sources: ONS & BEA via Ecowin.

A large fall in business cash flow is necessary if the UK and the US fiscal deficits are to be reined in. But it is likely to be impossible for the full burden to fall on business and an important contribution will be needed from an improvement in external trade deficits, which would have a double benefit. First, it would reduce the extent to which business cash flow had to fall for any given improvement in the fiscal deficit and, second, it would shift the burden towards investment and away from profit margins.

As Chart 34 illustrates, the current account balances of the UK and the US are heavily negative and their elimination would allow their fiscal deficits to fall by around 3% of GDP. Were this to be achieved, it would greatly reduce the extent to which an improvement in the fiscal balance would throw the burden on the business sector. If most of the impact falls on companies then sustained recovery would be highly improbable. A marked improvement in the external sectors of the UK and the US is thus an essential condition for sustained recovery.

3

Alternative Explanations for Today's Low Business Investment and High Profit Margins

The trend decline in business investment can be explained by the change in the way that management is paid, but there are other possible causes.

It may have been due to declining confidence in the prospects for growth. This cannot be measured, but until the financial crisis confidence about the growth of both economies was generally thought to be high. Chart 35 shows that, while growth was quite volatile and seemed to be trending downwards a bit in the US, there was no apparent reason to take a dim view of prospects before the financial crisis in either the UK or the US.

Another possible reason is that the returns on investment may have fallen. The return after tax on net worth in the US is shown in Chart 36. Using either of the two definitions of profits used by

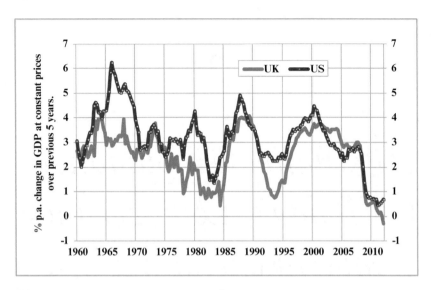

Chart 35. UK & US: 5-year Growth Rates.
Sources: ONS & NIPA.

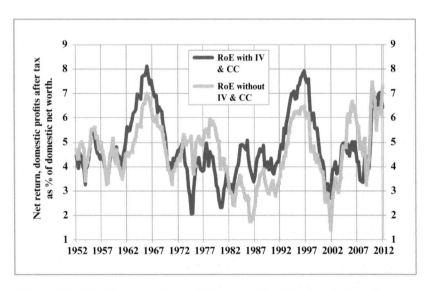

Chart 36. US: Return, Net of Tax, on Net Worth of Non-financial
Companies.
Sources: Z1 Tables B.102 & L.102 & NIPA Table 1.14.

the US national accountants, the domestic profitability of US companies was 40 or 67% above average in Q1 2012.[1]

UK returns on capital are not as high as they are in the US, but as Chart 37 illustrates they show no sign of being under pressure despite the weakness of the UK economy. In fact, they seem remarkably high given the apparent weakness of the economies.

The return on capital for UK non-financial companies, shown in Chart 37, was in Q1 2012 almost exactly at its average level since Q1 1989, which is when the data series start.

The high returns on equity in the US (Chart 36) would, according to standard economic models, be expected to lead to high levels of business investment, and are thus inconsistent with the decline shown in Chart 13. Even the average levels of return in the UK (Chart 37) provide no explanation for the very low level of investment (Chart 13).

Investment in the Anglophone economies may have been depressed, even with their high returns, if it was thought that potential returns elsewhere were more attractive. This assumption cannot be tested directly as there is no way of measuring such expectations, nor do we have good data we can use to compare returns on investment between countries. It is common to read in the financial press of comparisons being made between equity returns in different countries, but these are based on the data published by companies and should not be used for international comparisons or even within countries for comparison over time. When corporate data are used, the comparisons can only be made on book values, which are misleading because the difference between the replacement and book cost of assets varies from country to country depending on their past level of inflation. In a country like

---

[1] The only data available on UK profitability that include Q1 2012 are the "return on capital" as defined by the ONS and shown in Chart 37. The returns cannot therefore be compared directly with the US returns shown in Chart 36, which are very much lower in absolute terms. Both series are, however, comparable over time and can therefore be compared with their own averages. The difference between the returns of 40 and 67% for the US arises from the two different ways profits are calculated in the national accounts. The inventory (IV) and capital consumption (CC) adjustments are made to allow for the impact of inflation on inventory values and depreciation.

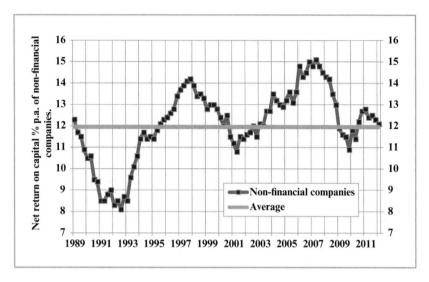

Chart 37. UK: Net Return on Capital of Non-financial Companies. Source: ONS via Ecowin.

Japan, which has had mild deflation for many years, book values may overstate the replacement cost of assets, whereas in the UK or the US the opposite will be the case. Even if profits were calculated on the same accounting principles and the return on assets was really the same in all three countries, Japanese returns would show up on book values as being lower than in the UK or the US. In addition, however, as I shall be explaining at greater length later, the accounting methods used in different countries are massively different. In order to see whether expected returns have been higher in foreign countries than in the US and that this has shifted corporate investment, it is necessary to look at data other than those published by companies.

Chart 38 shows the way in which the net worth, measured at constant prices, of US companies' foreign subsidiaries has been changing since the end of the war. The chart shows that far from accelerating in recent years the trend of growth has been falling and has been lower over the five years from 2007 to 2012 than it was after the war. As the data are only available for the net worth of the foreign subsidiaries, the growth of total investment could have been rising if the leverage of these subsidiaries had been rising.

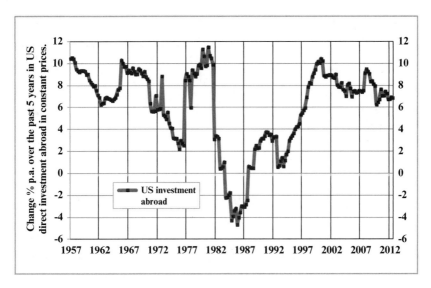

Chart 38. US: Changes in Non-financial Direct Investment Abroad. Sources: BLS & Federal Reserve Z1 Table L. 102.

Anecdotal evidence suggests that this is highly unlikely.[2] It is generally believed that the leverage of US companies' foreign subsidiaries has been falling as tax disadvantages have encouraged companies to return cash abroad rather than remit it to the US.[3] If this anecdotal evidence is correct, US companies' investment abroad has been growing even more slowly than the trend in Chart 38 shows. There is therefore no evidence that the disappointing level of business investment in the US can be ascribed to a recent preference for investing abroad rather than at home.

Another reason for thinking that the lure of foreign markets has not been deflecting business investment away from the US is that the great bulk of foreign investment is in the developed world,

---

[2] The BEA also publishes data on the value of US direct investment abroad. These include financial companies' investment and seem to cover a short period, but show the same trends, with the value of US direct investment in constant prices having risen by 7% a year in the five years to 2011 and by 5% over 2010.

[3] The decline in the real value of US foreign investments after the oil shock shown in Chart 38 and Chart 39 seems likely to reflect the nationalisation and other forms of sequestration which hit the oil majors, and some others, in that period.

Table 3. Income from US Direct Foreign Investment (Source: BEA latest available data 2009)

	$bn	% of total
Total	900.47	100.00
Developed world	592.75	65.83
Non-Japan Asia	97.90	10.87
Latin America	167.52	18.60
Other	42.31	4.70

where past growth and probably future expectations of growth are no better than for the US. Table 3 shows that investments in the rapidly developing parts of the world, where anecdotal evidence points to strong expectations of high returns, were relatively insignificant even in 2009, which is at the end of the period we are considering. Measured by income, two-thirds of US foreign direct investment was in the developed world and only 11% in Asia, excluding Japan.

Neither poor expectations of growth for the UK and the US nor high expectations of competing opportunities seem therefore to provide an explanation for the disappointing level of UK and US business investment in the run-up to the recent recession. The change in the way management was paid therefore looks the best available explanation, though it seems likely that the weakness in the recovery has dampened companies' investment spending. The impediment to growth provided by the change in management behaviour will thus have added a negative cyclical effect to its structural impact.

I have pointed out that the change in management remuneration provides an explanation as to why business investment has been low and why profit margins have been high. Other explanations for current high profit margins have also been put forward, particularly by those working in financial services who have an interest in the continuance of high margins, as they believe that it is easier to sell a bullish story than a bearish one and that in general business flourishes more when profits rise than when they fall. This view seems to have some justification. Chart 39 shows that the strong rise in the volume of business on the New York Stock Exchange was reversed for a while after the fall in profits in 2000 and again dra-

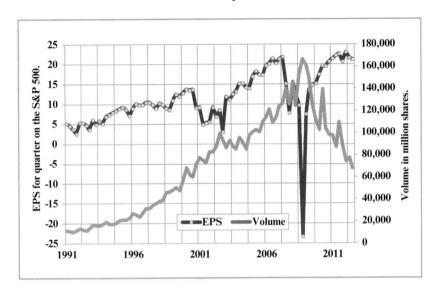

Chart 39. US: NYSE Volume & S&P 500 EPS.
Source: NYSE & Standard & Poor's via Ecowin.

matically after the fall in 2008. Investment bankers therefore want
the recent rise in profit margins to be a permanent rather than a
temporary shift and the assumption that the bargaining power of
labour has fallen on a permanent basis fits with this hope. Attempts
to explain away the threat posed to future profits by the high level
of current profits have included the claim that margins have risen
because "the bargaining power of labour has waned as the membership and aggression of trade unions has fallen".

It is reasonable to argue that trade unions increase the individual
cost of those employed by pushing up unemployment and thus
reducing the supply of labour. But their ability to cause rising
unemployment is, fortunately, limited. As the numbers of unem-
ployed grow they will lower wages in those industries where unions
cannot prevent employers from hiring labour at lower cost. This will
make labour cheaper to hire per person and would encourage more
employment in industries that are not affected by union restrictions.
Trade unions' ability to raise labour costs should therefore rise and
fall with the extent to which their control extends over the economy.

I show in Chart 40 that both the proportion of employees that
were members of trade unions and their militancy, as measured by

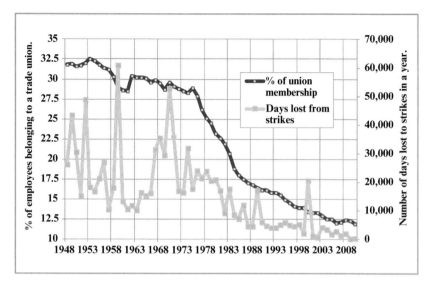

Chart 40. US: Unionisation & Strike Action.
Source: Department of Labor.

strike action, has fallen steadily since the end of the war. If this is compared with profit margins, as shown in Chart 41, it will be seen that there is no apparent relationship whatever. Profit margins tended to fall from the end of the war to 1980 while union membership and militancy fell steadily. From 1980 onwards, however, when union membership and militancy continued to fall, profit margins rose.

The data therefore provide no support for the claim that the undoubted decline in union membership, or labour militancy and bargaining power, which has occurred since the end of World War II, has had any influence on profit margins in terms at least of their trend changes over time.

Another reason for the rise in US and UK profit margins, that has from time to time been put forward, is that it is the result of globalisation, or more precisely from the entry of China into the world economy. If capital is scarce relative to labour then profit margins, which are the share of profits in total output, will be higher than normal. This was the situation in Japan at the end of World War II, as can be seen from Chart 20. Although profit margins subsequently fluctuated with the cyclical strength of the economy,

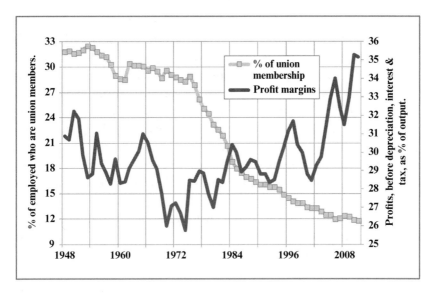

Chart 41. US: Profit Margins and Union Membership.
Sources: BLS & NIPA Table 1.1.4.

they started at a very high level at the end of the war, then came down steadily over the next 30 years and are now below US margins. When in the late 1970s China decided to open itself to the world economy, it had a huge workforce that, relative at least to its standard of living, was well educated. It was thus similar to Japan in the 1950s in having a shortage of capital compared to labour and a similar pattern was thus likely to be seen in Chinese profit margins. It was therefore probable that margins would be high when China first opened its doors to the world economy and would then fall if, as would be expected, these high profit margins encouraged a high level of investment.[4]

This was not only the pattern that should have been expected but the pattern that has been seen, at least according to strong anecdotal evidence, and is probably a key reason for the poor returns

[4]This pattern is generally accepted with regard to open economies with the Stolper–Samuelson theorem as the standard model. Even though the world economy is far from open to movements of labour, some impact from China's development on profit margins seems likely.

that investors in Chinese shares have suffered in recent years.[5] The narrowing of profit margins in China would presumably have had a similar impact on the world economy if there had been no barriers to the movement of labour and capital. Even without this proviso, it is reasonable to assume that profit margins would have been affected and would have risen in the early years after China opened itself to the world economy and would have then tended to fall back with those in China.

But profit margins in the UK (Chart 18) and US (Chart 17) have in recent years been tending to widen rather than narrow. It is not sensible therefore to assume that globalisation, or China's opening in particular, have had a major influence on those margins. It is also improbable that globalisation should have had a different impact on profit margins in the UK and US to that which it has had on margins in France and Japan.

The OECD is among those who have sought to blame technology for the rise in profit margins. It argues that "the spread of information and communication technologies have created opportunities not only for unprecedented advances in innovation and invention of new capital goods and production processes, thereby boosting productivity, but also for replacing workers with machines for certain types of jobs, notably those involving routine tasks". The report starts by claiming that "during the past three decades, the share of national income represented by wages, salaries and benefits – the labour share – has declined in nearly all OECD countries". The report subsequently points to the way in which this approach is bedevilled by measurement issues.[6] These may be

---

[5] According to Edward Chancellor, "The real return to investors on Chinese shares since the early 1990s has been minus 2.5%." Financial Times' Fund Management Supplement (4th March, 2013).

[6] "In many industries outside the business sector, measurement of value added is problematic. For example, the value added of public administration, as measured in national accounts, is often dramatically inflated in the public sector . . . the share of self-employed varies significantly across industries as does the compensation of employees, therefore imputation rules based on average compensation in the whole economy can be misleading both in terms of levels and trends." Labour Losing to Capital: What Explains the Declining Labour Share? Box 3.2, Chapter 3, OECD Employment Report (2012).

explained, in less technical terms than those used in the report, by pointing out that the decline in the share of national income shown in national accounts may be the result of changes in the relative importance of the output of either the public sector or from those who are the self-employed, rather than to any change in profit margins. There have been significant changes in the public sector's output, in response to attempts to reduce fiscal deficits, and the rise in unemployment has encouraged the growth of self-employment. These caveats therefore mean that changes in the ratio of labour incomes to GDP do not provide us with useful information about the labour share of output in the business sector.

Looking at labour incomes as a percentage of GDP is not therefore a sensible approach for those seeking to investigate changes in profit margins. These measurement problems, to which the OECD has itself drawn attention, mean that conclusions should be based on the share of labour income in business output rather than in GDP. Although the OECD accepts this and has looked at trends in individual industries across many countries, it does not seem to have considered the data for the non-financial corporate sector of the economy, which, as I pointed out, are available for four of the G5 countries. Had it done this, the OECD would have noticed that France and Japan are markedly different from the UK and the US. I have already pointed out that, as Charts 19 and 20 show, profit margins in France and Japan have been on declining trends relative to their output gaps, whereas the UK (Chart 18) and US (Chart 17) have been on rising ones.

An adequate explanation of the way profit margins have changed differently in different countries must involve an explanation that is specific to individual countries. Changes in technology or in globalisation, which apply worldwide, would therefore only provide a satisfactory explanation of the way in which profit margins have changed if those changes had been common to all G5 countries, which they have not been. But this objection does not apply to the impact of changes in the way managements are remunerated as this varies from country to country, with the problem of the bonus culture being effectively confined to the UK and US.

In an article in the New York Times, Paul Krugman claims that antitrust enforcement largely collapsed during the Reagan years and has never really recovered.[7] He quotes Barry Lynn and Phillip Longman, of the New America Foundation, whom he finds persuasive when they argue that increasing business concentration could be an important factor in the stagnating demand for labour, as corporations use their growing monopoly power to raise prices without passing the gains on to their employees.[8] The evidence does not suggest that the demand for labour is stagnating. Indeed, quite the contrary as it appears that business currently prefers to employ more labour rather than more capital when it increases output. Nonetheless, a rise in monopoly power could explain the high level of profit margins, though it provides no explanation for the disappointing level of business investment.

The argument for increased monopoly power is the best that I have encountered, next to the change in the way management is remunerated, for the change in corporate behaviour in the UK and US with regard to profit margins. Companies have a great deal of monopoly power in the short-term. Unless there is lots of spare capacity, buyers of goods and services cannot easily move large amounts of their purchases in the short-term from one supplier to another. Managements are thus always making judgements when they make decisions about the prices they charge. The risk they take if they keep margins up is that they will increasingly lose market share over time. The risk they take if they allow margins to narrow is that they will make lower profits in the short-term. They have to make similar judgements when taking decisions about investment. The decision not to invest increases their long-term risks of having higher production costs than their competitors. The decision to invest involves the probability of lower profits in the short-term, because of the cost of finance and the rise in the charge for depreciation. Another factor is that money spent on investment cannot be spent on buying back shares, so that investment has the added opportunity cost of reducing the scope for raising profits per share. The bonus system encourages management to accept higher long-term risks but to avoid, if possible, the shorter-term ones. It is in

[7] *Technology or Monopoly Power?* by Paul Krugman, New York Times, (9th December, 2012).

[8] *Who Broke America's Jobs Machine?* by Barry Lynn and Phillip Longman, Washington Monthly, (March/April 2010).

effect a way of encouraging management to exploit more aggressively than before their companies' shorter-term monopoly power.

The effect of the bonus system and a rise in monopoly power are thus very similar in several ways. In both cases profit margins will be higher than they would otherwise have been. In the case of a rise in monopoly power, there will also be no incentive to invest more. Investment will not rise proportionately to the rise in profit margins, as these will tend to be improved with regard to the existing capital stock and not necessarily with regard to additional capacity. The effect of the bonus system is to actually discourage investment. The weak level of investment is thus explained by a change in management remuneration but not by a change in monopoly power.

There are also reasons for preferring the impact of the bonus culture as an explanation for why profit margins are so high as well as investment low.

- The evidence for an increase in monopoly power must apply to both the UK and the US as it is needed to explain the change in corporate behaviour in both countries. As far as I am aware there are no claims of such a change in the UK, but only in the US. Even in the US the evidence for less competition is the evidence that profit margins are oddly high given the relative weakness of the economy. The argument is thus circular and involves adding something to explain the evidence rather than, as in the case of the impact of the bonus culture, noting the existence of something for which the evidence is independent of the phenomenon. The accepted scientific principle of parsimony, also known as Ockham's razor after the 14th-century philosopher and theologian, should therefore lead us to prefer the bonus culture as the preferred explanation.[9]

- The bonus culture encourages management to report highly volatile profits. There is no similar incentive arising from a rise

---

[9] In this instance Ockham's razor, "*Numquam ponenda est pluralitas sine necessitate*", as paraphrased by Bertrand Russell, fits particularly well. "Entities are not to be multiplied without necessity." *A History of Western Philosophy*, George Allen & Unwin Ltd, (1946).

in monopoly power. The dramatic rise in the volatility of the reported profits of listed companies compared with profits in the national accounts (Chart 12) is thus another reason why the bonus culture is the explanation that should logically be preferred.

This does not of course mean that there may have been a reduction in competition and that this change may have added to the rise in profit margins. Changes can have multiple causes and it may be that in addition to seeking to change the bonus culture, policy-makers would be sensible to put renewed attention on reducing monopoly profits and increasing competition.

4

Forecasting Errors in the UK and the US

Additional evidence for the importance of the change in management remuneration is provided by the way in which those forecasters who have ignored the change have made exactly those errors in their forecasts that they would have avoided had they made allowance for the way in which the behaviour of companies has altered.

In his recent revision to previous forecasts, Robert Chote, who is Chairman of the UK's Office for Budget Responsibility (OBR), expressed surprise that inflation had been higher than he had expected and investment weaker. The Bank of England has also been persistently too optimistic about inflation and output. In its Inflation Report of November 2012, it discusses the way that employment had risen unexpectedly fast compared with output, so that productivity has been poor. As Chart 42 shows, measured from Q4 2010, the output of the UK has fallen but employment has risen so that productivity, measured as output per person employed, has fallen by 3%.

In the previous forecast to which Robert Chote referred, the OBR had expected that the UK economy would grow by 5.7% from Q1 2010 to Q2 2012, whereas the outturn has been only 0.9%. Consumer spending, business investment and net exports were all weaker than expected and "all contributed roughly equally to the unexpected weakness in growth". The OBR attributed the

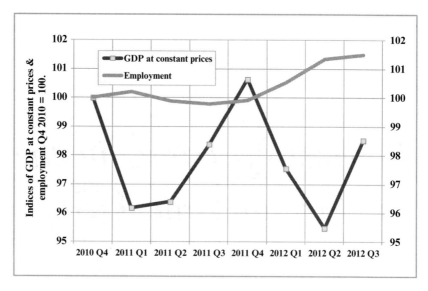

Chart 42. UK: Output & Employment.
Source: ONS via Ecowin.

weakness in consumer spending to the fact that inflation had been higher than it anticipated.

There are often multiple causes for unexpected changes in the economy, and to some extent it is likely that several things have contributed to these forecasting mistakes. There is, however, one single change that would naturally cause each of these errors to occur. Invoking again the principle of parsimony,[1] the generally accepted point in science that simple explanations should be preferred to more complex ones, the explanation that all the errors can be attributed to the change in management behaviour deserves to be given particular attention. It is also the only broad macroeconomic explanation that I have encountered. Most explanations have either been an amalgam of differing microeconomic justifications or assumed that the data need to be revised to accord with the forecasts, rather than that the forecast methods need to be revised in the light of the data.

---

[1] In the sciences, including economics, the principle is generally known as that of parsimony, whereas in theology it has been called, with accidental irony, the principle of economy.

The change in management behaviour is my broad explanation for all these forecast surprises. As explained I attribute this alteration in behaviour to the impact of changes in incentives arising from the way managements are paid with an increasing proportion of their income coming from bonuses and options rather than as fixed salaries. As a result profit margins are higher than they would have been in the past under similar economic conditions, investment is lower and companies will prefer to increase output by adding more labour rather than more capital. The economic results are:

- Consumer prices are higher than expected, particularly where companies are not exposed to international competition. When forecasters fail to allow for this, they will tend to underestimate inflation.
- Investment is lower than was expected by those who failed to allow for the change in corporate culture.
- Employment rises relative to output. With the rise in bond and equity markets, the cost of capital has fallen rather than risen for companies. But the perceived cost from managements' perspective has risen, because they benefit when cash or debt is used to finance buy-backs and suffer when they are used to finance investments in plant and equipment. The natural impact of this rise in the perceived cost of capital is to make management prefer to use more labour rather than more capital to achieve a given output. In terms of economic theory, the coefficient of substitution has changed and this has the result of pushing up profit margins.

Both higher than expected inflation and lower than expected investment reduce demand and thus account for the excessive optimism that the forecasters have had regarding growth. All the forecasting errors that we observe can therefore be ascribed to the natural and economically perverse consequences of the change in management incentives.

A similar tendency for productivity to disappoint has been seen in the US. After a good improvement in the early stages of the recovery, output per hour has fallen. As Chart 43 illustrates output per hour worked has been unchanged or fallen over the previous

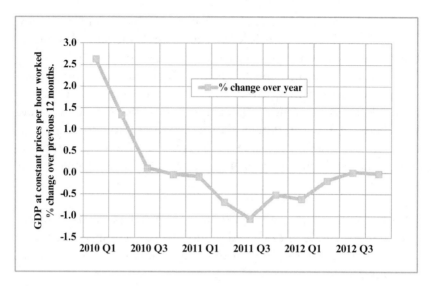

Chart 43. US: Change over Year in Output per Hour.
Sources: NIPA Table 1.1.6 & BLS via Ecowin.

12 months in every quarter since Q4 2010 and fell by 1.3% from
Q4 2010 to Q4 2012.

In both the UK and the US forecasters employed by central
banks have been surprised by the strength of employment relative
to output: "the gap between sluggish economic growth and rapid
falls in joblessness has puzzled the US Federal Reserve".[2]

US inflation averaged 3.3% from 2005 to 2008 and was on a
rising trend, but this was halted by the recession. As measured by
the CPI, inflation is volatile, as Chart 44 shows, and it is therefore
difficult to be confident about any underlying trend. The chart
shows, however, that service inflation varies much less from month
to month and it has clearly been creeping up. Nonetheless, the
Federal Reserve regularly expresses confidence that inflationary
expectations remain low. I think that this is a reasonable judgement
today, though it owes a great deal to the cuts in the US fiscal deficit

---

[2]"*US confidence hit by fiscal fears*" by Robin Harding, Financial Times, (7th
December, 2012).

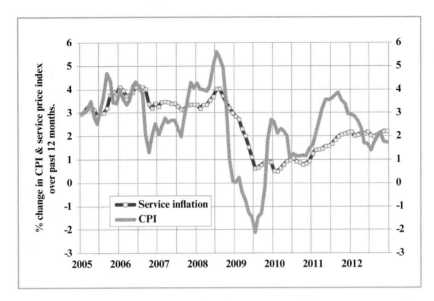

Chart 44. US: CPI & Service Inflation.
Source: BLS via Ecowin.

for 2013, without which the economy may well be strengthening to the point at which a rise in inflationary expectations would have become a significant risk.

In the absence of a change in inflationary expectations economic theory holds that inflation should fall if there is an output gap. If the Federal Reserve is correct in assuming that these are not a current problem, it is disturbing that US inflation has been on a rising trend since the beginning of 2010 and they should be worried by this. As Chart 45 shows, the current rate and trend of inflation, in the absence of any rising fears of inflation, appears inconsistent with the assumed existence of a sizeable output gap.

As Chart 17 showed, US profit margins are at their widest recorded level. They are, for example, 4.4 percentage points higher than they were in Q1 2008, when the recent recession started. I have shown that in the past margins fluctuated with the output gap, but this has changed with the "short-termism" induced by the bonus system. Had the pattern not changed, profit margins would, if the estimates of the output gap were correct, now be below rather than

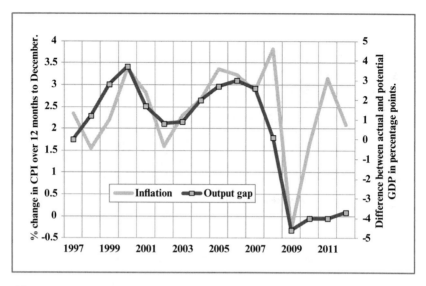

Chart 45. US: Output Gaps & Inflation.
Sources: OECD Economic Outlook Vol 92 & BLS via Ecowin.

above average. If profit margins were at average levels they would
be 6.4 percentage points narrower than they are and, as corporate
output is just over 50% of GDP, the current price level would be
3.2% lower than it is and if spread over the past three years inflation
would have been 1% lower and the trend would have been falling
rather than rising.

In the light of the assumed output gap the level of US inflation
has therefore been, like US productivity, disappointing. As I have
explained, with reference to similar disappointing results in the UK,
both the higher than expected rate of inflation and the weaker than
anticipated data on productivity are the natural result of the change
in management behaviour, which results from the bonus culture.
Even in an economy that is stagnant overall, there will be some
companies and industries for whose output demand rises. From the
viewpoint of management, bonuses drive up the cost of capital.
Companies thus prefer to increase output by the addition of labour
rather than capital. (In technical terms the coefficient of substitution
has changed.)

As inflation has been on a rising trend in recent years and policymakers argue, reasonably in my view, that inflationary expectations remain low, they have a choice:

- They can assume that there is no output gap and that stimulatory policies should be reined back.
- They can assume that the change in management remuneration is keeping inflation much higher than it would otherwise be. To avoid a revival of inflation, stimulatory policies should therefore be kept in abeyance until changes in the bonus culture have been effected.
- They can ignore the evidence and continue with stimulatory policies, thus risking a vicious circle of rising inflation and inflationary expectations.

In the US the Federal Reserve is taking the third choice. For example, the Reserve's vice-chairman, Janet Yellen, announced that she saw "the evidence as consistent with the view that the increase in unemployment since the onset of the Great Recession has been largely cyclical and not structural".[3] This argument seems designed to avoid rather than address the issue. As we showed in Chart 43, US labour productivity has been very poor over the past three years. Compared with output, unemployment is therefore unexpectedly low and evidence of the cyclical or structural nature of the current malaise is not likely to be found in unemployment data. Anyone undertaking a serious consideration of whether the current weakness of demand was primarily cyclical or structural would surely be looking at output, investment, productivity and inflation. These data, rather than those about employment, are where the disappointment lies and where the evidence points to structural rather than cyclical problems.

The evidence that the change in management remuneration is holding back the economies of both the UK and the US from utilising their untapped resources of labour and capital equipment

[3] *"A Painfully Slow Recovery for America's Workers: Causes, implications, and the Federal Reserve's Response"*, remarks at A Trans-Atlantic Agenda for Shared Prosperity conference sponsored by the AFL-CIO, Friedrich Ebert Stiftung, and the IMK Macroeconomic Policy Institute, Washington, DC, (11th February, 2013).

is in a sense encouraging. At least it is better than the alternative explanation, which is that inflation has failed to decline because we do not have spare output capacity. This deeply depressing alternative seems to me, fortunately, to be unlikely. But if the Bank of England and the Federal Reserve wish to share this optimism, they need to explain rather than ignore the disappointing data on inflation, investment, profit margins and productivity.

5

Cyclical or Structural: The Key Issue for Policy

Until there is a change in the way managements are paid, those companies which operate under the current bonus system will continue to prefer the long-term risks of losing market share rather than the short-term ones that would come from allowing margins to narrow and will continue to buy shares in preference to spending money on new equipment. But the combination of high margins and weak capital spending is at the heart of our current economic malaise, as it boosts the intended savings of companies and depresses their intended investment. According to standard economic theory, the correct policy response to an intended surplus of savings over investment is for the government to run a budget deficit. This has the effect of reducing the intended savings of the economy as a whole. When a government spends less than its income, it saves; when it spends more than its income, it has negative savings, i.e. it "dis-saves". By running a budget (i.e. a fiscal) deficit, the government's negative savings offset the surplus of intended savings over intended investment in the business sector.

After the event the amount of savings in the whole economy has to match the amount spent on investment. If there is a mismatch between intentions to save and to invest, the economy has to adjust.

If the intentions to save are greater than those to invest, the adjustment takes the form of a fall in incomes and output, so that the intentions to save are thwarted. By running a fiscal deficit, the government prevents this from happening and thus saves the economy from a painful and unnecessary rise in unemployment combined with falls in income and output.

The UK and US governments have increased their budget deficits sharply to prevent unemployment being even higher than it is, and this action has in my opinion been correct and sensible. We are, however, now facing the longer-term problem of bringing down the deficits, which are currently around 8% of GDP in both countries. This longer-term problem has for many years been at the heart of those economists who have been critical of Keynesian economics. Keynes's reputed reply to how to deal with this long-term problem was, "In the long term we are all dead." This amounted to a tacit admission that he had no real answer to the question and it is reasonable to worry that, in this sense, "We are now living in the long-term."

This long-term problem has not arisen before in practical terms. If budget deficits arose before World War II, it was because demand was weak not because governments were deliberately using fiscal deficits to stimulate their economies. These policies have been exclusively a phenomenon of the post-war era and, until the current recession, the result has invariably been successful with the world economy duly recovering in response to fiscal stimuli so that deep recessions were avoided and the world economy bounced back quickly without budget deficits having to remain at unsustainable levels thereafter. The assumption that we will have another similar recovery from the recent recession is, I fear, misplaced. It is clear that it hasn't happened as yet. If, as I claim, the problem is structural rather than cyclical, neither monetary nor fiscal stimuli are going to reduce the current surplus in the business sector whereby savings exceed investment. The surplus is the result of a change in the way companies behave and does not arise from the losses of confidence and the dampening of the animal spirits of entrepreneurs that has produced the earlier and milder recessions of the post-war era.

Today, most economists, whether they emphasise the importance of monetary or fiscal policy, are assuming that the savings' surplus in the corporate sector is a short-term cyclical one rather than the semi-permanent structural one that is a consequence of the change in corporate behaviour. The assumption is seldom set out clearly by those calling for more fiscal or monetary stimuli and this probably reflects, in many cases, a failure to realise that the assumption is being made. A welcome exception to this can be found in an article claiming that the "textbook prescription – followed successfully by the 1992–97 government – [is] that deficit cutting should follow, not precede, sustained recovery".[1] Only if the problem were cyclical and thus temporary would sustained recovery arrive simply by increasing the deficit and waiting, like Mr Micawber, for something to turn up.[2] Unfortunately, as the problem is structural and semi-permanent, delay on its own will simply make the matter worse. A sustained recovery will not arrive until a new policy is introduced to deal with the fundamental problem. During a long delay in which enthusiasts for fiscal stimulus await the recovery, there is a risk that inflationary expectations will mount as the ratio of national debt to GDP climbs. This danger will become particularly worrying if it is thought that there is no credible policy for containing the rise in national debt, let alone bringing it down. As I will seek to show in more detail later, a rise in inflationary expectations is probably the worst risk that we face, as the cost of bringing such expectations down again in terms of lost output and higher unemployment is likely to be greater than the costs that we have already had to meet as a result of the financial crisis.

Other economists put their hopes on monetary policy and presumably expect that business will be happy to switch from buying shares to investing in equipment if only the cost of finance is reduced by quantitative easing. These hopes do not seem to me to be realistic, because they share with the fiscal enthusiasts a failure to address the

---

[1] "*UK should have waited to enforce austerity*", Jonathan Portes and John Van Reenen, Financial Times, (2nd August, 2012).

[2] "I have known him [Mr Micawber] come home to supper with a flood of tears, and a declaration that nothing was now left but jail; and go to bed making a calculation of the expense of putting in bow windows to the house 'in case anything turned up'." from Chapter 11 of *David Copperfield* by Charles Dickens.

key problem, which is that the change in business behaviour is not a short-term one that results from a loss of confidence but a more fundamental one that results from a change in management incentives. Whereas low interest rates would have been likely to stimulate investment in the past, by lowering the cost of capital, the impact is different today. The cost of capital, as perceived by management, is not reduced but the cost of buying back equity is. Lower interest rates thus encourage more buy-backs rather than more spending on capital equipment. This change is unlikely to prove a permanent one, but it is likely to remain important for some years to come and thwart recovery unless economic policy is adjusted to tackle the problem.

The longer we delay introducing policies to deal with the change in corporate behaviour in the UK and US, the greater the risks we run of either toppling back into recession or having a rise in inflationary expectations. If the latter occurs, we will suffer first from a bout of stagflation, during which inflation picks up while output stagnates or falls. Inflation will then continue to rise until expectations are deflated by another recession, probably even more severe than the last one.

Worldwide we probably need more rather than less fiscal stimulus in the short-term, but we need it in countries that do not already have excessive fiscal deficits. Japan, the UK and the US are thus the most inappropriate countries to add to their current budget deficits, but it is only in this "Keynesian trio" that Keynes's advice to use fiscal stimulus when economies are weak seems currently to be accepted. The rest of the world seems to be unwilling to use fiscal deficits to stimulate their economies, even when, as in the eurozone, these seem so badly needed. The immediate risk is that additional fiscal stimulus is now necessary and will not be used in the short-term. As I write, this is becoming acute as fiscal policy has been tightened. We may therefore already be heading for the next recession and need fiscal stimulus to avoid it, or we may be teetering on the brink and any additional tightening will be sufficient to push us over. The longer-term risk is that, even if the world economy muddles through for the time being, the failure to reduce budget deficits and the massive size of national debts will cause inflationary expectations to rise and we will return to the stagflation of the 1970s and early 1980s.

I am not alone in seeing the change in the way the managements of companies are rewarded as damaging the US economy. In December 2011 the Federal Reserve Bank of New York published a paper on the way the change in management remuneration was likely to be seriously detrimental to the economy.[3] The authors have produced a theoretical model which leads to very similar conclusions that I have drawn from analysis of the data. The change in the way US managements are remunerated has been truly dramatic and the paper starts by drawing attention to this by highlighting the way bonuses have become much more important than basic salaries as a proportion of total remuneration. They quote other economists who "report that for the period 2000–2005 options and other long term incentive pay averaged 60% of total executive compensation; in 2008 the salary component had fallen to only 17% of average total pay."[4]

The essence of the argument set out in the New York Fed's paper, which as usual in academic economics involves much algebra, can be explained in non-technical terms. In good years salaries are a small fraction of the money executives are paid and the bonus element rises dramatically with profits. This is described technically as a "convex contract" and the paper points out that in practice "convex contracts may induce a self-interested manager to adopt investment policies that drive his firm's equilibrium (equity) capital stock to zero". A convex contract is one in which mildly good profits will produce a useful rise in total remuneration, but the impact becomes massive if profits per share, or the return on corporate equity, are a bit better still. One result is that managements have a strong incentive to reduce the equity capital of their companies.

While models, such as this one, may appear complicated because of the mathematics involved, they are necessarily simplifications of the real world. This is true of all models, as only through

[3] *Some Unpleasant General Equilibrium Implications of Executive Incentive Compensation Contracts*, John B. Donaldson, Natalia Gershun and Marc Giannoni, The Federal Reserve Bank of New York as "Staff Report No. 531". (2011).
[4] "*CEO Compensation*", C. Frydman and D. Jenter, Annual Review of Financial Economics 2(1): 57–102. (December, 2010).

simplification can we separate the fundamental issues from the noise that comes with the data and thus understand how things work. It is, however, probably true that filtering out the noise is particularly difficult for economic models, which depend on human behaviour. The simplifications necessary for building models are nonetheless essential, if we are to understand the workings of the economy. Once a model is constructed it has to be tested, and the authors of the New York Fed's paper tell me that they are planning to do this. On the basis of the evidence I have set out it seems likely that their model will prove robust when tested.

The paper's model leads to concerns which are strongly supported in practice by the evidence that I have set out. For example, the conclusion that today's managements have a strong incentive to reduce the equity capital of their companies is supported by the evidence set out in Chart 11, which shows that companies in recent years have preferred buying back shares to investing in new plant.

I am pleased that the authors of the New York Fed's paper should have looked at this problem, as it is encouraging to find that others besides me are worrying that the change in management incentives has become very damaging to the economy. Another economist who has expressed concerns on these lines is Bill White, who writes in a recent paper: "A third reason for continuing low investment seems to have been a secular trend on the part of corporate managements of AMEs [Advanced Market Economies] to maximize cash flow. The incentive for this 'short-termism' could be that it allows for larger payouts for both salaries and dividends, also raising equity prices and the value of management options into the bargain."[5]

Bill White lists the wish to maximise cash flow as the third of his reasons for low investment after general uncertainty and the

---

[5] *Ultra Easy Monetary Policy and the Law of Unintended Consequences* by William R. White, The Federal Reserve Bank of Dallas Globalization and Monetary Policy Institute "Working Paper No. 126" (2012). The author is chairman of the Economic Development and Review Committee of the OECD and previously Economic Advisor and Head of the Monetary and Economic Department of the BIS.

growth of anti-business rhetoric. In my view it is the key reason, as it is sufficient on its own to have constrained investment and has been an important contributor to both general uncertainty and the growth of anti-business rhetoric. I would also add that the incentives for the "short-termism" given to corporate management, to which he refers, encourage share buy-backs even more than higher dividends and this aggravates the problem of excessive corporate savings.

There are, no doubt, other economists who have similar concerns, but if so I have not, to my regret, encountered their work. The more that is written on this subject, the less it is likely to be disregarded. It is difficult for new ideas to get aired, for both good and bad reasons. The good one is that many are nonsense. Economics vies with medicine as the science most liable to attract views that are frankly bonkers, and economists and financial journalists cannot give time and press space to all views. They are therefore forced to dismiss some ideas without careful analysis. The bad reason for the difficulty of getting new ideas aired is that they are an irritation to many, unless the ideas are their own, and those who are most likely to be irritated by new ideas are those least likely to have them. New theories may prove wrong, and indeed are bound to do so in some respect, as they are never the last word. They must therefore be debated. Of course, it is unfortunate if some new ideas do not stand up to the test, but it is far worse if good new ideas, which would pass the test, are ignored, especially by those who have neither thought of them nor found holes in them.

The current weakness of the recovery requires more attention than is habitually given by those who assume that it is a cyclical rather than a structural problem. Among those who recognise this, a frequently encountered explanation is that recovery is being held back by "deleveraging". The proponents of this view hold that the private sector in the developed world found with the financial crisis that they had too much debt. According to this theory the private sector is seeking to use the strong cash flows, which are the counterparts to fiscal deficits, to repay their debts rather than investing in new plant and equipment (in the case of companies) and in new houses (in the case of individuals).

Chart 46 shows that balance sheets have improved slightly since 2008, but very little of the improvement seems to have come from

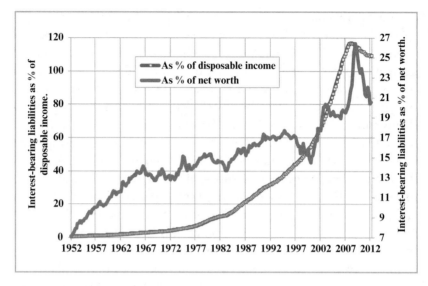

Chart 46. US: Household Leverage.
Source: Z1 Table B.100.

an increase in household savings. Debts can fall because they have been repaid or because the borrower has defaulted. This happens when individuals become bankrupt or when they simply walk away from their debts and banks and other creditors have to write them off as "defaults". The recent improvement in household balance sheets seems to owe much more to a rise in defaults than because debts are being repaid. The proportion of loans on residential property that banks wrote off (the charge-off rate) rose by 35 times between June 2006 and the end of 2012.

Balance sheets have been improved by a combination of reluctance and inability to take on more debt. Households have been deterred from buying houses, because the terms for mortgages have become less absurdly easy than they were and, until very recently, because house prices have been falling, particularly in the US.

Household savings are currently low in both the UK and the US (Chart 9), which is difficult to reconcile with claims that demand is depressed because households are striving hard to reduce their debts. While household balance sheets are highly leveraged and this is likely to depress household spending over time, the wish to reduce debt seems to be either non-existent or has been postponed in the hope that it will not, when the economy recovers, require a cutback in living standards, just a slower improvement in expenditure compared to incomes.

Companies, as well as households, have highly leveraged balance sheets, a point that I will investigate in more detail later. It is often claimed that business is, as a result, bent on deleveraging and cash is therefore being used to reduce debt rather than being spent on new investment in plant and equipment. An odd feature of this argument is that those who hold that companies are constrained from investing by the wish to deleverage are often those who claim that US companies' balance sheets "are in good shape". In fact, neither of these popular assumptions are supported by the data, which show that leverage is high, and despite this companies are far from seeking to improve their balance sheets. If they were, they would be repaying debt, but in practice they are choosing to spend their cash flow *and* any new debt that they can borrow by buying back their equity at a rapid rate.

Not only are companies increasing their leverage by buying back shares, they have been the only major group of investors who are buyers, both over the past 20 years, as Chart 47 for the long-term and Chart 48 for more recent years show. In Q3 US companies were buying shares at over $400 bn a year.

This is not unique to the US: the same phenomenon is found in the UK (Chart 49). The most recent available data are for 2011, when UK non-financial companies were net buyers of £47 bn of equity, which was 3.1% of GDP and thus proportionately even higher than US net buying, which was equal to 2.7% of GDP.

As I showed in Chart 11, the proportion of cash generated from depreciation and profits after tax that is currently being invested in plant and equipment is the lowest in the US that it has been in the post-war era and the proportion returned to shareholders is nearly 55%. These data clearly show that it is not a wish to deleverage that holds back investment, but a preference for buy-backs.

Debt deleveraging following financial crises seems to have often held back investment and demand in the past, but the data do not support the idea that it is the cause of our current problems. It is sadly typical of much economic analysis today that deleveraging

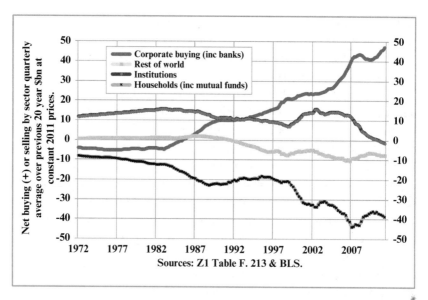

Chart 47. US: Net Buying of Shares by Sector.
Sources: Z1 Table F.213 & BLS.

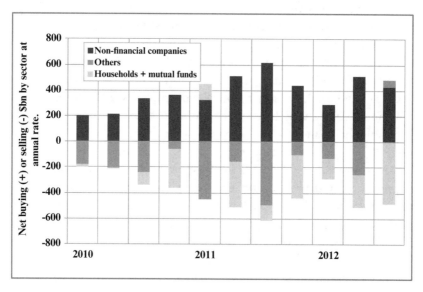

Chart 48. US: Companies Keep Buying.
Source: Z1 Table F.213.

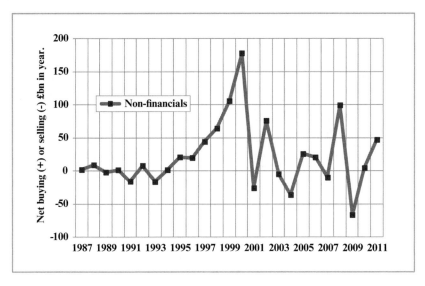

Chart 49. UK: Non-financials Net Buying.
Source: ONS (NESH & NEVL).

is nonetheless frequently put forward as a major problem.[6] This illustrates what will be a recurring theme of this book, which is that economists all too often rely on their preconceived and theoretically-based views about the way the economy works and are unprepared to revise them when the evidence is inconsistent with their preconceptions.

---

[6] As an example see *"Explain the disease to help US citizens"* by Richard Koo, Financial Times, (5th November, 2012).

6

The Particular Problem of Finance and Banking

The authors of the New York Fed's paper point out: "Financial firms seem particularly prone to lavish convex compensation practices. We are reminded of the financial crises surrounding the collapse of LTCM. In the year preceding its bankruptcy, the partners took the deliberate decision to reduce the firm's capital, as a device for maximising returns."[1] The fact that the distortions of the bonus culture are particularly acute with regard to financial companies aggravates the way in which business has sought to increase its cash flow. This is because financial companies are not likely to invest heavily in new physical equipment, even if they are exceptionally profitable. As I show in Chart 50, their share of business output is much higher than their share of business investment.

The problem for the economy that has arisen because of the rise in the cash flow of the business sector comes from the combination

[1] *Some Unpleasant General Equilibrium Implications of Executive Incentive Compensation Contracts*, John B. Donaldson, Natalia Gershun and Marc Giannoni, The Federal Reserve Bank of New York "Staff Report No. 531". (2011).

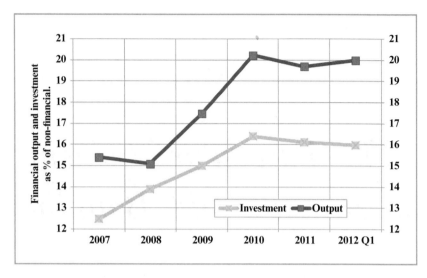

Chart 50. US: Financial and Non-financial Investment & Output.
Sources: Federal Reserve Z1 Tables F.101 & F.107 & NIPA Table 1.14.

of higher profit margins and lower investment spending. Since financial companies invest less, relative to their output, than non-financial companies do, the problem is magnified if finance becomes relatively more important and, as Chart 51 illustrates, this is exactly what has occurred.

Trouble in finance is clearly more dangerous than problems in other sectors of the economy. This may not be a permanent state of affairs but it is likely to last for many years until there have been major changes in the way banks and large financial institutions are regulated. In particular the new rules require increases in the proportion of banks' assets that must be financed by equity capital relative to their deposits and other forms of debt. It is clear that if finance becomes hyperactive it is more likely to become a major threat to the stability of the economy than if the effulgence bursts forth in some other sector, such as electronics or steel production. Finance seems to pose a chronic source of instability, which readily becomes acute in the absence of watchful attention. We have recently suffered from one of the more dramatic upticks in its capacity to cause havoc and it is, I think, clear – and happily clear

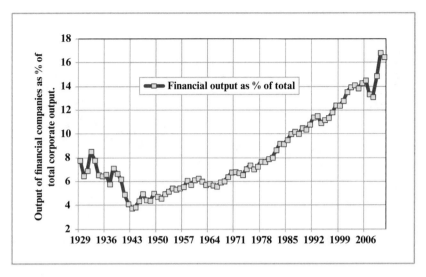

Chart 51. US: Financial as % of Total Corporate Output.
Source: NIPA Table 1.14.

to most people concerned with bank regulation – that this danger persists.

The dangers that arise from the growth in the importance of finance are also apparent when observed from a more theoretical perspective, as the New York Fed's paper by Donaldson, Gershun and Giannoni makes abundantly clear. They draw attention to the way in which the financial part of the business sector is particularly prone to damage the economy through the perverse incentives given to management. This is a welcome instance where the evidence supports conclusions based on theoretical analysis. Financial margins are exceptionally high relative both to their past history and to non-financial margins in both the US (Chart 52) and the UK (Chart 53).

The theory that profit margins are usually mean reverting seems too reasonable to be easily doubted and, when this theory is tested for mature economies, the evidence gives full support to the theory.[2]

[2.] As shown in Appendix 1.

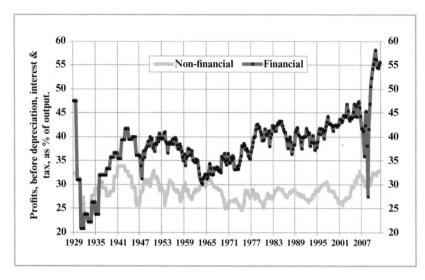

Chart 52. US: Financial & Non-financial Profit Margins.
Source: NIPA Table 1.14.

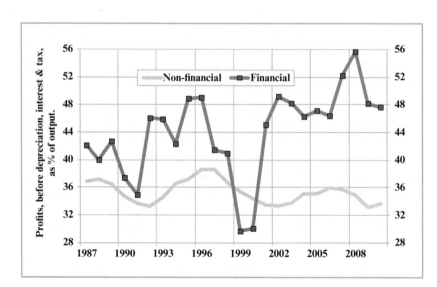

Chart 53. UK: Financial & Non-financial Profit Margins.
Source: ONS (FDBA, NHRE, NQNV & NRJK) via Ecowin.

It does not, however, follow that profit margins in finance and non-finance will, when measured separately, have the same characteristics. Indeed, it is highly likely that they will not, and this expectation is supported by the evidence shown in Charts 52 and 53, which show that in recent years the profit margins in finance have been persistently higher, in both the US and the UK, than the margins of non-financial businesses. In competitive conditions the return on capital must be similar in both finance and non-financial business, at least after allowing for risk, as otherwise capital would move to whichever sector gave the best returns. Whenever returns in one sector were higher than in another, capital would flow towards that sector and bring down the returns in it. While returns may be temporarily higher in one sector than another, this cannot last in a competitive environment. Returns on capital depend on profit margins and the output that can be produced from any given amount of capital. When an industry or sector needs more capital than the average, its profit margins must be above average in order for the return on capital to be average. Capital-intensive industries therefore have high margins, and if finance needs a lot of capital then its profit margins must be relatively high. The need for capital varies over time and relative profit margins must therefore also change. The rise in off-balance-sheet finance has reduced the need for capital in non-financial companies and increased it in the banks, which provide the finance. This will have tended to increase the relative profit margins of banks. Only if we measure the corporate sector as a whole should profit margins be mean reverting around a stable mean.

By moving debt off the balance sheets of the non-financial and household sectors onto that of finance, the interest costs associated with the debt will also have moved. To pay for these costs profits in finance will have to have increased relative to profits in non-financial businesses. Even if the plant, or aeroplane, is now owned by a financial company, the people operating it will still be working for a non-financial one. There will, therefore, have tended to be a much greater rise in the relative need for capital than labour in finance, and this will have to be reflected not only in profits but also in profits per person employed. The large growth of off-balance-sheet debt is likely to have made a major contribution to the growth in financial debt, which in the US has grown from 3%

of GDP in 1952 to 90% today. A major feature has been the growth of "Off-balance sheet leases, which have historically allowed firms to make fixed-cost capital expenditures without recognising them on the balance sheet [in the US] this source of fixed-cost financing increased 745% as a proportion of total debt from 1980 to 2007."[3] This dramatic change may well therefore provide at least a partial explanation for the way the gap between the profit margins of the two sectors has widened. Nonetheless, the way in which profit margins in finance have risen so rapidly to such heights makes it unlikely that the growth of off-balance-sheet finance provides a fully adequate explanation of the massive gap in profit margins illustrated in Chart 52 for the US and Chart 53 for the UK.

I have been unable to find good data from the national accounts with which to compare the returns on the capital employed in financial and non-financial businesses, and it will be clear from comments that I have made already, and will be amplifying later on, that companies cannot be relied upon to publish accurate data. Nonetheless, it seems clear that financial companies have become relatively much more profitable than others in recent years. This could have arisen either because finance business has become more risky and therefore needs higher returns on capital to compensate for the additional risk or because competition in finance has decreased. In both cases this poses a threat to the economy. Finance, as Chart 51 shows, has become more important to the economy. If it has also become more risky, it will have become an increasing threat to the stability of the economy as a whole. If it has become less competitive, it poses several other problems. First, an exceptionally profitable financial sector that invests relatively little in plant and equipment and pays out the same proportion of its profits in dividends as other companies will have an excess of savings over investment. This will make it more difficult to reduce the fiscal deficit without pushing the economy back into recession. Second, a large industry that produces excessive profits will wish to protect them and will spend money on lobbying politicians to discourage them

---

[3]"*Bringing leased assets onto the balance sheet*" by Kimberly J. Cornaggia, Laurel A. Franzen and Timothy T. Simin, draft paper available at http://papers.ssrn.com/sol3/papers.cfm?abstract_id=1680077, (accessed 5th June, 2013).

from introducing measures that enhance competition. This problem is particularly worrying if the industry is subsidised. Banks are heavily subsidised by taxpayers through the guarantees that they give to depositors, since it reduces the cost of borrowing to banks.

Because we guarantee bank depositors against loss, we enable them to borrow more cheaply than would be the case if these guarantees were not there. These guarantees are, therefore, a form of subsidy and we are, therefore, in effect, currently subsidising bankers to make political contributions aimed both at preserving their subsidies and their industry's ability to obtain excessive profits through inadequate competition. It would be hard to invent a more absurd arrangement or one more obviously contrary to the interests of taxpayers and more likely to bring both banking and politics into disrepute.

Within the financial sector, banks are particularly important not only because of their size but also because of the subsidies they receive through the guarantees given by taxpayers. As with any industry that is subsidised, the effect is to increase the size of banks and thus increase the danger that they pose to the economy. These guarantees are much greater in practice than they seem to be at first glance. There are specific guarantees that governments make on behalf of taxpayers, but the explicit amount for which individual depositors are guaranteed is limited in both the UK and the US. But in addition to these explicit assurances there are implicit ones. Taken together, the implicit and explicit guarantees are more important than the explicit ones alone. The implicit guarantee arises from the general belief that governments will either stop banks going bankrupt or, at the very minimum, bail out all their creditors whether or not they are covered by the specific guarantees for depositors.

Large financial institutions have become labelled as "too big to fail", on the grounds that the crash of any one of them would push the economy into recession. It is therefore assumed that governments cannot allow large financial institutions to go bust in the future, and the myth that surrounds the bankruptcy of Lehman Brothers has made it very difficult for government policy to defy this assumption. The Lehman Brothers myth is that its bankruptcy caused the financial crisis and that we would not now be suffering from its aftermath if only the US government had intervened to

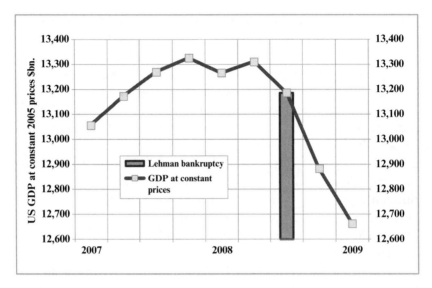

Chart 54. US: GDP & the Lehman Bankruptcy.
Source: NIPA Table 1.1.6.

stop the bank going bust. In fact, the Lehman bankruptcy occurred in September 2008 well after the US and world economies had started their steep descent into recession, as I illustrate in Chart 54. US GDP started to fall in Q1 2008. The recession did deepen in the two quarters after Lehman Brothers collapsed, but output was growing a year later. It is possible but far from certain that the recession would have been less fierce if the company had been bailed out. No one can tell what would have happened, but on these occasions myths are more important than facts and this myth makes it more difficult in the future for governments to allow major bankruptcies to occur. As it is very important for the health of the economy that financial companies should be allowed to go bankrupt, it has become all the more important that no financial company should be "too big to fail". It is uncertain whether the bankruptcy of Lehman Brothers amplified the weakness of the economy, but the recession was certainly not caused by the investment bank's collapse.

It is also widely believed that banks were responsible for the financial crisis. My own view is that the crisis would not have occurred if central banks and particularly the Federal Reserve had not fuelled the rises in debt and asset prices by foolish policies. The Fed's actions were the fundamental cause of the problem because its "easy money" policy failed to restrain banks from excessive expansion of their balance sheets. Rapid expansion of balance sheets always appears profitable until the resulting bad debts rise. Bankers seem unable to resist such rapid expansion unless they are constrained by monetary policy. History suggests that banks will invariably behave badly if encouraged to do so by the follies of central bankers. It was famously said by William McChesney Martin Jr., a former chairman of the Federal Reserve, that the job of central bankers is to take away the punchbowl before the party gets going. The Fed, and to a lesser extent other central banks, singularly failed to act up to this job description in the run-up to the financial crisis.

To explain this point more clearly, a parallel may usefully be drawn between the behaviour of banks and burglars. A rise in the incidence of burglaries can clearly be blamed on burglars, but as burglars will always steal if they can, an increase in their activities is likely to have a more fundamental cause than a drop in their morals. A rise in burglaries is likely, for example, without any change in the ethics of the criminal community, if there are fewer policemen or the police become less efficient and catch fewer thieves. It is equally true that no decline in the ethical standards of bankers is needed to explain a rise in the foolish risks taken by them, if the monetary policy of central banks allows greater scope for their follies.[4]

While the fundamental cause of the crisis was bad central banking, the visible agents were the commercial banks, and they can no more be held blameless than burglars can be excused for their thefts. Equally, however, it is foolish to assume that a rise in burglaries or banking problems can be blamed on a deterioration in the morals of bankers or burglars. Peter Lilley, who was a member of

---

[4] For a fuller description of the follies of central bankers over rises in debt and asset prices see "*Stock Markets and Central Bankers: The economic consequences of Alan Greenspan*" by Andrew Smithers and Stephen Wright, World Economics 3(1): 101–24, 2002; and *Wall Street Revalued: Imperfect markets and inept central bankers* by Andrew Smithers, John Wiley & Sons, Ltd, (2009).

the select group who warned that regulatory changes were increasing the risks of a financial crisis,[5] gave a succinct demolition of the widespread claims that the financial crisis was caused by the behaviour of bankers, when he remarked that "a change cannot be sensibly blamed on a constant". Unless one assumes that there was a sufficient fundamental deterioration in bankers' morals, the financial crisis must have come from a change in the circumstances under which they operated. My view is that the rapid rise in private sector debt and the huge expansion of banks' balance sheet, which were allowed by the monetary policy of central banks and eased by poor regulation, were the fundamental causes of the financial crisis and that the sharp change that triggered the crisis was the fall in asset prices.

Myths are common with regard to both the demise of Lehman Brothers and the role of banks in the financial crisis. But myths are a powerful influence on political decisions. These particular myths increase the attention that policymakers give to banks and add to the misinformation about the dangers they pose to economies and the ways in which they should be regulated.

Banks have changed. Their traditional activities of taking in deposits and lending the proceeds have lost their primacy. Banks have greatly increased their profitability and the increase has been driven by rises in the importance of their non-traditional activities, such as dealing, the sale of new and complicated financial products and fees for advice. Among these, dealing is probably the greatest contributor to profits.

Chart 55 shows the marked change in the return on equity of UK banks. From 1921 to 1971, the average return was 7% and it was then 20% from 1971 to 2009.

In the US the situation was similar, though not quite as marked. Chart 56 shows that, on average, from 1934 to 2012 the real return on bank's equity was around 6%, which is similar to the long-term

---

[5] Even more presciently, Peter Lilley cautioned in 1997: "With the removal of banking control to the FSA it is difficult to see how and whether the Bank remains, as it surely must, responsible for . . . preventing systemic collapse", *Battle starts for the new Governor* by Philip Aldrick, Sunday Telegraph, 16th September 2012. Peter Lilley, PC, Conservative MP, was at the time Shadow Chancellor of the Exchequer.

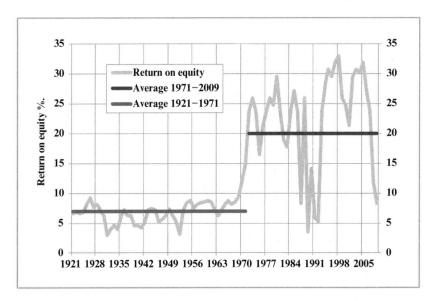

Chart 55. UK: Bank's Return on Equity.
Source: Bank of England (Allesandri & Haldane).

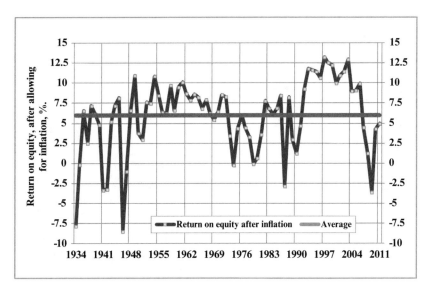

Chart 56. US: Bank's Real Return on Equity.
Sources: FDIC & BLS.

real return on equity for all companies, but averaged over 10% in
the two decades before the financial crisis. The return on bank
equity is probably understated in this chart by the inclusion of
goodwill in the equity of banks. If this were deducted, as it should
be, the real size of the returns would rise. I don't have long-term
data on the goodwill element and so have been unable to adjust
the returns to allow for it. The FDIC does, however, publish data
and these show, for example, that the return excluding goodwill was
four percentage points higher than the published figures from 1997
to 2007. It tells us a lot about banks' accountants that they should
believe that banks in aggregate are in a position today of good-
rather than ill-will.

The high returns recorded in both the UK and the US from
1996 to 2006 cover too long a period to be easily attributed to
chance. It seems likely that there was either a rise in the riskiness
of banking or a reduction in the competition. As I will seek to show,
there is a strong case that both changes occurred. As the change in
profitability was more marked in the UK than in the US, a satisfactory explanation must include reasons for this difference.

Evidence that the riskiness of banking rose from the 1970s in
the UK and from the 1980s in the US is shown in Chart 57. In

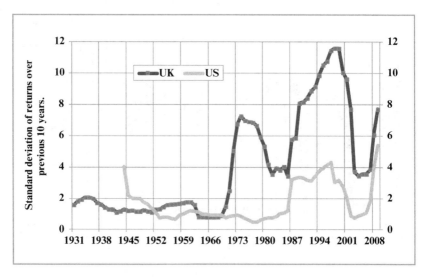

Chart 57. UK & US: Volatility of Bank Returns on Equity.
Sources: Bank of England & FDIC.

this chart I employ a commonly used measure of volatility, which is the standard deviation, and use it to measure the volatility of profits by the extent to which the returns on bank equity (net worth) varied over the previous 10 years. In the UK this measure started to rise sharply from 1970 and in the US from 1987. It is reasonable to attribute the high volatility of US returns on the decade ending in 1944 to the exceptional level of bankruptcies experienced in the 1930s. The high volatility of returns before World War II is therefore a measure of the riskiness of the economy at that time rather than of the banking industry considered in isolation. As this measure of volatility shows the riskiness over the preceding decade, changes will have tended to occur around five years before the dates shown on the chart.

On the evidence of Chart 57 it seems reasonable to conclude that:

- Banking became a riskier activity in the UK from the late 1960s and in the US from the mid-1980s.
- The rise in the volatility of returns after 2008 and in the 1930s can be attributed, at least in part, to the rising risks of the economy and not solely that of banking.
- Banking in the UK has become a more volatile business than in the US, which fits with the probability that dealing profits have been more important for British banks.

The rise in the return on banks' equity can therefore be reasonably attributed in part to a rise in the riskiness of banking. There is also strong evidence that banking has become less competitive. Chart 58 shows this for the US in two ways. The left-hand scale shows that the importance of individual banks has grown relative to the economy, by around three times since 1990, having been unchanged over the previous 60 years. At the same time, as shown on the right-hand scale of the chart, the assets of the three largest banks have grown from 8 to 40% of the total for the industry. Competition is weak when there are barriers to entry. Numbers will therefore tend to fall if declines owing to bankruptcies and takeovers are not offset by new entrants. Industries with marked barriers to entry will therefore tend to be increasingly concentrated. A key sign of inadequate competition is therefore that the number

Chart 58. US: Rising Importance of Large Banks.
Source: Bank of England.

of companies in the industry has tended to fall over time, and studies show that this has been a feature of banking in the UK as well as the US.[6]

Many of the problems posed by banks have been well debated. These include a general agreement that banks need a great deal more equity capital both because their vestigial current ratios pose a major threat to the world economy and because taxpayer guarantees, which enable banks to operate with such low amounts of equity, distort the economy and are without a compensating economic justification.

There is, however, a problem that arises from the market-making activities of banks, which are also sometimes described as dealing for their own account. This does not seem to me to have yet been properly debated or adequately understood. This is why we need to

---

[6] For a detailed examination see, for example, *Firm Stability and System Stability: The Regulatory Delusion* by Geoffrey Wood and Ali Kabiri, a paper for the Conference on Managing Systemic Risk, the University of Warwick, (7th to 9th April, 2010).

separate the dealing and market-making activities of banks from their more traditional activities. The current lack of understanding was illustrated with sad clarity in a leading article in *The Economist*. This called for an end to the attempts by regulators to separate the dealing activities of banks from their deposit taking and lending businesses, and failed to mention the key issue, which I will now seek to explain.[7] Today market making is mainly confined to banks and is an important part of their activities. This may, without exaggeration, be described as a kind of doomsday machine in which regular collapses are highly likely and almost inevitable and in which each collapse is likely to be larger than the last. This is clearly a foolish arrangement and, to make it even more absurd, it is one that is currently subsidised by taxpayers.

The LIBOR scandal revealed that banks had conspired to mislead the world about the rates at which they could borrow in the wholesale money market. This reinforced demands that banks should be split up, with the old-fashioned business of taking deposits and lending separated from the market making and other riskier activities of banks. Such a step is essential for the future stability of the world economy, but the inherent danger of having market making included in the activities of banks does not seem to be generally understood.

Market making needs to be separated from other activities. The size of individual market-making firms must be kept down and their numbers kept up. The reason for this is that market making is a risky activity that will produce regular bankruptcies. The scale of bankruptcies rises with each crisis, and each crisis will, if the current system is left unchanged, produce an even larger crisis than the last and have an even more damaging impact on the economy. To prevent this doomsday process from causing crises, individual bankruptcies need to be kept small, which means that the companies which are involved in market making must not be "too big to fail". Market making needs to be separated from banking so that this dangerous activity is not unnecessarily expanded through being subsidised and because the bankruptcy of banks is more disruptive to the economy than the bankruptcy of market makers.

---

[7] "*Sticking together: Breaking up universal banks is a bad idea . . .*", The Economist, (18th August, 2012).

The reason why market makers tend to get bigger and bigger is a combination of two factors, one of which is a piece of simple mathematics; the other is the way this is reinforced by the advantage given to size. The mathematical point is known as the Law of Large Numbers (LLN), for which Encyclopaedia Britannica Online has the following entry: "law of large numbers, in statistics, (is) the theorem that, as the number of identically distributed, randomly generated variables increases, their sample mean (average) approaches their theoretical mean."[8] This theorem can be usefully applied to games, such as poker, which combine skill with random fluctuations due to chance. If the participants in the game have equal skill, their results will be solely down to the random fluctuations. The wealth of the individual players will fluctuate and every so often one will go bust and have to withdraw from the game. The most likely loser is the one who starts with the least amount of money. Periodic losses are the inevitable result of the random fluctuations and if those going bust are not replaced by new entrants the average wealth of the remaining participants in the poker game will rise as their numbers fall.

Market making is a business that combines skill and random fluctuations. The skill consists in using the information provided by order flow to gauge the direction in which prices are moving, and the luck lies in the fact that the future is unknowable. Without order flow, market makers, however inherently skilful, cannot exercise their expertise. Orders are received by market makers before the impact of those orders are reflected in prices. Except where prices are the result of computer matching, in which no human skill is involved, order flow provides inside information to market makers prior to prices being determined.

The value of order flow varies between different markets. Well-organised markets, such as those for equities on the London or New York stock exchanges, publish the prices at which deals are made and the activities of those operating in them follow rules that render these markets more "transparent" than others. At the other end of the scale, much of the deals in derivatives and debt are made at prices that are not published, but known only to the dealer and the

---

[8] http://www.britannica.com/EBchecked/topic/330568/law-of-large-numbers, (accessed 29 April, 2013).

client. The information conferred by the flow of orders is greatest and most valuable when information about prices is restricted. This accounts for the perennial opposition of banks to the creation of transparent markets where these do not already exist.

But even if the market makers are skilful, they will be subject to luck. Every so often a large fall or rise in the prices of the assets being traded will cause large losses. If all market makers are equally skilful, the incidence of these losses will be random. Every so often one participant will lose all his capital and cease trading. According to the LLN, the most likely loser is the market maker with the least capital.

When the numbers involved in an activity decline, competition becomes less and the returns rise for the remaining participants. This will encourage new players to enter the industry. If entry is easy, the loss of one market maker will be readily replaced by a new entrant and competition will keep the return on equity down. If there are barriers to entry, the numbers of players will fall and while the returns will show cyclical fluctuations they will exhibit a rising trend over time. In both the UK and the US the numbers of banks have been falling. At least until recently, this was despite a large rise in the returns on banks' equity. Rising returns and falling numbers indicate an industry into which entry is difficult, where monopoly power is growing. As crisis follows crisis, each bankruptcy is likely to involve a larger company than the last one and to cause greater disruption to the economy.

As I showed in Chart 58, there has been a marked degree of concentration in the US banking industry. The size of the average commercial bank was stable, relative to GDP, from 1934 to 1994 but has since tripled and the proportion of bank assets held by the three largest banks has followed a similar pattern, having been stable at between 10 and 12% until 1994 and then tripling. A similar concentration has occurred in the UK banking sector, with the largest bank having had assets equal to 50% of GDP in 2000 and 140% in 2007.[9]

[9] The data for Chart 58 and for the concentration in UK banks are taken from *The $100 Billion Question* by Andrew G. Haldane, Bank of England, (2010).

This concentration was not due to banks being driven to leave the industry owing to poor returns. The real long-term return on equity has been stable at around 6%, and, as Chart 55 shows, the return on UK bank equity was similar to this, averaging 7% nominal from 1921 to 1971 and then averaging 20% from 1971 to 2009. Returns in the US have shown a similar though less exalted pattern (Chart 56).

As there is an advantage for size, the need to raise a very large amount of money in order to compete acts as a barrier. But this on its own should not deter those in other industries who have access to massive financial resources from entering an industry with high returns. However, the advantage conferred by size applies to the scale of order flow as well as to the scale of capital. As there is also skill involved in market making, a potential new entrant will have difficulty in recruiting those with skill if they do not have a large order flow, as the skills cannot be properly exercised without the flow.

The tendency for market making to have high and rising returns will not necessarily apply to banks' other activities. Banks will therefore tend to increase the proportion of their capital deployed in market making. This will reduce the speed at which competition falls but increase the exposure of banks to market crashes.

The high returns on banking in the recent past could be attributed either to the high risks being run or to limited competition. Both explanations are likely to have been important and both underline the need for change.

If the returns were solely a consequence of high risks, well-informed shareholders might like to restrain management from excessive risk taking. This could be done by increasing equity capital ratios, which would reduce both risks and returns. But shareholders, at least as represented by fund managers, and the management of banks both strongly oppose rises in equity ratios. This is even quite reasonable from the viewpoint of shareholders. "Limited liability" means that the value of the shares in any one bank cannot be negative, and shareholders are unlikely to find that governments will permit several large banks to be liquidated at the same time. This limits the likely losses on a portfolio of banks' shares more than it limits the likely profits. This effect is amplified by the subsidies provided to banks by taxpayer guarantees. These guarantees reduce the funding costs of banks and remove the market from applying limits to bank leverage, which is therefore solely determined by regulation.

It is widely known that most market returns are not symmetric, as they would be if the returns were above average half of the time and below average half the time. In practice most of the time returns from equities and other financial markets are above average with occasional periods of sharp losses. The remuneration of dealers and senior managers depends on their results and is often a multiple of their basic salary. As the salary is fixed, but the bonus will usually rise at least proportionately with profits, their total remuneration rises far faster than profits. Shareholders bear the losses and dealers take a large slice of the profits. The compensation packages are therefore structured to reward risk taking in an activity where risk taking pays most of the time, at the cost of occasional heavy losses, which, for the most part, do not fall on the dealers. It is therefore rare for managements either to wish or to be able to restrain the risks that their dealers take. Even if shareholders were able to instruct bank managements to limit risk taking, it is unlikely that their orders would be obeyed.

Banks receive a large subsidy from taxpayers. These are explicit in many countries, including the UK and the US, through the guarantees given to depositors. But in a world in which there are financial institutions that are considered too big to fail the subsidies extend implicitly rather than explicitly to all the debts of banks and large institutions. So long as banks are free to make markets in securities and deal in them for their own account, we will be in the ridiculous situation of not only allowing a highly risky activity, which becomes increasingly dangerous to the economy over time, to be part of banks, but also subsidising the process.

Market makers will go bankrupt from time to time. We cannot and should not try to prevent this. But if we are to avoid future financial crises, we need to make sure that when the bankruptcies occur they do not cause the economy to suffer because the supply of credit and business confidence collapses. We therefore need market makers to be kept small and unsubsidised. For both reasons they need to be kept separate from banks.

There are many ways in which this could be achieved. I am doubtful that regulating the activities of banks will provide a long-term answer, though it could be a useful way of reducing risk over the shorter term. One problem with regulating activities is that the regulators never know as much as those regulated and cannot therefore keep up with the ways businesses find to circumvent detailed regulations. In addition we don't only need to separate market making and dealing from banks: we need to ensure that market makers are kept small. It is only when they become large that they pose a problem when they go bust.

In the London market before "Big Bang", when the Stock Exchange was forced to abandon its control of the commissions charged by stockbrokers, market making was restricted to jobbers, one of which, Akroyd & Smithers, was founded by one of my great-grandfathers. Until the 1970s jobbers had to be partnerships and the partners were at risk for any losses made. This restricted their size and controlled the risks they took. The risks did not then have the asymmetric nature to rewards that came when jobbers were allowed to be companies with limited liability. While they were partnerships, the partners were fully exposed to the losses as well as to the profits. The need for mutual trust limited the number of partners, which, together with the need for those retiring to withdraw their capital, resulted in the size of jobbing firms being effectively limited. When jobbers were permitted to operate under limited liability and some, including Akroyd & Smithers, became listed on the Stock Exchange, the previous limits on size ceased to operate and by the time Big Bang arrived three firms – Akroyd & Smithers, Wedd Durlacher and Smith Brothers – dominated the business of market making in London.

It is probably impossible to return to a world in which market makers have to be partnerships. This is equally true of banks, though the idea that this would solve the problem of banking crises has been suggested by some. The most likely solution, which has had the approval of many, including the IMF and the BIS, is for banks and possibly other financial institutions to need proportionately more equity capital relative to their assets the larger they are. For example, a bank with total liabilities of $1 bn would be required to hold equity equal to 10% of those assets (i.e. $100 m), and one with liabilities of $11 bn would need equity not just of 10% but, say, 11% (i.e. $121 m and not just $110 m). This would not only reduce the risks of large firms going bankrupt but also provide a disadvantage that would increase with size. As the growing concentration of banks seems to be based on the advantage of size, it will require a compensating disadvantage to offset this, which increasing minimum capital ratios with size should provide. It would not be necessary to decide initially how rapidly the capital requirement would increase, but if banks did not decide to split off these activities from the traditional ones, it would be clear that the disadvantage for large banks arising from their need for additional equity capital would not yet be great enough and a further increase in the equity ratio of large institutions would still be needed. In time the minimum degree to which capital ratios would need to rise with size in order to keep dealing away from retail banking would become clear. It would be a market-based solution and thus free from many of the complaints justifiably made about regulatory systems.

The reasons why the dealing activities of banks need to be hived off are not widely understood, as an article in *The Economist* underlines.[10] There is, nonetheless, considerable pressure for such reforms. This was shown in a somewhat half-hearted way by the report from the UK Commission on Banking, which wanted dealing split in operational terms from deposit taking and lending but to continue under the same ownership.

There is an international agreement, known as Basel III, which requires banks to increase their capital ratios, but banks have been effective in resisting the immediate and full implementation of the agreement. Bank equity ratios can be increased either by increasing their equity or by cutting back on their balance sheets. The delay in forcing banks to have more equity arose because of fears that a more aggressive requirement would cause banks to reduce their lending and thereby inhibit growth. This problem could easily have been circumvented by requiring banks to have an adequate equity ratio which was measured against their balance sheet totals in, say, 2010 rather than their current ones. Banks could then improve their equity ratios by adding to their equity capital but not by shrinking

---

[10] "*Sticking together: Breaking up universal banks is a bad idea . . .*", The Economist, (18th August, 2012).

their balance sheets.[11] This was not, however, done – though it still could be. The required ratios have been based on current balance sheets and, since banks dislike adding to their equity capital either by new issues, lower dividends or reduced bonuses, the result has been that banks have been cutting back on their balance sheets. This is widely, and perhaps correctly, seen as inhibiting recovery.

The regulators have blundered and banks should be required to increase the amount of equity they hold and thereby to improve their ratios faster and further than currently proposed without, initially at least, being allowed to do so by reducing their lending. There is widespread agreement among economists that the under-capitalisation of banks continues to provide a massive subsidy to the industry and leaves the world unnecessarily exposed to another banking crisis, particularly in the eurozone. It seems that the UK is planning to change its regulations in a sensible way by deciding on the amount rather than the proportion of equity capital that banks will be required to hold. This is a step forward and needs to be followed by increasing the amount of equity that banks need.[12]

If the equity of banks is to be increased, this must either involve making new equity issues, retaining more profits by paying lower dividends or using shares rather than cash to pay dividends and bonuses. As most banks claim to be profitable and pay large bonuses to their employees, one or other of these methods could be readily used to raise more capital. But as shareholders and management dislike new capital being raised, this obvious truth is consistently, blatantly and absurdly denied.

Despite their absurdity, the denials are also accepted by many politicians at face value. When the crisis occurred, the response of politicians was to seek advice on what to do and they sought this advice from bankers, who are the most unsuitable people they could

---

[11] This point has also been made in leading articles, for example "Capital require-ments must be enforced in absolute euro terms, not only ratios, so that banks cannot meet them simply by deleveraging." From *"Banks' continuing to damage Europe."* Financial Times (27th August, 2012).

[12] According to the article *"FSA eases bank rules to boost lending"* by Brooke Masters, Financial Times, (10th October, 2012).

have chosen. They have massive conflicts of interest and their past behaviour suggested that they have little understanding about the causes of the crisis. While there were probably bankers who had some clue about the mess they had got themselves into, they must have been a small and sadly ineffective minority. In the run-up to the crisis, banks' managements had been suffering from a process known to economists as adverse selection. A banker of good understanding and principles would have been increasingly unhappy about the activities of his bank in the years before the financial debacle and most would have been pushed out as uncomfortable colleagues who were a drag on profits, as measured at the time, while others would have left of their own accord. As a result there were, and still are, few bankers from whom it was sensible to take advice about how to resolve or forestall the next crisis.

In addition to their naivety, it seemed natural to politicians to turn to bankers because they knew them. The high profits that bankers had made during the decade in the run-up to the crisis rendered them a large potential source of political contributions. As they wished to preserve these profits and this required political support, they were a ready as well as a large source of money. Their high profits were mainly the result of taxpayer subsidies and inadequate competition. It was in the public interest, but not the bankers', that these should be reformed. Political contributions were thus readily available as bankers sought to preserve their excessive profits and the excessive level of remuneration that went with them by lobbying against the public interest.

When excessive profits can be earned by an industry or an individual company, this is known to economists as rent extraction or, more colourfully and equally accurately, as rent gouging. Because political contributions will be made in attempts to preserve rent gouging, it is extremely important that such conditions should not be allowed to continue for a country's political as well as economic health.

In the run-up to the crisis there was also a marked increase in the development of new products. Of course innovation should be encouraged in most industries, but there are strong reasons for thinking that this is not necessarily the case in finance. Bankers often object to regulation on the grounds that it will inhibit innovation. Even if this were true, it is not necessarily a case against the regulations because analysis shows that innovation in finance can be against the public interest by encouraging rent gouging.[13]

Franklin Roosevelt's success in reorganising US banking in March 1933 stands in marked contrast to the poor policies pursued in the aftermath of this crisis. There was a sharp recovery in both banks and the economy, which dates immediately from the introduction of the 1933 Bank Act. As Tony Badger shows in his history of the period, the one group from whom Roosevelt did not take advice was the bankers.[14]

In the eurozone the political clout of bankers appears to be great for somewhat different reasons. In Germany the *Landesbanken* (or state banks) have a large and important role and are owned by the local authorities who have strongly and effectively opposed requirements for greater capital ratios. In France, a major obstacle to reform comes from the intellectual predilections of bureaucrats and politicians, who prefer *dirigisme* over markets, and their consequent preference for banks, which are amenable to political direction, over investors, who are not. This has been reinforced by a desire to blame the financial crisis on the attitude of Anglo-Saxons. Eurozone politicians have sought to load regulations on credit agencies, short-sellers and hedge funds who cannot reasonably be blamed for the financial crisis, rather than on banks, which cannot be exculpated. This approach seems to have been exemplified by Michel Barnier, the French European Commissioner for Internal Market and Services, who regularly sought to load regulations on credit agencies, short-sellers and hedge funds, the relatively innocent bystanders to the crisis, and protect banks, who were at the centre of the trouble. He announced, just in time for the absurdity of his claim to be demonstrated by events, that European banks had adequate capital and that individual countries' regulators must not require higher standards. According to the Financial Times, M. Barnier's comments drove Lord Mervyn King, the Governor of the

---

[13] *Innovations, rents and risk* by Bruno Biais, Jean-Charles Rochet and Paul Woolley, Paul Woolley Centre, (2010) Working Paper Series 13, Discussion Paper 659, http://www2.lse.ac.uk/fmg/researchProgrammes/paulWoolleyCentre/working Papers/dp659PWC13.pdf, (accessed 5th June, 2013).

[14] *FDR: The First 100 Days* by Anthony Badger, Hill & Wang, (2008).

Bank of England, "who is not known as a man given to shouting", into doing just that.[15]

In the UK the key objection to banking reform is that it will be bad for the UK and, at least on a temporary basis, there is a reasonable if rather cynical case to be made for this view. Financial services are extremely profitable, probably because competition is limited. Looked at from a national viewpoint, the ability of one industry to extract rent from others is bad for the economy. It encourages resources of skilled labour to be misdirected. It does social damage by aggravating disparities of income and encourages political contributions to prevent necessary reforms. For an individual country, in particular the UK, it can, however, be justified on the grounds that a significant part of the rent gouging is at the expense of foreigners. Its justification is thus the same as that which has been used for piracy in Jamaica and Madagascar in its heyday, or put forward for Somalia until very recently. The UK currently has a net surplus on its international trade in financial services and it is likely that if this were a more competitive industry the surplus would be smaller and the change would reduce the UK's GDP.

---

[15] *"Barnier vs the Brits"* by Alex Barker, Financial Times, (8th November, 2011).

7

Japan Has a Similar Problem with a Different Cause

Japan is similar to the UK and the US in that its corporate sector is also running a large cash flow surplus. As Chart 59 shows, prior to 1993 Japan's business sector habitually ran a cash deficit, as it invested more each year than it saved through the combined resources of depreciation and retained profits. Since 1995 it has persistently run a cash surplus and this amounted to 7.5% of GDP in 2011 which matched nearly all the fiscal deficit of 9.7% of GDP.[1]

In Japan's case, however, the reason for the corporate sector's cash surplus is very different from that of the UK and the US. The main problem in Japan arises from the amount that companies are allowed for tax calculations to deduct from their profits for depreciation. There is no evidence that management remuneration has changed in a way that has changed business behaviour and Japan's problem thus had a different origin from that of the UK and US.

[1] As the cash surpluses and deficits do not always equal zero in aggregate, as they must in the absence of statistical discrepancies, I have taken the cash flows from the fiscal deficit, household savings and the current account surplus, and taken the figures for the business sector as the residual. The actual figure recorded for the business surplus in 2001 was 7.5%, while the figure used in Chart 59 is 7.3%. For earlier years the data are derived from the national accounts.

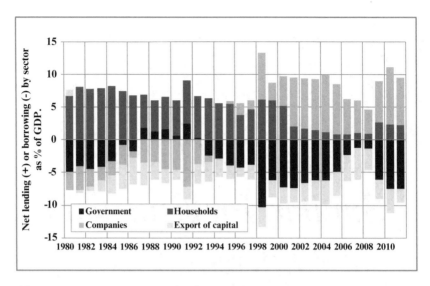

Chart 59. Japan: Sector Cash Flows.
Sources: Cabinet Office data for 1980 to 2000 are from the National Accounts for 2003 & for 2001 to 2011 from the National Accounts for 2011.

As Chart 60 shows, depreciation was sufficient to finance less than half of Japanese companies' investment spending in the 1950s, but since 2010 depreciation has covered more than 100% of their capital expenditure. This means that companies don't need any additions to their equity or their borrowings to finance their current level of investment. They could keep investing at the current rate and pay out all their profits as dividends and their leverage would be unchanged as they would need no new debt.

In the third quarter of 2012 Japanese output fell and it will probably have done so in the fourth quarter as well and will thus have fallen back into recession. The cause has been a sharp decline in its exports, not only to China, with whom Japan is in dispute over the ownership of the Senkaku Islands, and the eurozone, which is in recession, but more generally. Before this setback, however, Japan had been growing both in terms of its actual GDP and its potential GDP. In its May 2012 Economic Outlook, the OECD was expecting the economy to expand by 2% that year and 1.6% the next. The recent weakness of the Japanese economy is thus the result

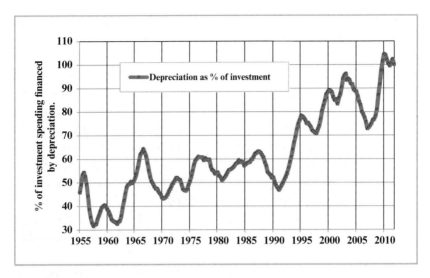

Chart 60. Japan: Non-financial Companies' Investment Spending & Depreciation.
Source: MoF Quarterly Survey of Incorporated Enterprises.

of weak demand. Its output potential is growing and the economy would grow if demand were adequate. At current levels of investment it could increase output in line with the OECD's pre-recession expectations and, following the recent weakness of the yen, its chances of doing so have greatly improved. This is not surprising. Although business investment in new capital has been slowing, its level is still well above that of the US, it currently amounts to 13% of Japan's GDP and only 10% of that of the US. If the two countries' abilities to grow were simply determined by the amount they invested, Japan would have the capacity to grow 30% faster than the US. Even allowing for the fall in the numbers of those of working age, the current level of investment is clearly adequate to finance a reasonable rate of long-term growth in GDP. If the data were correct then Japanese companies would be able to finance a steady expansion of their domestic output without the need for either any additional equity or any new debt.

If companies could really expand their output in this way, they would also be able to expand their profits, unless 100% of output was paid to employees. Output is for someone's benefit, it goes either to employees or to profits and if output grows then the sum of profits and labour incomes must also rise. If we accept the accuracy of Japanese data, and as we know that all output does not go to increase wages, we would be in a situation where profits would rise without any new capital, net of depreciation, being needed. The return on investment to companies depends on how much output rises in response to a given amount of capital spending and the proportions of that output that go to employees or to profits. If, as the data show, output rises without any new investment after depreciation being needed, then zero investment, net of depreciation, will produce a rise in profits unless employees receive 100% of the benefit from the rise in output. Thus, if profits take any share of output, the net return on investment will be infinite, as any number must be when divided by zero.[2]

As I am confident that the net return on new investment in Japan is less than infinite, it follows that the data must be wrong. I hope and expect that my confidence, in this instance at least, will be shared by readers.

The level of new investment is readily measured and its accuracy is subject to the checks that national accounts provide because GDP and its constituent parts can be measured in terms of expenditure, income and output. Significant errors are unlikely so long as these different methods of measurements agree with each other. There are, of course, small differences (termed statistical discrepancies) between the different estimates. The calculation of depreciation has none of these aids to precision and checks on its accuracy. In Japan, where companies must by law publish in their own accounts the same figure for depreciation and tax as they agree with the tax authorities, the charge for depreciation depends solely on the allowance that the tax authorities permit. As companies don't wish to pay more tax than they need to do, companies generally depreciate as fast as the tax authorities will allow them to.

---

[2] Using the conventional symbols, the return on capital is equal to the profit (Π) divided by the capital employed (K) so that the return $= \Pi \div K$. Output (Y) depends on the amount of capital needed to produce it, which is the capital/output ratio $K \div Y$. Output is divided between labour and profits, so that the return on capital must equal the profit share of output ($\Pi \div Y$) divided by the capital/output ratio, i.e. $\Pi/K = (\Pi \div Y)/(K \div Y)$.

Japanese practice is very different from the US, where there is no requirement that companies record the same level of depreciation in their published accounts as they claim for tax.

Japanese companies are thus, on the basis of current accounting practice, making an infinite return on their new capital expenditure and would do so whatever the division of output made between employees and profits, provided that the profit share is above zero. But this return on new investment does not appear in company accounts. If all new investment is financed by depreciation, there will be no additions made to the value ascribed in company balance sheets to plant and equipment. If the profit share of output falls, as Chart 20 shows that it has done recently, then the profitability of investment will appear to fall, even if it has "really" risen (i.e. it would have been shown to have risen had the accounting method used been less perverse).

It is, I think, clear that the allowances for depreciation in Japanese company accounts are far too great. This distortion has arisen because the allowances have not been altered over time, which they should have been in order to adjust for the marked change that has occurred in Japanese labour productivity.

Depreciation is often misunderstood. It is not, as seems often assumed, the costs involved in maintaining machinery in good working order. This is a separate charge that is part of the running costs of a business. But keeping plant in good working order will not stop it becoming less profitable and thus less valuable over time. The profitability of a piece of equipment falls because it embodies in it the technology of the time when it was installed. It is often possible to improve the efficient use of plant once it is installed as those using it learn on the job. Such improvements are, however, comparatively limited. The main way in which productivity improves is through investment in new equipment that incorporates improved technology. In general, therefore, it takes the same number of people working on an old piece of equipment to produce the output that can be derived from it. But over time wages rise and, as they rise in real not just nominal terms, they increase faster than prices. It therefore follows that the faster real wages rise the faster must be the rate at which depreciation should be charged.

As Chart 61 shows, real wages in Japan were rising at nearly 4% a year in the late 1980s but have not been growing at all recently.

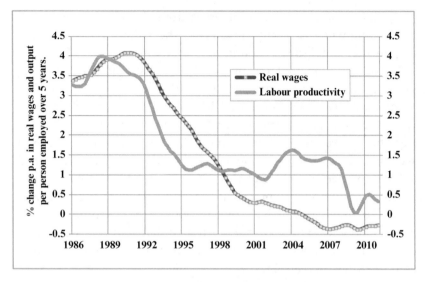

Chart 61. Japan: Real Wages and Labour Productivity.
Sources: MIC & Cabinet Office.

The main determinant of real wages is the growth in labour productivity, and where the labour share of output is stable productivity
and real wages grow at the same pace. Although there have been
changes in the labour share of output, the decline in labour productivity has moved in a similar pattern to the speed at which the
growth of real wages has decelerated. Real wages and labour productivity do not necessarily move together in the short-term, as the
labour share of output fluctuates and the costs of employment
depend not only on wages but also on contributions for pensions
and health insurance. We cannot know how labour productivity and
profit margins will change in the future. This unpredictability means
that the correct rate of depreciation cannot be known in advance.
We can, however, be sure that if the rate of depreciation used in
the 1980s was correct, when productivity was growing at between
3 and 4% a year, it is most unlikely to be correct today, when it is
probably growing at no more than 1.5% a year, even if due allowance is made for the impact of the recession.

Determining the correct rate at which depreciation should be
allowed as a cost before charging corporation tax is even more

complicated in practice, because it is not just determined by the speed at which real wages rise. Other important factors include inflation and the amount of capital, in addition to plant and machinery, such as land, inventories and net trade debtors, which is needed for output, and although we know their current values these change over time and their future values are thus also unpredictable.

If the prices of equipment rise then the cost of investing in new equipment will be higher than it would be if prices were stable. Depreciation is, however, charged on the basis of the book cost of the equipment. Even if depreciation were correctly assessed on the basis of stable prices, it would be too low if prices rose. Equally, it would be too high if they fell. As the prices of equipment in Japan were increasing in the 1980s, but have been falling for the past 15 years, an adequate rate of depreciation in the 1980s will have become too high now, not only because of the fall in labour productivity but also because of the change from a period when equipment prices were rising to one in which they have fallen.

Neither productivity nor inflation can be predicted, but their marked fall since the 1980s indicates that a marked fall in depreciation allowances should have occurred, and no changes have been made to them. Since the current accounting rules show that the return on new capital investment is infinite, we know that it is wrong. To avoid this absurdity the current allowances for depreciation need to be sharply reduced. We not only know, from the changes in labour productivity and inflation, that such a change is necessary but also know how the mistake has happened.

The excessive amount of depreciation charged to companies in their accounts reduces their profits, which are therefore understated. The extent of the decline in labour productivity points to the reduction being a large one, which means that the extent to which Japanese profits are now understated is also large. In Table 4, I show that if the ratio of profits to depreciation were the same for quoted companies in Japan as it is for those in the US, and the cash flow was unchanged, then published profits in Japan would rise by 77%, owing to a fall of 42% in the charge for depreciation.

I am not suggesting that a fall of 42% in the charge for depreciation would be the correct amount needed to bring down Japanese depreciation to its economic level. This would only be correct if the amount that US companies charged for depreciation in their

Table 4. EPS & Cash Flows for the Non-financial Companies Listed on Japanese and US Stock Markets 4th June 2012 (Sources: Nikkei & Standard & Poor's)[3]

	Earnings per share	Depreciation per share	Cash flow per share
Nikkei 225	581.9	1067	1648.9
S&P 500	87.18	52.26	139.44
Nikkei 225 (assuming unchanged cash flow and US ratios)	1030.917	617.9827	1648.9
Resulting increase in Nikkei profits	77.2%		

published accounts were correct, and it is almost certainly too low. We know for several different reasons, each of which supports the other, that US companies have historically overstated their profits and undercharging for depreciation is highly likely to be a major source of this overstatement.

US profits have over the long-term been overstated on average by around 10 to 15%, and the current degree of overstatement is likely to be more than this, as I shall explain later. While we can be confident that the extent to which Japanese profits are understated is likely to be large, it is probably less than the 77% that is suggested by a comparison with published profits of US companies. Manufacturing is more important among Japanese quoted companies than it is among US quoted companies and as manufacturing requires more investment in plant than is needed for the same level of output in services' industries this will probably mean that the depreciation should represent a higher proportion of the profits of quoted companies in Japan than in the US.[4] Nonetheless, Table 4 shows that

[3] I don't have direct data on the cash flow per share for the Nikkei 225 or for the S&P 500. I have therefore used the ratio of cash flow to earnings of listed companies from the Tokyo Stock Exchange to estimate the ratio for the Nikkei 225 and the ratio of cash flow to earnings of the constituents of the S&P 500 to estimate the cash flow of that index.

[4] Evidence that there is a large difference in capital requirements between manufacturing and services is set out in Appendix 2.

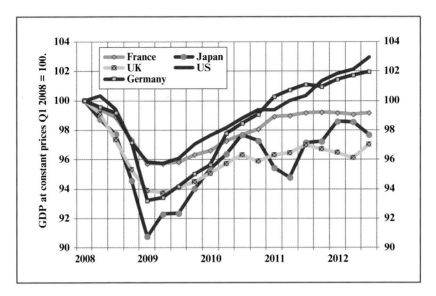

Chart 1. The Weak Recovery of G5 Countries.
Sources: National Accounts via Ecowin.

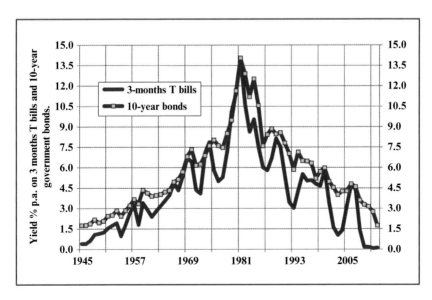

Chart 2. US: Interest Rates & Bond Yields.
Sources: Federal Reserve & Reuters via Ecowin.

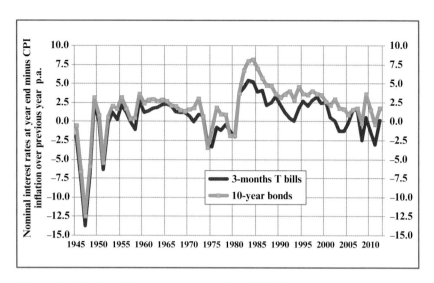

Chart 3. US: Real Interest Rates & Bond Yields.
Sources: Federal Reserve, Reuters & BLS via Ecowin.

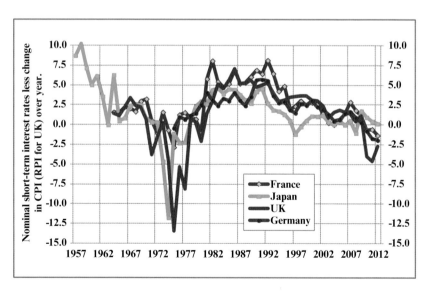

Chart 4. France, Germany, Japan & UK: Real Short-term Interest Rates.
Sources: Reuters & Federal Reserve via Ecowin.

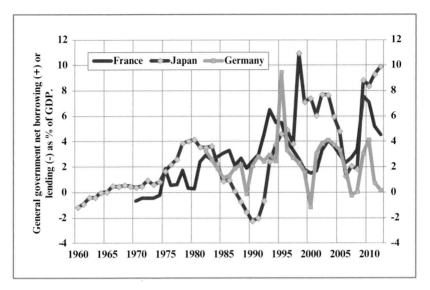

Chart 5. France, Germany & Japan: Fiscal Deficits.
Source: OECD via Ecowin.

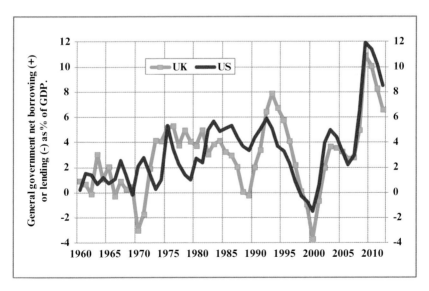

Chart 6. UK & US: Fiscal Balances.
Source: OECD via Ecowin.

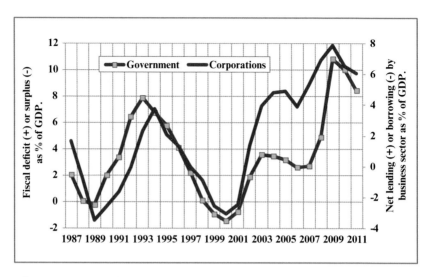

Chart 7. UK: Budget Deficits & Business Cash Surpluses Go Together. Source: ONS (EAOB, NHCQ & YBHA).

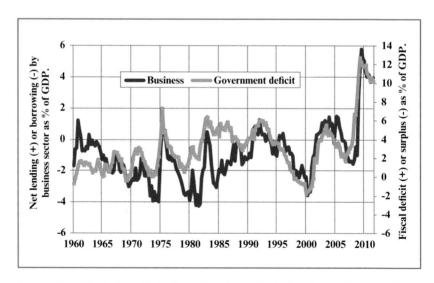

Chart 8. US: Budget Deficits & Business Cash Surpluses Go Together. Sources: NIPA Tables 1.1.5 & 5.1.

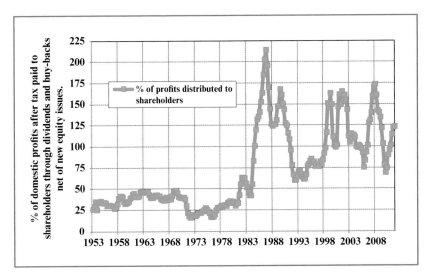

Chart 9. US: Percentage of Profits after Tax Paid to Shareholders through Dividends & Buy-backs.
Source: Federal Reserve Z1 Table F.102.

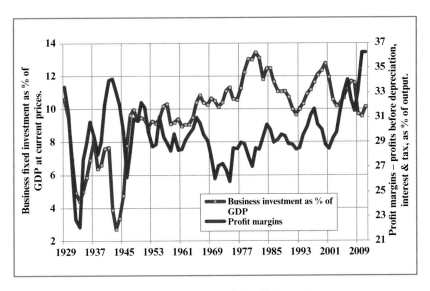

Chart 10. US: Business Investment and Profit Margins.
Sources: NIPA Tables 1.1.5 & 1.14.

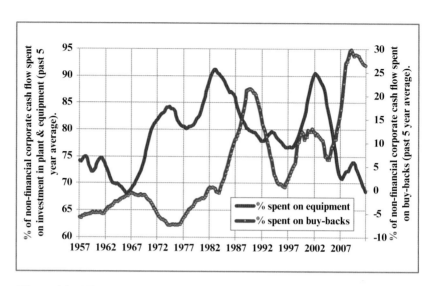

Chart 11. US: Management Prefers Buy-backs to Investment in Plant & Equipment.
Source: Federal Reserve Z1 Table F.102.

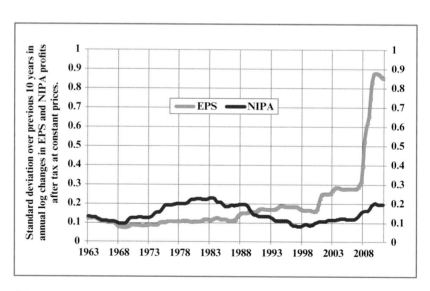

Chart 12. US: Volatility of S&P 500 EPS Compared with Volatility of NIPA Profits after Tax.
Sources: Standard & Poor's, NIPA Table 1.14 & BLS.

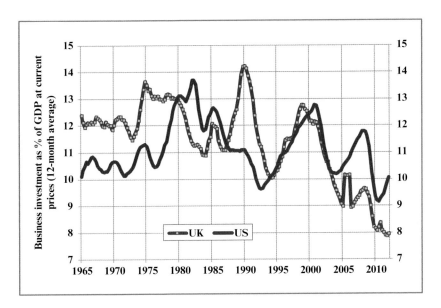

Chart 13. UK & US: Business Investment.
Sources: ONS (NPEK & YWBA) & NIPA Table 1.1.5.

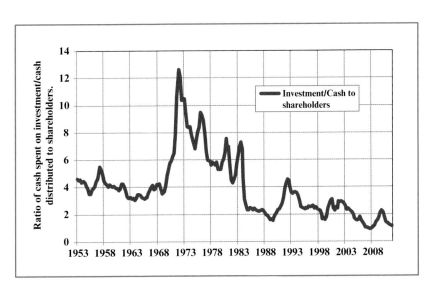

Chart 14. US Non-financial Companies: Management Horizon – Long-term vs Short.
Source: Federal Reserve Z1 Table F.102.

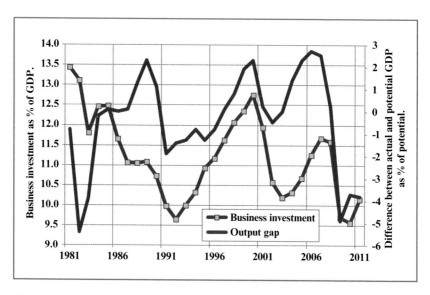

Chart 15. US: Business Investment & Output Gaps.
Sources: OECD Economic Outlook Vols 64 & 90 & NIPA Table 1.1.5.

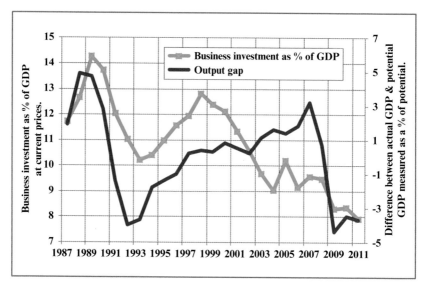

Chart 16. UK: Business Investment & the Output Gap.
Sources: ONS & OECD Economic Outlook Vols 68 & 90.

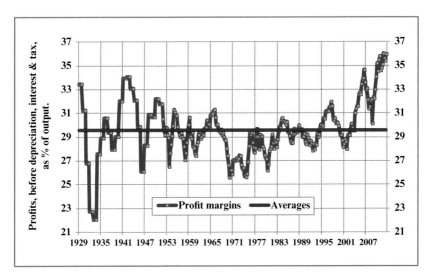

Chart 17. US: Profit Margins 1929 to Q3 2012.
Source: NIPA Table 1.14.

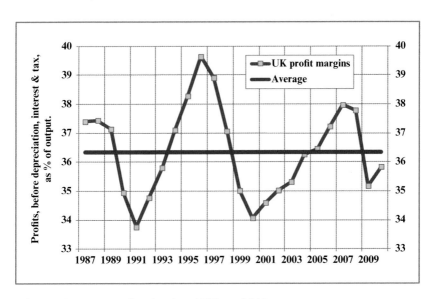

Chart 18. UK: Profit Margins 1987 to 2010.
Source: ONS via Ecowin.

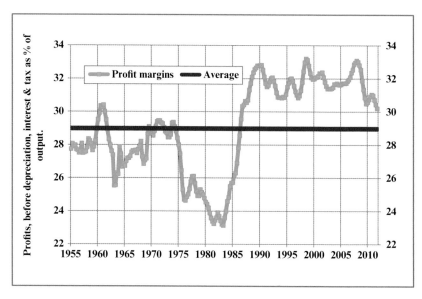

Chart 19. France: Non-financial Profit Margins.
Source: INSEE via Ecowin.

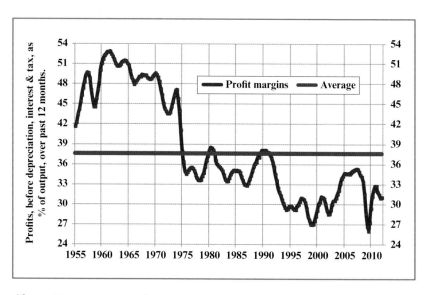

Chart 20. Japan: Non-financial Profit Margins.
Source: MoF quarterly survey of incorporated enterprises.

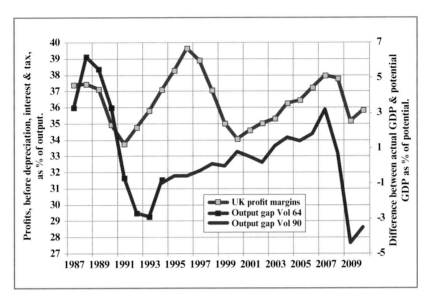

Chart 21. UK: Profit Margins & the Output Gap.
Sources: ONS & OECD Economic Outlooks.

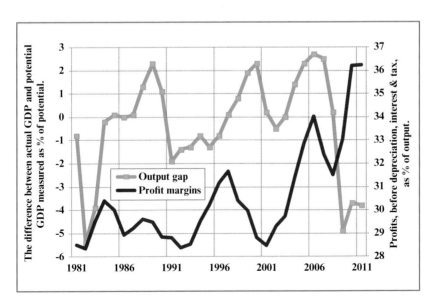

Chart 22. US: Profit Margins & the Output Gap.
Sources: NIPA Table 1.14 & OECD Economic Outlooks Vols 68 & 90.

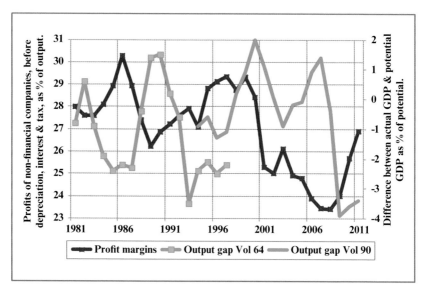

Chart 23. France: Profit Margins & Output Gap.
Sources: INSEE via Ecowin & OECD Economic Outlooks.

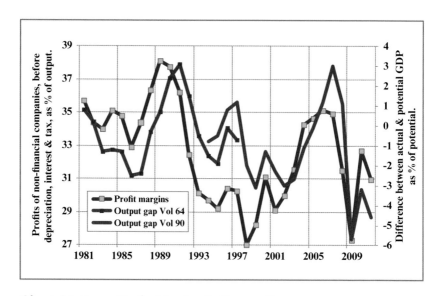

Chart 24. Japan: Profit Margins & Output Gap.
Sources: MoF Quarterly Survey of Incorporated Enterprises & OECD Economic Outlooks.

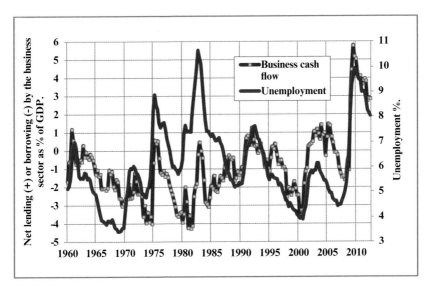

Chart 25. US: Business Cash Flow & Unemployment.
Sources: NIPA Tables 1.1.5 & 5.1 and BLS.

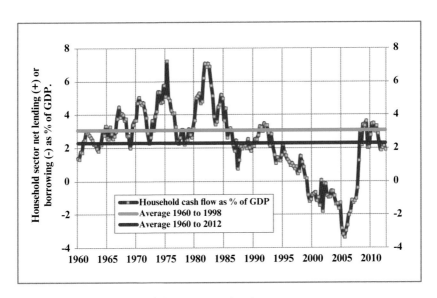

Chart 26. US: Household Sector Cash Flow.
Sources: NIPA Tables 1.1.5 & 2.1.

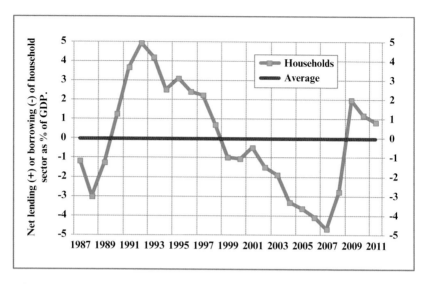

Chart 27. UK: Household Net Savings as % of GDP.
Source: ONS via Ecowin.

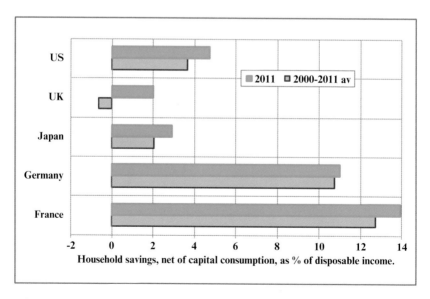

Chart 28. G5: Household Savings.
Sources: OECD Economic Outlook Vol 91 & ONS.

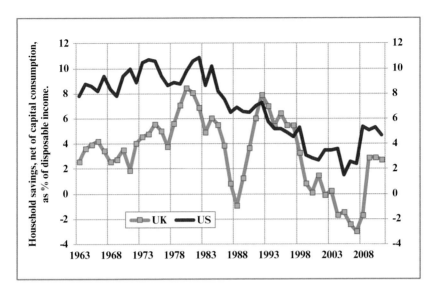

Chart 29. UK & US: Household Net Savings.
Sources: ONS & NIPA.

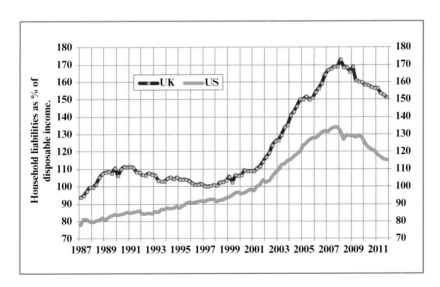

Chart 30. UK & US: Household Liabilities as % of Disposable Income.
Sources: ONS & Federal Reserve.

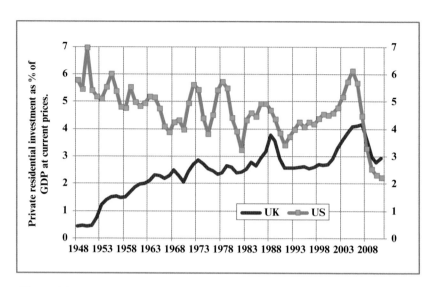

Chart 31. UK & US: Household Residential Investment as % of GDP. Sources: ONS (DFDF & YBHA) and NIPA Table 1.1.5.

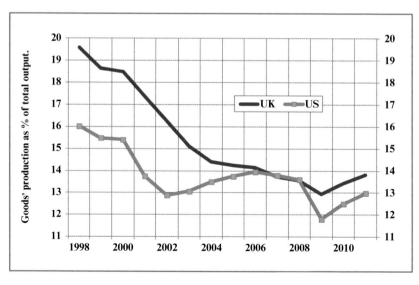

Chart 32. UK & US: Goods' Output as % of Total. Sources: ONS via Ecowin & NIPA Table 6.1D.

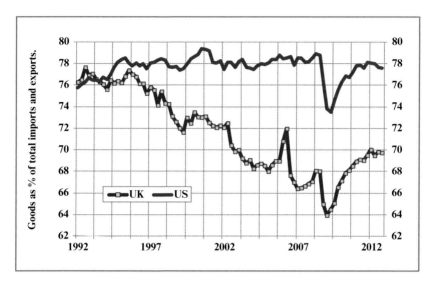

Chart 33. UK & US: Goods as % of Total International Trade.
Sources: ONS via Ecowin & NIPA Table 1.1.5.

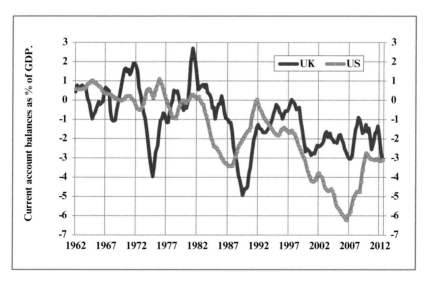

Chart 34. UK & US: Current Account Balances.
Sources: ONS & BEA via Ecowin.

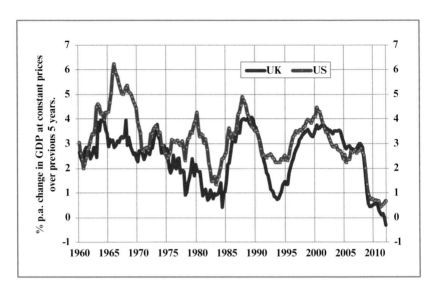

Chart 35. UK & US: 5-year Growth Rates.
Sources: ONS & NIPA.

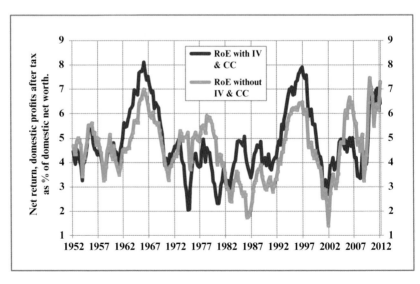

Chart 36. US: Return, Net of Tax, on Net Worth of Non-financial Companies.
Sources: Z1 Tables B.102 & L.102 & NIPA Table 1.14.

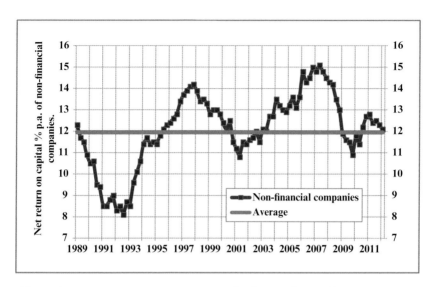

Chart 37. UK: Net Return on Capital of Non-financial Companies.
Source: ONS via Ecowin.

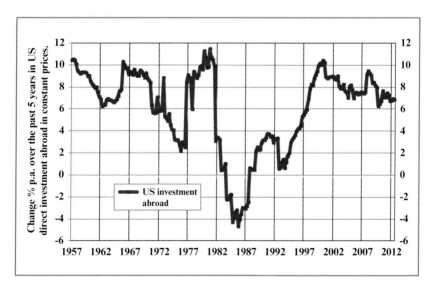

Chart 38. US: Changes in Non-financial Direct Investment Abroad.
Sources: BLS & Federal Reserve Z1 Table L. 102.

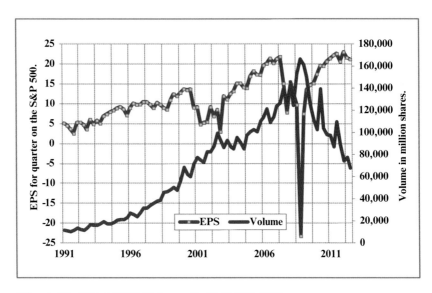

Chart 39. US: NYSE Volume & S&P 500 EPS.
Source: NYSE & Standard & Poor's via Ecowin.

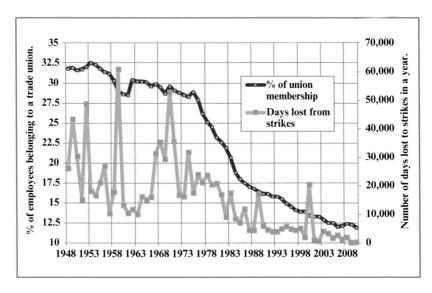

Chart 40. US: Unionisation & Strike Action.
Source: Department of Labor.

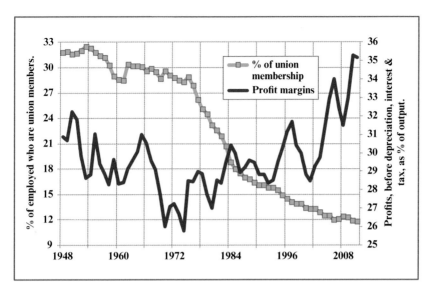

Chart 41. US: Profit Margins and Union Membership.
Sources: BLS & NIPA Table 1.1.4.

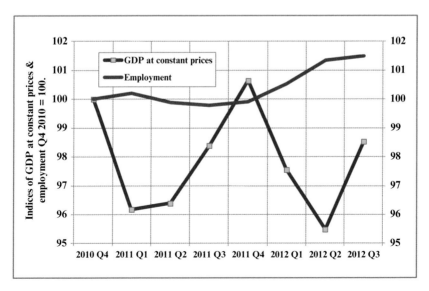

Chart 42. UK: Output & Employment.
Source: ONS via Ecowin.

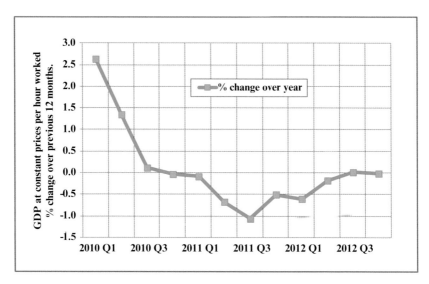

Chart 43. US: Change over Year in Output per Hour.
Sources: NIPA Table 1.1.6 & BLS via Ecowin.

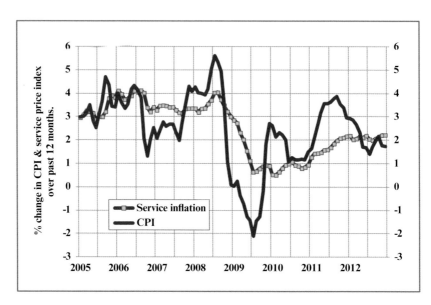

Chart 44. US: CPI & Service Inflation.
Source: BLS via Ecowin.

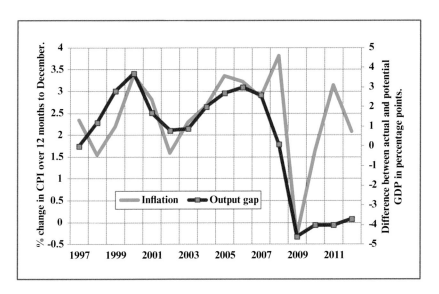

Chart 45. US: Output Gaps & Inflation.
Sources: OECD Economic Outlook Vol 92 & BLS via Ecowin.

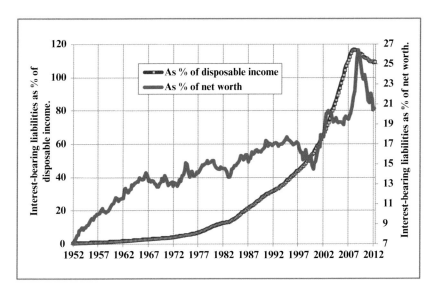

Chart 46. US: Household Leverage.
Source: Z1 Table B.100.

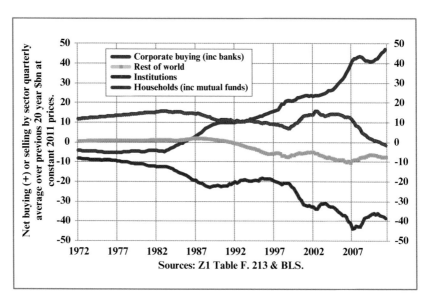

Chart 47. US: Net Buying of Shares by Sector.
Sources: Z1 Table F.213 & BLS.

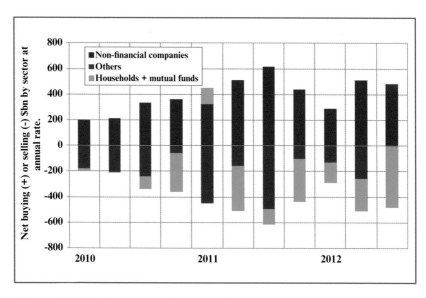

Chart 48. US: Companies Keep Buying.
Source: Z1 Table F.213.

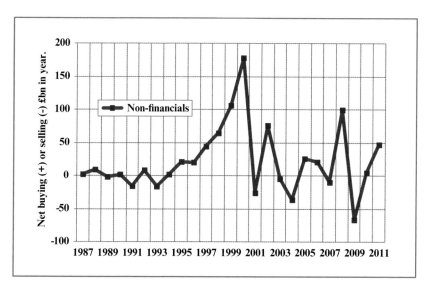

Chart 49. UK: Non-financials Net Buying.
Source: ONS (NESH & NEVL).

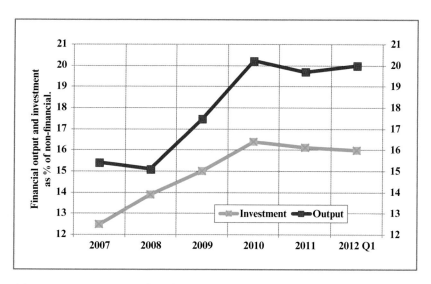

Chart 50. US: Financial and Non-financial Investment & Output.
Sources: Federal Reserve Z1 Tables F.101 & F.107 & NIPA Table 1.14.

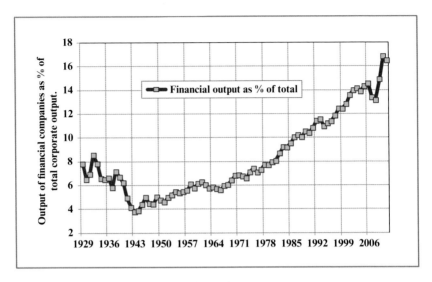

Chart 51. US: Financial as % of Total Corporate Output.
Source: NIPA Table 1.14.

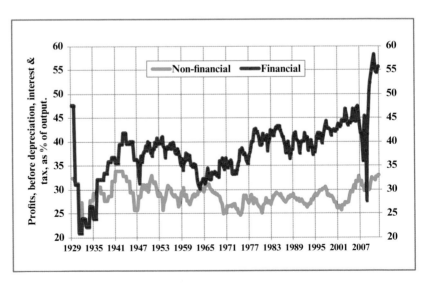

Chart 52. US: Financial & Non-financial Profit Margins.
Source: NIPA Table 1.14.

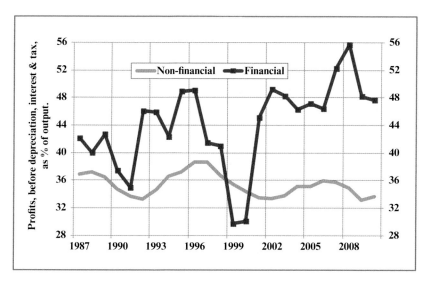

Chart 53. UK: Financial & Non-financial Profit Margins.
Source: ONS (FDBA, NHRE, NQNV & NRJK) via Ecowin.

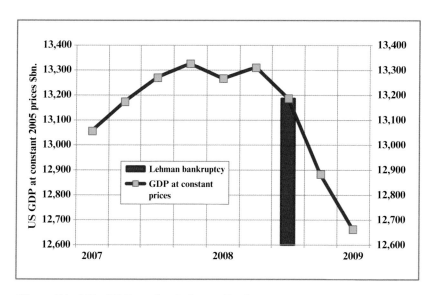

Chart 54. US: GDP & the Lehman Bankruptcy.
Source: NIPA Table 1.1.6.

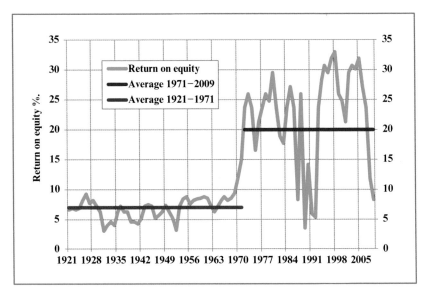

Chart 55. UK: Bank's Return on Equity.
Source: Bank of England (Allesandri & Haldane).

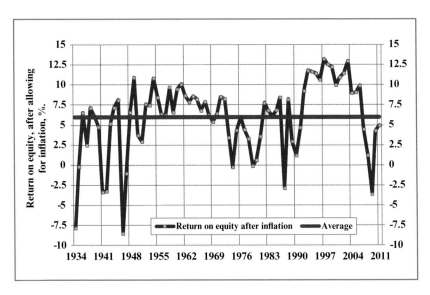

Chart 56. US: Bank's Real Return on Equity.
Sources: FDIC & BLS.

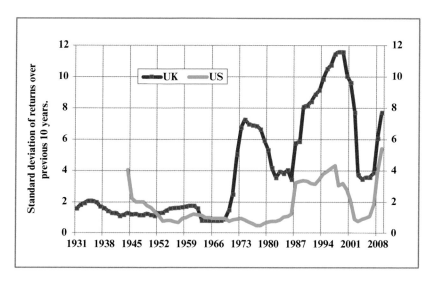

Chart 57. UK & US: Volatility of Bank Returns on Equity.
Sources: Bank of England & FDIC.

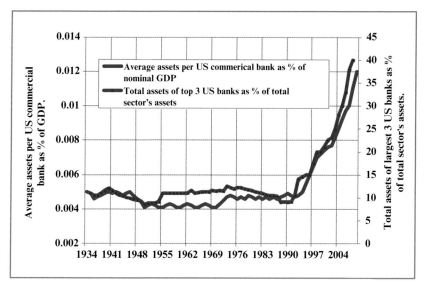

Chart 58. US: Rising Importance of Large Banks.
Source: Bank of England.

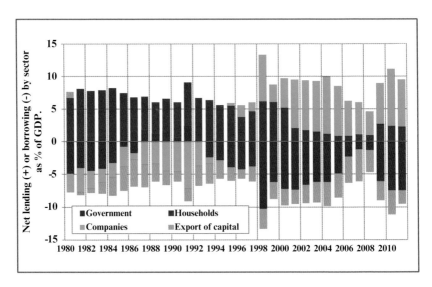

Chart 59. Japan: Sector Cash Flows.
Sources: Cabinet Office data for 1980 to 2000 are from the National Accounts for 2003 & for 2001 to 2011 from the National Accounts for 2011.

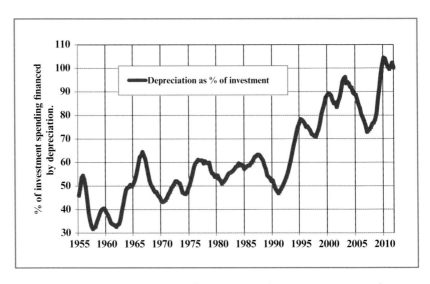

Chart 60. Japan: Non-financial Companies' Investment Spending & Depreciation.
Source: MoF Quarterly Survey of Incorporated Enterprises.

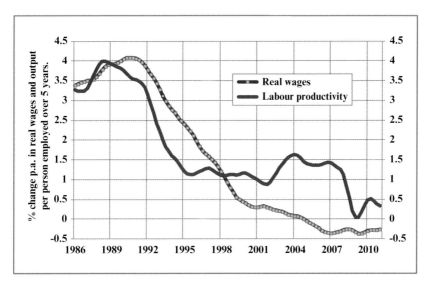

Chart 61. Japan: Real Wages and Labour Productivity.
Sources: MIC & Cabinet Office.

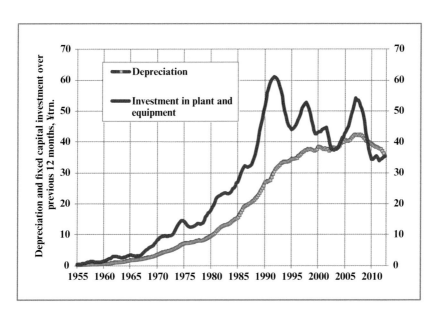

Chart 62. Japan: Corporate Investment & Depreciation.
Source: MoF Quarterly Survey of Incorporated Enterprises.

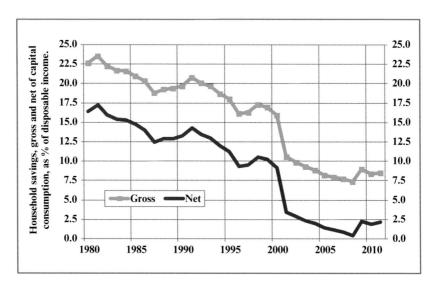

Chart 63. Japan: Household Savings.
Sources: Cabinet Office website for 1980 to 2000 from National Accounts 2009 & for 2001 to 2011 from National Accounts 2011.

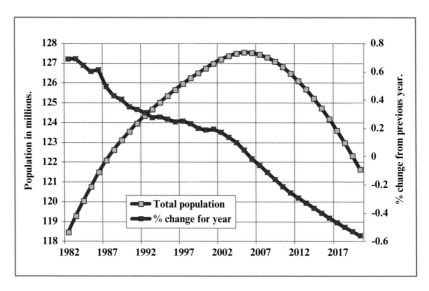

Chart 64. Japan: Population.
Source: MIC.

depreciation is nearly twice as great as profits after tax for companies in the Nikkei 225 index while it is not much more than half the profits after tax for companies in the S&P 500.

We cannot of course be sure that US profits are not substantially more overstated today than they have been historically, and the increase in the volatility of published profits in the US compared with those in the national accounts, which I illustrated in Chart 12, provides cause for concern. Even if we allow for depreciation being understated in the US and for the greater importance manufacturing in Japan, it seems overwhelmingly probable that both the extent to which the charge for depreciation in Japanese accounts is overstated and the consequent understatement of profits is large.

An important consequence of the overstatement of depreciation in their accounts is that Japanese companies distribute less of their real profits than they would if those profits were more accurately recorded. The payout ratio, which is the proportion of profits after tax that companies pay out as dividends, is lower in Japan than in the US, as Table 5 shows. This is interpreted by many analysts as indicating the lack of importance that Japanese management place on the interests of shareholders. I have, however, shown in earlier chapters that US managements appear to place their own interests well above those of shareholders. I think it is fair to say that managements in neither country seem to place much emphasis on the interests of shareholders. The difference is that in Japan the long-term interests of the company and its employees seem the key consideration for managements and in the US the short-term remuneration of managements dominates their concerns.

It is quite likely, however, that the high level of depreciation has the impact of reducing the payout ratio of profits as published and not just reducing the ratio of dividends to "real" profits. This is

Table 5. Payout Ratios on Non-financial Companies in the Nikkei 225 & S&P 500 Indices (Sources: Nikkei & Standard & Poor's)

	Earnings per Share	Dividend per Share	Payout Ratio
Nikkei 225	581.9	192.2	33%
S&P 500	87.18	35.66	41%

because profits after tax, which are the resources from which dividends are paid, will be more volatile, relative to the same change in profit margins, if there is a large charge for depreciation. Since companies are reluctant to cut dividends, the greater the volatility of profits the more managements will need a safety margin when declaring dividends. It therefore follows that the higher the depreciation charge, the more volatile profits will be after tax and the lower dividends will be as a ratio of published profits. The excessive charge for depreciation thus serves to keep down dividends and therefore increase corporate savings in two ways, both by causing profits to be severely understated and by discouraging a higher payout ratio even on the basis of the published figures.

The excessive allowance for depreciation also encourages a higher level of domestic investment than would otherwise have occurred. As Japanese managements are usually concerned to assure that their companies flourish over the long-term, they are biased towards spending the funds representing their current depreciation on new investment, as they will otherwise fear that they are running down the business over the long-term. They will also tend to see depreciation as a form of free money in the sense that it involves no borrowing cost.

Reducing depreciation allowances can therefore have an adverse short-term impact on demand, by discouraging investment. But it can also raise profits and dividends, which would increase shareholders' income and thus encourage consumption. A sharp rise in profits is also likely to produce a rise in the stock market, which seems to be currently depressed by the fact that profits are really much higher than those published. The rise in share prices should thus be a long-lasting one rather than a temporary blip and give a boost to confidence in an economy where that attribute seems to be in permanent short supply. Current depreciation is largely determined by past investment, so a fall in depreciation allowances is likely to give a long-term as well as an immediate boost to published profits.

Over time the level of domestic investment in Japan is likely to fall, as we can be reasonably sure that it is far too high in terms of the benefit that accrues from it. From the viewpoint of the economy as a whole, investment is justified if the loss of current consumption, which it entails, is offset by increases in future consumption. To balance the value of future consumption against today's, one has to discount the future at some rate of interest. It seems likely, though of course it cannot be known, that Japan's growth would be no slower if investment were, say, one percentage point of GDP lower than it is today. If that were the case then at any discount rate the loss of potential consumption today would have a greater value than a non-existent rise in future consumption. In the terms used by economists, Japan's welfare would increase if investment were a lower proportion of GDP and consumption a higher one than it was today.

Currently, business investment in Japan is three basis points higher as a proportion of GDP than it is in the US (i.e. it is 30% higher). Japan's population of working age is falling and that of the US is rising, with the difference between the two being 1.5 to 2% a year. As productivity is rising at more or less the same pace in both countries it is clear that either investment in the US is too low or it is far too high in Japan.

In practice both are extremely probable. US companies are likely to be underinvesting simply because this is the result of current management incentives. The level of investment in the US has been falling since around 1980, as Chart 15 shows, and the growth rate of the economy has been on a declining trend, as Chart 35 shows. It is probable, though such things are far from certain, that investment needs to rise in the US as a proportion of GDP if this decline is to be halted. But even if, for example, US business investment were to rise by three percentage points of GDP it would be no higher than the current level of investment in Japan. If this were sufficient to stabilise US growth around 2% a year, it would be likely to have a trend growth rate, which was rather better than that of Japan, which would be investing the same proportion of GDP. It is therefore very hard not to conclude that Japan's current level of investment is too high even though that of the US needs to rise if current hopes for the country's long-term growth are not to be seriously disappointed.

As the current level of investment in new plant and equipment in Japan is uneconomically high, it not only needs to fall but will almost certainly do so over time. Unless this is offset by some other form of demand, it will depress the economy. At the same time the budget deficit is also unsustainably high and as this falls it will also need to be offset by some other form of demand.

Considered individually, either falling domestic investment or a lower fiscal deficit would be sufficient to push Japan into recession. If they happened together, the impact would produce something approaching a depression. To avoid what would otherwise be, at the very least, another major recession, it is essential that other sources of demand rise strongly. There are only two candidates. These are a rise in the current account surplus, which would have to be driven by a rise in Japan's net exports, and an increase in consumption. Both will no doubt have to make large contributions. But a rise in Japan's current account would depress output in the rest of the world. To some extent this must make an essential contribution to the rebalancing of the country's economy, and if the rest of the world were booming this would happen without causing undue problems. But the world is not in this happy situation and seems unlikely to be so for some time. It is therefore essential that a rise in consumption as well as in exports should make an important contribution to offsetting the impact of falling investment and a narrower fiscal deficit.

Consumption can rise either because household incomes rise or savings fall; as the savings' rate is already rather low, a rise in household incomes as a proportion of GDP is essential to boost consumption. As the labour share of output has risen so much already, there seems little room for further increases, which means that rises in household incomes need to come from higher dividends and interest rates. As interest rates rise, so will the fiscal deficit. In our search for a source of rising demand to meet the required fall in the fiscal deficit, rising interest rates will thus be no help and we must look to rising dividends for a solution to the need for additional demand, and this should readily follow from a reform in depreciation allowances and the rate of corporation tax. It would be overoptimistic to assume that such reform would be adequate on its own. Nonetheless, it seems reasonable to assume that the contribution that it could make would be an essential ingredient in achieving the required rebalancing of the Japanese economy, which would otherwise depend too much on an improvement in the country's net exports and thus would simply increase the burden on other countries.

As depreciation is a function of past investment, the level of corporate savings derived from depreciation falls, with a time lag, as

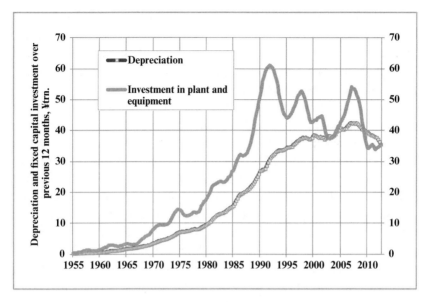

Chart 62. Japan: Corporate Investment & Depreciation.
Source: MoF Quarterly Survey of Incorporated Enterprises.

the level of investment falls. I illustrate this in Chart 62. Because it is currently too high, the level of Japanese domestic investment seems bound to fall over the years ahead and, as it does, so will the rate of depreciation, with a time lag. Provided that net exports or some other source of demand rises to offset the fall in investment, falling investment will over time cause profits measured after depreciation to rise relative to the level that they would otherwise have. For example, at unchanged profit margins a lower charge for depreciation would produce a rise in profits after tax, which in turn should produce higher dividends and higher household incomes.

A fall in depreciation allowances would speed up this process. It would reduce the tax benefits from new investment and thus encourage a reduction in the level of investment. It would also reduce the level of corporate savings in two ways. The fall in investment would reduce depreciation over time and the fall in allowances would have an immediate impact and, by raising the level of published profits, would encourage a rise in dividends. Higher dividends would increase household incomes; if the rate of the sector's savings were unchanged, this would boost consumption. If the level of household savings were unchanged or fell, the increase in consumption would be even greater. As a rise in published profits should help push up share prices, and thus encourage a rise in optimism, a fall in the savings' rate is more likely than a rise.

The short-term overall impact of such a change is uncertain and could be either positive or negative, depending on whether the boost to consumption was greater than the fall in investment. Over the longer term, it should be unequivocally positive since investment should fall anyway and by speeding up the growth of dividends it will improve living standards with the rise in household incomes and should do so permanently with little if any reduction in their future growth. The case for such a reform in corporate tax is massive. It should stimulate consumption, which provides the only internationally satisfactory route by which the longer-term negative impact on demand from falling investment can be offset. The only other route is to have a rise in Japan's international current account surplus, which increases the problems faced by the rest of the world.

A reduction in depreciation allowances would, in the absence of other changes, increase the revenue from corporation tax. It could be offset to be tax neutral by reducing the rate, which at 40% is high by international standards. Japan's Ministry of Finance could thus use tax reform as a way of stimulating the economy or as a way of reducing the budget deficit.

Some decline in the household sector's cash surplus is likely for the same reason as a long-term fall is likely in the corporate sector. Although, as I mentioned before, household savings in Japan are low, this is more obvious when savings are measured net, which is after capital consumption (i.e. depreciation) than it is when they are measured gross, which is before capital consumption is deducted. Unincorporated enterprises are included in the household sector and are more important in Japan than in other developed economies. The sector's capital consumption is over three times its net savings' rate, as I show in Chart 63, whereas in the US it is 30% less. As investment by unincorporated enterprises falls, the household sector's gross savings will fall even if the net savings' rate is unchanged.

The total contribution from the household sector to offsetting the required fall in the fiscal deficit is, however, likely to be small.

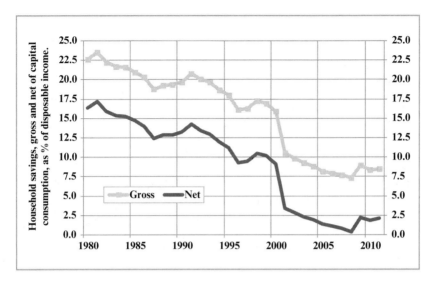

Chart 63. Japan: Household Savings.
Sources: Cabinet Office website for 1980 to 2000 from National Accounts 2009 & for 2001 to 2011 from National Accounts 2011.

Investment in housing is unlikely to rise much, given Japan's falling population, though given the crowding that still exists in major cities it seems unlikely to fall much for many years. Gross savings will only decline slowly because falling investment by unincorporated enterprises will only be reflected in declines in capital consumption with a time lag. As the net rate of savings is already low, it is unlikely to make much additional contribution. Household savings should fall over time, but the decline is likely to be slow.

Japan's tendency to run a cash surplus in its business sector is not solely due to the distortions of the tax system. It is also driven by the way the country's demography has a different impact on business savings and investment.

Japan's population has already started to decline and the rate of decline is expected to accelerate over the next decade, as I illustrate in Chart 64. Japan will need to keep investing in order to keep up with changing technology, but in other respects the country will need less capital as the population declines. Japanese business seems at last to be adjusting to the fact that an ageing and declining population

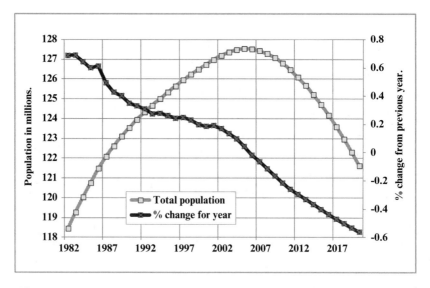

Chart 64. Japan: Population.
Source: MIC.

will need less production in the future of such things as toys, cars, houses and beer. The level of investment in Japan will therefore tend to shrink over time.

Because the population is ageing, there will also be some tendency for savings to fall, but those economic forecasts, of which there have been many, that assume that national savings will fall in line with the demographics have proved to be wrong in the past and these errors are likely to continue. A major reason is that business, as Chart 59 shows, is a far more important source of savings than individuals are. It is currently three times as important. If individuals were the major source of savings, it would be reasonable to assume that the personal and national level of savings' would fall in a similar way as the population ages. But the savings level of Japanese companies is decided by Japanese managements rather than by its ageing population, and as the age at which managers retire does not rise fast enough to keep pace with the speed at which the population ages, the average age of those employed is not ageing as fast as the population. In addition corporate managers seem to look upon their companies as perpetuities. Japan is said to have more 100-year-old businesses than anywhere else in the world. Companies are seen as having a life of their own rather than being extensions of the interests of their ageing shareholders.

If companies' behaviour reflected the wishes of their ageing owners, they would probably be paying out much higher dividends and shrinking their capital stock. In practice, however, their behaviour reflects that of managers, who see themselves are custodians of an enterprise which has a life and purpose which is different from that of its owners. This is known to economists as "the corporate veil" and is one reason why forecasts of future national savings based on a simple approach to Japan's changing demography have been and will continue to be so wrong. The existence of the corporate veil and the fact that companies are the main source of savings must be taken into account when forecasting Japan's future level of national savings.

In the very long-term the effect of the corporate veil on keeping up the national savings' rate of Japan is likely to dissipate through a change in the ownership of Japanese companies. The proportion of shares held by foreigners is likely to rise and rise faster than the proportion of foreign companies' shares owned by Japanese shareholders. The international diversification of portfolios is increasing the importance of foreign holdings in all markets, but as the population is ageing and falling more rapidly in Japan than elsewhere, this will tend to cause the ownership of foreign companies by Japanese shareholders to rise more slowly that the ownership of Japanese companies by foreigners. As a result dividends paid by Japanese companies to foreigners will rise faster than those received by Japanese from abroad. This will cause a mild reduction in the ratio of national savings to GDP.

The trend for Japanese companies to increase their foreign profits faster than their domestic ones tends to push up the national savings' rate. An increased foreign ownership of Japanese companies has the opposite effect. It will take time before the rise in foreign ownership matches the rise in Japanese companies' foreign earnings. For many years ahead, therefore, the existence of the corporate veil is likely to continue to inflate the level of Japan's national savings and thereby add to the distortion that arises from the impact of excessive allowances for depreciation.

Several American academics have published papers telling the Japanese how badly they have mismanaged their own economy.[5] US academic economists seem generally to agree that the mistakes of Japanese policy consist of being insufficiently expansive with their fiscal and monetary policies, with the aim that Japan should end deflation and stimulate domestic demand through higher investment and consumption. In my view this is a compound of the unlikely with the unwanted. Investment is already too high and it needs to fall in order to reduce the depreciation charge, which is the largest cause of excessive savings, both in the corporate sector and, through the large numbers of unincorporated enterprises, in the household sector. Neither investment nor consumption is likely to be stimulated by more quantitative easing and although they may be boosted by fiscal easing this is the opposite direction to which Japan needs to go, as it already has a budget deficit of 9.9% and a gross national debt ratio of 214% of GDP. What Japan needs is a lower real exchange rate and reform of its tax structure. While a lower nominal exchange rate is needed to get the real exchange rate down, thereafter continued deflation or at least near zero inflation is needed. Japan is a slow-growing economy and so, according to the accepted economic theory known as the Balassa–Samuelson effect, needs a falling real exchange rate to remain competitive with China and other rapidly growing countries in East Asia. As China unfortunately resists rises in its nominal exchange rate and, sensibly, resists rapid inflation, the only way to have the steadily falling real exchange that it needs without the international problems of currency intervention is for Japan to have no inflation.

Japan receives a barrage of bad advice from foreign economists, who seem to me to have an insufficiently detailed knowledge of the peculiarities of the Japanese economy to understand why the policies that they have persistently recommended have not worked. They assume that this is simply because the policies have not been tried hard enough and seem unable to consider the possibility that these policies are ill designed to deal with Japan's problems.

[5] See, for example, A. Posen, *The Realities and Relevance of Japan's Great Recession* talk at LSE (2010) in which the author refers to several other American academics as agreeing with his analysis, including Lawrence Summers.

8

The End of the Post-War Era

The recession that followed the financial crisis is not only the worst that we have suffered in the post-war era: it foreshadows the end to that era. Whereas in the past the US, with recently some help from Japan and the UK, has borne the main burden for keeping the world economy moving forward, that burden will now have to be more evenly shared. This will require a major change in the economic policies of China and Germany, among others, which unfortunately they appear unwilling to contemplate.

For the past 50 years or more the US has aimed to avoid recessions by using both fiscal and monetary policy and has used them too eagerly. Whenever it appeared that weakness in domestic demand was leading to falls in output and rises in unemployment and defaults on debts, the US administration and central bank would boost the economy by stimulatory policies. Until the financial crisis the results of this policy were beneficial in the short-term in so far as recessions were mild, but it caused two major long-term problems.

The willingness of Japan, the UK and the US ("the Keynesian trio") to use fiscal stimulus has reduced the pressure on other countries to do the same and as the Keynesian trio cannot do more, it is essential that others learn that they must make a greater contribution to the success of the world economy than they have been prepared to do in the past. The other problem arose from the encouragement that the excessive eagerness to prevent even mild recessions gave to the growth of private sector debt, which consequently increased to dangerous levels. It will take years for this debt to be reduced to comfortable levels without a depression, which would result in widespread default, or hyperinflation, which would destroy the real value of the debts.

At the end of World War II the US was the world's dominant economy. It was said that when the US sneezed the rest of the world caught influenza. But this also meant that the rest of the world would boom when the US recovered. With the US leading, the rest of the world followed and learnt that it could have the benefits of steady growth without the problems associated with fiscal deficits. This left the US with the burden of taking the primary responsibility for demand management on behalf of every other country.

Until the financial crisis the recessions of the post-war world were shallow. This was due to both fiscal and monetary policies, though the former has, at least recently, been largely confined to Japan, the UK and the US. The eagerness with which the US sought to mitigate recessions reduced the need for similar policies to be employed by other countries. And so the US current account moved from a surplus of 4% in 1947 to a deficit of 4% of GDP today. No gratitude was shown by those who gained. The beneficiaries saw no need to use fiscal deficits to boost their economies and in Germany their avoidance seems to be considered not only wise but virtuous. This has added to the problem. It is always difficult to persuade people that their views are wrong, particularly when they consider them to be not only intellectually correct but also the result of virtue.

We currently have structural cash surpluses in the business sectors in each member of the Keynesian trio. To generate recovery in the face of these surpluses, the world probably needs more fiscal stimulus, but four changes in the world economy limit the chances of this happening and increase the risk of recession should the US decide in its forthcoming budget to undertake a significant degree of fiscal tightening.

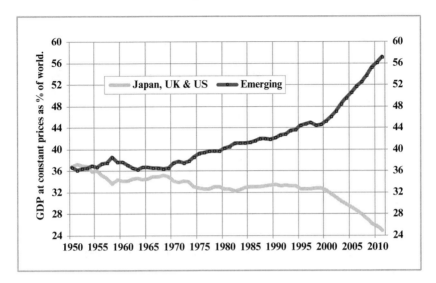

Chart 65. Relative Size of "Keynesian Trio" & Emerging Economies, as % of World GDP.
Sources: Angus Maddison 1950 to 2008 updated to 2011 from IMF & national accounts.

The first of the four changes is the decline in the importance of those countries where fiscal stimulus is a readily accepted policy, which I illustrate in Chart 65. In 1950 Japan, the UK and the US amounted to 37% of world GDP and although there was then a slow decline, the Keynesian trio still produced 33% of world GDP in 2000, but as Chart 65 shows, it has since fallen sharply to only 24%.[1]

The second change that has limited the willingness of the Keynesian trio to boost the world economy by their own efforts comes from the rise in the importance of international trade to their economies. This means that a boost to domestic demand gives much

[1] The data are drawn from the standard source, which is that of Angus Maddison. Such measures depend on the system of measurement used, particularly with regard to the way adjustments are made for changes in real exchange rates. Other approaches will give different relative levels of GDP, but the trends shown are likely to be common to all.

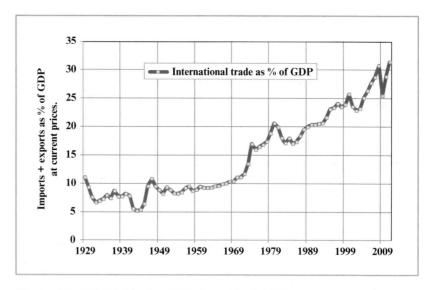

Chart 66. US: International Trade as % of GDP.
Source: NIPA Table 1.1.5.

less support to domestic output than before, and a much greater stimulus to the output of other countries. As Chart 66 illustrates, the combined value of exports and imports has risen from 6% of US GDP in 1945 to 31% today. International trade is equally important for Japan and even more for the UK, where the sum of exports and imports is currently equal to 65% of GDP.[2]

The third key change is that the fiscal deficits of the Keynesian trio are already so huge and their national debt levels so large, as I show in Chart 67, that it is increasingly doubtful that it will either be possible politically or wise economically to increase them any further.

The fourth change is the way in which these deficits have become structural and semi-permanent rather than cyclical.

[2]The only data we have for the value of exports and imports is their sales, which should not be compared directly with GDP, which is a measure of output. Countries' international trade measured in sales can therefore amount to more than 100% of GDP. Nonetheless, we can be confident that the importance of international trade in terms of GDP has risen hugely and to a reasonably similar degree to the increase in the ratio of exports and imports to GDP.

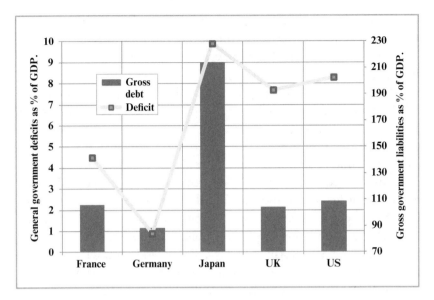

Chart 67. G5: Government Deficits & National Debt.
Source: OECD Economic Outlook Vol 91 Estimates for 2012.

These changes have greatly reduced the ability of Japan, the UK and the US to generate growth either for themselves or for the world as a whole through stimulatory fiscal policies. But these inhibitions are confined to the Keynesian trio. Other countries could boost world demand by additional fiscal stimulus. Unfortunately, they show, in general, a marked antipathy to doing so. In some cases, such as Germany, this seems to be based on a scorn for neoclassical economics, which is not based on the faults of that consensus but stems from a contempt for those parts that have proved sound. Other countries, with China as the outstanding example, have preferred to use exchange rate intervention in the past to boost demand. While this has often been successful for that country in isolation, it provides, unlike fiscal stimulus, no help to world demand as a whole. There is also the more general problem that standing to one side in the past and letting the US bail out the world economy has been a sound if selfish policy. Large fiscal deficits and high national debts create long-term problems for the countries that use them. Countries that have been able to reap the benefits of the fiscal stimuli of the Keynesian trio without having to burden their economies with more debt have appeared to be twice blessed. Convincing these fortunate countries that this is no longer an option is difficult and thus increases the risk that policy errors will push the world back into recession.

The UK, the US and even, to a lesser extent, Japan have a vibrant financial press, where policy is actively debated, though naturally enough it is usually conducted within the limitations that have become imposed by the inflexibility and aprioristic bias of most academic economists today. This debate has an important influence on the economic policies of governments and central banks. Elsewhere it is less common to find these issues debated in the same intellectual context, either with a similar degree of public attention or with the same likely impact on policy. Among the major economies, only the Keynesian trio have deliberately embraced massive public sector deficits as a solution to the great recession which followed the financial crisis. Elsewhere, Keynesian theories are ignored or even, as they are sometimes in Germany, scorned. The only purpose for which Germany has been prepared to run massive fiscal deficits over an extended period was to pay for the costs of reunification. From 1991 to 1998 Germany's national debt rose from 38.8 to 63.2% of GDP and then fell for the next five years. There was a sharp, albeit inadvertent, rise owing to the world recession in 2009 and 2010, but Germany's national debt ratio has since been flat to mildly falling, much to the detriment of the rest of the world and, in particular, to other members of the eurozone.

Even in the US, the standard views of modern economics are contested by many, including some who hanker after a return to the gold standard. In the unlikely event that their advice is taken, it would heavily limit the extent to which the US could use either fiscal or monetary stimuli. Support for a return to the gold standard reached the level at which the Republican Party's platform for the November election could have included "a commission to look at restoring the link between the dollar and gold".[3]

The eagerness with which the US embraced fiscal deficits to boost its economy has not been generally followed by other countries. Germany appears to think that they are damaging in nearly

---

[3] *"Republicans eye return to gold standard"* by Robin Harding and Anna Fifield, Financial Times, (24th August, 2012).

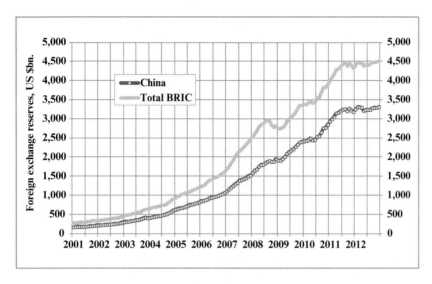

Chart 68. BRICS: Foreign Exchange Reserves.
Sources: National data via Ecowin.

all circumstances and the eurozone crisis has allowed it to impose fiscal retrenchment on an economy two-thirds the size of the US. Elsewhere, there is less disdain but no enthusiasm. China has preferred to use currency intervention rather than budget deficits as a tool of demand stimulation and its example has been followed by other developing economies. As Chart 68 shows, over the first decade of this century China's intervention in currency markets has resulted in its foreign exchange reserves rising by $3 trn and the other BRICs (Brazil, Russian, India and China) have increased theirs by a further $1 trn.

In addition to its unhappy impact on economic policy in the rest of the world, the overuse of fiscal and monetary policy in the US led to an excessive build-up of debt and to asset bubbles in equities and houses. Private sector debt grew in the post-war era from 33% of US GDP to 250% today. While lenders were exposed to the risk of default by specific individuals and companies, the risk of a large general rise in bankruptcies was limited by the speedy recoveries engineered by the stimuli given to demand. Lenders retained the specific risks, but they were largely insured by government policy from the systemic risk of a significant general rise in defaults. This naturally encouraged the excessive rise in debt. "Moral hazard" is defined as the result of insurance encouraging inappropriate behaviour. The too-ready protection by the US authorities against the systemic risks of lending provided such insurance and caused a large, though unintended, increase in moral hazard. The excessive ease of monetary policy assisted the rise of asset prices, and when they broke we had the financial crisis. Despite desperate attempts, monetary policy now seems incapable of generating recovery.

Since the end of World War II, economic policy in the UK and the US has been based on the belief that recessions are undesirable and should be stifled early if they show signs of arriving. Both fiscal and monetary policies have been used to achieve this and the results were generally perceived to have been successful until the oil shocks of the 1970s. The major Anglophone economies were then subject to rapid inflation, as I show in Chart 69. From March 1973 to June 1976 inflation averaged more than 9% in the US and 15% in the UK. Over the same period, however, output fell in both countries. Another further burst of inflation in 1979 and 1980 was also accompanied by stagnant or falling output.

A new word, "stagflation", was coined for this combination of high inflation and weak or falling output. Many economists had previously thought that this combination was impossible for any length of time, as inflation was meant to decline when the economy was operating with unused resources of capital and labour. However, this theory had to be discarded when, as Chart 70 shows, both unemployment and inflation were on a rising trend in the 1970s.

Before economists were forced to revise their theories in order to allow for the existence of stagflation, it was assumed that inflation would decline if there were spare resources of capital and labour, and that it would only pick up if there were a shortage of these resources. It was said that there was an "output gap" if spare resources existed, which was defined as the difference between current GDP and potential GDP. If, for example, actual GDP was 98 and potential GDP was thought to be 100, then the gap of two was expressed as minus 2%.[4]

---

[4] Potential GDP is subtracted from actual and the result is −2; this is expressed as a percentage of the potential GDP and thus $-2 \times 100 \div 100 = -2\%$. When, for example, the OECD shows a minus number for its estimate of the output gap, this shows that it estimates that a gap exists, not that it doesn't.

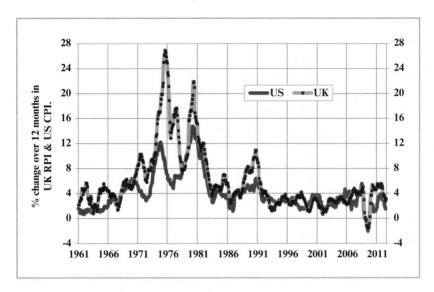

Chart 69. UK & US: Inflation.
Sources: ONS & BLS via Ecowin.

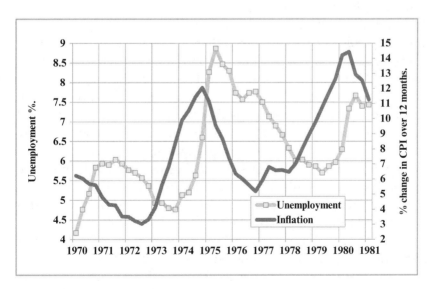

Chart 70. US Stagflation: 1970 to 1981.
Sources: NIPA Table 1.1.6 & BLS.

In the 1970s high unemployment and underutilised plant capacity showed that there were plenty of spare resources, but inflation was nonetheless rising to 12% in the US in 1975 and to 25% in the UK. The theory therefore had to be revised. This was done by including the impact of expectations. Business decisions are based on managements' views of the future. If they think that inflation is going to rise, they will push up their own prices more vigorously than before and will be less resistant to increases in the wages that they pay. If wages don't rise as fast as prices they will fall in real terms and this will tend to depress demand. If governments and central banks are anxious to avoid recessions, they will act to stimulate the economy to offset any weakness in demand and thus help to keep wages rising at least in line with prices. Workers will, when they think that inflation is picking up, be even more than usually exposed to a failure of nominal wages to rise and thus particularly anxious to secure higher wages. They will therefore in these conditions also press harder than usual for higher wages. A rise in inflationary expectations thus tends to be self-fulfilling. Inflation rises because it is expected to rise and this encourages expectations to rise again, and the self-reinforcing cycle will continue until halted by some shock.

A rise in inflationary expectations thus changes the way inflation responds to an output gap. If there is no change in expectations, inflation should fall back if there is an output gap, but this will not happen if fears of inflation are rising. This can easily produce a major problem, as a rise in inflationary expectations followed by a rise in inflation will usually lead to another upward jump in the expected and actual rate of inflation. Among economists it is now generally accepted that a rise in inflationary expectations is very dangerous and will tend to produce a self-fulfilling upward spiral unless the expectations are crushed, and that the only way to do this is to create a much larger output gap than would otherwise be needed to keep inflation under control.

A rise in inflationary expectations is thus one of the worst problems that can hit an economy, as it is agreed that the only way to bring them under control is to provide a sharp shock, which will probably result in a worse-than-usual recession. Since inflation only falls back slowly, these are particularly unpleasant and difficult times in which unemployment rises, output falls and inflation remains high. Central banks are therefore now concerned to try to measure people's expectations of inflation and regularly refer to their assessments, as the Federal Reserve did on 13th September 2012 when the new programme of quantitative easing ("QE3") was announced.

Today's theory is that inflation should ease if there is an output gap and "inflationary expectations are well contained". In practice, however, there are lots of problems. Central banks can try to measure expectations in a number of ways, but even if these are assumed to be correct expectations can change sharply. Economists have also shown that there are great problems with measuring output gaps, at least without the benefit of hindsight.[5] Despite these troublesome issues, much economic theory revolves around the idea and there is widespread agreement that the concept of the output gap is useful, even if it is very difficult to measure its current size. But the instability of expectations combined with the uncertainties that surround the level of the output gap mean that inflation can pick up quickly and unexpectedly. A rise in inflation leads all too easily to a self-fulfilling rise in expectations, and because the cure for this is so unpleasant economic policymakers need to take great care to keep inflation and its expectations subdued.

In the early 1980s the shock that was needed to contain inflationary expectations was provided by the Federal Reserve, whose board of governors was chaired at the time by Paul Volcker. Under his leadership, the rate of interest on 3-months Treasury bills rose to 15.5% in February 1982 and this depressed the economy to the extent that the output gap was estimated by the OECD at 5.6% in 1983, and unemployment rose to 9.6%. In terms of the OECD's estimate of the output gap, the US economy was more depressed in 1983 than it was in 2009. This seems reasonable as the level of unemployment was the same in 1983 and 2009, which suggests that there was a similar level of spare capacity in terms of labour and there was probably more spare capacity in 1983 than in 2009 in terms of capital equipment. It is reasonable to think that at the same

---

[5]This was notably set out in *The Unreliability of Output-Gap Estimates in Real Time* by Athanasios Orphanides and Simon van Norden, CIRANO working paper (2001) and subsequently in the MIT Press Review of Economics and Statistics, (November, 2002).

level of unemployment there should have been more excess capacity in 1983 than in 2009 because investment was much higher as a proportion of GDP in the run-up to the recession of 1983 than in the early years of the 21st century. This suggests not only that there was relatively more unused plant and equipment but also, as I shall explain later, that any given amount of capital investment was capable of producing more output in the early compared to the later period.

The sharp rise in interest rates in the early 1980s and the increase in unemployment that followed provided a severe shock, which proved successful in breaking the rise in inflationary expectations. Paul Volcker's policy shock of putting interest rates up to over 15% was successful and the next 25 years were a period of steadily falling inflation.

The period of falling inflation from the early 1980s until the financial crisis was also a period in which the fluctuations in the economy became less marked and more moderate than before and thus became known as the great moderation. In 2004 Governor Ben Bernanke claimed some credit for this change on behalf of central bankers and thus by implication for himself. "My view is that improvements in monetary policy, though certainly not the only factor, have probably been an important source of the Great Moderation."[6] Events then followed the classic pattern of a Greek tragedy. After this exhibition of pride, termed hubris by the Greeks, we had the inevitable retribution (Greek nemesis) of the financial crisis. So far this retribution has fallen on the world rather than on Dr Bernanke, though we may not yet have witnessed all the acts in the tragedy. My view, which I have set out before in more detail,[7] is that the policies of central bankers were largely responsible both for the great moderation and for the subsequent crisis and that the same policies were responsible for both. As the crisis has brought far more pain to the world than any benefits that can reasonably be ascribed to the great moderation, it seems to me that central bankers need to be far more apologetic than they have so far been

---

[6] "*The Great Moderation*", remarks by Governor Ben S. Bernanke at the meetings of the Eastern Economic Association, Washington, DC, (20th February, 2004).
[7] *Wall Street Revalued: Imperfect markets and inept central bankers* by Andrew Smithers, John Wiley & Sons, (2009).

about their past policies. Acknowledgement of past errors is usually necessary to avoid their repetition.

The fundamental post-war policy aim of keeping recessions as mild as possible was therefore punctuated by Paul Volcker's interest rate shock, but not ended. The negative impact of high interests on US output was also offset by President Reagan's stimulatory fiscal policy. Despite the recovery of the economy, which grew at 3.2% a year over the decade, US budget deficits averaged over 4% of GDP in the 1980s.

The successful "Volcker attack" on inflation proved a brief interruption rather than a fundamental change in policy. Thereafter, both fiscal and monetary policy were used to stimulate demand as soon as, or even before, there were any signs of weakness in the economy or that debtors were having increased trouble meeting their obligations.

There are therefore two key changes needed in the management of the world economy if we are to have a stable and satisfactory rate of long-term growth now that the post-war era is over. Debt must be brought down and the burden of stimulating the world economy must not be left to the fiscal policies of Japan, the UK and the US. Neither of these will be easy, but the change in international attitudes needed to achieve the second makes it particularly daunting. Two particular changes are needed. The Keynesian trio must reduce its fiscal deficits, and if monetary policy is ineffective and worldwide demand inadequate this means that other countries must be more willing to run fiscal deficits than they currently seem to be.

The policies being tried in the eurozone at present show how great a change in attitude is needed. In general the aim in this book is to draw attention to the failures of economic policy that come from the weaknesses of current economic theory. The failure of economic policy in the eurozone does not fall into this category: it comes from a political failure to understand and apply sound economic theory, but it is important to understand the issues as the eurozone's follies act to magnify the risks of mistakes elsewhere.

The problems of the eurozone that usually hit the headlines arise from the threats to bonds' markets and banks. Crises succeed one another as the strength of these threats rises and then falls as money is thrown at the markets and the banks. Chart 71 illustrates

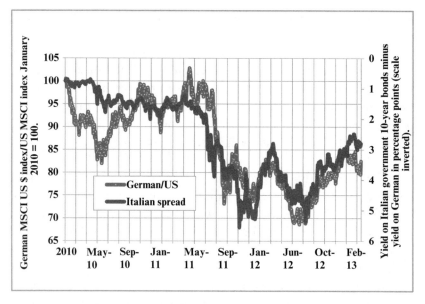

Chart 71. German/US Equities Move with Italian Bond Spreads.
Sources: Reuters & MSCI via Ecowin.

how the fluctuation in Italian bonds is treated by markets as a key
indicator of confidence even for Germany. In this chart I show the
difference in the yields on Italian and German government bonds
on the right-hand axis and invert the scale so that the chart rises
when confidence improves, and vice versa. On the left-hand axis I
compare the relative performance of the German and US stock
markets. The close way in which the two charts move up and down
with each other shows how confidence in the future of the eurozone and its members fluctuates with the premium that the Italian
government has to pay to borrow compared with the German
government.

Confidence in the eurozone thus varies with the bond yields
of its weaker members, and this in turn varies with the support
given by the ECB, which is prepared from time to time to buy
bonds. But the fundamental problems of the eurozone do not rise
and fall with the bond market and, unlike many observations in this
book, my views on this accord with the consensus of most economists. The problem is that labour costs in Greece, Italy, Portugal and

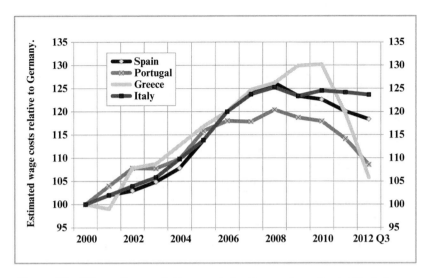

Chart 72. Wage Costs of Greece, Italy, Portugal & Spain Relative to Germany.
Source: The Economist 2000 to 2010 updated from national data via Ecowin.

Spain ("the garlic belt") are too high relative to more northern members of the zone ("the butter belt"), with France being both economically and geographically between the two. Garlic belt wages therefore need to fall relative to those in the butter belt. If garlic belt countries were not in the eurozone this could be achieved by devaluation. So long as this is not possible, the relative fall in wages must come from either inflation in the butter belt or deflation in the garlic belt.

It follows that, so long as Germany rejects inflation, nominal wages in garlic belt countries must fall so long as they remain in the eurozone. How much nominal wages must fall is, of course, unknown, but the consensus among economists is that a fall of around 20% is needed, and I show estimates in Chart 72.[8]

---

[8] According to Lorenzo Bini Smaghi, the figures in Chart 72 probably understate the scale of the problem. According to this former member of the ECB's executive board: "Since the creation of the euro, Italy's unit labour costs have risen by about 30% more than the currency area average." "*Italians need more than the old politics*", Financial Times, (17th January, 2013).

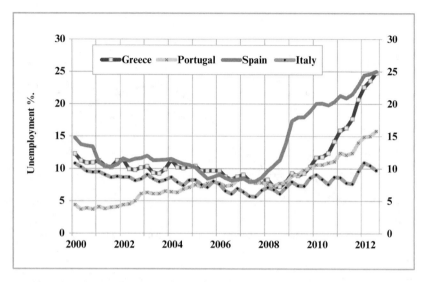

Chart 73. Greece, Italy, Spain & Portugal: Unemployment.
Sources: National data via Ecowin.

Getting wage costs to fall is very difficult. As Chart 73 shows, unemployment has already risen to 25% in Greece and Spain and the process of forcing down nominal wages will presumably require the loss of even more jobs. If the rise in unemployment is successful in causing wages to fall, it will raise the ratio of debts to incomes and GDP and this applies to private as well as public sector debt.

Debt ratios are already very high, as Table 6 shows, and the greater the success in lowering wages, the greater will be the level of bankruptcies, which in turn will risk increasing the severity of the recession and the level of unemployment.

No one knows what will happen, but what is clear is that the problems of the eurozone are not those which have the attention of its leaders. However much money the ECB and eurozone politicians throw at bond markets and banks, the threat to the zone's existence comes from the voters in the garlic belt. The Governor of the ECB, Mario Draghi, gave huge encouragement to the bond market when he remarked that the ECB would do "whatever it takes" to preserve the eurozone. This was, however, an idle boast from anyone who cannot control 50% of the votes in the threatened

Table 6. Ratios of Debt to GDP (Source: IMF Financial Stability Review)

	Greece	Italy	Portugal	Spain
Government gross debt	166	121	106	67
Households' gross debt	71	50	106	87
Non-financial corporate gross debt	74	110	149	192
Financial institutions' gross debt	22	96	61	111
Gross external liabilities	202	140	284	212

countries. Voters may be prepared to support governments that accept rising unemployment as the cost of staying in the eurozone or they may revolt. What voters currently want seems clear. They wish to remain in the zone and have falling unemployment, and what they want they can't have until Germany agrees to change the policy of needless austerity. The future of the eurozone depends on how long the voters in the garlic countries are prepared to put up with rising misery.

It has been argued that the German economy has suffered rather than gained from membership of the euro and it is even possible that voters in Germany will get fed up with a succession of bailouts whose rising costs seem to produce no lasting solutions.[9] So long as voters continue to support current policies the eurozone will remain a drag on the world economy. If they revolt, the break-up of the eurozone may well set off another financial crisis. A possible solution, other than break-up, would be for Germany to embrace Keynesian economics and introduce a massive tax cut, thereby boosting its own and the whole of the eurozone's economy. Germany can afford to do so, as it has almost no fiscal deficit, but there has as yet been no serious public debate in Germany of such an idea.

It is possible that the eurozone will manage an orderly rather than a disorderly break-up. At the moment this seems, sadly, unlikely; perhaps there are politicians and bureaucrats in the zone who are working out ways in which this could be done but are working in

---

[9] *"Germany should not, and maybe cannot, afford the euro"*, Charles Dumas, Lombard Street Research Monthly Review, (31st August, 2012).

secret. If it were known that such plans were being seriously considered, it would be reasonable to fear that this would precipitate the crisis. Even those favourably disposed to the eurozone have argued that a temporary managed exit is the only likely way in which Greece can regain competitiveness while avoiding massive bankruptcies.[10] I fear, however, that no such planning is taking place.

The mess in the eurozone increases the likely cost of policy mistakes elsewhere. The main threat is that voters in the garlic belt will become fed up with austerity. This risk naturally rises if the world economy as a whole is weak. If the eurozone breaks up, the shock that this will have will probably be sufficient to reduce world demand. This reduces the chances that the next recession would be mild. A weakness in world demand that would otherwise produce a gentle drop in output would, if it led to one or more countries leaving the zone, probably turn a mild recession into a deep one.

Despite its severe costs, the eurozone crisis could bring major benefits to Mediterranean countries that have suffered from governments creating monopolies to gain support for the political party in power. For example, Vicky Pryce records that, in Greece, "There are 580 hardship professions that have been created by decree over the years, allowing those in them to retire early with full benefits because of the particular hardship of their professions. They include everything from tuba players to hairdressers . . ."[11] Mancur Olson argued that the growth of special interest lobbies was a key cause of national decline. If these examples of rent gouging can be abolished, the prospects for the Mediterranean countries will be greatly improved and they will be less obviously among those identified by Olson as likely to decline.[12] The problem is, however, deep seated, as the opportunities for rent gouging arise from the structure of the political parties who have used their periods in power to create supportive client groups. Reform thus needs a political revolution to end the control of these "clientist" parties, and we seem as yet a long way from this.

[10] *The Euro in Danger* by Jagjit Chadha, Michael A. H. Dempster and Derry Pickford, Searching Finance, (2012).

[11] *Greekonomics: The euro crisis and why politicians don't get it* by Vicky Pryce, Biteback Publishing Limited, (2012).

[12] *The Rise and Decline of Nations: Economic growth, stagflation and social rigidities,* Mancur Olson, Yale University Press, (1982).

There is a huge need in the new post-post-war era for countries other than Japan, the UK and the US to become more willing to use deficit financing, but the policies imposed on the eurozone by Germany show that we are a long way from this need being satisfied.

The other area where a marked improvement is needed in international economic cooperation is over exchange rates. Some countries have used massive interventions to boost their economies, as I showed in Chart 68 for the "BRICs", while Germany has been a major beneficiary of the weakness in the euro, as I show in Chart 74, which has been set off by fears for the break-up of the eurozone. We have recently experienced a fall in the yen and this was quickly condemned by German economists and politicians, thus illustrating that having gained an advantage countries are loath to lose it. An even more outlandish example was recently given by China. "Beijing has issued a new warning against competitive devaluations by rich countries."[13] China has increased its foreign exchange reserves by

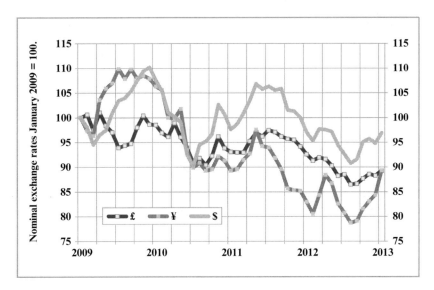

Chart 74. Euro: Nominal Exchange Rates.
Source: Reuters via Ecowin.

[13] *"China warns over fresh currency tensions"* by Leslie Hook and Simon Rabinovitch, Financial Times, (9th/10th March, 2013).

$3 trn over the past decade, as I showed in Chart 68, so this warning seems the equivalent to Germany blaming the outbreak of the First World War on Belgian aggression. Current international comments on exchange rates seem to be similar to the less sporting forms of rugby football, where the aim is to "get your retaliation in first".

It is essential for the UK and the US to reduce their external deficits. This would usually require a fall in their real exchange rates. It should surely be internationally recognised that countries with large fiscal deficits can be justified in seeking to have lower real exchange rates. Sadly, there is no sign that there is currently any movement towards an international acceptance of this. As Chart 75 shows, Germany stands out among the major developed economies as having the least helpful and cooperative international policy. It has virtually no fiscal deficit and a huge current account surplus.

Looking ahead, the US may solve the problem of its trade deficit without the need for devaluation, because net oil imports currently amount to 1.7% of GDP, which is more than half the current account deficit. As Chart 76 shows, the US dependence on oil imports has been falling steadily in volume terms, but the benefit has been more than offset by rising prices. With the exploitation of

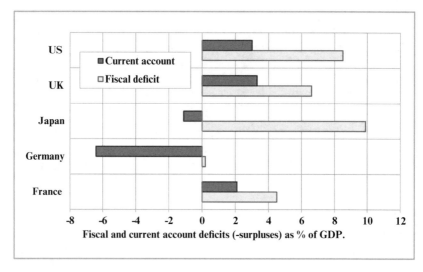

Chart 75. G5: Current Account & Fiscal Deficits (Surpluses). Source: National Accounts via Ecowin.

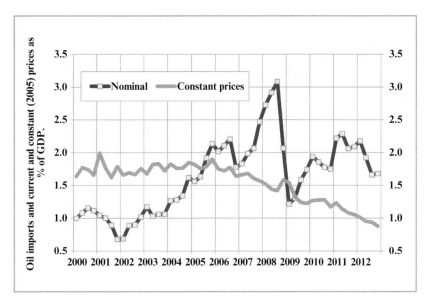

Chart 76. US: Net Oil Imports.
Source: BEA via Ecowin.

previously unconventional sources of oil and natural gas, the US is expected to become self-sufficient over the next one or two decades.

The UK, on the other hand, is in the exact opposite position of being a country with a rising deficit that is expected to rise further (Chart 77). If the UK is to succeed in reducing its current account deficit, it will need to improve its trade balance. As I showed in Chart 33, the UK's international trade is predominantly in goods rather than services, and an improvement in the current account balance will thus mainly depend on a rise in the production of goods, which will only occur if this is adequately profitable. Chart 78 shows that this is not currently the situation. Services have average returns, despite the weakness of the economy, but the returns on goods' output are at their lowest recorded level. I can see no solution to this other than a fall in the nominal, and thereby the real, value of sterling.

There is clearly a need for greater international cooperation with regard to having worldwide levels of fiscal stimulus adequate to keeping the world economy growing, but it is equally clear that

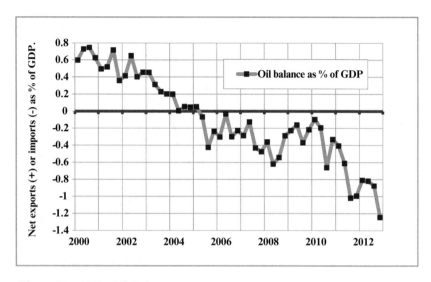

Chart 77. UK: Oil Balance.
Source: ONS via Ecowin.

Chart 78. UK: Returns on Capital in Manufacturing & Services (excluc-ing Finance).
Source: ONS (LYRB & LYRP) via Ecowin.

this must be achieved by sharing the burden more equitably. We need to combine the same overall fiscal stimulus that we have today while reducing the existing overdependence on Japan, the UK and the US. It is equally essential that there is international understanding and acceptance that this requires the Keynesian trio to have improving current account balances, which may in turn need intervention in foreign exchange markets. It is equally and sadly clear that we are a long way from having these issues sensibly discussed, let alone agreed on.

If countries with large fiscal deficits seek to reduce the real value of their exchange rates they will meet international opposition. They will, however, be amply justified in ignoring this and if they succeed, as Japan has recently done, they will be helping the world economy. Currency adjustments are an essential step towards reducing the international disequilibria that are helping to constrain worldwide recovery.

Proposals to reduce real exchange rates where these are clearly needed are often greeted with the objection that this is a beggar-my-neighbour attitude which cannot have a beneficial impact on the world economy in total and which is therefore referred to as a zero sum game on a worldwide basis. This is, in my view, extremely naive. A rebalancing of the world economy is vital and it is countries like Germany, which combined large current account surpluses and low fiscal deficits, that are beggaring their neighbours.[14] It is essential that these policies change and, as those with the surpluses seem immune to persuasion, the steps to rebalance the world must be taken by the countries with large fiscal deficits through exchange rate intervention. If these are successful in reducing trade imbalances, they will weaken the economies of those countries that are currently running surpluses and, we must hope, lead them to take more stimulatory policies. Sadly, it does not seem that persuasion is effective, and in its absence countries with large fiscal deficits both need and are entitled to intervene to depress their exchange rates.

The other issue raised by the end of the post-war era is the need to bring down debt levels.

---

[14] For an example of this naïve attitude, see *"Beggar-my-neighbour is wrong game"*, by Desmond Lachman of the American Enterprise Institute to the Financial Times, (28th February, 2013).

9

Misinformation as a Barrier to Sound Policy Decisions

I showed in Chart 12 that profits as published by US companies have recently become far more volatile than those published in the national accounts and pointed out that it is likely to amplify the dangers which a fall in profits poses to the US economy. The volatility arises from published profits being habitually overstated and for this to be partly offset by periodic bouts when they are understated through write-offs. Other examples of misinterpreted data are Japanese accounts, in which profits are seriously understated, and claims that company leverage is low in both the UK and the US. These are examples of a more general problem, which is that there is a great deal of misinformation that gets widely circulated. This poses many problems for the management of economies in two ways. One is that much of the misleading information is widely publicised by those who benefit from it. Another is that policymakers naturally tend to assume that they can rely on published data. But as the data often differ from one source to another, it is easy for policy decisions to be based on misleading data. A general problem is that the users of economic data are seldom driven by the pursuit of truth. Investment bankers are in pursuit of business, politicians in pursuit of votes and journalists in pursuit of news.

Probably the single most significant source of misinformation today is to be found in the balance sheets and profit and loss accounts of listed US companies. It's important to understand how this has arisen and it is vital for future prosperity that the shortcomings of company accounts should receive widespread attention. So long as the figures published by companies are treated with a respect that they do not deserve, economic policy is likely to be influenced by misleading and poor-quality data.

According to the national accounts (NIPA) data, in 1932 and 1933 US companies in aggregate made losses, but no loss was recorded in any quarter in the aggregate published results of companies included in the S&P 500 index. The published profits of quoted companies in the depression were thus less volatile than the profits of companies as shown in the national data for the economy as a whole. In the recent recession US companies continued to make profits after tax, according to the NIPA data, at the rate of $400bn a year (3% of GDP) at their lowest level. Profits fell but remained strongly positive. In sharp contrast aggregate losses were published by companies in the S&P 500 index in Q4 2008. It seems therefore that quoted company profits have now become more volatile than those of the economy as a whole. I showed in Chart 12 how this change could be demonstrated statistically and it shows that the profits which companies report have become startlingly more volatile than the profits which are shown in the national accounts. I have described how the change in relative volatility is the natural result of the change in the way managements are remunerated. But the extent to which profits are currently overstated, and the incentive to alternately over- and understate them, increases the risk that when the next downturn in profits arrives it will be exaggerated in the figures that companies publish.

If assets can be recorded in balance sheets at their assumed market value, then profits will rise and fall with the values attributed to them. If, as is the case more often than not, these market values are matters of judgement then they can be written up or written down as circumstances and judgements fluctuate. Profit volatility can then easily be generated by adjusting up or down the prices of assets. As bonuses usually depend on changes in profits, companies' managements will usually be able to benefit from both over- and understated profits. When profits are overstated, they will rise more than they otherwise would have done and bonuses will rise with them. When profits are understated in one year but not the next, the rise in profits will also be exaggerated, together with their associated bonuses. Managements therefore want profits to be volatile. As management gets what management wants and what management wants is greatly eased by marked to market accounting, the result has been the growth of periodic "write-offs".

The greater the contribution that changes in asset prices, either positive or negative, can make to the published profits of companies, the greater will be their volatility. Even with the contrivance of the most amenable accountants, asset prices cannot rise indefinitely and so after a period in which they boost profits they will at some time have to be written down and cause profits to fall to a greater extent than would have occurred had they not been written up before. Write-ups followed by write-offs will thus occur regularly and will enhance profit volatility. Should corporate managements wish to have volatile profits, and with current methods of remuneration this is exactly what they do wish, modern accounting practices allow even greater scope for generating such volatility than the more old-fashioned sort. Assets are therefore periodically written up or written down. The associated write-offs are either an admission that profits have been overstated in the past or a promise that management will try to overstate them in the future. Writing down the value of assets that have previously been overstated need not hit published profits if the adjustment can be made to the balance sheet rather than to the profit and loss account. This will be advantageous if bonuses are linked to the return on equity or total capital. The presentation of the figures can thus be adjusted to create profit volatility or high returns on equity, and so managements have considerable flexibility to choose the most advantageous presentation for the purpose of maximising their incomes.

The marked way in which profits published by companies have differed from those in the national accounts can only be possible because of the great flexibility that managements have when deciding on figures that they choose to publish as their companies' profits. To some extent managements have always had a considerable amount of leeway. For example, auditors are unlikely to quarrel with chief financial officers who suggest that the value of their companies' plant or inventories should be written down. Writing down the value of assets will depress current profits and boost future ones. The level of pension contributions is another matter of judgement. Increased contributions will reduce profits and reductions boost them.

A major difference between profits as published by companies and those in the national accounts arises from intercompany asset transactions. Sales of assets between companies are likely to produce profits for the seller without a compensating loss being recorded by the purchaser. But since neither output nor income from employment rises with intercompany asset transactions, they will not cause profits in the national accounts to rise. A flurry of dealings between companies will thus tend to increase published profits of companies without having any positive impact on those in the national accounts. As these rises have no real substance or counterpart in the output of the economy, it is probable that they will in due course have to be reversed by write-offs.

While it has always been easy to flatter or depress profits in the short-term, the scope for published profits to diverge from those in the national accounts has become significantly greater in recent years. This is due to the change in accounting from "marked to cost" to "marked to market". Companies' net worth can change from buy-backs and new issues of equity capital or from operations. When changes come only from operations and profits are marked to cost, they are, if correctly measured, equal to any retained profits, and profits in total will equal this increase in net worth plus the dividends paid. When marked to market accounting is used, there is an additional element of volatility that depends on short-term fluctuations in the value ascribed to assets and liabilities. GDP could be measured in this marked to market way, but it would be seen as absurdly volatile if it were. I illustrate this in Chart 79, which compares real GDP, as published when measured at constant prices, with real GDP if it were measured on a marked to market basis, giving allowance for the changes in the value of equities and houses owned by US nationals. The absurdity of this approach is shown by the fact that GDP in constant prices would have risen by 95% in the 12 months to 30th September 2009.

The return that an individual investor receives from owning a bond will vary not only because of the interest on the bond but also because of changes in its price between the time when the

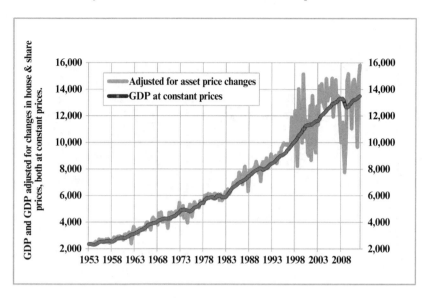

Chart 79. US: GDP as Published and Adjusted for Changes in House and Share Prices.
Sources: Z1 Tables B.102 & L.213 & NIPA Tables 1.1.4 & 1.1.6.

bond was purchased and when it was sold. But for all investors in aggregate, the gains and losses arising from the profits and losses made by individual buyers and sellers will cancel out and the total return to investors will be the same as the interest rate when the bond was issued, which is also the cost that will be incurred by the issuer. This identity is equally true for equity investment. The return to investors in aggregate must be the same as the return earned by companies on their equity, which is also called their net worth.

The long-term real return on US equities has been stable at 6 to 6.5%, as can be seen from Chart 80, and, as a consequence, PE multiples, which are the ratios of share prices to the earnings per share, must and do rotate around their average level. Another identity, which applies over the long-term, is that the return which investors receive must be the same as the earnings' yield (i.e. 100/PE) on the shares they buy. Virtually all corporate equity has been accumulated by the retentions of past profits. The stability of the long-term real return on equities must therefore be matched by the

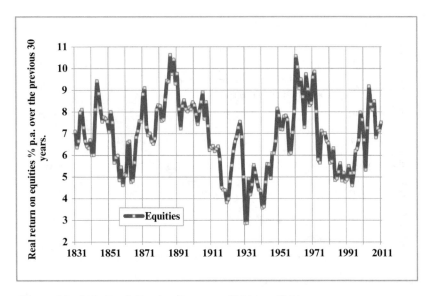

Chart 80. US: Real Equity Returns 1801 to 2011.
Sources: Jeremy Siegel 1801 to 1899 & then Elroy Dimson, Paul Marsh & Mike Staunton to 2011.

same return applied to the amount of money that comes from the reinvestment of retained profits. As the long-term return is stable, the growth of real dividends per share must therefore depend on the proportion of profits that is reinvested. As the current dividend depends on the amount of profit that is paid out and not reinvested, it follows that the growth of dividends will depend on the payout ratio.[1]

If the data are accurate, there must therefore be four identities: (i) the return to equity investors, (ii) the return on corporate equity (net worth), (iii) the earnings yield (which is 100/PE) and (iv) the dividend yield + the dividend growth rate (the dividend and earnings are the next 12 months' figures), i.e. the return to equity investors = the return on corporate equity = the earnings yields = the dividend yield + the dividend growth rate.

---

[1] As the return on equities depends on the dividend yield and the rate at which the dividend grows, it is thus independent of the payout ratio, as shown by the Modigliani–Miller theorem.

In fact, these identities do not quite match, if we use the figures for published profits, and we can show from the discrepancies that profits as published by companies are habitually overstated.

One way to show this is to look at the return on corporate equity, which is available from 1952 onwards, though only for non-financial companies.[2] These data show that the average return on corporate equity has been 4.5%, which is far too low for the figures for profits and corporate equity (net worth) to be accurate. The net worth figures are derived from the data on retained profits, with adjustments for inflation. The extent to which retained profits are overstated is much greater than the extent to which profits are overstated before the deduction of dividends. For example, if "true" profits are 10% below those published and 50% of published profits are paid out in dividends then retained profits will be overstated by 25%.[3] As net worth represents, for the most part, the accumulation of past retained profits and these are boosted proportionately more than profits before dividends have been deducted, the overstatement of net worth is proportionately greater than the overstatement of profits. The overall result of overstated profits is to depress below their true level the published return on net worth. The average long-term return on corporate equity, shown by comparing the profits of non-financial companies in the National Accounts (NIPA Table 1.14) with the net worth of companies shown in the official Flow of Funds Accounts (Z1 Table B.102), is only 4.5%. As we know that the return to investors has been 6% or more, this tells us that the published figures for profits and net worth have both been overstated.[4]

Another approach is to compare the average earnings' yield on US stocks with the long-term return to investors. From 1871 to

[2] The data on profits are available from NIPA Table 1.14 and those on corporate net worth from the Flow of Funds Accounts ("Z1") Table B.102.

[3] "True" profits of 90 after deducting a dividend of 50 will leave "true" retentions of 40 compared with published retentions of 50, and 50 is 25% greater than 40.

[4] Because of this habitual overstatement of profits and net worth, the *q* ratio averages 0.65 rather than 1. As retained profits equal profits after dividends are deducted, the overstatement of retained profits is greater than the overstatement of profits after tax. Because net worth depends on the past level of retained profits, the overstatement of net worth is proportionately greater than the overstatement of profits.

2011 the earning yield averaged 7.27%, which is substantially higher than the real return to investors over the same period, which was 6.59%. The anomaly can most readily be rectified by assuming that published profits have been habitually overstated.

Because there are three identities, we can also gauge the extent to which profits are overstated by looking at the growth of real dividends per share, which have only grown at 1.23% a year since 1871. The average payout ratio has been 58.6% and if profits had been correctly stated this would have meant that dividends would have grown at 2.7% a year.[5]

An examination of each of these relationships thus produces the same conclusion: profits, as published by companies, have been habitually overstated.

There is an important check on the validity of profits published in the national accounts, at least when measured before capital consumption, which is the equivalent in the national accounts of depreciation in company accounts. GDP, which is measured gross and thus before any deduction for capital consumption, can be measured from the data on incomes, expenditure or output, and, while the results from all three approaches may differ, the differences, which are termed statistical discrepancies, are small. If they were not, the national accountants would need to revise their data. There is no similar check on the validity of the aggregate profits published by companies. It is therefore reasonable to consider that the figures published in the national accounts, before capital consumption, are much more likely to represent the "true" profits than those published by companies.

We know from Chart 12 that published profits are now much more volatile than those in the national accounts are. We also know that US published profits have been habitually overstated in the past, but it is unlikely that the degree of overstatement can be constantly increased over time. We must therefore expect that published profits will rotate around a level which is on average above but parallel to their "true" level.

---

[5] A payout ratio of 58.6% means that 41.4% of profits have been ploughed back and if these had been invested at the same rate as the real return to investors of 6.59% from 1871 to 2011 the growth of dividends would have been 6.59 × 41.4 ÷ 100 = 2.7% a year.

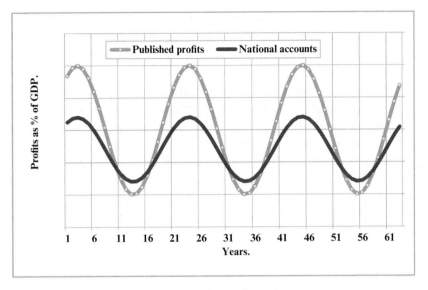

Chart 81. Representation of How Published and National Account Profits Appear to be Related.

In order to present this in diagrammatic form, I illustrate in Chart 81 how, on these assumptions, published and national accounts profits would have been related if "true" profits rotated evenly around a stable proportion of GDP. In Chart 81 published profits are, on average, higher than those in the national accounts, but they are lower at troughs. The swings between peaks and troughs are also much greater for the published profits of companies than for the profits published in the national accounts.

Two data sources shed light on the difference between national account profits and those published by companies. The first is to be found in the data on corporate balance sheets in Table L.102 of the Flow of Funds Accounts of the United States ("Z1"), which is published by the Federal Reserve. In this table are to be found miscellaneous assets and liabilities that are "calculated residually". From email correspondence I have had with economists at the Federal Reserve, it seems reasonably clear that the words "calculated residually" mean that these unidentified miscellaneous items are the difference between the value of assets and liabilities that can be identified – such as plant and equipment, property, inventories, foreign investments, cash, interest-bearing assets and liabilities – and the value of the assets and liabilities that corporations publish in their accounts.[6]

The assets which the Federal Reserve's accountants cannot identify probably don't exist or represent misvaluations of those that do. Overstated profits will produce overstated assets and neither the profits nor the assets as valued will "really" exist. As companies overstate their profits, they will normally also overstate their net worth in a similar way. Changes in the value of the unidentified miscellaneous assets should therefore provide a guide to the way in which the published profits of companies will differ from those in the national accounts, at least over relatively short periods of time and when inflation is low.

Profits in a given year will, if correctly measured, be equal to the change in net worth from operations (i.e. excluding net issues or buy-backs, plus dividends). Changes in the value ascribed to the unidentified miscellaneous assets, expressed as a percentage of net worth, should therefore provide a guide to the extent that the published profits of companies will differ from those in the national accounts, and I therefore show how this has varied in Chart 82.

With the change in accounting from "marked to cost" to "marked to market" the impact of changes in the values ascribed to assets will have risen. In addition the incentive to management to inflate or deflate profits will have varied with the level of the stock market. It is therefore natural to expect that changes in the level of unidentified net assets will tend to move with the stock market.

---

[6] The *Guide to the Flow of Funds Accounts*, Board of Governors of the Federal Reserve System, (2000) explains that "Unidentified miscellaneous assets, which are calculated residually, may include such items as deferred charges and prepaid expenses, goodwill, other intangible assets, and intercorporate holdings of corporate equity. Intangibles can include such items as copyrights, patents, distribution rights and agreements, easements (gas, water and mineral rights), franchises and franchise fees, trademarks, and client lists. Unidentified miscellaneous liabilities, which is also calculated residually, may include such items as unfunded pension liabilities of corporations and loans from private equity funds and hedge funds."

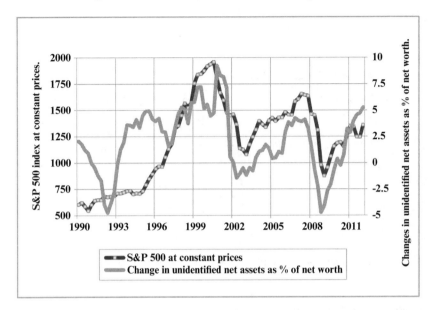

Chart 82. US: Fluctuations in the Stock Market & the Value Ascribed to Unidentified Net Assets.
Sources: Z1 Tables B.102 & L.102 and BLS.

Changes in unidentified assets as a percentage of net worth should provide us with a guide to the difference between the profits that companies publish and those that are recorded in the national accounts. If this assumption is correct, it is likely that the changes In unidentified assets will tend to fluctuate in line with the stock market and, as we showed in Chart 82, they have.[7]

Chart 83 shows that changes in unidentified miscellaneous assets added 5% to net worth over the past 12 months, whereas in 2008 they caused a reduction of 5%. These data suggest that published profits over the past 12 months have risen by significantly more than they would have been had they been produced on the same basis as the national accounts and that profits published in 2008 were significantly depressed compared with their "true" level. This

---

[7] From 1997 to 2012 the correlation coefficient between changes in net unidentified assets and the level of the stock market was 0.76. The data on net worth allow for the impact of inflation, and in order to compare like with like I therefore also adjust the stock market for inflation.

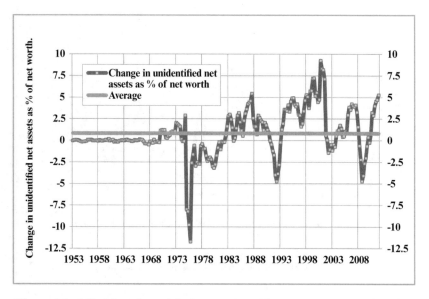

Chart 83. US: Non-financial Companies, Change in Net Unidentified Net Assets as % of Net Worth.
Sources: Z1 Tables B.102 & L.102.

conclusion fits with the otherwise anomalous way in which the aggregate losses were recorded by the constituents of the S&P 500 Index in Q4 2008, while large profits were still being recorded in the national accounts.

Chart 83 also shows that the adjustments for unidentified net assets have been positive not only over the past 12 months but also over the past five or 10 years. It is therefore likely, though far from certain, that the profits currently being published are above their "true" level by more than their usual degree.

Another way of comparing the national account profits with those of published companies is by using the ratios of depreciation to profits shown in both, using the data from the S&P 500 Index. At the time of writing, the latest data that are available for Japan in terms of the income estimates of the national accounts are for the year ended 31st March 2011. This is happily a very good period for comparing Japanese and US accounting for non-financial companies as the profit margins in both countries were almost identical, being

Table 7. Depreciation (Capital Consumption) and Profits after Tax for Japanese and US Non-financial Companies Comparing Published Data from Listed Companies with Data in the National Accounts[8]

	Profits after tax (A)	Depreciation (B)	(B) % (A)
Japan-listed companies	¥14.2 trn	¥26.7 trn	189%
Japan national accounts	¥38.4 trn	¥63.9 trn	166%
US-listed companies	$249 bn	$160 bn	64%
US national accounts (with IV & CC)	$692 bn	$865 bn	125%
US national accounts (without IV & CC)	$755 bn	$864 bn	114%

32.79% of output in Japan compared with 32.82% in the US. At that date, domestic business investment was 38% greater in Japan than in the US as a proportion of GDP and with the same accounting treatment depreciation would be higher in Japan than in the US by a similar proportion.

I set out the comparison in Table 7. The ratio of depreciation to profits in the case of Japanese non-financial companies is very similar, and indeed a bit higher, than the ratio for all non-financial companies in the economy; in the case of the US, it is around half. Far and away the most likely explanation for this massive discrepancy is that US profits in the year to 31st March 2011 were heavily overstated by making insufficient allowance for depreciation. (I showed earlier that Japanese depreciation is overstated in both the national and company accounts.) The gap may have narrowed since but it is still likely that US-listed companies are currently overstating their profits by even more than usual.

---

[8] The data sources for Table 7 are for the 12 months to March 2011. For Japan, Pelham Smithers Associates has provided the data for all non-financial companies in the TOPIX, and the national accounts for 2011 are from the Cabinet Office website. For the US, Grantham Mayo van Otterloo has provided the data for all non-financial companies in the S&P 500 Index. The national accounts are from NIPA Table 1.1.4.

It seems clear from the above analysis that:

- US profits as published by companies have been habitually overstated.
- The degree of overstatement has probably become worse in recent years.
- This overstatement alternates with short periods of understatement, so that published profits have been and will probably continue to be much more volatile than those in the national accounts.
- The overstatement of profits causes retained profits and thus the net worth of corporations to be even more overstated.

I mentioned earlier that investment bankers are fond of claiming that US corporate balance sheets are "in good shape". As the validity of this misconception is not often challenged, it is often repeated in the financial press and by bankers, economists and policymakers. The claim is invariably based on the published accounts of US companies. There are a few reasons why it is misleading:

- The overstatement of published profits, leads to the even greater overstatement of retained profits and thus of net worth.
- The published balance sheets of companies are based on book values. When inflation is high, the real values of assets are well above book values, but the gap narrows when inflation falls. As inflation over the past 20 years has been much lower than it was in the 1970s and 1980s, this means that ratios on today's book values might show that leverage had fallen even if it had really risen if allowance were made for the changing impact of inflation.

The composition of indices, such as the S&P 500, changes over time. When companies leave or join, an adjustment is made so that there is no distortion in the price series. But only one adjustment can be made. It is not therefore possible to avoid distortions occurring in the debt ratios. One result is that if a highly leveraged company is removed from the index and is replaced by a less leveraged one, the debt ratio appears to change without any change taking place in the debt ratio of companies in aggregate. A recent example is provided by General Motors. The share price of this highly-leveraged company fell after the financial crisis to the point when it was withdrawn from the S&P 500 and ceased to be a constituent of the Index. The impact of this was to reduce the leverage ratio of the Index. However, no reduction in the leverage of US companies occurred simply because the constituents of the Index changed. Changes in the debt ratios of companies in the Index do not therefore represent changes in the debt ratios of companies in general. Highly leveraged companies are more likely to drop out of the Index than join it and, as a result, the changes in the leverage of companies in the index will tend to understate over time the rise in the leverage of companies in aggregate.

The debts of the US business sector have risen dramatically relative to GDP, as Chart 84 illustrates, and, as far as I am aware, those who claim that corporate balance sheets are in good shape do not deny this: they just ignore it and must therefore be implicitly assuming that improving balance sheets in the corporate sector are compatible with rising debt relative to GDP. This is possible under certain conditions but these are unlikely and, if they occurred, would be extremely worrying. The proportion of GDP produced by companies has not changed very much. It follows that if debt

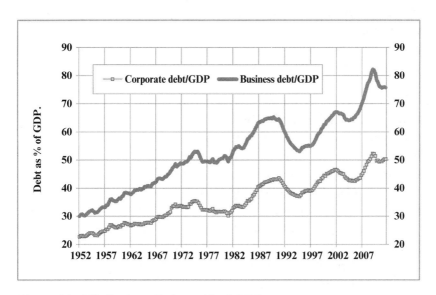

Chart 84. US: Business Debt as % of GDP.
Sources: NIPA Table 1.1.5 & Federal Reserve Z1 Table B.102.

has fallen relative to assets but has risen relative to output, which is measured by GDP, then there must have been a dramatic deterioration in the efficiency of capital. This means that more and more capital must be needed to produce growth and without a rise in the proportion of investment to GDP the ability of the economy to grow will have been steadily deteriorating. I shall show later that with regard to plant and equipment, which is an important part of business capital, there has been some deterioration, but this has been far less than the dramatic decline which would have to have occurred to justify the claims that corporate debt ratios have been falling in recent years and that balance sheets are consequently in good shape.

If we ignore the totally misleading data that investment bankers derive from the published balance sheets of listed companies and look at the official data published, we will see that US company balance sheets have been steadily deteriorating during the post-war period and that their current leverage approaches the highest and thus most dangerous levels so far reached.

Corporate output is around half of total output (i.e. GDP) and the ratio fluctuates, but it has been reasonably stable in the post-war period. It is therefore to be expected that the rise in corporate debt relative to corporate output, like debt to GDP, will have risen strongly over the post-war period, and Chart 85 shows that this expectation is fulfilled. Corporate debt, relative to output, is nearly at the maximum level it has reached in the post-war period and after a brief initial decline following the financial crisis has recently been rising.

Chart 86 measures debt in relation to assets, excluding those which cannot be identified and, I assume, arise from the past overstatement of profits. The growth of debt relative to output and that relative to assets is similar but less marked. The difference must arise because assets have risen relative to output. This, as I will discuss in more detail later, represents a problem for the US economy, because it indicates that it takes more capital today than it did in earlier years to produce a given increase in output and means that US growth will slow unless the ratio investment to GDP rises.

The distortions in both the profit and loss accounts and balance sheets that feature in the annual accounts of US quoted companies have disturbing consequences for the stability of the US economy and increase the risk of another financial crisis. By overstating

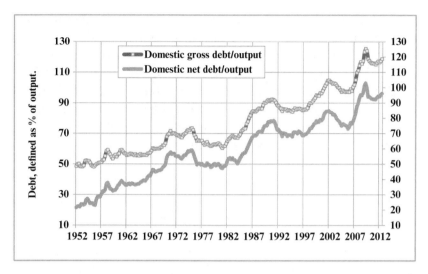

Chart 85. US: Non-finanancial Corporate Debt as % of Output.
Sources: NIPA Table 1.14 & Federal Reserve Z1 Table B.102.

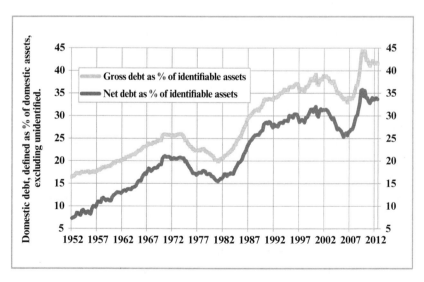

Chart 86. US: Non-financial Companies' Debt as % of Physical and Indentifiable Financial Assets.
Source: Federal Reserve ZI Table B.102.

profits, the ease with which interest payments can be readily afforded is exaggerated and the overstatement of assets means that in the event that assets will have to be sold to meet debts their realisable value is likely to disappoint. These distortions are particularly worrying when interest rates are so low that they cannot fall further. In the past, difficult times when profits fall have been accompanied by falls in interest rates, but this cannot happen in the future and the risk of bankruptcies when profits fall will therefore be even greater than it has been in the past.

When the credit agencies assess the risks that companies will default on their debts, they apply labels to various bonds and loans. The terminology varies between the various agencies, but in broad terms the less risky are "triple A" and then, via "Bs" and "Cs", we come to junk. In making these assessments the agencies tend to concentrate on two ratios. The first is the extent to which the interest on the debts is covered by profits and the second the extent to which the amount of the debt is covered by assets. It seems to me sadly unlikely that on making these assessments the credit agencies allow for the extent to which profits that companies publish are overstated, the degree to which this overstatement varies from year to year or the extent to which the value of company assets is overstated.

This has an important consequence for economic policy. It seems likely that the degree to which businesses are leveraged is being seriously understated by the credit agencies. As their evidence on leverage is taken seriously by central bankers and other policymakers, there is a tendency for the dangers of high debt to be underrated. As the risks of another financial crisis are heavily dependent on the level of debt, I fear that these risks are greater than is generally understood by central bankers and others who are concerned with financial stability.

Another problem that comes from the mis-statement of profits and assets is that the returns on equity which companies, investment bankers, fund managers and financial journalists assume to be reasonable are overstated to the point of absurdity. For example, this comment appeared in the Financial Times: "Average return on equity for the top 200 companies in the TOPIX is a woeful 9% . . ."[9] As Japan has had mild deflation for the past 20 years this return would

---

[9]The quotation is from the Financial Times Lex Column, (5th March, 2013).

be a bit more than 9% in real terms and around three percentage points or 50% above the long-term real return on equity. Far from being woeful, the return would, if correctly measured, be extremely high. As it will be difficult for companies to distort their profits up and their investment down sufficiently to make future returns appear much better than the long-term equilibrium return of 6%, the widespread and absurd belief that 9% is "woeful" is likely to discourage listed companies from investing even when the prospective return on new equipment is likely to be well above the historic returns. This problem is less likely to affect Japan, where companies appear sensibly indifferent to the comments of investment bankers and the financial press. It is, however, likely to be a problem in Anglophone economies, where managements are attentive to such criticisms and where such sensitivity seems to be particularly prevalent among bankers. One result of the pursuit of unrealistic returns on banks' equity is that it encourages excessive risk taking and inhibits commercial lending at economic interest rates. Lord Salisbury is reputed to have remarked with the onset of universal male suffrage that "we must educate our masters". Now that bankers are reputed to have become "the masters of the universe", we need to apply this precept to the whole of the financial services industry, and to the politicians and central bankers who appear to take their views seriously. It is very important that the financial services industry should be better educated in finance than seems currently to be the case.

10

Avoiding Future Financial Crises

Recovery is stalled because we suffer from structural rather than just cyclical constraints on growth. Current economic policies are ill-conceived and need to be changed and this should be the major priority for policy. But we must at the same time avoid policies that precipitate another financial crisis. The creation of massive fiscal deficits was successful in moderating the impact of the last one. It is politically improbable that we could introduce another large increase in these deficits were we to hit another crisis and it is doubtful whether this would be sensible in economic terms. We have also reduced interest rates to near zero and, although the unorthodox monetary policy in which central banks buy bonds may have helped, there are widespread doubts both about its continued benefits[1] and its possible risks.[2] While it should always be a major aim of policy to avoid financial crises, the need today is greater than

---

[1] C. A. E. Goodhart and J. Ashworth "*QE: A successful start may be running into diminishing returns*", Oxford Review of Economic Policy 28(4): 640–670, (2012).
[2] *Ultra Easy Monetary Policy and the Law of Unintended Consequences* by William R. White, The Federal Reserve Bank of Dallas Globalization and Monetary Policy Institute "Working Paper No. 126" (2012). The author is chairman of the Economic Development and Review Committee of the OECD and previously Economic Advisor and Head of the Monetary and Economic Department of the BIS.

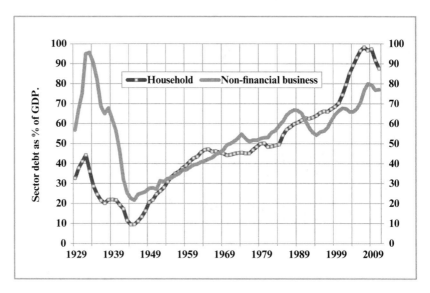

Chart 87. US: Non-financial Business & Household Debt.
Sources: Bureau of the Census, NIPA Table 1.1.5 & Z1 Tables B.100 & B.102.

ever as the ammunition that was used to mitigate the consequences of the last one has been expended and is no longer available. It is therefore essential to analyse the causes of previous crises so that we do not repeat the errors that led to them.

There have been three, and happily only three, examples of financial crises in the past 100 years that have caused severe and sustained losses of output. They were the slump of the 1930s, which followed the Wall Street crash of 1929, the stagnation of the Japanese economy, which followed their stock market crash of 1990, and the recent recession and subsequent economic weakness that followed sharp falls in shares and house prices. Each occasion had its own individual characteristics, but they were all marked by the existence of high levels of private sector debt and were triggered by sharp falls in asset prices.

Chart 87 and Chart 88 illustrate the way the debts of households and non-financial businesses were rocketing up prior to their crises in both the US and Japan.[3]

[3] I have been unable to find data for Japanese household debt levels before 1985.

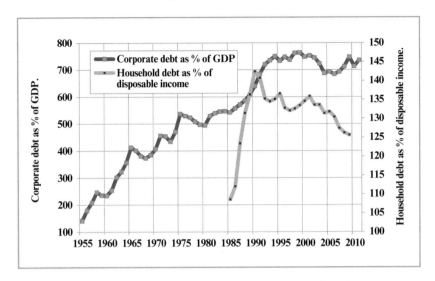

Chart 88. Japan: Non-financial Business & Household Debt.
Sources: MoF Survey of Incorporated Enterprises, Cabinet Office & OECD.

Prior to each of the three financial crises, there was a large increase in debt. Chart 87 shows that in the US the total amount of both business and household debt peaked in 1930, but although it then fell, measured in dollars, it continued to rise relative to GDP because the fall in output in the depression was so great. Debt fell rapidly but GDP fell even faster. As a result the ratios of debt to GDP did not fall until 1934 for households and 1935 for business.

After these crises had passed, the debt levels in the private sector, which include both households and businesses, fell or at least stabilised. It would seem that debt prior to the crises had become "too high", but it is far from clear how high debt has to be to have become "too high". For example, US non-financial business debt in 1929 was 58% of GDP in 1929 but reached 80% in 2008, and if other private sector debt ratios are used, such as those for households or financial business, the rise in leverage was even greater.

A common feature of both the US crises and the Japanese one was a major fall in asset prices; on all three occasions this happened

Chart 89. US: House and Share Prices 1925 to 1932.
Sources: Robert Shiller & the Bureau of the Census.

in share prices and in two of them in house prices as well. In
September 1929 the US stock market crashed after rising dramatically but, as I illustrate in Chart 89, house prices were flat in the
US both before and after 1929 and seem to have been barely
affected by the stock market. From January 1990 there was a similar
crash in Japanese shares; which preceded the weakness of the
economy from 1992 onwards, as Chart 90 shows, the fall in the
Tokyo stock market preceded the subsequent fall in house prices
by 18 months.

Chart 91 shows that in the recent crisis US house prices started
to fall before share prices and, presumably because recent events are
more vivid and seem more important than those of the past, there
has been a tendency among commentators, including some economists, to overweight the importance of house prices and under-
weight that of shares. It is therefore worth emphasising that the US
1929 crash was purely a stock market affair and did not involve
house prices and that the fall in house prices in Japan lagged by 18

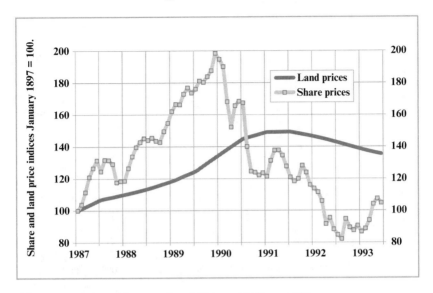

Chart 90. Japan: Share & Land Prices 1987 to 1993.
Sources: Japan Real Estate Institute (urban nationwide index) & Nikkei 225 via Ecowin.

months the fall in share prices. From past evidence, therefore, we have no reason to assume that the prices of houses are more important than those of other assets. We should also avoid assuming that we should place all our attention on share prices. As debt levels are high today, another financial crisis may well be triggered by falls in the overextended prices of corporate or government bonds, or in commercial property. Once we accept the importance of asset prices and have rid ourselves of the myth that they cannot become overvalued, we should take care to observe any danger signals from them and not restrict our attention to one class of assets such as house or share prices.

It also seems likely that the fall in US share prices in 2001 (Chart 91) would have had a more serious impact on the economy than that which duly occurred had there not been a sharp tax cut introduced in November 2000. This was not introduced to avoid or mitigate the weakness in the economy, which was not generally

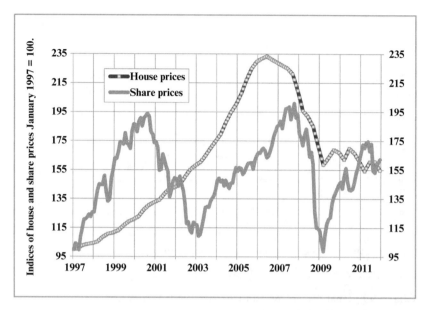

Chart 91. US: Share & House Prices 1997 to 2012.
Sources: Case-Shiller and S&P 500.

anticipated,[4] but seems to have been inspired by the wish of the
Republican party to gain popularity and forestall the risk that some
future Democratic Congress would take advantage of the fact that
the budget was then in surplus to increase expenditure rather than
cut taxes (as Republican orthodoxy demands). The result was a boost
to the economy that had the accidental and unanticipated benefit
of limiting the unexpected recession. Given the high levels of debt
and the trigger provided by the fall in asset prices, it seems highly
probable that the recession in 2001 would have been severe rather
than mild but for the fiscal stimulus provided by the tax cut.

[4]The Economist (January, 2005) reported that "In a survey in March 2001, 95%
of American economists said that there would not be a recession. One of the few
exceptions was the Economic Cycle Research Institute [ECRI], which that month
correctly forecast, on the basis of its leading economic indicators, that a recession
was unavoidable." Lakshman Achuthan of the ECRI points out that "GDP revisions in late 2002 showed three successive down quarters of GDP, but that more
recent revisions have reduced this to one negative quarter. However, the US
economy lost 2.7 million payroll jobs during and in the months following the
recession – one of the largest job losses associated with any postwar recession."

While the result was thus beneficial in the short-term, it created a problem for the future. When an even greater stimulus was needed to mitigate the 2008 recession, this arrived when the deficit had already risen through the earlier tax cuts, and to sustain the economy after the crisis the budget deficit rose above 10% of GDP. In 2012, the latest data we have, it was well over 8%, and if another fiscal stimulus were needed to meet another recession it has become politically as well as economically difficult to introduce one.

We cannot tell from past history how much debt will in retrospect prove to have been too much and it is equally and unfortunately true that the speed at which debt is growing has also failed to provide a guide to past crises. I show in Chart 92 how rapidly private sector debt grew relative to GDP in the US since 1930 measured over both one year and three years. The chart shows that there was no acceleration in the growth of debt before the recent crisis. The problem has been that in all but a few years debt has persistently grown faster than GDP, so that the rise in the ratio of private sector debt to GDP has been insidious rather than dramatic.

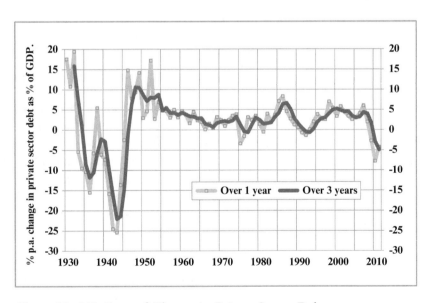

Chart 92. US: Rate of Change in Private Sector Debt.
Sources: Bureau of the Census & NIPA Table 1.1.5 & Federal Reserve Z1 Table D3.

Neither the level of debt nor the rate at which it has grown has provided warnings of an imminent crisis.

Fortunately, we can measure the degree to which the US stock market is over- or undervalued and, while this does not provide a guide to the imminence of a crisis, it presents, in a way that debt levels and growth have not, an important guide to the current level of risk. Stephen Wright, Robert Shiller and I all wrote in 2000 about our ability to judge the extent to which we were in danger from an overvalued stock market.[5]

It is important to stress that while the extent to which the dangers of a crisis can be assessed, the timing of a crisis cannot be known. The failure to understand this vitally important point was illustrated by the widespread, but possibly apocryphal, story that after the financial crisis broke, the Queen asked, "Why did no one warn us?" In fact, many of us had warned of the growing risks, but we could not forecast when the crisis would hit. As a fall in asset prices appears to be the key trigger to financial crisis, it would only be possible to forecast the timing, as distinct from the growing risks of a crisis, if it were possible not only to measure asset prices but also to forecast the time when overpriced assets would start to fall. If such a forecast were possible, markets would never become overvalued. Warned of an imminent fall, investors would sell and stop the market from rising. It is therefore a necessary condition for the existence of financial crises that we can warn of their rising risks, but we cannot predict their timing. In an attempt to make the difference clear, I wrote a letter at the time to the Financial Times in which I pointed out that Cassandra had the three typical attributes of a sound analyst. Her forecasts were correct, she made no claims about their timing and her views were invariably ignored, including her warnings about the wooden horse. But I added that, while she was too used to this to be upset by it, what made her hopping mad was a headline in the Troy Times: "Queen Hecuba asks: 'Why did no one warn us about the wooden horse?'"[6]

---

[5] See *Valuing Wall Street: Protecting wealth in turbulent markets* by Andrew Smithers and Stephen Wright, McGraw-Hill, (2000); and *Irrational Exuberance* by Robert Shiller, Princeton University Press, (2000).
[6] "Take heed of Cassandra's warning against imminent ruin", letter from Andrew Smithers, Financial Times, 24th April 2009.

As we have, happily, had only three major financial crises we cannot base policy on statistical analysis, as this requires a much greater wealth of data than can be supplied by something that has only happened three times. A sensible approach to avoiding a repetition of the recent catastrophe must therefore be primarily pragmatic rather than theoretical. Nonetheless, past crises have enough similarities to provide warnings, which it would be folly to ignore. From our past experience the following guides to policy seem clear.

- We should seek to avoid high debt levels and, if we have them, seek to bring them down. This would require us to acknowledge that we already have this problem today.
- We should avoid policies that encourage debt growth or rises in asset prices, unless prices can be shown to be depressed. This again would require us to be willing to acknowledge that important classes of asset prices today, including US bonds and equities and UK house prices, may be dangerously high. It would also argue strongly against "quantitative easing", which involves central banks buying assets and thus pushing up their prices.
- We should not assume that the signal of an imminent crisis would be given by an acceleration in debt growth. An excessive level of debt, not a rapid growth in debt, has been the necessary condition for past crises.
- We should note that the trigger for each of the three past crashes has been falls in share prices, with house prices having also been important in the lead-up to two, but only two, of the three crises. It is vital to recognise that, while equities and house prices have indicated looming problems in the past, bond or other asset prices may do so in the future.

11

The Current High Level of Risk

Monetary policy in Japan, the UK and the US has become based on quantitative easing, which involves the expansion of their central banks' balance sheets through the purchase of assets. The full impact of this policy is not known and cannot be, because this is the first time that it has been pursued as a deliberate attempt to stimulate the economy. Expanding central banks' balance sheets to finance government debts produced the hyperinflations found in Germany and Hungary after World War I and more recently in Zimbabwe, but these results seem to have been accidents rather than deliberate attempts to create the catastrophes. But partly because of these examples, quantitative easing has been attacked as a route to certain disaster. I do not share this view. I see no reason why quantitative easing could not have been beneficial as a temporary measure, though in conjunction with large budget deficits it will surely lead to inflation if it is treated as a semi-permanent policy tool and it increases the risk that a sharp fall in asset prices will trigger another financial crisis.

Since we have so little experience of quantitative easing, we cannot be sure of either its efficacy or its side effects. I am particularly concerned about the latter, and this is a concern that I share with others, including Bill White and Charles Goodhart. The former has warned that it will have unintended and undesirable long-term effects.[1] While Charles Goodhart warned at a conference that quantitative easing "may contribute to keeping the economy trapped in a low growth equilibrium" and that "lower yields are putting significant pressure on pension funds . . . Corporate pension contributions hit new highs in Q1 2012 and the risk is that money could potentially be increasingly diverted away from business investment."[2]

There is a measure of agreement, which seems to me to be reasonably persuasive, that quantitative easing has so far helped the world economy. By buying government bonds central banks have pushed up their prices and brought down their yields; they have also increased the quantity of money in their economies. Those taking out new mortgages in the US constitute one group that has clearly benefited from the lower yields on government bonds, which has been one consequence of quantitative easing. In the UK most mortgages vary with short-term interest rates, but in the US the majority are linked to the rate of interest on 10-year government bonds. Had the Federal Reserve not bought government bonds, the cost of mortgages would have been higher than it is. As a consequence it is likely that the fall in house prices would have been even greater and there would have been even less investment in house building.

It is also likely that if quantitative easing helped limit the fall in house prices that this would have had the additional benefit of limiting the fall in consumption. The more house prices fall, the more worried and cautious people become, and this encourages higher savings at the expense of household spending. As Chart 93 shows, household savings are strongly correlated with the value of

---

[1] *Ultra Easy Monetary Policy and the Law of Unintended Consequences* by William R. White, The Federal Reserve Bank of Dallas Globalization and Monetary Policy Institute "Working Paper No. 126" (2012). The author is chairman of the Economic Development and Review Committee of the OECD and previously Economic Advisor and Head of the Monetary and Economic Department of the BIS.

[2] Comments at a conference organised by Fathom Consulting, (2nd November, 2012) by Charles Goodhart, Professor Emeritus London School of Economics and formerly chief economist of the Bank of England. For details see C. A. E. Goodhart and J. Ashworth, "*QE: A successful start may be running into diminishing returns*", Oxford Review of Economic Policy 28(4): 640–670, (2012).

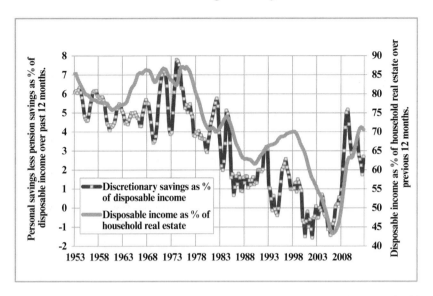

Chart 93. US: Personal Savings (excluding pensions) and Household Real Estate Wealth.
Sources: NIPA Table 2.1 & Z1 Tables B.100 & F.100.

houses. The richer people believe themselves to be, the less they feel the need to save, and the less they save, the more they consume.[3]

Lowering yields on government debt has the additional advantage that it usually reduces the cost of borrowing to companies. In the past this would have encouraged higher business investment. Today, unfortunately, any impact appears to be small or even non-existent. Owing to the change in corporate behaviour that has bedevilled the UK and US economies in the 21st century, low interest rates today seem to encourage companies to buy their own shares or those of other companies through takeovers, rather than to increase their capital spending on new plant and equipment. The ability to raise debt cheaply increases the attractions of both fixed-capital investment and share purchases. It verges on the tragic that

---

[3] The savings' rate shown in Chart 93 excludes savings made via pension funds, which respond more to changes in share than house prices. The correlation coefficient between savings as defined here and the value of the housing stock is 0.83.

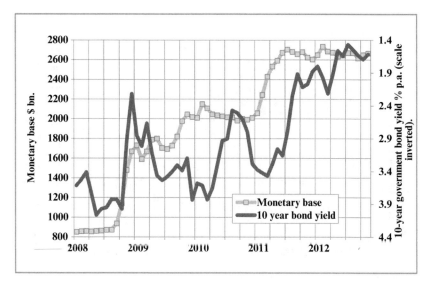

Chart 94. US: Monetary Base & Bond Yield.
Sources: Federal Reserve & Reuters via Ecowin.

the latter should now be preferred by business, at a time when the
stimulus to demand which comes from higher investment is so badly
needed.

When a central bank buys bonds, or other assets, its liabilities
expand, thus causing the size of these liabilities, which is the monetary base, to grow. In Chart 94 I compare the size of the US
monetary base with the yield on 10-year government bonds and in
Chart 95 with the level of the stock market. This does not prove
that quantitative easing has pushed up bond and stock markets, as
many other influences affect their levels. It is, however, reasonable
to believe that under recent conditions this has been the impact.

It thus seems probable that quantitative easing has had a positive
impact on demand through its impact on asset prices. But the higher
asset prices are, the more they are likely to fall. Past financial crises
have come from the combination of high debt levels and sharp
falls in asset prices. Debt levels are still extremely high, as Chart 96
shows, for US business and personal debt and are even more extreme
if financial debt is included.

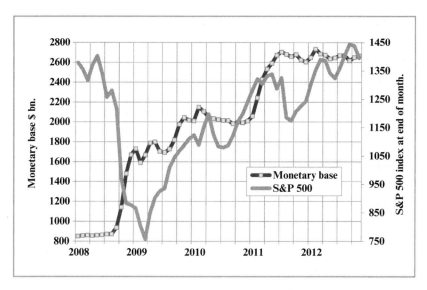

Chart 95. US: Monetary Base & the Stock Market.
Sources: Federal Reserve and Standard & Poor's via Ecowin.

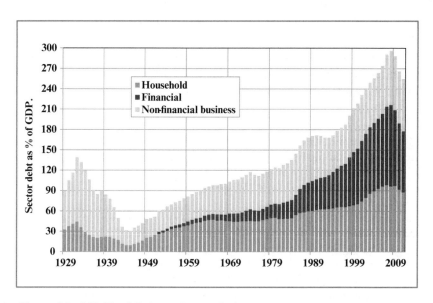

Chart 96. US: Total Private Sector Debt.
Sources: Bureau of the Census, Federal Reserve Z1 Table D3 & NIPA
Table 1.1.5.

It is common practice for companies to obtain finance in ways that avoid the debt having to appear on their balance sheets. Individuals can do much the same by leasing automobiles rather than by borrowing to buy them. Such debts are termed off-balance sheet and should be included in data for financial debt.[4] It is therefore important to include financial as well as non-financial debt when assessing the risks that economies are running as a result of leverage. If financial debt is ignored, the risks being run in the private sector, for both business and households, will be understated.[5]

Ireland provides a superb and sad illustration of the importance of private sector debt levels. Prior to its recent crisis, the data showed that it had a relatively low level of national debt, at 28% of its GDP, and was running a fiscal surplus. But it had and still has huge debts in the private sector. When the financial crisis hit, the Irish government had to bail out its banks to prevent the economy from collapsing. The cost was so great that it pushed up the national debt to 109% of GDP and caused such weakness in the economy that GDP in Q4 2011 was 12% below its level in Q4 2007.

As the risks of high debt levels have become increasingly recognised the IMF has started to publish data on countries' private sector debt as a regular matter. I showed in Table 6 the high levels of debt in Greece, Italy, Portugal and Spain, but Table 8 shows that although Ireland stands out as having massive problems the debt levels of other G5 countries are on the whole no better than those of the US, which, as Chart 96 shows, appear to be dangerously high.

---

[4] It seems that this is not always the case. A former Chairman of the International Accounting Standards Board, Sir David Tweedie, is reputed to have said that one of his ambitions was to ensure that all the debt in an economy appeared on at least somebody's balance sheet. It seems that he retired with his ambition unfulfilled.

[5] PricewaterhouseCoopers in "*The future of leasing*" (April 2010) concluded that interest-bearing debt would be 58% higher and leverage up by 13 percentage points if leasing debts were brought onto balance sheets. The survey covered 3,000 companies worldwide, and it seems likely that US companies would be particularly exposed if the proposed change in accounting standards were implemented. See also "*Bringing leased assets onto the balance sheet*" by Kimberly J. Cornaggia, Laurel A. Franzen and Timothy T. Simin, http://papers.ssrn.com/sol3/papers.cfm?abstract_id=1680077, (accessed 5th June, 2013).

Table 8. Gross Debt to GDP % 2011 (Source: IMF Global Financial Stability Report)

Country	Household debt	Non-financial corporates	Financial institutions	Total economy external liabilities
US	92	90	94	151
Japan	77	143	188	67
UK	101	118	547	607
France	61	150	151	264
Germany	60	80	98	200
Ireland	123	245	689	1680

It is also clear that the UK remains vulnerable because of the high debts of its financial institutions.

The major US financial crises of the past, which hit in 1929 and 2008, have been followed by severe recessions, and Japan's post-1990 crisis was the start of a period of prolonged stagnation. Large falls in asset prices appear to provide the trigger for the crises, while the fundamental problem has been excessive debt. The risk of large falls in asset prices naturally mounts the more overpriced they are. As reducing debt without catastrophe is a long-drawn-out process, it is important to avoid having assets overpriced.

At least three groups of asset prices appear to be dangerously high today: US equities, bonds everywhere and UK house prices.

As Stephen Wright and I have shown, there are two valid ways of measuring the degree to which US equities are over- or under-valued. These are the q ratio, which compares the stock market value of non-financial companies with their net worth, after allowing for the impact of inflation, and the cyclically adjusted PE.[6] These must, of course, give the same answer, as sound approaches to valuing the market cannot give different ones. As I write, the S&P 500 Index is around 1500, and these two indices show that the US market is

[6] See *Wall Street Revalued: Imperfect markets and inept central bankers* by Andrew Smithers, John Wiley & Sons, Ltd, (2009); and *Valuing Wall Street: Protecting wealth in turbulent markets* by Andrew Smithers and Stephen Wright, McGraw-Hill, (2000).

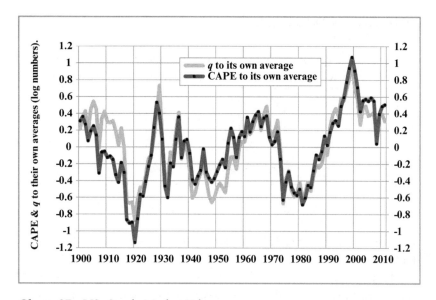

Chart 97. US: Stock Market Value.
Sources: Stephen Wright & Federal Reserve for *q*, Robert Shiller for CAPE.

around 50% overpriced. As Chart 97[7] illustrates, this degree of over-valuation is way short of the extremes reached at the year ends of 1929 and 1999, but it is similar to the other major peaks of 1906, 1937 and 1968. Each of these was followed by prolonged and nasty bear markets and weak economies.

PEs based on the earnings over the past 12 months, or over the next 12 months, are among the criteria that can easily be shown to be worthless as guides to the current value of the stock market. As can be seen from Chart 97, the US stock market hit dangerously high peaks in 1909 and in 1937; in September 1906 and May 1937 the stock market was selling at a below-average multiple and on each occasion subsequently fell by 40% and was followed by serious

---

[7] Chart 97 compares the value of the US market at the year end. By the end of December 1929 US shares had fallen by more than 30% from the end of September. The degree of overvaluation in September 1929 and August 2000, when the S&P 500 hit its bubble peak, were much more similar than the impression given by the year end figures.

recessions. Not only did low PE multiples serve to disguise seriously overvalued stock markets, the opposite also applied with some of the cheapest markets on record occurring when current PE multiples were well above average. In June 1933 the stock market had fallen to as near to the cheapest level as it has ever reached. Nonetheless it was selling, on the basis of the past 12 months' earnings, on a PE which was 72% above average. It is worth noting that even on the basis of the next 12 months earnings, which were of course unknown to investors at the time, it was selling but at a PE which was 65% above average.

Despite the clear evidence that it is nonsense to value the stock market in terms of past or forecast PEs, Janet Yellen, vice-chairman of the Federal Reserve, has used this approach to dismiss worries about overvaluation.[8] It would take an intelligent person who studied the data no more than half an hour at most to realise that using PE multiples based on either past or assumed prospective earnings per share is absurd. It appears that Dr Yellen and her colleagues at the Federal Reserve have not been willing to spend the time required and are prepared to announce views on matters that they have been unprepared to study. I think, and hope that readers will agree with me, that this is quite simply irresponsible.

In this respect the situation in the UK is better than in the US. The Bank of England publishes a Financial Stability Report every six months. In its June 2011 edition (No. 29), there was a table No. 1.21 labelled "Equity Price Valuation Measure". The authors of this table appeared to have read the guide to how not to value equities, which Stephen Wright and I set out in *Valuing Wall Street* and then proceeded to follow that guide as if it were an instruction as to how, rather than how not, to do so. Stephen and I had shown that among the commonly used but invalid approaches were the use of current dividend yields, PEs and price to book values. We had also shown that it was essential to use really long-term data covering 100 years or more in order to be able to compare any given ratio with its historic average in a useful and valid way. As if striving to do things badly, the Bank of England's table included the criteria

---

[8] See "*Assessing Potential Financial Imbalances in an Era of Accommodative Monetary Policy*", speech by Janet Yellen, International Conference: Real and Financial Linkage and Monetary Policy, Bank of Japan, Tokyo (1st June, 2011).

we had shown to be invalid, had ignored long-term data and used only the past 10 years' averages for their comparison. In addition it failed to mention either of the valid criteria that we had shown could be used for valuing equities.

I was therefore less than polite about this document when lunching with Andy Haldane shortly after it appeared. Andy is a member of the interim financial policy committee and, as the director of the Bank of England for financial stability, has a particular responsibility for the Bank's Financial Stability Reports. Happily, Andy Haldane is not someone who dislikes new ideas; indeed, he is a fount of them. He responded to my comments with an invitation to Stephen Wright and me to discuss our objections with a group at the Bank. At this meeting we remarked that we were pleased that the importance of the issue of equity valuation was acknowledged by being included in the Financial Stability Report and appalled at the way in which it had, so far, been approached. It was easy for us to show that neither the ratios chosen nor the period of comparison could be used by a sensible person as a guide to equity market valuations. I hope that our criticisms will lead to an improvement in the way that future financial stability reports will treat the key issue of asset valuations. The result so far is that the subject has been dropped.[9]

I show in Chart 98 that real returns on bonds have not rotated around their average in a similar way to equities and, as a result, they are less easy or perhaps even impossible to value. But bonds have only rarely given negative real returns and at current levels both in the UK and in the US inflation-protected bonds give zero or even mildly negative real returns. It is possible to imagine situations which are so bad that the negative returns on these bonds are superior to even worse returns on other assets and those that buy them today might be able to sell them at a profit at some stage in the future. It is nonetheless, clear that current yields assure investors that they will in aggregate have very bad returns by past average standards and it is, I believe, sensible to hold that these assets are ridiculously overvalued.

[9] I had a second important objection to Stability Report No. 29, which included a claim that US companies' financial positions had improved. This was based on a common and highly misleading claim made by several investment banks, on which I have already commented.

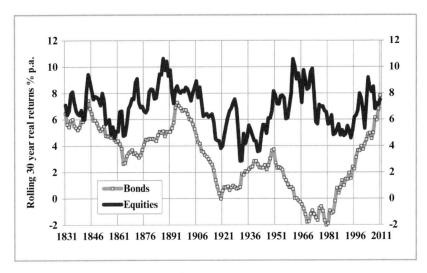

Chart 98. US: Real 30-year Returns on Equities & Bonds.
Sources: Siegel 1801 to 1899 & then Elroy Dimson, Paul Marsh & Mike Staunton via Morningstar to 2011.

The real returns that investors will receive on nominal bonds depend on the future rate of inflation, which is unknown. If investors had been good at forecasting the level of inflation, we might have reasonably assumed that the low current return on nominal bonds was justified by the low level of future inflation, but investors have proved to be very bad at forecasting inflation as the real return achieved by bond investors has been low when inflation has been high and vice versa.[10]

When investors have not made large errors about future inflation, the real returns on bonds have in the past been around 4%,[11]

---

[10] Statistically, the extent to which two series move together is measured by the correlation coefficient. When there is no fit, this measures zero and 1 when the fit is perfect. The correlation coefficient between real returns on US government bonds over 30 years and inflation, measured from 1801 to 2011, is −0.7.

[11] See *Appendix 6: Errors in Inflation Expectations and the Impact on Bond Returns* by Stephen Wright and Andrew Smithers, from *Wall Street Revalued: Imperfect markets and inept central bankers* by Andrew Smithers, John Wiley & Sons, Ltd, (2009).

and over the 210 years for which we have reasonable data US bonds have given an average real return of 3.5%. Inflation-protected bonds currently have negative yields and the traditional ones which are not protected against inflation have yields varying from under 2% for 10-year maturities to 3% for those of 30 years. If we have stable to falling consumer prices over the next 30 years, then long-dated nominal bonds will give real returns that match historic averages. Given the Federal Reserve's apparent wish to have inflation that is not less than 2%, it seems to me highly likely that another very deep and unpleasant recession will be needed if we are to experience the low rate of inflation needed to justify current nominal bond yields.

As the economic conditions that would render either inflation-protected or nominal bonds reasonably priced today are so unpleasant, I hope that they will prove to be badly overpriced. The problem with this hope is that it implies that we will at some stage have a large drop in the prices of bonds and this is likely to have a very bad impact on the economy if it happens quickly.

Not only does it seem likely that bonds are massively overpriced but we can be reasonably sure that a likely cause of this is the fact that the Bank of England and the Federal Reserve have been buying them heavily. I showed in Chart 94 the apparent connection between the yields on US government bonds and the expansion of the Fed's balance sheet due to the scale of its bond buying. Only those who have faith in the efficiency of financial markets can surely expect that massive buying of bonds by central banks will not push up their prices and will probably push them up to absurd levels. Faith in the efficiency of financial markets at pricing assets is, in my view, absurd and although it is probable that few economists now continue to hold such views, those who have held them in the past have done a great deal of damage. It is reasonable to hold that bond markets are today absurdly overvalued and that we know why this has occurred. It is also reasonable to contend, to judge from Chart 95, that the bond buying by central banks has added to the risks that we suffer from an overvalued bond market by contributing to the overvaluation of the US equity market, which I illustrated in Chart 97.

UK houses are another group of assets that appear dangerously overpriced. As Chart 99 shows, houses in the UK are roughly three

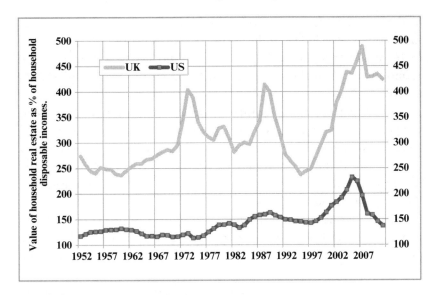

Chart 99. UK & US: Housing Affordability.
Sources: ONS (+ other sources for ealy data) & Federal Reserve.

times more expensive than those in the US relative to household incomes and, unlike US house prices, they have barely fallen from their peak levels. The reason for the relatively high cost of UK housing is not the cost of materials or labour; it is the price of land, and the price of land is high because of planning restrictions. It is the intention of the UK government to ease planning restrictions sufficiently to allow a significant rise in house building. If this actually occurred there would be a large fall in house prices, but change is unlikely to be effective in practice. Development is strongly resisted locally and by many Conservative members of parliament under pressure from their constituents. The declared aim of those opposing development is to preserve the countryside and their achievement is to keep up house prices. The Council for the Preservation of Rural England is a most effective pressure group and may reasonably be renamed the Council for the Preservation of Rural House Prices. If house prices fell sharply, it is likely that UK banks would find their bad debts rising. There are two other ways in which house prices may fall sharply: one is a recovery in the economy accompanied by a rise in interest rates, and the other is a further weakening setting off a rise in unemployment. None of these looks very likely at the moment, but it would be foolish not to recognise that the high price of UK houses is a danger to the economy and that the danger is amplified by the weak capital basis of UK banks.

As the prices of US equities as well as bonds seem to have been driven up by the purchases of government debt by the Federal Reserve, as suggested by Charts 94 and 95, I am worried that many other assets, including commercial property, may also have become overpriced. I am not, however, aware of any valid way of measuring the value of these assets.

Past crises have arisen through a combination of high debt levels and falling asset prices. It is clearly important to understand the way in which this dangerous association has produced such damaging results.

Much of the world's debt is secured against assets, and, when extending credit, lenders generally assume that the value of an asset is unlikely to be very different from its current price. The past attachment of economists to the Efficient Market Hypothesis (EMH) has encouraged such folly. When the prices of assets fall, these assumptions become questioned, and when large falls occur, they appear downright stupid. Lenders then become reluctant to extend new credit and are anxious to be repaid. Borrowers then have good reason to doubt whether they will be able to refinance their debts by additional borrowing. Fear of lending and fear of reduced access to borrowing combine to make companies and individuals cut back on their spending. They want to save more and invest less, thus causing a recession.

Hyman Minsky is among the well-known and respected economists who have questioned the neoclassical consensus. He has described three stages in the pattern of borrowing that involve increasing risk. In the first stage debtors expect to be able to pay the interest and repay the principal from the cash flow they reasonably expect to obtain from the investment the debt has financed. In the second stage debtors are only concerned to be able to meet the interest payments from the cash flow and hope to refinance the debt when it falls due by raising new debt. In the final stage the interest on the debt is not even expected to be covered by the earnings generated. Borrowers expect that the value of the investment will rise over time and can be sold in the future to repay the debt and make a profit. Regarding stage one Minsky, writes: "A unit that expects its cash receipts to exceed its cash payments in each time period is engaged in what we will call hedge finance." In describing the final stage he writes: "an organisation from which the contractual cash flow *out* over a time period exceeds its expected cash flow *in* is engaged in either speculative or Ponzi finance".[12] Sooner or later, and often later than may reasonably be expected, this house of cards collapses. The faith in the future evaporates and, in the rush to sell assets, prices fall, creating a "Minsky moment", which sets off a recession.

History shows that relatively minor changes in asset prices have an important impact on both savings and investment. The eagerness of companies and individuals to invest ebbs and flows with the optimism described by Keynes as the "animal spirits of entrepreneurs" and rising asset prices provide a wonderful tonic for optimism. Even small changes in asset prices can thus have an important impact on demand and output. Large falls in asset prices don't just have a greater impact than small ones: their effect is proportionately much greater. For example, if one assumes that a 10% price fall produces a loss of 1% in demand, a 20% fall is likely to produce a fall of much more than 2%. A reasonable degree of economic stability does not therefore require us to prevent small fluctuations in asset prices, but rather to avoid large ones. Small fluctuations in output as well as asset prices could only be avoided if our expectations about the future were always correct, or that our ability to value assets was totally precise and unaffected by future events. As neither can or could be so, the economy and financial markets are bound to fluctuate. But the economy is always adjusting and does so pretty well most of the time. The aim of policy should not be to avoid these small fluctuations but to avoid the big ones. The way to do so is to avoid high debt levels and overpriced assets as the risk of financial crises increases more than proportionately as they

[12] *Stabilising an Unstable Economy* by Hyman P. Minsky, Yale University Press, (1986).

rise. Success in dampening fluctuations reduces the risks inherent in lending, so successful attempts to reduce economic volatility to very low levels encourage more debt and thereby lead to financial crises and deeper recessions. Policymakers must recognise that attempts to make the economy stable will, if overdone, cause much greater instability than would otherwise be necessary.

12

Inflation

The stagflation of the 1970s and early 1980s produced a major change in economic theory. Whereas it had previously been assumed that inflation would fall if there were spare capacity in the economy, it is now agreed that this will not occur if expectations of inflation are rising. In these conditions we can have that extremely unpleasant combination of a weak economy and increasing inflation, which is known as stagflation. It has also become generally agreed among economists that in order to halt rising inflationary expectations a shock in the form of a sharp rise in interest rates is needed. As today we have high debt levels and asset prices, I fear that a sharp rise in interest rates would precipitate another financial crisis.

Current views on inflation cover a wide range. To some it is seen as the inevitable result of today's huge fiscal deficits and massive national debt ratios, to others as a solution to the overhang of excessive debt and to others and me as a serious threat.

History does not support the claims that inflation is inevitable when deficits and national debts are high, as both Japan's and the US's experience show. For example, Chart 100 shows that Japan has had rising deficits and falling inflation over the past 20 years.

Over the past 100 years there have been three sharp rises in US budget deficits and national debt ratios. The first occasion was set off by the US entry into World War I, when the deficit rose from 1.4% of GDP in 1917 to 11.8% in 1918 and then to 15.9% in 1919. There was also a surge in inflation, but it is clear that this was not set off by the rise in the deficits but by the outbreak of hostilities

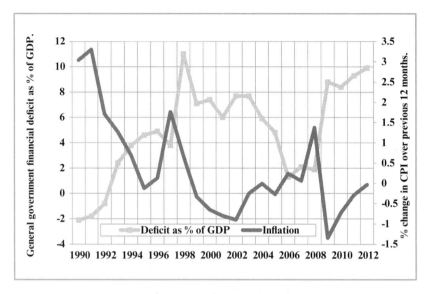

Chart 100. Japan: Falling Inflation & Rising Deficits.
Sources: OECD Economic Outlook Vols 78 & 92.

which occurred before the US entered the war in 1917, and the fiscal deficits ballooned. Inflation rose well before the deficits. Inflation rose sharply in 1916 to 12.6%, the year before the US declared war and two years before the deficits took off. Inflation was only 2% in 1915 before rising to 12.6% in 1916 and then to 18% in 1917 and 20% in 1918. Thereafter it fell sharply and in 1921 consumer prices fell by 11%.

There was no connection either in the 1930s between deficits, which rose sharply, and prices, which fell. On the other hand, the experience during and immediately after World War II gives some support to those who connect inflation with deficits. Prices rose by 9% in 1942 and 1943, as the deficit rose from under 4% of GDP in 1941 to 12% in 1942 and 30% in 1943. However, the introduction of price and other controls limited the rises to 2% in 1944 and 1945, though deficits remained over 21% of GDP, before moving to surplus in 1946. As controls were eased after the war, inflation jumped to 18% in 1946 and, while falling back, was 9% in 1947. Thereafter deficits and inflation were contained until the latter increased sharply with the oil shock, while deficits were still low.

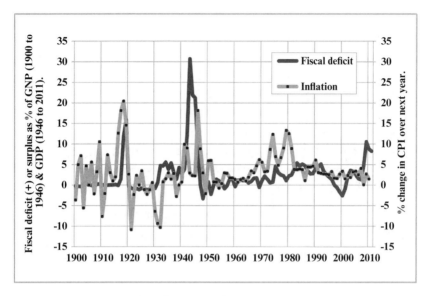

Chart 101. US: Fiscal Deficits & Inflation.
Sources: Bureau of the Census, Z1 Table D3, NIPA Table 1.1.5 & BLS.

Inflation rose to a peak of 10% in 1976 and averaged 8% throughout the 1980s. Deficits were relatively subdued in the 1970s, as Chart 101 shows, but were higher in the 1980s, when inflation fell back.

There is therefore no necessary connection between fiscal deficits and inflation. Nor, as can be seen in the case of the US from Chart 102, has there been any apparent relationship between national debt and inflation. US history therefore provides no support for the claim that high deficits inevitably cause inflation. But it can nonetheless be argued that inflation will be the outcome on this occasion, either because it will be the choice of policymakers in response to the perceived wishes of voters or the accidental consequence of their policy errors.

Some reputable economists have proposed that inflation targets should be raised to help boost demand.[1] This case can be argued in a number of ways:

---

[1] For example, *Rethinking Macroeconomic Policy by* O. Blanchard, G. Dell'Arricia and P. V. Mauro, "IMF Staff Position Note SPN/10/03", (2010).

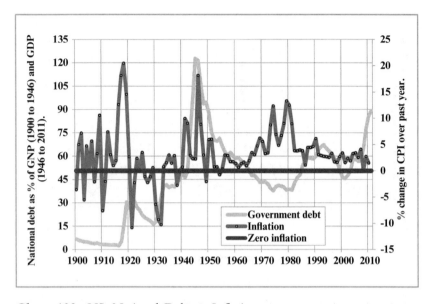

Chart 102. US: National Debt & Inflation.
Sources: Bureau of the Census, Z1 Table D3, NIPA Table 1.1.5 & BLS.

- We suffer from excessive levels of debt and, as inflation destroys the real value of debt, a rise in the rate would ease this burden.
- The private sector, including both companies and households, now recognises that it is over indebted and therefore wishes to deleverage, which deters spending.
- As interest rates cannot fall below zero, at least without great difficulty, real rates of interest can now only be brought down through higher inflation.

It is probable that private sector debt was relatively high by historic standards prior to the depression of the 1930s and again before the recent recession, as Chart 102 shows. But as debt was so much higher recently than in 1929 we cannot judge how much debt is "too much". Nor, as I showed in Chart 92, was the growth in debt more rapid in the run-up to the financial crisis than it had been for many years before. We cannot therefore judge the tipping point at which debt becomes "too great" either by its level or its speed of growth.

It thus seems likely that the rise in private sector debt was the fundamental cause of both the great depression of the 1930s and the recent great recession. In each case the immediately preceding falls in asset prices determined the timing of the financial crises, which were the proximate cause of the major losses of output and welfare that followed. Getting debt down, in order to reduce the risk of another crisis, should therefore be an important aim of long-term policy. It is, however, far from clear that a moderate rise in inflation of the sort advocated would provide any significant help.

A bout of unanticipated inflation reduces the real value of debt incurred in the past. But once expectations catch up, neither theory nor history suggests that there will be any benefit. Chart 103 shows that debt in the US grew faster than GDP without a break from 1951 to 2009 despite an inexorable rise in consumer prices. Chart 104 shows that the relationship between inflation and debt has been irregular. For example, debt, as a percentage of GDP, was falling rapidly up to 1937 and then rose to 1947, while inflation was picking up during both periods.

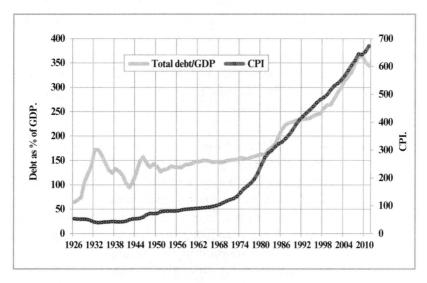

Chart 103. US: Debt & Consumer Prices.
Sources: Bureau of the Census, NIPA Table 1.1.5, Z1 Table D3 & BLS.

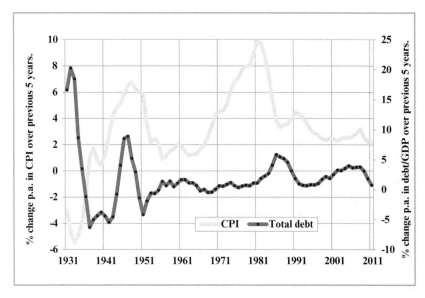

Chart 104. US: Debt/GDP & Inflation.
Sources: Bureau of the Census, Z1 Table D3, NIPA Table 1.1.5 & BLS.

The instability of the relationship between inflation and debt growth is shown in Table 9. I have divided the whole period for which we have data into three equal periods. Over some periods there is a positive correlation and over others a negative one.

In the absence of any stable relationship between debt growth and inflation, it would be senseless to try to reduce debt by increasing inflation unless there were clear benefits to the economy in other ways.

Although inflation does not have a stable relationship with debt, it could nonetheless encourage spending. US households (Chart 105) are highly leveraged, and it is widely assumed that they are deterred from spending by a desire to reduce this debt burden. The advocates of inflation assume that this would reduce leverage or make households less concerned about it and that this would encourage them to spend more on either consumption or housing.

Chart 105 shows that US household balance sheets have improved slightly since 2008, but it is improbable that this is due to a fall in inflation. Households have been deterred from buying

Table 9. Correlations between Log Changes in CPI & Debt as % of GDP (Sources: Bureau of the Census, Z1 Table D3, NIPA Table 1.1.5 & BLS)

	1926 to 2011	1926 to 1954	1954 to 1982	1982 to 2011
	Changes over one year			
Total	−0.39	−0.49	0.05	0.10
Private sector	−0.25	−0.33	−0.40	0.10
Government	−0.32	−0.39	0.23	−0.05
	Changes over five years			
Total	−0.32	−0.45	0.16	−0.04
Private sector	−0.28	−0.43	−0.62	−0.17
Government	−0.20	−0.23	0.67	0.18

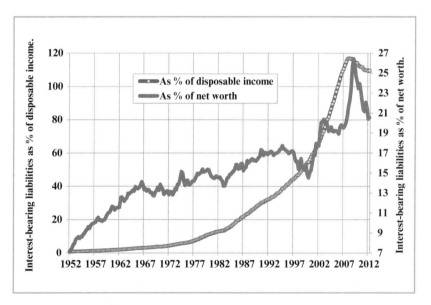

Chart 105. US: Household Leverage.
Source: Z1 Table B.100.

houses because the terms for mortgages have become more difficult, or less absurdly easy, and because house prices have been falling.

Household savings are currently below their post-war average level (Chart 106), which suggests that even though household balance sheets are highly leveraged, households are not striving hard

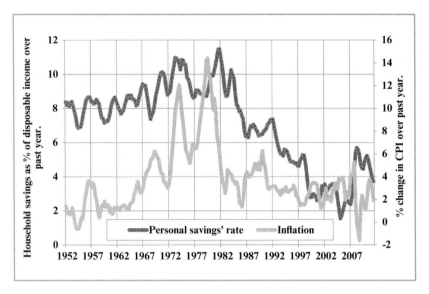

Chart 106. US: Inflation & Household Savings.
Sources: NIPA Table 2.1 & BLS.

to improve them. Chart 106, however, also shows that household savings tend to rise rather than fall with inflation.[2] History therefore suggests that a rise in inflation is more likely to have a negative than a positive impact on household spending.

As inflation is associated with a rise in household savings, it is likely to dampen rather than boost consumption. If house prices rise, this would probably encourage buyers, but there is no reason to assume there would be any impact from higher consumer prices.

As a rise in inflation is more likely to depress than stimulate consumption, the only way that it could encourage household spending is by boosting residential investment. This is, however, improbable. As Chart 107 shows, there seems to be no relationship at all between inflation and house building.

Companies, as well as households, have highly leveraged balance sheets as I showed in Chart 84, Chart 85 and Chart 86, and it is

[2]The correlation coefficient between the savings' rate and the level of inflation is 0.42 and between log changes in the savings' rate and the CPI over one year is 0.04.

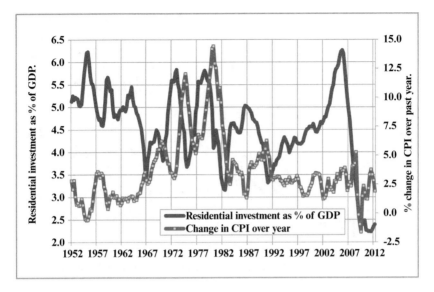

Chart 107. US: Residential Investment & CPI.
Sources: NIPA Table 1.1.5 & BLS.

often claimed that business is also bent on deleveraging and that this is holding back non-residential investment. I have pointed to an odd feature of this argument, which is that those who hold that companies are constrained from investing by the wish to deleverage are often those who claim that US companies are "in good shape". In fact, neither of these popular assumptions is supported by data. If companies were anxious to improve their balance sheets, they would be issuing equity rather than reducing it.

Not only are companies increasing their leverage by buying back shares; they have been the only major group of investors who are buyers (Chart 47 and Chart 48) and in Q2 and Q3 2012 were buying at over $400 bn a year.

Historically, however, there has been a positive relationship between inflation and business investment, which we illustrate in Chart 108.[3] This is not a relationship on which policymakers can

---

[3] The correlation coefficient between business investment as a percentage of GDP and the level of inflation is 0.53 and between annual log changes in business investment as a percentage of GDP and the CPI is 0.69.

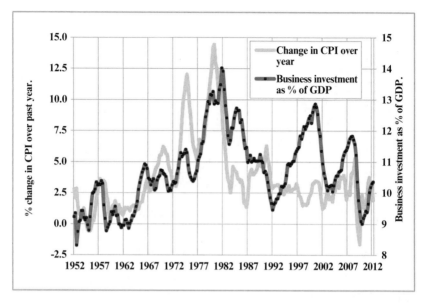

Chart 108. US: Business Investment & Inflation.
Sources: NIPA Table 1.1.5 & BLS.

afford to rely. As a rise in inflationary expectations would be seriously destabilising, it is only sensible to consider the impact on investment of periods in which inflation rose but was still moderate. As Chart 108 shows, there have been two such periods after the war: 1952 to 1968, when gently rising inflation was accompanied by rising investment, and 2002 to 2008, while inflation was rising but investment fell.

If we assumed that these past relationships between inflation and spending by households and businesses would continue, there would probably be no impact on spending from a rise in inflation, with lower consumption from the rise in household savings offsetting any rise in business investment. In practice we think that inflation would be even less helpful for demand by tending to increase household savings without encouraging business investment. This is because corporate behaviour has changed over the past decade and current remuneration practices discourage investment, so that the combination of rising inflation and falling investment shown from 2002 to 2008 is likely to be a better indicator of company behaviour today than the relationship shown from 1952 to 1968.

Not only is a pick-up in inflation unlikely to boost US domestic demand; it is likely to have a negative impact on international demand for US goods and services by pushing up the real exchange rate of the dollar. The argument here is the same as that I applied when arguing that the aim of achieving inflation in Japan was singularly ill judged. As I mentioned in Chapter 7, the Balassa–Samuelson effect holds that the exchange rates of the currencies of the developed world need to fall in real terms compared to those of the more rapidly growing emerging economies, and this theory is supported by history.

Chart 109 shows how closely changes in the real exchange rates of the yen and dollar have moved with changes in the relative growth of productivity for Japan and the US, and Chart 110 shows the same pattern for the UK and the US. This is, therefore, a gratifying example of economic theory proving to be robust in practice.

If, as seems overwhelmingly likely, the emerging economies continue to grow more rapidly than the developed ones, the real exchange rates of the dollar, euro, sterling and yen will all need to

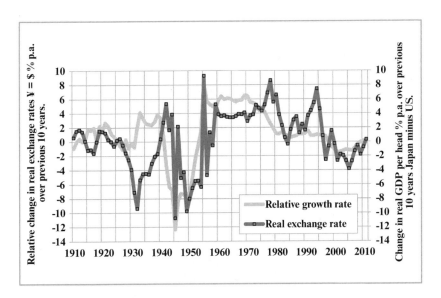

Chart 109. Japan and US: Relative Productivity and Exchange Rates. Sources: Angus Maddison to 2008, then National Data to 2011.

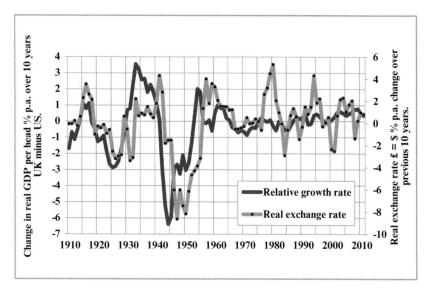

Chart 110. UK and US: Relative Productivity and Real Exchange Rates. Sources: Angus Maddison to 2008, updated from National Data to 2011.

fall relative to the real exchange rates of Brazil, China, India and other emerging economies.[4] This can be achieved either through changes in nominal exchange rates, which the emerging economies tend to resist, or through differences in inflation. For this to be possible, the inflation rates of the developed world need to be lower than those of emerging economies, which also, in this instance for good reason, resist high rates. It follows that the higher the rate of inflation in Japan, the UK or the US, the more difficult it will be for their international trade balances to improve.

There are four ways in which a country can attempt to raise the level of inflation:

- Intervention in the exchange rate.
- Protectionism.

[4] Real exchange rates are too volatile for relative productivity to be used to predict rates in the short-term any more than purchasing power parity can be used as a guide for countries with similar changes in productivity. The relationship between changes in productivity and exchange rates is probably not linear, as shown by the difference in the scales used for comparing Japan's faster growth and the UK's slower growth with that of the US.

- More fiscal stimulus.
- More monetary stimulus.

Exchange rate intervention would be relatively easy for Japan and the UK, but much more difficult for either the US or the eurozone. It would, in my view, be a very sensible policy for both Japan and the UK. As I write, both the yen and sterling have weakened, and if this continues this may make intervention unnecessary. While, like any possible policy, it involves some risk, it is the only available one that seems to me to combine a moderate level of risk with a reasonable expectation of success. If the nominal exchange rates of the yen, sterling, euro or the dollar can be lowered, this will push up their inflation rates. But if, as is generally assumed, these countries have plenty of spare capacity in terms of both capital and labour, then the rise in inflation will be limited and will allow the real rates of exchange to fall almost as much as the nominal ones. With unchanged demand worldwide, weaker real exchange rates would help stimulate output in Japan, the UK and the US at the expense of others. Although there would be no net benefit to the world economy, this would nonetheless be helpful because it would encourage countries that can afford to increase their deficits, like China and Germany, to do so. In a world which seems to suffer from an inability to stimulate demand through monetary policy, i.e. one that suffers from a liquidity trap, it is important to shift the burden of fiscal stimulus from those who cannot afford to do more to those who can.

Direct protectionist moves to improve the current account balances may seem quite similar to exchange rate intervention, but they are not. First of all, exchange rates are constantly adjusting to bring them into line with the competitive positions of different countries, which are constantly changing. Changes in nominal exchange rates are thus part of the normal and essential process of rebalancing the world economy. Second, the impact is spread widely and evenly over all the goods and services that are internationally traded, whereas protectionist measures are necessarily specific. Their impact is thus to shift output from countries which have a comparative advantage in that area to those which lack it. As a result they raise world prices and lower world output. The third difference is that exchange rate intervention can be carefully calibrated and, as it occurs all the time, is unlikely to cause the sort of marked impact that raises the political temperature and leads to reprisals.

Fiscal stimulus seems to be highly desirable in the world today, provided it is conducted by those countries that can afford it and not by Japan, the UK and the US, who can't. For them it is counterproductive because the intended savings surplus[5] of business sectors in these countries is not, as seems to be assumed by those who favour stimulatory policies, a cyclical problem but a structural one. If these countries were to engage in more fiscal stimulus, the benefit to the rest of the world would probably equal that of their home economies and their longer-term problems would mount because they would have even greater fiscal and international trade deficits. Such action would also reduce the pressure on those who can afford fiscal stimulus to do so and would raise, perhaps to breaking point, demands for protection.

There is therefore a strong case for reducing fiscal stimuli in the Keynesian trio and increasing it elsewhere, and this is reinforced by the risk of a rise in inflationary expectations. This risk is much higher in Japan, the UK and the US, with their massive deficits and debt levels, than it is, for example, in China and Germany. Unfortunately, the likelihood of switching the source of fiscal stability away from those with high fiscal deficits towards those with low ones currently seems as improbable as it is desirable.

The only remaining policy option is that of additional monetary stimulus, and this is the one on which the Federal Reserve is currently relying in the form of quantitative easing, which involves the US central bank buying assets. These have so far been mainly bonds, and although it is proposed that the most recent programme, which is known as QE3, will include a sizeable number of mortgages, the impact on the economy is unlikely to be noticeably different.

The Fed's balance sheet, and thus the monetary base, expands with purchases and contracts again when bonds are sold or repaid at maturity. The size of the monetary base therefore provides a measure of the extent to which quantitative easing has occurred and has not been unwound. The data show that quantitative easing has

---

[5] Intended savings' surpluses are designated by economists as being "ex-ante", because after the event, i.e. "ex-post", savings have to equal investment for the economy as a whole.

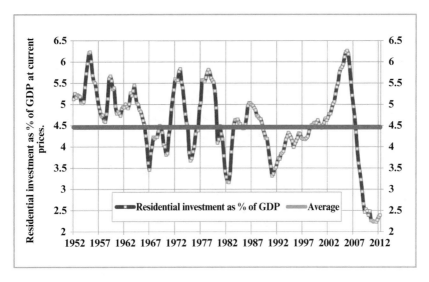

Chart 111. US: Housebuilding.
Source: NIPA Table 1.1.5.

been accompanied by rises in both bond (Chart 94) and equity prices (Chart 95), and there seems little doubt that it has made a major contribution to those increases.

So far the policy has had both good and bad results. On the good side it has helped support demand, in two ways. As I showed in Chart 93, households' discretionary savings move with house prices, and quantitative easing has helped moderate the previous rise in savings and encouraged the recent fall.[6] As the chart shows, however, discretionary savings have recently fallen back relative to the value of household real estate and there is therefore no reason to assume that they will fall from their current level, even if house prices now stage some recovery.

The reduction in mortgage costs has also helped demand by containing the fall in house building. This is now so low (Chart 111)

---

[6] The correlation coefficient between the discretionary savings' rate over the previous 12 months and the value of house real estate compared to disposable incomes is 0.83 from Q1 1952, when the data series start, to Q3 2012, the latest currently available.

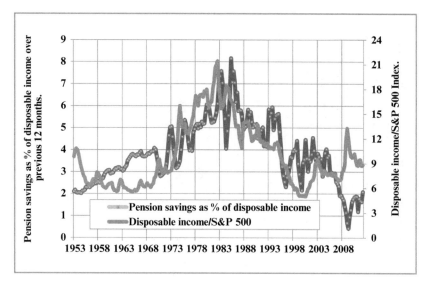

Chart 112. US: Pension Savings & the Stock Market.
Sources: Z1 Table B.100 & F.100 & Standard & Poor's.

that some recovery is likely, particularly as house prices seem to have stabilised and even risen slightly.

Pension savings have averaged rather more than half of total household savings in the post-war period. Swings in pension savings are thus very important in determining swings in aggregate household savings, and quantitative easing both encourages and discourages them. It discourages savings by pushing up equities, which, as Chart 112 shows, have had an important impact in the past.[7] On the other hand, the fall in bond yields has increased the value of the liabilities. This is because the current value of any liability to pay out money in the future, be it a bond or a pension obligation, rises as the rate interest falls and with it the discount rate at which future liability is measured to give its present value. Pension savings are rock bottom by historic standards and contributions are likely to continue their recent rise in order to reduce the massive deficits currently found in both public and corporate pension schemes. The

[7] The correlation coefficient between pension savings as a percentage of disposable income over the previous 12 months and the level of the stock market relative to disposable income is 0.63.

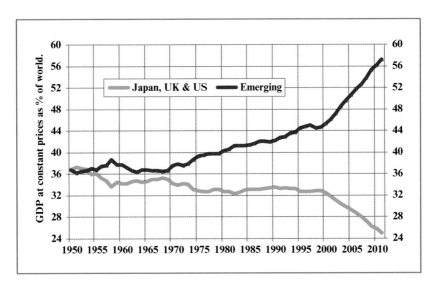

Chart 65. Relative Size of "Keynesian Trio" & Emerging Economies, as % of World GDP.
Sources: Angus Maddison 1950 to 2008 updated to 2011 from IMF & national accounts.

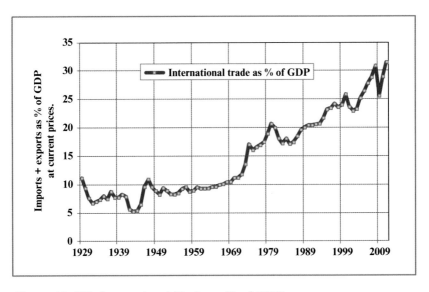

Chart 66. US: International Trade as % of GDP.
Source: NIPA Table 1.1.5.

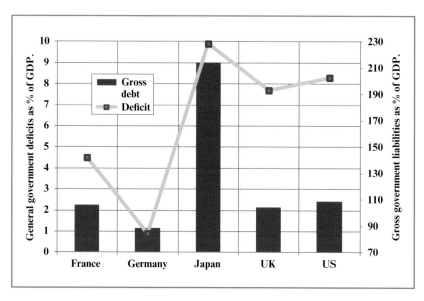

Chart 67. G5: Government Deficits & National Debt.
Source: OECD Economic Outlook Vol 91 Estimates for 2012.

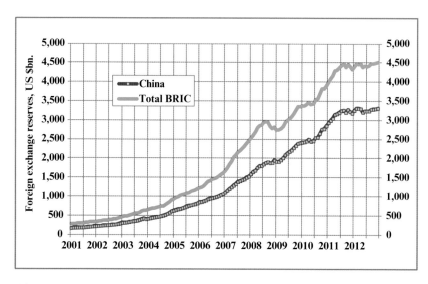

Chart 68. BRICS: Foreign Exchange Reserves.
Sources: National data via Ecowin.

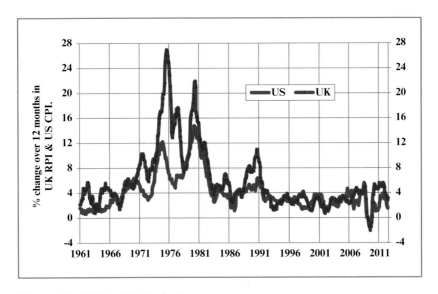

Chart 69. UK & US: Inflation.
Sources: ONS & BLS via Ecowin.

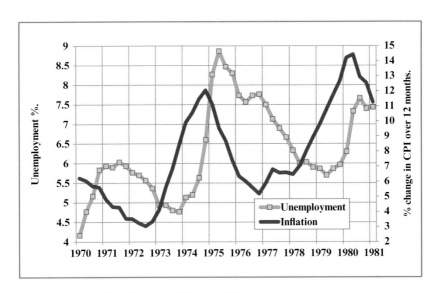

Chart 70. US Stagflation: 1970 to 1981.
Sources: NIPA Table 1.1.6 & BLS.

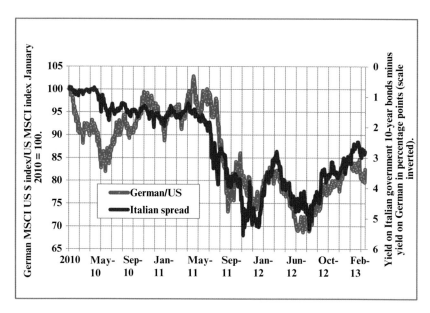

Chart 71. German/US Equities Move with Italian Bond Spreads.
Sources: Reuters & MSCI via Ecowin.

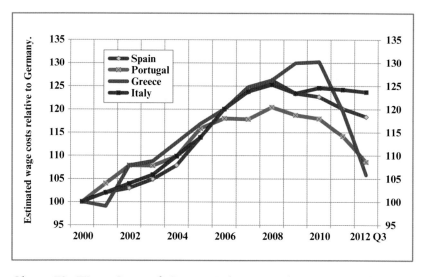

Chart 72. Wage Costs of Greece, Italy, Portugal & Spain Relative to Germany.
Source: The Economist 2000 to 2010 updated from national data via Ecowin.

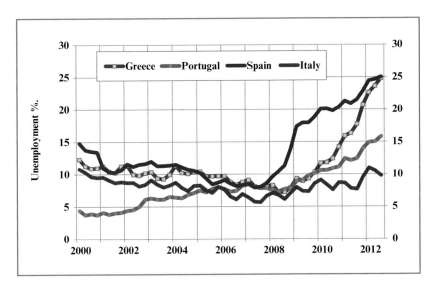

Chart 73. Greece, Italy, Spain & Portugal: Unemployment.
Sources: National data via Ecowin.

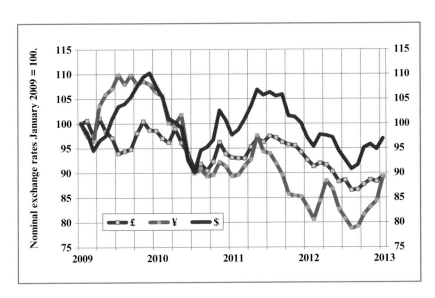

Chart 74. Euro: Nominal Exchange Rates.
Source: Reuters via Ecowin.

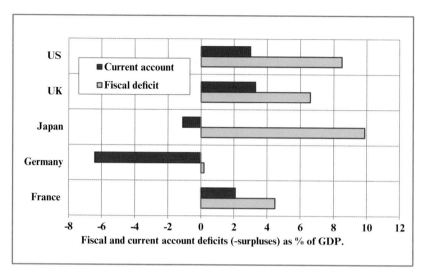

Chart 75. G5: Current Account & Fiscal Deficits (Surpluses).
Source: National Accounts via Ecowin.

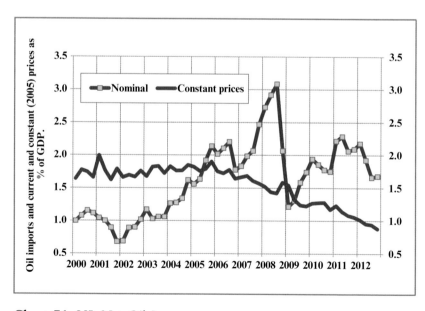

Chart 76. US: Net Oil Imports.
Source: BEA via Ecowin.

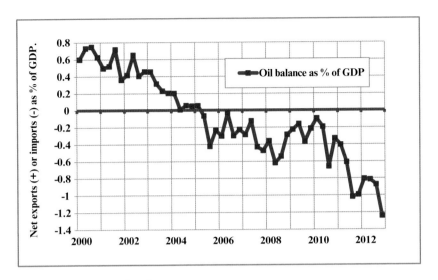

Chart 77. UK: Oil Balance.
Source: ONS via Ecowin.

Chart 78. UK: Returns on Capital in Manufacturing & Services (excluc-ing Finance).
Source: ONS (LYRB & LYRP) via Ecowin.

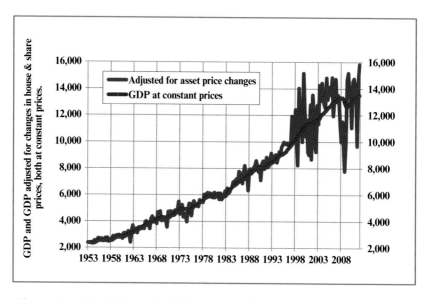

Chart 79. US: GDP as Published and Adjusted for Changes in House and Share Prices.
Sources: Z1 Tables B.102 & L.213 & NIPA Tables 1.1.4 & 1.1.6.

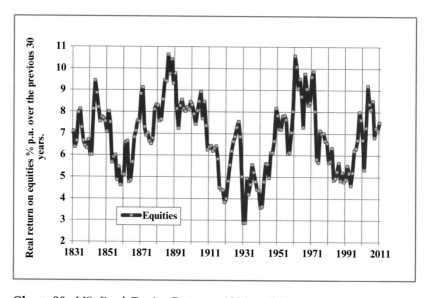

Chart 80. US: Real Equity Returns 1801 to 2011.
Sources: Jeremy Siegel 1801 to 1899 & then Elroy Dimson, Paul Marsh & Mike Staunton to 2011.

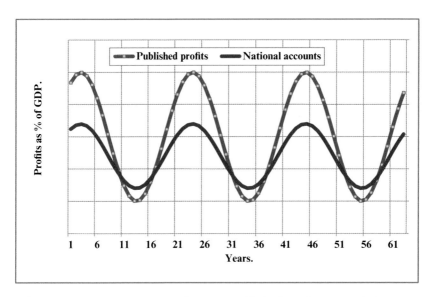

Chart 81. Representation of How Published and National Account Profits Appear to be Related.

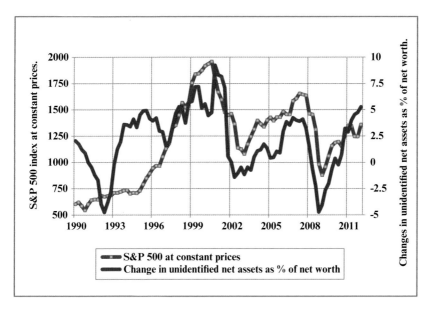

Chart 82. US: Fluctuations in the Stock Market & the Value Ascribed to Unidentified Net Assets.
Sources: Z1 Tables B.102 & L.102 and BLS.

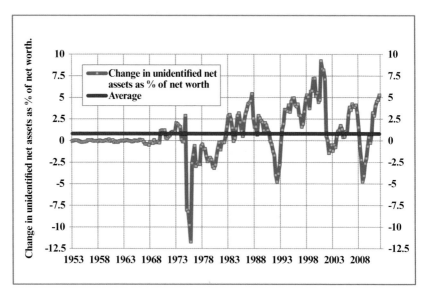

Chart 83. US: Non-financial Companies, Change in Net Unidentified Net Assets as % of Net Worth.
Sources: Z1 Tables B.102 & L.102.

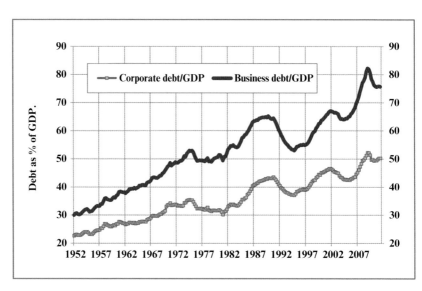

Chart 84. US: Business Debt as % of GDP.
Sources: NIPA Table 1.1.5 & Federal Reserve Z1 Table B.102.

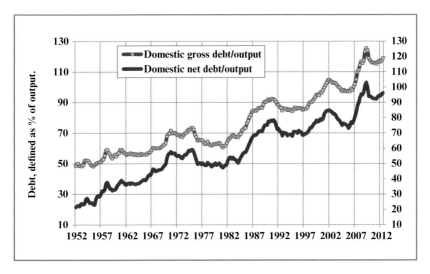

Chart 85. US: Non-finanancial Corporate Debt as % of Output.
Sources: NIPA Table 1.14 & Federal Reserve Z1 Table B.102.

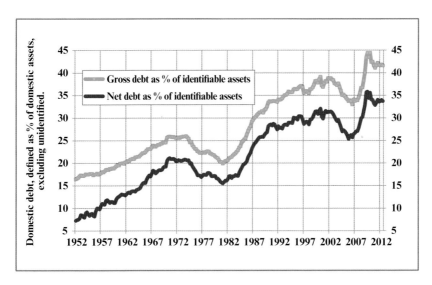

Chart 86. US: Non-financial Companies' Debt as % of Physical and Indentifiable Financial Assets.
Source: Federal Reserve ZI Table B.102.

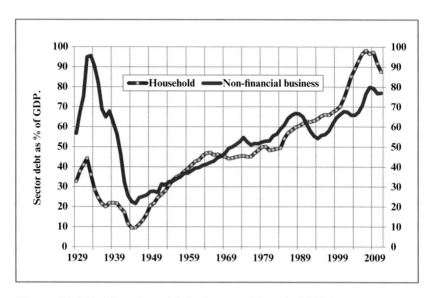

Chart 87. US: Non-financial Business & Household Debt.
Sources: Bureau of the Census, NIPA Table 1.1.5 & Z1 Tables B.100 & B.102.

Chart 88. Japan: Non-financial Business & Household Debt.
Sources: MoF Survey of Incorporated Enterprises, Cabinet Office & OECD.

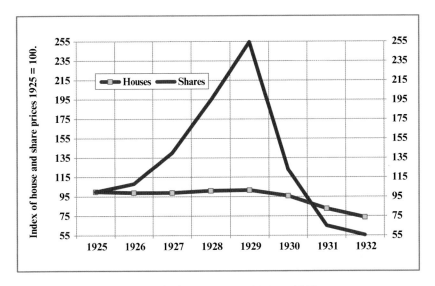

Chart 89. US: House and Share Prices 1925 to 1932.
Sources: Robert Shiller & the Bureau of the Census.

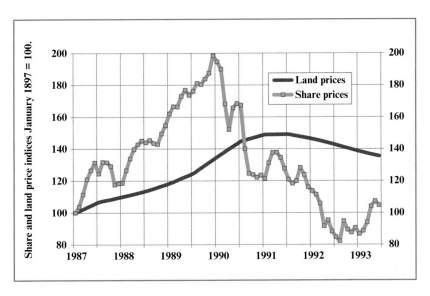

Chart 90. Japan: Share & Land Prices 1987 to 1993.
Sources: Japan Real Estate Institute (urban nationwide index) & Nikkei 225 via Ecowin.

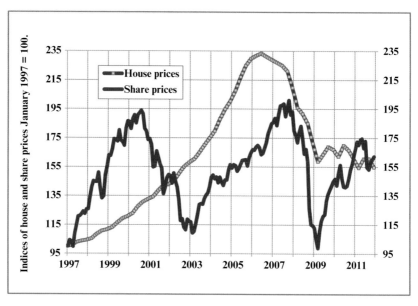

Chart 91. US: Share & House Prices 1997 to 2012.
Sources: Case-Shiller and S&P 500.

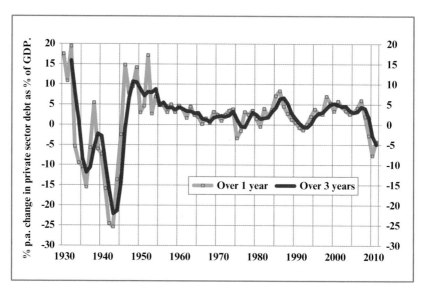

Chart 92. US: Rate of Change in Private Sector Debt.
Sources: Bureau of the Census & NIPA Table 1.1.5 & Federal Reserve
Z1 Table D3.

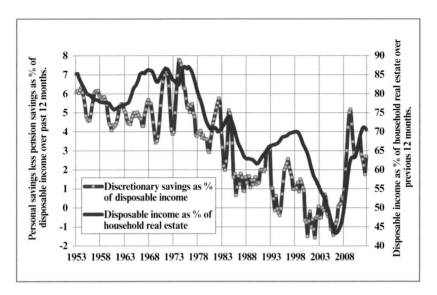

Chart 93. US: Personal Savings (excluding pensions) and Household Real Estate Wealth.
Sources: NIPA Table 2.1 & Z1 Tables B.100 & F.100.

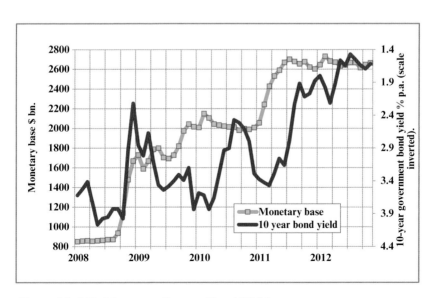

Chart 94. US: Monetary Base & Bond Yield.
Sources: Federal Reserve & Reuters via Ecowin.

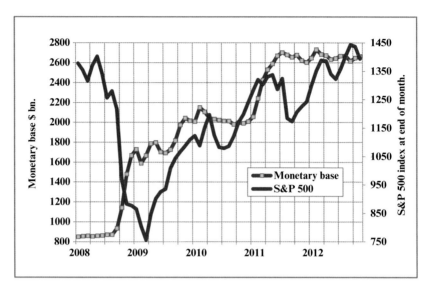

Chart 95. US: Monetary Base & the Stock Market.
Sources: Federal Reserve and Standard & Poor's via Ecowin.

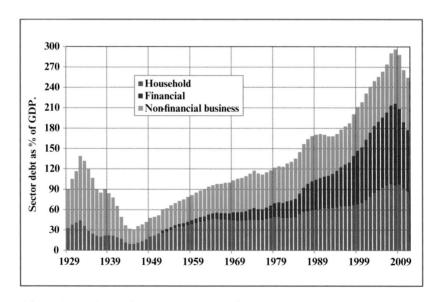

Chart 96. US: Total Private Sector Debt.
Sources: Bureau of the Census, Federal Reserve Z1 Table D3 & NIPA Table 1.1.5.

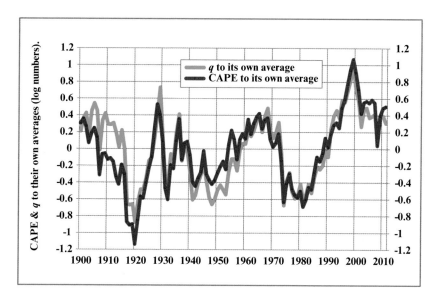

Chart 97. US: Stock Market Value.
Sources: Stephen Wright & Federal Reserve for *q*, Robert Shiller for CAPE.

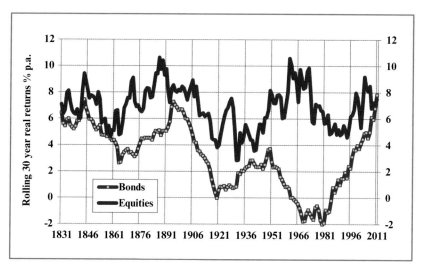

Chart 98. US: Real 30-year Returns on Equities & Bonds.
Sources: Siegel 1801 to 1899 & then Elroy Dimson, Paul Marsh & Mike Staunton via Morningstar to 2011.

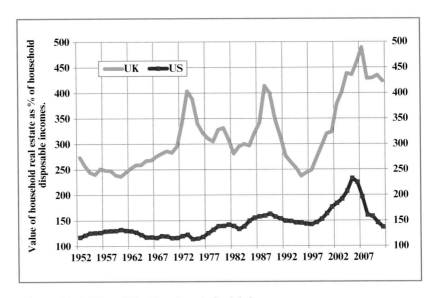

Chart 99. UK & US: Housing Affordability.
Sources: ONS (+ other sources for ealy data) & Federal Reserve.

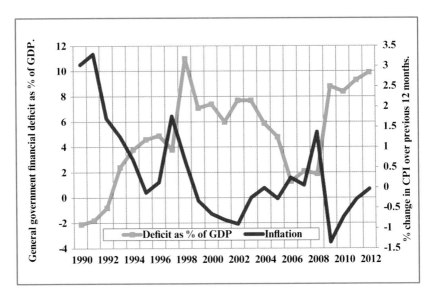

Chart 100. Japan: Falling Inflation & Rising Deficits.
Sources: OECD Economic Outlook Vols 78 & 92.

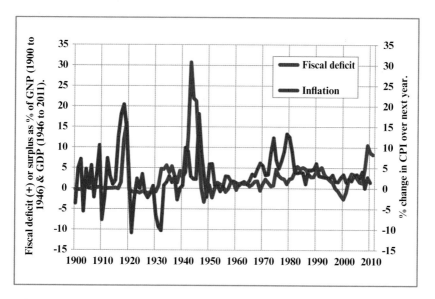

Chart 101. US: Fiscal Deficits & Inflation.
Sources: Bureau of the Census, Z1 Table D3, NIPA Table 1.1.5 & BLS.

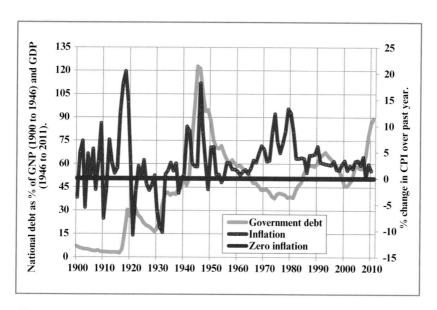

Chart 102. US: National Debt & Inflation.
Sources: Bureau of the Census, Z1 Table D3, NIPA Table 1.1.5 & BLS.

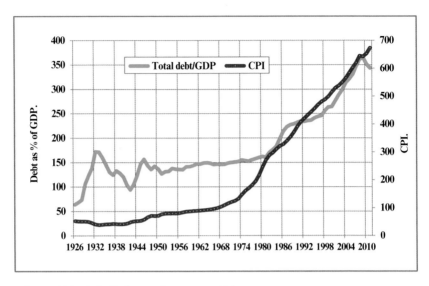

Chart 103. US: Debt & Consumer Prices.
Sources: Bureau of the Census, NIPA Table 1.1.5, Z1 Table D3 & BLS.

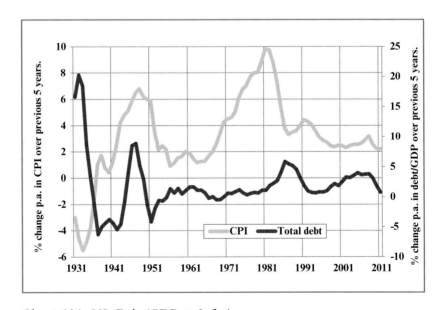

Chart 104. US: Debt/GDP & Inflation.
Sources: Bureau of the Census, Z1 Table D3, NIPA Table 1.1.5 & BLS.

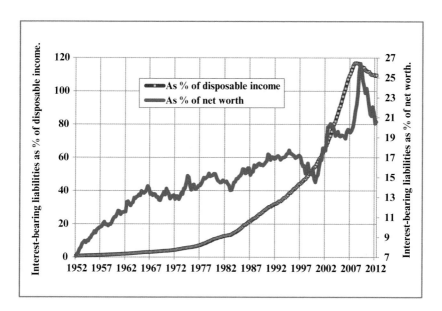

Chart 105. US: Household Leverage.
Source: Z1 Table B.100.

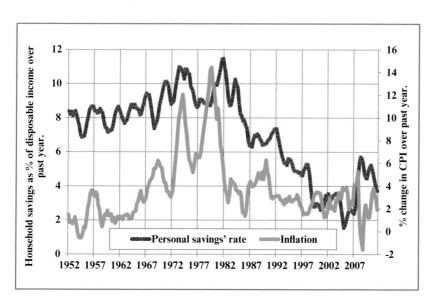

Chart 106. US: Inflation & Household Savings.
Sources: NIPA Table 2.1 & BLS.

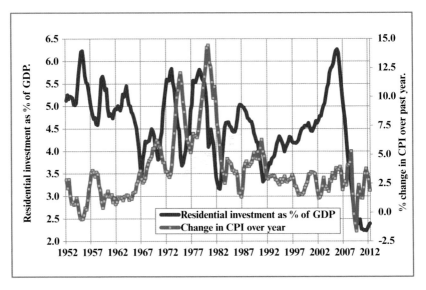

Chart 107. US: Residential Investment & CPI.
Sources: NIPA Table 1.1.5 & BLS.

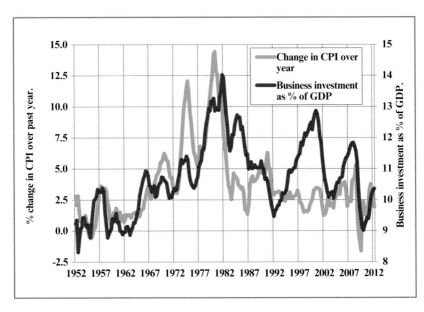

Chart 108. US: Business Investment & Inflation.
Sources: NIPA Table 1.1.5 & BLS.

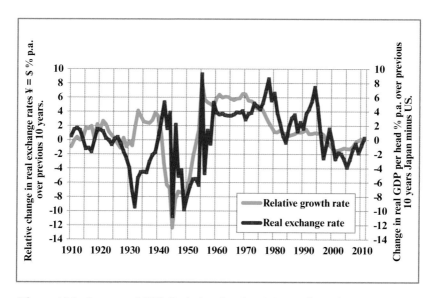

Chart 109. Japan and US: Relative Productivity and Exchange Rates.
Sources: Angus Maddison to 2008, then National Data to 2011.

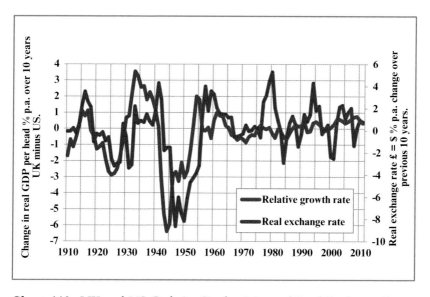

Chart 110. UK and US: Relative Productivity and Real Exchange Rates.
Sources: Angus Maddison to 2008, updated from National Data to 2011.

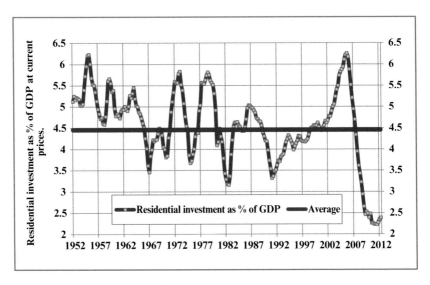

Chart 111. US: Housebuilding.
Source: NIPA Table 1.1.5.

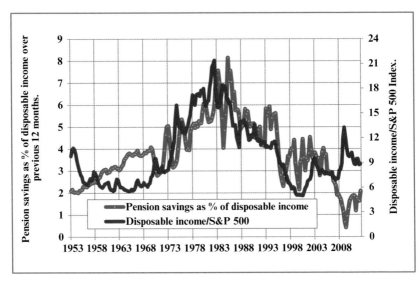

Chart 112. US: Pension Savings & the Stock Market.
Sources: Z1 Table B.100 & F.100 & Standard & Poor's.

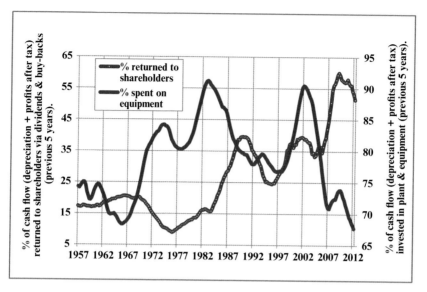

Chart 113. US: Non-financial Companies' Use of Cash Flow.
Source: Z1 Table F.102.

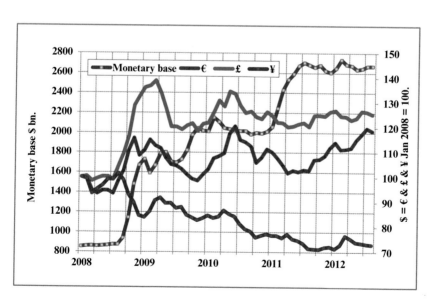

Chart 114. US: Quantitative Easing & Exchange Rates.
Sources: Federal Reserve & Reuters via Ecowin.

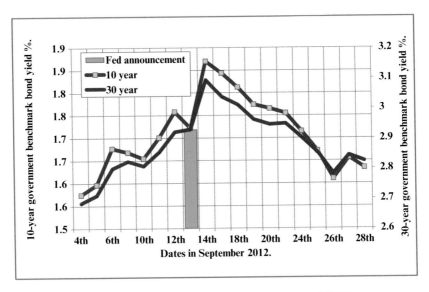

Chart 115. US: Bond Yields & the Announcement of QE3.
Sources: Federal Reserve & Reuters via Ecowin.

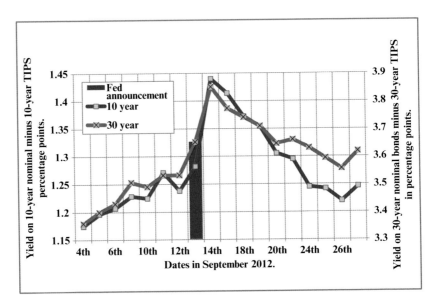

Chart 116. US: Inflationary Expectations Measured by Differences in Yields between Nominal Bonds & TIPS.
Sources: Federal Reserve & Reuters via Ecowin.

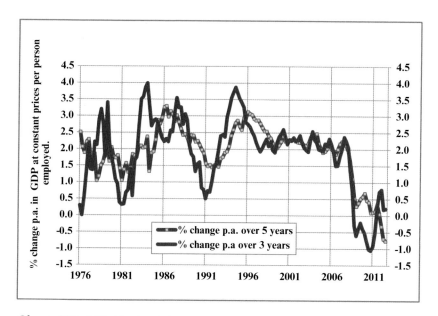

Chart 117. UK: Productivity.
Source: ONS via Ecowin.

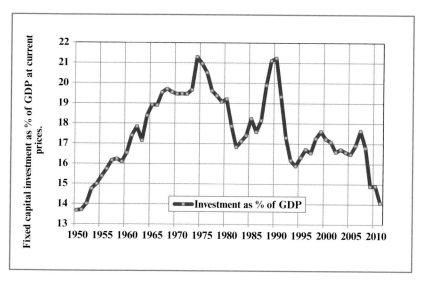

Chart 118. UK: Fixed Investment as % of GDP.
Sources: C. H. Feinstein & ONS via Ecowin.

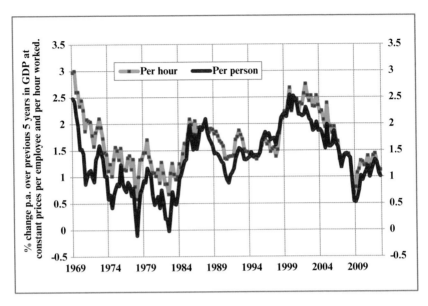

Chart 119. US: Productivity per Employee & per Hour.
Sources: NIPA Table 1.1.6 & BLS.

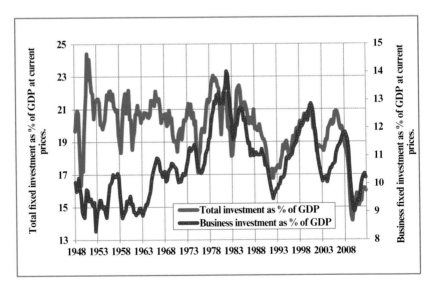

Chart 120. US: Investment as % of GDP.
Sources: NIPA Tables 1.1.5. & 3.1.

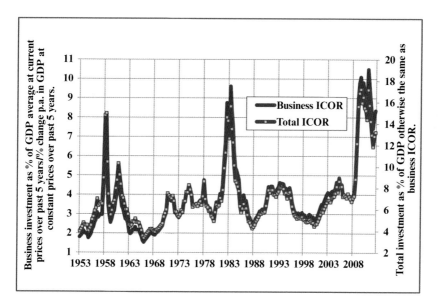

Chart 121. US: ICORs Adjusted for Recent Output Gap.
Sources: NIPA Tables 1.1.5, 1.1.6 & 3.1 & OECD Economic Outlook
Vol 91.

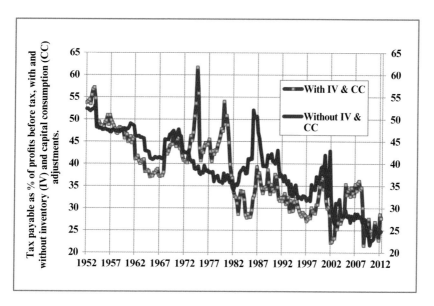

Chart 122. US: Effective Rate of Corporation Tax.
Source: NIPA Table 1.14.

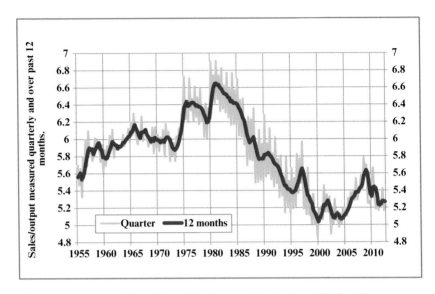

Chart 123. Japan: Non-financial Companies Ratio of Sales/Output.
Source: MoF Quarterly Survey of Incorporated Enterprises.

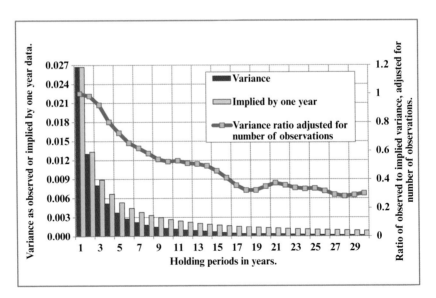

Chart 124. US: Variance Compression of Real Equity Returns 1801 to 2011.
Sources: Jeremy Siegel 1801 to 1899 and Elroy Dimson, Paul Marsh & Mike Staunton via Morningstar 1899 to 2011.

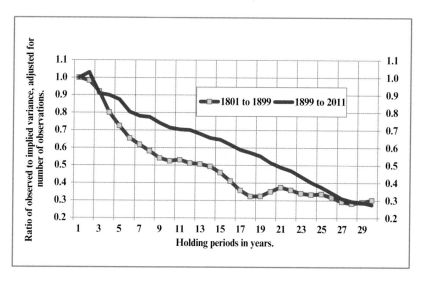

Chart 125. US: Variance Compression is a Common Feature of Both 19th & 20th Centuries.
Sources: Jeremy Siegel 1801 to 1899 & Elroy Dimson, Paul Marsh & Mike Staunton via Morningstar 1899 to 2011.

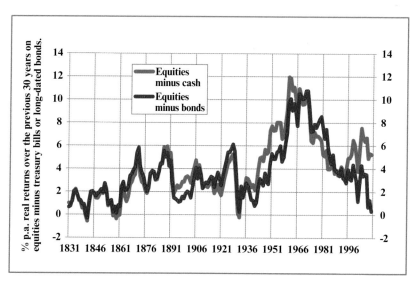

Chart 126. US: Equity Returns Minus Cash & Bond Returns.
Sources: Jeremy Siegel 1801 to 1899 and Elroy Dimson, Paul Marsh & Mike Staunton via Morningstar 1899 to 2011.

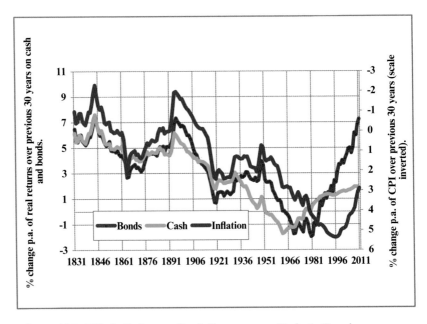

Chart 127. US: Inflation & Real Returns on Cash & Bonds.
Sources: Jeremy Siegel 1801 to 1899 and then Elroy Dimson, Paul Marsh & Mike Staunton via Morningstar to 2011.

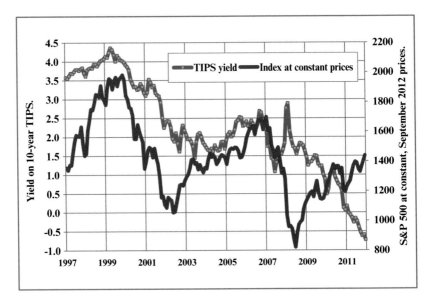

Chart 128. US: TIPS & S&P 500.
Sources: Reuters, BLS & Standard & Poors via Ecowin.

impact on pension schemes is important in the US as well as in the UK. As Chart 112 shows, pension savings, are near their lowest ever level. They are also likely to rise as corporate, state and local government schemes are all massively underfunded.

State schemes alone are estimated to have deficits of $4.43 trn, which is equal to 28% of GDP.[8] Unless it is assumed that state governments will default on their pension obligations, these are debts and if included in debt ratios would increase the US government debt from 109.8% of GDP (OECD estimate for 2012) to 138%. If additional contributions to the pension schemes were introduced, this would increase the state fiscal deficits with a matching increase in household savings. Fiscal deficits include the deficits in State and Local Governments as well as those incurred at the Federal level. If taxes were raised or other expenditures curtailed so as to avoid a rise in the fiscal deficit as pension contributions were raised, the net impact would simply be to increase household savings.[9] The deficits are rising each year, but if we ignore this and simply assume that they will be reduced to zero over 20 years then this process will cause household savings to rise by $220 bn a year, which is 1.4% of GDP.

The fall in the bond yield is now likely to have a greater impact on raising pension savings than in lowering discretionary savings. Because pension deficits are massive but not addressed quickly, pension savings respond less quickly to the fall in interest rates than the discretionary savings. The impact of quantitative easing on lowering "discretionary" savings is thus probably behind us, and the longer-term impact of raising pension savings is still to come.

Because of the change in corporate behaviour, it is unlikely that business investment has been boosted by quantitative easing and highly improbable that it will be helped by QE3.

[8] "Using zero-coupon Treasury yields, which are default-free but contain other priced risks, promised liabilities are $4.43 trillion. Liabilities are even larger under broader concepts that account for projected salary growth and future service", from "*Public pension promises: How big are they and what are they worth?*" by Robert Novy-Marx and Joshua D. Rauh, Journal of Finance (forthcoming).

[9] Although the national accounts would show a rise in household incomes and savings, there would be no visible increase in either, nor would households be able to spend the apparent rise in "disposable" income without having to borrow to do so.

In aggregate therefore the impact of quantitative easing on demand has probably been mildly positive in the past through reducing household savings, but I am one of those who think that from now on a further boost seems unlikely.[10] As is widely recognised in economic theory, low interest rates tend to have a two-way effect on savings. They boost asset prices and thus reduce the need for those with wealth to save more, but they increase the rate at which those with few assets have to save to provide an adequate income in retirement. Low interest rates thus benefit the elderly compared with the young and thus cause a transfer of wealth between generations. The effect of rising asset prices and lower interest on savings is thus both positive and negative, but the two impacts do not occur at the same time. It seems to me probable that the positive impact of higher asset prices on US demand is over and the negative impact is now likely to dominate.

There also appears to be a correlation between quantitative easing and commodity prices.[11] This does not of course show that there is a causal connection, but it is inherently likely that one exists, because easy monetary policy both reduces the cost of holding inventories for those who expect raw material prices to rise and increases expectations that a rise will happen.

Rising prices of raw materials are likely both to encourage more general expectations of rising inflation and at the same time to be a drag on demand. The mechanism for the impact on demand is well known in the case of oil, but probably applies more generally. When raw material prices rise, the revenues of exporting countries increase without any short-term compensating rise in their expenditure and the net impact is thus, on a worldwide basis, to tighten fiscal policy and so slow world demand. This would be offset if the rise in prices encouraged new investment, but producers are cautious when they see the price rise being driven by a rise in inventories rather than a rise in consumption and this has been the recent

---

[10] Others include Charles Goodhart and John Ashworth as set out in *"QE: A successful start may be running into diminishing returns"*, Oxford Review of Economic Policy 28(4): 640–670, (2012).
[11] See *"For a true stimulus, the Fed should drop QE3"* by Ruchir Sharma of Morgan Stanley, Financial Times, (11th September, 2012).

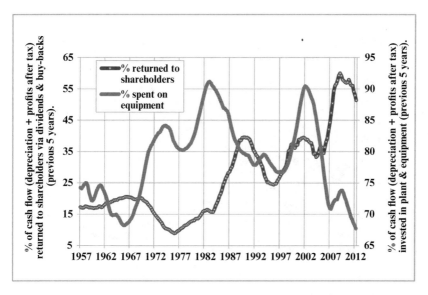

Chart 113. US: Non-financial Companies' Use of Cash Flow.
Source: Z1 Table F.102.

reaction. "'We are not investing until we see that inventory coming down,' says a senior executive at a big aluminium producer."[12]

Near-zero interest rates should have stimulated corporate investment as the required return on new projects should have fallen with the reduction in the cost of capital. But it appears that the recent fall in interest rates has failed to encourage investment as companies have preferred buy-backs to investing in new plant and equipment, as Chart 113 shows.

Quantitative easing is also likely to have an impact on exchange rates, and this seems firmly believed by the Brazilian finance minister who reacted angrily to the announcement of QE3. It does not, however, appear to be nearly as important as other influences and will of course be offset if other countries also engage in quantitative easing or intervene directly in currency markets. Its lack of any apparent contribution to depressing the US dollar's nominal exchange rate

[12] See *"Aluminium bears hold sway despite sharp price rally"* by Jack Farchy, Financial Times, (18th September, 2012).

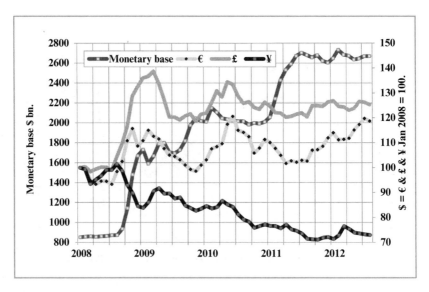

Chart 114. US: Quantitative Easing & Exchange Rates.
Sources: Federal Reserve & Reuters via Ecowin.

is illustrated in Chart 114. Following the initial introduction of quantitative easing, the monetary base doubled from August 2008 to
January 2009, but this was a period when the dollar strengthened
against both the euro and sterling, though it did weaken against the
yen. It remains probable that in the absence of offsetting intervention
in other countries QE3 should help the US economy, but it will
not be very important and any help that it provides through weakening the dollar will, of course, have an equally negative impact
elsewhere.

The impact of quantitative easing on the bond market is mixed.
The buying of bonds naturally pushes up their prices and lowers
their yields, but rising fears of inflation, which are also stimulated
by the monetisation of government debt that quantitative easing
involves, have the opposite impact.

As Chart 115 shows, bond yields were rising in the run-up to
the announcement of QE3, and initially rose again after the
announcement, implying that fears of rising inflation outweighed
the expected help from bond buying. The differences between the
yields on nominal and inflation-protected bonds (TIPS) also rose,

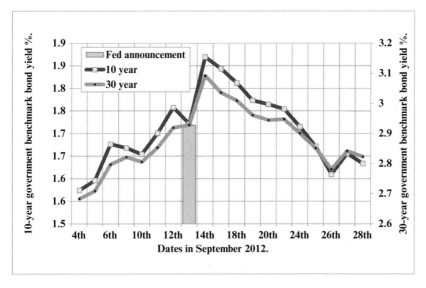

Chart 115. US: Bond Yields & the Announcement of QE3.
Sources: Federal Reserve & Reuters via Ecowin.

as Chart 116 illustrates, clearly implying that inflationary fears had risen.

The rise in inflationary expectations implied by Chart 115 and Chart 116 occurred in the run-up to the Fed's announcement on 13th September. Despite this, the Fed's foresight was sufficiently rose-tinted for the announcement to include the claim that "Longer-term inflation expectations have remained stable." This statement seems to me, therefore, to contain more information about Dr Bernanke than about inflation expectations. A predisposition to assume that inflationary expectations are low in the face of conflicting evidence aggravates the risk that policy will not act early to contain such a rise, and a greater shock in the form of higher interest rates than would otherwise have been necessary will then be required.

Although the statement about inflationary expectations made on 13th September strikes me as disingenuous in the light of the data then available – and the initial reaction disquieting – the subsequent fall in bond yields and the spread over TIPS suggest that investors are more concerned in the short-term about weakness in

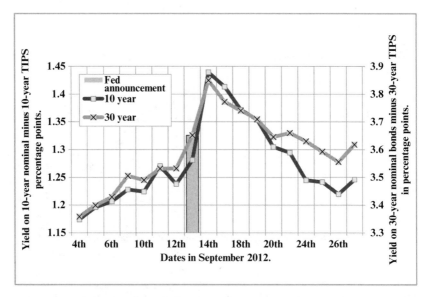

Chart 116. US: Inflationary Expectations Measured by Differences in Yields between Nominal Bonds & TIPS.
Sources: Federal Reserve & Reuters via Ecowin.

the economy than about inflation. A dangerous rise in inflation expectations would probably be set off by a rise in inflation, and although this could occur through rising raw material prices, the risk will be greater if it comes from more general increases in consumer prices, particularly if this is combined with some pick-up in the economy. QE3 seems unlikely to succeed in boosting demand, but it has increased the risks that the Federal Reserve will be forced by rising inflationary expectations to stifle such a recovery at birth.

Massive quantitative easing has not yet produced sustained recovery and it is likely that any help it has given to demand will now fall away and could become negative. As quantitative easing has increased the prices of bonds and equities, it has increased the extent to which they are likely to fall and thus to the negative impact on demand which such a fall has. It has also increased the likelihood of a sharp drop in the bond market by increasing fears of future inflation.

As quantitative easing has not been tried before, the result of the policy is even more than usually uncertain. Many economists are even more worried than I am. Bill White has expressed grave doubts about the "unintended consequences" of current policies.[13] He quotes Leijonhufvud's[14] contention that the results of such credit-driven processes could be either hyperinflation or deflation, with the outcome being essentially indeterminate prior to its realisation, and that Reinhart and Rogoff (2009)[15] and Bernholz (2006)[16] indicate that there are ample historical precedents for both possible outcomes.

Owing, perhaps, to my habitual optimism, which perceptive readers will have noted, I think that hyperinflation is unlikely. Deflation seems to me less likely to damage the economy than a rise in inflation would. Happily, the dangers of a rise in both inflation and its expectation are likely to have retreated, at least temporarily, now that US fiscal policy has been tightened and the deficit is expected to fall in 2013. The risk of inflation would have been amplified, had there not been such a reduction, in two ways. It would have made a strong economy more likely and reduced hopes that the deficit would be brought under long-term control. A rise in inflationary expectations seems to me highly likely if inflation itself picks up, with current fiscal and national debt levels. If the nominal dollar exchange rate were then to fall, this would create a self-reinforcing cycle of rising inflation. However, as many countries would resist a weak nominal dollar exchange rate, the real dollar exchange rate might rise, with the result that the US current account would

---

[13] *Ultra Easy Monetary Policy and the Law of Unintended Consequences* by William R. White, The Federal Reserve Bank of Dallas Globalization and Monetary Policy Institute "Working Paper No. 126" (2012). The author is chairman of the Economic Development and Review Committee of the OECD and previously Economic Advisor and Head of the Monetary and Economic Department of the BIS.

[14] "*Out of the corridor: Keynes and the crisis*" by A. Leijonhufvud, Cambridge Journal of Economics 33(4): 741–57, (2009).

[15] *This Time It's Different: Eight centuries of financial folly* by C. M. Reinhart and K. S. Rogoff, Princeton University Press, (2009).

[16] *Monetary Regimes and Inflation: History, economic and political relations* by P. Bernholz, Edward Elgar, (2006).

deteriorate and constrain domestic output. Combined with a weak dollar, the result would be a rising cycle of inflation that would need the shock of a sharp rise in interest rates to halt. In the absence of currency weakness, stagflation would be the likely outcome. As both results would be most unpleasant, avoiding inflation should be a key policy aim.

13

Prospects Not Forecasts

A dismal note has pervaded much of this book and this is, sadly enough, a fair reflection of my current assessment of the outlook for the world economy. But this is not because I am confidently expecting disaster. The course of the economy cannot be sensibly forecast and the fact that attempts to do so occupy such a large proportion of the money spent by governments and central banks on economic analysis is simply an example of waste. It would be desirable for more resources to be devoted to risk assessment and less to forecasts of future output. The physicist David Deutsch claims that poor philosophy is today at the root of much bad science[1] and this is, I think, particularly true of economics. The attention given to economic forecasting is an example of this. Deutsch writes that "some philosophers – and even some scientists – disparage the role of explanation in science. To them the basic purpose of scientific theory is not to explain anything, but to predict [the] outcomes".[2] It is common to read claims that economics is not a science because it is unable to make correct predictions. This claim can be shown to be wrong in many ways, one of which I have illustrated with

---

[1] "These misconceptions are rooted in philosophical doctrines, such as logical positivism, that were popular during the period when physicists developed and honed the theory." From *"Beyond the Quantum Horizon"* by David Deutsch and Artur Ekert, Scientific American, (September, 2012).
[2] *The Fabric of Reality* by David Deutsch, The Penguin Press, (1997).

the relationship between growth and real exchange rates. But it is in any event nonsense to assume that reliable predictions are the test of whether an activity falls within or outside the boundaries of science. Economics can be conducted scientifically or unscientifically, but predictability is not the test. Quantum theory is not thought to be unscientific when it claims that outcomes cannot be predicted but only observed and it is scientific to assert that the level of stock markets cannot be precisely predicted, provided that this claim can be tested. This philosophical error, which assumes that prediction is the purpose and demarcation of science, is known as instrumentalism and I do not propose to commit it. But an inability to predict the course of the world economy does not involve an inability to warn of the risks that current policies incur and to explain how different policies would reduce these risks and should therefore be followed.

Successful management of the world economy would produce sustained growth combined with low inflation. Failure, on the other hand, could take several forms, including another severe recession, another financial crisis and rising inflation. There are many who would consider that a rise in inflation would not, by itself, constitute failure. But it will be a failure of major proportions if it takes the form of stagflation in which rising inflation is combined with stagnant or falling output, or if it is accompanied by a rise in inflationary expectations, which results in a vicious self-reinforcing cycle that can only be broken by another and probably even more severe recession.

In order to achieve sustained growth at a level sufficient to satisfy the expectations of voters, it will be necessary to do more than avoid the types of failure I have listed. It will also be necessary for low inflation to be combined with a rate of growth which is similar to that achieved over the post-war era. It is important to assess the risks and obstacles to this being achieved rather than claiming to be able to forecast future growth rates. If this is done, the bonus culture can be seen as a problem not only because of the way it prevents the old-fashioned remedies of monetary and fiscal stimulus from getting us out of our shorter-term dilemma, but also because it has clearly had a very damaging impact on the UK and the US economies by depressing output and employment. Looking

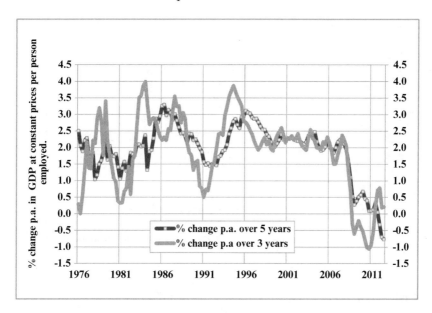

Chart 117. UK: Productivity.
Source: ONS via Ecowin.

ahead, it is probable that the change in corporate behaviour will cause sustained damage by the Anglophone countries' potential for long-term growth.

The productivity of labour has not only been weak recently in the UK, as I showed in Chart 42. It has also been on a long downward path, as I illustrate in Chart 117, and has been accompanied by a matching fall in investment, which I show in Chart 118. As investment is essential for growth, it would be surprising if these two trends were not associated, and I will seek to show that they are.

Productivity in the US has been very poor recently, as I showed in Chart 43; it has also been on a downtrend this century and perhaps since 1969, as I show in Chart 119.

Investment in the US has been on a declining trend (Chart 120) in a similar way to the trend in the UK, which I illustrated in Chart 118. In the US the impact on growth has been amplified by a decline in the efficiency of capital. This can be measured by comparing the amount of investment, as a percentage of GDP, with the growth of GDP measured in real terms. This ratio is known as the

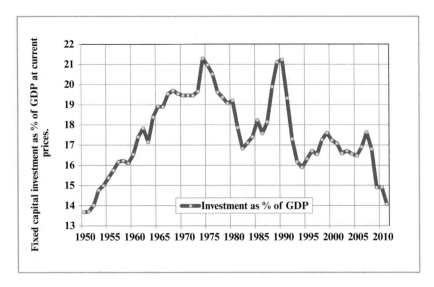

Chart 118. UK: Fixed Investment as % of GDP.
Sources: C. H. Feinstein & ONS via Ecowin.

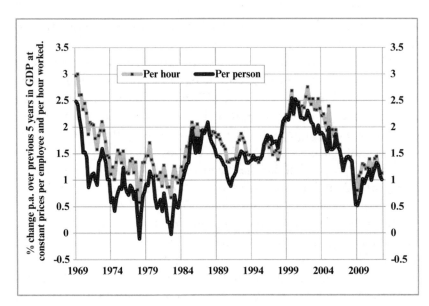

Chart 119. US: Productivity per Employee & per Hour.
Sources: NIPA Table 1.1.6 & BLS.

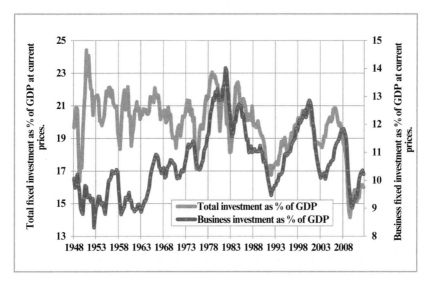

Chart 120. US: Investment as % of GDP.
Sources: NIPA Tables 1.1.5. & 3.1.

Incremental Capital/Output Ratio (ICOR). The higher the ICOR, the greater the amount of investment needed to increase output by a given amount – say 1%. A rise in ICOR is thus bad news. It shows that the efficiency of investment has fallen and that growth will tend to decline unless the ratio of investment to GDP rises.

If output is depressed by a recession, the ICOR will be pushed up and without an adjustment this will give an exaggerated view of the extent to which the efficiency of capital has deteriorated. The distorting impact that this has can be overcome, however, by adjusting the current level of GDP to allow for the extent to which it is estimated to be below its potential.

Chart 121 shows for the US that even with this adjustment ICOR has recently been at a higher level than ever before and that, even before its recent deterioration, it has been on a long-term rising trend. Whether the measure of investment is limited to business spending or all investment, including housing and government capital spending, it has been taking more and more capital to produce a given increase in output over time and there has recently been a sharp further deterioration.

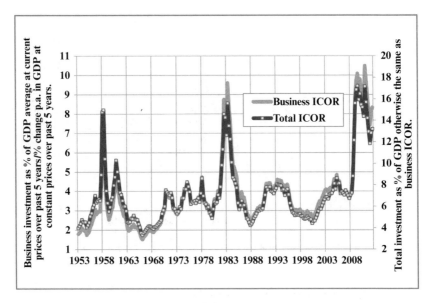

Chart 121. US: ICORs Adjusted for Recent Output Gap.
Sources: NIPA Tables 1.1.5, 1.1.6 & 3.1 & OECD Economic Outlook
Vol 91.

The productivity of both labour and capital has therefore been
deteriorating and these declines are associated. If it takes an increasing amount of capital to produce rises in real GDP, there must be
a rise in the proportion of GDP invested, or growth will slow. If
the speed at which growth slows is greater than the growth in the
number of people who wish to work, then there must be either a
rise in unemployment or a fall in labour productivity.

Unfortunately, there has been a tendency in the US for investment to fall rather than rise as a percentage of GDP, as Chart 120
illustrates. Without compensating changes, a rise in the capital/
output ratio would discourage investment by reducing the return.
But several compensating changes have allowed the return on corporate equity to rise to a point where it is between 30 and 60%
above its post-war average (Chart 36). These changes include a
decline in the rate of corporation tax, (Chart 122) rising corporate
leverage (Chart 84, Chart 85 and Chart 86) and high profit margins
(Chart 17).

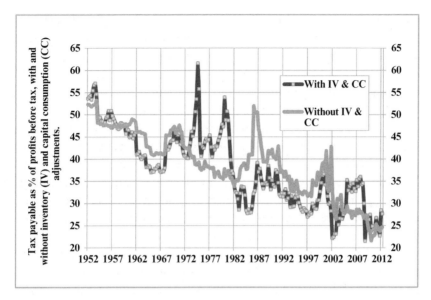

Chart 122. US: Effective Rate of Corporation Tax.
Source: NIPA Table 1.14.

If profitability were the driving force behind companies' capital-spending plans, investment today would be at record levels. Given that more investment is needed today than formerly to achieve the same trend rate of growth, higher investment seems necessary to avoid the ability of the economy to grow falling below expectations.

Unfortunately, the incentive to higher investment that would normally have resulted from high returns on capital appears to have been thwarted by the change in management behaviour. As business investment is currently 10% of GDP and the business ICOR, even when adjusted, is only 8, the implied trend growth of the US economy is only 1.25%.[3] If therefore the current ICOR does not improve and the level of business investment fails to rise, the trend growth rate will fall to only just over 1% a year.

As the US economy is operating, according to the OECD's estimates, at 3.9% less than its potential, there is no obvious reason

---

[3] This is because the investment ratio of 10% when divided by the ICOR of 8 equals 1.25%.

why short-term growth should be restricted to the long-term growth trend. Chart 121 shows that the business ICOR is volatile and on past experience seems likely to improve, but even if it falls back to its 2003 level of 5, the trend growth rate of the US economy at current levels of investment would be 2% a year, which is well below most current hopes and expectations.

The outlook for employment is, however, much less discouraging than that for growth. The preference of company management to use money to buy back shares rather than invest in new plant has the effect of raising the perceived cost of capital and thus to encourage managements to use more labour in preference to capital in order to increase output. (In the technical terms used by economists, there has been a change in the coefficient of substitution.) In the US labour productivity rose sharply in the early stages of the recovery from the depths of the recession but has since stalled, while in the UK it has been consistently poor both during the recession and afterwards.

The change in corporate behaviour resulting from the bonus culture is doing both short- and long-term damage to the economies of both the UK and the US. Its negative short-term impact is to produce the cash flow surplus in the business sector, which is the main reason why such huge budget deficits are needed, and so is inhibiting economic recovery. By depressing investment the bonus culture also threatens to slow the long-term growth potential of both countries. Without an unexpected, and it seems unlikely, improvement in their ICORs, it is likely that the UK and US economies will disappoint because investment is too low. It is unwise for us to rely on beneficial, welcome but unexpected, changes to occur. We should clearly seek to avoid the likely problems that will accompany poor growth rather than count on the problems disappearing by themselves.

The disincentive to investment, which is the key barrier to growth, is however, limited to large quoted companies in the UK and the US and does not apply to three other groups of companies: those that are not quoted, quoted companies that are dominated by individual shareholders and those owned by foreign companies. Managements are treating large-quoted companies as if they were oil companies or mines with a limited life. They operate them with the aim of extracting the maximum amount of cash. To keep shareholders sweet, the money is used to finance buy-back shares and, by doing this, managements are maximising their own rewards. Over time this process will cause these companies to lose market share in their industries. By exploiting their short-term monopoly power more aggressively than before, companies maximise their short-term profits, but become less and less competitive, as others who invest more will have greater success in reducing their production costs. The aggressive pricing policies that have pushed US profit margins to record high levels will also enable competitors to sell their goods and services at prices that are low enough to gain market share but high enough to produce sufficient returns to fund their capital needs. In time this process will undermine the bonus culture that causes the current structural savings surplus in the business sectors of the UK and the US. It would of course be better if the process were speeded up by reforming the perverse incentives of the present system and thus reducing the negative impact of both the short-term need to run up huge deficits and the long-term one of damaging future growth.

So long as the present system lasts, we will have a level of investment that is inadequate to meet the current hopes and expectations for growth. As we have underused resources of labour and capital, our ability to grow in the shorter-term would not normally be constrained by the longer-term problems. At the moment, however, it is unlikely that we cannot exploit these spare resources without pushing up inflation, as under the current bonus culture managements will seize any opportunity presented to push up profit margins.

The Federal Reserve and, to a lesser extent, the Bank of England favour a faster rate of growth than we have recently seen. As this slow growth has been accompanied by low but rising inflation, it is likely that any success in achieving more rapid growth will come at the cost of an acceleration in the rate at which prices rise. This carries with it the high risk that inflationary expectations would then pick up. Unless stamped on quickly, this would lead to the vicious cycle in which such expectations are self-fulfilling and can only be broken by a recession induced by a sharp rise in interest rates. As asset prices have been driven up by quantitative easing, they would then be likely to fall sharply and with debt levels still high the risk of another financial crisis is high, if inflation picks up.

The UK and the US would benefit from more rapid growth, provided that it did not lead to a rise in inflationary expectations or another financial crisis. The risk of a bad outcome depends to a large extent on the way in which growth is achieved. If fiscal deficits remain at high levels and there appears to be little prospect of national debt levels stabilising, the risk of a rise in inflationary expectations mounts, particularly if the debt is being financed with the help of quantitative easing rather than through the issue of long-dated bonds. On the other hand, growth arising from an improvement in the external trade balance and from more domestic investment is unlikely to raise concerns. Weak exchange rates by Japan, the UK and the US are likely to help in three ways. They should lead to an improvement in these countries' international trade positions. As I have shown, this should have a knock-on impact of improving domestic investment, because trade is concentrated in goods rather than services. In addition the negative impact on growth in the rest of the world should stimulate more fiscal stimulus where it can be afforded.

Recently, the world seems to have been lucky. The exchange rates of both sterling and the yen have weakened and, although this process probably needs to go further, the changes are in the right direction and should help the rebalancing of the world economy, whereby countries with large fiscal deficits will reduce their trade deficits and countries with low fiscal deficits will reduce their trade surpluses. We have also been lucky in that the oddities of the US budget process have produced a marked reduction in the fiscal stimulus, which should be sufficient to prevent the acceleration in demand, which policymakers are seeking.

Contrary to the wishes of the Federal Reserve, the US economy seems unlikely to accelerate in 2013 and this should help to keeping inflationary fears at bay and help towards the rebalancing of the world economy. The Federal Reserve has been trying hard to do the wrong thing and, fortunately, seems to be failing.

14

Tackling the Bonus Culture

Adam Smith taught us that qualities such as greed that are unpleasant at a personal level can be helpful for the economy as a whole. But this need not be the case in different economic environments. Clearly, it does not apply today in North Korea, where unpleasant qualities seem prevalent without any apparent help to the economy. However, we should not assume that individual greed, even if widespread, would be sufficient automatically to generate recovery in capitalist economies either. Businesses naturally seek to maximise their profits, and in order to have an edge over the competition they can create monopoly profits through new products or inventions that lower costs. To encourage this we allow their inventions to be protected by patents and copyrights, and there are concerns that this protection has become increasingly exploited by large companies to the point where it is inhibiting competition rather than encouraging progress. It is essential for the success of economies that we succeed in preventing the use of monopoly power to obtain "rents", which can be extracted by shareholders or employees. Electric power production, water and railways are often natural monopolies which need regulation to ensure that they are operated for the public good rather than for the benefit of their owners or, as we know from experience, particularly in the case of nationalised industries, for those who work in them. Rent extraction can be readily created by laws that limit competition, and these are a particular problem in Mediterranean countries where political parties have bought support from voters by giving groups special privileges. I have already quoted the absurd examples found in Greece. Mancur Olson argues that "Stable societies . . . tend to accumulate more collusions and organisations for collective action over time" and that "On balance, special interest organisations and collusions reduce efficiency and aggregate income . . ."[1]

A central thesis of this book is that we are currently allowing large quoted companies in the UK and the US to gouge rents from the rest of the economy and that corporate management is extracting huge benefits from this. In order to maximise the benefits to management this has created a structural savings surplus in the dominant form of business organisation that is found in the Anglophone economies. This rent extraction is producing two major problems. It has forced the UK and US governments to run huge deficits which are unstable in the long run and whose reduction is unstable in the short run. It is also inhibiting investment, which is reducing both countries' long-term growth potential.

It has been recognised for the last 80 years or more that the development of large quoted companies has resulted in the separation of ownership and control.[2] This creates an "agent/principal problem" because the interests of management and shareholders are different. Even if we assume that competition policy works well enough to ensure that profit maximising operates in the public interest, we will still need to avoid managements exploiting the capacity of the companies they manage to extract rent from the rest of us. One of the great ironies of recent years is that attempts to address this problem by "aligning the interests of management and shareholders" should have resulted in aggravating the problem to the point when it is the single largest problem for economic policy today in the UK and the US. The change from having senior company officials remunerated largely by salary to the present system in which the income is predominantly from bonuses and stock options was encouraged by business theorists who assumed that this

---

[1] These are propositions 2 and 4 from Chapter 3 of *The Rise and Decline of Nations: Economic growth, stagflation and social rigidities* by Mancur Olson, Yale University Press, (1982).

[2] For example, *The Modern Corporation and Private Property* by A. A. Berle Jr. and Gardner C. Means, Commerce Clearing House Inc., (1932).

would cause management and shareholders to have identical interests in profit maximisation. There is indeed a problem that the long-term interests of shareholders are in conflict with the shorter-term interest of managements. The proposed solution to this agent/principal problem has magnified the problem. The key error arose from the failure to recognise the difference in managements' behaviour when the balance changes between long- and short-term profit maximisation. For managements whose remuneration is based on short-term profit changes, the key to maximising their returns is to maximise the volatility of profits. The remuneration contracts are essentially options contracts and the value of options on those shares depends on the volatility of the share prices rather than their long-term returns. While for long-term shareholders the value of shares, if correctly priced, is the present value of future profits. The more volatile the profits, the greater will be the appropriate discount for valuing future profits. Under current remuneration contracts, the interests of management and long-term shareholders have been driven even further apart than before. Those seeking to justify high salaries for management have claimed, "If you want monkeys, pay peanuts." It would be more sensible to respond, "If you want volatility, pay bonuses."

The issue now is how to undo the damage that has been done. I think that there are lots of ways in which this could be done, and although I will now suggest some of them, I would like to emphasise that the essential contribution must come from having the issue discussed. At the moment the matter is discussed but only in an appallingly uninformed way. It either revolves around the particular issue of bankers' bonuses or focuses on social issues of perceived fairness. If we can move the discussion towards the central issue of the damage that current remuneration practices do to the economy, particularly through the creation of a structural savings surplus, the chances of a sensible reform will become far greater than they are at the moment, when ill-considered changes are more than likely to have a perverse impact. The damage done by those who advocated the move from salary to bonus-based remuneration should be a warning against ill-considered changes and the chances that they will have unanticipated consequences.

The key aim of reform must be to align the interests of managements with the economy as a whole. The essential and difficult task is to change the incentives so that they have a beneficial rather than a perverse impact on the economy. As we need more investment and lower profit margins, we should aim to make it in the interests of management that the companies they manage spend heavily on new capital and keep prices down in order to win market share. If that seems impossible, we should at least try to reduce the current incentives that encourage less investment and higher margins.

It is easier to design incentives that would be beneficial for the economy than to see how companies could be persuaded or required to introduce them. The current system rewards increases in profits per share. The details vary but the basic incentive is the same. If earnings per share, or the return on equity, or the share price, rise then senior management receive bonuses. This system encourages a short-term approach to the management of the business and thus to increasing the long-term risks to which the company is exposed in preference to reducing the short-term ones. This point is quite widely understood, and one unfortunately quite useless response had been to delay the date on which the benefits can be received with the assumption that this will make the incentives less short-term. This does not work. The benefits are still decided, and must be, by reference to the period during which the recipients are managing the businesses. As senior executives do not and must not have long-term contracts, they are still rewarded on the basis of short-term results. Delaying, for example, the time they must hold any shares they receive will not change the time horizon of the risks that the chief executives will consider important, but merely add an additional element of uncertainty to the likely rewards, which must then be even greater in the future to have the same value today.

If the bonus system is to be changed to modify actions that are detrimental and support those that are beneficial for the economy as a whole, then the criteria on which bonuses are judged must be changed. For example, in addition to profit criteria, bonuses could depend on growth in output or investment.

The principle is simple, but the application to any particular company raises many problems. Some of these are quite simple to solve. For example, companies are currently required to publish their sales but not their output. Only in Japan do we have data with which we can compare sales and output, and, as Chart 123 shows,

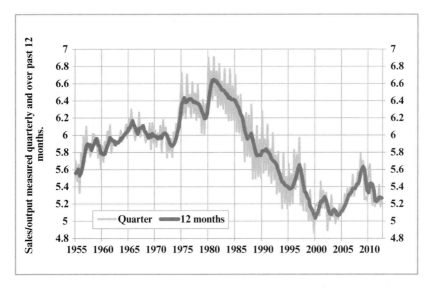

Chart 123. Japan: Non-financial Companies Ratio of Sales/Output. Source: MoF Quarterly Survey of Incorporated Enterprises.

the ratio between the two is not stable. It is only when profit margins are calculated as a percentage of output that the measure reveals any truly useful economic information. Investment bankers are fond of using profit/sales ratios rather than profits/output ratios. This only serves to confuse matters. Some cynics assume that confusion is the aim, while the more generous attribute the practice to a combination of ignorance and laziness. Profit margins related to sales serve to confuse because there is no reason to assume that they tell us anything about their likely future direction. It is only in terms of output that margins can be expected to be mean reverting.

The economy benefits if output rises but not necessarily if sales do. It would be ridiculous to use sales as a target to be achieved before bonuses could be paid. Sales ratios are unstable relative to output. They can easily be invented,[3] and even without manipulation

---

[3] If two Internet companies decide to advertise on each other's sites, they can both raise their sales by any figure they like, as long as they both agree on that figure. There are, of course, myriad other examples that could be given which are often less ridiculous than this but equally distorting in economic terms.

they vary over time with changes in the way businesses are structured.[4] Companies must know their output, as this is simply the sum of the profits they make, before depreciation, interest and tax and their employment costs. It would therefore be easy and virtually costless to require companies to publish their output figures.

Problems that are less easy to solve involve the need to have different targets for companies in different industries. It would clearly be wrong to require companies in declining industries to have the same output targets as those in expanding ones. I doubt whether these problems could be solved by laying down, for example, statutory requirements that companies must satisfy when paying bonuses. The most promising solution to this problem to my mind is that there should be an agreement on what constitutes "best practice", and where best practice is followed bonuses must depend not only on profits but also on changes in output and investment, which would thereby introduce incentives for management that would help the long-term growth of the economy. Being best practice rather than mandatory, the terms could be adjusted to the circumstances of different companies.

Among those who should favour such reforms are "tracker funds" (aka "index funds"), which invest their portfolios in the same proportion as the companies are weighted in the indices they choose to track. The current incentives encourage the management of listed companies to run them with the aim of extracting the maximum possible amount of short-term cash at the expense of longer-term returns. Actively managed funds, and those that invest in them, will assume that they can benefit from this by selling shares when the maximum short-term benefit from cash extraction has been achieved. Since companies are the only group of investors who actually buy shares, this assumption is reasonable so long as companies continue to buy. Tracker funds cannot, however, benefit from short-term selling and those which concentrate on the London and Wall Street markets will find that the short-term approach of company manage-

---

[4] For example, if the automobile industry in a country has independently owned distributors but then buys them out, sales will more or less halve without any loss of output − or, of course, double if the reverse process happens. One of the more persistent sources of error in the analyses of investment bankers comes from their habit of confusing sales with output.

ments in Anglo-Saxon countries will damage the long-term returns they achieve compared with those achieved by competing companies that are privately or foreign owned.

As the problem of perverse motivation applies to large quoted companies rather than more generally, an alternative approach could be to seek to reduce their importance in the economy. In the UK the rate of corporation tax applied to small companies is less than that applied to large ones. This could be extended, though there are obvious limits to the extent to which corporation tax could be raised on large companies because they would leave and move to more welcoming environments.

Corporation tax is economically undesirable for any economy that aims at growth. It is a tax collected by companies rather than paid by them. As a cost it can be passed on in a competitive environment and does not therefore fall on either shareholders or employees. All taxes fall ultimately on some form of expenditure, and as companies don't consume it must fall on investment, which is clearly undesirable in the UK and US today. Nonetheless, corporation tax is a valuable source of revenue. The vast majority of the tax comes, however, from large companies. Reducing the tax on small companies may therefore make a useful long-term contribution to the agent/principal problem posed by large quoted companies. If small companies are currently much more eager to invest than large ones, as the incentives make likely and which seem strongly supported by anecdotal evidence, tax changes favouring small companies seem sensible.

Another probably beneficial change in taxation would be to increase the depreciation allowances in the UK and the US in exactly the opposite manner that I have recommended for Japan.

15

The Need for Change in Economic Theory and the Resistance to It

Current economic policies seem to me to be both inadequate and dangerous. They are inadequate in that they have not produced a satisfactory recovery and are unlikely to do so. Advocates either of more fiscal or of more monetary stimulus are assuming that the current weakness in demand is cyclical. They assume that the failure of consumers to spend or businesses to invest is due either to deleveraging or to caution and that these inhibitions would be overcome by the same policies of fiscal and monetary stimuli that have tried and so far failed. They are convinced that their medicine is correct and that their patients will recover, provided they take even greater doses. I have argued that this view does not accord with the facts. Corporate buy-backs are inconsistent either with a wish to deleverage or with a cautious and fearful view of the future. If companies were nervous of their prospects they would be seeking to lower debt and conserve cash, rather than spend it on buy-backs. The same lack of attention to data is the root cause of the barrage of bad advice that has been given by many foreign, and some domestic, economists to Japanese policymakers. Arguments are said to be a priori when they depend on theory rather than evidence. But good theory is supported by data rather than being in conflict with them, so the accusation of an aprioristic bias logically requires that the theory on which the argument is based is unsound. Those who persist in recommending more monetary or fiscal stimuli are assuming that the current weakness in the economy is a cyclical rather than a structural problem. As the evidence is inconsistent with this assumption, they are, in my view, guilty of an aprioristic approach. They are therefore recommending policies based on poor theory and holding back the development of a less inadequate theory, which could be the basis for improved policies.

The current model on which economic policy is based is the neoclassical consensus, which has no room in it for debt and asset prices. Adherence to this paradigm rests on a similar aprioristic bias to that which inhibits most economists from even considering the structural nature of our current economic problems. The schoolmen of the 12th century based their arguments on assumptions that were, in turn, based on revealed wisdom. The scholasticism of that time is very similar to much of the academic economics of today. There are similar good qualities in the intelligence of the participants and the intellectual rigour with which they seek to derive their conclusions from their assumptions. But the benefits of these virtues are undermined by their defects. As the schoolmen before them, many academic economists today have constructed axiomatic models and, like all such models, they are valueless when the wrong axioms are selected. The aprioristic bias of so much of today's academic economics means that they are massively resistant to change that (inevitably) challenges their basic assumptions. It should, however, be acknowledged that those who seek to challenge the failed paradigm of the neoclassical synthesis are happily placed compared with those who challenged the theories of the scholastics. Today's iconoclasts are likely to be ignored and those who seek academic careers may find that tenure eludes them. But they should find consolation by considering that their 12th-century equivalents faced physical persecution.

The major problem for those who challenge today's failed orthodoxy is to get their ideas debated. Despite similar problems, we had a revolution in economic thinking in the 1930s and it is therefore instructive to see how this succeeded. In 1929 the economic theory of the time had no explanation for the financial crisis that hit the US, or any cure for the resulting depression. The event produced a revolution in thought as it was clear that the existing consensus, while it may have been satisfactory when applied to those small-scale events that are covered by microeconomics, provided little understanding of macroeconomics, which applies to the economy as a whole. The revolution was signalled by the publication in 1936 of John Maynard Keynes's *The General Theory of Employment, Interest and Money*, which provided both an explanation as to how the depression had occurred and a policy to mitigate the severity of the consequences. Over the next 60 years, economists developed and solidified the theories that this revolution had spawned, so that they produced over time one of those generally agreed worldviews, which are known as paradigms, that was termed the neoclassical consensus.

This new paradigm provided the underlying theory on which most economists have for many years been basing their arguments and policy proposals. Current scientific theories are, however, never the last word and are changed in one of two different ways. They can be accepted, strengthened and improved, or they can be discarded and replaced with a radically different theory. The historical pattern is for enhancement to be the main concern of scientists, and the development of the neoclassical consensus from Keynes's theories is an example of that process. From time to time, however, an upheaval is necessary and a new paradigm required. After the policy failure that led to the great depression the need for a new one was clear. The upheaval, from which the new paradigm of the neoclassical consensus emerged, was duly provided by Keynes's theories and policy proposals, which at the time were and had to be revolutionary. In economics the usual cause of such a major transformation is an event for which the consensus theory has no adequate explanation. This occurred in the "great depression" that followed the financial crisis of 1929 and has occurred again with the "great recession" that has followed the financial crisis of 2008. We are, I hope, at the beginning of a revolution in economic theory that will provide us with an explanation of what went wrong. We certainly need such a revolution if we are to have agreed policies that will prevent a repetition of the catastrophe.

Even before events demonstrate the inadequacy of an existing consensus, there are usually those who are dissatisfied with it. These dissenting voices are sometimes central to the creation of the next

consensus, but this is far from always the case. Opposition comes
not only from the thoughtful but also from those who would be
called dotty in England. Among the sciences, economics shares with
medicine the title of being the outstanding breeder of dottiness.
Those with strongly held and irrational views can be found in every
field, but economics and medicine attract dottiness like iron filings
around a magnet. My father was a doctor, who specialised in the
treatment of cancer by radiotherapy.[1] I used to discuss with him
which of our two professions was the most subject to strongly held,
irrational and ill-informed views. Medicine probably suffers the
most, but the competition is close. The similar attractions of the two
disciplines as dottiness magnets come from their shared characteristics. Next to personal relationships and occasionally even dominat-
ing them, health and prosperity are the two most important concerns
in most people's lives. Strong views about them are therefore natural
and it is equally natural that such views will depend on prejudice
and wishful thinking as much as on rational analysis.

For sheer dottiness the arguments of health nuts usually outstrip
those of their economic counterparts, but in the competition for
second place economics is well fancied among the connoisseurs of
folly. In my pantheon they rival those who claim that Bacon wrote
Shakespeare and those who believe that the future can be forecast
through astrology or from the measurements of the Great Pyramid.

In science the consensus is never the last word. We do not yet,
and presumably never will, understand everything. Pointing out that
the consensus view has faults is therefore to score an open goal. The
bald statement is bound to be correct and does not therefore have
any value in itself. In such a very general way negative criticisms
are almost bound to be right – even the dotty ones. But they are
only useful if they point the way to improvements and have a sound
logical and testable justification. Over the past 50 years economists
who have brought logically coherent arguments against the validity
or adequacy of the consensus have included a number of economists
to whose work I refer in this book. Each of them in very different
ways has pointed to problems with the consensus. Their criticisms
have such strength that when a new and improved consensus is

---

[1] Interested readers can find a short biography of David Waldron Smithers in the
Dictionary of National Biography.

developed it will need to satisfy their criticisms. At the moment their views are widely respected by most economists, but usually ignored when policy is discussed. This unsatisfactory situation is partly due to the sheer intellectual difficulty of producing a satisfactory model which incorporates their insights. But it is also because of the danger of the enterprise to budding economists. Only by working within the limitations of the existing consensus is a young academic safe. Questioning the accepted paradigm is a necessary condition for its destruction and the rebuilding of a new and less unsatisfactory one. But such questioning is disrespectful to authority and requires great confidence. It is not the way for undergraduates to pass exams or postgraduates to get their papers published in academic journals.

The philosopher and sociologist T. S. Kuhn has described the way in which paradigms can both advance and impede scientific progress.[2] When the paradigm is young, it can be very fruitful as scientists improve and solidify their models without discarding the agreed assumptions. But progress slows as the inadequacy of the fundamental model begins to restrict further advances. We now need the kind of marked change in theory, which Kuhn termed a paradigm shift, so that progress becomes possible again. This is difficult for both good and bad reasons. The bad one is the conservatism of elderly academics and their power over promotion and publication. This has produced the witty if uncharitable jest, which nonetheless contains much truth, that "science advances obituary by obituary". The good reason is that new models are difficult to construct and attempts to do so are likely to produce problems and errors. Scientific advance depends on discussion, debate and testing. It is right, as well as the way things are, that the promulgators of new ideas have to face much more robust criticism than those whose views follow familiar lines.

Many of the limitations of the neoclassical consensus were known and discussed before the recent financial crisis, but it is only now that their practical importance has been so sadly and dramatically demonstrated. Creating a new paradigm to replace it has become the key intellectual challenge that we face in economics. It

---

[2] See in particular *The Structure of Scientific Revolutions* by Thomas S. Kuhn, University of Chicago Press, (1962).

is urgently needed, not just because the consequences of the recent crisis were so painful but also because the medicine used to mitigate the pain has been used up. While the understanding provided by the neoclassical consensus was not enough to prevent the crisis, it was invaluable in moderating the cost of its impact on the economy in terms of lost jobs and output. The dramatic rises in government budget deficits and falls in interest rates, which served to reduce the pain of the last recession, will not be available again for many years and we will therefore be in dire straits if we face another financial crisis before fiscal and monetary policies can be used with the same vigour as they were after the financial crisis. The recent recession was the most severe faced by the world economy since the great depression, but it would have been much worse without the extreme ease of fiscal and monetary policy which was used to moderate the damage that it caused. Ammunition that has been used up is no longer available. Equally, monetary policy has become as stimulatory as is probably possible and quantitative easing now seems to be more dangerous than helpful.

The need for a new paradigm is, I think, clear but it is denied by those who seem somehow to believe that the crisis validated the old one. John Kay commented on this in an article in the Financial Times. "Inexplicably most supporters of that paradigm also feel that the crisis confirmed its validity."[3] He also touched on another point, which is one of the recurring themes in this book, remarking on the pressure on academic economists who wish to be published to conform to rather than challenge the established paradigm. John Kay highlights the way in which events are so often seen as reinforcing the writer's views. As I think that the crisis has vindicated the worries that I expressed before it happened, this book provides an example. I hope, however, that readers will, after reading it, find that I am a great deal more justified in finding the crisis to have confirmed my criticism of the neoclassical consensus than its supporters are in believing that events have supported it.

One reason that many economists have found difficulty in accepting the need for a new paradigm is the scale of the shock they have suffered. Before the financial crisis the majority view

---

[3] *"Why economists stubbornly stick to their guns"* by John Kay, Financial Times, (16th April, 2011).

among economic policymakers was that the major problems of managing the economy had been solved. This view was based on the neoclassical consensus and produced, before we were hit by the financial crisis, an outpouring of complacent views that made the crisis more likely by inhibiting serious discussion of the rising dangers shown by poor policy and wild asset prices. For example, Alan Blinder, a former vice-chairman of the Federal Reserve, claimed that "For the economy to go into a significant recession, never mind a depression, important policy makers would have to take leave of their senses."[4] Stephen Wright and I were among a number of economists who disagreed. We wrote in 2002 that "Time will tell whether Professor Blinder's confidence proves to be admirable or foolhardy".[5] Unfortunately, time has told.

The crisis, the recession and the weakness of the recovery have all caused grief and suffering to many and all have been unnecessary as well as disappointing. They were all caused by poor policies, based on inadequate economic theories. These events have shown that we face new problems and it should be no surprise that these require new solutions, which current economic thinking does not provide. New theories are therefore needed and, unfortunately, academic economics is currently better organised to resist innovation than encourage it. Change is never welcome in science, for good as well as for bad reasons, and sloppy explanations often take strong roots. I have already quoted the physicist David Deutsch's claim that poor philosophy is today at the root of much bad science[6] and remarked that I think that this applies as much, if not more, to economics as it does to physics. The branch of philosophy which deals with how we know things is epistemology. The most prevalent philosophical error, which bedevils much economic theory, and if Deutsch is right much physics, lies in a poor understanding of how we know things. Bad epistemology is common. The outstanding example of this has been the credence given to the Efficient Market Hypothesis (EMH),

[4] *"Keeping the Keynesian faith"* by Alan Blinder, World Economics, 2(2): 105-40, (April, 2001).
[5] *"Stock markets and central bankers: The economic consequences of Alan Greenspan"* by Andrew Smithers and Stephen Wright, World Economics 3(1): 101–24, (2002).
[6] *"Beyond the quantum horizon"*, David Deutsch and Artur Ekert, Scientific American, (September, 2012).

which has been a major barrier to the development of a less flawed model for us to use in trying to manage the economy. To do this we need to include the impact of debt and asset prices. These vital influences have no place in the neoclassical consensus that provides our current model. The EMH has been the major obstacle to the development of a more rounded view of how the economy operates, because it denies the importance of asset prices by its assertion that they are always correct.

The EMH holds that the market prices of financial assets are always correctly priced because, if they were not, well-informed investors would be able to profit from any divergence between price and value. The result would be that, subject to the necessary costs involved in research and management, price and value would have to be the same.[7] While it was never accepted by all economists, the EMH for many years dominated theory and had a major and damaging impact on central banking policy. The EMH had, of course, to allow for the fact that market prices were rather volatile, and this was accommodated into the theory by assuming that these price fluctuations were simply the result of new information. If, for example, it could not be known in advance whether a well currently being drilled would strike oil, it was natural and sensible that the share price of the company would change when the result was known.

The theory was not therefore inherently silly, and research into the way share prices moved provided strong evidence for it, provided that they were only applied to the relative value of assets of the same type. When, for example, the EMH was tested with regard to the prices of different shares relative to one another, a variety of tests were devised, and the theory passed the tests.[8] With regard to asset prices within the same asset group, the EMH was shown

[7] This limitation, that costs must be incurred in order for markets to operate efficiently, is not a fundamental objection to the EMH. This is set out in "*Index funds and capital market theory*" by Andrew Smithers, The Investment Analyst, (September, 1978). A subsequent and much better known version of the case is "*On the impossibility of informationally efficient markets*" by Sandford Grossman and Joseph Stiglitz, American Economic Review 70(3): 393–408, (1980).

[8] These tests, known as the weak, semi-strong and strong test, are set out in "*Index funds and capital market theory*" by Andrew Smithers, The Investment Analyst, (September, 1978).

to be scientifically acceptable, as it was testable and when tested appeared robust.

The evidence that the market determines the relative prices of equities in a more or less efficient way has led, sensibly, to the growth of "tracker funds", in which dealing and management costs are kept to a minimum by simply seeking to track the performance of an index. The proportion of equities passively managed in this way has grown steadily and if it expands further should end in what could reasonably be described as a genuinely efficient market, which would not only apply to the relative prices of shares but also ensure that financial services were efficiently priced so that the costs needed to achieve efficiency were not excessive. In these circumstances the average return on actively managed funds will equal, after expenses, the return on the indices they are seeking to outperform after allowance has been made for the costs and inevitable slight mismatch known as the "tracking error". At the moment more money than necessary is spent on the research and management costs than are needed to keep the market efficient. Too little could be spent, in which case the average performance of managed funds after expenses would actually be greater than that of the indices they seek to track. A truly efficient market would be one in which the amount spent on research, dealing and management costs was just that needed and no more, for the relative prices of shares to be efficiently evaluated by the market. At the moment the costs levied by the financial service industry for asset management, including dealing expenses, are excessive and needlessly reduce the incomes available to those who live on the assets they have accumulated for their retirement.

The deficiencies of the EMH became apparent, however, when the value of shares as a whole was considered, rather than their relative prices. If shares in aggregate were always accurately priced, their total value could fluctuate, but these fluctuations would have to come from new information. This could not be predicted in advance and would therefore be as likely to push the market up as to push it down. It was therefore naturally thought that if the EMH were correct then the returns from shares would vary in a random fashion. Investors don't, however, hold shares without expecting a return and, although the returns varied, investors required that the returns were positive on average. In technical terms this implied that returns should follow a "random walk with drift". That is to say the long-term real returns would be positive ("the drift") but actual returns would revolve around the average level, which would equal the long-term return, in a random fashion.

But when tested, this version of the EMH, known as the Random Walk Hypothesis (RWH), was shown not to work. If returns had to revolve in a random way around their long-term average, they would have done so in the same sort of way that operates under conditions of pure chance. When this happens the past has no influence on the future. It makes, for example, no difference to the chances of red coming up in roulette on any given turn of the wheel if it has come up every turn for the past 50 or if black has done so. Whether the past has had any impact on returns can readily be tested and when this is done with regard to the total value of stock markets we find that returns are not random, but that after periods of good returns we are more likely to have bad ones and vice versa.

If the returns from equities had followed the expected random pattern, then investors would have been exposed to similar risks if they held shares for short periods or for long periods. But there is clear evidence, which I illustrate in Chart 124, that this is not what actually happens. The chart compares, in the two sets of columns, the volatility of returns that investors have actually suffered with those they would have suffered had there been no reduction in their exposure to risk. The ratio of the two columns is the line, which declines markedly over time. If real equity returns followed a random walk this line would not decline but would remain constant around a value of one. As I show in Chart 125, the same result is found if we look just at the US in the 19th century or take the data since the beginning of the 20th, and it also applies to all the stock markets of different countries for which I have been able to find data since 1899.[9]

The EMH in its random walk form was thus a testable hypothesis that when tested was found not to work. Economists then had the choice of discarding the theory or changing it so that it was robust under testing in its new form. Attempts at revision have

---

[9] For a detailed description of the test see Chapter 7 of *Wall Street Revalued: Imperfect markets and inept central bankers* by Andrew Smithers, John Wiley & Sons, Ltd, (2009).

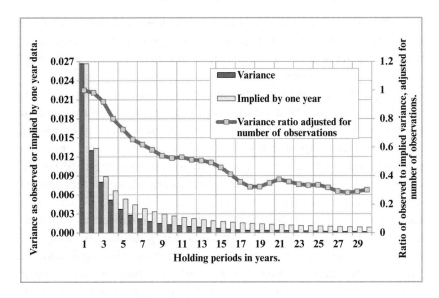

Chart 124. US: Variance Compression of Real Equity Returns 1801 to 2011.
Sources: Jeremy Siegel 1801 to 1899 and Elroy Dimson, Paul Marsh & Mike Staunton via Morningstar 1899 to 2011.

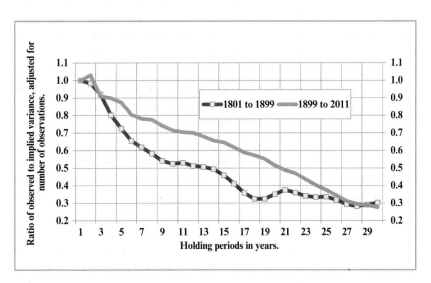

Chart 125. US: Variance Compression is a Common Feature of Both 19th & 20th Centuries.
Sources: Jeremy Siegel 1801 to 1899 & Elroy Dimson, Paul Marsh & Mike Staunton via Morningstar 1899 to 2011.

proved unsuccessful, so far at least. No one has yet devised a testable form of the EMH that is robust under testing and the hypothesis is therefore to be found on the wrong side of Karl Popper's demarcation between science and non-science.[10]

A frequently aired but in my view misdirected question is whether economics is a science. The answer is, of course, that it must be a science or it's nothing, except perhaps an elaborate and absurd confidence trick, but like any other science it can be pursued unscientifically. Those economists who still adhere to the EMH are being unscientific. This is increasingly accepted, albeit in a half-hearted way. We are currently in a kind of limbo in which open faith in the efficiency of financial markets is rare, but so is acceptance of the consequences. If markets are not efficient they can become misvalued and as it is hard to deny that financial markets have an important impact on the real economy, it follows that central bankers need to have a strong understanding of how markets can be valued and any significant over- or undervaluation needs to be taken into account when formulating policy, but they have proved to be extremely reluctant to accept this logic.[11]

Central bankers are not only alone in their wish to duck the serious issues that follow if the inefficiency of markets is accepted. The majority of papers published today on financial economics and the standard way in which the subject is taught in the finance courses suffer, in my view, from a similar myopia. The outstanding example of this is the way in which these papers and courses seek to explain the past returns or forecast future returns on equities by reference to past or expected returns on bonds. This relationship is known as the Equity Risk Premium (ERP) and in my view this is a hangover from the EMH, as in an efficient market the prices of bonds and cash would "efficiently" be determined and would provide a good guide to their future returns. The prospective returns on

---

[10] "Note that I suggest falsifiability as a criterion of demarcation but not of meaning." And "every scientific statement must be testable". From *The Logic of Scientific Discovery* by Karl Popper, Hutchinson, (1959).

[11] As I illustrated in the reference to "*Assessing Potential Financial Imbalances in an Era of Accommodative Monetary Policy*" speech by Janet Yellen, International Conference: Real and Financial Linkage and Monetary Policy, Bank of Japan, Tokyo (1st June, 2011).

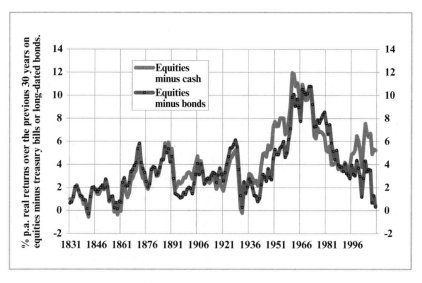

Chart 126. US: Equity Returns Minus Cash & Bond Returns.
Sources: Jeremy Siegel 1801 to 1899 and Elroy Dimson, Paul Marsh &
Mike Staunton via Morningstar 1899 to 2011.

bonds and equities would therefore be related and presumably have
some stable relationship.

As Chart 126 shows, however, there has been no stable past
relationship between the returns that have been achieved on equities, compared with either cash or bonds. As this has become, often
reluctantly, recognised, most enthusiasts who hope to find the ERP
a useful concept assume that there should be a relationship between
expected returns on the different assets but that forecast errors
destroyed any past relationship.

The assumption that investors are poor forecasters of inflation
is supported by the evidence, which I show in Chart 127. I show
inflation on the right-hand scale with the scale inverted so that a
rise in inflation can be seen to match falls in the real returns on
bonds and cash. Equities are titles to the ownership of real assets, in
the form of plant and property, so inflation has little impact on the
real returns from equities, but has a huge impact on bonds. It is
therefore not surprising that if investors are poor forecasters of inflation then any relationship between bonds and equity returns will
not show up from an analysis of past returns.

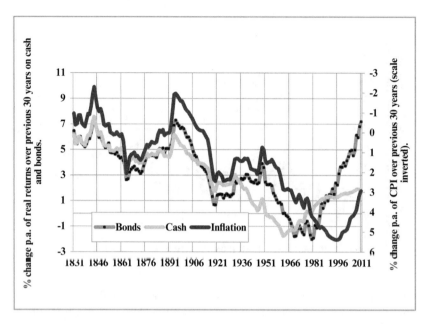

Chart 127. US: Inflation & Real Returns on Cash & Bonds.
Sources: Jeremy Siegel 1801 to 1899 and then Elroy Dimson, Paul Marsh & Mike Staunton via Morningstar to 2011.

The evidence that investors have been poor forecasters of past inflation makes it possible that even without any past relationship between bonds and equity returns there might be a relationship between the returns actually expected. But while it makes it possible that there is such a relationship it provides no evidence that it does exist.

The arrival of Treasury Inflation Protected Securities (TIPS) enables us to show that the evidence is against rather than in favour of such a relationship. Because the interest and the amount that will be repaid on maturity are linked to the rate of inflation, we know the expected return on TIPS in real terms. Chart 128 shows that since TIPS were first issued in 1997 the prospective real return on them has fallen sharply from between 3.5 and 4.5% in the first four years to a negative one today.

It can be shown mathematically from the variance compression shown in Charts 124 and 125 that past returns on equities have an

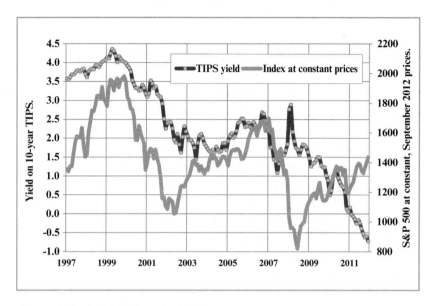

Chart 128. US: TIPS & S&P 500.
Sources: Reuters, BLS & Standard & Poors via Ecowin.

impact on future ones. If past returns have been good then future ones will be relatively poor and vice versa. This mean reversion of returns is also obvious to the eye when the historic real returns are shown as I illustrated in Chart 80.[12] It follows that when the stock market falls in real terms the prospective returns rise. Chart 127 shows that the prospective real returns from bonds have been falling since TIPS were first issued in 1997, while the prospective returns from equities must have been rising simply because the stock market has been falling when measured at constant prices. We have therefore evidence over the past 15 years that the expected returns on TIPS and equities have been moving in opposite directions. The chart also shows that over the same period there has been a large fall in the real value of US equities.

[12] The identity over the long-term between the returns earned by companies on their net worth, which is corporate equity, and the returns earned by shareholders means that both must be mean reverting, and for companies this is shown in Chart 36 and for shareholders in Chart 80.

In the face of this evidence there seems to be no justification for the assumption, regularly made by financial economists, that the ERP is a useful concept and this is true whether it is defined in terms of the return relative to bonds either on a historic or on a prospective basis. It may be that there is some relationship, which has so far eluded economists, between bond and equity returns, but in order to show that any exists it is necessary to state some testable hypothesis about the relationship and show that it is robust. In my experience those economists who write about the ERP make an a priori assumption that some relationship exists without producing supporting evidence. I have not yet encountered such a testable and robust model. The ERP is, therefore, in my view an example of the all too frequent failure by many economists to produce hypotheses that qualify as scientific statements in terms of Karl Popper's definition.

Asset price falls have in the past been the key triggers that have set off financial crises. A rational approach to asset pricing is thus essential if we are to improve our understanding of the economy and avoid future crises. If, as I claim, the majority of papers on asset prices and the way the subject is taught in finance courses is unscientific, this acts as an important and dangerous inhibition to the development of sound theory, and therefore sound policy.

The hangover from the EMH and its weak sister the ERP remains a limitation on the development of a rational approach to asset pricing among academics and central banks. I am one of many economists who argue that the outstanding defects of the neoclassical consensus are the failure of the model to include debt and asset prices. I think that an important contribution to this failure has been the poor epistemology of so many of those who teach financial economics. The faith placed on the EMH is the outstanding example of this, but much attention is still being given to the ERP, which seems to me to have the same faults. At the moment we have a situation in which the lack of market efficiency is usually given nodding acceptance that is ignored in most research and debate about the way asset prices are determined. Fortunately, a growing number of economists not only reject the EMH but also work on asset prices in a scientific manner. In this respect the Paul Woolley Centre for the Study of Capital Market Dysfunctionality and the anonymous donors who have set up The Keynes Fund deserve particular praise and attention.[13] Once it is accepted that financial markets are not fully efficient it is important not only to measure the extent to which they diverge at any one time from fair value but also to try to understand the forces that lead to over- and undervaluation. The Woolley Centre has already published several papers that shed light on the way in which assets are actually rather than theoretically priced and that are uncontaminated by the EMH or the ERP.[14]

I am therefore optimistic about the ability of economics to surmount the theoretical challenge and create a coherent, testable and robust model of the economy in which debt and asset prices are included. I am not, however, optimistic that we will get there quickly.

My central aims have been to explain how bad economics caused the financial crisis and is now inhibiting recovery and how bad epistemology has been the root cause of so much of the bad economics. I hope that we will now see an increasing willingness by academic economists to discard the errors of the past and help build a new paradigm in which debt and asset prices are accepted as essential parts of any model of the economy on which policy can be sensibly based. It is also essential that work on data should be valued in academia far more highly than it is today. Without good data it is impossible to test hypotheses and to discard them if they are not robust. Unless we give more value to data, academic papers will continue to be all too prone to fall the wrong side of Karl Popper's famous demarcation between science and non-science, by producing untestable hypotheses with their authors quoting them in each other's work as if the support from one untestable hypothesis could give validity to another. The importance of academic articles in economics is largely judged by the frequency with which they are cited in other articles, but this is often a barren and fruitless activity as non-testable hypotheses remain outside the boundary of science however often they are quoted.

[13] The Keynes Fund is organized in association with the Economics Faculty of Cambridge University. Its sponsors wish to encourage research that does not readily fit with current academic preoccupations and should not, if I have understood their wishes correctly, suffer from the epistemological limitations which this book attacks.

[14] For an example, see "*An Institutional Theory of Momentum and Reversal*" by Dimitri Vayanos and Paul Woolley, Review of Financial Studies (forthcoming).

16

Summary and Conclusions

The world economy is being held back by poor economic policy that is based on poor economic theory and analysis. The key mistake is the assumption that the current weakness of private sector demand is simply a temporary phenomenon. This leads to the expectation that demand will recover when entrepreneurs recover their animal spirits, consumption revives as households become less cautious and private sector deleveraging ends. As I have pointed out, this assumption and the expectation that follows from it are incompatible with the data. It is also sadly typical of the aprioristic bias of so many academic economists that they are either ignorant of the contrary evidence or choose to disregard it. The first essential step on the road to recovery is that the structural nature of today's recession is recognised and the data be given a proper consideration so that public debate can start as to how current obstacles to sustained recovery can be overcome. Only if this is done are we likely to be able to find ways to reform the bonus culture that is currently depressing demand in Anglophone economies and damaging their capacity to grow over the longer-term. In Japan there needs to be a similar public debate about the damage being done by excess depreciation allowances, so that politicians and bureaucrats can be persuaded to reform the structure of corporation tax. If we can get these matters aired rather than

255

ignored, I am confident that we can solve the obstructions they currently place along the road to recovery.

Equally, I fear that without public debate these key problems will remain unresolved and we will either suffer from years of unnecessary poor growth or have another financial crunch in which rising inflationary expectations force up interest rates. As we still have high debt levels and many excesses in asset prices, the conditions that set off previous crises are still with us, and a sharp rise in interest rates would probably be sufficient to precipitate another crisis.

Recognising that the current recession is fundamentally structural rather than cyclical, and that the combination of high debt and asset prices is dangerous, are the key economic challenges that we face. But we also need to deal with the international conflicts and misunderstandings. We may well have cyclical weakness in world demand that a rise in fiscal stimulus would alleviate. This seems to me very likely. The structural excess of savings over investment, which is the key imbalance in Japan, the UK and the US, probably has a discouraging impact and adds an element of cyclical weakness.

If we are going to have more fiscal stimulus it must come from those countries that can afford it and where it is least likely to create rising inflationary expectations. The only practical way to do this is, I fear, for the Keynesian trio to improve their current account balances to the point that those countries that have avoided fiscal stimuli, such as Germany and China, will be driven to pursue policies that are more internationally accommodating than those they have chosen so far. Even if the world does not need more fiscal stimulus today, the post-war era is over and at some stage in the future it will be needed. The task of managing the world economy must be spread more widely. I understand the viewpoint of those, such as Desmond Lachman,[1] who argue that currency intervention by the UK or Japan is unhelpful and uncooperative, but this seems to me to be simply naive. We will not persuade other countries that cooperation is in their interests so long as it is not.

---

[1] See "*Beggar-my-neighbour is wrong game*", a letter by Desmond Lachman of the American Enterprise Institute to the Financial Times, (28th February, 2013).

Sensible policies to address the structural cash flow surpluses of the business and foreign sectors in Japan, the UK and the US should be sufficient to allow these economies to combine adequate growth with the essential task of reducing their fiscal deficits to levels that allow long-term reductions in their national debt ratios. But this will still leave unresolved the problems of excessive debt, dangerously high asset prices and incompetently regulated banks.

The excessive level of debt that has built up in nearly all economies in both the private and the public sectors needs to be brought down. This could simply be done by massive default, which would produce a slump, or hyperinflation, which would be at least as damaging. We therefore need to produce this reduction slowly. Over time we need to change the tax treatment of debt, which encourages companies in virtually all countries today to have high leverage. In the US there is a similar encouragement to households as the interest on mortgage debt is a deductible expense for income tax assessments. This used to be the case in the UK, but this subsidy on debt has fortunately been abolished.

As the amount of debt relative to GDP builds up in an economy, the risks of financial crises rise. As these debt levels rise, the risk becomes greater, but there seems to be no precise level at which the rise in debt is sufficient by itself to cause a crisis. The build-up of debt creates the necessary conditions for financial trouble, but it requires a trigger to set off actual crises and in the past the trigger that has set them off has been a rapid fall in asset prices. We must therefore give proper attention to asset prices. We are still suffering from a hangover from the Efficient Market Hypothesis, which held that markets were always correctly priced. While this view is no longer widely held, it has deterred economists from giving proper attention to the mispricing of assets. A great deal of work is needed to improve our assessment of value in equities, property and bonds, and to educate central bankers and other economists on their importance. In the meantime central bankers and others concerned with economic stability must use, rather than continue to ignore, the work that has been done on asset values by Robert Shiller, Stephen Wright and myself. Where asset prices are already at dangerous levels, as they seem to be today in US equities, UK house prices and almost all bonds, policies are needed that will encourage them to fall slowly. In particular, quantitative easing, which encourages the overvaluation of assets, should be halted and slowly reversed.

None of these reforms is very difficult in theory, but in practice they are all quite daunting because the political understanding is generally lacking. Above all, therefore, this book is a plea for a willingness to debate the issues and consider the evidence, which I have sought to present, with Alice's comment about the uselessness of books without either pictures or conversation much in my mind.

Appendix 1

Mean Reversion of US Profit Margins

By James Mitchell

Using the annual data for US corporate profit margins, which we have from 1929 to 2011, the Augmented Dickey–Fuller (ADF) test statistic is − 4.683. This is a clear rejection of nonstationarity (the associated p-value is 0.000) and therefore indicates that US profit margins are mean reverting. While many statistical tests for nonstationarity, or indeed stationarity, exist, the ADF test remains an important benchmark. We operationalise the ADF test by using a statistical criterion (the Bayesian Information Criterion) to choose the lag length in the dynamic univariate regression underlying the test.

Appendix 2

Goods' Output Requires Much More Capital Than Service Output

Data for the capital/output ratios (COR) of different industries in the US are available. As Table A1 demonstrates, these show that output in non-traded sectors requires much less capital than that needed for traded goods and shows that the results are statistically significant.

Table A1. Average COR in the US Traded and Non-Traded Goods Sectors: 1998–2003[1]

		COR	p-value for Test of Mean Equality[2]
Traded	Manufacturing	1.560	–
Non-Traded	Construction	0.396	0.000
	Retail trade	0.977	0.000
	Finance, insurance, real estate, rental and leasing	1.095	0.000
	Professional and business services	0.553	0.000
	Educational services, healthcare and social assistance	1.342	0.001
Weighted average of non–traded sectors		0.919	–

It takes, on average, 70% more capital to produce output from manufacturing than it does from sectors that are primarily or exclusively non-traded. It follows that if growth is concentrated in the former there will be a lower required level of investment and savings for any given rise in total output.

[1] The COR is defined as the ratio of the current-cost net capital stock of private non-residential fixed assets to national income. The ratios are derived from NIPA Table 6.1 for national income by industry, and the "detailed fixed asset tables at replacement cost".

[2] This test shows that the differences in the COR are statistically significant. The p-values indicate the probability of accepting the hypothesis that the average COR in the selected industry is equal to the average COR in the manufacturing sector. The test is a so-called ANOVA test based on the idea that if the sub-groups have the same mean then the variability between the sample means (between groups) should be the same as the variability within any sub-group (within group).

Bibliography

A Note on Data Sources

The sources that I use for data are shown in the charts and tables, but readers may wish to understand a little more about them and why one source is used rather than another on different occasions.

Many of the sources are shown as being "via Ecowin". This is a data service to which I subscribe and from which I have downloaded much of the data used. Ecowin draws its data from a wide variety of sources and its service covers a large number of countries and contains the main data series published in the national accounts of the individual countries. This usually means that the detailed source is less precisely specified than when I download the data from the websites of the national sources. For example, the UK national data are published by the Office for National Statistics (ONS) in a variety of publications, such as the Blue Book (BB). As these data are often included in more than one publication, they are identified by a series of four letters (e.g. YBHA); these are known to the ONS as "signifiers", and I include these whenever possible.

My key source of long-term data for the UK is from *National Income Expenditure and Output of the United Kingdom: 1855–1965* by C. H. Feinstein, published by Cambridge University Press in 1972.

Most recent UK economic data come from either the ONS or the Bank of England. In Japan and the US the data sources are more varied.

In Japan the national accounts are published by the Cabinet Office, which has a website in English. Japanese national accounts are published quarterly and expeditiously on an expenditure basis, but those on an income basis are less timely, being as I write available 18 months behind today. They are not always updated for earlier years when first published and I have had therefore to link two different series of national accounts together, as, for example, in Chart 59.

Other important sources of Japanese data are the Ministry of Finance (MoF), which publishes, amongst other things, the Quarterly Survey of Incorporated Enterprises. The data included in this series are very similar, but not the same as the data on companies in the national income accounts. MoF data cover the *Kabushiki kaisha* (KK) but not the *Yūgen kaisha*, which constitute the smaller incorporated company sector, which comprises companies with a capital of less than ¥10 million. *Yūgen kaisha* are, however, relatively insignificant in total, whereas the non-incorporated sector is substantial and is included in the household sector.

Other important sources of Japanese data are the Bank of Japan (BoJ), the Tokyo Stock Exchange (TSE), the Ministry of Economics, Trade & Industry (METI), the Ministry of Labour, the Ministry of Communications (MIC) and the Ministry of Construction, all of which have websites and from which nearly all the data can be found in English. I have relied on Ecowin for stock exchange data published by the country's financial newspaper, the *Nikkei*, and data on land prices are available from the Japan Real Estate Institute.

For the United States, the Bureau of Economic Analysis (BEA) publishes a wide variety of data that can be readily accessed from its website. The BEA has published the data on the national accounts since 1929 in the form of the National Income & Product Accounts (NIPA). These are published in a number of tables in which the specific data series is indicated by the line number. For example, nominal GDP is found in Table 1.1.5 line 1. I try to specify NIPA and Z1 Table numbers in the charts and tables. The BEA also publishes data on the US's international capital position and domestic capital stock. The Federal Reserve is also an important source of data, not only for interest and foreign exchange rates and monetary data but also for its Flow of Funds of the United States (Z1). Detailed explanations of the way these data are compiled are set out in the two-volume *Guide to the Flow of Funds Accounts*, to which I refer in a footnote in Chapter 9. These accounts are particularly useful for balance sheet data and for the details of buyers and sellers of US equities.

Other important US data sources are the Bureau of Labour Statistics (BLS), which publishes the Consumer Price Index (CPI) as well as data on employment and hours worked, and the Federal Deposit Insurance Company (FDIC), which publishes data on banks and other financial institutions.

The key source for long-term US data is the historical *Statistics of the United States: Colonial Times to 1970*, published by the Bureau of the Census of the US Department of Commerce.

Angus Maddison's authoritative data, which cover a remarkable number of countries often over very long periods with regard to their GDP at constant prices and per head, are available from his website and, since his death, have been updated to 2008.

I have used the Organisation for Economic Cooperation and Development's (OECD) data from the Annex Table in its biannual "Economic Outlooks". I prefer to use these data, when available, for comparisons between different countries as the OECD seeks to make these comparable. In some cases I have had to make adjustments, notably with regard to comparisons of household savings' rates, as the OECD publishes some of these gross and some net and I have sought to make my comparisons using the same definition.

Other international comparisons are drawn from tables set out in the IMF's *Global Financial Stability Report*.

Standard & Poor's website contains a wealth of data, including those on the EPS on the S&P 500 Index. Long-term quarterly data on EPS can be found on Robert Shiller's website (http://www .econ.yale.edu/~shiller/data.htm). Jeremy Siegel kindly sent me his data series on US equity, bond and cash (short-term bond) returns starting in 1801. I have linked these with the series by Elroy Dimson, Paul Marsh and Mike Staunton, which can be purchased from Morningstar, which start at the end of 1899. This series is also useful for exchange rates and inflation and covers many countries. Other stock market data are drawn via Ecowin from Morgan Stanley Capital International (MSCI) and US house prices from the Case–Shiller index.

Further Reading

Badger A. (2008) *FDR: The First 100 Days*. Hill & Wang.

Baumol W. J. (2002) *The Free-Market Innovation Machine*. Princeton University Press.

Berle A. A. Jr and Means G. C. (1932) *The Modern Corporation and Private Property*. Commerce Clearing House Inc.

Bernanke B. S. (20th February, 2004) *The Great Moderation*. Eastern Economic Association, Washington, DC.

Bernholz P. (2006) *Monetary Regimes and Inflation: History, Economic and Political Relations*. Edward Elgar.

Biais B., Rochet, J.-C. and Woolley P. (2013) *Innovations, Rents and Risk*. Paul Woolley Centre, Working Paper Series 13, Discussion Paper 659, http://www2.lse.ac.uk.fing/researchProgrammes.paulWoolleyCentre/workingPapers/dp659PWC13.pdf, (accessed 5th June).

Blanchard O., Dell'Arricia G. and Mauro P. V. (2010) *Rethinking Macroeconomic Policy*, IMF Staff Position Note SPN/10/03.

Blinder A. (April, 2001) *Keeping the Keynesian Faith*. World Economics 2(2): 105–40.

Chadha J., Dempster M. A. H. and Pickford D. (2012) *The Euro in Danger*. Searching Finance.

Cornaggia K. J., Franzen L. A. and Simin T. T. (2013) *Bringing Leased Assets onto the Balance Sheet*, draft paper available at http://papers.ssrn.com/slo3/papers.cfin?abstract_id=1680077, (accessed 5th June).

Deutsch D. (1997) *The Fabric of Reality*. The Penguin Press.

Deutsch D. and Ekert A. (September, 2012) *Beyond the Quantum Horizon*. Scientific American.

Donaldson J. B., Gershun N. and Giannoni M. (2011) *Some Unpleasant General Equilibrium Implications of Executive Incentive Compensation Contracts*, The Federal Reserve Bank of New York Staff Report No. 531.

Duus P. (ed) (1988) *The Cambridge History of Japan Vol. 6*. Cambridge University Press.

Federal Reserve System (2000) *The Guide to the Flow of Funds Accounts*. Board of Governors.

Frydman C. and Jenter D. (2010) *CEO Compensation*, Annual Review of Financial Economics 2(1): 57–102.

Goodhart C. A. E. and Ashworth J. P. (2012) *QE: A Successful Start May Be Running Into Diminishing Returns*, Oxford Review of Economic Policy 28(4):640–70.

Grossman S. and Stiglitz J. (1980) *On the Impossibility of Informationally Efficient Markets*, American Economic Review 70(3): 393–408.

Haldane A. (2010) *The $100 Billion Question*. Bank of England.

IMF (2013) *Debt Bias and Other Distortions: Crisis Related Issues in Tax Policy* http://www.imf.org/external/np.pp/eng/2009/061209.pdf (accessed 5th June).

Kuhn T. S. (1962) *The Structure of Scientific Revolutions*. University of Chicago Press.

Leijonhufvud A. (2009) *Out of the Corridor: Keynes and the Crisis*, Cambridge Journal of Economics 33(4):741–57.

Lynn B. and Longman P. (March/April, 2010) *Who Broke America's Jobs Machine?* Washington Monthly.

Minsky H. (1986) *Stabilising an Unstable Economy*. Yale University Press.

Novy-Marx R. and Rauh J. D. (2011) *Public Pension Promises: How Big Are They and What Are They Worth?* Journal of Finance 66(4): 1211–49.

OECD (2012) *Labour Losing to Capital: What Explains the Declining Labour Share?* Employment Report.

Olson M. (1982) *The Rise and Decline of Nations: Economic Growth, Stagflation and Social Rigidities*. Yale University Press.

Orphanides A. and van Norden S. (November, 2012) *The Unreliability of Output-Gap Estimates in Real Time*. MIT Press Review of Economics and Statistics.

Popper K. (1959) *The Logic of Scientific Discovery*. Hutchinson.

Posen A. (2010) *The Realities and Relevance of Japan's Great Recession*. LSE.

PricewaterhouseCoopers (April, 2010) *The Future of Leasing*. PricewaterhouseCoopers.

Pryce V. (2012) *Greekonomics: The Euro Crisis and Why Politicians Don't Get It*. Biteback Publishing Ltd.

Reinhart C. and Rogoff K. S. (2009) *This Time It's Different: Eight Centuries of Financial Folly*. Princeton University Press.

Russell B. (1946) *A History of Western Philosophy*. George Allen & Unwin Ltd.

Shiller R. (2000) *Irrational Exuberance*. Princeton University Press.

Shirakawa M. (2012) *Looking through Prices in Financial Markets*. Paris Europlace Financial Forum, Tokyo.

Smithers A. (September, 1978) *Index Funds and Capital Market Theory*. The Investment Analyst.

Smithers A. (2009) *Wall Street Revalued: Imperfect Markets and Inept Central Bankers*. John Wiley & Sons, Ltd.

Smithers A. and Wright S. (2000) *Valuing Wall Street: Protecting Wealth in Turbulent Markets*. McGraw-Hill.

Smithers A. and Wright S. (2002) *Stock Markets and Central Bankers: The Economic Consequences of Alan Greenspan*, World Economics 3(1):101–24.

Vayanos D. and Woolley P. (forthcoming) *An Institutional Theory of Momentum and Reversal*. Review of Financial Studies.

White W. R. (2012) *Ultra Easy Monetary Policy and the Law of Unintended Consequences*, The Federal Reserve Bank of Dallas Globalization and Monetary Policy Institute Working Paper No. 126.

Wood G. and Kabiri A. (2010) *Firm Stability and System Stability: The Regulatory Delusion*, Conference on Managing Systemic Risk, University of Warwick.

Yellen J. (1st June, 2011) *Assessing Potential Financial Imbalances in an Era of Accommodative Monetary Policy*, International Conference: Real and Financial Linkage and Monetary Policy, Bank of Japan, Tokyo.

Yellen J. (11th February, 2013) *A Painfully Slow Recovery for America's Workers: Causes, Implications and the Federal Reserve's Response*, Transatlantic Agenda for Shared Prosperity Conference.

Acknowledgements

I have many to thank for the help that I have received in writing this book, because it is the result of long hours of discussion with a variety of people. First of all, my thanks go to Martin Wolf, who has so kindly and generously written the foreword. My particular thanks go to those to whom I sent a copy in draft; Bruno Biais, Simon May, James Mitchell, Jonathan Steinberg, Dimitri Vayanos, Martin Weale, Paul Woolley and Stephen Wright have all made very helpful comments as a result of which the book is considerably revised. Whatever its current defects, I am sure that it is much improved as a result of their kindness in reading the draft and suggesting changes and I am most grateful.

My thanks also go to my friends and colleagues at Smithers & Co and particularly to Vanessa Brown, Annalise Hamilton and Otis Stewart. My thanks go to Annalise for organising all the details needed for publication, to Otis for help with the data and above all to Vanessa, who as all those mentioned here will endorse, has borne the brunt of getting everything actually completed.

Index

Note: *Italic* page numbers indicate charts and tables